Praise for *The Fugitivities* and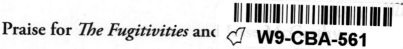

A *Kirkus* Best Book of 2021

"Virtuosic . . . [McCarthy's] prose, agile as a pianist in full flow, dances across the page . . . there are no conclusions, no resolutions to this fugue state, but there is something glorious in its exploration." —*The New York Times*

"Sensitive and sharp . . . " —*The New Yorker*

"McCarthy's captivating debut tackles race and the American dream . . . With its rich, lyrically drawn atmosphere and incisive commentary . . . McCarthy's tale maintains an authentic feel. Readers are in very good hands with this smart, empathetic, and soul-searching writer."
—*Publishers Weekly* (starred review)

"An acclaimed African American essayist puts forth a first novel whose quirky romanticism, vivid landscapes, and digressive storytelling owe more to classic European cinema than conventional literature . . . An intellectually stimulating fiction debut." —*Kirkus* (starred review)

"In his insightful debut, writer, editor, and Harvard professor McCarthy explores the tension between community and individual perceptions of Black identity in different cultures . . . Superb storytelling." —*Booklist*

"If you haven't already heard of Jesse McCarthy, you soon will! . . . [*The Fugitivities*] is best enjoyed by sinking into the ruminative prose and savoring the ride." —*Bookreporter*

"McCarthy is absolutely brilliant."
—Imani Perry, Hughes-Rogers Professor of African American Studies at Princeton University and author of *Breathe: A Letter to My Sons*

"*The Fugitivities* is a thrilling twenty-first-century sentimental education—a tale of black intellectual guilt and irrepressible wanderlust that follows a young teacher from disillusionment in Brooklyn to doubt and revelation abroad. McCarthy's spiraling, observant, exquisitely cadenced prose is a shot of adrenaline in a sea of laconic and episodic fiction. A powerful debut that is worldly in the most expansive sense—and with electricity to spare."
—**Julian Lucas,** *New Yorker* **staff writer**

"Jesse McCarthy is an artist of the ear."
—**Vinsom Cuningham,** *New Yorker* **staff writer**

"*The Fugitivities* is an ambitious debut novel that speaks to the deepest of vulnerabilities of the human condition: how we make sense of our identities as it relates to others and our stake and responsibilities in the world."
—**Morgan Jerkins, author of** *This Will Be My Undoing*

"A gorgeous, virtuosic novel. In exquisite, often ecstatic, prose, McCarthy gives us a portrait of the artist as a black man—or rather, as a set of young black men, brothers and friends and rivals. This is blackness as it collides with class and love. Blackness in its uneasy relationship to Europe and the Americas. Blackness in all of its inner intricacy, tension, and beauty. Blackness shattered from the inside, each facet spinning, in McCarthy's own words, in 'a hypnotic dance like shards in a kaleidoscope'."
—**Namwali Serpell, author of** *The Old Drift*

THE
FUGITIVITIES

THE FUGITIVITIES

JESSE McCARTHY

 MELVILLE HOUSE
BROOKLYN · LONDON

The Fugitivities

First published in 2021 by Melville House Publishing
Copyright © Jesse McCarthy, 2021
First Melville House Printing: June 2021

Melville House Publishing
46 John Street
Brooklyn, NY 11201
and
Suite 2000
16/18 Woodford Road
London E7 0HA

mhpbooks.com
facebook.com/mhpbooks
@melvillehouse

ISBN: 978-1-61219-977-1

Library of Congress Control Number: 2021932777

Designed by David Ter-Avanesyan/Ter33Design

Printed in the United States of America

1 3 5 7 9 10 8 6 4 2

A catalog record for this book is available from the Library of Congress

For my mother and fathers,
and all the foremothers and forefathers
who keep us in flight

They said a whale swallowed Jonah
Out in the deep blue sea
Sometimes I get that ol' funny feelin'
That same old whale has swallowed me
—J. B. LENOIR

Le voyage est une suite de disparitions irréparables.
—PAUL NIZAN

PART ONE

My best allegiances are to the dead.
—GWENDOLYN BROOKS

Your letter came today. I brought it with me to the Luxembourg Gardens and read it on the shaded path behind the tennis courts. Are things going very differently from the way you imagined? Or is it that your writing has changed since you moved? You sound more American now, I think. But there's something else too, a sadness that you haven't shared with me before. I'm glad that you found an apartment, and, if I read you right, a new friend. I liked the image of you and Isaac painting the walls, and of the group of black girls playing double Dutch on your street in the evening. I understand you're worried that they might soon disappear, but could Brooklyn really change that suddenly? I would have written sooner if I didn't keep falling behind at work. I get so distracted staring at the screen. Does it happen to you? I'll be clicking and tapping along and the whole thing weirds into daydreaming. I think it's the other half of my brain playing tricks on me—the part that wants to write songs. Sometimes I get into a panic, interrupt whatever I'm doing and throw down scads, a flurry of notes that I hope I might finish someday. Not even songs, just spots of emotion flaring up, like Sailor Moon in her ecstatic transformation. It's funny how I used to fantasize about being swept up in that tornado of light. I wrote something the other day that made me think of you. It's about the river by my grandfather's house. The smell of its mossiness. The cold licking at my ankles. Those spirals of snail-colored water under the neat lines of the poplar trees along the départementale. It reminded me of those ripples of river grass in the Tarkovsky film that we talked about at the café around the corner from Le Champo. I miss those days when we were always together. I guess I should worry about you—or tell you that I do. You say that maybe you're drinking too much, waking up suddenly in bars not knowing where you are and stumbling outside to hail one of those yellow taxis that have televisions in them now so that you don't have to look out the window. That many times when you wish you would pass out, you don't. I feel like

I can see you slumped in a musty back seat, hear the droning rush, and feel your loneliness as the car takes you over one of the great bridges, and for a brief moment you feel everything drop away. Like the city all around you is a distant star. I know better than to tell you what you need to do. But don't forget that you promised we'd keep writing, even in our delayed, interrupted way. Remember all the things you promised to tell me, and the stories we've only half told each other. I have my moments, comme tout le monde. I never told you about them, maybe because there would be too many other things to say. But I think that's what these letters are for. To make up for lost time with an unavoidable slowness, like a station where we always know we'll bump into each other. I wish I could tell you why I think of you when I think of my river. Or the smell of rain along the footpath behind our house. I would say it entirely in images like one of your favorite poets. But I can't right now. I still have two open reports to file and my mother needs me to help her with the telephone company. They're tearing up her street to install the fiber-optic. I'm going to Strasbourg tomorrow. I'll be sure to write you again from there if I can. I'm bringing your letter with me and will read it again on the train. I want to travel with it a while, stretch these words across space and time, unfold, read, refold. I want to hold onto you, to this.

—A

1

Perspiring, dizzy with heat and exhaustion, Jonah stopped at the corner of Underhill and St. Johns and plunked down the armchair he had trundled through the leafy streets of Park Slope, along the wide sunbaked extension of Flatbush Avenue, and, at Grand Army Plaza, around the imposing monument to the "Defenders of the Union," where bronze charioteers looked out over the construction of a condominium tower. The rich folk in the Slope had a habit of throwing out nice furniture in the summer, and he was determined to furnish his new apartment. The haul had been pretty good so far—a "reclaimed-wood" bookcase, a banker's desk lamp, a vaguely Oriental side table—with the only downside being that the crib now had the eclectic air of a showroom.

He was about halfway down the block when he took note of the commotion surrounding a double-parked Grand Cherokee directly across from his building. The vehicle was loaded down with equipment for living: a cream leather sitting chair crammed in at an angle, trash bags full of clothes, a plastic crate stuffed with video-game accessories, assorted lotions and hair products. Foodstuffs, cooking appliances, a bottle of Crisco, remained stranded on the sidewalk awaiting transport. A man carrying a stereo unit emerged from the brownstone across the street and hollered. At the boom of his voice, a somber boy in a durag, one earbud pendant, looked up. At the man's side stood a little girl with beaded braids, wearing a backpack; she saw Jonah and ducked behind her father's knee. "You heard him, go help your father," shouted a woman from the front passenger side, where she must have been trying to find more room. Her gaze passed over Jonah, assessing and dismissing in one sweep, before turning to the stoop as she called out the girl's name in a high sweet voice.

It took Jonah a moment to understand what he was seeing even though it was the simplest thing in the world. The expression on the face of the man carrying the stereo was concentrated and severe. He arranged the equipment in the back seat, then turned to go back in for whatever remained. The boy still stood curbside, staring blankly at nothing in particular. They would have been neighbors, but as it stood, Jonah was only a straggling stranger who happened to be moving in while they were moving out. There was no trace of sadness in the boy's face, no trace of fondness or regret for the street he was leaving, only an intimation that fairness was something he had never known and never would.

The scene stuck in Jonah's mind as he struggled with the chair up two flights of stairs to the apartment. Isaac was in the living room unpacking his records. Jonah shoved crumpled newspapers and packing materials out of the way and set the chair in the corner facing the window with the fire escape, then dropped his exhausted body into it. Focused completely on his own task, his roommate barely registered Jonah's entrance. The brother had more records than a DJ. Isaac wasn't actually that involved in the music scene; mostly he just listened to a small handful of albums on rotation. When they had first moved in, Jonah would find him there at all hours, sitting on the bare floor in the unfurnished room with his back up against the wall, one leg outstretched, locked in deep concentration, now and then murmuring a word or two, nodding his head in solemn agreement with the sound.

"Folks next door are moving out," Jonah said as he watched his friend digging through the crates, meticulously arranging his collection, unfazed by the room's stifling heat. Everything had to be strictly alphabetical—his Main Source record, with its splash of atoms, he held aloft momentarily like a rare talisman, before sliding it in next to Madlib and Mahalia. That was Isaac, cool as a fan.

"Oh yeah . . . it's gonna flip."

"I feel like I should say or do something, you know . . . and then I'm standing there looking a fool with this vintage armchair in the middle of the street . . . like I'm a harbinger of doom or some shit."

"Yeah, I don't know, man. It's like the migration all in reverse. Same old story though, chief. Black folk moving out, white folk moving in . . . you know the deal. They stay on top like an apostrophe."

The conversation moved on to a recent television show, dropping the issue without acknowledging they were doing so, though both were eager to change the subject for reasons they didn't yet feel they could share. There would, in any case, be no conclusions to *that* conversation, and the concrete reality they shared was the next day's dawn commute to another training session in Canarsie.

Jonah had met Isaac one month earlier at the orientation assembly for a teacher-training program at the Canarsie High School auditorium. They were around the same age and had followed the call to fill the ranks of the city's teaching corps, decimated by decades of decay and demoralization that had driven the most qualified teachers out to better, wealthier, and whiter districts, where the parents were on the right side of the law.

He found himself among a hundred or so would-be teachers crammed into the school's gymnasium. There was no ventilation and like the rest of the educator corps, Jonah sweated into his interview attire as he tried to make sense out of the raucous commotion, the bleating cell phones, the shouted orders and pleas for attention. A team of young folk in matching polos circulated frenetically through the rows of folding seats thrusting documents into people's hands. A beleaguered administrator shouted into a microphone until the hive cooled to a bearable hum. A series of officials took to the mic to enumerate rules and policies. They made frequent use of the words "rigorous" and "compliance." The intimidating legalism culminated with a deadline to report to the Department of Education on Court Street for fingerprinting.

Something about the way the brother seated next to him kept his quiet made Jonah think he must be there to teach math. After a quick glance and a hesitant pause, Jonah turned to him and they settled on an awkward dap. Jonah commented on the heat and the hectic crowd. If the teachers were this bad, Isaac said softly, he hoped the students would be saints.

When the teacher orientation broke for lunch, they went out together in search of a bite. Jonah was thinking sandwiches, but Isaac seemed to ignore that proposition and they ended up gravitating to a Crown Fried Chicken. After waiting in line and getting their orange trays with menu items #1 and #2, they secured a table of their own with a view looking out onto a set of mid-rise housing projects arranged like Tetris blocks along a stretch of Ralph Avenue. Over wings, Isaac mentioned that he had split up with his girl and needed a place. Jonah was living in a hostel and needed a permanent roof over his head too. They agreed to join forces and they were already discussing neighborhoods and rent when they returned to the gymnasium to fill out more forms.

The gears of metropolitan bureaucracy did their thing, and Isaac and Jonah were duly anointed with stamped (or photocopied) city certificates asserting their aptitude for pedagogical instruction in the public schools. A week later they were signing a lease. The rent was steep but between their two salaries they could afford a place within walking distance of Prospect Park. They would live together, but they would be working far apart; an obscure lottery system determined which schools they would actually serve in. When the numbers came up, Isaac was directed to a school in Brownsville—*Never Ran, Never Will*—and Jonah to a school in Red Hook, a neighborhood he associated mainly with *On the Waterfront*.

It wasn't until they were living together, going through some of the same experiences, that Jonah really got to know his new roommate. Isaac's folks had fled the chaos and violence in Detroit for the suburbs of Richmond where he grew up a little more isolated but a whole lot safer. It was the trade-off people had to make—the lucky ones, those who already had some-

8

thing going, a minister in the family, a funeral-home director, a mother who had broken into one of the public school systems. They took advantage of the affirmative-action door jimmied open ever so briefly after the riots, raised *Reading Rainbow* kids, and never looked back. That was basically, Isaac told him, how he'd ended up everywhere, in that sweet spot where admissions officers were always hunting for precisely his demographic, the ones who had been afforded all the benefits of a better zip code, but who would also color in the brochure and the website appropriately.

Jonah wondered, as he always did, how his own ambiguous but affluent upbringing would go over. A black dude *from* Paris? But his new friend was unimpressed, if interested. "That's cool. A brotha from *Paree*. They got barbecue over there?" Isaac had a line for everything, but nonetheless this underwhelmed curiosity pretty much summed up the attitude he held generally. Isaac had been all over the US, on school trips, to visit friends and family. But he had never left the country. He wasn't opposed to the idea; he simply never had the means, certainly not to go somewhere on his own. One time, his junior year of college, he had been on the verge of visiting a girlfriend in Jamaica, but they had broken up a few weeks before he was set to go. Now Jamaica was out of the question. Next chance he got, though, he was hoping to use his first paid vacation days as a teacher to go somewhere else in the Caribbean, maybe Trinidad or Barbados. "Frenchman, you gotta teach me to use them words the way you do," Isaac would say, screwing up his face. "L'amour, les misérables, les incompétents. Love them French horns, too. I knew a football player in high school named Terrence who played the French horn. He wanted to go to Virginia State and play for the Trojans, but he got injured in a practice senior year. He ended up dropping out and going into the military. Haven't heard nothing since."

In spite of the disparate slots and different ladder rungs Isaac and Jonah had alighted on, everything they learned about each other confirmed how significantly their trajectories converged once they graduated with their degrees. Jonah had attended an elite private college in New England, and

Isaac a public university in North Carolina. Yet they both knew former classmates who had started more lucrative careers in consulting or banking or found prestigious internships with distinguished institutions and nonprofits, while they were both now engaged in something like charitable work, in "giving back," as people said.

On balmy evenings, they'd sit with beers in the front room and share stories about hallway incidents. When Jonah was buying, he walked over to Flatbush to purchase one of the new floral microbrews; when Isaac was buying, it was always Miller Time. It was a mellow ritual. They listened to Isaac's favorite records, originally his mother's. There had been some tension around his acquiring them. Isaac had started a small collection of his own during his senior year of high school. When he came home from college over spring break of his freshman year, he wouldn't leave his room for days. He threatened not to go back and eventually showed his mother a note from the school therapist. They talked about it, and she made a deal with him. If he would go back to school and get his education, he could take some of her own records with him. It was, he said, just one of many ways in which she'd probably saved his life.

The poor righteous teachers sat back in their bougie furniture and talked about "the situation" as they half listened to the plush tones of the Emotions or seventies-era Bobby Womack. There was always music in the air. On Sundays, Jonah awoke to the Clark Sisters ringing all down the hallway and into his room. The scratchy records somehow thickened things, popping softly in the air while they bantered until Isaac, without interrupting his train of thought, switched them out.

"The situation" was everything and nothing in particular. Even though the friends almost never agreed on why, or what, it meant, or what was to be done about it, they agreed and mutually reinforced each other's opinion that something had gone fundamentally wrong. It was in everything. Language and manners, gestures and traditions, entire understandings could be hollowed out overnight. Things had gotten weird, glitchy, like the looping video of the second plane. Twisted creeps were coming out of the woodwork all across America. Berserkers armed with gleaming shotguns and tubes of K-Y Jelly slaying Amish schoolgirls. "Active shooters," in the new parlance, burning holes in the bodies of fellow college students cowering under their desks. Wars and shadow wars multiplying, mutating without a semblance of purpose. The inferno of Katrina. Corpses floating through the Ninth Ward. The Malebolge of the Superdome. The death of the oceans. Texaco dumping crude runoff in the rainforests of Ecuador. Jihadists slitting throats. Ice caps collapsing. Narco wastelands. The interfaces taking over. The death of the heart. Everywhere and in everyone, the situation was drawing out the worst; the sickos were gaining the upper hand.

On paydays, Jonah and Isaac walked to a new soul food joint on Franklin Avenue, run by a West Indian woman who had anticipated the changes coming to the presently less gentrified parts of Crown Heights. Isaac was offended by the lack of white bread stuck to the bottom of his wings, but the sauce wasn't bad, and over drinks they talked politics and traded gossip, arguing fiercely about the importance of various music critics they had, in reality, only just discovered.

In the dark on the walk back, they'd swagger, partly on account of the rum and sugar, but also because they felt the eyes of the battered neighborhood watching, and even though not a finger or even a holler was ever raised in their direction (although occasionally it seemed it might happen, and plenty of adventurous white kids, especially white girls, had gotten robbed in the area since their arrival), they knew with unspoken certainty that they were alien to these corners and that no amount of Garveyite pleading would ensure their safe passage should things take a different turn.

Early in the mornings, hungover or not, they left the apartment together, walking in hurried silence down to the subway station at Grand Army Plaza, where they split with a nod and took trains in opposite directions. The subway platform was quiet at those hours, and it wasn't uncommon to have to wait fifteen or twenty minutes before an arrival. The inbound trains coming from East New York and Flatbush on Jonah's side were always packed with black and brown faces. White folks started boarding in numbers just one stop farther in the Slope. The cars were so packed by then that they were often left stranded at the edge, with their wet hair slicked, earbuds in, staring icily at the compressed accordion of bodies. But before the crunch, in that precious time before the thundering clatter rolling up out of the tunnel announced itself, Jonah would head to the abandoned stretches of the platform where he could sit on the last bench (unless a homeless man was slumped there) and feverishly compile notes about the previous day in a teacher's journal that the school administration had recommended he start keeping.

In his first weeks as a new teacher, the thing that struck Jonah most about the students were the tattoos. They all had them. Gangs, he'd figured at first, or the usual rituals of adolescence. Boyfriend-girlfriend, signs and blessings for courage, fearlessness, spirituality. There were plenty of those. But they were not the most common ones. Those were the markings of death. Names and nicknames of friends, schoolmates, brothers, sisters, cousins. One of them Jonah recognized from screen-printed T-shirts he had seen students wearing in the hall. The face, name, and lifespan of a kid who must have been sitting in a classroom with whoever had filled Jonah's role the year before. This grim reaping, everyone agreed, was nonetheless a measure of progress. Things were far better than ten years earlier, in the terrible early nineties, when the death count had been much higher and even the school's principal of twenty-six years, Mr. Daly, was shot and killed in a burst of crossfire while out looking for a student who had been bullied. R. J. 1982–2000. Wade Never Forget 1980–1997. Antoine 1984–2004. Krystal R.I.P. in Heaven 1985–2001. Jermaine Noah Howard 1980–2002. The most beautiful, and the saddest, inked along a forearm in tightly bound cursive simply read, "Peace To All My Brothers Who Passed Away."

Teaching was, among other things, a high-wire act. Jonah learned to walk the wire, often by falling painfully from it. The hours of instruction sometimes felt like battle. Something about the collective charge of restless minds made endings, no matter how calculated, feel sudden and abrupt. The students rushed back out in a vortex, a few strays always lingering, sometimes out of curiosity, or kindness, oftentimes for protection. There was no silence like that of the classroom when one stood at the desk alone, wiping down the blackboard, gathering one's papers in a quiet shuffle.

The long commute home from Red Hook required a transfer from a bus, since the trains didn't run there. When Jonah got home, he often found Isaac as drained as himself. They'd barely be able to speak to each other, unless to relate what often sounded like war stories. Jonah hadn't necessarily expected his job to be what it was, but now he was knee-deep. Almost without realizing it, he spoke more to himself than to anyone else, and he did so in the pages of his journal. The weeks passed, and as he grew more practiced in the form, more accustomed to the rhythms of his own mind, the number of pages scrawled in haste every morning on the subway platform multiplied. So much so, that, more than once, he looked up in a jolt of panic to see the doors jamming shut in his face.

Lesson planning helped, but it could not save them. That was the conclusion that kept resurfacing in his notes as the days began to resemble each other more than they differed. He held a pivotal but tenuous role in the lives of the kids who came to him from the housing projects that sat between the long-defunct waterfront and the elevated tracks over the Gowanus canal. A stabbing incident involving a transfer student less than a month after his arrival concentrated these thoughts into an indissoluble fear. He felt it leeching his courage every morning as he approached the high walls and metal cladding of the school's fortresslike frontage. Once he got past the metal detectors and up the grand staircase, his classroom was at the end of the hall, a corner room on the fourth floor, which meant it got light and even a glimpse of the harbor where, though you couldn't see it, Lady Liberty watched over the endless rounds of the Staten Island Ferry.

He wasn't afraid for himself. What he feared was becoming attached to a student who might lose their life, or spend years in prison, or who might never leave these same blocks that formed everything they knew, and that they might not want to. The fear was that he would fail to reach them, founder in showing them how to remain on the narrowest of rising roads, the slim chance that maybe, if they went against everything, the most powerful forces in society and the most intoxicating impulses of puberty, if they persevered with unwavering tenacity and a near-military discipline, there was a chance they might slip through the bonds. This fear could be crippling.

The infernal contradictions between his hopeful expectations and the downward spirals of aimless and angry students deepened. He was locked in a struggle, but against whom? It felt like it was against *them*, the students who went off like bottle rockets without warning, were fine one minute, spazzing out of control the next. But it wasn't them, and he knew it. He told himself it was their parents. Or it was the administration; the school principal with her perpetually gleeful greetings and frizzy hair who had clearly decided she would rather be liked than respected. But that wasn't the truth. Nor was it the brand-new Barnes & Noble Classics he had purchased that sat untouched on the "reading shelf" he had set up along the back wall. It was none of those things, and yet in a way it was all of them. Everyone knew the rot had reached the core. Knowing didn't make a difference to what could be done. The acronyms, the tests, the teaching staff themselves; everything changed except for the thing they were all supposed to be achieving. The unspoken game was how to get credit for sweeping dirt under a rug. But then why should he have expected anything else?

From his pedagogical instruction, Jonah knew that he was never supposed to have a favorite. He knew it was unethical to think in those terms. But he did have a favorite. B., who usually came in with a hoodie, kept to herself, and pretended to be asleep at her desk. It had taken Jonah months to understand that she was too smart for the class. He hadn't connected the dots until she turned in a free-writing assignment not long after the Christmas break. It was an essay about discovering her aunt's fatal overdose. She wrote it in longhand with a glossy purple pen. Her prose was elegant and fluid. When Jonah handed her the paper and she saw the letter grade, she lit up. He told her it was exceptional, that she was talented, and he asked her if she had thought about going to go to college. She said she wanted to study fashion. He gave her a copy of *If Beale Street Could Talk*, and in the following weeks she would show up early to class every day and read alone at her desk, still wearing her puffer coat and cradling the book defensively like a treasure.

The possibility of her failing had never entered Jonah's mind. So, when B. stopped coming to class around Easter, he was genuinely shocked. Was there something more he should have done? Had he done all that he could have? If he were doing a better job with his classroom management would she still be there? He tried to hold the students in his mind in a loosely individuated whole, a kind of buzzing abstraction. But when bad things happened to them—and they did with alarming frequency—their fragile lives suddenly became very real and singular, unbearably so.

As the weeks passed, the possibility of her recovering or making up assignments and getting a passing grade faded and then finally evaporated entirely. Jonah thought he might not see her again at all, and he was told by other teachers that this was something that sometimes happened, and that one simply had to accept it. But at the very end of the year, on a bright summery day with light streaming in through the corner windows, B. appeared in the doorway after class and asked to speak with him. She apologized for her absence and told him the outlines of what he understood was an account of sexual assault. It might have been exceptionally allowable to give her a hug, but he did not think he could, so he told her gravely and emphatically how sorry he was and asked her if there was anything he could do to help. She told him not to worry about her. That she was more confident in her future than ever before. She said she had suffered more than anyone would ever be able to make her suffer again. She said she was sorry to have failed his class. He told her she hadn't failed. That so many people, and he first among them, had failed her. She told him not to blame himself. She wasn't angry anymore, she said. She said nothing could hurt her now. "Don't worry about me—Imma do for myself," she said. He told her it was a brave thing to say, that he was proud of her resolve. She said she was going to make her own way in the world, like she always knew she would have to. She thanked him for the novel, and said that Tish was her, that she had never connected with someone in a book like that before. He was going to say how pleased he was that she enjoyed the reading, but her friends were calling to her from the hall. She dabbed her eye, smiled, picked up her schoolbag, and hurried on her way.

2

eaching had not allowed for much in the way of frivolities but going out to film houses to lose himself in the dark was a vice Jonah couldn't shake. As long as he stayed in Brooklyn the unfavorable equation of public transport and distance usually led him to adopt the path of least resistance: ordering takeout and watching something random online. But in Manhattan, he gravitated toward indie screen institutions like Cinema Reggio down on Twelfth Street, with the old-fashioned marquee that reminded him of the rue Christine. One evening that spring, he ducked into the Reggio, mostly to get out of a sudden downpour. They were screening a restored print of Charles Burnett's *Killer of Sheep*—according to some critics, read the lobby notice, it was the greatest black film ever made but virtually unknown outside the indie film world, having disappeared from most screens for decades. He went to purchase a ticket.

Unmistakable. The lanky boyish shag of hair, the reedy voice, the thin delicate hands extended in Italianate gestures. The vendor working the booth was his former college classmate, the wild Cubano from B Dorm. Octavio Cienfuegos. In this serendipitous instance, Octavio was occupied with finessing the elderly couple in line ahead of him; the old man, visibly overwhelmed, was writing down his email address for the Reggio news-letter. Unbeatable discounts, exclusive VIP screenings, not to mention the privilege of supporting the seventh art—Octavio dispensed his assurances with charming conviction and more than a little free association. Once the couple had given up their email and fled in polite haste, Octavio seemed to just as swiftly become a statue again, an inscrutable Pierrot, his gaze fixated on a point somewhere in the middle distance, so that when Jonah got up to the counter and knocked on the glass, he nearly jumped.

"Oh shit! Oh, *shit*! Jonah? Qué bolá, asere?"

Octavio was visibly high.

"Nothing much, man, just come to see a movie. How the hell you been?"

"You see I'm working, right! Listen, Jonah, normally man, *for you*, you know I would hook you up, but I haven't been on the job so long, you know how it is, give me a few weeks, I'm gonna have my way around here, I'm seeing things *already*, man, I'm telling you, the way they run this rig, it's por la izquierda, you wouldn't believe it. Next time you come . . ."

"No worries, man," Jonah said. "I wasn't looking for the angle. I make decent money now, anyway. I'm teaching."

"Okay, Teach—get those tax dollars, but don't be a stranger, come see me after the film. Seriously. I'll be off by then. I want to talk to you. Some strategies I've been working on. Knight moves. Avanzadas. I'll explain. You gotta catch the flick, pero socio, find me later, okay? If you don't see me, just chill, don't ask around. Sometimes I duck out, you know, but I won't be far."

This conspiratorial tone and its implied precautions proved entirely unnecessary. After the film, Jonah found Octavio waiting for him outside in front of the theater. He was standing unperturbed under the marquee. The rain still coming down hard and blowing in sideways had left him soaked on one side, as if he had been standing there for a long time. Octavio handed him one of the cinema's upcoming events calendars to use as an impromptu umbrella. Jonah accepted it with thanks, and they ran, splashing, over to Heathers, a nearby bar, where Octavio was well known, and, as he put it, had "standing." Under Prince-purple fluorescent lighting, they reacquainted themselves with college anecdotes and a debate over whether *Killer of Sheep* was truly the greatest black film ever made. Without hesitation, Octavio said it was commendable but in no way superior to the best of Micheaux. Jonah hastily agreed, vaguely recognizing the name, though he had never actually seen a film by that director. Octavio had always already seen everything—working the Reggio "internship," which meant little pay and a lot of free films, certainly helped. Not that he needed rent money. He was living with his parents in the city to save money while he applied to art schools.

The job itself was a soft take. Do whatever management said needed to get done, be a jack-of-all-trades. He would fix the marquee, sell popcorn and tickets, and assist Benny, a Mexican dude from Aguascalientes, who cleaned all the surfaces and the bathrooms, and mopped the lobby. The Reggio management was Sal, a cigar-smoking Bensonhurst man built like a bouncer and notorious for his gator-skin loafers and low boiling point. Octavio put his Cuban heritage to good use when they hosted the Latino Film Festival, doing Q&As and the like. As long as Jonah kept a low profile, Octavio volunteered to sneak him into the festival when it came around.

Jonah found himself drawn to the air of intelligent mischief that he recalled admiring from a distance in college. Octavio was the kind of guy who cut it close and knew, maybe a little too well, that he was attractive, and that the relation between those things allowed for certain kinds of movement in the world, slippages and maneuvers available only to some. This meant that when he had an idea, he acted on it immediately, seemingly intuitively, although because the hidden ratio of calculation and impulse remained masked it was impossible to tell whether plans or impulses led the way, only that the end result was that he enjoyed a remarkable knack for merging with whatever currents were around.

So, when Octavio texted Jonah one evening in May to say that he had an idea that would change their lives, Jonah agreed to meet him the very next morning without giving himself cause to question the possible reasons or portents. The school year was in its last few weeks, and because Jonah still needed to make his way to Red Hook and Octavio was in Manhattan, it was suggested that they meet at the crack of dawn in the Financial District, where they could catch a ferry taxi over to the Brooklyn waterfront. The trip over, Octavio said, would give him all the time he needed to explain himself, and Jonah would get to class on time.

That morning, Jonah got up in the blue darkness and left the apartment while Isaac was showering and took the train to downtown Manhattan. The Fulton Street station hadn't reopened yet, so he got out one stop higher, grabbed coffee at the first Starbucks he saw, and headed down on foot. A good third of the district was still being excavated and repurposed. Construction workers cried out to one another over the chorus of chattering rock drills. Thunderous loads of concrete barreled into the tumbril of Mack trucks to be carted away. American flags were draped on machine pieces, decals adorning the countless work helmets of men whose booming Jersey voices seemed to hang and ring out longer in the dusty air. Forty stories above him floated the largest flag he'd ever seen, billowing out behind a crane operator, the long boom turning like a clock hand, sweeping across the brightening sky and over the massive hollow below.

Jonah crossed below City Hall in the shadow of the Woolworth Building, mostly east and south again, into the blue veins of New Amsterdam. He toyed with visions of the same streets in the first century of their existence, festooned at their ends with sail and riggings. The disembarked European tribes staking out street corners, scrabbling like dogs trained for the fight. The clank of continental commerce and the groan and shudder of titanic construction. Black dock workers signaling with their eyes and a nod of the head to the runaways not yet secure on the landing. Looking for agents on the path to the North. Those others had walked here, those persons whose cherished names and things had gone misremembered, unrecorded, or just overlooked, trapped in fine layers of archeological sediment, entire cities of the dead murmuring under the blab of the pave, like the African burial ground he had read about, discovered underneath a parking lot.

He imagined the perspective of someone who had worked in these environs for a living, maybe as a customs inspector. The comedy of summing up exhausted voyages, transoceanic in scope and plagued with a litany of troubles, all taken in under a looking glass, done up in fine penmanship, arranged for the benefit of the custom's house master, who requires neat columns on the page.

One hundred and fifty years later, the commercial ocean recalibrated and danced about him. Somewhere above the sea-level streets, the diversity-trained, indefatigable, and ruthless agents of white-shoe firms huddled in their war rooms, ready to think outside the box, to dismantle and repackage the world at will. In the blink of an eye, a tinkering of margins could send spasms across the globe, tremors registered in cable-news crawl picked up and translated into sports analogies by the screaming bald guy on *Mad Money*, another indefatigable prognosticator in the wilderness of mirrors.

Jonah passed the lines at the Dunkin' Donuts where black workers wearing hairnets took orders, looking tired of building someone else's civilization. He watched Bangladeshis manning their outposts in the early traffic, poking at hot dogs under their blue umbrellas. The storefronts were already open for business: gadget shops with their galaxy of cellular components; luggage vendors; and shoe stores with loafers 20 percent off. Above them, in a tinted haze, rows of high office windows transecting the sky in every direction conveyed a degree of the gray mystery of the general enterprise, as if the whole system generated a sweat, a mist burning off a dark river down which one had already been sold, without the friction of a public auction, and better yet with one's tacit consent, the human cargo happily surrendered, as though the end of all historical troubles and aspirations, centuries of subsistence, of slavery, of colonialism, of empire, of industrial totalitarianism, had contracted to the dim radiance of this null surface.

Jonah caught sight of Octavio ahead of him as he neared the water. He recognized the gait, the slim frame nimbly jaunting past some corporate art on the corner of Water Street, his presence made noirish by an orange-and-white Con Edison ventricle siphoning off steam that turned lavender, then green, in the traffic light. They went under FDR Drive and Jonah caught up just as they were turning on to the pier. Octavio swiveled and extended an arm in embrace without entirely arresting his motion, as though anticipating and absorbing the momentum of the encounter. They exchanged swift and somewhat severe greetings, before resuming the march down to the water. A foghorn sounded. At the far end of the dock, a water taxi was tying up. It was packed with business types all jockeying for positions at the exit. When the chain rope was pulled aside, they came pouring out in droves like extras from a Buster Keaton film. Octavio looked upon the scene with an enigmatic grin. When the commuters had disembarked, they made their leisurely way onboard.

The sun was hoisting itself over the deck of the Brooklyn Navy Yard. They stood at the prow of the water taxi, the spray of the East River prickling Jonah's shirt as his tie snaked in the snapping wind. The roar of the motor and the flapping gusts nearly covered their voices, so they ended up howling two feet away from each other, like floor traders caught in a five-hundred-point drop. Jonah had to concede the genius. He certainly wouldn't do it on an everyday basis, but this was a hell of a way to commute to Red Hook for work. Octavio gazed south to the Verrazzano Bridge lying like an open parenthesis on its back.

Octavio's impassioned hollers overcame the diesel motoring.

"We need to go south!"

"What, you want to get off in Sheepshead Bay?"

"No, I'm talking farther south, all the way south. Think big picture!"

"What, Florida?"

"No, man. I'm talking farther out. Past the Caribbean."

"You want to go to South America?"

"To Rio."

"Rio. If you want sand and bikinis, why not Orchard Beach?"

"Tss! No seas tan bruto . . . perdónalo dios, el caballero es flemático."

"You're losing me. Why Rio?"

"You remember my girl, Barthes?"

"Barthes?"

22

"Maggie Reynolds. Brunette, soccer team, she was the year above us. We both took lit theory our junior year. Every time she spoke, it was 'Barthes this' and 'Barthes that.' I used to tease her. The name stuck. Anyway, we had a thing, right, it was going pretty well too, but then we had to break it off when she decided to leave the city to work with favela children in Rio through one of those GlobalGiving NGO-type things. Anyway, the point is I have a plan. We go down there, we find her, we say what's up, you know, and she gets us connected down there—she'll have the whole place figured out, all we gotta do is take it all in. And she can put us up, I mean, she wouldn't refuse me; we have history at this point, I'm talking *romantic* history!"

"Yeah, I'll bet," Jonah scoffed. "You want to go all the way down to Brazil to rekindle a flame. That's romantic, that's cool, man . . . Maybe that'll be impactful on your life, but why do you need to bring me along? I'm not trying to play third wheel. Are you suggesting we're going to get work with Barthes's NGO or something like that?"

"Think bigger. We don't go to Rio, we *begin* in Rio. We take on South America! Brazil! Argentina! Bolivia! Peru! The Andes! The Amazon! The Southern Cone! I'm saying, let's get the hell out of here! It's about having connections on the ground, man. Once we do, we make our own NGO. Needs Getting Obliged. Anyway, who needs a reason? This country is terminal—it doesn't deserve saving. I wouldn't wish a life in Castro country on anyone. But if you think Miami is a paradise you're out of your mind! It's a drugged-out swamp with a Gucci store. A resort-world run by reactionaries, real estate barrons, and cartel lawyers. The population is lunatic ex-Batistas and a mezclado of non-white refugees who basically do all the shit service jobs in the tourism hustle where the overlords launder their money. Come on, man, don't act like you don't know what I'm talking about—it's the same everywhere. New York is a joke, a punchline in a tired Diceman routine. Have you listened to the way people talk? The writing is on the wall. We have to get out of here, see something else before it's too late! How can these people *live*—how can anyone live when it's like you can't breathe half the time?"

"But, so . . . what? You want me to just drop everything I'm doing and fly off with you," said Jonah, watching the terminal pier come into view. "I think I know what you mean, but even if I agreed, I'm not sure running off somewhere else solves anything. Plus, I can't just abandon my students."

The water taxi slowed, coming around the bend into the part of the waterway that fronted the ruins and relics of the Gowanus. There was a plan, much discussed at Jonah's school, to have large tracts of it converted into a furniture superoutlet. Furniture for the massive influx of white graduates fleeing the suburbs their parents had fled to, not for the kids in the Red Hook Houses, who had never gone anywhere, who had survived, and who now sat in Jonah's classroom daydreaming about driving a foreign super-car, or having enough money to buy a pair of limited-edition sneakers, or nodding off because of their meds or because they only ate one hot meal a day in the school cafeteria.

"Who knows what is important? All my life, I feel like people have been telling me what is important," Octavio was saying. "Everybody has a theory. God is important. Making money is important. Saving the environment. Ending racism. Changing health care. The church. It's Marx, or the Media. But none of those things ever felt important to me. People just *say* they are. Barthes and all her friends and all of us—all of us. Come on, man, you know it's all bullshit. Everyone wants what people have always wanted. They want to win. Why you think they sent us to that school? They only care that you're successful. Famous and successful. To do that, you need to be someone other than yourself. So now you get good at simulating. You hide all your feelings and beliefs and desires, which you didn't even know in the first place, and soon you can't tell the difference. But it's easier to believe in the you that does well in interviews, the you as corporate candidate, a good team player who knows how to display leadership and integrate criticism and bring the right kind of energy to the project and smile like the diversity hire they all hoped that you would be. And you must be right about everything because all these people want to be your friends, and you *deserve* to make more money in one year than your parents made working hard in a decade. And that's if it all works out, and odds are sooner or later it won't. How can we be part of any of this shit, honestly? Look at you. I mean, you're doing good. But tell me the truth. Dime la verdad. Do you want to be a teacher for the rest of your life?"

Jonah looked out at the hazy undefined Brooklyn skyline, the endless tumble of warehouses and cranes that made up the Red Hook waterfront. The rest of life appeared sprawling and unknowable.

"I don't know. Probably not, I guess," he said at last.

"So what are you doing here? What is anyone doing? Work? Nobody believes in work anymore! It's all a joke. A scam. You make a latte. You sign people up for forty bucks a month for free wireless and explain 'features' to them. You make a website that takes like two hours and charge for two hundred because these morons think making their Flash site is like building a cathedral. You look for things on search engines and add numbers to spreadsheets, then make new spreadsheets. You do all of this as part of an internship for which you are not paid, or only enough to pay for the commuting costs to get you back to your desk. Maybe you get the right kind of soy milk-substitute for the head of production and you feel gratified and tell yourself you're getting ahead when they take a minute to gasp about the latest episode of *America's Next Top Model*. No matter who you are or what you do or where you are, you spend the better part of your earthly hours staring at a computer screen and waiting to be free again. Period. Nobody works—they're tethered, bothered, harassed by tasks, all kinds of mindless drudgery. But in truth, the only people who work are immigrants and men in construction. Everyone else is either a technocrat or serving the technocrats. Why play these corny games? I say out. Out! Let this place go to pieces. Life is too short. Ask anyone. If you had time and money, what would you do? Their answer: travel. Get away from it all. There's nothing to figure out here. Nothing to solve. Get out! That's all that matters."

Jonah got off at the pier. He had assumed Octavio would follow him, but when he turned around, he saw that his friend was still standing on the deck and sending him an indecipherable sign. The lanky figure cupped his hands to his mouth. "Think about it!" Octavio shouted something more after that, but whatever it was got swallowed by the chugging growl of the ferry as it reversed course across the greasy waters.

Jonah turned into the pastoral calm of Red Hook's cobblestone streets. Little clumps of greenery and dandelions sprouted in the curbside. He passed old cable drums and warehouses with marine outfittings, their bricks glowing warm and pinkish in the sun. The kneading sensation under his dress shoes kept him awkwardly amphibious, dipping in and out of his thoughts, pausing to bask momentarily whenever a salty summery gust came in off the wharf. Despite ambling, he arrived at the school early enough to find his classroom still empty. Through the windows he watched as morning light poured down over the harbor and the island city. Octavio was over there somewhere now, walking among the skyscrapers. It was, just then, the wrong feeling, and he was aware of this without being able to shake its significance in his heart. Manhattan had never looked so alarmingly beautiful.

3

Summer had arrived, bringing with it hydrant games, daylong cookouts, and heated brawls. The first Monday after school let out, Jonah spent the day wandering uptown. He walked through Central Harlem, heading west. He stopped to see the cathedral where James Baldwin's funeral had taken place and then popped into a café across the avenue. He ordered coffee, secured a small table in the back, and ostentatiously pulled out his copy of Baraka's *The Dead Lecturer*. He seemed to be the only person there without a laptop. But his mind wasn't really in the poetry. It was on Octavio's offer. His phone vibrated with a text: Isaac in "the city" (code for Manhattan), wondering what he was up to. Jonah texted back saying he should join him uptown.

Whenever Isaac arrived somewhere, people took notice. The way the brother moved, like Morris Day, you knew what time it was. Entering the coffee shop, he gave the place a once-over, looking mildly irritated. A young couple stepped gingerly around him, offering an unnecessary apology. Only black men can unnerve a whole room so effortlessly, generating a sudden surface tension with only the faintest outward ripple. Jonah smiled. The waitress came by with fresh coffee, and Jonah launched right into it.

"Listen, man, I've been thinking. Octavio wants to go down to Brazil, and he thinks I should come along."

"You buy your ticket?"

"Not yet, I'm still trying to figure out what I can afford."

"Huh. Why?"

"Because there's nothing left! New York is dead, it's moribund, practically a Connecticut suburb at this point. It's getting to be like you can't breathe. And it's only going to get worse. The wars are never gonna end. The street shit is never gonna go away. And we're still young but it won't last forever, and I want to see more, you know, see the world before . . .before it's too fucking late and the whole thing is underwater or whatever."

Isaac considered this without skepticism or keen interest.

"Well, shit, man. You're Mr. International over here. If the shit appeals to you, go for it."

"I don't know, I mean it's crazy on one level, but what if I regret not doing something that I'll probably never be able to do again?"

Isaac looked past Jonah. For a moment he was completely still, even statuesque. Then he sat back in his chair and let out a loud breath.

"Listen, J., I think you alright, you have a good head on your shoulders— but you know Octavio is crazy, right? I mean, don't get me wrong, he's a great guy, but he's got a . . . man, I don't know . . . he's got this restlessness . . . that you'd best be mindful of. I'd say he needs you to go with him just to keep him from doing some crazy shit that will get him killed down there."

"Yeah, I know . . . I know what you mean. But I can handle it."

"You can handle it."

"I can handle my own."

"I don't doubt it—I'm just saying, with Octavio, it ain't about to be just a walk in the park . . . and to be honest it sounds like he probably has his own reasons that got nothing to do with you. It's like GZA says, 'I gotcha back but you best to watch your front.' That's your problem right there. Don't get me wrong, I like Octavio. But you know how he is. Trouble finds him. I'm talkin' some outlandish diplomatic-incident type shit. Brazil? Nigga, you be lucky just to make it to the airport."

Octavio and Isaac had met a couple of times, usually at whatever bar

Jonah had invited them both out to. In theory they should have vibed well, but more often than not Jonah found himself trying to mediate and preempt miscues between the three of them, the minefield of perceived slights or challenges that masculine conversation cannot seem to avoid. This often meant that even if he didn't fully perceive himself to be doing so, he was taking sides. Music was especially unforgiving territory.

As a New Yorker, Octavio felt a homegrown entitlement to hip-hop, a fierce pride that could abide no pretenders, and he brought up his favorites with a defensiveness that they didn't need. Isaac respected, even appreciated, the depth of Octavio's knowledge. But that was as far as he was willing to go. Because there wasn't nothing in the world like being born to it. Cradled and raised in it. He never missed an occasion to remind them that the real home of the music would always be the South. They heard about it all the time because apparently Isaac had never loved and understood what made him Southern until he got to the city. As he saw it, Octavio was like an ambassador of the city. Isaac had talked with Jonah separately about his problems with some of the black administrators at his school, the ones he sensed would have called him country if they could say it to his face. Who kept an attitude but played like it wasn't nothing, like they could afford to deny what they were made of, like it wasn't all those dusty front porches and tiny one-room churches across the South that their families had made their way through and left people behind in. Like the South wasn't the lifeblood that made everything how it was in the first place. He was always complaining to Jonah about the way they talked, the way they leaned over you with their corporate-seminar lingo. Isaac said he hadn't seen a square mile so ignorant, so dissonant and confused about how to live, as the core of the rotten apple between the bottom of Central Park and Canal Street. He wouldn't dispute Octavio's claims to NYC's hip-hop bona fides. But as far as he was concerned, the South was never wrong when it came to the sound. New York didn't know shit about drop-tops and candy paint. And there would come a day when the South finally had its say. When all that funk leaking out of Houston and Atlanta would bubble up like an unstoppable lava. Rising up out the Louisiana low-rises of Calliope and Magnolia. Pumping the full repertoire of low life into every nook and cranny of George Bush's patriot-acting U.S.A. Flooding it with criminal hieroglyphics and underworld lore cooked up in dank bedrooms and basements. Exorbitant odes to pimpology served up on mellifluous flows. Mortuary tales of the long drug wars of the nineties rattling a trunk on the outskirts of Memphis where a box Caprice with a pint of Crown Royal in the dash creeps through the twilight bumping Tupac's "Lord Knows." That bass turned all the way up, soaked in so much pain it slows the heart.

Despite their territorial and musicological disputes, Isaac and Octavio got along all right enough, and in certain moments Jonah even felt a spark of mutual understanding between them that *he* was fundamentally left out of. Sometimes they would suddenly lock in and start trading bars, flipping back and forth, sometimes pulling from tracks that he recognized, or thought he recognized, and sometimes breaking out into a mutual hilarity that Jonah couldn't parse. On the other hand, now and then Octavio would go out on a fiery tirade, causing people to stare and bartenders to call for the bouncer, and Isaac would always refuse to move, shake his head, directing a look squarely at Jonah like *this your man,* disowning any association with either of them. For Jonah they read like devastating verdicts on him as a person, throwing into question how he carried himself along and across the color line, a potential laser beam that could appear at any time, snapping subtextual lines of force together with sudden, icy coherence.

Isaac would switch off sometimes, his whole frame of mind gone to a place where he was only half in the room, following the scene from afar. Jonah could tire of Octavio's high-strung energy just as easily. But he also felt a special closeness there. They shared a fanatical love of film; besides, Octavio's eccentricity appealed to him, he interpreted it as an assertion of defiant personal freedom. It did not occur to him that Isaac might resent that very freewheeling quality as something he could not afford himself.

And this hairline fracture running beneath the surface of things extended to an unnamed reserve between Isaac and Jonah. It was never a resentment exactly, although Isaac hinted once that he might well have gotten his much tougher assignment, in a much rougher part of the city, on account of his dark skin—though of course it would be impossible for him to locate exactly when or by whom this calculation had been made. Isaac would just say stuff like that. "Color just has to be navigated, bro, it's sad but we got to face that shit." He told Jonah that it was like a student going to a math exam with formulas programmed into his advanced calculator. Like a cheat code that allowed you to skip certain levels, defeat seemingly impossible bosses. For Isaac it had nothing to do with sincerity, or even character. It was more of a naturally expected thing, like a weather pattern, something he felt he'd been primed his entire life to see and to recognize whenever it came across his path. The light-skinned ones. Always on their way, somehow effortlessly floating upward, buoyed by currents seen and unseen, sliding past the glass doors and showing up on the other side and waving back, always insisting everything was the same, even though everything was different—for them.

Isaac appeared to brood and consider the general mess of things. He was always the type who took his time while he searched for the right thing to say—so that when he had framed it for himself it ended up coming out blunt, not because he was imprecise, but because his tone always had an intimidating air of Solomonic judgment baked in. Tell it plain. That was his instinct, his way of keeping shit real.

"So you think I should go?" asked Jonah.

"I didn't say that. But I do think you've already made up your mind."

"And I can't convince you to come with."

"Shit . . . there you go."

"What? You're always talking about how you hate the city."

"Look, J., I'm an American. This is where I belong. I think you're used to existing between cultures. It's good for you. Traveling is a natural extension of that. But me, I got to fight on the home front. I know it's not glamorous, but it's real. It's real to me."

Isaac took a sip of his coffee. His composure was unwavering.

"You're not bored with this place? I mean, the same shit, the same violence, the same stories over and over?"

"Bored? I'm not bored. It's the rest of the country that's bored. They've all been shocked into numbness. We live in a blasé culture right now. Straight up. Turn on the TV any time, day or night, and prove me wrong. It's a way of protecting ourselves against something. I don't know what it is. But that's exactly why I need to be here. Someone has to fight back. And the truth is, it doesn't help anything, you leaving. You run away from your teaching, but also your friends, your people. I mean, call me old-fashioned, but I still believe in the struggle, and not in some bullshit flag-waving sense. I mean in that you build yourself around a community and take responsibility for it, own it, make a good old-fashioned contribution."

"I know what you're saying. And you're not wrong. But don't you ever feel suffocated? Like, it's too big, too vast for anything we do to count? Like the atmosphere is poisoned? It's not in one thing or one group of people. It's everywhere you look. And there's this feeling of 'Fuck it, man!' Just get out. See something new, be somewhere else."

"I see it another way, J. I mean for me, it's all right here. You can live a whole life right here in Harlem and never know the half of it. I mean, look at Albert Murray. My man is still living right here in the Lenox Houses. I don't need to go find the rest of the world, let the rest of the world find themselves . . . I'm trying to fuck with this music shit, and this is where it's at here, now, and it's about us, like it's always been, and the only place you can find the realness is in these same streets. In our history, J. There's so much richness we have that no one has even touched yet."

"Yeah, there's richness, and you know what we do with it, we throw that shit away like it don't mean nothin." We both know what happened in New Orleans. Gave this country our culture and they let us drown on live television! They Wolf Blitzer you and then it's so long, folks. Moving like piranhas. Feed on the body and they're gone. No one cares about our losses, and you can't make them.

"Hey man, Kanye said it." Isaac leaned back with his arms folded. "The president don't care about black folks. Like we didn't know already. So yeah. You right, so far as it goes. But who needs they opinion anyways? I don't need George Bush to care—I don't need none of these fools one way *or* the other. The way I see it the culture stands for me and I can stand on that. What you so upset about anyhow? Our shit has survived bigger storms than this. Our shit is official. Always has been. Official down to the bone gristle. Made outta gutbucket bayou back-porch church sweat and grease all up in it. Built hand to hand. Built outta nothing and no way. They tried to lock us up but we did it anyhow. Did for this country. And did for us. I seen niggas bounce back straight outta county and make that shit sound like a cool million. You understand what I'm saying. I ain't 'bout to start feeling sorry for myself now. Shit, with what ma dukes been through? Her mother, her grandparents? No hope, just run away somewheres? Is that what you gonna tell the kids you teach?"

Jonah, already defeated, interjected anyway: "I don't know *what* I'm teaching them. I don't know that anything I can teach them would even make a difference."

"You lying, bro. You know they watch and listen to every word come out your mouth. You just mad because you don't really want to be there."

Jonah winced and failed to make any reply. Isaac, seeing that he had hit a nerve, shifted away as if to indicate he wouldn't dwell.

"Listen, I'm just saying. How you know what's around the bend? What if the best days for New Orleans is yet to come? What if we only just getting started—only just starting to get the conditions we need to make this place really work out the way it's supposed to? You talking all this apocalypse. Everywhere I go it's the same racket. I got these *Wall Street Journal* dudes on the subway, breathing on me and shit, yakking about how we're under attack by 'Islamofascists,' whatever *that* means. Every Asian kid in the country is convinced it's the black kid done jacked his spot in college when we got more brothers in jail than finished the twelfth grade. Meanwhile everybody mad at the war. But only cause the Iraqis not takin' the ass-whooping and quick drive-by they was supposed to. So I'm not buying none of it. Maybe we're all just a little screwed-up right now. Maybe we grew up thinking we were special. Turns out we ain't. Now the whole world gotta catch hell, and even the Dixie Chicks ain't safe? Nah, I'm not having it. Say you're right, and we are the undertakers for this doomed country, and yeah, even this doomed planet. Well, a pallbearer should try to get the damn funeral right. I ain't running nowhere. And I'm not complaining neither. I got to build from what I know. I love my people, I love our music, the whole thing, man, my everything. Imma stand on that."

The coffee shop was filled with light bouncing off simmering coffee pots. The wide steel fan in the corner shuffled sticky air without providing any relief.

"Let's get out of here," Jonah said. "You want to go for a walk?"

"Sure. I don't mind heading down the West Side, but let's go up first so we can take that path, you know, the one that goes through the campus."

They walked together up Amsterdam Avenue along the outer ramparts of Columbia. The weather was cooling off into evening; fit young students jogged by or stood around laughing in small huddled groups. They cut into the main section of the campus and sat down on the steps facing Butler Library. The sun was going down to Union City. Warm rays bathed the library's massive frontal colonnade, catching the light like a massive neoclassical grill. They stared across the patchy turf where commencement tent poles had bruised the grass below the pantheon chiseled into the facade: Homer. Sophocles. Plato. Aristotle. White teeth. Washington's fake smile. Harvested out the mouth of his slaves. Jonah lit a cigarette.

"You know something?" Isaac said.

"What's that?"

"This is the only place, I mean it's the only thing, that could ever make me wish I were white. Nothing else. And I'm not saying I do. But I've felt it before. Man, when you first lay your eyes on a nice college campus, and you see the girls reading on the steps, and everyone's got this flair about them, like they belong there, like they've always belonged there. I look at it, and I wish, man, I wish I could feel that."

Jonah knew inexactly what he meant. He said nothing.

4

June was moving closer to July and Jonah still hadn't given Octavio an answer. It wasn't like Jonah was doing anything that required him to be in New York, but Isaac wasn't wrong in questioning why Jonah should spend money he didn't really have. Surely he could do something. When he wasn't writing in his journal now he was scribbling out a loony screenplay for a secret-agent spoof movie about black underground radicals with a plan to set up a revolutionary resistance base in Paris that gets foiled when they discover a time machine that would allow them to control the future but that they end up using against each other instead in a series of backstabbing leggy entanglements with white women. He would pitch it as Solaris meets Austin Powers, preferably to be directed by Melvin Van Peebles. He thought about asking Isaac to collaborate. Maybe he could do the soundtrack? But when Isaac did catch him typing away furiously in his room one evening, Jonah lost his nerve and made up a story about a set of school reports and self-assessments.

Summery days full of hypothetical promise flowed by uneventfully, until one morning Jonah got a call from his father in Paris. In a strained and uncharacteristic voice, he instructed Jonah to pack an overnight bag and meet him the next day at the airport rental lot in Newark. His father's brother, Vernon H. Winters, had died of a heart attack at his home in Pleasantville, New Jersey. He was flying home for the funeral, his father said. Home was a word he rarely used.

Jonah didn't know his uncle Vernon. "Vern," as his father referred to him, was unmarried and childless (a striking anomaly by family standards), and he and Jonah's father hadn't gotten along. But then, his father didn't seem to get along with anyone. Toward Uncle Vernon, though, Jonah suspected his father of harboring some degree of envy. Vernon was considered the successful sibling in the Winters family. He had worked his way up at a local division of Honeywell, one of the biggest employers in South Jersey. The only time Jonah had met him was also the first and only other time Jonah had been down to Pleasantville. It was for his grandfather's funeral. His uncle was one of the pallbearers, and he stood out to Jonah because he had never seen old-fashioned conked hair before. He remembered his uncle's long, thin frame, his severe expression, the sweat dripping down at his temple, and his thin mustache, wet with tears. Jonah was still a boy then, and had been completely overwhelmed by the event, by all the faces of family that he didn't know, by the rawness of the emotion and the clamor of the church, and also because it was the same week Tupac was killed in Vegas, and the two events had become linked as a period of deep confusion and mourning in his mind. Now it was Vernon's turn to be put to rest, and it would be Jonah's father shouldering the box of his estranged older brother. Jonah would take the train out to Newark and then they would drive the rest of the way down to Pleasantville together.

The next morning, he packed and made his way to Penn Station. In the New Jersey Transit lounge, swirling crowds of commuters struggled against the stale ventilation, dodging and slipping around ragged drifters, counterterrorism units patrolling in military fatigues, and deceptive low-pressure zones where bodies people had given up on lay slumped against the side of a wall or sprawled on the steps under faux mosaics memorializing the old Penn Station, the one modeled on the Baths of Caracalla that they tore down in the sixties. It occurred to Jonah that Vernon, as the older brother, must have walked through those grand archways as a boy, holding his parents' hands. Madison Square Garden, where Spike Lee watched the Knicks play, now stood in its place.

Once he was in the frigid railcar, everything was efficient and swift.

Only a few minutes from departure, they were rolling under the Hudson in a tunnel built under conditions he could scarcely fathom, but which must have cost untold lives for every yard he now traveled. The train banked up over the meadowlands and refineries and trucking depots around Secaucus, stopped in the brick carcass of downtown Newark, and then proceeded to the gray terminal complexes of the airport.

His father was waiting in the rental-lot complex. He was calmer than Jonah expected, as if the situation brought a kind of neutrality to their relationship that made it easier for his father to be around him. It helped that his father had logistics to keep him occupied. They got in a midnight-blue Ford Focus, looped through the interlocking airport clovers, and merged onto the Jersey Turnpike.

After they settled into the road, Jonah's father told him to reach into his travel bag and pull out a stack of CDs.

"Which one you want me to put on?"

"I don't own no jive records, boy. Just put one in. We gotta have *something* to make up for this bullshit ride they gave me. Five times I told them over the phone, I want a Lexus and I ain't payin no goddamn fees. Now Avis tells me all they have left is a Ford Focus. They got me paying for this golf cart when I was supposed to show up pushing a Lexus. Jonah, I'm telling you. Why you think I left this messed-up country in the first place? Why I left? Because a Nee-gro can't get a fair deal. I mean how—how? And see, they know I gots the mo-nay. They just want to ruin my day a little is all. But I ain't gonna let em. Boy, you listening to me? Don't ever let them ruin your day. Give an inch, and they will get you everytime. Not a thing, not a damn thing changed since I left. Rental man tellin me this the best-selling car in America. Like imma take advice *from you*— the guy grinning in my face cause he clocked in on time at the Liberty Hertz rental desk this morning."

"How 'bout this right here?" Jonah ventured.

A smile, the first he had seen since they had left the lot, beamed back at him.

"Okay. Now you talking."

As they pulled out of a tollbooth in the southbound lanes, the familiar piano chords of one of the Gap Band's Greatest Hits sent *soul-stirring* tremors through the little Ford. They nudged along for a while in heavy traffic, canyoned between big rigs, barracuda-grilled SUVs, Hummers fresh off the assembly line and ready for Baghdad beyond the Green Zone or a P. Diddy video shoot. *You light my fire . . .* The traffic thinned as they passed the gaslights and townships of the Jersey midlands with their names blazoned on the water towers *. . . I feel alive with you, baby . . .*

His dad was suddenly saying, "Your uncle Vernon could get down, boy, ooohhhweee, Jonah, when he was liquored up, like the time he started dancing at our wedding reception. Lord, I can see it now, like it was yesterday. He had your grandpappy's funky chicken legs, and he could work them things too. You had to see him out there, puttin' moves on 'em." Jonah saw a wet line on his father's cheek. The Band harmonized, urging someone not to *keep running in and out of my life."* Jonah lowered his window a crack and squinted at the road ahead. Warm soupy gusts of chemical fumes and car exhaust buffeted the soulful audio-love inside. They were hurtling toward the prickling points of holding tanks, pharmaceutical plants, the megalith forms of malls and factory-discount outlets, RKO-style radio masts rising into irradiant haze. Everywhere and nowhere, isolated suburban lights winked like fireflies as they sailed down the trunk roads of the Garden State through the summer dusk.

Pleasantville was a residential community that fed off the perpetual transit of gamblers, criminals, and retirees passing through on their way to Atlantic City. His father had booked a room for them in a budget motel in the shadow of the casinos. But with the roads increasingly snarled in beach traffic, they decided to take a break and stop for dinner at the Walt Whitman Service Area outside Cherry Hill before making the turn on Route 40 that would take them toward the ocean. Over fried chicken and curly fries, his father started loosening up.

"You know Vernon never married?"

"Yeah, I know."

"But he had a woman. I'm talking back in the day. Before you were born. Wonderful woman named Evelyn Jones. One of the strongest, most beautiful women I ever seen. You would have liked her. I know she would have liked

40

you. She was so damn smart. Her and Vernon met at night classes at Atlantic Community College. She came from poor folks, at a time when Atlantic City was beginning to decline, but she was doing good, you know, and she had a smile that just . . . it just had you wide open soon as she walked in the room. And your uncle Vernon was gone on this woman. But, you know, she was very proud . . . She had that poor working pride, tough as nails, boy. She wouldn't bend, and she never asked for help. Always figured things for herself, did things her own way. And that was okay with Vern, but what happened was she was so proud, she wouldn't say when she wasn't well. They had been seeing each other almost a year, and Vern is in the bathroom and sees some blood in the sink. Come to find out she'd been sick for months but hadn't allowed that she was, didn't want to bother him about it and figured neither of them could afford the doctor. Well, Vern loved this woman, Jonah. He says, 'You have to see the doctor. I'll pay for it.' Finally, he convinces her to go, and you know what, she has a cancer, but now they got it too late. And she got real sick, and Vern took care of her and then moved with her to be by her family. She died the same year. Like that. Wilted and all shriveled up . . . it was terrible. Your uncle, he never really recovered from Evelyn. In fact, he kind of retreated from the whole family, kind of like me, but in a different way. Threw himself into work. I would hear sometimes about a woman here and there, but it never lasted more than a few months. A few times I think because he was abusive, wasn't treating them right. Didn't treat himself right either. You know, I wasn't so surprised when I heard. He's had a lot of problems the last few years, gained a lot of weight, always seeing doctors. Tellin' him he has to exercise and all that. We had so many arguments about him needing to get better that I finally just gave up. I didn't want you to be around his troubles. For a long time, I was angry at him for having put the family through such concern about his well-being, for his refusal to get better, but as I flew over here, I got to thinking that maybe his depression went deep. For him, there was no light at the end of the tunnel. It was like he only had that one love, and that was it. And that loss came between him and the world, and between us, and now . . ."

His father made a gesture to finish the sentence. They sat for a while in silence, watching the crowds circulate through the eatery line with their trays.

His father snapped back into logistical mode. "Come on, I want to get us to the motel early so you can get a good night's sleep. I want you up and sharp for the service tomorrow."

The following day, under the beleaguering Jersey mugginess of an overcast summer's morning, Jonah and his father joined the rest of their kinfolk in a long shimmering line of wide-crowned brims, flitting fans, tie clips, pocket squares, brooches, impeccable footwear, peppery wafts of cologne and grand-motherly jasmine, that overflowed the parking lot and spilled over onto the corner of Elm Avenue. Muted gasps of delight rose in the air as cousins and elders exchanged strong effusive clasps. As with all large families, a peculiar energy hovered over any Winters reunion, and it gained in strength now, as the reunited prepared to enter Mount Zion Victory Baptist Church for Vernon Winters's homegoing.

Since the time of Grandfather Earl's passing, they had multiplied consider-ably. Jonah had no idea he had so many cousins, aunts, folks who had driven all the way up from Florida, from the Carolinas, from DC and Baltimore, down from Mount Vernon and New Rochelle. And Vernon was beloved by the people of Pleasantville. A city councilman, members of the local school board where he had donated heavily to after-school programs; even two or three white folks showed up from the Honeywell office and were greeted just as warmly.

The whole service, Jonah was in a daze. The minister spoke. The siblings gave testimonials. They sang "Lord Keep Me Day by Day" because it was known to have been one of Uncle Vernon's favorites. The piano and the choir led the assembled, old folks and young, family and friends, neighbors and coworkers, in sending Vernon Winters home.

> *I'm just a stranger here*
> *And I'm traveling through this barren land*

Rapturous vowels thundered around their heads and the rolling march of foot stomps charged the air with the acknowledgment of the one whose journey was won, who watched them now, from a building not made by hand.

Then it was announced that a young lady, Jonah's cousin Esther, would line a hymn she had practiced for the occasion: "A Charge to Keep I Have." Little Esther couldn't have been more than sixteen or seventeen, and her range and tone weren't perfect or even sweet exactly, but she laid it out. Everyone was on their feet and called back to her. *Go 'head.* They clapped her on. *Lord, Jesus.* The voices raised the hymn together until its unearthly roar was only praise and the praise took the body before it took the voice.

> *To serve the present Age*
> *My calling to fulfill*

From out her tiny frame, songful Esther moaned the lines with utter ferocity. No one could deny. She was there with him, and she brought the church with her in her singing. Jonah felt all the hairs on his neck stand on end and the shivers run down, and he saw that even his father was crying.

> *O may it all my pow'rs engage*
> *To do my Master's will!*

Esther stretched it out. *Mmmhhhmmm. Yes, Lord.* She stretched it out. She left nothing, allowed no one to feel they were not hand in hand with the one they had come to see off to the other world. *Somebody give Gawd some praise for that one,* someone shouted. And the church gave forth.

When the pallbearers emerged, the sun had broken through and glinted off the chrome trim detailing the hearse, and off the waiting Cadillac Escalades and Lincoln Town Cars and the sunglasses of so many men in dark suits you would have thought a statesman were passing through. They had lined the street and spilled over into the parking lot of the Rite Aid, which faced the church. Uncle Vernon was buried just a few minutes away in the family plot at Greenwood Cemetery, a modest burial ground between Washington and Martin Luther King Jr. Avenues. They had a spot for him next to the elders, Earl and Liza, who rested together. After the burial, there was a reception at his aunt Ella's house, and Jonah found himself pressed into a near-continuous embrace as paper plates piled high with a seemingly never-ending procession of sweet potato pie and oxtail and fried chicken and peas and greens and all the cake you could eat to feed the riotous laughter, tale-telling, well-wishing, and greetings and goodbyes. It was moving and exhausting all at once.

When they finally left a little after midnight, Jonah's father, who'd had a bit to drink, asked him to drive, which he did, rolling very precisely within five of the limit at all times, the music soft and no words between them, all the way back to Atlantic City. When they got to the motel, instead of getting out of the car, his father rolled down the window and lit a cigarette. After a moment, Jonah took one from his own pack, and they sat that way in the motel parking lot, looking like a couple of gangsters. Jonah's father looked like he had something to say, and Jonah waited for him to say it. Finally, his father took an envelope out of his coat and placed it on the dashboard.

"This is for you, from Vernon. He left you and all your cousins, each and every one of them, a portion of what he had, what he made for himself. That's a remarkable thing. A great gift, and I don't want you to take it lightly. There are a lot of ways to go about life. No matter which way you go, you're gonna need money. And, more importantly, you're gonna need to know how to handle money. When he was sick, your uncle decided to make some decisions about what he wanted for after he was gone. And he wrote it all out. Take that envelope, it's yours. I have no control of what you do with its contents. But as your father, I'm asking—no, I'm telling you, son, think on it. Think on it careful now. Remember, this man worked hard for that money. Nothing came free to him in life. Nothing comes to no one free."

With that, his dad stepped out of the car, leaving Jonah with the envelope. He thought about opening it there but felt no rush to do so. He exited the vehicle and locked it for the night, then headed toward the waterfront.

The boardwalk was eerily vacant. Down the shoreline, the lights of the Taj Mahal loomed in the murky distance like an anglerfish. A woman rolled by in a Power Chair, indifferent to his gaze. He had walked a bit down the boardwalk before he gave up and headed back inland. On Atlantic Avenue, he came to the Breezy Point, a tiki-themed joint just off the strip. It was almost as devoid of people as the boardwalk. The lounge area had big bay windows facing the Econo Lodge Riviera, and he took up a seat there. Kanye's "Gold Digger" was playing at a tepid volume on speakers behind the bar. A suite of large, muted television screens were running SportsCenter highlights, while the screen farthest away, at the end of the bar, showed a news story about a unit of marines getting ambushed in the Korangal Valley. A waitress appeared to take his order. A Braves tomahawk was visible above her tiki-themed apron, and she had a tattoo of an ankh on her inner wrist. She was too attractive for Breezy Point, but perhaps not attractive enough—or, rather, light enough—for the casino floor, especially at the Taj Mahal.

"What can I get you?"

"Do you have something not too floral but not too bitter—actually, forget it, do you have Budweiser?"

"Is that a question or an order?"

"Maybe both?"

She smiled forgivingly and walked away, leaving Jonah to turn his attention to the envelope in his hands. Inside there were two separate sheets. One was a letterheaded set of instructions to get in touch with Rhonda Rollins, a Philadelphia-based attorney. The other was a plain paper letter autopersonalized to his attention, evidently formatted in an outdated version of Microsoft Word. As he looked these over, the waitress returned with his beer. He thanked her and looked around. As far as Jonah could tell, he was her only customer. He could tell, too, that she was watching him examine the materials in his hands. It didn't matter. He took a sip and began to read.

To my nephew, JONAH WINTERS,

If you are reading this, I have passed. Attached to this letter, you, like all of your cousins, will find instructions with my lawyer for how to retrieve the inheritance I have left you. Since I love all of you equally, it is my wish that you all receive equal shares. Since there are many of you, this means nobody is going to walk away with a fortune. I do feel it's best this way. I would have liked to leave you each $10,000, but with the tax and the lawyers and fees that must be paid, it could not be that much. Instead, you are each receiving $6,500. Whatever you may think, this is a very great deal of money. If you are wise, any one of you can use it to build a company or start a family or get an education. Yet these are not conditionals. Only YOU can decide how best to use these funds. I believe in hard work, and I hope all of you do too. I believe in education, and I hope all of you will try to go to college and make your parents proud. I also believe in offering a helping hand. And so I want to leave you, instead of with more instructions, with a little story, a true story from my childhood.

When I was a boy, your grandfather (my father), Earl Winters, worked in the casinos in Atlantic City. It was a grand destination back then, not the seedy place it has become. But back then, things for us were also harder. In the summer, me and my brothers used to pick up white folks at the Steel Pier and push them around in rickshaws for a nickel. I went to the Indiana Avenue School, which was for colored students only. I liked school, but I was often in trouble. When we'd get into trouble, sometimes we'd have to go sit or stand in the hallways with the school janitor, a big man everyone called Pop. One day, because I had been bad, I was sent to "cool it," and I found myself sitting with Pop and talking. He wanted to know what was bothering me. I told him these kids were bugging me, that I felt stuck here. And he said, "Well, you can't let these things get you down. You can't let things stand in your way." He said, "You know, if I'd been that way, I never would have become a ballplayer." Well, I had no idea Pop had played ball. But Pop's real name was John Henry Lloyd, and he was one of the greatest baseball players to ever play the game. He was a real legend back in the days before Jackie Robinson, when black folks played in the Negro League. I was stunned.

"And now you're here?" I asked him. I was a kid, so I didn't know any better, and that must have hurt him the way I said it. But he wasn't bothered by it at all.

"Sure, I'm here," he said. "But I've also been there. I did those things. I set those records. I heard the crowds shout my name. No one can take from me what I done. Where I've been. What I seen. And even if all the records of all my games were lost, and nobody even remembered my name, God would know, and I would know, and I am well with him. You see boy, time is like God's great wax cylinder. He keeps track of everything, and what I've done and who I am are fixed that way for good, like a line engraved in God's hand." Pop had huge hands, and after that talk, he got up and took my little one in his, and he walked me back to class. To this day, I have not forgotten that. Make your lives whatever you will with where my helping hand will take you. Don't go making excuses. Work hard. Do something righteous with your life.

Faithfully,

Your Uncle Vernon

They drove back to Newark the next day and dropped off the car at the airport lot where they had picked it up. His father was very agitated now, and he ended up arguing with the clerk about the cost of the rental. Then suddenly it was time to part, and they were hugging warmly, Jonah assuring his father he would stay in touch. He felt a sense of relief once he was on the train heading back to New York, but when he did finally reach Penn Station, a terrible sense of emptiness overwhelmed him, a void in the midst of the surging crowds. Back at his apartment, he found Isaac eating takeout and listening to records. They talked a bit about the funeral. Isaac's grandparents were still living in Detroit.

"So I guess you haven't gone through it like that," Jonah said.

Isaac looked away toward the window with their fire escape. When he answered, it was without looking back and in a tone of voice Jonah hadn't heard before.

"Nah, I been to a lot of funerals. Too many."

Jonah had willingly let his phone battery die on the trip and hadn't charged it for days, so he assumed he would have a million messages and reminders waiting on him. It turned out, apart from reminders to pay his phone bill, the only one trying to reach him was Octavio, who was trying to get him to confirm he was down for the trip to Brazil. He must have left thirty messages ranging from one word to rambling non sequiturs to just random background scratches and a huff.

"So what's the word?"

Because Jonah hadn't replied, Octavio had followed with, *"I'm going to assume this is a no."*

Jonah rang his number, not expecting him to pick up.

"Yo. Why've you been avoiding me?"

"I had some family stuff to take care of. I'm in, actually. Let's do this."

Jonah could hear Octavio's voice change from grim to glorious as he first sputtered disbelief before whooping his enthusiasm.

"Alright, then, alright," said Jonah, trying to calm his friend down. "So when we leaving?"

"How's July 1?"

"'Til?"

"Open ticket."

"Open ticket?"

"Yeah man, we come back when we're done, not when we feel like we're supposed to. I can even get us tickets through my friend's mom, who's a travel agent. You good to pay me back?"

"Yeah, I'll cut you a check next I see you. When can that be?"

"There's a launch party for a literary journal this Friday," Octavio replied. "A couple friends are in the first issue."

Jonah could imagine the kind of time he'd have. Literary parties were infamously the worst gatherings of any kind in New York City. You could guarantee zero dancing, stilted conversation, nasty sexual tension, quipsters, conservative outfits, liberal politics, and much playing at being adult. There would be enough booze to get everyone seriously sloshed, but not enough of a good atmosphere for anyone to willingly want to be there. Token minorities were de rigueur.

"I don't know. Could be a drag."

"C'mon, man, these parties are for networking. I'm doing you a favor. Plus, you're the one who wants to be a writer. It'd be good for you to meet real ones."

Octavio's dig was a shot that should not go unchecked, but he didn't have the energy to take up the fight. Besides, a night out would take his mind off the funeral, the money, the command of little Esther's voice, the solemn charge to keep.

"Alright then," he said. "I'll be there."

5

In New York everything that matters occurs as part of a "scene." Octavio had made inroads in the film scene and these networks overlapped significantly with the adjacent literary one. Jonah would pick him up after his shift got out at the Reggio, and they would fortify themselves at a local dive before making an appearance at an apartment in cozy book-lined apartment in Cobble Hill or Fort Greene or a chic loft in Tribeca. One of the bigger events of the season was the launch party for a new lit mag with a radical name and a sleek green cover. Octavio was tight with one of the founding editors whom he had known from his school days. The comrades funding the publication and staffing the key positions on its masthead reflected the city's supercon-ducting private school to Ivy League pipeline. The word on the street was that the most talented writers would be gravitating to its pages, attracted by the considerable sums on offer for fairly predictable content and by the "hot" interns prominently featured on the magazine's elegant, minimalist website.

The launch took place at the magazine's new offices, located in a refash-ioned Greenpoint warehouse right on the East River. Octavio and Jonah rolled up a little after eleven, entering into a scene that was sumptuous and well attended. The guests were balkanized into tiny groupuscules, each in their corners, accentuating the negative space of the floor plan, which in city psychology was also, of course, a supreme assertion of luxury.

All around the open cross section of the loft were the faces of the sad young literary men, each in their own way terribly preoccupied with the unbearable whiteness of being. Jonah knew them. Not personally, but almost by osmosis; and he felt a measure of ironic sympathy for their plight. They had self-consciously constructed themselves as a force for good. They had good politics, went to good schools (where he had first crossed paths with the tribe); they were good readers of the best reviews (which they hoped to emulate and rival), copies of which further advantaged a vintage mid-century credenza. They all wanted change and hated racism: principally in politics, and geographically in the vast hinterlands (starting in Long Island and New Jersey). The greatest shame of all was the racism in their own families. Sometimes, a good few drinks in, they wanted to confess those unpardonable horror stories in hot breathy convulsions that Jonah had some practice in compassionately, but firmly, evading.

He felt for them because what could be wrong with them, really? They wanted what he wanted, more or less. To see good ideas and good art triumph, especially their own. The only problem was that the ascendant power blocs didn't seem to care a whit what they said. Those with the real power—the consulting firm types, the I-Bankers, the DC apparatchiks and the math majors gone to Wall Street that they knew from college—wanted art, if they ever thought about it at all, to be a larger, more expensive version of a desktop background. They were too busy rigging up massive systems that would liquidate the old printing-press jobs to worry about what was being said by the last cohort to have them.

The sad young literary men were the most despised men of their time. They held a declining share of even those few perches they had once held like grand viziers in the days of the Plimptons, the Mailers, the Updikes; when shuttling between mistresses in Connecticut and dipping down to Greenwich Village to drink with famous war correspondents was all in a day's work. Most of the top jobs in their circles were held by women now, and the proclivities associated with fashionable narcotics were starting to be scrutinized and sometimes even openly deplored. There was still money, of course, but without status it was an enfeebled collateral glare. They formed, ironically enough, a genuinely besieged class; and presumably in their minds they constituted an oppressed one too, since whatever largesse and goodwill among the Midtown Maecenases remained was reserved strictly for identities that would appear charitably treated upon its disbursement. Since they would never be in that number, the spoils of a wilting branch had to be fought over ever more bitterly. It was the main reason such events were to be avoided. Over a shitty mixed drink, the knives come out: friends and colleagues cruelly humiliating each other while desperately trying to appear relaxed and popular. There was no direct danger to Jonah in this; he would be safely ignored. Unless he spoke up. But to what end? It was perfectly typical for him to spend a great deal of these tense soirées finding ways to say nothing at all.

Instead, he listened. To the cornered woman agreeing overenthusiastically; to the political argument; to the chopped ticker-tape phrases indexing the fait divers of industry gossip. Apparently, African child-soldier narratives were trending and there was speculation that one of them might snag a Pulitzer. The perennial topic, however, remained real estate. And on this point, there was much woe. For it is a truth generally observed that everywhere white money moves, it does so in the same settler-colonial pattern. Like so many before them, the sad young literary men had attempted to desert from the advancing army. They had crossed the river and set up camp in the desolate streets of postindustrial Brooklyn, only to find like *Dances with Wolves* that the army was close on their heels. Within a few years, the frontier would be closed. The chill of enclosure and amenities would dominate this once savage ground. It would be ready for unparalleled comfort, saplings and lit walkways, constant surveillance, delivery of goods and services, yoga studios, the good life in all of its passionless expenditure. The sad young men would have to decamp to a farther zone or give up the struggle and put their trust funds into homesteads of their own, get tattoos, strollers, take comfort in ethically sourced and shockingly expensive garlic scapes. Of all the seven and a half billion people in the world—who else carried such a burden?

On the other hand, didn't they, on balance, have a rather desirable existence? The things in this apartment *were* expensive and they *were* pretentious. But they were also nicely made; they looked cool, better yet they looked right. Hadn't Jonah, in truth, been trying to make his own apartment look essentially just like it, only on the cheap? And couldn't he, if he made the right connections, perhaps at this very party, have a loft of his own one day? Sure, it would mean living in a place where he'd have to turn the stereo down at ten o'clock or have the cops called on him for a noise complaint. And the cops might even be called on him as he was trying to enter the building, if, say, he decided to wear a hoodie. And it would mean having to listen to *This American Life* and other boring but *important* shows on NPR in order to make small talk over Pabst Blue Ribbon and hummus. But wouldn't that possibly be worth it?

Even in its decline, there was a lingering aroma of achievement in this lettered world. Its nicer and more adult clothes; its confident intelligence and cosmopolitan circulation. It would snugly envelop his life, like a boutique-hotel bathrobe, making it richer and ready to be enjoyed discreetly, without the loud vulgarity that some other lifestyles would necessarily require. And naturally he would bring to it just enough of a mocha touch, the crucial note, so that his own contribution would be immensely and inevitably appreciated, perhaps without him even having to try that hard. With the right glasses (those being naturally the correct accessory), he might pull off a move like his father had in the art world—propping himself up on the stepladder of white guilt and taking the journey for all it was worth.

Jonah was drinking steadily, standing next to Octavio, doing his best to look interested and supportive as they talked to Sasha, an attractive reader for the magazine. The three were comparing college experiences, and Sasha was explaining the "rapey" social scene and how many times she had blacked out at parties. They had moved on to a vividly confessional discussion about antidepressants and feats rumored to have been accomplished under the influence of Adderall when Jonah excused himself to make an expeditionary foray back to the beverage lineup.

By now he was three or four drinks in, operating with a pleasurable motion that felt more graceful than it looked. On his way back to Octavio, a curator from a swanky Chelsea gallery thought she recognized him. She wanted to know what he was doing these days. "Teaching," he said.

"That's great!" she said. And since it was clear she had made a mistake and that he had nothing to offer her, she immediately broke off, leaping like a salmon toward whoever had the real pull, maneuvering adroitly across the trench lines of her possibilities.

Jonah needed to get some air. Smokers were directed back to the landing and up an extra flight of stairs that opened to an expansive rooftop. The view was tremendous. Midtown in profile. Power suit lines cutting into the darkness, the whole fabric softly pulsating. There wasn't anyone around. Jonah lit a cigarette and walked to the far ledge.

He thought about Uncle Vernon's letter, what Octavio was saying about cutting out altogether, and what Isaac meant about making oneself responsible to something here, *now*, where it mattered.

His life was absurdly gifted with choices, and here he was, lonely, drunk, growing increasingly bitter. Just then, he felt a tap on his shoulder.

"Excuse me, do you have a light?"

The man asking must have come across the rooftop without a sound. He had what Jonah thought was maybe an Australian accent and fine, pale features that made him suspect the high station and poor diet of English boarding schools. His eyes appeared preternaturally fatigued.

"Yeah, I got you."

"Thanks, mate, so kind. I've been dying for a smoke, and I can't seem to find anyone who does. My god, it's ridiculous, you'd think at a launch party in New York . . ."

"Yeah, times change."

"So, what do you do?"

"I, uh . . . I teach."

"Oh, I see—like in bad areas type of thing?"

"Yeah, something like that. You?"

"I'm an editor at Minos Press."

"Oh. Nice."

"Yeah, I was in banking for years, and then I thought, '*What am I doing?*' You know? I've always loved books, loved reading. So I changed it all up and now I'm practically running the place. Hit the jackpot. You know Esteban Riocabo?"

"I haven't heard of him."

"You will."

"Oh."

"He's going to blow up, mate. Huge, and I'm the one that got him for us at Minos. The thing is, it's all about timing. It's a prestige economy, and what you do is you wait until these writers die, you know, and then their value explodes, right through the roof, man. He's dead, plus he's Latin American, like Uruguayan Mexican, so it's got all the mystique built in. The edge becomes the product, the whole package. Practically markets itself, really."

"Sounds like a good setup."

"Best thing about it is that we bought all the material, and now we can just trickle it out whenever we want, control the buzz around it and so forth, extend the life of the brand, so to speak, so it keeps generating revenue long-term. I expect we'll get about a decade's worth of earnings out of it by the end, if not more. Ah, it's a bloody great view, isn't it?"

Riocabo's editor gestured toward the scintillating skyline and aspirated violently on his smoke as Jonah pondered the view.

"Right, got to be off, then. Thanks for the light, yeah?"

Jonah watched him flick the butt in a high arc toward the street, and then the editor slicked his fingers through his hair as he marched resolutely back to the stairwell and down to the business below.

When he got back to the party, Octavio and Sasha were nowhere to be found. He made himself another drink, downed it, and drank another. People were staring; he didn't give a damn. He was going to get faded, and this shit was free. The luminaries of the literary world and their sour complexions felt as alien and irrelevant as the savage customs of some obscure tribe whose way of life only really tells you how you read your own, how you think, and what you care about—or what you don't care about. An ethnography of rarefied social gatherings in New York City could make an interesting volume someday. Or maybe it wouldn't.

He stumbled out into the night. Traffic honking, hipsters yelling on Bedford Avenue coming at him, nice white couple out on the town. Racist bastards. He hailed a cab and hoisted himself inside. Too hot. The West African up front asked too many questions. "Ay, yo, open the window! Turn the radio up, man! I said turn that shit up!" Hot 97, Funk Flex playing throwbacks. RIP J Dilla tributes still pouring in. Dilla dead at thirty-two. All that Motor City soul leaking out, all that warm fuzz on the tracks he blessed . . . so many things lost and found in hours of head-snapping beats, all those years knocking Tribe, *Illmatic, Only Built 4 Cuban Linx, Uptown Saturday Night*, scattered mixes taped off the radio, the nineties boom bap, with its Christmas chimes, clunky rhymes, and fat piano licks, blowing smoke over the yellow Discman with the skip protection, practicing gangster gestures with the earphones in . . . *Can it be that it was all so simple then?* . . . Mecca to Medina. Harlem to Brooklyn. Queensbridge. Exodus of the Afrocentric Asian. The Sunz of Man. Trife Life. Wu-Tang. The Chef. *Shine like marble. Rhyme remarkable. Time is running out* . . . Ay, man, I said turn that shit up! Rush of lights and blasted air like a wind tunnel . . . we moving. Through the night. Like Gladys. Singing "The Way We Were." *Can it be that it was all so simple then?* . . . What happened? What happened to all that was and all that was supposed to be? All that beauty. What did it all mean? And how would it ever all get remembered? My Nigga! My Nigga! *Time is running out* . . .

The cab hit the bridge, and the clunk knocked him back like a slug to the chest. He drank in the sheet of lights slashing from all sides now, the effect nightmarish, like the strobe of a muted television in another room. A swelling breathless rage seemed on the verge of splitting him apart. Then they were in city traffic again, lurching ahead violently in breakneck spurts. At a slow corner, he had the car pull over, ready to be sick. The cabbie demanded money. *Give him the money. Blood-thirsty vampires. Just needed another drink anyway, whatever was left. Whatever.* So many things incoherent. Like this other man sleeping behind the fucking Citibank planter. He entered another bar. Pricey, glossy sign, beefy arms. A Gorgon manned the cobra-headed taps. Music crashed overhead. Television aspirants, underage girls on safari, squealing, blurting obscenities, ordering Jell-O shots that cost twice what the Mexican barback would make in an hour washing their vomit off the floor later as they passed out in private cars on their way back to the upper echelons that flank Central Park. And then this moronic automaton shoving him out, ready to swing. Outside again, colder than before. Everyone in the street a sad clown. Everything *ugly.* Shrieking homeless man. Poor bastard shoving his raggedy-ass Rocinante under the aquiline noses of the Abercrombie & Fitch flagship. Pale mannequins floating in the twinkling windows. Unbothered as this wretched man, reeking of filth, howls and pounds his fists against the glass.

He was leaning heavily against a wall, breathing hard. Screaming into his cell phone. But there was no call in progress. Who was he dialing? Did he get her digits at the party? Sasha? He sat down in a damp cool place. Next thing it was like his head was leaking. Slush. Toppled, flattened out. The blur was general for some time, he had no idea how long.

A man appeared towering over him. For a moment he was sure it was Uncle Vern, but that couldn't be. Was it his father? No, it was Phineas! It was the jazz pianist! The genius of Phineas watching over, up above his head, playing sweet music in the air. And it was all rhythm. Rhythm! Flowing in time like a river. Like the whole frame, conceived in motion. America, a mighty river rhythm. World moving, pulling everything into its fated direction, debris digested, every broken limb jigged up, dead matter as welcome as the live, as likely to proliferate unspeakable wastelands of ruin as to float the delirious chandelier of a paddleboat. A river rhythm swallowing belly-up even its sucking countercurrents, its bubbling froth nurturing settlements of moss, loosely girdled banks soused in green shades, the long-bearded current animating the living underbelly right down to the bottom. Nothing on solid ground. Everyone floundering, everyone grasping like looters for whatever might be at hand. Not only the poorest but even the richest families in the land busy making a raft for themselves, doing their best to paddle along, facing the wilderness, knowing nothing of where they are, knowing nothing of the way back. Only the slaves holding a tattered map to join the sundered worlds—their vision grown deep. And here was one. Could it be? Yes, Phineas standing overhead, astonishingly tall, like some warrior god of Meroë enrobed in a pulsating sheet of blue light.

"Either he can walk and he goes with you, or we're booking him."

"You bastards! I didn't *do* nothing . . . I'm innocent . . . tell them they can't take me . . . tell them I have *rights* goddamnit . . . I'm a teacher!"

"Look, we don't want to waste our time, but he needs to get off the street."

"I understand the situation, sir, but it's okay, he's with me. I take full responsibility for him. Got my car right around the corner, he won't bother no one, I promise."

"You understand normally we would have to take him in . . ."

"Sir, I understand that perfectly, but I can assure you I can handle my baby cousin. You know how the kids is these days. Ain't like back in the day, right? Hey, you guys probably too young to even recognize me, but, you know, I used to ball back in the day . . . Yeah, in the league, check this one out right here, always keep it in my wallet."

"No shit, hey, check this out."

"So listen, I get this young fella home, and we're all good here, right?"

Phineas, sweet Phineas, always in time, just a little behind the rhythm so that it carries you ahead, carries you away until the level is passed, and the flood is everywhere, and the flood is all things.

6

Nathaniel Archimbald placed the boy on the couch in the living room with a pillow under his head. He went into the kitchen to make some energy drink. In the sink a frying pan streaked with grease lay stranded like a supertanker. No matter. Doing dishes, for Nathaniel, was a pleasing exercise, an operation that allowed him to ventilate his mind, to see before him those magic hands splendidly at work, the rhythm and practiced improvisation like smooth handles on the dribble. When he returned to the living room, the youngster was lying on the rug. *Now how in the hell did he end up on the damn floor?* The kid looked too clean to be a dopehead, dressed in that eccentric preppy style he often saw downtown or in Brooklyn. He found a teacher's ID in the wallet, though that hardly proved anything in New York City.

Nathaniel lightly touched his shoulder, not too hard, but with enough pressure to make sure the boy would feel his hand through his coat.

"Hey, kid."

The boy moaned.

"Look at me."

Jonah turned over, his face nearly plastic from dehydration.

"Where the fuck am I?"

"You in *my* house. So let's get one thing straight. You follow my rules. And I only got three. Rule number one: Watch your mouth. Only person that cusses in this house is me. Keep that up, and you'll find your way out my door with my foot in your ass. Rule number two: This ain't a flophouse. Don't mess with none of my furniture. You get yourself together and stay off my rug."

Jonah sat up. The full force of head-spin and nausea hit him with a wrenching dizziness. "Okay, okay," he said. "What . . . what's rule number three?" he asked, swallowing back a hint of bile rising in his throat.

"Rule number three: When I ask questions, I better get straight answers. I saved your ass from a long night in the Tombs—you can thank me later. For now, we gon' get you back on your feet so you can go about your business. And while we're doing that, you best keep in mind that you a guest in my house. I did you a favor, so you better do as I say. Don't give me no lip, and *don't* get any ideas. Here, take this Advil. Bathroom is down the hall on your right."

Jonah returned feeling less nauseated. His head raged with pain, particularly behind his eyes. There were other pains on his body too, bruising pains he'd have to locate later. His large host offered him a tall, greenish beverage.

"What is this?"

"That there is the good stuff. I call it Nate-o-rade, it's a secret recipe. Gets you squared away quick, never lets me down."

"And who are you?"

"Nathaniel. You can call me Nate. You're Jonah."

"How did yo—"

"Cause I'm Kojak, black. It's called photo ID. In your wallet."

"Right, sure. And you make your own Gatorade—you into fitness and stuff?"

"Fitness? Man, I learned to make this shit before Gatorade even existed. I was a pro athlete, fourteen years shooting hoops in the league. Didn't you notice?"

Nate gestured at the photos and plaques on the wall. Jonah had vaguely registered the museum-like clutter but hadn't mentally brought the content into focus. Now he stood up gingerly and gazed around the room. There his host was, in a Celtics jersey, suspended in midair, going for a layup, a defender with outstretched arms trailing behind him; and there, dribbling with spiderlike angularity; standing with fans and celebrities, holding a trophy of a man helping his teammate up.

"What award is that?"

"Teammate of the Year. Got that during my final year on the court."

"And when was that?"

"A long time ago."

"Why did you leave? You don't look that old."

"Blew out my knee. Any other questions?"

"What do you do now?"

"Coach."

"A lot of ballplayers seem to go right into coaching."

"This is more of a new development. I went overseas for a while after I retired."

"Where did you go?"

"France."

"No shit! Oh, sorry . . . I guess what's funny is that I'm from Paris . . . well, kind of. I mean, I'm American, but I grew up there."

"No shit? So what you back in New York for?"

"My life was too easy, I guess. I was just watching movies all day. I sort of had a girlfriend, but, well . . . it's complicated."

"Sounds cushy. Why did you leave?"

"I don't know. I mean, I do—but it's hard to explain."

"We got time."

As the young man got to talking, Nate examined him closely: the lightness in the eyes, his bony frame, the odd accent. *Jonah.* An errant prophet washed ashore. What had overcome him to pick this boy up and bring him home? Was it his spiritual thing, his compassion? Was it refusing to see another young brother get taken to jail like that? Whatever the reason, Nate concluded that Jonah's appearance was significant, a crosscurrent in the flow. It was instinctual; there was something about the young man that made him want to know more. He let Jonah talk (the brother loved to talk), and now he was going on about the situation he had left in Paris. And the things he was saying convinced Nate in the rightness of his thinking. Because the words spoken in his living room were taking him back, way back, across the ocean to that same city, to that place and time in his life that he could never entirely forget, but that he thought, at least he had once, that he'd left behind for good.

⁂

When Jonah spoke, the words rushed out of him and Nate struggled to keep pace as the young teacher bolted through sentences like hopscotch boxes, quick in his form, leaving a pattern in the air that was easy to see but hard to follow.

He told Nate about the work of a projectionist, the one who operates behind the scenes to bring the movie to light. There was always a moment before a screening when Jonah was alone. He would catch himself scheming, coming up with some fantastic occurrence that might indefinitely prolong his stay in the funk of the little booth. It was a space of half-lights, murky and warm. He enjoyed threading the film quickly and efficiently through its zigzag of sprockets and gates. If something went wrong, the film could get caught, a nightmare scenario that any projectionist worth their salt would prevent at all costs. Only when the picture was up could he feel his blood relax, and his mind begin to idle. In the booth he could see and not be seen. The eyes reached out across the dark where the stories rose and fell in the alphabet of variable light. A dry oven-like heat radiated from the lamphouse. The fractious chatter of rotors and film reels generated a gentle dharmic drone. The bulky frame of the mid-century projector loomed overhead like a mammoth lately fossilized; one of those vanished beasts that went down to drink of cool water at the Seine, whose bones came up when they dug out the tunnels of the Métro.

Jonah had taken the job fully aware of how it would look. Film was on its way out; the fact that it was dying gave it an old-world authenticity that

64

made it all the more attractive. He had been aware from a very young age that everything cool was archaic, defunct, retro. If it had handles, bulbs, dials, all the better. It was a way of styling yourself as not entirely on board with the futurists, the programmer dorks who had grown up friendless and who had since secured their revenge by ascending to positions of unfathomable power and wealth. They still couldn't dance, but it didn't matter. They were remaking the entire world in their image. They wrote the code and the rest would have to follow it. Like them, Jonah had been born just early enough to see something of the previous world before it disappeared, enough to have a nostalgic attachment that was useful only insofar as it could be converted into quaint mementos of that lost world, notes of tasteful decay or bygoneness. Landing a gig as a projectionist seemed like the most successful thing he could have done, at least in that regard.

But the job wasn't necessarily as easy as it looked. In the tiny Parisian movie houses, the projectors were cranky old machines, and one needed a nimble hand just to keep them going. The film came on platters like shellfish. He shucked them, holding the strips up like X-rays, pinching them carefully along the sides, looking for damage and dust, for splices or punctures along the soundtrack. There was an absorbed solemnity to the work. The ultimate test was in motion; he waited for the cue marks on the flying filmstrip, those bright cigar burns in the corner, enjoining the projector to bring two pieces of the story together. His heart rate slowed as the moment to change reels approached. He imagined a single frame on its Z-shaped voyage, around the big platter, up to the roller, then down to the film gate, where the intermittent sprocket held them, one by one, twenty-four times every second, each slice of light a still picture, like the frozen gestures of the saints projected daily by the sun through the oculi of the cathedrals.

One evening, he learned that his assignment was to project a documentary about an obscure jazz pianist. He had never heard of the film or the director or its subject; likely it had screened once at Deauville before getting dumped on them by one of those obscure cultural functionaries who followed the seasonal junkets across the globe. The titles scrolled, and the name of the subject appeared in a bold, modern font: *Quiet Genius: The Life and Music of Phineas Newborn, Jr.*

He checked his watch and called down to the office. They were ready. He set the action in motion. The film leader wound through the reel, sending a crazed scribble across the screen. With a soft pop, the picture came up.

Jonah squinted in the viewfinder and sharpened the focus. With a sudden self-conscious check, he realized he was looking into the grain of a black man's skin, right about his neck. He looked up from the viewfinder at the face staring back over the shadowy rows. On the screen he took in the man's smooth brown facial features, boyish, shy, an aristocratic demeanor and a faint trace of anxiety in the expressive eyes framed by a pair of thick, horn-rimmed glasses. A fine trace of sweat glistened on his brow. *Phineas.* The musician gazed down at his instrument, the flight of keys reflected in his lenses.

Just then the senior projectionist, a man named André, came in to check the feed on the projector.

"Salut, Joe," said André.

He called Jonah Joe, like so many other French people did—happily and over Jonah's objections. His passport read Jonah Raymond Winters. His parents sometimes called him Ray, and sometimes J.R. Joe was the diminutive of Joseph, not Jonah. André didn't seem to care.

André snapped some technical questions at him as he patted his rail-thin body down in search of tobacco. He wanted to know if Jonah knew anything about *le grand jazzman.* Without hesitating, Jonah lied. It was a reflex—he always lied if asked about something he didn't know about black culture. He knew they would never dare to call him on it. André invited him to come down to the lobby for a drink once the picture was up and running. Jonah quickly explained that he wanted to keep a close eye on the feed, which, truthfully, had been somewhat finicky that week. André appeared pinched, or simply baffled, and abruptly left.

Jonah trained his eyes back on the screen, where Phineas was now playing piano. From time to time, the camera cut to focus on his hands. Massive black fingers filled the screen, rising and falling on the ivories. A heavily accented voiceover described a tumultuous life in decline, a squandered talent. A montage sequence revealed the musician's unraveling, falling prey to inebriation, predisposed to mental breakdown. Still photographs drifted in hesitant suspension. Down and out in New York, Memphis, Philadelphia. In this sequence, there was no music, and the only sound in the theater was the flutter of the projector itself.

The movie ended with an interview, a coda of sorts. An interviewer with a thick Italian accent asked, "Mr. Newborn, you have many fans here in Europe. Tell us about your first solo European tour. What did you think of it?" Now Phineas spoke, and his granular Southern voice reached out and seized hold of Jonah in his booth.

> Well, I always did dream of arriving one day in a city. Some place far away from America. Some place where nobody would know my name and I wouldn't know nobody else and I could just be who I am, the finest pianist that ever came out of Tennessee. When I recollect those days, what I think of is how fast everything happened at that time in my life. Like I was no more than a little flea caught up in some mighty circus. That's how I think on it now. But you can't imagine the feeling, at the time, what it was to make that trip. Where I was coming from. I remember arriving in Europe. I can see it clear as yesterday. Boy, I knew I had arrived, too. I'd made it, and with a recording contract to my name. And over there, the women and the men all dressed so nice, but best of all nobody asked me my business like I had none. And no "colored" water fountains. I could walk down the swankiest boulevard just as tall as the next man. I really felt so blessed to be alive. But you know, I think maybe it's always like that when you arrive for the first time in a city, the shock of things could be different. Like

hearing Bud Powell for the first time. See, I never think of a city without thinking of music. For me there's no Paris without hearing Bud. So every new city is an opportunity to change your ear. You might catch the light in the trees more. The rhythms of life arrive with a strange off-kilter sensation, and the artist has to try and make something of this new arrangement, to catch the changing signs of the new world in their flight.

Could you tell us, Mr. Newborn, what year was this?

That was nineteen hundred fifty-eight. I had released *Phineas' Rainbow*, and the people at RCA wanted me to do a European tour to promote the album abroad.

What about your early life? You had a difficult relationship with your father, yes? Could you tell us some things about that?

My father was a musician. But my father used to say, "You got to walk the valley by yourself." I truly believe he hated the idea of me getting into music like he did, but I never had it in me to give something up if I liked it, and I loved playing music from the day I was born. I'd say I got my stubbornness from him. Sure, between us, it wasn't always easy, you know? But it wasn't in him to back down, to give up, to settle. He was the one who told me, "You just remember, boy, none of your forefathers never jumped off no slave ship." He was a tough man. Had to be. Born down in Georgia in the Reconstruction. A terrible time, and we see how it still is. The whites were stringing black folk up in trees and they might set you on fire for any damn thing. When I was a boy, I remember folks talking about Elbert

Williams. He had started working to help the blacks vote in our area and before long they found his body face down in the Hatchie. Well, I never thought about it as something that *could* change. Other than music it was all I knew. Father was a music man, a drummer known all round Memphis. Made a name for himself good enough that he figured mine should be the same as his. I remember how him and Tuff Green would come stomping through the house after a night at the juke and my mother would cuss the both of them out till they were forced onto the porch. They would keep on hollerin' back and forth for hours it seemed and I lay awake listening through the walls. They might be playing off the banister or a chair with a wooden spoon or just clapping their hands and that was better than transistor radio. Sometimes they would get to singing an old blues number or a jug-band tune. That was like water to me and I took to it. Beale Street was right there in my house. Jelly Roll was my little night music. My father he trained me to follow in his footsteps and work in his band. But I knew that I wanted to make my own way and to do that I would have to be better than good and get noticed out east in the big cities. So I put my two little hands together and I prayed. I asked the Lord if He would only let me I was going to become the greatest piano player Memphis had ever seen.

You mentioned Jelly Roll Morton. Who are some of your other influences?

How much time you got? Art Tatum, Oscar Peterson, Ellington. The great Ahmad Jamal. But of them all, I most admired Art Tatum. The only smart thing I ever heard a critic say—and this was a white critic, mind you—he said, "When you listen to Art, you feel like a bird-watcher who stumbles across a sky full of kingfishers." That stayed with me. Now, you know, Art was very nearly blind. From birth, I believe. But he could see music clear as sunshine. Far as I know he never practiced, never needed to read a sheet of music. He just sat down and played. It was like the notes were there for him all the time, like he could see them all at once. As a musician, you didn't want to go up after him. It wouldn't make sense. He didn't leave nothing for you. Anything you could think of he already knew it, and he had the sweetest rhythmic understanding of the instrument I ever heard. No one, I mean no one, could play like Art. I don't believe anyone ever will.

What about yourself? What is unique about your style?

Let me play you something, let's see . . . You hear that? That's Billy Strayhorn. See, I can get that color because Strayhorn is a genius and he's in love with the sound. Then all I need is for the keys to be ready, and then you've got to be ready for them. That ways you bring kindness to the hammers as they fall. You keep them yearning at all times. That's why the sound you hear is what we call lush, the way Billy wanted it. Now I could be playing in Rome or Los Angeles, it don't matter; when I'm ready, I'll always be sitting right there in my old house in Whiteville, Tennessee. Where you can hear the locomotives of the L&N goin' down the line and the voices of my aunties and uncles talking about the rent man and cooking up the fish fry. To me that's what style is. It's the presence that lives around the notes, the part of your playing that tells the listener this is how my music sees the world, how it lives in it. It's like what happened one night when I was playing a gig in Copenhagen. After the show, I see these two cats with horns waiting for me; it was Albert Ayler and Don Cherry. They had come to see me play so I invited them up. And I'll never forget this, Albert came on the bandstand and started doing a spiritual. And I heard this sound. It had that unbroken fire, the way before you become known, when you're still practicing, woodshedding as we like to call it, there's this naturalness, this fearlessness, before you're discovered by the commercial world and they put you in that whole mess. Well, I could hear it in the man's sound, all that love. And to me, it was like the Word came back, and I had that feeling of when I was very young and my parents would take us on Sundays to church. And it's this feeling you get in a Baptist, holy-type church, when everyone feels the Spirit in the room, and people become happy, they call it. And some people even speak tongues. But it's this feeling of the Spirit holding the room, and it happened that night with Albert too. He took hold of us. And I felt his Spirit, the world of the ancestors talking to us through him. And that's really what our thing is all about. Getting to that place where the sound touches you, and the shadows of the valley flicker, and you're moved, touched by the source of things, the love that brings all things back.

⊁⊰

Freeze-frame. That was the effect if he had to describe it, Jonah said. He was aware that the lights had come on, the cinephiles dispersed, the theater returned to entombed silence. But as he placed the film reels carefully back in their cases, he could feel the lingering presence of Phineas, his troubling voice and troubled genius shifting him off foundations he hadn't even known were there, something newly moving, like a pendulum at the instant when it has finally passed the point of its maximum amplitude. He hastily jotted down his hours and slipped out.

On the rue Christine, the air felt clean and cool. It was late in the afternoon and people strolled languidly, pausing to consider café terraces and their perennial cast of dilettanti. Sounds and images from the film trickled in his mind and mingled with anxieties that had followed him since his graduation. Folks had warned him that, after college, if he wasn't careful, he could be led into a dead-end job, that if he didn't keep his eye on the ball, he could be knocked off the course of professional and personal advancement and fall behind his peers, that it was too easy to lose all the hard-fought gains that a college education had provided, particularly (although he felt it didn't need to be repeated as endlessly as it was) for a young man like himself. One had to advance decisively.

This attitude (firmly adopted by his kinfolk) held a very dim view of the kind of reasoning that would consider an internship as a projectionist's assistant in a Parisian art-house movie theater an acceptable postgraduate term of employment. The suspicion was, depending on who he asked, that Jonah was either spoiled or a damn fool, or both. He didn't have a good counterargument. It *was* easier to view life than to experience it. At work, he sat in the dark, watching; at home, he flipped open his laptop and watched his friends' life-pages proliferating, streaming at an ever-increasing frame rate.

His own life, up to that point, had been, by most counts, "interesting," special, even singular—though to him it seemed primarily a matter of cushioned apartness. Boyhood brought to his mind mostly an impression of innocence suspended in a kind of fin de siècle phoniness, an unlikely life of privilege. The details he retained most vividly were sheltered and oddly abstract. The tinkle of pickup sticks; the loving rotundity of LeVar Burton's voice; clots of Nestlé powdered cocoa and the vibrant packaging of multipack breakfast cereal. At the time, it had seemed to him like an ideal upbringing. It could have occurred just as easily in one of those rare and famous wealthy black American enclaves that his father liked to crack awkward jokes about. But a black American in Europe? That was a weirder story, not without precedent, but not entirely relatable either. It was his father, Jonah said, who was the architect of this strange situation, who provided the illusion and snatched it away. "Remember this, boy," he'd say if Jonah upset him. "You're living a life other kids just like you don't have. You have no idea how good you have it, you never will."

Confronting one's history was important. His father talked a great deal about history and power. The limitations placed on men by its cruelty; the force of hatred in the world, which was oppressive and could strike anywhere at any time, which he should be prepared to face down as a special condition because it would inevitably target him. This was the most terrible vision. That history would come looking with special prejudice *for him*. Sooner or later he would confront a penalty, and it would be his responsibility to prove that he was not going to allow that penalty, however unjustly imposed, to hold him back. That he would use the extraordinary good fortune of his upbringing to make something great of himself and serve others, in spite of the inevitable swerve of history that would come looking for him and all who were darker than him, with intentions that were not to be trusted but nonetheless grimly confronted, surmounted with grace, without complaining, without under any circumstances allowing *them* to see the hurt.

Often, history was taught through the television, which brought its lessons—sometimes, and sometimes not, involving darker people—into the living room. But in his father's explanations, they all were versions of the same thing: the great contest between the forces that tried to pit man against man through hate, and the forces of quiet dignity that tried to resist this, but often failed and often paid a terrible price. The more terrible price was paid by women, who generally bore the scars of this great cosmic conflict twice over, and who were the ones left to tend to the wounds caused by male chaos, to weep at funerals, to care for and raise neglected children, to survive and patch together the human family while making a life for themselves as best they could.

On such occasions, his father adopted a tone of ancestral teaching, as if (despite his rather limited schooling) his paternal mission consisted of imparting the ways of the world from the standpoint of successes and failures not only his own but of mankind generally. His voice, always grave at the outset, could shift, depending on his humor, revealing unsettled edges like a graveled road. He was fond of marking dramatic pauses with a flick at the base of one of his blue packets adorned with an Asterix helmet. The little kick liberated a cigarette, whose consumption was momentarily deferred until oratorical triumph dictated it should be plucked and ignited to his satisfaction.

Through the gauzy spread of tobacco fumes, the Japanese television set transmitted the revolution in newscasting, a never-ending global drama beamed directly into the living room. Riots, earthquakes, rafts of the dispossessed, Ethiopian famine, the space shuttle, Nelson Mandela, Morgan Freeman, Michael Jackson, Whitney Houston. He remembered his father explaining the Berlin Wall coming down, the throng of fists and scarves and gloves parading, a chorus rising and roaring to garbled cheers and astonished weeping, a white man with a sledgehammer whacking away as slabs of gray matter yawned open. "You see, son," his father said, "this is what freedom means. Taking it into your own hands, making the arc of history bend to your will. Hell, that's what all great men want, and it's what all great artists do—*if*—if they have the *opportunity* and the God-given ability to meet the challenge that's in their path."

Jonah's father believed strongly in the greatness of art. He also believed, and for a time had convinced enough other people with the right connections, that *he was* an artist. He had come to this realization while studying for a degree in business communications. If he had learned one thing from those classes, it was the importance of seizing on opportunistic timing in a volatile market. He was well aware that, to some extent, he had taken advantage of a moment, after the assassinations of the sixties, when white liberals felt guilty about race relations and wanted to be seen endorsing, supporting, and promoting radical black art. This awareness didn't imply pure cynicism on his part. Especially in the early days, he had brought genuine anger and frustration to his work, and its expressionist élan reflected something bold and unnerving that caught the eyes of gallerists and the art press alike. He nurtured an Afrocentric brand and ran with the dashiki crowd, admired Ron Karenga, flirted with Islam, even seriously considered converting, but couldn't bring himself to give up swine. He also came to doubt (or confront) the reach of his abilities, seeing them for what they were, talents not gifts, unusual but not immeasurable, not genius beyond compare.

He liked to tell the story of an important showing of his work at a reputable gallery in Paris in 1977. He was particularly proud of a mixed-media portrait, a mural of sorts, that he called *Homage to Barbara Jordan*, which depicted the congresswoman as a towering figure of justice in the act of indicting Nixon, who appeared as a grotesque, pale gnome in the corner, part of his face spray-painted over with graffiti. The crowd at the opening gave it rapturous attention and adulation, and he basked in this glow, right up to the moment when he noticed, or came to the end of a long failure to notice, that he was the only black person in the entire room. "If you ever find yourself doing something and you're the only one there—you better check yourself," he would warn Jonah in his sternest voice.

His father was, according to himself, black in the right place at the right time. But it still felt wrong, like a bad joke. Like he was getting the pretend version of what he had grasped at all his life. Yes, he had faked it when he had to, in order to rise; but now that he really wanted it, or rather wanted to be real *in* it, every vernissage he showed up to was full of the wrong people, even though they were the same people from the years before, the ones who were always thrilled to see him, wanted him to drink at their tables, pose for pictures with them, and never gave a damn about a thing he had made.

It could have led to despair, and for a brief and turbulent time, it seemed it would. But his father was able to convert these frustrations into a desire to get over, to get the most, and his social connections blossomed accordingly. He was even more successful once he made it obvious and plain to them that he was scheming, that he was a needy and somewhat fraudulent hustler taking advantage of their thirst for his "urban" sensibility. It only made him more glamorous, more real, and a stream of increasingly prestigious "minority" and "diversity" fellowships, residencies, and keys to chateaus were never more than a phone call away. His plot against the white art world quickly turned into something of a perpetual-motion machine, as he dragged his family with him from position to position, always in search of a place where he could maximize his quality of life at minimum cost. The family bounced around overseas from one art-world metropolis to the next: London, Berlin, Paris.

Berlin Jonah remembered as gray blocks, gray skies, and snow. Deep drifts under the linden trees on Hölderlinstraße. And the beautiful girl, very blonde and porcelain, whom he met sledding somewhere in a forest clearing, her image set to rest at the very back of the mind like a snow globe waiting to be shaken. If he closed his eyes, he could remember the sound of her name, but not the name itself. He might not have remembered her at all if she had not formed an early taste of some unspeakable gulf between desire and detachment, something bitter, a cool remoteness that frightened him. Those were strange days, when the TV spoke in a foreign tongue and rosy-cheeked boys like cutouts from Kinder chocolate commercials stopped cheerfully to interrogate him, touching his hair, laughing. The girl and her sky-colored eyes had questioned him too, that day in the woods, not with any overt hostility, but with distance, as if he had appeared like a comet, a sight from another world.

When his father announced that they were moving to Paris, the change meant nothing more to him than another, hopefully more temperate city. On the overnight train he dreamt that the girl was hidden in his father's suitcase. He joined her there, and, in the darkness of the sealed luggage, she played with his hair. He told her to stop and slapped her. The trunk flew open, and she fled, vanishing into the silence and whiteness of German forests. He woke near dawn. Their carriage was flooded blue. The train clacked and screeched, gently rocking across the exchanges of a rail yard. Outside, the little balconies and the slate rooftops of Paris faced the pale sunlight.

They moved into an apartment on rue de Tocqueville, an unglamorous part of Paris near the rail yards, Jonah said, where switching tracks formed long radial chasms bisecting the Périphérique before sweeping out into the dreary suburbs to the north. The neighborhood shared the name of the little Square des Batignolles that stood beside the Pont-Cardinet station. If the weather was good, Jonah spent long afternoons in the park, where time was marked by the rumbling of the trains and the clean, cracking report of Pétanque players punctuating the gravel lots. A carousel turned, radiating a ragtime or an old song by Barbara, a sad woman who looked like a bird and sang like one too. Sometimes the race-car man had a set of wooden-pedaled soapboxes. If he was there, for five francs you could hurtle along into a halo of glory like Ayrton Senna, racing the commuter lines out of Saint-Lazare. That childhood experience of Paris, Jonah said, was impossible to evoke clearly. It had a shimmering, confectionary weightlessness; and yet it was also dense, a plenitude accumulated imperceptibly, like the leafy dust sagging in the green awning of the crêpe stand.

On the evening of the Phineas Newborn screening, he had come across an accident as it was unfolding on the boulevard Saint-Germain. A woman on a scooter had been struck by a small delivery van that had pulled out hurriedly into her lane. The woman was on her back in the street, and a small crowd had gathered around her. Passersby stopped, dumbstruck, some putting their hands to their mouths, others looking around anxiously or reaching for their phones. The woman was wearing a navy-blue business jacket, and Jonah could see her dark hair coming out of her helmet, which rested motionless on the pavement. It was impossible to tell if she was conscious. A wail came pulsing up the boulevard. Police arrived and began diverting traffic. With the traffic stilled, the plane trees appeared even more majestic, their crowns basking in the evening light. As the ambulance neared, some bystanders began to move again, but others just arriving now stopped, transfixed. The paramedics crouched over the woman's body. There was a shout, and a man in a light-blue shirt, holding a phone to his ear, ran up the sidewalk. He was sweating heavily, and everyone understood. He knelt over her, talking into the helmet and turning periodically to consult with the medics. And then Jonah could see a small heaving in the woman's chest. The man held her wrist. The medics brought out an orange canoe with straps and a pillow. The driver of the van hid his eyes with his hand.

Jonah waited a bit longer. Then, feeling vaguely irritated with himself, he turned and left the scene hurriedly. It was overwhelming, the touch of human stuff, the queer vastness of it colliding all around. Everyone knew all of it could, in the space of one head-on smash, come to a full stop. That there was a day, a definite one somewhere still in the future, full of the same buzz and pullulation of other people living and going on, when it would be someone else in some version of that crowd looking on at him, lying there, watching him exit the play with no more difficulty than the energy it took him to turn and walk away.

The accident had caused him to backtrack, reversing course along the opposite side of the boulevard as the summer evening deepened. At the Odéon intersection, looking more miserable than ever, Danton thrust his arm out over the loiterers assembled at the base of his socle. Jonah turned off the boulevard into the medieval passageways running down to the Seine. He passed art galleries with garish and austere baubles. Tourists fumbled with their digital cameras. At the angle of the rue Jacob, he thought he heard a piano playing. But it was only a waiter storing his silverware. He pressed on into the quiet

78

streets. On the rue Bonaparte he passed the cobbled courtyard of the École des Beaux-Arts and its Greek statues, and then the Tunisian greengrocer where he sometimes bought clementines in the winter. He kept thinking of Phineas. That image of Phineas Newborn at his piano, staring down at his own hands.

He arrived at the crossroads near the statue of Condorcet. To his right, the Pont des Arts stretched across the Seine to the Louvre. The bridge was peppered with young professionals and students. They lounged against the railings or formed circles around cheap bottles of wine and beer, laughing and rolling cigarettes. Dealers roamed their periphery looking for sales. Street vendors with key chains, plastic gadgets, and bottled water, button-holed tourists trying to pose for each other with a romantic view. A column of jolly Americans dressed in khakis and polo shirts rolled by on Segways, traversing the scene like a vaguely alien but benign patrol force.

Paris at the dawn of the new millennium. The softness of its way of life, its affordance and assumption of the artful enveloped them all like a delicate and indefinitely antiquated movie set. It was, Jonah said, almost sickeningly beautiful. He stood in it as one who had neither a place nor no place in it. He hadn't done nothing to nobody. But really, he had done nothing, could do nothing, other than grow more like the city around him. Become a waxy walker in the museum of nostalgia, a curious prop, seemingly borrowed from another set for the tourists to ponder with disinterested bewilderment.

What was *he* doing? Elsewhere life was happening, moving in some fateful direction. It might ultimately be catastrophic, but it was moving all the same. The decisive meanings would be discovered and won or lost there. His college friends, armed with their degrees, were moving to Brooklyn or out to Silicon Valley, where the future was being encoded as a set of calcu-lably diffusive effects presided over by a sempiternal abstraction devoted to watching, recording, and taking a cut. He knew he wanted no part of that. But what alternative vision did he have? These thoughts obsessed him as he walked back across the city to the rue de Tocqueville.

His bedroom was full of movie posters, most of them rolled up in tubes in a corner leaning against his desk. He got them for free on the job and had more than he knew what to do with. He had seen so many films, too many. Art films from small European countries that were younger than he was; obscure westerns that only the elderly came to watch, and usually dozed off to. Even the glorious Isabelle Adjani who stormed across the screen in her avenging genii, her Emily Brontë, her Adèle Hugo, her Camille Claudel; even Adjani's achingly romantic poses looked somehow hollow to him now. He was tired of watching. What was he really looking for? What did the watching conceal? He loved the movie theater; he loved working in the booth, feeding the reels and watching the platters turn. But how long would any of it last? What did it have to do with him? It came back to the same thing. The movies were his way of hiding. And he knew it. He just hadn't had the courage to admit it. Somehow Phineas had said it for him. Reached something vulnerable, something that was broken but not forgotten in the life that held the music forth like an instrument that played his unknown past and spoke of unknowable futures.

Phineas. Newborn. His voice was still going in Jonah's mind, tinkling as it receded like a caboose. How far back did one have to go to understand a man? He had seldom found a single word to fit his own question mark. Was there a way to the inner directness of the thing, the things that he had never found he could say? Shades of history and cries of a people. Was that what Phineas had finally moved into the light? Fear of the missed life. Like that of the Ex-Colored Man discovering one day he has chosen the lesser part? There was only one way to find out. Get out ahead of it. Complete a turn toward whatever was out there that he had yet to know. Grasp and hold. Or be held.

It was time to get real. Get a real job, deal with the real world. New York was a place where you figured some shit out, where whatever people could handle could be found, along with a good dose of whatever they couldn't. The force of a decision brought with it a fresh inlet of perspective. His room, when he finally got home, looked entirely different, Jonah said. The things in it were no longer just the haphazard accumulation of restless days. They formed an image of his life up to that point. The nobody he saw there bothered him.

He stared at the map on the wall over his bed. It was a gift from his mother. A Mercator projection, the Earth squared to the tidy scale of one to five hundred thousand. In the corner above the legend, the Air France Pegasus reared up with the national colors flaming in its mane. Air routes sprang from the world's magnetic poles—Paris, London, New York—and sailed off in falling parabolas to distant cities, crossing the time zones. Underneath the map was a wide and low bookcase that ran the length of the wall.

He pulled out a novel by Aragon and read the first sentence. It was as arresting as he had remembered. Arna had given him the book and he had promised her he would read it. He flipped through the pages, pausing over her elliptical notations. It was long and he had put off finishing it at some point without giving himself a reason for doing so. He could perceive now that it wasn't anything about the story or the style that had failed to enthrall him. It was something in the sadness of the fate gripping its characters that he wanted to avoid resolving. It was the implication of her deciding this particular story was one they ought to share. He had concealed this to himself and chalked it up to distraction. But the truth was that he was afraid to read too far, to accept an ending that her intelligence had absorbed, reflected upon, and deemed cautionary.

Arna Duval Fignolé. A name redolent of fronded colonial mysteries, some obscure relay between la France hexagonale and the American South (perhaps if it had never sold Louisiana to Jefferson after defeat at the hands of her revolted slaves), a combination that, for one reason or another, Jonah associated with Arna's equally unusual areas of expertise, such as how to knot a cherry stem inside one's mouth; how to split matchsticks into figurines; how to carry anime jingles with a boyish whistle before lapsing into an awkward, hissing laugh.

Despite these talents, Arna wasn't exactly popular, Jonah told Nathaniel. Outside of school, she wasn't easily reached. Jonah would call the landline. If her French father answered they would exchange the usual greetings, and then he would receive (crystallized in the impersonal politeness of French conversation) the default declaration that his daughter was unavailable. But if her American mother answered, it was another story. He would be quizzed on everything: school, his parents, weekend plans. Her mother spoke in high bursts of spirited Southern drawl that had been amusingly livened by a distinctly Parisian chirrup full of assumed common sense about the way things are done. If it was her mother, he would gladly talk all evening, because he knew it meant, sooner or later, she would pass him along. There would be a "Hey, hold on," and through the receiver the plink and clatter of the kitchen would yield to the thudding of footsteps and the snapping of coil on the cord as Arna yanked the phone back to her room.

In art class, he often sat behind her. The uniform-blue smock was tied in a bow at her back; her hair was the color of a chestnut you find in the yard and pocket for safekeeping. She was the beginning of poetry, and the idea of it spread contagiously to his tender nerves, like the smell of a face drawing near. Overnight, he was Lermontov. The great Russian poet, Jonah explained, whose very name (even if he was unsure how to pronounce it) had suggested the dashing sound of what poetry ought to be, and of all that it promised to do. Every sonnet smoldered, even the formidable Séyès lines of the composition books could not regulate them. The finest lyric achievements of an evening were delivered up the rows to Arna's desk the next morning. With respect to these strenuous developments, Arna maintained perfect inscrutability and a distanced cool.

While his fevers swirled inward, Arna was slowly but surely expanding her vision outward, primarily through her admission to the circle of the beautifully scarved elite, who gathered in the nearby Parc Monceau to smoke hashish after classes. One afternoon, after much pleading on Jonah's part, she allowed him to join her at a small gathering in a high-ceilinged apartment on rue de Téhéran where she taught him privately how to heat a stick of Moroccan hash with a lighter and fritter its crumbs into a bed of rolling tobacco. Hashish was Arna's oblique answer to poetry. She had accessed a different portal to knowledge, one she wanted to know of through her body, and that she had somehow, seemingly without his being able to detect when or how, confidently claimed as new territory for exploration. While he pretended to watch music videos on a television fitted into a Louis XV cabinet, she moved lithely from one body to another, laughing tipsily, then suddenly entwined in voluptuous and cryptic gestures. There were no rules, at least none he could detect; sometimes she was kissing boys, sometimes caressing girls.

Jonah worried that his wallflower inhibitions would mean losing Arna to the dizzying new world she had so swiftly, and apparently effortlessly, integrated. But, miraculously, even as he remained outside the inner circle, his skin color had come to take on new meanings, some of them positive, or at least it was made clear to him that his presence added something cool and desirable, like a prized and rare accessory. Most importantly, from his perspective, it ensured his continuing access to certain invitation-only parties at country houses in the "Island of France," that green Merovingian radial marked by all points, no less than half and no more than one hour's distance from the bell towers of Notre Dame.

To get there, Arna and Jonah had to prearrange rides. Things started in the back of seat of a Peugeot in whispers, a joint passed around furtively, burning at the lips. Circumflex accents in tight sweaters caught the eye and legs brushed together in the woozy sway and tip of the car, touching off tactile collisions. Sometimes there was "free" kissing, in that it didn't count. In the gardened manor houses, all vaguely alike, someone always put on the same album by the Doors, and Jim Morrison's oracular pronouncements licensed and promised a time in which anything could happen, and would happen, under the sign of eternal youth. The aroma of hash and spilled Malibu liqueur, of being seventeen, caused a permanent tilt, so that there was only the possibility of bodies moving toward each other or falling away into various degrees of paranoia. In the tense, hermetic daze of the country house and its many attic rooms, skin and color were complicating assets, and Arna took it upon herself to act as a kind of chaperone, keeping her eye on him, teaming up when necessary, so that he, too, could fleetingly let his guard down and succumb to the ambient goal of pursuing new sensations. She allowed him to kiss and to discover the surface of her body, only, or mostly, above the waist. She gave him hints of desire, but he understood that it was also an act of generosity, a tacit sign of the compact that she was engaging in to protect them both. In the morning, the stone houses were always incredibly cold. Three and four under extra blankets, they lay in bed virtually naked and feverishly hot. He listened to the birds sing in the blue darkness, unsure whether the spell had broken, how much longer they might touch that way before it was time to go.

With Arna things were never official. They weren't "going out," but they also agreed that theirs was a special kind of friendship. They haunted the record stores behind the Pantheon, watched Hitchcock flicks on the rue des Écoles, and posted up in cafés, bantering about movie stars and music and the hookup scene. Arna's hair was short like a boy's. She should have been a member of the group of girls from the good families, but those girls hated her. She was a transfer student and the shape of her eyes and her skin tone was held to be suspicious. Behind her back they called her "a Mongol" and the rumor was that Arna was a gitane. One afternoon as they waited in line for the bus, a group of girls got a chant going. Arna walked away, presumably to cry, but she reappeared moments later with a jar full of filthy water that she tossed in a girl's face, causing an eruption of hysteria. On one of their first hangs, Arna showed Jonah an impressive knife from her father's collection, a lissome folding blade. She liked to play with it over lunch after slicing vertices from her Camembert. It was Arna's idea to carve their names into the green plank of a park bench where they met sometimes after school. Their special friendship, which was always something more, but also less, went on this way until the afternoon Arna came over to the rue de Tocqueville.

Jonah had invited her before. This time she accepted. It was midweek and his mother had left her usual note reminding him she would be working late. They sat on the living room floor watching MTV Europe. MC Solaar, Massive Attack, heart-stopping Lauryn Hill, watery flashes of Kurt Cobain. Arna half watched as she flipped through a *National Geographic*. She was wearing her evergreen track shorts with the Adidas flower, and a white tank top. A new show came on, and they decided to move to his room. Arna sat on his bed, poring over an article on whaling in Iceland. He followed along over her shoulder. Her hair smelled like wet wood in the sun, like the bark of a tree hit by a sprinkler in the summer. She flicked through the pages for a while, then, with a sigh of boredom, stretched out on the bed. He picked up the magazine, pretending to read in silence. Arna said something muffled into the pillow, and he heard her pull off her top and flounce back down. He waited a moment, then put the magazine aside and lay down next to her carefully, as if afraid of waking her. At first, when she touched him, he thought it must be an accident, but then he saw that her other hand had slipped under the elastic of her shorts. She stopped and gave him a long serious look. Then she rolled over, pressing herself on top of him. He felt her heat as she placed his hand. "I want to get this over with," she said. When it started, he felt like her body was squirming away. They thrusted in contradictory motions, meeting in tense shocks. When he shuddered, she jerked away violently. He apologized and she did not answer. They stayed that way for a time, breathing. At one point, he feared she was crying, but she wasn't. When she got up, she wiped the back of her thigh with his T-shirt. Suddenly, there was a sound at the front door. Arna bolted. Within seconds, she was somehow dressed again, her backpack slung over her shoulder, saying something to his mother with a quick laugh of surprise in the front hall as she slipped out onto the landing. Jonah went to the balcony. He watched her cross the street in a dash, walking, then running, as she turned the corner and disappeared.

That was the early summer of their graduation, as Arna was preparing to leave for England and he was waiting to go off to college in the States. She asked to meet him the day before she was set to go. They met for a coffee not far from the school, but ended up walking for almost an hour, down along the river and then through the hot, dusty Tuileries Gardens crowded with tourists. Arna was going to study politics, philosophy, and economics at Oxford, a compromise with her father, who had wanted her to follow the family tradition and attend one of the grandes écoles in Paris but consented to let her go abroad as long as she promised to return and not to study anything frivolous.

They ended up standing in the proscenium by the ticket booths at the entrance of the Métro station at Concord. The pneumatic gates of the turnstiles whooshed and clattered. Against the wall opposite the ticket booths was an old indicateur d'itinéraires, one of those connecting boards that lights up when a steel node is pressed down next to the label for a destination. Punch in Mairie des Lilas and a string of pale, green dots illuminate your trajectory across the city. Jonah and Arna took turns pressing possible destinations. The board lit up, dutifully, colored bracelets radiating outward in crossing paths.

Jonah had hoped at least for a warm farewell. Instead, they struggled to find things to say. Arna was distant. It became clear that there was too much they hadn't acknowledged over the years. As if they had crossed some threshold, run afoul of the obscure bylaw that states that past a certain point of ambiguity in a relationship, the real one can no longer be recovered. The realization felt strange, because the possibility that they would become vastly different from each other had never really occurred to him before.

Arna said she thought it would be a good thing to have some real distance between them. He quickly agreed. She gave his shoulder a gentle, playful nudge. Sweaty faces were streaming past them out of the tunnel. He thought to kiss her, but the jostling of the crowds, the heat, the noise, it was all so overwhelming that they briefly hugged instead.

It was Arna's idea that they should correspond, and he enthusiastically co-signed. They kept in touch "across the pond" while attending university. Though there was no positive sign of the romance that had made their friendship special, the letters, which increased in volume over time, took on increasingly intimate hues. He knew a good deal of what was going on in her life—at least, the portion she wished to share with him.

Jonah said he only saw Arna in person once during college, however, around the same time the following year back in Paris. On that occasion she was in town for a few days and said she could only do coffee. They met at one of the large corner-sweeping brasseries by Courcelles. Even though it was a little windy, they sat on the terrace in rattan chairs, not facing each other, but side by side, oriented outward toward the traffic of the boulevard and beyond it, the high gates sealing off the cool verdant mass of the Parc Monceau and the plump facades of the grand villas overlooking its "English" gardens.

Arna told him she was seeing someone, a guy who went to the London School of Economics, who played in a band and was studying to be a human rights lawyer. She spoke well of him, without particulars, but added that she wasn't sure it was going to work out on account of her plan to take a post-graduate fellowship with the Directorate-General for Regional and Urban Policy under the European Commission. In theory, it was based in Brussels, but in practice she would travel almost the entire time, all across the Union, gathering statistical data and meeting with local and regional political actors to gauge various measures of compliance. She would essentially be "taking the temperature of the European project," as she put it. Once people could see the numbers, she explained, recalcitrant populations that were being manipulated by local politicians would realize the many benefits that they were ignorant of or took for granted. She had learned at Oxford that a totally politically integrated Europe was now only a matter of time, possibly less than a decade away, and it was crucial to martial more popular support for the supranational conception of citizenship that it would entail. She was animated about her looming professional debut, and it struck Jonah, as he in turn explained to her something about his dismay at the decline of the film industry, that their conversation in person was far more formal and stilted than in their letters.

"Ack, I'm sorry. I hate it. This will just take a sec."

"No worries."

She was responding to a text message. *From the guy*, Jonah thought, although it would turn out that she was actually making plans with her mother. Jonah reflexively felt in his pocket for his own phone. He had text messages from his parents too. His father wanted to know if he had seen the latest news about the torture scandals from the war. He had heard about them, seen a handful of the images. But it was the last thing he wanted to think about just then.

In college, a friend had urged him to join a small group gathered in a dorm room to watch the beheading of a Jewish journalist. He had gone to check it out, and then, as the tape began, excused himself. It wasn't only the gore that he sought to avoid. Or even the dissociation of being a random onlooker watching this snuff film from Karachi on a laptop in snowy western Massachusetts. There were those who whispered that, like the September attacks, this was one of the signs of the coming "clash of civilizations." Jonah didn't have the courage to face that bleak possibility, nor could he imagine what confronting it would require. He hated conflict and didn't have the stomach for it, even if it was inevitable. But he also, more reservedly, couldn't comprehend the self-evidence of that phrase to many of the students around him. To him, if anything, there was a clash of barbarisms, and the barbarians could be found just as easily in Columbine, or Howard Beach, as in Baghdad. What truly made the video impossible was the foreknowledge that there would be so many more like it; that this spewing taste for cruelty and hatred was just the beginning of a long death-spiral that would shroud the future in its cold spell. That their future had already disappeared.

They both looked up from their phones. Arna was wearing a handsome jacket, and Jonah complimented her on it.

"Thanks! Mariam helped me pick it out from this great little shop in Notting Hill. You would love her. Actually, I'm hoping she will come with me, you know, when I start. She's got this consulting thing based in London—I think I told you about how she was freaking out when going through the interviews. But they need her to do liaising with the offices in Frankfurt and Paris, and she speaks like seven languages or something, so I'm thinking we can coordinate some time to get away together. Plus, I feel like we would travel well together."

He picked up on the "get away," but it was taking him a moment to place the name. She had come up in their correspondence, but not as a main character; a friend she had gone to a karaoke night with, who was busy and ambitious and funny, spoke with a posh accent, and was involved with the

Oxford African and Caribbean Society. And possibly she had said something about a talk they had attended together on gender and queer studies?

"She sounds great. I hope I'll get to meet her one of these days."

"Me too. Look at these."

She showed him a sequence of pictures taken at a house party (lads, glitter, Smirnoff) where Arna and Mariam appeared always together amid others, whom she pointed out and named. Arna appeared happy and flushed. In one picture she was smooshed against her friend's face, the pair sticking their tongues out for the camera. Mariam was obviously fun and hot; she wore a stud in her nose, defiant punctuation on an almond-toned and -shaped face, South Asian, he guessed; more attractive than he had imagined.

"She's the best. I wish she didn't have to spend so much time at her job. I know she hates it. But we're both planning on doing these gigs for now to get started, you know, see where it takes us. Oh my god, look, I'm a mess in this one!"

"You guys look great together—like you're having so much fun."

Was she *with* Mariam? Arna wasn't exactly saying one way or the other. Possibly she hadn't decided, or maybe it wasn't a thing one did decide, or, at least, broadcast like the result of an election or a soccer match. It wasn't really any of his business. He wasn't hurt at all, except insofar as he felt he should have known, and thought she would have been more explicit with him about her feelings. But even as he thought this, he realized how stupid it was, how many good reasons she might have for not wanting to tell him everything about whom she was sleeping with.

The waiter came by to see about another round, but Arna, with the precise, almost sculptural language of gesture that Parisian women use, expressed her desire to pay for the drinks, explaining that she had to go see her parents while she was in town. Jonah thought about protesting but knew better than to insist. The entrance to the Métro was at the corner and they walked together to the steps. He went to kiss her on the cheek, but she pulled him to her intimately. She made him promise to keep writing to her. He promised he would. She looked at him, considering; she kissed him on the neck, once, just below the ear, then turned away and descended below ground.

Whatever he had known up until that point now strengthened his new resolve. In a sense, it was simple. He had wasted too much time already.

Jonah's mother accompanied him to the airport. On the train they slid past the familiar panorama of the banlieues, the peri-urban sprawl, feeder roads swooping under a Samsung Electronics billboard, container shipping facilities, grim little roundabouts, a dingy café de la gare. A Gypsy player with a young boy came into the car and started playing a ballad. The young boy sang and walked up and down the car with his cap out. No one gave him any coins. A mute woman came by and placed a key chain with a little note on top of one of Jonah's bags. He didn't touch it, and eventually she came by and picked it up again. His mother noticed that he was quiet and asked how he was, if he had everything he needed. He said he was fine. She asked if he was still friends with Arna. He said they were still close, that they were staying in touch. She told him a story about when he was a boy, one they both knew and that she always retold whenever they were about to part. Her eyes were very clear and light. There were deep wrinkles between her eyebrows. He could feel the exact length and depth of those ridges because he frowned in exactly the same place. Suddenly she had a coughing fit, and he frantically got a water bottle from his backpack. Her lungs weren't what they used to be. *She's growing old*, he thought. He couldn't sleep on his flight.

8

Laura Petrossian had not ruined Nathaniel Archimbald's life, but she had come close. She had overthrown his sense of himself, given of herself to him and taken from him in ways he had not recognized, and then vanished, leaving behind a gap like a vacant lot. He never entirely believed that her intentions were bad, though to the end they remained inscrutable. Still, he had to concede that even the pain she had caused had been a kind of good fortune. She had helped him to see what was worth saving in the world and forced him to think seriously about what he could do about it.

He had started thinking of Laura as Jonah described his relationship with Arna. Of their paradoxical combination of openness and elusiveness. Nathaniel thought of that openness now, of how happy it would have made Laura to know he had gotten this lost young man out of his fix. He thought of the face she would make if he told her the story. And it reminded him of her other face, the one she made when she was sleeping. The unvarying coolness of her voice when they were naked a long time in her bed. Of midafternoons in the little apartment on the rue des Cinq-Diamants.

Nathaniel leaned back in his chair, stretching out the red and green of his tracksuit with his albatross wingspan. He regarded Jonah intently now, appealing to the grown man in him.

"And you haven't spoken to this woman since?"

"We write to each other. She's always traveling. I get letters and postcards from the cities she's visiting on account of her government job, you know, collecting research about economic development, that kind of thing. We try to do mail the old-fashioned way, and it means that we have this slow-motion conversation over time. I think about her a lot, but then I'll save the thought and write it down, and then when I have some time it turns into something more, it grows into a letter, and then I send it."

"Now hold on, that's the word right there. This sending. Because I got to ask myself who sent you. See, I've been sitting here listening to you, and it's like this weird thing I've been running in my mind. The way I make sense of it is, maybe I saved you. Maybe something even worse was about to happen to you last night and we'll never know it. You don't realize how lucky you are. Only reason I was even downtown was to support a buddy of mine who is trying to get clean and has this meeting he goes to in Chinatown. I heard some stuff in the meeting that was so hard, I had to walk it off and ended up way over off East Broadway. I come round a corner, find you lying on the ground, down for the count and still acting all belligerent, and I seen the cops rolling up, and well, shit, I just acted on it. And I don't even know you. So why did I do that? Had to be a reason. And I been sitting here listening to you and I'm thinking I see what it was. I'll be damned if you aren't some kind of messenger. Universe trying to tell me something. You just might be a sign I got to revisit some shit I've been trying to put behind me for years."

"How do you mean?"

"Well, I'll bet you would never guess I was in a situation just like yours. *Long* time ago. My Paris days. Damn. You know, I haven't been back since. Don't plan to neither, to be honest. Feels like it was another life. It was another life, a whole other world. My first life was hoops. I guess you could say my second life was this love story that didn't pan out. I figure I'm in my third now. At least I'm happy where I'm at. I thought I put that whole Paris thing behind me; now you show up, and it brings it all back. Man, she had me *wide* open. Had me learning my words all over again, and in French. What a crazy time that was. Brings back memories, man, even after all these years."

"What was her name?"

"Laura."

Saying it aloud was like a conjuring. Nathaniel gave himself a few moments to recollect as he struggled to find the right words to describe her. There was the way she looked at a man. The defiantly brash eyeballing of a woman who had ceased to be a girl early in life. *Like so many sisters he had known coming up.* She had this toughness; she frowned more than she smiled, but when she did, she lit up the room.

"Tell me about her," Jonah said.

"I will. I'm thinking on it now. I have to get in rhythm when I'm storying. I'm not usually the talking type like you. But don't be thinking that means I ain't got a whole lot on my mind. Because I do," Nathaniel said.

There was a point in his life, Nathaniel said, when he noticed a shift happening around him. He could feel it happening, not just to him but to everyone. At first, he chalked it up to a frustration that he didn't have the championship rings he had always dreamed of winning. The hard facts of age and injury had dimmed that prospect, even as he battled the pains that became more frequent and that he refused to acknowledge. But it wasn't just his body. The game was changing. It was glossier, louder, bigger somehow. The splash of money was in your face, and it changed attitudes. On the court, in the locker room, but most of all in everyday life. Things that weren't done in his day were becoming common, some of them rumored, but a lot of them showing up in the newspaper and sometimes on the six o'clock news. He felt cut out, as if the segment of history to which he belonged had been dropped from the big board. He spent more and more of their games watching from the bench. He saw a shadow in his future, a time beyond the game that only recently had been unthinkable to him. How would he fill it? He thought about going back to school. He had always felt he had to hide his love of school. He never talked about it. But the truth was that he regretted how little he actually read in college. He had barely gone to class. If he had more time, and eventually he would, he could read whatever he wanted. He always had so many questions that lurked in the back of his mind. But the game was everything, his career, his future, how he put food on the table. He had pushed those questions out of bounds.

But he had always felt a deep desire to learn more about history. He knew his people were from the Carolinas. His grandfather had moved the family to New York in the migration. And he knew that his mother's side had roots in Haiti. At least that was what they always said. In fact, his mother had even sung some Creole lullabies to him as a child. The little bird, *ti zwazo*, going where he's not supposed to. When his mother sang it fired his imagination like the sun. It was all that kept him and his sister alive in those early years, the worst years, after his father left with no news until they learned he had been charged and locked up in another state.

Nathaniel had been hotheaded from the beginning. What his father called "a knucklehead." The Bronx streets never gave an inch. In the static there was no other way to be. He'd seen his first body when he was eleven. A Puerto Rican boy only a few years older than himself in Echo Park with a hole in him and no one coming to help. He had seen the pimps handling the streetwalkers, and the women lined up and fondled by the cops on Southern Boulevard. By the time he was fifteen he had scrambled in and out of hot rides, seen a kid lose one of his eyes to a brass knuckle, had a knife pulled on him by a man twice his age who pulled him into an alley and told him he was going to die that day. If it wasn't for his sister, Naia, who knew how to talk sense into him, he almost certainly would have ended up dead or behind the wall like his old man. It was really only by chance—and the fact that his high school coach took a liking to him—that he started playing ball. Discovered that he was unguardable off the dribble; could shoot the lights out when he wanted to. They let him know if he wanted to keep playing, he had to get his grades right. He was never happy with schoolwork, though. The desk chairs gave him cramps. In class, the way people snickered and put eyes on him when he spoke made him feel stupid. But he loved to read the paper, something he could remember seeing his father doing when he was a little boy. Especially the sports section, where alongside the gray columns and score boxes were pictures of the greats immortalized in their action. The Big Dipper rising for a layup, skywalking like a graceful astronaut.

He never had too many illusions about the business side of basketball. The trades, the scouts, the college reps, the coaches. He knew it all came down to the numbers: his stats, their cash flow, being docile, telling them what they wanted to hear, getting minutes. The only thing he cared about was getting a chance. He was good and he knew it. If he got the right opportunity, he could take over a game. They would see what he could really do and then it would be set. He would be able to provide for his mother. With his success he could give her the protection he had always dreamed of as a boy. He could move his mother out to Jersey. And not a day too soon. The block wasn't just bad. By then, it had become apocalyptic.

He got his break and pressed his advantage as best he could. The years in the league flew by in a blur of sweat, bright lights, adrenaline highs, and crushing blows. He would never have believed the rise and fall through the seasons could happen so fast. He could replay entire games, or parts of them, in his head. Feel the gruel of a walk to the locker room. Hear the ecstatic roar of big wins. He had played alongside and against heroes and legends, guys who had changed what the game could be. Dr. J in Philly, Magic on the Lakers, Earl the Pearl with the Knicks. He was proud just to have been there, to have been part of the generation that brought swagger and soul to the game. He had walked with giants. Fourteen seasons. All, in one way or another, good. Except the last one.

The last year, his mother's sickness meant, for the first time, she couldn't come to his games. Then, shortly after an away game in LA, she died of heart failure. She was sixty-three. He was devastated. For all that Nathaniel had accomplished, he felt he hadn't done enough to do right by her. To make good on the hardships of her life. Women never get the credit that's due them, Nathaniel said. How little they get recognized. And by folks that's closest to them, who really, truly know what it took to bring another generation through. The world is what it is. Women who make everything, who allow themselves to become life itself as it passes through to the future, have the harder road. And who could deny that more often than not, it's a road paved by a man without the slightest notion of where he is trying to go. Losing his mother was a nightmare, Nathaniel said. The dreams of basketball, even if he had won a championship, could not compensate, not even come close. Nothing else had ever anchored his life. She had held his hand for days, refused to leave his bedside when he had to have knee surgery. Now he would have to continue alone.

Staring into the future was like staring at a wall. He had made and saved enough money to not worry about bills. He could pay for the hospital, for the funeral. If need be, he could support Naia; she didn't need him, though—she had graduated from nursing school and was living with a court translator in Montclair.

He was thirty-six years old and in reasonable shape. Yes, he had started to feel his age when he played, but in his mind, in some ways he'd never felt younger. The passion for learning that he had buried for years returning like a tide, rising up to roll back feelings he had locked up in a single word: ignorant. Even the sound, the way some folk said it, made it seem like just a different word for that other one.

His mother would have wanted him to go back to school. Basketball had been his world; looked at one way, that might seem like a good deal, and it was, especially for a black boy from the Bronx. But basketball was also a self-enclosed sphere of existence that could be suffocating. Besides, he could see that the sport was beginning a new chapter, one that Michael Jordan was going to make his own. The pages had already turned. He was a figure from the past, he never had a sneaker deal, didn't know you could have one. Give it a few seasons and the kids would barely recognize him or his name. The machine was moving on, into an Olympic stratosphere of international celebrity and wealth he had never conceived. He still felt lucky. He'd had a good run. He had made the best of the gifts of his body. The question was: What could he do with the other thing? What about the *mind*?

When he and Naia had gone through their mother's things, they had found, besides a study Bible, only two books. One was *The Bluest Eye*. Naia wanted that one, and it seemed natural he should take the other. It was an anthology with a strange title that appealed to him. *The Negro Caravan*. Flipping through it he found only one marking, beside a poem by Langston Hughes, where his mother had penciled in the words *what I want to know* next to the lines

> *When love is gone, O,*
> *What can a young gal do?*

He had never thought of reading poetry, and he felt a flush of shame that he didn't know it was important to his mother. Shame that he had never heard of most of the names in the *Caravan*, who had written all kinds of books, not just poetry, but stories, essays, theater, history. He resolved to get his learning, if he could.

He found a night-school program at City College. At first, it was very hard. He hadn't been in a classroom in so long and hadn't liked it the first time around. He worried that he would stick out, possibly even be recognized and embarrassed by professors or the other students. But the students in the class and the professors at the chalkboard didn't know who he was. They all knew he hooped. But that was on account of his height, not from having watched his games.

History was captivating. Nathaniel learned in detail about slavery and the Civil War, events and epochs he'd only ever had the vaguest notions about. He discovered that there were black writers and thinkers who had studied these things. He was genuinely astonished, and angered, that he had never heard of them before. While he was preparing his final paper, he discovered a history book in the library called *The Black Jacobins*. Something about the image of the black general on the cover intrigued him. He quickly realized from the first few pages that there was too much he didn't know for him to properly understand this Haitian hero, this clue, he thought, to his mother's heritage. The void created by her passing still lived within him. He found himself up late at night, pacing his room. He would stop and stare at the color photograph of himself that he kept on the wall over the TV. In the image he was suspended in air, driving to the hoop, his clover-green jersey rippling, his knees and arms held almost as if in a flying prayer, small beads of sweat on his forehead, his face locked in an expectant grimace. He couldn't stand to look at it anymore. He wanted to change everything, to be someone new. The Haitians had taken the French ideas and the French language and set themselves free. They had thrown the slave masters out and set about making a new world. He wanted to understand that, he wanted to get to the source of things. His stack of books grew, and his learning deepened. He enrolled in an intensive French language course at NYU and read history books as he rode the express trains up and down the length of Manhattan.

He had always wanted a reason to get out of the Bronx and see how things looked from somewhere else. Why not go to Haiti? As it happened, the island was in the news and the news wasn't good. He followed the coverage but couldn't understand enough of the politics to make sense of why there was so much chaos. US soldiers were leaping out of choppers and running through Port-au-Prince like they were still in Vietnam. It wasn't a time to visit. From his language class he learned that, if he paid a fee, he could enroll for a semester as a foreign student at the Sorbonne, in Paris. Obviously, he had the money. And the destination was romantic, an old ideal. It was where the Negro Caravan stopped on its voyage through the desert wilderness. He knew James Baldwin had gone there, Richard Wright, and others. Why couldn't he?

His first days in France were unpleasant and lonely, Nathaniel said. Perhaps, in retrospect, the loneliest days of his life. His classes had not yet begun, and in that first month he mostly encountered American tourists as he made pilgrimage stops at the city's famous monuments and museums. The Parisians were apparently elsewhere. Maybe on one of the far-flung, turquoise-ringed possessions advertised in the Métro that promised all-inclusive packages and discount airfare. The Americans dressed like they were going to the mall. He noticed that waiters, bus drivers, ticket booth operators, and strangers assumed that he was African. They always changed their expression when they heard his accent. Their faces brightened and relaxed as if a stink was gone. Apparently, in Paris his blackness was an African problem. They weren't afraid he was a criminal; they were afraid he was colonial. Never in his life could he have imagined constantly meeting people who were relieved to discover that he was a nigger.

Nathaniel had taken up residence in a small but comfortable room in a three-star hotel on the rue de Rivoli. He wanted to live in style, to have a place that did justice to his vision, or, since he had never before really entertained fantasies of living in Europe, to what he thought his friends and family back home would imagine when they pictured him living abroad in Paris. The image relayed back home and the need to control and manage it was important to him, even if it was unpleasant to think of it that way.

Still, living detached left him prey to certain doubts that had never crept to the forefront of his mind before. He thought of his mother often. Some days he woke alone, consumed with the fear that he was becoming ill. It was a new experience. Although he had suffered injuries, even a serious injury to his hamstring that the doctors thought might keep him out of the game, he had almost always enjoyed optimal health. He took pride in his physical form, in those indomitable qualities that he deployed at will to shake his adversaries. He had always been strong. But ailment was not the same thing as injury.

The only remedy he knew was the rope. He had used the same jump rope since he was sixteen years old. He got it from the manager of a boxing club that no longer existed, a dank, funky old place near the ballpark that was always incensed with a combination of cigar smoke, Pakistani leather, and freshly spilled sweat. People said Joe Louis had practiced there, and Sugar

Ray too. There were two sounds that attracted young Nate as boy on the streets. The whap of gloves rapping on the bags, and the crisp, metallic snap of skipping rope. Before long, he and his rope were virtually inseparable, his nirvana instrumental. Once he got started, he could keep time like a Rolex.

He never would have guessed his training would come in handy in Paris, but it did, one memorable day in September. After his last class of the day, he had tried to take the RER B, which he understood to be like an express train, back to his apartment. But he had ended up taking it in the wrong direction. He didn't realize his mistake until the train was pulling out of the Port Royal station, outbound towards the periphery. A crew had boarded at Port Royal and immediately headed for the far end of the carriage where he was sitting. One was black, three others Arab, the last one possibly Arab or white, it was hard to tell. They were obviously riled up, perhaps not unusually rowdy, but deliberately imposing on the other passengers. Just as the train pulled out of the following station, one of the posse members said something to a young woman who was facing away from them. After a moment the crew burst out laughing, and the same guy got up and stood over her.

There was time for Nathaniel to evaluate the situation. He was outnumbered, but he was also older and stronger than any of them individually by the looks of it. And he was black. Now the same kid was shouting at the woman, obviously telling her to answer him while she sat frozen and looking straight ahead. Furious at her defiance, the kid raised his hand to her, not with much force—more like a humiliating pat on the cheek. He was laughing. Instantly, she threw her arm up and hit him back. Stunned, he came back across her face, hard enough this time that her head audibly cracked as it met the thick plexiglass window of the train.

Nathaniel jumped out of his seat. The other travelers gasped and turned, pretending to see the situation for the first time. He marched right up to the kid so that anyone in the crew would have to get through him to the girl. "You need to back off, now," he said in English, putting a deep *Don't fuck with me* into it. The English surprised the kid, and he seemed to take a second to reconfigure the scene in his mind. "You heard me, step off." The crew was reacting with a mix of incredulity and hilarity, but they were also signaling that they were ready to back their words. Nathaniel readied himself for a blow. In a flash, the kid spit in his face. Nathaniel was so startled that he was slow to react to the first punch. It was a weak one, but the action had signaled the game on, and they jumped over the seats and started pummeling. Nathaniel lashed out, landing confused blows, trying to keep his eyes open, looking out for a knife. He cracked the tallest one with an elbow to the nose. But they surrounded him, kicking him on all sides so he couldn't get to them. The train was slowing. They all started shouting at once. The kid who had accosted the girl did exactly what Nathaniel had feared. He pulled out a knife. Nathaniel tensed, backing against the door-way. The black dude was telling his friend to chill with it. Nathaniel could see the plan forming. They'd stick him just as they pulled into the station, then book it. But they didn't have him pinned down; his chances were still good. Maybe he'd only get grazed. The brakes were whining. The whole train was coming to a nauseatingly slow stop on an embanked curve. The kid was still holding the knife pointed at Nathaniel's midsection. All he needed was a good lunge.

"Je vais te niquer ta race," the kid shouted, laughing and waving the blade. Then suddenly before the doors could open, he reached over to the girl and thrust his left arm out, putting her in a stranglehold. He put the blade up to her face. Nathaniel had seen enough to know what was said by tone. The put-down that compensates for what the knife won't do—this time. "Vas-y, je te laisse cette fois, t'es belle, petite salope." The doors opened. He let the girl go, and the whole crew jumped out. Nathaniel looked at the girl, then bolted. His heart was pounding. He could see them at the far end of the tracks turning off into a corridor. He sprinted as fast as he could, cursing between clenched teeth. He turned at the corridor; it was a long underground passage-way. He could hear their shouts echoing from the far end. It was a straight line, nobody in the way. He put the run on like Jesse Owens, ducking his head, pumping. He reached a staircase leading up to the turnstiles. At the top of the stairs directly in front of him were the swinging pneumatic doors. He burst through them, ready to let all hell break loose. As he came out panting, he noticed figures in blue sweeping in from his peripherals. Two men with gloves and clubs tackled him from behind and sent him smack against the floor. They immediately kneeled on his back, pinning his chest to the ground so that he could barely breathe. One of them started beating him, cracking the baton over his legs and arms. They held him on the ground and told him to shut up while one of them spoke into a crackling radio. Nathaniel could feel the blood from his mouth pooling the cheek pressed to the ground and spilling out onto the cold floor in front of him. Out of the corner of his eye he could see the sneakers of the other members of the posse. They were lying facedown, side by side, with their hands behind their necks. Some more cops showed up with dogs, muzzled German shepherds yanking on their leashes. Commuters walked by, glanced without slowing down. Still more cops arrived, and long discussions ensued; everything was conducted in a dispassionate, even subdued manner, as if each of them really wished they were somewhere else. Finally, it was decided that the posse would be cuffed and taken out in a van. Then they cuffed Nathaniel and walked him out of the station, ducked him with great difficulty into the back of their blue Renault and took off.

At the police station Nathaniel couldn't do anything right. At first, he was so furious at being taken in at all that he refused to even try to speak in French and cursed loudly in English, at which point they threw him in a holding pen and told him he could wait there indefinitely for a translator. After a few hours, since no translator materialized, they decided to try again, and this time, Nathaniel, using his broken French, gave them his basic information. This only seemed to make them even more suspicious, convinced that he was an African trying to pass himself off as an American to avoid having to confess his illegal immigration. He wasn't carrying his passport, but he did keep a New York driver's license in his wallet. The officers passed the little plastic card around, making faces. No one asked him about the events on the train. They asked him about drugs. Then they simply told him he was going to continue being detained until they cleared things up and he was sent back to his holding cell.

He put his head in his arms and tried to sleep. He couldn't. Never in his whole life had he gone to jail. The only time he had ever even seen the inside of a police station was when he was seventeen and had gone with his mother down to the Forty-Second Precinct on Washington Avenue to pick up his uncle, who had been taken in on a domestic abuse complaint. His mother had told him then and he had never forgotten it: "Boy, don't you ever do anything in this city that might land you anywhere near a police station. You can't afford it. People disappear in this system. Don't matter what you did or say you did. Once they have you, they can make you go away. We love you. But we won't be able to do nothing for you. Once you in their hands, you belong to 'em. Right and wrong ain't got nothing to do with it. That's just how it is."

But that was before he became a star. He found himself laughing uncontrollably. These bastards have no idea, he thought. They've arrested an innocent man, an innocent black American who also happens to be a famous basketball player. And they had busted him for trying to be a Good Samaritan! If only he had a Topps card. He was detained for three more hours until finally an officer came in and led him out to the reception area. The girl from the train was standing at the desk talking to one of the officers. When she saw Nathaniel come out, she was visibly moved. After hearing her story, the police captain said he was satisfied that the man they were holding was not a criminal, but that he still needed to clear up some issues about his identity and background. The young woman told them she refused to leave until he was released. She insisted he be let out from the holding cell, so they moved him to a bench in the hall. She sat down next to him. It was then he realized that she looked familiar.

"Thank you," she whispered in English. "I'm sorry about all this."

"It's okay."

"Do you recognize me, from the university?"

"Yes, it's you—I've seen you, well, I saw you outside the tabac, the Ravaillac."

"Ah yes, everyone goes there . . . except you. I guess you don't smoke."

"Hell no! I'm an athlete—or I was—I seem to be out of shape. A few years ago I would have caught those guys easy. Taught them how we get down in the Bronx. I used to play basketball."

"Of course."

"Of course?"

"You're so tall. You stand out in the amphitheater. I'm not the only one who noticed. All the girls talk about you."

"Is that a fact?"

"This is so terrible. I'm so sorry they are treating you so bad. Nothing like this has ever happened to me before," she added after a moment. "My name is Laura. Laura Petrossian."

"Nathaniel Archimbald," he replied. "You can call me Nate. Hey, you know, your English is really excellent," he added after a moment.

She burst out laughing.

"Your French is very bad!"

⁊ß

The university courses took place in a grand amphitheater with a waxy fug. A professor would stand center stage and discharge the lecture in rolling waves of latinate complexity. Laura's attendance was irregular, so Nathaniel never knew if he would see her. He was learning about the history of France, and Napoleon's conquests were carefully and rather lovingly examined for their triumphs of grandeur, cunning diplomacy, and personal hubris. Inevitably, Haiti came up, though more as a footnote than a fatal and world-altering check on French dominion. Nate was primed for this and eager to intervene. But this was not allowed of him, nor of any of the other students around him, who dutifully took down their notes in the same bemused, impassive way they took down everything else. But just hearing about the treacherous and dishonorable treatment of Toussaint Louverture made Nathaniel's blood boil. Every day after class, he needed a couple of hours just to decompress. He found a corner of the Tuileries Gardens where he could stretch and skip rope in the evening. His shoulder blades flexing, his posture proud and linear like one of the Louvre's Egyptian statues, his feet tapping like a ballerina, Nathaniel would skip rope staring with a severe, disciplined intensity. He strengthened himself in rhythm, murmuring to himself the names of his mother's ancestors, the heroes and generals of the Haitian Revolution. François Mackandal. Georges Biassou. Cécile Fatiman. Capois-La-Mort, the Black Achilles.

It was after such a session, returning in the evening to his hotel suite, when Nathaniel first met Claude, the new desk clerk on the nightshift. At first, Claude's English was so good it had Nathaniel suspecting he must have an American parent or attended an international school. But Claude smiled and insisted he had only taken the usual classes in school. Everything else he learned by listening to hip-hop.

When Claude learned that Nathaniel was from New York City, he was ecstatic. His whole face, round as it was already, glowed with excitement and admiration. His questions were endless. Nathaniel couldn't make an inch through the lobby without a symposium on the state of hip-hop, the situation in New York, the possibilities for blacks in America. Did he have a position on West vs. East? Biggie vs. Tupac?

The night clerk's queries took Nathaniel back. All the way back to the distant memory of his father's voice, and the voices of his friends scrapping around the blocks of Morrisania and Melrose, the Hub off Willis and 149th Street, the dead buildings that scorched the neighborhood, barbecues and summer jams, block parties. Night games on basketball courts where every drive to the hole was also a shot at someone's character. The rattle of subways and the smell of peanut butter crunch and musty bodegas. The sound of a watermelon-red Buick guzzling up Third Avenue, and girls in high-tops sitting on stoops, laughing, calling out his name. Nathaniel spent more and more evenings hanging out in the lobby with Claude late into the night. Within a few weeks, Claude had convinced him to leave the expensive hotel and move in with him and his friends in Maisons-Alfort, a suburb to the south of the city.

Nathaniel knew what living in what they called the banlieue meant. It was basically the hood. But he wanted to be around skinfolk at least some of the time he was abroad, and that was where they were at. It would also mean spending a tiny fraction of what he was spending on hotel luxuriance and room service. It was time to see what the Other Paris was about.

Claude was renting an apartment with two other West African friends on the eighth floor of a housing block. Their unit was in the bottom half of an L on the far side of six identical buildings that made up the Cité Lamartine. The buildings were joined by a barren concrete esplanade, along which several rows of scooters were always parked, and where there had once been a low-rise frontage for shops (most boarded up and closed down) and a kind of gravel extension where kids played soccer. In fact, there was only one business still open—Faisal's, a kind of café or tea shop run by Ahmed, an Egyptian, that served as the informal meeting room for the men of Cité Lamartine.

It was at Faisal's over Moroccan tea that the new roommates all met for the first time. Claude introduced Nathaniel as his American friend, which drew large smiles. He was introduced to Ghislain, a young man from Cameroon who worked as a cook in a Senegalese restaurant in the Marais. Then to Apollinaire, a slightly older Senegalese man, nearer to Nate in age, who had arrived in Paris almost ten years before, and who had a job working as a sanitation worker for the city. And Claude explained finally that he was French, born in Sarcelles, but that his parents were from the French island of Martinique. They toasted to a new beginning.

The apartment was small but functional. Nate had his own room, as did Claude, while Apollinaire and Ghislain agreed to share a room and pay less for their share of the rent. Nate had a window that faced out onto the scrubby outskirts of Maisons-Alfort, which consisted mostly of a car-and-motorcycle dealership, more apartment complexes, and a low, flat, boxy building, which turned out to be their local Leader Price grocery store. Claude's window faced the inside esplanade of the Cité, and in front of it, he had set up his decks, his mixer, and a synthesizer he had hooked up to a PC. His bed was often covered in clothes that he would mix and match, crisp outfits that he kept meticulously ordered in his mirrored closet. The rest of the room was devoted to his records and to the neat rainbow rows of a nice sneaker collection.

With his new friends and warmer living arrangement, things were falling into place. At the university, Nathaniel's heart always jumped when he spotted Laura entering the amphitheater. She would come over to him and meet his cheek with a warmly perfumed *bise*. They often paused to chat before class in one of the grand stairwells, a flirtatious islet in the hubbub of students streaming in and out of the lecture halls.

He continued to struggle with his coursework. His French was still pretty bad, as she had pointed out, although he found he could understand a good deal more than he could speak. But the professors certainly didn't make it easy. They had a way of talking about an idea or an event without ever really saying what they thought about it, or what had happened.

The history of Iceland, one professor seemed to argue, was crucial to understanding the origins of the French Revolution. Nathaniel had never thought about Iceland in his life, nor the people that lived there, and it occurred to him that had he not taken this particular course he most likely would have gone to his grave without ever even once having considered them. The professor said that one of the great human tragedies of the modern era took place on this tiny North Atlantic island. A period known as the *Mist Hardships,* which followed the eruption of the volcano Laki on June 8, 1783. This massive eruption, the professor explained, produced the closest thing to nuclear winter that anyone had ever experienced until Hiroshima. In Iceland, anyone living at that time would have believed it was the end of the world. Clouds of poisonous sulfur and ash blotted out the sun. Rivers of fire and falling molten rock set fire to the villages. The clouds of death spread to Europe. In London the fog of noxious gases made navigation of the Thames impossible. Laki's pall of doom generated extreme weather that spread chaotic and toxic conditions around the globe. In the winter of 1784, as far away as North America, the Mississippi froze at New Orleans, with icebergs spotted by bewildered slave and sugar traders in the Gulf of Mexico. The extreme weather lasted until 1788, when disastrous hailstorms put the final nail in the coffin of Europe's peasant underclass, causing widespread famine, notably in France, where passions stoked by the Jacobin intelligentsia set the house of Europe on fire, igniting a revolution that forever changed the course of history. Geography. Meteorology. The seasons of the Earth are as much an actor in History as any other force, the professor claimed. Even the origins of the French Revolution could be traced and explained, at least in part, by a spell of bad weather. A change of climate issuing from a dismal and humiliated island in the North Atlantic that no one cared about. History, the professor concluded, is a deep ditch of diabolical misfortune, out of which Man has always struggled to climb by filling the cavity with the bodies of other men somehow unlike him and using them as a ladder, only to discover that the bodies and the ditch are one and the same thing, and that nothing is more like oneself than one's enemy.

∗∗

Nathaniel had recounted his story with Laura to his roommates. They listened and they offered their advice. "The women here are not trustworthy," Ghislain said. "You have to be very careful. Don't get involved in something you can't control, or you'll have problems and the police will come and deport you if they can, and if they can't, they will harass you so much you'll want to leave anyway." Apollinaire said that he had never been with a white woman, that he wasn't interested in white women, that every time he had ever interacted with a white woman it had only further confirmed his feelings. Ghislain passed around a joint. Claude said women were not something you could know about one way or the other. You had to accept that and flow with it day by day and not judge them because, in the end, you can only judge yourself.

One evening, Laura invited Nate to dinner at her new apartment, a fifth-floor walk-up in an old building on the rue des Cinq-Diamants. You could see most of the place from the entryway. It was more of an attic with a kitchenette and a shower. She had a little oval window with a view of rooftops and potted chimneys and a patch of sky. It reminded Nathaniel of a painting that he had seen at the Musée d'Orsay.

Laura made grape leaves stuffed with ground lamb and rice in a mint yogurt sauce. They drank a bottle of burgundy with the meal, and a second one kept them talking late into the night. After clearing the dishes, she went over to the window where he stood and put her hand on his back. As he turned, she raised herself on her toes, leaned forward, and kissed him. It was a good kiss. Nathaniel found himself surprised at how safe he felt. He had wondered if he would actually be capable of feeling at peace in her arms. But he did. He had also feared a certain intimidation on her part. But she was without hesitation, as if the pleasures she would give and receive would have always been self-evident. If anything, he was the one who was slightly intimidated by her feistiness. How she strapped herself around his torso, pressing her dark nipples to his chest, nipped him with puckish kisses, came with unassuageable ferocity.

When he woke up, Nathaniel felt a cold breeze running along his arm. Laura was asleep, curled under the blanket like a teardrop. He got up. It had rained, and there was a puddle forming along the wall and the baseboard. He closed the window and glanced around the apartment. He ran some water and did the dishes. Then he brought the wine bottles down and slotted them one by one, with shattering cries, into a giant municipal-recycling container. He spotted a bakery. Laura looked confused when she opened the door to let him back in. "I brought you some breakfast," he said. He took the warm pastries out of their paper pouch and set them on the table. They spread spoonfuls of confiture along the innards and talked.

They decided to go for a walk in the Parc Montsouris. Nathaniel was convinced that the people they passed were staring at them. He thought for a long time about how to put this to Laura and wondered whether she was seeing the same thing. But by the time he had put together the words to ask her, they had crossed all the way through the park and arrived at the station where he would have to take the train back out to the suburbs. The way she held him as they kissed made putting it off indefinitely desirable.

"No life is really meaningful without good food. Without eating well. Without fish and rice and mango and okra, the world would be a mistake," Ghislain said. "There is no greater food to be found anywhere than in Cameroon, a land, thank god, blessed with the best fish and the freshest fruits in all of Africa. I must teach you how to cook real dishes from Yaoundé, which, if you prepare them only once for your lover, she will never leave you. Like Roger Milla, you will score every time!"

"What Ghislain is saying is wise, leke mo bax," said Apollinaire, "but not entirely true. The greatest food in the world, it is well known, comes from Senegal, which makes the finest sauces and the most raffiné cuisine in all of Africa. And the real way to a woman's heart is to make yassa with fresh catch from the Casamance caught by the excellent fishermen of Ziguinchor. Or a chicken mafé with a spicy peanut sauce that they also love in Mali. Or a delicious lamb dibi if she is more of a city girl and you want to show off the savors of the capital. Basically, love in a marriage should resemble a long meal, pleasantly sauced and served with care. That is, grosso modo, all there is to the good life."

"Taking a woman out to dinner can be expensive," said Claude. "If you cook for her you will save money, but she will also love you more because good in the kitchen means good appetite, which means good sex and good health, and if you can have all those things in your life at once then you must be doing something right with your life, because God bestows his favors and blessings on the just."

Nathaniel and Laura spent many nights together. And many days too, days when they were supposed to be in lecture but remained marooned in her blankets pleasuring each other in the quiet part of the afternoon when folks were still at work, and the traffic was light, and they could hear the leaves outside whisking greenly. He would hold the curves of her belly. Smell her olive-black hair, pressing into the pillow beside him like his picture in the history book of an old Roman aqueduct.

One day, on a square near the Métro Jourdain, he came upon a large poster on the side of a building of a starving African child. The eyes were sunk deep in their cavities, and the skin around the mouth was so taut to the jawbone that the expression was fixed in a tawdry, heinous smile. The slogans asked passersby to give, to fight, to support, to end hunger. He froze for a moment before the black-and-white advertisement.

Why was it always like this? A nameless starving African. And people going to work averting their eyes, the message assimilated, quietly disposed of. How much had really changed? The agency behind the poster had probably hired a marketing team to produce their campaign. They had offices in London, Geneva, Paris, and New York, and employed wealthy and upper-middle-class whites who could afford to live in the great cities and chose to take up more attractive volunteer work. The life behind the starving face had no substance or will. A fly crawling over the mind of Europe.

Nathaniel felt a swelling rage. There was such a vast canvas of injustice, bigger than he had ever previously imagined, worse the more he learned. All the knowledge he had acquired since he had moved abroad was coiling together, glowing hot as his own sense of futility increased. It was like the time when he stood in that awesome hallway in the Louvre, nearly deafened by the massive paintings on all sides, furious at the hollering mobs of tourists knocking into him with flagrant fouls. He was surrounded on all sides by pinkish angels and Madonnas and bearded saints with their marks of holiness, their place in history. But nowhere, in the entire palace, could he find a celebration of the goodness, the power, the intelligence, the glory of anyone who looked like him. Not one instance in all the sacred imagery of the Occident of a black man crowned with power and holiness.

And yet he felt especially peculiar, perhaps more alien than ever, when he passed the groups of young black teenagers huddled together in the gray wastelands in the city center at Les Halles. Boys who looked so familiar to him, and yet who regarded him with a wary curiosity. And he couldn't deny that this was, at least in part, because they (like whoever had built the hideous shopping-mall complex where they copped their cheap Euroburgers and chased skirt) seemed astonishingly indifferent to the flying buttresses of Saint-Eustache. A building whose old stone arches and spires filled him with awe.

At the top of the rue du Transvaal, there was an esplanade from which one could see the whole city spread out below. It was lovelier than the Bronx. It had art and aspiration. But did it have *soul*? Did it have a place for *his* arts? *Would the mind of Europe ever be able to incorporate him?* Just then, as if to banish any further thoughts, an overwhelming need to urinate came over him and he marched furtively down into the sketchy park below. There, he found a suitable tree and released a torrent which, in an alternate universe, he would have made gargantuan enough to drown every embassy, every sleek arms-dealing bureau, every petroleum office tower, every pompous government office building in the city of light.

The questions nagged at him. Could he love the woman and not her city? Could she ever love him across the vast gulf of experience that separated two people like them? What was it in her that he couldn't reach? What filled her with the sadness that he had detected from the very start, but that she wouldn't reveal or hadn't yet? He had seen the traces of that sadness. They could show themselves in anything or nothing at all. In the way she said, "Toss me a cigarette, I think there's one in my raincoat." Or those odd moments, he noticed, when she stared absently at her own hands. Sometimes when they fucked, he would catch a glimpse of her mouth biting at the air, uttering words that he couldn't understand, that he supposed were

Armenian, or maybe not even words at all but a lost or alternative alphabet accessed only in those fleeting moments when sex makes language strange again, keeping a part of the world secret, sacred, free from the will of men.

One night as they left a café in the Latin Quarter, Laura pulled on Nathaniel's arm, and said she wanted to talk. They moved off the boulevards and took the narrower, older streets. They came to the fountain square at Saint-Sulpice. One of the bell towers of the church was covered in scaffolding, the clasped fingers of planks and girders covering its massive, ghostly presence in a loose skin that rippled and ballooned gently in the wind.

Laura said she was thinking a lot about her brother, Mehdi. Nathaniel felt as if a jab had caught him in the ribs. "I didn't know you had a brother," he interrupted, stopping in his tracks for emphasis. She had never mentioned him before.

Laura stared at the pavement as she fished through her bag. "I'm sorry, I thought you would be overwhelmed because Mehdi adds a layer of complication to my life. He's really only my half brother, and he's Muslim. He stayed in Lebanon with an uncle. I haven't seen him since we left Beirut. We were very close before my parents took us away. I get letters from him sometimes, very beautiful letters in Arabic. He's a great writer. So good." She paused to light a cigarette. "My parents won't talk to him. My father never got over his decision to stay in Beirut or his disdain of science. Mehdi embraced religion and totally rejected Paris and the studies that my father wanted him to pursue. He said he didn't need the French to understand his place in the world or the universe that Allah set in motion. Sometimes I think he was right to want to stay. When I read his letters, I think about how long it's been since I've seen an olive tree. Just sunlight and an olive tree in a garden. The smell of cypress and lavender and the wooded closeness of earthly things."

They walked slowly up the rue Férou. Laura continued. "I thought God was real when I was little. One summer, my parents took us on a trip to the Sinai. We stayed with Bedouin in a camp by the Red Sea. In the distance on the water there was a city we were forbidden to go to. At night, one of the old Bedouin men took us away from the campfires and up into the dunes. His blue shesh was wrapped under his chin and his hands were very bony and strong. We rested on one of the highest dunes overlooking the camp, with Mehdi on one side of the old man and myself on the other. 'Look up,' he said. We looked into the deep and all that was there were the stars. The old man said, 'Look close,' and he lifted a hand into the darkness above. 'Do you see it?' And Mehdi said yes, he did. And I asked, 'What are we looking for?' And the old Bedouin laughed and tousled my hair roughly and then took my hand and made an arc with it through the middle of the sky. And then I did see it. A trail, a phantom plume like fog on a windshield. 'What is it?' I asked. The Bedouin said that it was the fingerprint of God. And then he said something that I didn't understand, but that Mehdi nodded to in agreement. He told us that men's fates were written in the stars. And then he coughed loudly and spit in the sand. He told us not to live dangerously. That danger was always a sign your life was out of balance. He told us to love life and to love Allah, who gave us the chance to know Him. Then he put his bony hand on my thigh and held it very hard, which scared me. He said it was necessary to live very close to Allah. 'In the cities, a life in accordance with the will of Allah is impossible,' he said. 'Only the desert nomad knows his ways and does not stray from the righteous path.' It was one of the most frightening experiences of my life," Laura said. "But I think about it often. And when I do, I think of Mehdi."

Back in the apartment on the rue des Cinq-Diamants, Laura undressed in the bathroom. When she came out, Nathaniel was lying naked on his stomach. She slipped down next to him and kissed him gently between the shoulder blades. Their bodies wanted as immoderately as ever. But something was there that was also different. The distress of brittle sex that is not as it once was.

9

The central stairwells of the Cité Lamartine formed a vertical chorus. All through the day, the crying of children, the muffled shouts, the scurrying whoops and shrieks of schoolchildren, the racket of scooters coming in through broken windows, the laughter and ritual greetings saturated the life on the landings and even in the spaces between them. Sisters, mothers, neighbors from every corner of the former colonial world raised up a babel from their impromptu salons, chatting, gossiping, arguing as they braided, twisted, brushed, picked, locked, roped, pressed, and prodded.

Behind this polyphonic hubbub, Nathaniel recognized a recorded music that amplified as he rose toward the upper floors. It was coming from the apartment next door, and he knew from his time at Faisal's that it was the extraordinary voice of Umm Kulthum. She sounded to Nathaniel like a blues singer. When he asked his African friends about her they told him, only half-jokingly, that her voice was the only thing the Arabs agreed upon. An experience of transcendent beauty that some, in moments of weakness (and near blasphemy), said even rivaled the surahs of the Qur'an. If the windows were open, and he knew that on a day like this they probably were, her call to her lover, her habibi, would carry out over the balcony, a faint wail reaching the ears of the kids playing soccer in the concrete lot.

Ghislain was cooking, and throughout the apartment there was a heavy aroma of okra stewing in peanut sauce. Nathaniel dropped two grocery bags in the kitchen and exchanged greetings with the chef. When the food was ready the four men sat down and ate by hand from a large bowl set in the center of the table equidistant from each of them. At first, they all ate in silence. Then they discussed their plans for the evening. Each of the roommates desired to know how Nathaniel's affairs were progressing with Laura, and if he had yet considered marriage. Ghislain produced cups and boiling mint tea, which he poured from very high without losing a drop. For a time, they drank in silence as they listened to the faint voice of Kulthum through the wall. "Nathaniel," Claude asked suddenly, changing the subject, "do you think one day there will be a black president of America?" Nathaniel felt as if he should have anticipated the question, even though he had no prepared thought on the matter. He looked around at the other men. They met his gaze gravely in a way that suggested they expected him to take some time to answer.

Nathaniel closed his eyes. For a moment his father's voice wavered in his mind. The time he had talked about Malcolm. Nathaniel was twenty the year they shot King down in Memphis. And the poet Henry Dumas just a month later, right there in Harlem. He hadn't taken it as badly as others had, certainly not as badly as his father. But that was before. That was then. Now he had taken more time to learn, to think and reflect. When he thought on it hard what he saw in his mind was dishonor. Too many nameless dead. Ship holds. Coffles. The deaths he had seen in his own lifetime. At Orangeburg over a bowling lane. At the hands of the police. He thought of the years of lynching. The faces smiling under the charred flesh of Jesse Washington down in Texas. He thought of the Freedmen betrayed in the Reconstruction. The long centuries before then, all under the whip of the founding fathers, as they took in their immeasurable lucre, built their empire westward, fiddled in their private Monticellos. He thought of all the brothers behind bars. The acquittals of officers, as regular and predictable as tides. Nathaniel opened his eyes. It was shocking to realize how powerfully he missed home. How the catalog of infamy that he had wanted, consciously or unconsciously, to run away from for so much of his life, to somehow ignore or work around, was still not powerful enough to keep him on the run forever. How strange it was to be here in this other land, in so many ways a better one, where he was seeing and understanding more than at any other time in his life, and yet his experiences, his study of history, all of it was only solidifying an itch he had repressed: a need to get back, to return home.

"No," he said finally, looking over at Claude, "I don't think there will be a black president in my lifetime." He thought a moment and added, "But that won't keep us from trying."

Of the three friends from Cité Lamartine, Apollinaire was the one Nathaniel had gotten to know the least. Yet the week before it all came to an end, they had shared a most intimate moment together, one that Nathaniel could never forget. Apollinaire had insisted they go for a drive. Nate had to practically crouch to get himself in the little green Simca, but once they were packed in they peeled out marvelously, swerving out of the projects with a beastly guzzle, accelerating along the wide boulevards extérieurs, crossing the arm of the Seine at Bercy, switching lanes, the suspension yawing as they darted through traffic. A wooden cross on a string of colored beads jangled in a syncopated dance over the dash.

"Open the glove box!" Apollinaire ordered, as he imperiled their lives in an attempt to light a pungent cigarillo. Nathaniel popped the notch and instantly, an avalanche of papers began flying into the back seat. Nathaniel quickly shut it again, but not before having nabbed one of the pages as it whipped past. Compiled with a wobbly ballpoint pen was a list with the heading *The Plot Against Africa*:

Jacques Foccart / François de Grossouvre / Paul Barril / Bob Denard / Étienne Léandri / Charles Pasqua / Félix-Roland Moumié / Bolloré / Outel Bono / Eduardo Mondlane / Herbert Chitepo / Amílcar Cabral / Dulcie September / Steve Biko / Patrice Lumumba / Thomas Sankara / Aginter Press / Robert Sobukwe / Union Minière du Haut-Katanga /

"Don't worry about that," Apollinaire said. "Just some research of mine. Look in there for my OK Jazz." Nathaniel rummaged through the papers at his feet and pulled out a plastic cassette box. *Franco et le Tout Puissant OK Jazz Band, Paris 1984.* The tape was a mess, looping out in a crazed tangle. Nathaniel stuck his pinky in one of the eyes, felt the teeth pinch his fingertip, wound it back till it was tight again, then shoved it in the car deck between their knees.

The twang of African guitars and Lingala poured out of the car stereo. Electrified guitars clanging Franco bellowing out with his chorus chiming in behind—*LIBERTÉ*—the guitar ringing out *eh pa! OK Jazz en forme* Apollinaire agreeing slapping the gearbox through second and third and fourth up the boulevard Leclerc—*LIBERTÉ*—Franco insisting on it the guitar chimes spilling over with a shattering clarity like diamonds in a briefcase on a flight from Goma to Kisangani to Antwerp like earrings chilling a glass countertop at De Beers—*LIBERTÉ*—Apollinaire gliding the whip expertly round the Place de la Nation the tires of the Simca skittering over the neatly combed cobblestone the two friends leaning magically in time muziki na biso—*LIBERTÉ*—in their wake the frown of disbelieving Gauls bopped on the head by the swinging congas of the Simca this African parrot green and raucous and loud her chassis screeching in bittersweet spasm—sweet *LIBERTÉ!!!*

"Ah voilà, mon ami. Nous sommes arrivés." Apollinaire brought the car to a stop by the side of the road just off the roundabout at Porte Dorée.

"My friend, I wanted to bring you here to tell you a story, to illustrate to you so you might know my situation. You see that telephone booth over there. That one. I used to sleep in it. No money, no job, nowhere to go. It was a very bad time. That café over there, I would go in there when they were closing and offer to clean their toilet in return for some bread and a glass of wine to help me sleep. At first the waiters just said no. But I came back again, and the barman who was very nice, he said okay, but just a few times, a week maybe. Then I had to go elsewhere. I was very scared. It was a very hard time. And then, my friend, a miracle happened. I met a woman. Here, right here, where we are now. Her name was Florèse. You see over there that great building? That is the Tropical Aquarium of Paris. That was where she worked. One evening when she came out, she saw me, and she saw how I had nothing. How I was scared. My friend, I was so ashamed. That was the first day, the first day of my life, I really began to believe in God. Florèse took me home with her. She lived just around the corner in a tiny room on the rue de l'Alouette. You know, I had not washed and I smelled so bad. But she didn't say anything. She gave me soap. I thought I was in heaven. I was so happy. I was sleeping on her floor. And I would lie there and think, this is the greatest gift God has given me. Florèse gave me life again, and I began to fall a little bit in love with her. During the days I would look for work. I found some small jobs but always in the evening I would come back. And I asked, 'Florèse, what can I do for you?'

"She had pain to her back when she worked. So she'd take me some evenings into the aquarium, secretly, when it was closed and there was no one. And I helped with her job. I was doing cleaning, washing things so she could rest. It was water all around us. We were alone under the ocean. Florèse knew all the fish and she would name them to me, like a goddess: gourami fish, green and pink Malabar fish, Picasso fish, Blue Hamlet fish. We would walk together and talk this way. And little by little I came to see two things. That Florèse was very intelligent, like a scientist or a saint. And that she was a woman who loved women. She was always talking about her lover. And even so, I know it's crazy, but I found myself falling deeply in love. I hid my feelings, of course! What could I do? Besides, we became good friends. It was Florèse who introduced me to the music of Franco and the Orchestre Kinshasa. And it was Florèse who opened me to poetry. She was always writing on her days off, and sometimes, if I was helping her, she would write during her shift while I mopped. She encouraged me to make my own poems. She said it helped when you were hungry. She said that when you write you do not feel the time so much, and I discovered this is true.

"Florèse gave me books to read and she taught me many words. I was changing and becoming better in many ways that had escaped me in my past. But the burning inside of my love would not go away, and I did not know what to do. Florèse wrote poems in Lingala for her lover who lives in Saint-Denis and is married to a very religious man. She would read her poems to me and try to teach me words from her language. And it stung me more than you can imagine, because I wanted to learn everything from Florèse. I wanted anything that was drawing us nearer to each other. It was Florèse who introduced me to Rabearivelo. Jean-Joseph, *mon frère austral*, who changed everything in me, whose poems I drank *coup sec* like cups of coffee at six in the morning. I would be hauling trash or moving crates in a warehouse and my mind would drift to the palm beaches of Madagascar, to campeachy trees and willowy filao, to the bars and taverns of Antananarivo. Florèse would read to me from his journals. And I suffered with him the pain of wanting to get away, to get to Paris at all costs, and yet desiring the fragrance of home only the more with each passing day. Florèse told me that it was Rabearivelo who gave her the courage to continue writing in the face of everything. Florèse was a great poet too. But she was hopelessly in love with a married woman. I knew from the tone of her poems, even though I couldn't understand most of them, that I would never be able to reveal my feelings for her.

"Then one day, the immigration police came and arrested her, right in front of everyone, all of her colleagues at the aquarium. It was terrible. Of course, there was no way I could see her, or find out if she was alright. I had to think of my own problems. Through contacts I learned that they had deported her. She had been working with false papers. Some people said that she had gotten them through Papa Wemba. I don't know if it is true. What I do know is that she made it back to Kinshasa, because about a month later a person from the community found me at the café and gave me a letter from Florèse postmarked from the Congo. In the letter she asked me to act as a courier, to discreetly forward her poems to her lover in Paris.

I wrote her back and promised her that I would take this job. Soon letters began arriving regularly from Kinshasa. Nathaniel, would you believe, to this day they come in thick envelopes with many stamps. And every couple of months I meet a woman I know nothing about, only her first name, and we always meet at the same café. I wait at a little table with letters from the woman I love in my hands, and her lover comes in and joins me. We talk about the weather and such things. She leaves a coin for the coffee, takes her packet, and leaves. This is what I owe Florèse. I have to do this for her. She saved me, out of the goodness and the strength of her heart. This is how I live, my friend. It is hard, very hard to live away from the people and the places that you know and love. My heart is not broken, but it is heavy. It is far away in the Congo where I know the most wonderful woman in the whole world is writing poems and love letters, but not for me."

⁂

Life in Paris came abruptly to an end. But when it did, Nathaniel did not find himself entirely surprised. It was as if there had been an off-ramp he knew was coming, and perhaps had even somehow wished into being. Still, he was deeply hurt that Laura never came to say goodbye. It was a friend of hers who delivered the message one day after classes. She simply said she was charged with telling him that Laura would not be coming to classes anymore and handed him a letter written on a loose sheet of quadrille paper. He knew what that letter meant even before reading it. And he had resolved, even before hearing out its arguments, to leave the country.

It turned out she was not only leaving him. Laura said in her note that she was heading to South America, that she needed to get away, and it was a trip she had always wanted to make. He took no comfort in her faint apologies, but he couldn't bring himself to hold the decision against her. After all, he had felt the same urges and made his own moves when he had the chance. Coming to Paris, he had wanted to acquire knowledge that he felt he lacked. He had learned enough. The affair with Laura, the life at

Cité Lamartine, the stories of Apollinaire, all the recent past took on the force of wisdom, the last of it dashed with pain. The whole freewheeling world be damned. He knew where he belonged. He wasn't going to hit the hardwood again. He was too old for that. But he could take the young boys from his neighborhood and teach them to play ball. He could live in the streets of New York with his people and hear those voices again and share those burdens and make something out of the places that made him. Mixed with the hurt that she didn't have the courage or the desire to confront him in person was an ironic sense of relief. He had lived the dream of a black man abroad in Paris. Now he had to complete the other half of that curious pilgrimage: return to the native land.

10

Under the high ceilings of a Tremont Avenue duplex, the young teacher and the retired hooper examined each other closely. Both had listened; both had talked. They enjoyed sharing memories. Across space and time they were connected by so many experiences that connected at odd angles, like crooked street corners. Nathaniel had let the floodgates open within. Talking brought relief and even a little thrill from realizing how crisp his recollection of those days remained.

They had indulged their inward feelings and most private remembrances in the manner of people who believe they will never meet again. Now there was a hesitant energy of expectation between them.

"I'm supposed to go down to South America soon," Jonah said suddenly. Nathaniel squinted, as he gauged this new knowledge.

"You serious?"

"Next week. Flying down to Rio with a friend."

"You mean for the summer?"

"I don't really know. I didn't buy a return ticket. I think what I want right now is just to get away from it all, just sort of be invisible . . ."

But he stopped because Nathaniel was chuckling to himself.

"You want to take off somewhere for a bit. Okay, and then what? It's chess out here, you gotta have at least one or two more moves than that!"

Jonah rubbed his temples.

"I mean, truthfully, I don't know that I'm cut out for this teaching thing. And there's all these places I never been before. I feel like if I don't get to them now, I never will. I'll get stuck in something, maybe something I don't even really like but that I feel like I *have* to do."

"I hear you. That's what *you* want. But just remember, at some point it's not going to be *about* you. At some point you're gonna have to make it about something bigger than that."

"Why?"

"*Why?*"

"Yeah, I mean no disrespect, but like, *why?*"

Something in the tone of this set Nathaniel on a different track. It wasn't that he didn't have enormous sympathy; in a way he'd been just the same even if their life chances had nothing to do with each other. But he couldn't shake the feeling rising in him now that this brother was off course.

"I'll tell you why. Because there's a city right here that needs help. There are children born in this city everyday who are being thrown to the lion's mouth. No education. No opportunities. Damn near half the kids who grew up on my block either dead or in jail, and everybody's lives scarred. You don't really know nothing about that, do you? You don't know what it feels like to look out every day on the same broken streets and know that if you can't play ball or rap, you never going nowhere. What you know about that?"

"I ain't arguing that though."

"You ain't arguing but you ain't saying nothing neither. And I'm calling you on your bullshit, pardon my French. You've had this amazing life. You've had this perspective. You have it all—the sheer *possibility* to do and be anything you want. Now you telling me all you can do is go hide somewhere with your Ellison blues? You gotta own up to some things. You a grown-ass man. It's time to take a look around and take this thing seriously, figure out the reality of the moment. I know that ain't easy. Trust me, I get it. It took me coming back here, back home, to see how privileged I was, and how much trouble my people, our people, are in. And it's deep. I know you're smart enough to *see* that. But do you *know* that?

"Well, I totally get where you're coming from, but see I feel like—"

"Excuse me, brother—but you educated. Not just educated, but worldly in ways most of our people will never get to be. Don't you see how important it is that you share that knowledge with a younger generation?"

"But that's the thing, why does it have to be *me*? You got the media, the corporations, the politicians—what the hell can I do? Nothing's gonna make a difference, so why not just get the hell out, at least go see something else before it all goes to shit, before like everyone in this fucked-up country, I lose my goddamn mind!"

"What I say about that cussing in my house?"

"My bad."

"That's okay, it's a fair point. You just wrongheaded about it is all. Are people's heads all messed up? Yeah. But that's exactly why you got to speak the truth. Why you gotta give it to 'em raw, uncut, straight to the gut—no bullshit. You got to call out the folks you know is wrong when they wrong, and do it right where you are, right *here* in the community, where it matters, where it *can* make a difference. It's like how I teach when I'm coaching. Talking to the kids about how you got to keep your head straight out here, think for yourself, respect yourself and your community. You don't think it matters that they see someone around them who has that message?"

"But they can't hear that message though."

"Nah, *you* the one not hearing the message. The truth always comes out on top. The best players can go cold, but they don't lose their shot. If you have it, soon enough it will manifest, and when it does, it's a wrap. These phony rappers out here today, flashing they cash and don't have no talent—they can't win the battle for these young minds forever. Not if you show them what else is possible."

"Yeah, but they got money and in this world that's all that counts."

"In the short run, yes. In the long run, no. Ask folks around here, they all want money. But there are lots of other things they want too. Lot of folks want to see they family together again. People want to feel respected and useful. Lot of folks want to see a world where children can be children and never worry about nothing bad happening to them. People want a place to honor their dead. Or make something beautiful that will last beyond their own life. There's all kinds of things."

"Then why does it all feel so hopeless?"

"I don't know, Teach, you tell me! All I know is that nothing good happens when you have no sense of history. No independent sense of values. When you caught up in the propaganda. Don't be fooled when they sell you on that 'We can do anything now' line. We can have all types of achievement. We always have. But it still don't shake out *for the people*. What that tells you is they got us in a funhouse. That tells me, if we're not careful, *we're going to lose our form. Because it can be lost. You feel me? I'm talking 'bout the things that give us shape, substance, form.* You know what I see when I look around? I see black jelly. All this rawness, all this raw energy that's beautiful but got no *direction*. Smuckers, motherfuckers. And you know what I think? I think that's exactly what the Man wants. He don't want you *thinking*. He don't want you knowing too much. Getting your bearings and deciding, on another level, how to *live*. No. He wants the formless energy of our blackness, seedless, no substance. Without form, without agency, without *power*."

"Black power—right, and how we supposed to get that? We've already seen how the Panther picture show ends."

"Well, the first thing is to stop abusing each other. The first thing would be committing ourselves to the point where we are incapable of taking each other's lives—because we *need* each other and *love* each other more than any differences that have come between us. We gotta quit playing ourselves. We gotta come together block by block and city by city to to work this thing out. We all agree that doing whatever it takes to change the basic situation is what needs to be done. And that's where *you* come in. That is exactly where you have a role to play."

"Wait, wait. But why *me*?"

"You a teacher, a natural. I've listened to how you talk. You have the ability to reach these kids. I can *see* it."

"They didn't hire me for my ability, they hired me 'cause no one else wants to do the job! They hired me because it looked good on an Excel table in an email someone had to forward to someone with the power to fire them. And, look, man, I don't even know that I'm *good* at it!"

"But you are *doing the right thing*! Instructing our young men and women. Giving them the understanding they need to get themselves up out of the mess they living in right now, the damn lies and confusion, all the media hype and the garbage that's being thrown at them and they don't even have a chance to form their own damn minds! Only reason I'm here is I was lucky enough to have talent. A rare gift, and then lucky to have all the breaks work in my favor. You have gifts too, and you have this great chance to make a way for others. Who's gonna do it if not you?"

"I don't know."

"*I don't know* . . . You scared. That it?"

"Nah, it ain't that. Like I said I just want to get out. I want out. Isn't that what you did?"

"It is what I did. But I also came back."

They both paused over this last point, which held different meanings for both of them.

"Listen," Nathaniel continued, "why don't you work *with me*? You can help me *right here* in the Bronx. I've got a nice program going. We coordinate with the schools, get the kids out playing ball in the sunshine, keep them away from the dope, the gangs, and the guns, all that shit. I could use a young guy like you, smart, fresh, ready to make a difference, to help out a little bit around here, you know."

"All that's fine, Nate. It really is. I really admire your program and what you're doing, and I do think it's important and all . . . but really . . . why does it have to be me? Why do I have to be the one to do it?"

"Simple. You have to take responsibility for your blackness."

"But . . ."

"You have to take responsibility for *our* people! If the ones like you that have it all won't do it, then no one will. Can't you see that?"

"But I don't want to! I don't want to do any of that! I don't want to be responsible, I just want to live my life!"

Nathaniel let this go without reply and an uncomfortable silence settled over them. In spite of what he was saying, Jonah thought of his students. He thought of B. and her dreams of getting into a fashion school and all the others who would have to continue without him, who would once again feel rejected and abandoned by the people they were told to trust. There was no way to say it, but he knew Nathaniel was right. He *was* scared. He just didn't know what he was scared of or why.

Nathaniel hadn't meant to get so worked up. "Hey, listen, Jonah. We not gonna solve the world's problems in a day. And nobody's saying it's *all* on you. Shit, I didn't mean to make it sound like you the Messiah, cause you damn sure ain't that!"

"I know, I'm sorry, I feel confused is all. I want to do what's right, it's just that . . ."

"Look, man, life will take its course. You're gonna do what you think is best for you, and that's okay. I'm just trying to give you some perspective from where I'm coming from. To remind you that at the end of the day we all gonna have to answer for our choices, what we done, and what we didn't choose to do. I'm just reminding you that you have the choice, the privilege and the choice, to do a lot of good, and if you don't know, well, now you know. All right?"

"All right."

"But yo—don't let me catch your faded ass downtown no more. I find out your black ass is still knockin' back drinks when you supposed to be teaching kids, it won't be no cops. I will come down and give you an ass-whoopin' myself! Fair?"

"Fair. I really do appreciate it, man. Getting me out of there."

"Ain't no thing, I know how to handle that type of situation. It's always nice to play the famous-ballplayer card on some city cops."

Jonah said that he should probably get going. Nathaniel didn't answer him immediately. He got up with a sigh and moved to the window. He stared out at the sky. It was a marvelous deep blue. The planes were shifting east over Queens; others were coming out of Newark flying up the West Side. So many planes, even now, he thought. Grains of light were prickling the dusk over the five boroughs, and the forked tongue of the Cross Bronx Expressway flickered more brightly. The Harlem River quivered. A line about the riverside from one of the hymns his mother loved came to him. *Old ship of Zion*. Old songs. Why did they always sound like history calling?

Nathaniel went into his office and pulled out a small paper envelope. It had lain there in a corner of his desk drawer for a long time. For a long time, he did not know what do with it, or why he had even composed it in the first place. But maybe it was for a moment just like this. He brought the unsealed envelope to Jonah and placed it carefully in his hands.

"Here, take this with you," he ordered. "You going anyway, so do me a favor and take it. If you find Laura somewhere down there, you'll give it to her. Most likely of course, you won't. And in that case, you can bring it back to me. That way I know I'll get to see you again. And you'll remember that you always have a reason to come back."

Jonah didn't refuse. He was moved by the gesture, by the great dignity in this man who had rescued him. It was an intimate gift, and even though it was awkward, he felt that he understood it in light of the stories and conversation they had exchanged on this extraordinary day. He understood that Nathaniel wanted to mark the occasion with some material token of its significance. It was a gesture of nobility and hope, and he felt unworthy of its aspirations.

"I'll hold on to it," he said simply.

They shook on it, and Nate gave him a bottle of water and an extra Advil for the long ride back to Brooklyn.

When he was alone again, Nathaniel would stare out at the city once more. He would think of what Laura would make of all this if she knew—how this kid had brought back to his mind with such force what they had shared, how close it all still felt, after all these years. But it was getting late. He still had phone calls to make and a late dinner to prepare. He had a group of kids to shepherd and tend to in the morning. The encounter with the lost Jonah would leave him feeling both young and old. Why this pull of remembrance? Why now, when he was past the time of life when it is possible to sincerely believe in new beginnings? But all beginnings are uncertain and hard to see. The coming of the night is not.

Back in the borough of Kings, Jonah pressed his key into the lock and stumbled wearily into the apartment. He knew before he had turned the corner into the living room that Isaac was around. He could hear the soft scratch of a record playing, something mid-century and bluesy. The mournful whine of a trumpet. Isaac was deep in the chair by the window, his chunky Dell laptop casting an eerie moonlit glow on his face.

"Hey man, I don't mean to get all on you and shit, but rent is due *to-morrow*."

"You're right. My bad, I'll get on it."

"Oh, and before I forget, you got another letter from that French girl—excuse me, *pardonnez-moi*, from your *mademoiselle*."

"Oh, yeah."

"Yeah, I put it on the desk in your room. You musta put something special on her, boy—she's really feelin' it, you got her jonesing for you long-distance. I mean, how many times she gotta write you before you go over there and do something about it?"

"Nah, man, it ain't even like that."

"Oh yeah, what's it like then?"

"Man, I don't know. If I did, I would tell you . . . Hey, is this Miles?"

"Nah, this Booker Little. My uncle Darren played trumpet for a while, knew all about the music. Always told me Booker was his favorite. No one knows how great he was, or how great he might have been 'cause he died so young. 'Bout our age, come to think of it. Cut some beautiful records before he left, though. Contributed his one little piece to the edifice, to the tradition. Played his part. See, I knew you would like this one."

"Oh yeah, how's that?"

"It's all about *you*, chief. It's called 'Man of Words.' And that's you, brother; just listen to that *there* . . . Now that's a blues for ya. A blues for the man of words."

PART TWO

Era bom
Aquele tempo em que eu vivia junto de você
Aquele tempo que se foi
—ELZA SOARES

I'm writing to you from the Hotel Rubens in Antwerp. Mariam came to visit me here last weekend. She wanted to party, so I took her out clubbing and we took ecstasy together. I'm still trying to process the whole experience. At one point we were dancing, touching each other's faces and laughing hysterically in a kind of feverish game. The music was shit but it didn't matter because I felt lucid and uncomplicated and happy. I didn't want it to stop. At first, I wasn't sure if Mariam wanted to go as far as I did. Only that we kept having this magnetic sense of wonder at each other's bodies. It was so hot and there were too many creeps trying to hit on us, so we left and walked back to my room. I never felt so beautiful. It wasn't just the sex, it was this energy ringing inside of me, this need to tell Mariam things I've never said before. I think I may have frightened her a bit. We didn't sleep at all, just stayed up in our bathrobes talking for hours. When it was light out, we went looking for breakfast pastries and ended up walking together through Nachtegalen Park in a cool leafy blur. I had this overwhelming desire to tell Mariam that I loved her. It's so hard to know what it would mean to be worthy of that word. I wondered whether our experience was honest, or if rolling together had created an artificial paradise that would evaporate as soon as she got back to London. I still have this unshakable worry that I'm not on Mariam's level. She always knows exactly what she wants. It's what makes her so hot. But she is so confident that it's hard for me sometimes to assert myself. I can tell she thinks she has to educate me. It angers me because I can show her things too. It's just that I'm too much in my head, always composing instead of playing. I'm under no illusion that Mariam couldn't get any lover she wants. But I don't want to be settled for. I don't want to be the one she's with just because I'm smarter than her other girlfriends—because I read books and they just watch television. I want her to want me because I'm desirable in every way. But should I have to prove it? If that's what it takes, I need time. But that's the problem.

I don't know if I have enough time before she loses patience or interest in me. And then I'll lose her. If things don't work out, it will be my fault. Do you think I'm afraid of letting myself truly have what I want? Am I sabotaging and dodging the very thing I seem to be pursuing? I ask you because I know you will answer me in your own sweet way by talking about something else. It's funny how the two of us are alike and also so different in our muddles. No one knows you like I do. I hope it's okay for me to say it like that. I feel like you will understand. You and I have this ability to talk across the world to each other, across everything that makes us so distant. I will always value that. But I also know there are some things that are only mine to discover, and some that are only yours. I need to find out what I really believe. I've got to find out about living for myself. I want to know how much of this world can be mine. I want to live all that I can. And if you still love me, you'll understand this, and you will know how to think of me no matter what.

—A

11

Closing your eyes when a jolt of turbulence rocks the cabin makes it worse. When the sucking feeling in his chest came, the temptation was to go dark, but he refused. Below the belly of the plane was the black Atlantic. According to the in-flight map, the little islands of Cape Verde and the tip of Africa at Dakar were somewhere out his window. They were crossing the great slave-shipping lanes now, cruising swiftly over the swollen past, the vast stretch of black-and-blue veins that sealed the fortunes of the Americas. In the greatest empire the world had ever seen, he had paid two hundred dollars for a tourist visa at the Brazilian Consulate on Forty-Second Street.

Jonah put down his book. At his side, Octavio was snoring peacefully, his eyes covered with an airline-issued sleeping mask. A paisley tie was flicked back over his shoulder and splashes of a lasagna dinner bloodied his shirt; on his lap, a weathered copy of the war diaries of José Martí was propped up on its pages like a general's tent.

Jonah had paid for the airfare with money from Uncle Vernon's will, but how long would the rest last on the ground?

A stewardess came up the aisle. There was another jolt, stronger this time, and Jonah flinched. His eyes were squeezed shut. He prayed, in the most secular way, for time to pass. Into his unpeaceful mind came a vision. At first, he thought it was the spirits of the holds, of the drowned, rocking the plane. But this struck him as an absurd, primitive fear. The spirit level, if it existed, wouldn't stand a chance against the computer-assisted engineering of Boeing. So why then, of all things, was he moaning? Why did his moaning seem not his own as it swelled? He felt a cold heat starting in the pit of the stomach and rising up through his chest. Let it be. A surrender of the body, the pure flame giving up. For a moment it was the peace of weightlessness. And then, against every conviction, he felt them as they passed through, rushing onward in a shimmering grotesque and clanging with languages he had no tongue for. They passed eastward into the night leaving behind a cavernous emptiness. Their fading cries, sending for him, sounded like warnings. Against what? The unavoidable, for it was too late. She was already upon him, moving out of the roiling depths, a giant shadow living within the shadows. Her great rim closed in overhead and the ocean gave way to a living hold. A home within the darkwater.

He came to in a fright. The plane was still. He was safe. Around him rows of bodies were slumped in their cushioned seats, absently focused on pale screens. There was a soft ping. Seatbelt lights.

On the ground, Rio de Janeiro was a new world. Verdant pockets of lush floral beauty smashed into the concrete of mid-century bank towers, which in turn towered over baroque colonial ruins. The street life was teeming, overflowing, hot; a bouillon concentrated in the countless outdoor bars, cafés, and hole-in-the-wall eateries where raucous Cariocas gathered around glasses of beer served bem gelada from tall garrafas sweating in their cold sleeves. Jonah noticed the abdundance of popcorn carts, little trolleys in the zany intersections attended by sad-faced men. The sound of Portuguese was almost unbearably sweet, like a caramelized French. Jonah scrambled to jot down lists of words as they came up—pipoca, "popcorn"—but the new language poured easily through Octavio. He churned it right back out, a bit choppy, but alive to its unique rhythms and intonations.

Octavio had directions for how to get to the apartment where Barthes was staying, but they were clearly wrong. Someone had cherry-picked the intelligence. A thrashing rain started coming down and it was getting dark, so they ducked into a bar to wait out the worst of it and give Octavio some time to try and formulate a better plan. Plump men idled at the counter, scanning the street front or watching the mounted television in the corner. Jonah watched the flickering box, inferring content from the images. Commentators were shouting hysterically over soccer replays. Then a news segment came on about an upsurge of violence. A "pacification" operation was in effect across the city and state in support of the Pan American Games. The toll was apparently high, several police injuries and many deaths among the traficantes, drug dealers. Octavio had figured out how to get a telephone card and ducked out to use one of the Skittle-colored booths to call Barthes. He came back with a confident swagger, proud that he had gotten them back on track.

The new orders involved a long walk, at one point taking them along a highway, which cut underneath a mountain covered in shantytown constructions that Octavio pointed out to him were the "favelas." They followed a narrow walkway caught in the violent tangerine glare of oncoming traffic. By the time they emerged the rain had finally passed, and you could see the stars again, pinholes in the tropical night.

They came to yet another beach, long and brightly lit like a bracelet studded with empty café tables facing the ocean. There was a faint smell of rotting fish in the air. On one of the beachfront terraces, Jonah watched a middle-aged American couple as they struggled to order their drinks. Splotches of rose branded their arms and calves. It was the first time, he realized, that he was somewhere nobody would find his complexion remarkable. Now *they* were the minority, pinkish flotsam in a sea of honey, brown, and black.

Dark-skinned women in heels walked distractedly back and forth in front of the hotels. Street vendors hawked anything on which they could print a Brazilian flag. A group of younger men came up from the beach laughing loudly and jabbing at each other. Hotel staffers in drab uniforms wandered in and out of their establishments, verifying things, making rounds, and scanning the beachfront expectantly. Begging children came asking for money and food. A shirtless boy in ragged shorts asked Jonah for a cigarette. He hesitated, then gave him one.

Barthes had a room in a condominium tower on the rua Gustavo Sampaio in what appeared to be, from what they had seen, one of the ugliest parts of the city. When they rang her bell, she cracked open the door and then, seeing it was them, threw her arms around Octavio, greeting them both in the familiar, bubbly Esperanto of American collegiate irony.

Jonah recognized Barthes immediately, right down to the way she swept her sandy blond hair under a bandanna. She had worn one around campus, as he recalled, a sign of alternativeness balanced out by pastel monochromes from American Apparel. Her place in Rio was really a studio, which meant the guests would sleep in a corner that Barthes had padded with some blankets and sleeping bags. Octavio noted that her minimal adornments to her pad reminded him of the tribal-patterned accent pillows and throws she had used to disguise the institutional prefab of her dorm room. Barthes said something sharp in Portuguese that Jonah didn't understand. Somewhere along the line, she had acquired a confidence that Octavio hadn't counted on, one that could not be reconciled with the geeky moniker he had pinned on her.

Back home, she was Maggie Reynolds from Newton, Massachusetts. But in Rio de Janeiro, she went by her middle name, Grace, converted locally to Gracia. She seemed not entirely displeased to have Octavio and Jonah visit. Aside from the ex-boyfriend situation. The history with Octavio—or what remained of that history—was likely to prove "complicated." Already, they were reprising a familiar game with each other, their banter sandpapery, with quips and ripostes over small talk that were clearly arbitrating much else besides.

The studio room only had one window and it faced the favela of Chapéu Mangueira. During the day, music and the sound of construction work on a little botequim, a bodega that sold dry goods and fresh tropical fruit,

142

came up from the bottom of the hill. The first time Jonah heard gunfire he almost convinced himself it was a firecracker. But the report was too acute, and it happened too regularly, rhythmically even, so that eventually you could even decode warning shots: a sharp pop with a loud echo shattering the night, then one shot in reply, then silence.

Barthes was always up at dawn and heading out to far-flung corners of the city for her work. Octavio and Jonah would wake closer to noon, and usually began the day by roaming in search of a place to eat. At first it was difficult to get around, on account of the complexity of the bus system and the perilous street traffic. But once they learned how to give and receive the thumbs-up, a gesture of subtle significance and usage, everything else about the city became strangely logical. In Laranjeiras they spent an afternoon going down the menu of one of the thousands of juice bars, many of which offered fruits they had never heard of before.

Barthes only worked three days a week, so on her days off she showed the boys around the city. Octavio refused categorically to be taken anywhere "touristic," nixing the Sugarloaf, the *Christ Redeemer*, and the grand beach at Copacabana. This was agreeable to Barthes, and she walked them instead through random commercial shopping centers, and through the dense streets and public squares behind the old theater in the city center. They were a trio now—a bande à part, Jonah thought—living beyond the reach of family, of internships and institutions, beyond responsibility. That was how he wanted to see it.

One day they took a commuter bus out across a long causeway to Niterói, a neighborhood on the eastern shore of Guanabara Bay. Octavio and Barthes sat next to each other, arguing; really Octavio was arguing while Barthes looked away furtively in despair. Jonah sat behind them gazing out over the traffic and the fast-food chains and the ocean. He was keenly aware that things were not as simple as Octavio had claimed they would be. Like all ex-lovers, these two were united in an unhappy need to pluck at the strings of the other's desire. Octavio was constantly teasing, but Barthes parried handily. It looked like no matter which way things went, Jonah was going to be left holding the candlestick, as the French liked to say, a result he had dimly predicted without ever resolving what to do when it came up.

The beach at Niterói faced back toward the city, so you could make out all the different neighborhoods with their cream-colored high-rises tucked between the green mountains, and the reddish bric-a-brac of the favelas atop the green. Octavio spread himself facedown in the sand while Barthes installed herself on a beach towel and opened a tome on microcredit financing in the developing world. Jonah had with him a pocket-size volume of poems in Portuguese by João Cabral de Melo Neto that he had picked up in a bookstore in Centro.

He was fairly sure that the poem that had caught his eye when he was browsing, and that he now turned to again, was about the world coming to an end. Melo Neto said the world would end in a melancholy of indifferent men reading newspapers. One line was clear to him: "the final poem nobody would write." But what was the final poem? Was it the melancholy world itself? Was it the words in the newspapers read by indifferent men? Was it some other poem entirely, one written for whatever people were left, who didn't read newspapers but still wanted to get the news from poetry? Perhaps the world ended within the poem and the reader was one of the melancholy men waiting for something that has already happened?

When his eyes tired of the page he watched the ocean. A Petrobras supertanker showed its stenciled letters against a block of orange rust. Octavio ran down to the water and dove in, his body splitting the blue like a porpoise. Barthes applied sunscreen. After a moment, she looked over and pointed the bottle in Jonah's direction.

"No thanks, I'm good for now."

"No, dummy, on me. Get my back."

She presented herself to his touch and pulled down her straps. As he was finishing, a group of European-looking young women set up their towels and beach chairs nearby. Reclining on his side, ostensibly keeping his eyes on the book lying on the towel, Jonah tried to identify what language they were speaking, but their voices were carried downwind and he couldn't make it out. He tried to read more poetry. The poet was like an engineer, said Melo Neto, or the poem itself should be neat and clearly delineated like a tennis court, or perhaps it was precisely these things that poetry was not.

Octavio was rejuvenating himself in the sea. The salt on his shoulders flashed in the sun as he thrust himself through the waves. A Brazilian man had joined the European women near their spot. He laughed with them while he took off his shirt. He was wearing a black Brazilian-style Speedo that ended at mid-thigh, and, around his neck, a thin gold chain. He stood watching over the women with his arms crossed and his feet planted beneath his shoulders, like a lifeguard. Jonah had never seen such a perfect man, not in the sense necessarily of absolute beauty, but of masculine ideal. He was chiseled, his hair cropped and trim, his skin dark—darker than Jonah's and with a glowing vermelho in it. Handsome in the inimitable, charismatic way of black men. Barthes was looking at him too, over the spine of her textbook. Jonah glanced at her breasts. They were small, not flat really, but diminutive. She still had an adolescent figure. Just then Octavio came crashing into view, dripping all over Barthes's books and tearing towels away to dry himself. Barthes looked up from her reading.

"How was the water?"

"Spectacular," said Octavio. "You need to stop all this reading, it's unhealthy, we're in Rio, try and act the—"

"The water is filthy," Barthes cut in. "They drop raw sewage in there for miles up the coast, so do me a favor and don't touch me." Instead of following her orders, Octavio came after her. Barthes refused to scream as Octavio wrestled and tussled with her in the sand and Jonah remained neutral until they kicked up sand in his face. He noticed the Brazilian man looking over. He didn't seem bothered at all, just indifferent, as if he expected the foreigners to be exactly what they were.

On the bus on the way back Jonah felt sick. The couple sat in front of him bickering. Or at least Jonah thought they were bickering. But then after a while, to his astonishment, Barthes's head was resting on Octavio's shoulder, and he had placed an arm around her and was whispering something, or really kissing her softly, his face buried in her hair. To feel alone in the company of quarreling lovers is not the worst kind of solitude, Jonah thought. But few things are more grating to the demands of ego than to be alone in the presence of their reconciliation.

12

About a week after their arrival, Barthes invited them to a beach picnic her NGO had organized for her students. When Jonah and Octavio arrived, they found the young woman everyone called Gracia surrounded by a circle of kids and assistants handing out pieces of fruit, small sandwiches, and potato chips. Barthes was radiant. The sun was shimmering in her hair; she seemed less pale and twiggy, full of a raw vitality she hadn't yet fully displayed in their presence. She was wearing bangles and colored bracelets and she laughed easily with the kids as she played with them, chasing them around in the sand. Jonah and Octavio joined them and ate hungrily like little boys, and then Octavio got a game of soccer going.

The three friends played against five younger and more skilled kids who threw themselves across the sand diving and dribbling while the Americans tried to keep up. Octavio scored just enough to keep them in the game. After one goal Jonah saw him looking at Barthes and thought he saw a glimmer of relief, a look that said—*Why haven't you always been this way?*—and—*I knew you were like this all along*—and—*This is how I like you*—and for the first time it was clear to him that their abrasion against each other had also polished them like lenses. This in no way assured they would always be together, or even that they would always be there for each other in times of need; but it had fostered in them an inconvenient conviction that no other person would ever understand them so well, that all other relationships, even happier ones, must suffer a little for their comparative misalignment.

It was getting dark, and Barthes announced that she would be accompanying two of her students, Taìs and Angelica, back to their homes in the favelas. Octavio quickly insisted on joining them, which meant that Jonah would have to go as well. They all caught a van on Avenida Atlântica and headed north in rapid bursts, swerving over as the fare handler threw open the door, crying out a string of destinations, and hustling more rides. Along the way, Taìs and Angelica quizzed the young men on their sightseeing accomplishments and were tickled that they had been in Rio for weeks without visiting the *Christ Redeemer*, or the famous Lapa steps where Snoop Dogg and Pharrell filmed the music video for "Beautiful."

By the time they reached their stop night had fallen. In the increasingly narrow lanes where they were walking, the streetlights either hadn't come on yet or someone had disabled them so that they never would. Barthes was walking ahead with Octavio and Taìs, who had taken him by the hand, while Angelica walked quietly at Jonah's side. A moped driven by a young man, carrying an older woman with some grocery bags behind him, squirreled past noisily. Octavio was becoming quieter as Barthes, ever sure-footed, marched them up to what they could see was the beginning of the favela. They climbed a long flight of stairs in near darkness. At the top Jonah looked back and saw the twinkling lights of the city strung out below in undulating waves. They had passed the first low brick constructions when he heard the click. Two boys came out of the shadows with long guns dangling casually at their sides. Their faces were sullen. Barthes was pointing at the Americans, signaling they were her friends. One of the boys lifted his weapon at Octavio's head. Then he swiveled and pointed the muzzle into Jonah's face. He stared at the mouth of the gun. A half inch squeeze of a finger the only thing it needed. Here it was, Jonah thought. The end of the world, and it would be their own names in the newspapers being read by indifferent men. Jonah couldn't understand the gun boy's words, but he understood what he was saying perfectly. *You shouldn't be here.* Then Octavio spoke up. Instantly the barrel swiveled upon him.

It seemed something bad might happen then; even Barthes began to lose her composure, her voice breaking into a panicked plea. But the boys, excited by the presence of Americans, were tripping on Hollywood now, calling Octavio "Taxi Driver," toying with the muzzles as they cackled to an improvised version of De Niro's lines. Perhaps Angelica felt how stricken Jonah was with fear, or perhaps she simply felt momentarily more mature than the clearly floundering adults around her. She must have passed through checkpoints every day of her life, and here these Americans couldn't even do it once. She grabbed Jonah's hand, gripped it tight, and spoke to the gun boys in a tiny voice. When he heard her name, the boy with the gun shouted in surprise and lowered the Kalashnikov enough to signal a détente. Angelica talked with the boys for a minute. They were asking about her family. After a moment, they shrugged, gave a thumbs-up, and waved them all through, laughing.

Jonah's legs felt heavy; his jaw clenched. His hands were trembling, but he focused on his pace, on keeping it even and rigid. Tripping over a stone, making any false movement, anything unpredictable or unexplained might set off a nervous trigger finger attached to a boy who was high and hearing things. It was worse with the boys behind them now. The feeling of a gun possibly aimed at the back of one's head.

They moved deeper into the favela, rising along narrow streets that were lit in spots and where there was more life and the sounds of children and babies crying and hundreds of families preparing dinners. They dropped Taìs off first, and then made their way to Angelica's home.

Angelica's mother, who addressed Barthes as though she was part of the family, insisted they all stay for dinner. An aunt was helping to cook some chicken and rice. In the far corner Angelica's older brother was sitting on a wooden stool watching a soap opera about drug lords and their love lives on Globo, apparently the only television station in Brazil. Angelica helped her mother and her aunt and brought them soft drinks. The older women spoke with Barthes as though she were saintly. Not a spiritual saint, not a figure of salvation, but *saintly* in her ability to do no harm, to say nothing wrong, to bring only good. Did Barthes feel that way? Sometimes it seemed to Jonah as if she was driven by a tremendous guilt that she had recast in an armor of irreproachability.

While the visitors ate, Angelica looked up from time to time and asked the Americans to teach her new words for the things they were eating. Octavio talked animatedly with Angelica's mother, showing off his Portuguese and trying to make a good impression. Despite the terror of the ascent, there was a spectacular peacefulness in Angelica's home. It looked out over a ziggurat of corrugated roofing and down to the bright lights of the city below. A balmy breeze lilted inland from the ocean.

After dinner, Angelica and her mother thanked the visitors profusely for coming to visit and made them promise to come back. When they stepped back into the alleyways, Jonah noticed that his eyes had adjusted to the darkness. The favela cascaded down below like a river winking with isolated lamps. Somewhere farther above in the honeycomb, the distinctive propellant of American rap sent down snapping echoes of growling bass and syncopated voices interlocking call and response.

They followed Barthes back down a different path that took them into a gully and then across a narrow walkway made of wooden planks and back up a new set of stairs as they made their way along the side of the neighboring hill. They came up to a small roundabout with streetcar tracks. Largo das Neves. The Square of Snows. A strange name for a roundabout in these parts, Jonah thought. The night, with its sudden brushes with death and pockets of eerie tranquility, had turned surreal. His mind jumped from Nas rapping from the point of view of the gun to Villon's *mais où sont les neiges d'antan?* Criminal lingo for those in the know. Bold steel shoved in your face runs the blood hot; the mind ice-cold. Enough of this, Jonah thought, and Rio would get to feeling like Paris in January.

They were ambling gingerly now through streets marked by snaking entranceways to baroque and once ornate villas that were now caving in on themselves and smothered in knotted arboreal growth. They passed a disquieting mauve facade. Barthes said it used to be a dance hall where people came for the Samba de Gafieira and stayed late into the night. There were plans to reopen it, she said, as a hookah lounge.

Eventually they arrived in the neighborhood of Catumbi, where Barthes's friend Teresa lived. Barthes had met her at the Universidade Federal, where she took her language classes, and Teresa had more or less become Barthes's best friend in Rio. Teresa's house was set back from the road and covered with a fragrant mousse of flowers. Laundry was hanging from the fruit trees on her porch. Inside, an older man with a wizened head of dreads pulled back tightly in rows was rolling a joint on a mouse pad. Teresa introduced him as her boyfriend Lazaro. He was studying sociology at the State University, trying to document the living conditions of street kids. He smiled quickly and easily and talked in measured tones, often lingering on phrases in English, which he spoke quite well, as he worked the green buds between his thumb and forefinger.

The friends made a small circle on the floor, and Lazaro slid in a CD on his computer and lit up the joint as the samba of Cartola filled the room. Octavio asked Lazaro if he could recommend any Brazilian writers for them to read. Lazaro went into his bedroom and came out with a novel by Clarice Lispector for Octavio and one by Machado de Assis, which he handed to Jonah. *Memórias póstumas de Brás Cubas.* Lazaro explained that Machado was one of the greatest Brazilian writers. A black man. Jonah looked up, met the other man's fixed gaze, and nodded with grave approval.

This ceremonious moment led Lazaro to initiate a long conversation about Brazil and the way it had become a lagoon within the ocean of world literature. He was also deeply versed in candomblé and explained that he had written a paper about Nina Rodrigues's anthropological studies on the religious practices of the Africans in Bahia, but so far had been unable to publish it. Given his paltry understanding of the deities whose exotic names Lazaro invoked, Jonah could barely make out what he was saying. But Octavio was deeply enraptured and kept pressing Lazaro for more, occasionally exclaiming in Spanish as he recognized the equivalent of a certain figure or ritual he knew by a Cuban alias.

Teresa held the joint precariously and learnedly, tilting her neck way back, as she steered their talk back in a direction Jonah could more readily follow: the Brazilian cinema of the sixties and seventies, the brilliant madness of Glauber Rocha. The Americans listened intently, and Lazaro nimbly set about preparing more smoke. By the second round, the conversation had gotten predictably hazy and garbled. Teresa, Lazaro, and Barthes were slipping more and more back into Portuguese. Octavio seemed annoyed at his inability to keep up. He started tugging at Barthes's sleeve and when she pushed him away, they got into a playfully sloppy tussle. Teresa started hooting and yelling at them to get a room already. Everyone was high.

A long report of gunshots crackled through the house. There was a second of silence. Then more gunfire, louder, traveling in bursting echoes. Lazaro shoved the Americans to the ground. There were two loud bangs, then the sound of cries and the helter-skelter of human feet as a new hail of machine-gun fire sweltered the air with deafening metallic impact. People were screaming. Single shots ricocheted, loud enough to come through distinctly above the fray. Jonah looked over at Octavio. He was holding Barthes against him, covering her head with his hands. He looked over at Lazaro, who said something, but the gunfire came again even louder, and he couldn't make it out. There were more screams, some close and some distant, disconnected, lost to each other, coming from indeterminate corners of the night. Then it got quiet. Lazaro looked over. "Catumbi," he said, without lifting his head.

A tinny voice barked through a loudspeaker. It was coming from the top of an armored vehicle, climbing like a beetle up through the favela. They could hear crying now. Above all, they heard the voices of women screaming, calling names. The armored car was close, and they could hear the heavy diesel motor changing gears. The samba was still playing, and Cartola continued his song:

. . . Mas o pranto em Mangueira
É tão diferente
É um pranto sem lenço
Que alegra agente . . .

Jonah thought of Angelica hiding on the floor clasped in her mother's arms. Of her being shot, or, more likely, it occurred to him, her brother being shot. Was this the cleanup operation for the Pan American Games? There was an astonishing quiet for a time, with only sporadic, isolated shouts. But as the machinery of the military police receded again, someone somewhere in Catumbi turned the rap back up.

Barthes, who hadn't quite lost her composure, said calmly that they should go home. The acrid smell of the firefight was in the air, and there was an ambient tension all around them. Men shouted at each other in the darkness, and the sudden beam of search-patrol lights and gleaming muzzles clasped by paramilitary forces in balaclavas seemed to emerge from the darkness swift as roaches. Jonah and Octavio walked directly behind Barthes single file, at her own recommendation, as she was least likely to trigger a nervous shot. She had dealt with patrols before and she had a set pattern of phrases in both Portuguese and English to signal that they were American tourists. The soldiers barked at them and instructed them to proceed in the direction they were already heading. The sound of children crying came from the maze of shadows.

It was dawn by the time they got back to the rua Gustavo Sampaio. Coconut vendors were setting up their stands and adjusting their displays. Joggers headed out for their morning runs on Copacabana Beach.

13

T wo days later, Teresa invited the three friends on an outing to an area south of Rio that was renowned for its beaches and popular with the locals, who preferred to avoid the iconic waterfronts like Ipanema. Everyone agreed it would be good to get out of the city.

They piled into Teresa's blue Volkswagen Beetle and headed south on the highway, rounding the favela of Rocinha, then jetting past unfinished condominiums, the New York City Center on the Avenida das Américas, and the guarded entrances of gated communities built on the landfill of a newly dredged lagoon. The road broke away into higher altitudes as they followed the coastline, and the massive relief of the land came sharply into view. The green counterforts and protrusions guided them along, thumbing grandly into the glittering sheen of the ocean. The magnificent voice of Elza Soares and her bossa negra poured out of the car stereo hooked up to Teresa's new iPod. Barthes's spangled hair kept flicking past the headrest. The sun rushed the windows. Below them the ocean spread to the horizon, and they descended gradually toward it.

When they arrived at the far end of a mostly unoccupied beachfront, Lazaro went down to the water with Octavio and Barthes, leaving Teresa and Jonah to set up the picnic. As they were waiting on the blanket with the spread, she suddenly turned to him and asked in her broken English, "So, what you think of Brazil?"

He had sensed a question like that coming but didn't have a good answer worked out.

"I love it," he said after a moment.

"You love it."

"I mean, I love the atmosphere, I guess. The people, the life."

"The shooting, you love it too?"

"No. It's true, that was pretty bad."

"For us, it's like this . . . from forever. We are more used to it than you. I saw you were very afraid. Yes, you were very afraid. It was a lot of shooting for you, I think."

They had finished setting up the spread and Teresa was sitting in lotus position now at one edge of their checkered blanket, rolling trees.

"It was a lot; I'm not going to lie. I was scared—weren't you?"

"Mmm, yes . . . but, how you say . . . I'm coming from here, so it's my home. I know the favela . . . I know what can happen, but I am always walking in my beliefs. Like God, he is watching for me . . . Look, you see how it says?"

She was pointing now to a tattoo done in an italic script running along the inside arch of her foot.

"In faith."

"Faith? Yes, I am walking always in faith . . . I have it here with me. And I am not afraid for this. But *for you*, I think, I am afraid."

At this she laughed, and he felt the playful warmth of it rousing him.

"Are you believing?" she asked, grave again, but looking past him toward the shrieking and laughter coming over the waves. "Are you walking with God too?"

This brought him up sharply, and he considered whether to take the time to ask himself and then tell her what he genuinely believed, or to tell her what he thought she would want to hear, except that he realized he couldn't entirely know what that was, or indeed if she would care to the degree that it would be worth maximizing or minimizing the accuracy of his response. Fortunately, Teresa was just then preoccupied with lighting up, tilting back, taking in the sun and the fragrant smoke with her eyes closed to the world. When she opened them, she was looking straight at him. With a soft smile, she reached out to pass him the joint. The hot smoke rushed in, its peppery fumes watering his eyes. Teresa watched him struggling with his composure and laughed.

"It's strong," he said. "I don't know . . . I might have to go easy on this one."

"Yes, it's strong. Here, I will take some more, but . . . you still haven't asked me my question."

"Asked your question?"

"Are you believing in God?"

"Ah . . . well, I guess I believe in the universe, you know, everything all around us, I feel like I believe in that . . . but I don't really go for, like, a church thing. But I would like to think that I walk with faith . . . I just think for me it's more of a personal thing, you know?"

Teresa was smoking pensively and examining him. Her attitude suggested that his answer had not impressed her, and he wished that he had formulated a better reply, something perhaps closer to a useful lie.

"You don't believe—you are like my old boyfriend. You want things to be easy, you have answer for everything, but . . . when it is the bad times, when it is not so good for you, when an evil comes. Then you are scared. You say everything to make everyone happy. You say this to me now because you are wanting to make me happy. You want to get what you want . . . but you don't want to trust. That you cannot do, you could not go that far, not for God, not for me. So you believe in everything . . . but that way you can get nothing. Can you be happy with nothing?"

Jonah guessed that the tone of her last question was harder than she probably intended, but he wasn't sure.

"I know I don't have a good answer. But I don't think it's nothing—at least I hope it's not nothing. I try to be in the moment, to believe in that. Like right now, here with you, in this beautiful place, I feel like I can believe in the importance of this, even if I can't say for sure that it means what God means for other people."

"But how you can love this place? You don't know Brazil. You don't know even Rio. You don't know me. There are tourism where I live. With guides they come up into the favela to look at us. Like we are animals. But what do they know? They want to enjoy Brazil, like you. They want to have their photo and see Copacabana and see football and maybe sleep with Brazilian girls. What makes you different from this tourist?"

He didn't know what to say to this. She had caught him in a crosshair he couldn't dodge.

"Maybe you too . . . you want to sleep with Brazilian girls?"

He didn't answer.

"Don't be sad," she said, cocking her head. "I am making you feel sad?"

"No, no . . ."

"Don't worry, Jonah! I am liking you very much . . . Don't be sad!"

She repeated this last point again in her own language. The tone in her voice had stung him, but to his astonishment and relief there was also more than a hint of a smile in her face. It was a mocking smile, but it wasn't cruel. It left him no room for escape—but whether instinctively or in accord with her beliefs, it also afforded grace. What saved him, however, was the raucous return of the others traipsing up the beach, their shoulders glistening with salt water.

They ate sandwiches and drank beer that Lazaro had brought for the occasion. There was no talk of the police raid, other than a passing reference by Barthes to the fact that she still hadn't heard from some people that she wanted to check in on. The others had tired themselves in the ocean, and after eating there was a certain cozying up between the two couples, and Jonah felt increasingly awkward in the arrangement. He let them know he was heading out for a swim.

The water was colder than he had expected, but the waves were not rough, and he easily made his way through the breakers to a place deep enough to tread fully immersed. He enjoyed swimming alone, the solitude and sense of space. He relaxed his body upward in the water so he could stare into the brightness of the sky.

Teresa's body was magnificent, her color, everything. Her voice, the words she had said expressly for him: *eu sou muito apaixonada pra você*. He wished Isaac were with them, that he could talk to him about Teresa. He would have to write to him, describe all the crazy things that he had lived through since arriving. It was as if the place had intoxicated him with equal measures of nightmare and fantasy. Visions of being randomly shot and dying in the street, but also of a life far away from America, with a woman exactly like Teresa, living in one of the little houses in Santa behind a wreath of tropical flowers. Teresa reclining with her back against a shutter, reaching for a joint resting on the little yellow serving dish, taking a hit and waving off a spiral of smoke before stretching out her dark legs in the sunshine as she listened to the sound of the tram going by on its way to the Largo das Neves. Its lilting grumble showered in the cries of schoolchildren jumping on and off the sides, chasing it down the street. *Eu sou muito apaixonada pra você . . . você sabe isso . . .* The weight of her breasts, the heat of them chest to chest. The blue Fusca parked outside under a palm tree. A world of cold beer and trips down to the ocean on any given day, the breath of solar splendor and the beauty everywhere of colored bodies like his own; the sweat of lovemaking in the afternoon.

Barthes was shouting his name down the beach. The crew was ready to head back. He stumbled out of the water and Barthes came to him with a smile and a towel.

"How was it?"

"It was great. The water is fantastic."

"You looked like you were having a good time out there. I was watching you."

She gave him a look, and then they were interrupted by Octavio shouting about wanting to avoid traffic. Barthes was already heading back. Jonah dried and toweled in a dopey run up to the car that Lazaro already had revving and ready to go.

Teresa was in the driver's seat, beaming as usual, adjusting her headwrap and setting her playlist. She eyed Jonah in the back through the mirror.

"Someone has been smoking too much today, even when he's gone swimming, that one still looks like he's stoned! Octavio, your friend, our marijuana is too strong for him I think."

"Nah, he's all right, we do more than this in New York on a long night—*caballero, mi socio*, how you doing, man? I swear he's getting skinnier though! Man, you need to eat more—I need to get you back to the city for some churrasco or something."

"Truthfully, I feel good, man. I feel good, don't mind me. I'm just taking it all in. The sand, the water, the sun. It's just beautiful to be here."

The colors in the sky over Rio were beautiful, and everyone was somewhat fatigued. Lazaro and Teresa sang along with each other to the sambas. The Americans each basked alone in their thoughts.

The next morning they learned that Taìs was in the hospital. From what they could gather, she had been hit in the head with the butt of a heavy rifle. It was unclear whether the gun belonged to a police officer or a drug-gang commando. By the time her mother had gotten her to help it was too late. There was heavy hemorrhaging and she had slipped into a coma.

Barthes was furiously making phone calls all through the morning to people who worked for her NGO. She set up a meeting with Angelica so they could go to the hospital together. Octavio and Jonah asked Barthes if she wanted them to go with her. But she simply packed an overnight bag and left without an answer.

There was nothing to do but wait and pray. To the universe, if that was what might rescue her, although Jonah felt keenly how much better it would be to walk, as Teresa did, with a deity one believed would deliver. He could remember only sparsely what he had read of the Bible. Now, involuntarily, he thought of an image that had bothered him when he first read it in the Book of Job. It was the line about the human body being crushed like a moth. He had been a boy when he first heard that passage and had seen himself trapped under a boot, his slim chest crumpling like a chocolate wafer. He was so seized by the image that he looked it up online when they went to check their emails. He had basically remembered it correctly, but it was the lines that followed that now struck him viscerally, with an almost unbearable realism. *They are destroyed from morning to evening: they perish for ever without any regarding it.*

Jonah thought of the students he had left behind in Brooklyn. He tried to think of something else.

The weather was gorgeous, the city humming with life. Octavio and Jonah wandered, saying little, trapped in a daze. Eventually they ended up in a café in Copacabana watching a telenovela called *Paraíso Tropical*. That night Barthes didn't come home. She left them a message saying she would be at the hospital and that she didn't know when she would be back. The next night there was no word from her, and they assumed she was staying on at the hospital. Octavio got in touch with Lazaro, and he invited them to come watch a soccer game. Jonah hoped Teresa would be there.

The night was warm and the doormen of the edificios they passed were sitting on the edge of their swivel chairs, their shirts opened a button or two even more than usual, their heavy gaze not sunk into the surveillance monitors but riveted on the Japanese handheld radios broadcasting the Flamengo vs. Vasco da Gama match. You could follow its progress as you moved from building to building, bar to bar, corner to corner; it blurted out from passing taxis, from the corner grocers, seeping out of the living fabric of the city itself. Team flags and pennants appeared in windows; every other person in the street was wearing the anarchist colors of Flamengo.

At the bar they found Lazaro drinking with a group of friends and cheering on the squad. Flamengo had already opened with a scorching, if opportunistic, golazo by Renato setting the Maracanã Stadium on fire.

Octavio was in his element, and immediately fell in with the group, yelling about the qualities of the various players, annotating the progression of the play with his sweeping gestures, entering into passionate dispute with anyone and everyone, singing the heroics of Ronaldinho and the young Argentine Lionel Messi, poised to bring glory to Barcelona. Teresa wasn't there.

Jonah pretended to be involved, but he couldn't match Octavio's fluency, and in its presence he had a creeping sense of isolation. In the dance halls, when the sambas came on, the dividedness only deepened. On the one hand, the rhythms connected; a wall of sound, the battery of drums crashing with a relentless, implacable sweep. The whole thing was suffused with African synchronicity. But the vocals were another matter. It was as if each and every song were a national anthem, and every person in the crowd lifted their voice on cue. Everyone knew the words, everyone loved the same songs and sang them with the same passion, the same understandings. To be surrounded by this ecstatic chorus, and be left unsinging, was an insurmountable indicator that you were a gringo. Without the words to the sambas, without a soccer team, without becoming one with the spirit of the people, there was no way to truly be a part of the city, to be whatever it meant to be Brazilian. *Eu vou torcer*. He had asked Octavio to translate the words from Jorge Ben's song for him. They meant, he explained, *to cheer for*, the way you cheer for a team, but more than that—because in Brazil a team is more than just a team, and soccer is more than just a game. One cheers not just for the team, but for the hope of goodwill, for peace and comprehension among men, for the beauty of women, for the garden that is the city, for the seasons and celestial science, for the green beauty of the sea, for the haven of the human heart. Jonah felt the soulfulness of this. He was in awe of its expression. But he was not of it. He could not make it his own.

14

The burning sensation of cachaça coated the back of Jonah's throat and his head was pounding when he woke to the sound of Octavio and Barthes arguing. He was too groggy to care about the details, but her tone conveyed displeasure. He heard Octavio leaving the apartment. There was quiet for a time, and then a long strip of light along the floor coming from the bathroom. Barthes was in the shower. The room was dark. Someone had closed the shutters and the apartment was still cool, but he could see through the small slats that it was bright outside. He half dozed that way for a time, listening to the ceiling fan overhead and the shower spraying with a lulling flush.

When he opened his eyes again, he saw Barthes, or rather Barthes's wet feet and ankles. She was wrapped in a beige towel and her hair was dripping. The air was pungent with the aroma of her soaps, and he could smell her body. The towel fell. Before he could make sense of it, she was down beside him. Running her fingers over his legs. The tips of her wet hair stringing along his chest. She whispered and he nodded. She took him in her mouth, and when he was ready, she sprang up and went to the bathroom and returned with a condom. She kissed his shoulder as he rolled it on. Her body was frailer and bonier than he had imagined. The sex was uneven, and because it was going that way it was not easy. He felt as though he had to prove something to her, perhaps something he would have wanted to prove, but not just then. And he was too conscious of wanting to be away, anywhere else, and with anyone else. He was also disconcerted by not knowing the sincerity of her desire for him, or her motivations, which in that moment seemed the same thing. To satisfy a curiosity, to attack her lover, or simply because she felt like it—these were not the reasons he wanted her to have, but not reason enough for him not to go along with it. Since it was happening, if it was to go that far, what he now wanted was to make Barthes come. To see something, anything, through. But her moans remained deeply ambiguous, the tow of her pleasure rising and falling away again, her breath vacillating so that he wondered if the either of them would make it. And in the very moment of wondering he felt an iron tenseness in her arms that was not pleasure but panic, or rather instinctive fear, as they heard Octavio's voice rising in the hallway.

The first blow came in the ribs. Barthes was screaming. Two more blows came to the shoulder, the jaw. Octavio was kicking, trying to stomp the shit out of Jonah and hold off Barthes at the same time. He managed to roll away and get up. Barthes was screaming at both of them. With the towel in one hand, Jonah was trying to reason with Octavio, insisting that they take it outside. But now Octavio had turned on Barthes and was all in her face. When she refused to answer him, he tried to slap her, but she anticipated it and blocked the blow. That got Jonah back in the melee, the two struggling in a wrestling hold. Barthes joined in, kicking at them as she screamed in the center of her tiny flat, "GET OUT! The both of you! Just get out of my LIFE!"

They gave up the struggle, exhausted, and looked up dazed at Barthes, who was still trembling with rage.

"The two of you. Spoiled brats, two pathetic kids so full of themselves you don't even see what's going on around you. You're an egomaniac, Octavio. And Jonah, Jesus, you're a loser—all you do is follow him around. What are you even doing, like, with your life, other than being mopey, acting cool and shit? You're insane. Both of you. Why did you even come here? I never asked you to come. I never asked you to visit. I never called for you to come down here and just take over my life. I've been making a life, my own life down here! I've been trying to accomplish something. Which is more than either of you ever could imagine doing for anyone!"

There was a pause. Barthes pushed her way between them and threw Octavio's arm violently away when he reached for her as she passed. She had moved to the window, and she threw it open. The sounds of light traffic, birds chirping, and children playing flooded in with the fresh air. Her tears started to flow, which they could see made her angrier. She wiped them away before turning back to face the two still standing motionless and mute, as though waiting for her further scolding. She steadied herself.

"Do you know I made a website for the kids in my classroom so they can share their art with the world? Do you? Do either of you have any idea what it is I even do? Do you even care? Christ, you could at least have pretended to care! I learned Portuguese. I made friends, and guess what? I've had plenty of lovers. All of them better-mannered, better in bed, better than either of you. God. Get over yourselves. You hear me? Get over yourselves; in fact, get out of my apartment!"

At this last, Barthes crumpled down in a corner, heaving. Octavio, ignoring her command, kneeled down beside her, trying to give her his hand. She pushed him away.

"No . . . it's over. I'm sorry, but it's over. I'm leaving," she said. "I'm leaving you and I'm leaving Rio."

"Pero no me puedes dejar así. Mi amor. No seas así," Octavio was saying.

"No . . . no, no. I can't. I don't want to do this anymore. I don't want to do this. Anymore. I'm leaving."

"But I love you," Octavio said, now in English.

"I don't," she said. "I'm sorry. I'm so sorry. I did, I did at one point, actually, at several points . . . but I don't anymore. I don't know when it happened, please don't ask when . . . or why . . . I don't think . . . I don't think that would be a productive conversation."

Barthes got up and went over to her laptop. She opened a few windows on the screen and then began typing. Jonah looked at Octavio who had rolled over onto the floor with his back against the wall, his hair falling over his reddened eyes. His face was pathetic. He could not compose himself. There was a menacing sense of cruelty in the air.

"You know, I was just considering not even telling you, but you might as well know. Taìs died last night," Barthes said, without turning away from her screen. "I watched her vital signs go flat. Her whole family was there, watching. There wasn't a damn thing anyone could do. I've never heard . . . I never heard anyone scream like that. She was eleven. The NGO people think it was a drug soldier who did it . . . possibly unintentionally. Either way, it doesn't matter now. They're probably gonna torch the guy they think did it in a pile of tires up in the favela. That's what I've been dealing with. That's how things work around here."

There was nothing to say. The little ball of life from the soccer game, from their walk up through the crooked streets, who was an entire world of joy in the present and full of promise for the future, was going to be buried before her twelfth birthday while they lived on. Felled for no reason, for no purpose or motive other than the fact of exposure. The misfortune of having being born in a time and place where the risks to her life were infinitely and unfairly grave, even compared to that of some other girl living in a doorman building within spitting distance from the favela Taìs had called home, who might at that very moment be watching a popular movie about the elite squads fighting the drug wars or playing with friends in her private pool.

They had no standing to give Barthes comfort, certainly not to attend the funeral. They were strangers passing through, and they had outworn their welcome. Suddenly, Barthes was banging on the hard plastic of her keyboard.

"I have to get out of here . . . goddammit, I have to get out of here . . . Shit. Shit. Shit. I'm leaving. Don't you get it? I hate you, both of you! You bastards! I'm leaving."

Two days later everything was settled. Maggie Reynolds's parents eagerly paid for her ticket back to Boston. The month's rent on her sublet was paid for in advance but Barthes insisted on leaving extra money to have the place cleaned up. The elderly lady she was renting from came by to wish her well and when they embraced Barthes began to apologize and then burst into tears, and then apologized for her embarrassing display. The old woman hugged her, patted her back, and told her not to worry.

Octavio wanted to take Barthes to the airport, but she refused. They helped her pack her things and carried her luggage down to the taxi waiting on the rua Gustavo Sampaio.

When the taxi was out of sight, the hapless Americans walked to the Avenida Princesa Isabel and stood with their bags on the corner. They were homeless, they had nowhere to go. Octavio peeled a banana. Jonah felt in his pocket for a lighter and lit a cigarette. To their left the beach stretched out to meet the waves. The crowds were coming out for the afternoon, and most of the people heading up the Copacabana strip were giving themselves to the sun. A light breeze rustled the awnings of the coconut-vendor stands. To their right the wide avenue of commercial banks and hotels on Princesa Isabel led to the ugly yellow mouth of a tunnel.

"What do you want to do?" Jonah asked.

"We follow the plan. We'll go south."

"What plan? South where?"

"Florianópolis. Porto Alegre. I'm not going to let this define me. I have come too far, and I intend to go farther."

"Don't you think we should go back? What's the point of going on now?"

"You can go your own way if you want. I don't need you."

"I'm sorry, Octavio."

"Cállate! I refuse to talk to you about that. Do you understand? In other circumstances I would have you tried like Che did the counterrevolutionaries at La Cabaña. But now is not the time for tribunals. Now is the hour for decisive action. We must go like Martí to the Battle of Dos Ríos. To meet our fate."

"You mean we're going to die?"

"No. I mean we still have a reason to live."

"What—"

"Too many questions! We'll need to conserve our resources. Or find a way to make some quick easy money. I'm running low on funds. An intolerable situation, especially in our precarious position, which you put us in!"

"Well, I can loan you some money if—"

"Excellent. Buy my bus ticket and we'll call it even. For now."

PART THREE

Nous avons goûté, aux heures de miracle,
une certaine qualité des relations humaines:
là est pour nous la vérité.
—ANTOINE DE SAINT-EXUPÉRY

I'm in Berlin, writing to you from my favorite café on Weichselstraße near the canal. My work meetings are dull and endless, of course; but as soon as they end, I become an enchanted wanderer in this city. I sail down the hushed boulevards of Kreuzberg. I stand in awe before the Gates of Ishtar, visit with Tiye and Nefertiti. Even the bone-headed students from all over Europe spending their Erasmus money on cheap beer and techno have a cheerful innocence about them. Everyone clicks along in a timely fashion like the yellow cars of the U-Bahn on their viaducts. And yet nobody ever seems rushed to get anywhere or do anything. There's a kind of parallel time here, a gritty but lovable heart murmur that everyone agrees not to notice, like an underworld in daylight. A realm of libertine nights. I've been wanting to tell you about how I slept with another girl. Does it surprise you? I mean, my acting this way? I don't even know her name. I met her at a new club they've set up in the old gasworks. We were both smashed. She had this wonderful deep voice, and she was saying all this stuff to me in German, which I was too out of it to really understand. She was cool with leaving together. We walked, I swear it felt like miles, and at one point we ran into some friends of hers. I thought they were her friends but then it seemed like she was going to get into a fight, and I realized it was because they were making fun of me. We stopped at this sausage place and I needed to pee, but they wouldn't let me in, and she started yelling at them and we ended up getting thrown out and peeing between some cars. When we finally got back to her place it turned out to be gorgeous, full of plants and mirrors, and these big atelier windows that she nudged open, letting in the plush summer daybreak. I was thinking we would pass out, but she lit a cigarette and watched me and waited. Right away it was more intense and very different from what I've known with Mariam. In my mind it went on for hours—who knows how long it really was—but eventually I blacked out. When I finally came around, I knew I was going to be sick. Ran to what I thought was the bathroom but was actually the kitchen and heaved all over her sink. It was bad! I was shivering, trying to get it together, and all I could think about was Mariam. Trying to compose a text message to her in my head to send later. But for a split second I didn't know at all who I was. I did know, but it also felt like I didn't. And I stumbled around this apartment getting my things together, and there's this stunning girl lying naked in her bed. I'm looking at her and I hate myself because I know I'm hurting Mariam even if she never knows. And I'm walking out on this girl I just met. Would you blame me? Did I screw up? I swear I'm ready to be in love. I used to think I didn't want it to happen, I mean the confusion and neediness of it. But I'm feeling more and more that it would be better than the confusion that I feel without it. What I'm afraid of is letting myself make it that serious, of taking it there with Mariam, especially if she won't feel the same way. I worry she won't. I worry that she sees me as a fun thing, not a life partner. But how can anyone know? I'm ready for a change, I just don't want to ruin what's good about my life already. What do you think I should do? If you were here, I know we would walk through the city and talk it out. I would show you the trams rolling past Zionskirchplatz, and the little bridge in Neukölln where the swans come to sleep at night. The green water in the canals. They remind me of my Indre. If I could, I would bring you there one day and show you the bridge outside the town that my grandfather lined with dynamite in the summer of '44. My Indre, moving so slow you can follow a leaf on foot. As I send you this letter, I think of its waters as a poem, a hymn to the globe between us. My sweet Jonah, you are always so far away. I imagine you bounding across the great southern night like Saint-Ex in his aeroplane. But I can always recognize the lonely boy that I know, the little prince who is still probably madly in love with me despite everything. Look at the two of us, in love with our idle, fickle wanderings. Sometimes I wish I could do or be one thing sincerely. Have my motion fixed in space. Like the Indre, which goes only in one direction and takes its time and knows its place and is loved for some reasons that we can say, and some that we can't.

—A

15

Thick rolling forests of palms, large patches of them charred and covered in chalky stumps of ash, yielded to flatland, then badland, horizon-spanning swatches of rust-red earth stretching out to mountains that must have formed when the ocean shoved the continents apart and the land bid farewell to Angola, home of the human cargo who would journey back across the waters in chains. The wheezing bus advanced, road conditions worsening as it plunged farther south, the monotony of travel hours bleeding out.

When Jonah woke it was raining. Curtains of water swept across the windows of the bus as it sloshed through murky streets. They had arrived overnight in another distant city. He clenched his teeth and stared out the dark window. Beside him, still curdled with Barthes's contempt, was Octavio, his body wracked by spasms of inconclusive origin.

They were in Porto Alegre, the capital of a federal state called Rio Grande do Sul. The Great Southern River. They had traveled to a city they did not know, with no plan for where to go, without a friend to call, or a reason to stay. In the fetid air of the crowded bus station they studied a cheap and poorly printed tourist map they'd bought from a black boy in a Yankees baseball cap. Octavio decided they should aim for the Albergue Rialto, located close enough to what appeared to be the city center.

At the Rialto the rates were cheap, made even more so by the favorable exchange rate, and they took a room with two cots, a sink with a mirror, and a small table desk. Most important and improbable of all, there was a "business center" in the hallway with an old desktop that provided internet for guests. The room had a window that opened onto a courtyard with some trash cans, an old wall covered in growing vines, and the hanging laundries of an adjacent apartment block.

Octavio was feverish, and for the first time during their trip Jonah began to worry about him. Even though the weather was temperate, the man was pale and sweating and refused to eat. Jonah went in search of soup and juices and when he returned some hours later, he found that Octavio had gone down the street and procured his own medicine of choice: yerba maté, or chimarrão, as they called it locally. He had bought the necessary gourd and was imbibing the stuff like a hydrating sports beverage. Having commandeered the desk, he spent hours hunched over it like a scrivener, muttering phrases that sounded like incantations in Spanish, Portuguese, and French, followed by a nasty suction upon the gourd's metallic straw as his sallow cheeks puckered, the bitter green flowed, and his addiction grew. Octavio's physical state, to say nothing of his mental condition, made further planning impossible, and they agreed to stay put at least until the end of the week to see if his condition improved. Jonah was concerned for him, but no matter how much he wanted to help, Octavio was verging on unbearable. He moaned and talked to himself in different languages through the night; worse still, he was constantly rising with sharp cries of pain and stumbling in the dark to urinate with loud splashy relief.

Between the two of them they had already amassed a small library of Brazilian poetry, though most of it remained unread. Jonah had hoped to practice occasional translation to acquaint himself with the words, but Octavio was becoming obsessive in his feverish way. He would lie in bed all through the morning reading slim, often incredibly rare volumes that Lazaro had recommended to him. Lazaro knew book dealers and handlers who operated from their homes, and against Jonah's advice to remain in bed and rest, Octavio insisted on going out into the city alone to make specific purchases, as though dealing in highly sensitive contraband. He seemed to have gotten it into his head that he should have an edge on Jonah, and he made cryptic maté-fueled warnings to the effect that the books were his personal property, and he hoarded them accordingly, stuffing them under his shirts at the bottom of his travel bag. In just a few days Octavio had snagged a rare printing by the black poet João da Cruz e Sousa, one of Lazaro's recommendations, an obscure Symbolist of the late nineteenth century who died of consumption in poverty and neglect. The next day he was obsessed with a volume of tropical haikus by Paulo Leminski, who wrote a biography of Trotsky and translated Bashō before drinking himself into oblivion. But his most revered discovery was a rare collection by Ana Cristina César, who threw herself out of a window in 1983 in the nineteenth year of the dictatorship. The same year and month, Octavio noted, that he had been born at Saint Vincent's Hospital in Manhattan.

Jonah decided to do his best to steer clear. He spent late evenings online in the "business center," writing emails to Arna and Isaac and reading up on news from home.

It was uniformly depressing. The war in Iraq was going badly. Even the stalwart bureaucrats and blabbering policy wonks grinning their way through the morning shows were starting to admit that they were wrong. They had miscalculated. They had lied from the beginning through Colin Powell, who had done the state some service. His loyalty was exploited and he was being forced to take the tarnish as the story fell apart. This was the news—avarice and hubris smothering the future like burning oil wells. In New Orleans the black neighborhoods drowned by Katrina were still in ruins, most folks still displaced across neighboring states, some still in shelters, the stench of needless death extended by a spiking murder rate. The bumbling president was still insisting the government had done everything it could to help. The number of controversial police shootings was growing. Another kid had gone berserk and shot up a college campus, leaving scores of dead bodies in classrooms and hallways. It was said to be the worst shooting of its kind in American history. Talking heads warned there would be more to come as "copycats" stocked up their weaponry.

Arna was in Poland, according to her typically brief email update. Reading between the lines, it sounded like the first hairline fractures of disillusionment with her job had started to appear. The email didn't suggest she was unhappy, but possibly that she had a better sense of the difference between what she had expected the job would be and what it actually was. He would have to wait until he could read one of her real letters to find out more. Isaac's email was characteristically laconic. His take on the media frenzy over the massive school shooting: "Nothing new under the sun, chief—just another day in America."

Jonah was often up late clicking aimlessly through screens that loaded with a sluggishness that made the experience brutally hypnotic, so he tended to wake up late, sometimes around noon when Octavio was already gone. He left behind the traces of his ongoing mania. A mound of reeking maté filled the trash can. Greenish-yellow dribbles keyed the sink. Normally, Octavio stashed his writings away with his books in his personal affairs, but one morning Jonah woke to find Octavio's journal still resting on the little desk. Checking the hall to make sure he wasn't around, Jonah returned and rifled through some pages. With a sense of curiosity and some alarm, he skipped back to the first one, squinting hard to decipher the dense Vesalian microscript.

Perhaps it is my turn. The hour of my madness. Santa Yemanja! She has brought me to this—to this!! *Te acalma, minha loucura,* I hear you, Ana Cristina. But is it even my fault? From my Asturian forefathers who came for the money. Who came feverish for cruzeiros. Didn't I inherit? A case of King George's disease? Across the world for money. *Oro y plata* for a Habsburg plate. Silver and gold for a Habsburg jaw. O yes! Cienfuegos men and women. My people in the centrifuge of history. Navel of Las Américas. Immortal Martí standing at the waters of the Contramaestre, the blood of the soldiers Quintín Bandera and Antonio Maceo, son of Mariana, mother and warrior, Paulina Pedroso "madre negra" de Martí, patriots of 1895, of the Grito de Baire, forged in Santiago, raised out of the generations that came in chains in the galleons and brought the African gods of the slaves Xangô and Ochún and Obá into the green hills of Guantanamera where the flowers of the virgin Guadalupe come into the songs of the people and inspire the feast days of San Juan, the tumbadoras calling forth the dancers into the square . . . *ay, que linda la mélodia,* sweetness of the rumba flaring like the heat of a wound in the open sea, *el mar, el mar* . . . *elle est retrouvé* . . . *moi* . . . *l'éternité* . . . for what was I a century ago? what am I today? *Vagamundo.* I only understand revolt, my voice planted in its wild survivors, the whole island entire, planted like Virgilio Piñera says, *los pueblos y sus historias en boca de todo el pueblo* . . . so what do I care if I come from an inferior race? A race blasted by science, a race the technocrats will always want to do away with, just as even now, someone, somewhere, is scheming to rid the world of blacks. To rid the world of all tropical tribes, to do away with once and for all those who refuse to be regulated, who refuse to work, who refuse to behave, who refuse the orders of the police, refuse the orders of the Big Men. Barthes could know nothing of this, she could never understand . . . I lost my mind for her anyway. And yet how she stays! *O cheiro inebriante dos cabelos* . . . O Ana Cristina, she has destroyed me so wonderfully, so exquisitely . . . I call on Cruz e Sousa, *coração, tristíssimo palhaço* . . . the heart a sad clown. But I go to Martí again . . . as one must . . . *para aquel que ha logrado imprimir su pensamiento en la mente de los hombres, la muerte no existe, la muerte es un galardón*—for he who has imprinted his thinking on the minds of other men, death does not exist, death is a wreath of honor. Will I go too far one day? I will go too far. Then they will come for me. Power always does. I will tell them what they cannot hear. I am the wild one. The Savage. The Poet. The Last of the Last. What could I do? Was it not the madness, the malady of kings, of my—

"Pinche pendejo!"

Octavio had opened the door before Jonah had time to put the journal away. "What's this shit about, Octavio?" he said, brazenly.

"What's it about? You steal my girl, now you spy on my work! You're so jealous of my success that you can't help yourself? You can't even mind your own business?"

"I'm traveling with you. You are my business. Look, man, I'm getting a bit worried about you."

"You should be worried about yourself. I should beat you then leave you by the side of the road!"

Octavio snatched his journal back and glared at Jonah like he would hit him. If it was going to come to blows, Octavio would have the upper hand.

"Calm down. Look, man, you're unwell, I don't just mean with a flu or whatever it is—you're a mess, I mean look at you. Your skin is practically the color of that shit you're drinking. C'mon, man, let's get out of here and go see some sights along the river. That's what we're here to do, isn't it? Maybe there's a bookstore where you can re-up on some poets. I'll *buy* you a poetry book. Whatever you want as long as it's not more Rimbaud or any other tragic poet who died young. Just, let's go, yeah?"

Octavio looked at Jonah and then back at his journal. He flipped through a few pages, then tossed it on the desk.

"All right then, a truce, but don't think I'm not gonna remember this, Jonah. Don't think you can just slip out of this shit, *cabrón* . . ."

In Porto Alegre the jacaranda trees were in bloom and puddles of purple blossoms rounded the dark trunks all along the quiet streets of Bom Fim. Jonah and Octavio strolled around a park and examined the area around the university before turning and making their way back to the city center. There, close to the banks of the Guaíba River, they came across the semi-enclosed terrace of a grand former waterfront hotel—the Majestic. The building was an art-deco palazzo painted pink, spruced up and converted into a cultural center named for the poet Mário Quintana, with a café, a cinema, a book-shop, and a multivalent space for contemporary artists. Jonah examined the movie-house marquee. They were showing a film by one of the old French New Wave directors who was still alive and working, a nostalgic black-and-white remembrance of Parisian youth and revolutionary aspiration in the heady days of May 1968. Jonah was pleased to see that it was being projected on thirty-five-millimeter film. They paid forty-five reais each and went in.

The theater was empty. They decided to sit three rows from the screen, dead center. As the dark and grainy images swept over them, Jonah felt the languor of Paris. A jump cut between worlds. The lead actress, who played a young sculptress more in love with her art than with politics, had a mischievous intensity that reminded him of Arna. Octavio was entirely entranced by the actor who played her love interest, a morose *poète maudit* whose death was the inevitable and symbolic price to be paid for the tattered dreams of a failed revolution. When the lights came back on, they made their way up the aisle past the only other person in the theater, a young woman who must have entered late and taken up a seat in the very last row. They exchanged glances, but she remained seated, her eyes returning to the rolling credits.

They were sharing a cigarette outside the theater when she emerged. From the way she dressed, Jonah figured she was an art student. She spoke to them in Portuguese and Octavio answered "Pois não," and handed her a smoke. She said something back to Octavio in Portuguese, which erupted into a discussion that Jonah struggled to follow. Then Octavio gestured at Jonah and himself. "New York," he said.

The woman started sputtering scattershot words in English that had the lovely and strange coloring of her Latin cognates. It was obvious that her English was as poor as Jonah's Portuguese. She smiled gallantly. She said something to Jonah in Portuguese, but Octavio beat him to a reply. "I told her you don't speak Portuguese very well," he said. Jonah attempted to rebut this claim with some imitations of the native tongue. Her smile turned into a concentrated frown. Octavio again came to his rescue and translated for Jonah as they attempted to discuss the film they had just seen. It wasn't until Octavio told the woman that Jonah had also lived in Paris that they found a common tongue. "*Tu parles français, alors,*" he said.

"*Oui . . . mmm, un peu,*" she said. At that, they both burst out laughing.

The three of them entered into a conversation where everything had to be translated to someone, and eventually the person least translated to was Jonah.

The woman was slightly older, he guessed; it was hard to say because her features were youthful, but something around the eyes and about the way she carried herself suggested her age. She was dark-haired and rocked gently on her feet when she talked. He could see Octavio picking up on the same things. In fact, he seemed enthralled, if somewhat subdued. Octavio was trying to summarize what they were doing in Porto Alegre, and he was struggling because she seemed only increasingly puzzled, if also amused, by these wayward Americans.

"Tourism, tourism." She kept nodding and pointing at them.

And Octavio, in a panic, kept trying to nuance the label. "Traveling," he said. *Viagem.*

She didn't seem to buy it, but she didn't mind either. She turned to Jonah directly and surprised him with an entirely different question: Did he like

Beyoncé? She was a huge fan of American music. Jonah wearied of being the ambassador for black America, but he was happy to indulge her.

"She's our queen," he said with a smile. "Tell her," he relayed to Octavio, "that to paraphrase the great Keith Murray, when we see her shine we feel like we're all the most beautifullest person in this world."

Octavio gave him a look and was coming up with a deflection that would bring things back to him, but she looked straight at Jonah with a smile and simply said, "I understood you are saying . . . I think so too." This placed the momentum back with Jonah, who now took a different line but one he hoped would make clear something about where they were coming from.

"Tell her," he said to Octavio, "that when you are coming from the United States, being in South America can feel like visiting the scene of a crime."

Octavio was game, and she absorbed this even more intently, her attention now fixed on Jonah.

"Tell her there is no place in Latin America where it can feel good to be a gringo," he said. This led to an awkward pause between the three of them.

Then she spoke, but too quickly for Jonah to make it out. "What did she say?" he asked Octavio.

"She said Americans are imperialists who have a lot of blood on their hands. But a lot of that blood is at home and not just abroad. She respects the black people of America because they have been so strong in the face of everything. She says they are an example for the world, and that is why she, like everyone, turns to them and loves their culture."

"Tell her I appreciate that," Jonah said. He did appreciate it; he also noticed that she was still looking at Octavio in a way that was different, that meant something more, and he decided to make the diplomatic move and excuse himself. "I'll catch you back at the Rialto," he told Octavio. To the woman he gave a simple *salut*, but she insisted on pulling him toward her and kissing him on the cheeks and, as he leaned in, his nose got caught up in the fragrant mass of her dark curls.

It was late when Octavio returned, and Jonah was now the one reading poems in bed. Octavio unpacked his washing kit and prepared to shave. Since leaving Rio, Octavio had let his beard grow, and now he seemed to take pleasure blading it off in front of their small mirror.

"You have a good time?" Jonah asked casually.

"With Francesca? Yeah."

"Francesca, got it. What did you all get into?"

"We had coffee in the café at the cultural center. She was over the moon when I told her I had been reading Clarice Lispector, her favorite writer. She even bought me a copy of one of her books right there at the store."

From a bag, Octavio pulled out a green book with the illustration of an undersea coral on the front and handed it to Jonah. He opened it up to the title page, where he noticed that Francesca had written her full name, Francesca Meireles, followed by her digits. He flipped to the first page and read aloud the Portuguese: "É com uma alegria tão profunda. É uma tal aleluia."

Octavio's face had regained its color, and now he even seemed to be glowing. "*It's with such profound happiness. Such a hallelujah,*" he translated proudly.

"Sounds amazing," said Jonah, a little more flatly than he intended.

"Francesca?"

"Yeah."

"She's more than that! She's . . . well, you know what, man, you can find out for yourself. Because she's invited us, both of us, to a gallery reception at the Pinacoteca tomorrow."

The next evening, they met Francesca on the second floor of a beautiful open-plan art gallery. Octavio and Jonah both wore ties, but the effect didn't come off as classy as they had hoped. Their accessories had been hopelessly creased in their luggage, Octavio's shirts were lightly stained, and neither of them had jackets. Francesca didn't seem to mind. She spoke in Portuguese, with a sprinkling of French art terms, as she walked them around the room, pointing out prints, acrylic paintings, installations that merited attention.

Her own work was on display in one corner. She had cut out speech bubbles from local comic strips and used a magnifier to blow them up to canvas size before filling them with a collage of images of politicians, pop and movie stars (there was Beyoncé), newspaper clippings, old maps, sea charts, fashion icons, parts of wild animals, and zigzagging lines of pastel coloring that connected or bisected the fragments so that the whole thing had a kind of televised talismanic quality. She was proud of her work, and when she explained it to Octavio, their glances would invariably latch onto each other and she would turn away hurriedly and show them another piece. The place was crowded, and eventually they all ended up separating so that Francesca could greet people while Jonah and Octavio wandered on their own.

The show presented artists from all across the Southern Cone. An Argentinian had cut up a map of Buenos Aires so that only the cemeteries were left visible; a Chilean had created a wall of faces out of thousands of passport photos of the desaparecidos. There were international stars present as well. A famous white South African artist had a video installation that took you on a parallel voyage to the moon, an affectionate pastiche of Méliès, full of silvered light, scratchy Victrola piano, and a rocket fueled by unrequited love. Francesca found Octavio and Jonah there, loitering on the lunar surface. She suggested that the two of them join her on a cigarette break. Octavio agreed, and Jonah, sensing that his friend wanted to have her alone, declined.

"You sure?" said Octavio.

"Yeah, I'll catch up with you later."

Jonah watched the two of them gliding down the stairs of the Pinacoteca together. He felt happy for his friend, and envious too. Maybe he'd have the same luck too if he stuck around the opening. But with everyone speaking in Portuguese he just felt lost. On the other hand, he had nothing better to do, so he upgraded from white wine to a glass of champagne and made another tour of the show, trying to take an interest in the labels. But his glass was very soon empty. No one had come over to take an interest in him, and there was no sign of Octavio and Francesca. He looked around for somewhere to leave his plastic flute, smiled at an elderly gentleman he didn't know, and completed his desultory retreat from the gallery.

Ravines of gray and pink high-rises dominated the scuzzy streets around the Pinacoteca, but the older street-level shops, many of which were closing, spackled their bases with a dusky warmth. He walked back toward the Rialto with the discomforting feeling he was being watched, even though he knew it was really the opposite—he was insignificant to everyone he passed. At a corner, by the large roadway that marked the transition out of the historical city center, he passed a McDonald's. He hadn't eaten anything substantial all day. He looked around. What were the odds Octavio or Francesca would see him if he slipped in?

Everything was the same: the smell, the cold lighting, the demographic combination of working-class families and friends at recreation, and under-class drifters or loners camped out at the formica tables. The girl behind the terminal was dark-skinned with a lively, trained smile. He pointed to the image of the chicken tenders above her and she laughed and helped him through his order. He considered a seat by the large plateglass window overlooking the thoroughfare but opted instead for a booth closer to the condiment dispensary. Maybe it was only fair given the whole situation with Barthes. He hadn't wanted that, of course; if only Teresa had been available it would all have been different. Was this what it all came down to? There was a tap on his shoulder. The girl from the register was holding a soda out for him. He had forgotten to take it off the counter with his order. Embarrassed, he blurted out an awkward obrigado, which made her quiver with laughter. Her lip gloss sparkled as she said something he didn't understand beyond its sisterly compassion. She sauntered back to her station. He hadn't finished his meal, but he was so flustered by the interaction that he wrapped the remaining chicken to go and took off.

When he got back to the room, Octavio was there, his maté gourd in hand, bouncing off the walls with frenetic energy.

"Hey, I figured since I didn't see you guys come back for a while that maybe you had, you know, gone somewhere, so I . . ."

"What a woman! Jonah—I'm telling you—this is tremendous, she's devastated me, there is nothing else to say, no other way to put it!"

"Okay, chill . . . What happened? What did you get up to?"

They had talked about Francesca's life in Porto Alegre, about her family. Her parents were involved in city politics but had separated when she was still a teenager and only saw each other when necessary. He also learned that she was a mother. Divorced from the father now and raising the child on her own. A little girl named Paolina. They lived with Francesca's grandmother, who watched the girl when she went out. She wasn't from the city originally but from the mountains to the north. Her father was from the nearby city of Alvorada. Apparently, they were both invited to a family dinner at her grandmother's home that Sunday. Octavio had already said yes, that they would go. He described how as they walked back down toward the gallery she stopped and demanded that Octavio tell her if he had intentions. He said that he did. She demanded that he kiss her so that she could decide if he was worth it. She had approved. The next thing he knew they were back in the champagne chatter of the gallery looking for Jonah.

"When we realized you had gone, Francesca was very upset, actually. I told her it was fine, that you wouldn't mind at all, but she was all bent out of shape about it. She really likes you. But I'm warning you—don't get any ideas. Don't even think about it. This is not a game. I won't tolerate any more acts of treason."

16

T he following Sunday in the waning afternoon, they made their way to see Francesca Meireles at her grandparent's apartment on the Travessa da Paz, a tiny street just off the city's largest park, the Parque Farroupilha. Octavio and Jonah were pleased with themselves for managing to arrive on time, bottles of wine in hand.

Francesca's grandfather answered the door. He was tall and ushered the Americans in with a small grin and a tilt of the head. He had great Ellington pouches under his eyes, and his hands trembled when he held them up. He coughed and laughed a little as he gave the guests warm hugs. His eyes were sea-greenish like his granddaughter's and what was left of his hair frayed outward at the sides like the head of a well-worn toothbrush.

Then they saw the girl, a little bundle with a Tintin cowlick, curled up against Francesca's grandmother, Antônia, a small woman with graying hair in a chignon. They were watching television on a brown couch in the living room. Antônia smiled and pointed at them as she nudged the girl in their direction.

"Paolina, diga olá para nossos convidados."

Octavio was transfixed, and Jonah responded for both of them, putting forward his best Portuguese. Paolina looked at them wonderingly and half waved before returning her attention to *Procurando Nemo*, the adventures of the pixelated fish who was blubbering on the screen in dubbed Portuguese.

Francesca was in the kitchen preparing a bottle for her daughter. They all embraced and set about working on trimmings for the roast beef and drinks. They were expecting her father, Euclides (her mother couldn't come because of a political engagement), and her younger brothers, Carlo and Theo, both still in school and, Francesca noted proudly, avid salsa dancers. So eight people in all, plus Paolina, who would nibble from her mother's plate. Octavio got to entertaining her grandparents in the living room with tales of their travels, with an emphasis on the marvels (and an elision of the perils) of Rio de Janeiro.

Euclides arrived next. He was a bald-headed bull of a man who clearly had downed more than a few drinks before arriving. Her father gave each of the guests a bear hug—in Octavio's case, one that looked a little too intense to be comfortable. But when Euclides learned that he was Cuban, he was immediately bellowing and roaring with approval, demanding to know why Francesca hadn't told him so in the first place. Now the drinking began in earnest, and even Francesca's grandmother had a full glass of wine. Around eight o'clock, as everything was nearing completion, the brothers arrived. Carlo and Theo came in together in mud-streaked soccer jerseys, declaring themselves victorious and tramping about the apartment singing their club's fight songs. They barely noticed the Americans as they swept up their grandparents in their arms, dancing around the living room, tossing Paolina in the air, and romping all over the furniture. Euclides barked at them to get in the shower. Francesca shouted from the kitchen that they smelled. And without any further prompting, like a passing cyclone, they disappeared to get changed.

When everyone finally sat down to the family meal, Octavio was seated between Francesca and her father, while Jonah was placed in a corner seat next to Antônia. They all took each other's hands around the table to say grace. Francesca's grandfather intoned the benediction in a soft near-whisper. Jonah closed his eyes. Antônia's hand was buttery smooth like a leaf of chard.

The dinner could begin. Euclides carved with pomp as he quizzed Theo and Carlo on the details of their match. When everyone had been served, they all began eating and there was a general silence until from across the table, Francesca's grandfather addressed the guests in a quaint English:

"So, my boys, what are you doing in Brazil?"

Theo and Carlo chuckled to themselves. Octavio decided to take it on.

"We are traveling. We came to visit a friend, but some of our plans had to change, and we realized it was a chance to see more of this beautiful country, and to delay going back to the United States."

"Are you with some kind of an exchange program?" her grandfather pursued.

"No, not exactly. My friend Jonah is a great teacher, and I am . . . a poet . . . and I am on a mission, an expedition, I have come to understand, to learn, to discover the true materials I need for my poetry."

Theo and Carlo burst out laughing at this point and would have continued unrestrained if it not for Euclides's admonishing glare.

"They come all this way to see us, isn't it wonderful, and what do we have to show them—a country bankrupted by violence and corruption, our whole society a charade for these rotten politicians to plunder at will . . . a carnival, yes, a carnival of greed, and with the Party as—"

Francesca, who had been spooning rice for her daughter, jumped in with tender exasperation.

"Papa, please!"

At this her grandmother advised Francesca not to raise her voice, and then asked the table at large if maybe a discussion of politics could be left for another more appropriate occasion. Everyone fell into a cumbersome silence. The brothers suddenly declared that they had to go, the weekend had landed, they explained, and they were going out dancing. They cleared their own plates and gave a hasty salute as they bolted for the door. After they had gone, Euclides struck up a conversation with Jonah about politics, but kept his voice down.

Octavio asked Francesca if he could give Paolina a present, a book he had bought on Jonah's recommendation. He wanted to inscribe it, and Francesca helped him write a note.

When he showed Paolina the book, she pried it open cautiously and mussed a few pages before looking up.

"What is it?" she asked.

"It's *The Little Prince*," he said. "A book for you."

The girl looked down again, this time at the cover, which showed a French boy with hair the color of stars, wearing a bowtie and a flared pistachio jumpsuit, standing on a lonely planet. "But he's not a little prince," she said decisively. "He's a big king!" Octavio knew better than to argue with that.

Euclides insisted that if his guests had come this far to see the real Brazil, they must see his mountain cabin before they left. He explained that he would have business in Alvorada for the next few days, but that he could pick them up the following Friday and drive them to the Serra. Francesca urged them to come. They enthusiastically agreed.

Jonah saw less and less of his roommate that week, and spent more and more time wandering alone around the city or drifting through slow-motion cyberspace at the hostel. With nothing in particular to do, he felt a new kind of freedom, and as his Portuguese improved, he was getting better at navigating the small necessities of everyday life. It was pleasant to be untethered to, and unencumbered by, Octavio; he even enjoyed his best-friend role as he got daily news of increasingly romantic and intimate encounters. Best of all, it gave him time to write to Arna, and he spent more than one late night writing up his impressions of the new city, telling her about Octavio's manic episodes and his maté binging, the strange but oddly beautiful poetry of his journal, and their new adventures in the art world.

He told Arna about the things Octavio was relating to him about Francesca. How they would meet in the little barzhinos in Cidade Baixa with Francesca's small band of rowdy friends and go out to tightly packed spots where they danced to the slinky languor of forró. How late into the night, they would follow the other couples spilling out of the clubs and drift down toward the love motels in Menino Deus. How returning to the Rialto at dawn, he passed teams of black boys collecting trash by hand and filling carts pulled by donkeys on their morning rounds.

On the appointed Friday, Euclides appeared at the Rialto to pick them up. Octavio and Jonah clambered in the front of an aging Ford truck. Inside it smelled like old tennis balls, and the engine roared and groaned as he handled the staff of the gearshift.

Their first stop was a discount grocery store where Euclides ordered the boys out to get supplies. The truck loaded, they drove out of the city, north and slightly west. When they turned off the highway half an hour later, they passed over a drainage ditch filled with garbage and then onto an unpaved road that led through an extensive network of dilapidated and unfinished housing. The place was teeming with life. Francesca's father pulled over to talk to a young man who was kicking a soccer ball around with a little boy. An older woman came out of her home, shouted greetings, and went back inside. They continued farther into the settlement. "Where are we?" Octavio finally asked.

"This is Alvorada," Euclides said. "My hometown, my baby, my district, my jewel . . . It's a good place, good people. Some problems like everywhere, but good people, you know. Everyone you meet here, I know them. Everybody is who I work for. They know, I am the one."

He insisted on taking them to see some of the things that he was responsible for. The first was the site of a five-story housing project unit. The building, a gray affair that sternly blockaded the horizon, was obviously in disrepair. He explained how he had fought off the speculators and owners who had tried to have the building razed so they could sell the land. How he had organized resistance groups that infiltrated and sabotaged the wrecking crews that came to do their bidding. The second site was a vague patch of land with a partly caved-in warehouse. Some gravel, dripping puddles of mortar, and loose bricks had been poured on the ground. The better part of it was covered in sprouting weeds.

"This," Euclides announced, sweeping his hand over the spilled gravel like a wand, "will soon be Alvorada's first youth sporting complex . . . my dream—and I've had to fight for it, but you know, we have to do something for the youth. Look around you . . . who else will do it? The politicians? You know what they are: pickpockets, my friends; thieves! They line their pockets and then put their smiling face on a billboard over the highway . . . ha! I spit in their eyes. Always watch the generals, I tell you. In this part of the world, it's always the generals . . . Nothing that way has changed, nothing."

When they arrived at his home, Euclides pulled up to the curb and honked the horn with two fierce jabs. Children were coming in and out of the house and chasing one another through the front lawn and down the street.

"I'll stay in the car," Euclides said. "You go in and get Francesca and help bring out her things."

Jonah heard Francesca shout somewhere deep inside the house. From the doorway, he could hear through the living room to the kitchen, where someone was chopping vegetables. Paolina looked up at him from the floor by the television and continued ironing the rug vigorously with her wooden toy plane. It was a red airplane about the length of a pencil, and it had a slender white propeller. Just then Octavio stepped in the doorway. Paolina's gaze fixed and widened, and the airplane stopped mid-flight.

Francesca came swooping into the room, taking the girl up in her arms, balancing travel bags and packs in her free hand.

"I'm glad you came," she said, kissing Octavio on the cheek. "Paolina. Say hello, give the boys a kiss."

The girl was reluctant, but her mother coaxed her. Jonah got a kiss first. Octavio got one too, and for the first time, Jonah saw him blush.

The truck climbed steadily and gruffly into the mountains. They were long off the highway now, climbing narrow switchbacks on a path of ochre-red dirt. Octavio sat in the front with Euclides, discussing soccer. The patriarch was recounting the glory days of the Colorados: the forties, a golden era when Internacional crushed Grêmio, their bourgeois Porto Alegre rivals. But, Euclides moaned, those days were past. Now the Gremistas were in a seemingly unstoppable ascendancy, a shift that could not be dissociated from the virulently bourgeois ideology of the present epoch, the grave malaise of the social situation; and one would have to mention the increasingly clear sense that even though the PT had come to power—and perhaps even for that very reason—the tide of class warfare had markedly turned in favor of the bourgeoisie. How could it be! When the Left came to power, they implemented the program of the Right. Madness. Under Lula the speculators in São Paolo had seen their fortunes inflate. The poor, of course, were being pushed down, shoved under the rug to make way for upscale shopping complexes, ostracized from the same cities they had built, cast out to the periphery, to places like Alvorada.

In the back seat, Francesca and Jonah had Paolina tucked in between them. Mostly she asked her mother about Jonah. Was he from Africa? He said no, that he was from America—*North* America. Paolina told Jonah that he should look out for the lions and zebras. Francesca was embarrassed and told her that she was confusing America and Africa. Paolina looked at Jonah and insisted on her cautionary note anyway.

"Does she know about dinosaurs?" he asked Francesca.

"A little bit, we haven't learned their names, but she knows about them."

"Tell Paolina we don't have lions and zebras in America, at least not anymore. But a long time ago, Africa and America were actually all one big piece of land stuck together, and back then we had some of the biggest animals that there ever were: the dinosaurs. They were ferocious but they all died when the Earth got hit by a large rock from space."

This took Francesca a while to relate but it seemed to leave a strong impression on the child, and she remained quiet for a long time. Her doughy legs were draped over his thigh and her wondering head rested on Francesca's hip.

They were climbing through green mountains. They passed a small white church and a long wooden-slatted hall, and then turned up a smaller dirt path that led up to a large sort of bungalow and, beside it, a stable. "We're here," Euclides announced with magisterial authority. "In the arms of the Serra do Mar."

Euclides had built the house himself. He showed them where he got the wooden beams for the frame from a grove of faveira trees. He had used a large trunk that fell in a storm to build a support for his veranda. The whole house had more or less the shape of a wide boot, with a roof patched together from different materials that sloped upward, culminating in the kitchen in the back and its stove-pipe chimney. In the entranceway there was a vestibule stocked with riding gear: saddles, harnesses, heavy wool wraps, stirrups and packs, leather boots and spurs, and embroidered Paraguayan blankets. At the other end of the room there was a shrine for Euclides's patron saints: Jesus, Che Guevara, and Lenin. Euclides had a small bookshelf as well, upon which were mounted several distinguished volumes, including books by Eduardo Galeano, the poems of Langston Hughes, *The Count of Monte Cristo*, and an elegant clothbound edition of *Memórias póstumas de Brás Cubas*. The Americans made a point of showing their familiarity with the great Machado de Assis.

"One of the great black writers of all time," Euclides mused, gazing lovingly at the tattered spine. "But," and now he turned, with special attention to Jonah, "not a great writer of blackness. No . . . not a writer of blackness at all. The greatest Brazilian novelist—a black man born half a century before the abolition of slavery in his own land . . . and what does he write about? The flings and pangs of aristocrats . . . the little underwear affairs of the empire! Yes, I'm afraid it's true! Nothing on the enslavement of his forefathers! A man of magnificent, innovative genius . . . maybe the only thinking man to emerge from that slumbering sick empire in exile . . . and he could not even talk . . . about himself. What he might have done with Palmares! What a *Monte Cristo* we could have had if he had looked to Zumbi for a hero! If he had the courage . . . to imagine the free slave societies of the Quilombos! I tell you, my friends . . . I have thought on these things a long time. A hero must have his labyrinth . . . a true hero struggles through one alone. But I have come to the conclusion that the labyrinth of the black hero has no exit."

Before preparing dinner Euclides took them out to the stable to see his horse. As they approached, the animal became very agitated. But Euclides cooed and sweet-talked his way inside. It was dim in the stable and the only thing you could see was a giant watery eye staring out of the darkness. It belonged to a dapper chestnut criollo named Garibaldi. They stood and watched as Euclides brushed down Garibaldi's neck, soothing him until only a little wreath of steam periodically appeared from his gray nostrils.

"I have always believed that a man is made complete by a horse," Euclides confessed. "I can't help it. In my blood, in my spirit, I am a gaucho. Sometimes I feel that I am even a horse myself," he said laughing.

They heard a shout and turned to see an old black man walking up the path toward the house carrying an enormous bundle of branches. He was wearing a tattered poncho and walking steadily in dust-colored sandals. As he neared, they could see that the bundle he was carrying was lashed together with rope that rose almost four feet above his head and extended behind and over his back so that he looked almost like a snail in its shell.

"*Oi*, Orígenes!"

The two men engaged each other in a hearty greeting. Francesca looked on attentively. Jonah looked at Octavio, who looked back to confirm that he could not understand a word the old black man was saying. His words slurred into each other in a way that made his speech impossible to follow. After a moment it was clear that Orígenes wanted to ask Octavio something. But Octavio didn't understand, and so he smiled, and the two became stuck in each other's perplexity. Euclides explained that Orígenes wanted to know if he and Jonah were brothers.

Octavio looked at Jonah. "No. No, we're not brothers. We're friends. We're visiting Francesca. We have been traveling through the country."

Orígenes looked incredulous. He started to laugh and wheeze as the branches creaked over his back. Euclides invited the old man to join them for a beer, but Orígenes declined, saying that he had more work to do, that a drink was a bad idea for him, that he had stopped drinking, more or less. More or less? Euclides prodded. Mostly chimarrão now, Orígenes clarified. Euclides nodded approvingly. And with that Orígenes moved off into the dusk, climbing up the hill behind the house along a line of cashew trees.

That night they cooked together, raising a hot ruckus in the kitchen. They were making a feijoada. First off, the sausage bits. Euclides cut the slices roundly, their faces mottled and rouged. Francesca cut up morsels of beef and oxtail, peeling away translucent strips of fat. Octavio worked on chopping onions, peppers, and garlic, and Jonah peeled carrots and potatoes. Paolina sat on the counter and, in her own manner, exhorted the workers to greater productivity. When the stew was ready, a small dune of farofa was added to each plate and served hot.

After dinner Euclides produced a bottle of clear cachaça and held forth on his two favorite subjects, politics and the past. He described his efforts to promote land reform laws that would eventually allow Orígenes to own a portion of the land that he had worked his whole life. But he explained that there were complications in the contracts of land ownership and inheritance that he had so far not been able to overcome. A second story was about his father, whom he referred to as Francesca's grandfather. The old man had been an important figure in the movement, and fairly radical. The military chief in charge of her grandfather's region had leftist sympathies. He arranged for sentences to be lightened or commuted. He wanted order, but he wanted his orders executed cleanly, without blood. So, at first, her grandfather was placed under house arrest.

"I could tell you a thousand stories about that time," Euclides said proudly. "The greatest stories are all from those days. How he fooled the guards to attend secret meetings using coded language on the telephone, signals and messages passed in toothpaste . . . It became almost like a game. But eventually the leadership changed and sometime around '78 they decided a heavier hand was necessary. A new station chief was brought in from Brasília. They started to torture people. He would never talk about it, but I know from people who went in with him, the ones who came out . . . They strapped him to a bed frame in a basement of the police station. They brought in a little generator and a voltmeter. Then they taped electrodes to his testicles. My father was tortured like this. You have to understand, when you go through something like that . . . you never forget."

Euclides was a man who took great pride in telling tales the way they should be told, at length and with notable digression, with recurring motifs and luminous surprises. But women always had the best stories, he said. Best because they were all true. They were the only ones who ever knew the truth, and who could still remember the stories of their mothers and hand them down in ways that allowed their truth to pass on—just enough truth, passed down through the generations so that the crookedness of men would never completely triumph.

After she had put Paolina to bed, Francesca joined Jonah for a cigarette on the veranda. Octavio was exhausted and had decided to turn in; he agreed to keep an eye on Paolina, who was still whimpering a little.

They sat smoking under the moths gathered along the sides of the house and over the screen door. The view on a clear night up in the Serra do Mar was sublime. Francesca moved away from the lights of the house and Jonah followed her. The grass was cool and dry underfoot. When they were far away enough, she motioned for him to sit down with her. Orion was lifting a leg over the ridgeline. Cool air passed over their bodies, and in the dark, he felt her hand feeling its way to his and then up to his arm. But she wasn't pulling him to her. It was more, he realized, that she was holding onto him, almost for support. She spoke very slowly. "I am thinking . . . he will go away again . . . you too . . . and . . . I will be in pain when he goes . . . I'm afraid for this."

Jonah thought on this carefully. "Yeah, I gotta go sooner or later—

probably sooner—but Octavio, I don't know . . . I can't speak for him." He watched her face, gazing out into the inky darkness of the valley below them.

"I have already had some man leaving me. I want to be happy . . . and Paolina . . . I don't want her to see always men coming and going." She dropped her head for a moment, but she raised it again. He couldn't tell if she was crying.

"I think it would be better if I left Porto Alegre," Jonah said.

She seemed to think on this gravely. And then said, "But then he will go with you . . . you will leave me both alone."

"No, it doesn't have to be that way," he insisted. "I just think it's probably best for me to give you space to be together, if that's what you want."

There was no reply to this, and they stayed that way a long time staring into the starry night, until with a start she leaned over, kissed him softly on the cheek, brushed his face with her hand, and walked back to the house without waiting for him to follow.

17

When Jonah awoke, he could hear Octavio singing Spanish in the shower. He found Francesca and Paolina in the kitchen making breakfast together and talking. They had been out that morning in the orchards and they had gathered a bowl of black marbles that turned out to be jaboticaba berries. There was a glowing force that radiated in Francesca when she was caring for her daughter. He was struck by her fearlessness, if that's what it was—some deeply humane folly. Parenting was the most common activity in the entire world, happening all the time, and yet he couldn't fathom how or where a human got the courage and the mental resiliency to keep track of all the possible risks, monitor and arrange for every contingency and danger, know how to do what Francesca did every day.

Jonah thought of his own mother and father. They hadn't spoken since he had left New York. He knew his email inbox was full of pleading emails from his mother, and threatening emails from his father, demanding to know his whereabouts. But he never responded. He simply read them and kept going. Eventually they sent fewer missives. He still regularly received junk mail, mindless top-ten lists, scam promotions, links to humorous headlines and videos. His father forwarded or copied him on increasingly bizarre and angry letters to gallery owners, accountants, and tax attorneys, or on salacious jokes between old buddies who had washed up like him and were angry at the whole world. He couldn't help but feel that the voiceless emails and the forwarded flotsam actually made them feel more distant. The concerns of their world, the one that he was really from, sounded trivial and more annoying than ever. The tone of things was increasingly ferocious and tinny, the content derisory and manic. His folks had their faults and contradictions, but they had also come up with these huge revolutionary clashes to fight over and take sides on, and rightly or wrongly they had lived under the sway of a historical dynamic that seemed to matter, that you could understand and take a position on. He had grown up knowing only different things, and they stayed apart, fragmented.

Everyone he knew was like this—busy trying to figure out some way through the web, barely taking the time to know each other. But the real time, the clock of the world, ticked off the hours indifferent to their confusion. Life was what it was, no longer or shorter or richer or sweeter here or anywhere else but made up only of what you had really touched, known, believed, sweated your tiny cup of being into. Francesca and Paolina were each other's world, and had to be, at least for now. But what a rich life they had. Francesca refused to let mothering stand in the way of her enjoyment of whatever she wanted in her life, whether it was her friends, her art (even if it wasn't likely to lead to a career), seeking out men and sleeping with them if she pleased. It was impossible to be indifferent to this prowess, her ability to burn with a soft, ribbonlike flame. To find the path that took in more with less.

The next day Euclides took Garibaldi out riding and left a note saying that he would return by nightfall. The day was open to them, and they decided to go for a walk in the mountains. They started up the hill behind the house, passing under the cashew trees and winding up a little mountain pass. In places the climb was steep and rocky, and Francesca carried Paolina on her shoulders. She picked her way around loose rocks, hiking uphill with her daughter's little hands wrapped around her forehead. She moved with serene confidence, talking to her daughter the whole time, pointing out flowers and beetles and bees as they went along. They passed over a ridge. On the far side sugarcane fields extended on a long descending slope as far as the eye could see. The green stalks sashayed under the breeze, rustling like water.

Francesca guided them down along the side of the field. Ahead, they could hear the *tack-tack* of a machete and the hiss of falling cane leaves. It was Orígenes. They stopped to say hello. Jonah and Octavio still couldn't understand him when he spoke. Francesca explained that Orígenes was saying again that the two Americans were brothers. Octavio said that perhaps because they had been traveling together for some time, they had acquired that kind of knowing way about each other that siblings have. Orígenes considered this and then spoke.

Francesca said that Orígenes understood this, but that all the same he could see they were brothers. What were the chances, he said, of the two of them being here, and all of them meeting on the mountain, in the scheme of the world made under God's vast heavens?

Octavio nodded in solemn agreement.

Orígenes continued after a moment, and, for a while, Francesca went on translating haltingly. Jonah tried to follow as best he could. Orígenes was talking about souls, the soul having clothes, or not having them . . . or souls needing clothes when they got too far from the heat of the creator . . . souls putting on bodies the way people put on different coats in the winter . . . going from one body to another . . . to animals too . . . everything going back to where it came from. Then Orígenes stopped and looked at them expectantly.

"What was that last thing?" Octavio asked.

Francesca thought for a moment as she translated in her head. "Orígenes says that even the most wayward souls come from God and so even the most wayward souls have to go back to Him, and so there is a confusion—or, how do you say—contradiction, in the idea of Hell . . . because God is all-powerfulness and infinite love, and so it must be that *all* souls go back to Him. All souls are eventually saved, he says, even the Devil's. All souls are brothers, you two and all of us here together share of the same soul. And all of it will be saved, he says, at the end of time."

Paolina wanted her mother to let her down, but Francesca felt they should move on. Octavio wanted to try cutting a sugarcane stalk. Orígenes showed him how to cut the end of the stalk and chew out the juice.

With that, they thanked Orígenes and he shouted farewells as they moved on deeper into the valley. As they marched Octavio sang in Spanish for Paolina. She squealed with delight when he sang, and as soon as he ran out of steam she demanded more, clapping her hands wildly as Francesca tried to concentrate on walking.

They came to a field of tall grass. Francesca put Paolina down and let her chase Jonah around in a game of tag while she and Octavio held each other and kissed. Suddenly Paolina was wailing. Jonah crouched beside her, awkwardly patting her back. She had a small cut on her forehead, a streak over her eye. It was a fine, superficial cut. Francesca licked the blood away, laughed, and soothed her. Paolina soon calmed, looking into space for a while, a little stunned.

Jonah was mortified. "I've hurt her," he kept saying. He was overreacting. Octavio knew why and he tried to reassure him. They were thinking of Taís. They had talked about her only once since leaving Rio de Janeiro. They never would again.

Octavio gave Paolina some sugarcane to chew on. Francesca disapproved but didn't say anything. They stopped on the way home to pull up wild garlic for dinner. Paolina demanded more and more sugarcane to suck on, and Octavio shaved off more pieces and obliged sheepishly. By the time they got back and started cooking, Paolina not only sang but also banged on everything, shrieking repeatedly in her mother's face even when she was told not to. Francesca seemed exhausted. Jonah struggled to keep Paolina distracted and out of the way. Euclides had not returned. Francesca told them that it was normal, and that they shouldn't worry. Sometimes he decided to camp out on his own on the mountainside. Sometimes he went to find one of his women. He would be back sooner or later.

After dinner Francesca tried to put Paolina to bed, but it was useless. The girl would start bawling and wouldn't stop unless her mother came and stayed by her side until she fell asleep. When she finally could get away, it was late and chilly outside. She joined Octavio and Jonah on the veranda, and for a time they huddled and chatted together like old friends. It was hard not look up at the stars, so clear at this elevation. To think of the world, and the sky, all those colorful spinning tops Jonah knew from the Hubble foldouts in *National Geographic*. He had read that the spiral arm of the Milky Way would one day reach the bend of Andromeda, and the two great puddles of stars would commingle a while, before returning into a void with no boundary at all, only an infinite thicket, like a wild jaboticaba tree climbing the visible realm, its billions of candescent branches fanning out through space and time. Perhaps Orígenes was right. On the other hand, he was still a black man laboring in a sugarcane field, most likely as he had been his entire life. As though even in all the immensity and beauty of the universe his world had no exit, no line of flight.

They heard Paolina whimper through the wall. Jonah decided to give the lovers some space and went inside to check on her. Later, when he overheard the muffled sounds of their lovemaking, he realized, to his surprise, that he didn't mind. He was happy for them. What kept him awake was not the grating loneliness of hearing others consumed in pleasure, but the deepening shadow of self-doubt. He thought of Nathaniel's words, and Isaac's, and he knew he had no better answers to any of the points they had made. And he knew moreover that he would have to leave his present situation, and soon. That he was not really *doing* anything, despite the fact that everything in the world was seemingly free for him to choose or take, most of all the freedom itself, which was in the scheme of history both an incredible accident and a miracle, but which he had, to his mind, so little to show for.

When they got back to the city, Jonah told Octavio that he was leaving Porto Alegre, that he wanted to see Montevideo and Buenos Aires, that there was no reason for him to stay any longer. He asked Octavio whether he wanted to join him or stay and explore his budding relationship with Francesca. Octavio asked for the night to think it over.

Jonah was packing and nervous about missing his overnight bus to Uruguay the next day when Octavio showed up.

"I'm staying," said Octavio. "Actually, I'm going to stay with Euclides for a while in Alvorada, and then we're heading back up into the mountains with Francesca and Paolina, possibly for a week or more. You're invited, of course, if you want to postpone that bus ticket."

"I'm good," replied Jonah. "You go have fun. Where's Francesca?"

"She's still packing. I came to get my stuff."

"I left you my portion for the Rialto," said Jonah.

"Cool, you'll keep in touch? Maybe if I can swing it, Francesca and I will come find you later on."

"Yeah, I'm sure we haven't seen the last of each other."

"I'm sure we haven't," said Octavio. "*Sin duda*. You take care of yourself."

"I will, compañero, I will. And listen, man. Whatever the case, be good to Francesca. Do right by her, if you can."

On this unexpected and yet vaguely anticipated comment, Octavio reflected solemnly but gave no immediate response. "We'll go with you to the bus station when you're ready."

At the bus terminal where they had disembarked, it now seemed, so long ago, the two friends embraced. Francesca was more emotional than Jonah had expected, and he felt almost immediately regretful that he was leaving. Francesca explained that she had a gift for him and extracted from her bag a little blue journal and a book of poems by Mário Quintana. Inside she had inscribed three words to him: *Sul. Sorte. Saudade.* "If never I see you again," she said, carefully, as she handed it to him. He thought she misspoke and meant to say, "I hope to see you again." But she shook her head and said it again in her own language using the word he knew meant what it did, but not what it would always mean to her. And when she tried again very softly, almost without sound, it was: "If I hope then never I will see you again." He knew that it was true. She put her arms out and they embraced. Then he stepped up into the idling bus, giving a faint wave through the bubble of glass as he found his way to an empty seat. He held close the gifts he had received as the rumbling behemoth lurched forward and pulled away.

PART FOUR

I run, but time's
Abreast with me
—COUNTEE CULLEN

A letter to you from home. I'm resting for a few days. Came down with one of these flu things. Got it on the plane, I think. The delightful side of this is that now I have an excuse to lie around in bed catching up on my reading and writing to you! I suppose the first thing to tell you is that Mariam and I are now officially "on a break." We're still texting, but I know inside that it's probably over. I'm unhappy with myself for not handling it better. The fact that she's in London right now is probably for the best. But I miss her terribly. What if I've screwed up a relationship with the one person who could make me happy? How do you ever know for sure if a relationship is the one? I think I wanted so much to fall in love, to be in love, that I panicked when it felt like it might really be happening. The smallest things seem to make all the difference, the slightest alteration of a day's plan and entire stories we might have lived just evaporate or materialize out of the void. For at least a week, I had this notion in my head that we would get married. We could go to Amsterdam, or Brussels, where it's legal, and be part of this beautiful new era that's opening before us. I sometimes have to stop and think about how extraordinary it is, what a time to be alive. All these new freedoms for love and acceptance expanding the picture of what a life could look like, what my life could be. The chance to be part of a historic moment. But I'm clearly not ready yet. Isn't it strange? It's like everything is possible now, there's never been a better time, there's never been so much hope, it's never been so easy to communicate and travel, to have fun and meet people from everywhere. And yet, I still feel somehow trapped. More unsure and frustrated than ever, more afraid that things aren't adding up toward something that will last. I secretly worry whether what I'm doing will be worthy of everything my parents and their parents did for me. Maybe there will never be an answer. It does feel good to be able to write to you about all this, though, because I know you'll read this and smile when you think of me, so serious and philosophical-like, laid up in my bed with all these balls of tissue and my endless cups of tisane, writing feverishly to you while the dreary rain taps on my window. I suppose if all else fails, the one thing I can say is at least I have you. In our own way, at least we've had each other.

—A

18

J onah stared out at the trucks passing by on the broiling highway. Little dust tornados swirled over the copper-colored land. Then, abruptly, grayish-green fields of corn or maize sprouted out of the baked earth. Occasionally they passed low gray factory complexes with corporate names stenciled on windowless facades. They slowed to a stop next to a truck-servicing station. From his window, Jonah watched sex workers in nylon shorts take languid steps back from the asphalt as the bus passed them by. The driver loudly announced "Trinta minutos" and stepped off. In the convenience area, there were various food stalls and aisles of packaged snacks, all with unfamiliar designs and names. Jonah picked up a bag of Yokitos and stared at the alligator apparently wearing a ball cap made from a leg of ham. The thought of ham-flavored potato chips made him slightly nauseous. He felt homesick. For New York. For Paris. For familiarity of any kind. His heart rose when the cashier told him where to find a computer with internet. He quickly checked his email. Arna had not written him back, and he wondered if something he said in his last email had put her off. He wrote a short note to Nathaniel Archimbald.

> Dear Nate,
>
> I know this will seem kind of random, but I'm writing you from a service area not far from the Brazilian/Uruguayan border. Rio was crazy, amazing, dangerous. My friend Octavio

who was traveling with me fell in love in Porto Alegre, a city in the South, and now I'm continuing solo toward Montevideo, a bit of a relief as I have a stronger grasp of Spanish than Portuguese. Listen, man, I still have your letter to Laura, but I don't know what to do with it. You and I both know the chances of me finding Laura are as likely as finding a lost penny on the beach. I don't even know what she looks like, you know? Anyway, this next phase of my travels could be pretty unpredictable, and I don't want anything to happen to the letter, so if you remind me of your address, I'd be happy to send it back.

Un abrazo from a lost brother,
Jonah

Back on the bus, Jonah's window was now dark with night. He tried once again to sleep, and this time he succeeded. He dreamt that he was in Paris, in the projection booth. Yellowed movie posters floated in the darkness. The actors and actresses with their beautiful teeth no longer stared at each other full of rapture; they were staring at him, like a circle of mute lawyers. The Kinoton and its black snake whirred to life. A stock of silvery, crackling light wobbled against the screen, patiently clearing into the shape of Phineas sitting with his legs crossed, smoking a cigarette.

"Where am I going?" Jonah asked him.

Phineas took a drag but did not respond.

"What happened to you? Why did it all go south?"

Phineas looked out to a point in the near distance.

"It's all in the way it bends," he said. "It bends toward the heart, *always*."

"But how do I *know* . . . how do I find it?"

"The ear bends to the heart, brother, when you play everything *rightly*."

"Just play it right?"

"Play *all the notes* . . . Don't skip none now . . . You gotta let each one know they *already there* . . . show they was ready to begin with . . . the thing is . . . if I messed up it wasn't cause I didn't love the music . . . my spirit was always right with the music . . . whatever I got to answer for . . . please let them know brother . . . that every note I played . . . I did my best to play it rightly."

Jonah awoke with a start. He was in another country.

⁂

The trees were snowing in Montevideo. A dandruff of silky pollen came off the branches along the avenues, along all the hushed boulevards running down to the ocean. Jonah advanced in a daze, happy just to be off the bus. A bright pan of sunlight rinsed over the squat buildings that lined the boulevards, its warmth cut by the icy quills of the Southern Ocean. He leaned into the wind and the tumbling tufts of pollen flew in his eyes.

To Jonah the trees felt oddly familiar, their arrangement and disposition, the personality of their crowns. They looked just like French plane trees, and in fact the whole city seemed carved out of some idea of Paris in the late nineteenth century, as though a fragment had set sail and washed ashore at the mouth of the Río de la Plata. Like the French, the Uruguayans were fond of their cafés and bookstores, tons of them it seemed, especially for a country that was probably by population about the size of Queens. Inside a *librería* in the Ciudad Vieja he quickly discovered they were proud of their poets too. Perhaps the trees were a token of gratitude on the part of the French, in exchange for all the morose and maleficent Uruguayan exiles and dandies who pollinated their poetry—Lautréamont, Supervielle, Laforgue—who tasted the ozone of these austral latitudes.

Not far from the Rambla he entered an empty tavern where the bartenders looked like toughs from a Jean-Pierre Melville flick. The local whiskey seemed to be the thing. It went down fiery and marine. When he eventually stumbled out again, he was filled with hunger. In his sullen march for food and lodging he passed through the Parque Rodó.

The grounds of the park were impeccably kept and desolate. Making his way under the tall green palms, Jonah arrived before a huge obelisk done in Eurofascist thirties-style concrete. It was dedicated to Uruguayan writers and artists, and to the youth of Latin America. Dusk was enclosing the greenery around him in a canopy of chittering twilight. He turned from the monument in a mummified stupor. He was trying to gauge the quickest path back to the street, but he couldn't make it out. He felt like a feral spirit stranded on an island in someone else's world. And for a flickering moment, he was certain some oppressive force would try to keep him there, holding him in a state of wild captivity, solitary and enslaved, a native hypnotized into submission by a colonial magician. But the queasiness passed, and he eventually made his way down along a lake lined with eucalyptus trees, before finding his way out onto yet another avenue that abutted the park. A few streets farther on, he turned and came upon a catacombic alley illuminated by a single bulb of light. Jonah followed it like a beacon and came to a small pensión where the words EL VASCO had been lettered in green and red on the window. Without so much as a glance at the menu, he walked in.

Behind a lectern stood a man dressed in a frumpy tan jacket and drooping bowtie, his hair slicked back, his thin moustache regularly agitated by a twitch in one eye. The impression was of a slightly shabby and possibly shifty variation on the standard model.

"Hola," said Jonah. "Por favor, quiero una mesa para cena y una cama para la noche. Es posible?"

The man did not reply but instead looked around the room then up the stairs behind him. The tiny restaurant only had four tables. They were all empty. Four keys hung from hooks untaken by guests. He turned back to Jonah with a strained look, as if he were trying to dislodge a crumb scratching in his throat.

"All our tables and rooms are booked this evening," he said in unmoved Oxfordian English.

"Okay, so . . ." Jonah switched to English while steadying himself against the implication he was beginning to recognize. "Well, look, can I at least eat? I can be quick if the reservations aren't until later. Or . . . is there a problem here?"

The maître d' shook his head, expressionless. "The chef has not yet started to cook. By the time he begins, the guests with reserved tables will have arrived." He raised his hands in a slight shrug. "I'm afraid you will have to find somewhere else to eat."

The maître d' was now staring at him coldly, as if he were trying to glare him out the door. Jonah was trying to make up his mind on how far to take it. He was hungry, and now he was pissed too. On the other hand, he was a stranger in a strange land a million miles from home, and it was probably not the best time to test out the response time of the local cops.

From the kitchen came a sudden and loud clatter of pots and pans along with a shout of "Maldita!" The kitchen doors opened and a man with a chef's hat emerged, the cap ill-suited to his rather enormous head. The maître d' rushed over to him, initiating a ping-ponging of excited Spanish between them. Then the chef looked over at Jonah. His countenance changed from one of annoyance to glee.

"Miguel!" he said, slapping the maître d' on the chest. "No me dijiste que teníamos un invitado!"

Jonah couldn't understand what the chef was so happy about, but he sensed that his luck was about to turn.

"Muchacho! Estas aquí para cenar?"

"Sí."

"Sí, cómo no!"

The chef shook his head at the maître d' and they exchanged a few more agitated words that Jonah couldn't make out, but he gathered by the chef's hand gestures toward the upstairs and back to the restaurant tables that he was arguing for Jonah to remain as a guest. Finally, the chef approached him, flashing a grin.

"Perdónanos. El restaurante no está abierto aún para la cena. Pero Miguel lo llevará a una habitación en la planta superior donde puede ducharse y cambiarse sus camisas. Alguna comida y bebida le estarán esperando cuando baja."

Jonah was lost in the chef's flurry of Spanish.

"Lo siento, pero mi español es muy pobre."

The chef slightly raised his eyebrows. "Qué idioma hablas? Your language?"

"English or French."

"Ah, bueno. Where you from?" the chef asked.

"New York."

"New York? New York! *Newww Yawk Citayyyy! Qué suerte!* Do you remember when we went to New York, Miguel? And now, New York, she has come to us! Welcome to Montevideo, Yankee! My name is Oscar, and this is my *pareja*, Miguel. I was saying to you that we are not yet open for the evening. But it's okay. Miguel will take you to a room while I begin preparations for the dinner. After you shower and change your clothes, you will come back here, and there will be a table with food and drink waiting for you."

"*Que bueno*. Gracias, Oscar."

Oscar disappeared into the kitchen; with a lethargic flick of the wrist, Miguel gestured for Jonah to follow him upstairs.

Oscar's partner had not entirely warmed to Jonah, but he was more welcoming after Jonah spruced himself up. They had laid out for him a platter of meats, cheeses, and bread, along with a glass of wine. Miguel left Jonah alone to eat, but he was prompt in suggesting and pouring more red. There was only one other diner in the room: a woman, who sat facing away from him. She and Miguel periodically exchanged chitchat, laughing under their breath. Only when Oscar himself came to check on Jonah's satisfaction with the food did the woman turn to look at him. From her glance, he was able to discern that she was she was a little older than him, with features that lent her an enigmatic, foreign flair. From the kitchen doorway, Oscar appeared, and with a loud exclamation, greeted the woman, kissing both cheeks and exchanging pleasantries. Oscar asked if Jonah wanted anything further, but Jonah, apologetically declined, citing his exhaustion.

"Then tomorrow, we shall have a bigger meal. Something special for our Yankee friend."

Jonah slept fitfully. He seemed to be the only guest and sat alone with a breakfast of toast, jam, and coffee, served by Miguel, who said that Oscar had departed early to get to the seafood markets. Jonah observed Miguel at his lectern, seemingly waiting for guests that showed no signs of coming. Other than the maître d's distaste for colored folks, he wondered what it was about this particular pensión that caused people to avoid it. Certainly, in a city as generally pale-faced as Montevideo, his attitude wouldn't be the problem. Besides, the place wasn't without its old-timey charms. Jonah's eyes settled on the photographs that littered the wall, pictures of fútbol players and local celebrities from bygone eras. He noticed a newspaper photograph of what appeared to be Fidel Castro wearing a blue suit and being served food at an expensive restaurant. He thought he recognized the waiter, and, giving him a closer look, realized it was none other than Miguel. When he came to clear Jonah's plate, he asked about it.

"Oh yes, that really was something. I was chosen to be part of the wait-staff for the state dinner to honor Castro when he visited Montevideo in '95. Naturally, I more or less detested the Castro regime, but some of my dear friends still tease me and call me a Communist because I once served El Caballo. What do you want? It was a job."

Miguel gave a shrug much like the one he had given Jonah the night before. He seemed to be a man who kept his true opinions and those he shared in casual conversation in separately marked boxes. Jonah didn't push him and instead inquired whether Miguel knew of any independent theaters in Montevideo.

"Independent. What do you mean?"

"A theater where I could watch local Uruguayan movies or art films."

"I don't know, but maybe Cinemateca Pocitos. At least, that's the most famous one."

Following Miguel's rudimentary directions, Jonah walked all the way down to the waterfront. Cinemateca Pocitos was only a few blocks up from there. A film festival was under way, and people were congregating. He looked closely at what was being screened and was shocked to find *him*. Phineas stared back from a poster box. It was as if the places and cultures Jonah was from, that he had made all the effort he could to escape, were actually being reproduced everywhere he arrived. To move away from the center was to drag the center to the periphery. He had made efforts in that direction and what did he have to show for it? All too soon, he reflected, these circles would converge and there would be no outside, no elsewhere. No need for a future version of himself to travel at all. By then his failures would become like Phineas himself. Bowdlerized for passive consumption; languishing in the vast lot of the unfinished and unlamented. One more entry in the encyclopedia of black failure to achieve the greatness that black hope demands.

Spooked, he considered buying a ticket, but finally did not. Instead, in a kind of disoriented panic he picked a film called *Tango Amoroso*, the poster for which was peppered with award medallions. He settled down in his seat, wanting something to distract him from a creeping sense of anxiety, a dread that he was being followed, not by a sinister force or a surveilling state, but by the swirling accumulation of his own evasions coming to account. He could understand almost none of the dialogue, but that hardly mattered. The film was a documentary about tango dancers, about bodies in their color interlocking in the swiveling pattern that sailors and dockworkers, the sons and daughters of Africa and Italy and Spain, had invented on the shores of European outposts in America. But much of the film wasn't explanatory. It was simply a recording of human bodies expressing desire with extraordinary beauty. The smile of one dancer to another in motion. It summed up everything, it said it all. The pleasures of human dance swept over him. Everything about it effortlessly repulsed the very notion of cerebral tics, malaise, disgust with life. It was like a vision of all that he felt he was not. He found himself on the verge of tears and unable to move. He didn't want the movie to end. He wanted to hide, and when the last of the colorful bodies had dipped and the fade to black surrendered them to the theater's soft lights, he had to gather all his force to move on.

Outside, the city's nocturnal rhythms were beginning to take hold. Pockets of laughter and conversation reverberated under the pale evening sky. The thought of ambulating alone any longer, any farther, brought a leaky lightness to his bones. He leaned against a patch of wall between two posters for coming attractions and pretended to himself that he was merely catching his breath.

What was in reach? Across the way, directly in his line of sight, glowed the neon trimming of the cinema's Hollywood-themed bar. Before he knew it, Jonah had downed two, then three whiskeys, the slender bartender dispensing each shot and slinking off to the far end to continue conversing with a pair of older gentlemen with portly bellies and stylish glasses. From where he was sitting, he could watch folks exiting the theater. A porter opened the door and walked in with a broom. A few people staggered out, couples, students. Behind a small group, a woman in a dark coat emerged and moved swiftly past him toward the exit, and he had the fluttering sensation that it was the woman from the previous night at El Vasco, but he wasn't sure. He thought he should follow her, but he hadn't paid his bill, and in his excitement, it took him even longer than usual to get it settled. By the time he emerged on the pavement she was long gone.

In a state of anxious bewilderment, compounded by drink, he thought he must find an internet café and write to Arna and to Isaac to tell them about this lonely stretch of a trip that had taken him to a city in which he had never imagined setting foot. And then, if he was sober enough, he would find out about the most reasonable flights back to New York. He marched himself up to the more heavily trafficked city center and entered the first place that he found. When he opened his inbox, he saw a short note from Isaac telling him that he'd received a raise at his school and was happy about it, but not sure if it would be enough to keep him around for more than another year or two. But there was another bold line in his inbox that grabbed Jonah's attention. Nathaniel had written him back.

Dear Jonah,

It sounds like it's complicated out there, but look, man, don't think I don't envy your travels, it's a great chance that most of us never get. I am glad to hear you are okay. About the letter, it would mean much to me if you could hang on to it, at least while you are in Montevideo. I know you will make the most of your time, and even the thought of both of you being somewhere down there makes me feel hopeful somehow. I'm attaching a scan of one of the only photos I have of her—of us, actually. Paris, 1994. She was a beauty, man, and now I can see that I was looking pretty damn good then too. I wonder if she saw me now if it would even go the same, but you know, we'll always have Paris, like the movie says. And that's okay. I'm feeling more myself these days than ever, other than getting old and the fact that my jump shot ain't right, I'm what you might call a satisfied man. You can't imagine how great it is when one of my kids graduates, and I get to hug everyone in the family. Truth be told, I never had so much fun hooping as I've had coaching, even though our record isn't exactly pretty. Every time I see those eyes light up when I rap to them about this crazy world we're living in, well, it just makes me feel good, man. I mean sometimes we get to conversating *and* I can see it's connecting, how it's about the bigger picture, how the world is really theirs if they are willing to make it. But now you got me carrying on about myself again. Listen, be well out there, young brother, and remember to come back—that's why I gave you the letter too, because you can always come home again. We all got peoples who need us. We all got to find our own way to do good. So do your thing, man. Enjoy that life. I hope to hear from you again somewhere down the road.

Peace,

Nate

Jonah clicked on the photograph. Nathaniel did look terribly happy and handsome in the image. They looked very much like a couple in love. And Laura. Could it be her? The woman he had seen at the theater? The woman he had seen at El Vasco? She would be older now, so there was room for some difference, but the face was so strikingly similar; it felt uncannily cosmic, as though the universe were walking him to a crossroads. It seemed unlikely that she would return to the same restaurant two nights in a row. But Oscar and Miguel seemed to know her.

Jonah anticipated the evening playing out much like the one before it, with Miguel paying him little to no attention. But when he arrived for a table, he noticed that Oscar and especially Miguel were in noticeably good spirits. Miguel tapped his fingers to the music playing from a little Toshiba stereo, his hostility all but evaporated.

"Ah, muchacho. Good, good, you are here. Tonight we celebrate the feast of Saint James, the patron saint of the Basque people. I make piperrada y bacalao. Muy rico." Don Miguel led Jonah to the same table he had eaten at the night before, only this time, without prompting, he returned with a bottle of Uruguayan Tannat, a wine made from an Uruguayan red grape, as he explained while pouring a generous glass. "Compliments of the chef," he said, before returning to his hawkish perch at the lectern. A bark broke through the music and a whimpering short-haired wiener dog came waddling over the tiles to Miguel.

"Garufa!" he said. "Go say hello to the guest!"

When the dog refused, Miguel grabbed the Tannat and walked back to Jonah's table, coaxing Garufa to follow by patting on his thigh. To Jonah's surprise, Miguel took a seat, grabbed himself an unused glass from the table and, filling it, took a pleasured sip. Neither of them spoke. Jonah turned to look back at the photographs on the wall, many of which showed Miguel and Oscar on ports with cities spread out behind them. He came across a portrait of Miguel with Oscar's arm over his shoulder, the two of them dressed in overly heavy coats with the wintry skyline of New York in the background.

"So, tell me about your time in New York," Jonah said.

"Ah yes. The Big . . . Apple. Well, it came about as a result of our both doing a tour in the Merchant Marines," said Miguel, whose decent English now sounded tweaked with a James Cagney-like nasal snarl. "It's how we met, traveling the world together. I would say we've known all the major ports of the world. Buenos Aires, of course; Sydney; Singapore; Shanghai; up to New York; over to Dublin; down to Bilbao—the best of all; down even more to Cape Town, which is on the same latitudinal line as Montevideo, you know."

"Why was Bilbao your favorite?" asked Jonah.

"Have you been to the Basque country? It's beautiful for the people, an unconquered tribe. It's where Oscar and I . . . well, let us say that it has become like an adopted home. We have since been back many times."

Miguel waved his hands at the flag and jersey Jonah had noticed earlier. "That's the jersey for the Athletic Bilbao. Oscar is a big fan, as is Garufa. Aren't you, Garufa?"

Miguel reached down to give the dog a scratch. Jonah noticed that Garufa's collar was in Athletic Bilbao colors.

Oscar came out of the kitchen with the piping hot peppers, set them down, and poured himself a glass of Tannat. "A break now until the next guests arrive," he said, glancing at the door. But no one showed up.

Miguel put in a new CD and returned to the table to pour himself another glass of wine. The restaurateurs listened to the aching voice of the tango singer, and at times joined their voices to his song, gazing into each other's eyes with wonder and an insider's deep satisfaction.

"Who is this?" Jonah asked.

"Carlos Gardel. Uruguay's greatest."

Miguel pointed at a sepia-toned photograph of a man who looked like a South American Humphrey Bogart.

"I thought tango was Argentinian," Jonah said.

"What? Absolutely not!" Miguel hissed. "The Argentines are always claiming things that are not theirs. They even think Gardel is Argentine." Miguel gave Jonah an icy glare. "It's as if all good things that develop here must be taken from us. All our beautiful men leave for Buenos Aires, all our writers and artists leave for Paris, all our riches leave for foreign accounts in Switzerland or Brazil or up north. We were once the richest nation in South America until those Tupamaro bastards came along and ruined everything. And now this country is being run—into the ground, if you ask me, by those crooks."

"Now, come on, Miguelito, you're getting all upset over nothing."

"No! I won't calm down!"

No one spoke for a moment, and Jonah realized that Gardel was no longer singing. His music had been replaced by a song in a language he didn't recognize.

"What's this playing now?"

"Ah," said Oscar. "This is Evert Taube."

"What language is Señor Taube singing in?"

"Swedish," said a female voice. Standing in the entranceway was the woman from the theater, the woman from the previous evening.

"Señora Aussaresses, que bueno verte!" Oscar leapt up to kiss her hand and welcome her.

"I didn't mean to interrupt the conversation with your guest," she said in soft, French-accented English.

"Not at all," said Oscar, also switching to English. "You're welcome to join us if you like."

Miguel was at the table, pouring her a glass of Tannat. Evert Taube's lilting sea-captain Swedish sounded out like a bard's tale, full of roving wanderers and unhappy endings.

"Señora Aussaresses, this is . . . eh . . ." Oscar paused. "You know, I don't think I've asked for your name, muchacho."

Jonah stood up and extended his hand, which she took gently. "Jonah."

"These gentlemen call me Madame Aussaresses, but you can call me Laura."

"Jonah is here from New York City," said Oscar with a boastful note.

"I have always wanted to visit that city. I was once in a relationship with a man from New York, but that was a long time ago in another place. Now I live in Montevideo."

It *was* Laura. C'est pas possible.

He had whispered it softly to himself, but she had picked it up immediately.

"Ah, but how are you speaking French?" she demanded to know.

"I'm actually from Paris," said Jonah.

She gave Jonah a look that he found hard to interpret, something between suspicion and relief. "Très bien, then you will understand why I come and eat here nearly every night. It is so hard to find a decent place to eat in this town. All Uruguayans eat is steak, steak, steak. But these gentlemen, Oscar and Miguel, fellow wanderers and exiles like myself, they always make good company and good fun, and they have the most wonderful collection of music. You picked this place out of all others, so you must have an eye for good things too. So, why don't you tell me: What brings you here?"

"I'm thinking now that it must be fate," Jonah said faintly.

"Fate . . ." She turned to the Basques. "You hear that, Oscar? This young man seems to think he knows a thing or two about fate."

They shared a laugh at Jonah's expense. As easily as he had seemed to win over Miguel's approval, now it looked as though he were losing it just as quickly.

Laura stood up again, seeming to take note of the intensity in the young man's gaze upon her.

"Well, I'll leave you to your food . . . and fate."

"Vous devez m'excuser, je suis impoli," Jonah broke in.

"Alors vous êtes vraiment français . . ." Laura said, still skeptical.

"Oui, enfin, plus ou moins."

Oscar and Miguel had to attend to other guests, but Laura demanded to know more. She wanted details, the whole story, and with his permission, she joined his table, poured herself a glass, and listened. Jonah began at the beginning, as he had with Nathaniel. He tried to explain himself as best he could.

"And what about you?" Jonah asked, when he had finally come full circle to the present evening. "What is your story?"

"It's like yours," she said. "Made of so many threads and wanderings I never know where to begin."

19

"**M**aybe with a question," she said. "Because who I am is not so simple, and even very difficult to say if one expects the name of a country to suffice. For instance, I am Armenian by heritage. Born in Beirut. Speak French and Spanish and Arabic. You could say I am a métèque, like Moustaki says in his song. My education was French. I was a student at the Sorbonne before I left it all. I lived for three years in Mexico City where I fell in love with a young lawyer who wanted to marry me. Another man I had to desert. I returned to France to be with my family."

She tended to her father who was dying a long time. And then her mother, who started to decline soon after. She cared for them with the help of Rosemarie, a Catholic from Guyana who came by to help before her night shifts at the hospital. After her mother's death, she fell into a depression. She took up part-time work at a travel agency. They were very nice and did their best but she was a terrible employee and they fired her soon after. She wasn't working for the money anyway. Her parents had left her enough, not a fortune, but more than she had expected, especially once she sold their apartment.

That was the beginning of the second fugue. A flight to Buenos Aires, with vague plans to stay for a few months. The men she met there were intolerable, and most of the women too. But then in Quilmes she met two friends who were different from the others, who she discovered were not porteñas at all, but Uruguayans who lived in Buenos Aires where they could find work. They insisted she should discover their hometown. Her initial impression of Montevideo was that it was the ugliest, saddest-looking city she had ever seen. Nothing in its appearance should make one want to stay. And yet, for the first time in as long as she could remember, she started to feel alive again. Something about the city's unrelenting air of sadness alleviated her own. For so long she had stopped trusting the faces of men. As the fog of depression lifted, she could see them again, but differently. She felt at ease and no longer sorry. She enjoyed defying them. The roughly whiskered drunks in their caps who inched along through the market streets of the Ciudad Vieja or sat on the seawall along the Rambla staring at the long breakers. She felt neither fear nor desire as she crossed paths with young men shouting and knocking into each other. Their world was so gray and melancholy that her own life in comparison stood tall. The weightlessness of afternoons became addictive.

Still, it might not have lasted. She had, in fact, been considering returning to Paris and would have if she hadn't entered one night into a tavern called El Vasco for a late meal. "That was where I met him," she said. Salvador Aussaresses. When she took a table, he was already quietly dining by himself. He was at first glance fairly ordinary in appearance, though she could tell from his brightly colored scarf that he liked to dress. When her food arrived, he rose in a grand manner and approached her without an invitation. "Forgive me, but a woman should never dine alone," he said, in Spanish, and she knew immediately from his accent that he was Argentine. His attitude was off-putting, but charming enough that she felt it unnecessary to dress him down. He ordered more wine for the table and introduced himself as a successful local painter. He was disappointed that this information left her unimpressed. But when he learned that she was from Paris the conversation lit up. He knew it well. Had many gallerists who carried his work there over the years. Had not been back for at least a decade but had an undying admiration and love for the French and their art. He was a man who had been very handsome once, even if something had worn in the better features she could tell he had once possessed. When the proposition that she pose for him came, there was no naivete in her casual affirmation that she would consider it. "Come for a session," Salvador insisted. "If you don't like the experience, you can leave," he added, and slipped her his card. He paid for her meal.

When she decided, two days later, to go and see his address, Salvador seemed to anticipate her arrival. Before she had a chance to decide whether she would ring he had sprung outside coming into the street to greet her. Solemnly, he ushered her inside for tea. The house was large and well appointed. Salvador's taste in beautiful things was refined and one could tell that he took pride in their display. They took tea in the kitchen, which was tiled with smooth warm-colored tomettes like those she had loved as a child in her grandparents' house. Afterward, he took her to his studio. It was a beautiful open space, with old windows facing the inner courtyard. At first, she was very stiff. But the sound of the charcoal became soothing and after a time she got used to it. When the session ended, he pressed a pile of bills into her hand. It turned out to be an extraordinary sum, so much so that her worry about ulterior expectations nearly brought things to a halt. But the experience had not displeased her, and there was something about Salvador that she found unexpectedly attractive, she said. So, she returned. By the third week, she was posing entirely nude. At the conclusion of a long evening session, when he made a proposition, it was not the one she had prepared herself to answer. Salvador said that he was going to be away in Argentina for several weeks, that if she wished she could stay at his place. He would leave money and keys and she would agree to care for the house until his return.

That was how it began, she said. Having such a beautiful place to herself for long stretches of time, totally independent and with no concern for money, meant she could try something she had been thinking about all through her depression: the idea of writing. Now she had the means and a place to do so untroubled, in a city that she had fallen, however oddly, in love with. Salvador was aloof, an aesthete, but mostly harmless. Besides, he would regularly go away for weeks at a time, and when he came home, all he would ask of her was to sit for him so he could paint. She had so much time to herself. In the courtyard she could sit by the lemon tree in the sunlight and read books for hours without hearing a word or a sound besides the chittering of the birds and the lives of the insects. Salvador was often her only regular companion. Despite passing time together, she was never sure she knew him well. She had worried that he would ask her for sex. But he didn't, and after a while she stopped worrying that he would. Sometimes he had other models come to the studio, always young women, sometimes young in a way that made her uncomfortable. But artists are wont to surround themselves with the beautiful. The girls who came to the studio were certainly that. She knew he liked to gaze. Sometimes she would catch Salvador watching her from another room. One time over coffee, he said that she had a mannish quality to her face, that she reminded him of a close friend whom he had lost in the Falklands. She wanted to ask more about it, but the way Salvador spoke she thought it better not to.

Her writing continued to fill up her journals, she said, and the time of the world slipped away. Everything would have been perfect if it hadn't been for the nightmares. They were always similar and very regular now. It started with a conviction that Salvador was at the door watching her sleep. She would feel a deep powerlessness, her body paralyzed, and then wake up in a cold sweat. She always checked to see if Salvador was in the room or lurking outsider her door. But he never was. Outwardly, there was nothing wrong, as far as she could tell. But increasingly, she noticed that people fell silent around Salvador in a manner she had not noticed before. Worse, she said, sometimes she found herself doing the same thing, as though merely being in his presence made her lose her voice. Or she would become uncertain as to whether or not she had spoken. And she began to get visits at night from a tall blue bird. It would land on her head and grip her skull with its talons. She would stay very still and beg that it go away. But the sharp talons dug in. Just when she thought she couldn't take it anymore the bird would take off with a clapping thunder like the sound of a helicopter, and sometimes she was convinced it *was* a helicopter, or a great plane passing low overhead and moving out to sea. Then she would wake. People looked at her funny in the street, she said. As if they knew something about her, as if she was guilty of something terrible. "But all I'm guilty of is wanting time," she said. "Of needing space. Does anyone know how hard it is, even in this day and age, for a woman to live free of any attachments? Free of the need to work? To have a good place to live and write and not owe a man anything, not money, not sex, not the raising of children, nothing!"

There was a momentary quiet. By now the few other diners had long gone. Miguel was standing at his lectern nearby, but Jonah couldn't tell if he had he been listening. Oscar was somewhere in the kitchen, presumably washing up.

Laura was looking directly at Jonah. Their eyes lingered on one another's.

"I'm sorry if I've frightened you," she said after a moment.

"No, not at all."

"I thought, I don't know, there's something about you. I think you remind me of a friend I once knew, a dear friend from long ago. I hope you won't mind me saying this. But I almost never see black people here, you know."

"I can imagine."

"Please, I know it's sudden, but would you come to see me before you leave?"

"I will if you want me to."

"I do. Come see me tomorrow. I will introduce you to Salvador. I think he may like to meet you."

She asked Miguel for a menu and, to the maître d's obvious displeasure, wrote down her address on the back with a rough little map to show him.

"I will see you tomorrow, won't I?"

"Yes, I'll be around," Jonah said.

Satisfied, she left. Jonah immediately ordered another drink. But the bitter sea air in its bite was not enough. The winds had crossed him with Nathaniel's Laura. There could be no doubt. Indeed, he didn't dare doubt it, because it was already as if he had spoken too loudly and been overheard. And now the infinity of the world was answering his rudderless drift by crashing him into the rocks.

20

J onah spent the next morning anxiously going over the whole thing in his mind. On the one hand, he thought of heading immediately to the internet café to send a message to Nate. On the other, he thought about what the meeting Laura had demanded might promise—what was unspoken but powerfully felt in the way she had looked at him. The thought of her desiring him was troubling in the best and the worst way. Telling Nate would have the effect of collapsing the possible future course of his actions. Postponing that revelation would allow him to make discoveries, to inquire more about Salvador, for instance, which might be important in any report he sent back. But he was sufficiently torn that he made his way to Ciudad Vieja to check his email anyway and at least consider sending a note.

He looked first to see if there was any news from Arna, but there was none. On the other hand, there were several emails from Isaac, one being a short letter and the others containing links to news reports from different outlets. Isaac sounded characteristically grim, but there was a hint of anxiety in his tone that was even more alarming to Jonah than the aggressive graphics in the news clips.

There had been another ugly police shooting, this time in Brooklyn. In fact, it was only seven or eight blocks away from the apartment on St. Johns and Underhill. A team of undercover officers had come up to a young couple leaving their wedding party at a club and for reasons that still remained unclear had shot them as they were getting into their car to leave. The number of shots fired was incredible. As Isaac put it, "They just lit the car up like they were at a shooting gallery, for no reason." The head of the Patrolmen's Benevolent Association had put out a statement to the effect that no investigation would be necessary, it was a tragic incident of mistaken identity, the couple had acted suspiciously and failed to comply with police demands. The man was a local party promoter and the woman a nurse at Woodhull Medical Center. They were both pronounced dead at the scene, but there was additional controversy over whether or not the officers who riddled their bodies with bullets had bothered to call in a timely manner for an ambulance, with some reports indicating that the ambulance had actually responded to calls from others in the wedding party who were in the parking lot and witnessed the shooting. Three of the officers involved were white and a fourth was Hispanic.

There was already a fury in the streets because of the intensification of a campaign to randomly stop and frisk anyone coming in and out of the projects, and the city was now on edge as calls for revenge on the police were being circulated online and peaceful demonstrations in the neighborhood were overtaken by increasingly violent clashes. The police were responding with more brutality, more tear gas, and mass arrests. The images were out of a dystopian nightmare. Phalanxes of cops in military-grade body armor, mounted officers raising batons and smashing their shields into faces in the crowds on the dark streets of Brooklyn. Hundreds had already been arrested, the president had given a speech calling on "the better angels." But the raw anger in the streets and the grotesque disproportion of the police response were feeding a hopeless downward spiral. Isaac was still supposed to go to work and teach his third graders, but many parents were refusing to even let their kids leave the house as long as the threat of a wider riot was still heavy in the air.

By the time he had digested the news and realized he would have to compose some kind of note to Isaac, Jonah was utterly demoralized. What was there to say? Telling him about his adventures and discovery of Laura in Montevideo seemed somehow both unseemly and vaguely unkind. He wrote and deleted and rewrote several times what amounted to only a three- or four-line email, with banal phrases telling his friend to "stay safe" and "stay strong." Any thought of writing to Nate evaporated. He couldn't think straight, and besides, it wasn't the right time. But when would the right time be?

Outside in the cool breeze, he walked along watching the people of Uruguay go about their tranquil lives. How different it would be to live in some small country like this—with its own complicated history, no doubt, but where, at least at present, one might grow up without ever really thinking that anything one's country did or failed to do mattered, apart from occasionally making it to the World Cup finals. No foreign wars. No racial conflict spilling into the streets every day, no mass shootings, no sudden world-altering terrorist attacks would come screaming across the sky. Also, no black people. Which meant no place he could ever really be. Well, almost none. Once Jonah saw a glimpse of what appeared to be a drumline parading down one of the avenues. It was brief. He came around a corner and saw in the far distance a group of black men, one of them waving an albiceleste flag with a black diagonal stripe. But they were walking away from him and the music faded. He had asked Oscar about it, and had learned that there was in fact a small community of blacks in Uruguay, the descendants of slaves who had escaped south from Brazil, where emancipation didn't come until 1888, a full sixty years after the Uruguayans had fought their way to independence from the Portuguese Empire. The diaspora was always larger than one imagined. But whatever the situation of the black folk in Montevideo—and he guessed it probably wasn't magnificent—could it be as bad as Brownsville? As the bloody streets of Baltimore? He walked in a daze of muted anger. At what, he didn't know exactly, mostly at himself. He felt guilty and stupid for being where he was. For having it so easy, but also for not having an answer, something that would justify his trajectory. While in this state of agitation he found himself, having wandered a good deal farther to the north than he had anticipated, standing outside the green entrance of the colonial solare that Laura had described to him. It was late in the afternoon by the time he arrived on the beautiful, tree-lined street, which showed no signs of life other than the occasional car or small truck thudding along under a light load.

Laura met him at the door and led him in through cool dim hallways to a spare living room. A neoclassical mold stood in one corner, a large palm by the window fronded a passage to an inner courtyard, and in the middle of the room a long, heavily worn-in couch, dark and sea green, faced a small fireplace flanked on both sides by towering bookcases. Glancing over them, he noted artist monographs, old volumes of classical literature in Spanish, and moderns like Borges alongside names that Jonah didn't recognize, that he guessed were Argentine or Uruguayan writers of decades past.

As he was taking in the room, Laura brought a bottle and two glasses in from the kitchen.

"Will you drink with me?" she asked.

"Avec plaisir."

"Ah, tant mieux. I've been waiting for an occasion to have someone to drink wine with—you know they love their whiskey here. I hope you will be pleased with the vin de maison—naturally it's Argentinian."

"Honestly, I'm not picky. Besides, I think I can trust your taste."

She uncorked and poured them each a glass, then turned to him again.

"Do you mind if I ask how old you are? You look . . . very young, you know."

"Old enough."

She smiled at this. "Ah! Well, cheers to that. I enjoyed our talk. I realize I did most of the talking. But you put me at ease in a way I haven't felt in so long. I think I told you . . . you remind me . . ."

"Of someone you knew, someone from years ago in Paris . . . a black man."

"Did I say all that? Well, it's true enough. He was special to me . . . Something about him was different from all the others."

"And I remind you of him?"

"In some ways, yes."

He was very conscious now of controlling his voice, every intonation, of the way his hands were placed and more still of how her eyes fell on them at times as though quietly imbibing something there at the surface that she wanted to keep for a later time.

"Do I make you nervous?" she asked.

"No, only a little, maybe."

"I hope you don't mind if I say this. I can't help it, I'm always very direct. But you have the air of a young man who doesn't stay anywhere for too long, or with anyone for too long. Are you still planning on leaving Montevideo very soon?"

"Yes, I can't stay much longer . . . I think I've started to realize that there are a number of things back home that I really need to get back to."

"A girlfriend perhaps."

"No, actually. Not that."

"Are you sure? I would be surprised if there wasn't more than one you might have left behind."

"You seem to see more in me than others. I wish it were true in a way, but it isn't."

"Well, I feel lucky then to have caught your eye while you were passing through."

"Did you catch me? I feel like it's more that I've . . . found you."

"You've found me at an interesting time. I feel more myself now than I've felt in years, almost as if I'm coming out of a deep sleep."

"Tell me, what was he like?"

"Who?"

"The man you knew in Paris."

"He was a beautiful man. Handsome, athletic, darker than you—very intelligent and kind. He knew how to make love in all the ways that matter. What about you? I think you are probably too young to have such experience."

"I haven't got as much as experience as I would like."

"You wish you had more?"

"Yes. If I were with someone who wanted to give me the chance, then yes."

Instead of responding to this directly, Laura rose from her end of the couch and walked into an adjoining hall. He heard the creak of a faucet. A moment later, she reappeared in the living room, lifted her drink, and took a sip while looking upon him, and sat down again.

"I'm going to take a bath. Would you care to join me?"

Her gaze was steady, and he met it as he thought carefully about his answer. She was older, of course, and rounder and heavier than in the picture Nate had sent along. In the picture she still had a girlish prettiness, but also a blankness to her features. Now she was a woman, her body thicker and more attractive, her face more expressive, beautiful in a way that the image he had seen was not. She had grown her hair out very long, and now as she waited for his reply, she had taken some of it in her hands.

"I think I will, yes. If that's all right with you."

"Good. I would like that."

She put down her drink and moved across the couch, leaning in over him so that her hair was falling over his arm.

"Don't move."

"Okay."

She put her lips to his softly. And as he started to kiss her back, she took his hand in her own and placed it against her breast. When she had felt what she needed, she got up and led him to the bathroom where they undressed. She held him against her body as they waited for the water to rise. When it was ready, she turned off the faucet, threw down a pile of towels for her comfort and, having smoothed them to her satisfaction, turned to confront him with her sex. Afterward, they slipped into the hot water; the tub sang like a whale as they slid against its hull.

It wasn't until they were drying off that Jonah even thought to inquire about Salvador, and he was alarmed to learn that the owner of the house had been there the entire time, painting in his studio upstairs. Laura was nonchalant.

"I told him you might come by and he agreed to meet with you if you did. Why don't you go upstairs and you two can get acquainted? I'll be ready and have something for us to eat this evening when you come down."

After he'd dressed again, Laura led him through the inner courtyard, and over to a stone staircase that wound around itself. The air outside was immensely pleasant, and dramatic pinkish light was coloring streaks of high cloud above. She motioned for him to go up, then turned and headed back inside the main residence.

The studio of Salvador Aussaresses occupied an entire wing on the second floor. Jonah found himself on a landing with a small window adorned with a box of bougainvillea. He made his way across a short hall and found himself immediately facing the great open space of the studio itself. The chipped ceramic floor tiles were covered in rust-colored drips, and on what looked like a drafting table there were piles of soiled canvas rags. Paintings in various stages of completion were stacked together haphazardly along the walls. The stinging smell of oils hung in the air.

In the very center of the room, a man sat on a thick wooden stool squinting at the mounted canvas before him. He wore a pair of khaki shorts with a braided leather belt, flip-flops, and nothing else. He was tanned, the effect of his tall, angular build somewhat belied by a leathery neck and tufts of white hair sprouting at his shoulder blades. The column of his spine popped out to accommodate his spry corpulence as he leaned forward to apply the nib of his brush. Directly in his sights was a very pale naked girl reclining on a taupe divan, one arm draped along a wad of ragged throw pillows.

Jonah instinctively froze in his tracks and was about to turn and back out when the artist, without turning to acknowledge him, made a loud snort and motioned him in with the back of his free hand. The reclining model tried to look over at Jonah with her eyes, but at the quiver of her neck Salvador made an abrupt hissing sound and she became fixed in stone again. Jonah could tell that she was an adolescent, perhaps sixteen or seventeen. She had a mousy face, concentrated in an expression that might have been intended to convey coquetry but that suggested something more like masked terror. The artist continued his work uninterrupted. The model tried to sneak another look.

"Mírame," Salvador muttered under his breath. But the incident had broken his momentum. "Please sit down, pull up a chair," he ordered without taking his eyes off the canvas. His English was impeccable, with a touch of Oxbridge in the accents. There was a stool by the wall. Jonah pulled it over and sat toward the quarter of the room behind the painter so that they both faced the scene of subjection.

"So . . . you are the young man my Laura has been telling me about. I'm glad you came. I knew from the moment she told me that you would. As I'm sure you can see, Laura is a beautiful woman. We have a good understanding, she and I. She knows my nature, and I, in turn, know hers."

He paused at this, considering the exposed model on the makeshift couch.

"Tell me, young man, do you care for painting?"

"Painting? Sure."

"What part of her do you like best? What part catches your eye? Do you like her breasts? It's okay, you know, you can say so."

"I like the hands."

"Ah! The hands. Good, that's very good. Did you know that human hands are the hardest thing to paint? One hand alone, if a painter wanted to get it perfectly done, would take a year to paint . . . Even Rembrandt struggled to paint a good hand. But, the hands of the father in the *Return of the Prodigal Son* . . . now *there* is a hand painted in pure truth, the truth of our greatest fear . . . the fear of our own choices. I will tell you a little secret. Do you know which Rembrandt contains the greatest hand of all?"

"No."

"*The Slaughtered Ox*. Musée du Louvre, in the Richelieu gallery. A genuine masterpiece. Maybe his greatest work. True, it not a painting of a human hand. It is far greater, more ambitious than that. It is a painting of the hand of God."

The poor model, who hadn't moved an inch, sneezed. The light in the studio was failing. She must have been getting cold. Salvador dipped his brush in a jar of water and wiped it down carefully in a cloth. With a nod of the head, he dismissed the girl. It took her a moment to get up. Her legs seemed to have fallen asleep and she stumbled like a lame animal to a corner of the room and began hurriedly dressing. Salvador Aussaresses now turned his attention fully upon his visitor.

"Egon Schiele. There is a great painter of hands! I'm very fond of Austrian art, you know . . . Before I found this place, I thought about moving there. Had quite a few friends who left for Austria in '83. But I haven't kept in touch. I just want to paint. I just want to live quietly and enjoy the time that I have left. You'll see, when you get to be my age, you see things differently. I'm more sensitive to time now, how little of it there truly is. And I've become greedy, in a way. I want to be surrounded by beauty. I want to paint the perfect hand, a hand so sublime that one day it will hang in the Museo Nacional!" Salvador laughed, so hard that it pitched him into a brutal fit of coughing. Then he was composed again. "I'll be saved, you see," he went on. "I'll be saved by the curators. The critics. After you and I are long dead and gone, they will need careers and reputations, and then I will be *rediscovered,* celebrated—an overlooked, neglected master."

"Maybe, but then again, maybe not. I don't think my generation even believes in the idea of artistic greatness."

"You're a sharp little monkey, aren't you?"

"What did you say?"

"Don't think you impress me. You're still just a boy. I, however, am a man. I have struggled. I have known what it is to believe in something, to do whatever it takes even to achieve small, pitiful victories. You haven't struggled for anything in your life. It was all handed to you. And what have you done with it? Your entire generation . . . grown up with the whole thing handed to you. The war over, the dust settled. You're decadent, flabby. You forget that you are living in the world *we* won for you. *We* fought the Communists! We were the ones who eliminated them, so that you could come of age with all the world at your fingertips, playing with your new gadgets, shopping, living it up. How old are you? What do you know about anything?"

Jonah got up to leave, but the old man surprised him, crying out for him to stay, pleading with him pathetically over a sudden coughing fit. As Jonah wavered, Salvador fished under his easel amid a pile of rags and produced a bottle of whiskey. He took a couple of jars over to a sink in the far corner of the room and rinsed them out. The studio was getting dark. Jonah felt paralyzed. He looked around for a light to switch on, or a lamp, but there was none. When Salvador returned, he poured them each a large glass and sat down again in silence. Jonah realized he could barely see the painter's face now, just the deep bluish outline of his features, a glint of arctic sheen.

"Do you know what I like about painting?" Salvador began again, resuming his philosophical tone. Jonah put the glass of whiskey to his lips as Salvador continued.

"I like its faithfulness. All a good painting requires is faithfulness. Looking steadfastly at the abyss and accepting the world for what it is. Not just tolerating it. Weak men can do that. But taking it whole, as the greatest artists do. I have struggled my whole life to do it. But I have not yet succeeded. Now I have so few years left. One day, you will understand this. Or perhaps you won't. I was born in a time of war. I lived the wars of my time. There is only one law of human life. The permanence of war. And I faced it. I didn't grow up behind a screen."

Salvador carefully lit the end of a cigarette. The hot eye drifted in the gloom as the old man took a deep drag. He offered one, and Jonah accepted. When his own smoke was lit, he was ready with a reply.

"Maybe there's something more powerful," Jonah said. "Something real in the world, that escapes your law of war. Always and everywhere. And maybe it's just that you need to believe in war because the things you needed to figure out in your life, you've always left empty."

"Ah, you think perhaps I am merely a doddering old man. You have the idealism of youth, and yet your life, just as mine was, will be dominated by power. Even more so, yes, even more so. Ha! Look at you! A Negro, or what do you prefer we call you now? Black? You know, I've always been curious . . . how does it *feel* to be a *black*? I have often wondered. It seems like it would be quite terrible, if you don't mind me saying so. It seems like a cruel joke. One even feels sorry for you, *up to a point*. A people have to know when they are defeated. The Indios, the slaves. You can't unwrite the history, can you? It isn't *my* fault, is it? What has come to pass. You can't fight the nature of men. The war between us is permanent. Look how your towers have fallen. Dirty wars. Who has the dirt on their hands now? We laugh at the pictures of Abu Ghraib because you Americans are stupid enough to take them. You know what has to be done but you have no maturity, no stomach, no seriousness of purpose. I see by the look on your face that you are shocked by my words. But it is *you* who is not living in the real world. The real world is the law of violence: directed, organized by the will of men. The strong take violence into their own hands, lead history like a naked man on a leash—when the man yanks, smack him with the stick, and soon enough he learns. The Arabs are stubborn as mules. I admire that. I admire men who are not persuaded by anything but death. Mark my words, the day the terror stops, you will miss them, your Arab terrorists. War is without end. It is also without limit. You will see. These tools will be turned on you and your neighbors. The soldiers will come home and turn on each other. The drones will patrol Colorado and Texas and Virginia. For the blacks, well, I'm sure you can guess how it will go. I'm not fooled, I can see it all clearly. Thank god, I'll be long gone by then. In my day we fought for principles, for a way of life. But what do I know? I'm just an old painter. I only want the peace of an old man to live out his last days."

The old man drank for a time in silence. The studio had slipped into darkness. Jonah could barely make out his own glass.

"I hear Laura met you over at the Basques'?"

"Yes, Miguel and Oscar . . ."

"Did you enjoy their company?"

"Yeah, sure."

"Did they enjoy yours?"

"I'm fine with where I'm at, if that's what you're asking, but frankly I also don't plan on sticking around much longer."

"Oh no, what about the cuisine—great cooks, eh? Their kind always are, no? Didn't you like their food?"

"Yes."

"Good, I wouldn't want to have to tell them that you didn't. Hah! The Basques—they're liable to blow you up for far less. No, but I like them, I really do. In fact, I fully support them. Lots of good people around here do. They've got no better base anywhere in the world than right here in Uruguay. The Spaniards will never conquer the Basques, never I tell you. Spanish intelligence is a joke. Don't you think so?"

"I don't know what you mean."

"Of course they're a joke. You ever hear of the Spanish Air Force? You can't have good intelligence without a good air force. As an aviator, I had to learn how to dominate my instincts, in an environment where the slightest mistake, the slightest miscalculation, can be fatal. Omniscience is essential. Perfect eyesight, solid minds that stay cold. The same goes for the other game. We got our terrorists because we understood how to handle them. We wiped them out so badly it will probably be a hundred years before they ever come back. And it would be suicide even then. But something tells me they will come back some day. Those people have a death wish."

"No, you have a wish to kill. Because you're not just a painter, are you? You're ex-military."

"And proud of my service. Proud of my country. When I was a boy, even younger than you, I grew up dreaming of Jorge Newbery. The aviators were admired in those days, they were our celebrities. By the time I joined we were already in the process of national reorganization. The Communists were crawling all over the place like roaches. It was our chance to do something for our country. I volunteered for the counterterrorism missions, most of us did. I operated the Hercules, the C-130s, those big whales we got from America. We would fly out of Morón and hop down to Mar del Plata. We would land before dawn and the jeeps and trucks would come out to meet us on the tarmac. The Hercules is a magnificent aircraft. Up in the cockpit the airframe is so wide you feel like you're at the helm of a flying cathedral. At Mar del Plata we refueled, and they loaded the cargo. I was always in the cockpit. It was cold out there with the sun about to rise, and cold gusts from the Atlantic pouring over the airfield. I went through my checklists, chatted with the ground crews on the radio. The loading took a long time. Sometimes I would see a chaplain in black robes walking around, talking to the officers on the ground. Everything was very orderly. When I got the signal to go, we would rev up the engines and barrel down the runway straight for the ocean. I would set a cap due east and we would fly out two or three hundred miles. That's when the second officer would give the signal to take us down on a low pass over the water. I would straighten us out at twenty-five hundred feet. The cargo officer would open the payload doors and then he and some of the Naval Intelligence guys would go into the hold. My job was to keep the plane steady, and that's what I did. We would fly like that for twenty minutes or so. Then the officers would come back into the cockpit and strap in, and I would take us in a long loop, circling back over the drop zone but this time headed back toward Mar del Plata. There were always dark shadows in the water there, and when I asked the Navy boys about it, they said they were sharks. We did the same sorties two, sometimes even three times a week, for a while. It became routine, boring. On the flights back, we would often discuss the Malvinas and how the war was going. Everyone found positive things to say, but we all knew it was hopeless. England was too powerful, and probably the most stubborn nation on Earth, more stubborn than even the Arabs. One day, when we got back to the base in Morón, as I was heading into the barracks, I realized that I had forgotten my sunglasses in the cockpit. Since the hold was open, I went up through the belly of the plane to get them. The belly of the Hercules is like a train tunnel. I found my glasses in the cockpit, but on my way out I stopped in the hold again to marvel at its size. I shouted a little to hear the echoes. Then I noticed something by my feet. Along the bottom of the hold there were locking gears and grappling hooks for securing cargo to the floor. Tangled in one of the hooks was a large clump of hair. I could tell right away that it was a woman's, by the length, by its luster and curl. I'm a painter. I've always been a close observer of these things. I could tell it was the hair of a young brunette. And as I kept walking, looking closely, I found more clumps of hair caught in the riggings. Hair of different colors, some men and some more clearly women. That's when I knew. I mean, I knew before then. But that's when I knew for sure. An officer appeared on the ramp; he must have heard me shouting. He asked me what I was doing. I told him I was just getting my sunglasses and I quickly made some joke and we walked back across the tarmac together laughing. No one ever asked me any questions. Not until years later."

"What did you say when people did finally ask?"

"Some reporter found me in 1991. He came looking for names. He wanted to know about what he called 'the death flights.' I wasn't concerned. The president pardoned everyone. I was untouchable. But that's not the reason I kept my trap shut. The reporter offered me money in exchange for names, good money too. But those people don't get it. They don't understand there's no price you can put on loyalty. I'm not a mercenary. I can't be bought. I faced the reality of my time and I chose sides. And they were believers too. We were all wolves. Was it bad? Yes. They were alive when we dropped them. Drugged but alive. Our will was stronger. We had the virility of youth. We had the great forces of order, the state and the church, and the military on our side. The nation was imperiled. We had to clean our house . . . We had to reorganize . . . We had the will and it was a time of wolves when anything was possible and we were young and history was on our side and every sensation every action was vivid and extreme . . ."

The artist trailed off and there was an interminable silence. Jonah thought he heard the crack of a door slamming shut somewhere in the courtyard, but it could have been a branch snapping from a tree or a heavy book landing on a tile floor. The jolt should have prompted him to get up, but his muscles locked. The old man stared serenely across the darkness, his quivering lips parted ambiguously, expectantly, faintly amused.

21

What Salvador said of him was true. Jonah had never felt touched by the chill of evil. Atrocity and human suffering were spectacles that befell others. They came to him as breaking news, they bothered him, troubled his nerves for a time, but did not even come close to bringing him to the point of naming or even acknowledging anything like a willful, metaphysical malice that might at any moment take the form of a human face committed to irreversible destruction. He had never had a cousin gunned down, lost his family to a local warlord's political ambitions, a passionate campaign of slaughter, a posse of racists on the hunt, or a man so broken he would put you in the dirt for four hundred dollars, for bragging rights, to defend his wounded honor. Yet these were the most obvious features of life for most people everywhere. Far more obvious than whatever enemy he conjured for himself when he invoked the specter of "late capitalism," which was the nearest phrase to which he could affix the largest share of blame for the ills of the world while dimly perceiving that it also assured his own procession through it. The wheel of fortune had spared him from having to do truly ugly things. Many ugly things were done on his behalf. And many had also been endured. His body the gift of colossal, unending histories of violence. Salvador knew this, and he reached through the darkness to take Jonah by the hand and show him.

Before he knew it, Jonah was bounding down the stone stairs and making his way back across the courtyard and into the house. Laura was singing to herself, and he followed her voice to the kitchen where she was preparing dinner. As he entered the singing stopped. She could read on his face the end of a line of thought.

"You're not staying."

"No, I'm sorry, I have to go."

She did not appear wounded, but moved into a suspended pause of judgment, a stay against a blow.

"I should have . . . I should let you out then."

"Laura, I have to leave tomorrow. Could I see you once more before I go? Tomorrow morning. Please. It's very important."

"What for?"

"I have something. Something important to give you. I don't have it here with me. If you can meet me tomorrow morning at the Basques', I can leave it with you. And also, I want to get a chance to properly say goodbye."

"You could say it now. You are saying it now."

"I know, I'm sorry to be like this. I'm confused, really, I'm afraid . . ."

"You're afraid. Well, I'm glad you could at least say it. Go on, then, I have things to finish up here. I'll show you out."

She walked him back out to the front and for a moment stood regarding him out on the street.

"Will you promise me to come tomorrow, at nine o'clock?" he asked.

"You don't have to worry about it."

"So, you'll come?"

"I always come for the men who deserve it."

She had no more words for him, and he found himself drifting down the foreign streets alone, one cigarette after another lighting the way to his relative shelter.

When he got back to his room at El Vasco, he couldn't sleep. He opened a page in his travel journal and started writing a long letter to Arna. When he looked up, pale dawn was already in the window. He went down into the waking streets and made his way to the only internet café he knew in the old city, hurrying in case Laura decided to come early. He wanted to check his mail and look up as much useful information as he could find about Buenos Aires. He wondered how Octavio was doing. There had been no word since his arrival in Montevideo.

His inbox was overflowing, mostly with the usual spam. There were several emails from his mother and one from his father but he did not want to deal with anything from his parents right then, and he did not open them. More pressingly there was an email from Nate and an email from Isaac. With a sinking heart, he saw that Arna had not written him back.

Jonah considered writing her a brief note. He opened Isaac's email instead.

Sorry to break the news this way, man, but I've had to make some choices. With the way things are I've come to the decision that New York just isn't for me. I haven't told you about everything that's gone down at the school but suffice to say I'm done with that. I'm just not happy in the work, and everything with the shooting and the protests and all the crazy shit that's popping off in this city—I'm done with it, man. I don't want no part of it anymore. Also I've been talking for a while now with this sister I met online. She's from Atlanta, works for this label down there and she's been trying to get me to come down and see her for like forever, and last week while the shit was hectic I decided to take off and see her. And, you know, she's right. It's beautiful in the ATL. Reminds me of home, except the music scene is off the charts right now. A nigga could really get somewhere if he put his mind to it and had the right connections, and I'm feeling like I want to give this music shit a real chance. It's always been something I've loved and I feel like I have what it takes to do well in the business, especially right now, working with artists, scouting talent, maybe even producing records. So, I know this is kinda sudden, but I've decided to move down there. I've already put in notice at work. Lease is up soon, and the demand is so high here—I've talked to the management and they can't wait to get rid of my black ass. Not sure when you'll be back, but the one thing I wanted to touch base about is these letters, man. Your French girl been sending you mad longhand correspondence. I know you'll want those so I was thinking I would forward them to your place in Paris. So, send me your address when you get this. Hope all is well otherwise with you. I'll miss our times hanging out, man, I really will. But when you get your shit together, come on down to the real South America to see a brotha. You'll always have a place to stay with me. And I can show you a good time too. There's a whole world down there y'all don't know nothing about.

    —Isaac

Thus he learned the friendship he had made in New York was dissolving. There should have been nothing terribly dramatic about it. It was, from a certain point of view, logical and maybe even predictable. Friends moved from city to city all the time, and people held on to friendships as they could. And yet the news brought a rush of sadness to his chest. He reread the email, stunned, and then sent a brief reply saying how cool it was to hear about the move, and that he was excited for him. He gave his coordinates in Paris and hit send. Caught in a blank anger, he went to sign off when he realized he hadn't checked the note from Nate. To his dismay, the missive was fraternal and warm, and it struck like a dagger.

    Good brother,

       I was thinking about you again today and wondering when you might be coming back. I don't know if you've heard about the shooting and the protests in the city, but you've been missing out on some amazing stuff. Folks are mad as hell and taking it to the streets in ways I haven't seen since like the seventies. I know a smart young cat like yourself could be involved in it. I wish I could be, but honestly, I'm too old for this mess. Besides I got my hands full with my after-school ball program and all that. My offer still stands—would love to have you up here working with me. It could even turn into like an internship, a hoops fellowship. Kinda like the sound of that! Are you still in Montevideo? I can't lie, I do still wonder sometimes if she's really out there. I gotta stop with these fantasies. But what can we do? It's like Janet says, that's the way love goes . . .

  —Nate

Jonah felt his head spin. He knew he had to tell Laura to leave Salvador. He had to give her Nathaniel's letter. And he knew that as soon as he did, he would have to leave Montevideo.

Back in his room at El Vasco, he packed his things. Nathaniel's letter had gotten slightly crumpled in his bag. The envelope had not been sealed, and the fold lay flattened on its back, revealing a bit of paper marked with Nathaniel's handwriting. With a flush of shame, he pulled it out. There it was, his silent travel companion. He nervously unfolded the paper.

Dear Laura,

  I'll start this the only way I know how. I don't know if you will ever get this letter. Probably not. In a way, it's as if I'm writing to you from the past or maybe even a past life. I want to leave a record of my thoughts, so that if by chance you do read this, you will have some idea, at least some understanding of the man I am now. What can I tell you about that man? I'm writing to you today from New York City. From my desk in the heights of the Bronx, the city runs down the Hudson River away from me into steel and glass and fumes of Manhattan. It's not at all like Paris, which I can recall as clearly as this view. I can still see you standing outside the tabac, your hands moving as you talk at a café table, the shape your body made under the sheets, your books, the smell of cigarettes and plaster on the rue des Cinq-Diamants. That was Paris. It was our city, but it was your home. This is mine.

If you came you would find it's too hot in the summer, and too damn cold in the winter. It's too crowded and too poor and too rich . . . and every year it seems like things are getting worse, although, in truth, things always seem to be about the same. This is where I was raised, not just in the Bronx, but the whole city. I love the sound of a New York voice. I love the sound of helicopters in the sky, tugboats on the river, yellow cabs as they jump in and out of lanes, small talk at 125th Street and Lenox, night games at Yankee Stadium, girls in troupes cursing and singing and clapping, the beautiful sound of Spanish on Upper Broadway where they sell plátanos and sandía out the side of a Chevy, players pushing Fleetwood Cadillacs through the projects, bass booming. The smell of garbage and the hiss of frying meats, kids clowning around coming out of the corner bodega, brothers talking that talk on the corner, the subway rolling down the Jerome Avenue line. I love the sound of basketball courts at dusk. It's a sound that takes me way back . . . I'm talking back to the days of guys that used to play there that we gave names like Big Helicopter, Earl "The Goat," "Pee Wee" Kirkland, all these legends that I came up playing with in Rucker Park, a place where if your game was tight you went home feeling tall as Kareem.

I remember kids used to sit in the trees just to watch Julius Erving rise up through the air from the free-throw line, his arm carrying the ball like a torch of liberty. These things are the stuff my city is made of.

Laura, there are things I wish you could see. I have children now. Ones I'm teaching what I can in the hopes of doing something to make things change and come out right for once, to try and change the destiny of the kids who grow up on the blocks where I grew up, blocks where half the kids I grew up with are gone, dead, or doing bids upstate. I want so bad for these kids to have a chance to see what I've seen, to move through the world different, to see more and know more, and taste the kind of living that they struggle to imagine. And I can see it happen before my eyes one at a time. With all the love the folks in the community show me, I get new students to my basketball clinic every day. They come from all over the Bronx to learn how to play ball, how to improve their game. I always tell them: If you want to improve your game, improve yourself. You are the game. They don't know how literally I mean it. Sometimes there are fights, and sometimes the play is too rough. I remember how it was when I was coming up. I was small. I used to get knocked around a lot. Had to learn to scrape, had to be better. The game is intuition. You always know before you let go whether it's going in. You always know when to make the pass before you can think to make it. You know where to be, you feel the ball reach your hands at the top of the key, you fake, you whirl like Earl the Pearl, you open a notch and pop up, the ball is gone, it's over, sinking in, and you turn away because the game has already moved on. Everyone moves on, and the world doesn't slow for none of us.

The other night I went for a walk along the West Side

promenade. I stood at the edge of the Hudson and looked up. The lights of the George Washington Bridge parted the night. The sight of the bridge struck me like John Henry's hammer. I looked up and thought: What is this? What is this giant thing that I am made of? America, wading knee-high in the blood of its own children. Of the African slaves. Of Cherokee and Sioux. Union regiments and Confederate cavalry. Of sharecroppers and lynching blood on the leaves, railroad workers, field hands and migrant farmers, the children of Birmingham and the garbage collectors of Memphis, the people of Vietnam under our napalm and our flamethrowers, the blood of our own sons and daughters. The blood of my ancestors that flows in my veins. All that blood that I know we got to answer for. This imperial force more powerful than Rome. The George Washington Bridge is so awesome, so vast. It's got to mean something, to portend something that's still happening, something so big we'll never be able to imagine the end toward which it is pointing. And then I also feel there's something austere, even lonely about it. A Miles Davis kind of thing. For Baldwin it's where a man goes to jump when he can't take this life no more. I've seen people in my life go that way, and sometimes I've even secretly thought it myself. I think every American comes to that bridge at some point in their lives because how could you help it in the face of the sheer madness of things perpetrated on a daily basis? But I strive to see it otherwise. Call me a dreamer. Maybe, but to me that bridge could be my light, my lonely lighthouse, towering over Gotham, sending a bat signal so bright that you might see it round the bend of the world.

Laura, where have you gone? When will you come flying back to me? Your face peers into my dreams. How does it do that? Maybe because you are the one person I can speak deeply and freely with. I feel totally free when I write to you. Listening to music and watching the hand of time pass over the city. I like to listen to these jazz shows on WKCR when I write just to absorb some of that artistry. It's something in those brothers that moves me. I hear them playing like the only thing that matters is beauty. Even with all we going through. I hear them say, hold on now. Listen. How beautiful we are.

The other day I went downtown, found myself on Sixth Avenue. And truth be told, I had never thought of it before but we call it: Avenue of the Americas. The Americas. We should always use the plural, I think. What a beautiful ring it has to it. A life in the Americas. On every street corner and every subway car in New York City, the Americas. One island in the human archipelago. Headstrong and unstoppable, like the Staten Island Ferry, always chugging headlong into the looming shadows of the white buildings. Some folk stare up from the deck holding a paper cup full of coffee wondering if they'll ever catch a break. Me, I always preferred to stay apart from the crowd, looking back at the way we came over. You see, people always thought of me as just a body, a man they could use. But I got a mind, and my own philosophy. And being in the world a good number of years now, I have come to believe that it's in the nature of the human spirit to search. For a long time, I myself was on a search to understand where I came from and why, and what I ought to do with myself. And when I met you in Paris, I thought that maybe you were part of the answer. I guess I always thought the answer would be something new. But it's not. I understand why you left. I know you're searching for something too. Just remember that it might not be a new thing, but the old one to come back to that drives you onward again. I guess I've gotten carried away. It keeps happening with me now, when I sit down to write you. It's as if I need to get the whole world off my chest, and you, Laura, you are the only intelligent person left on Earth.

I've got to get down to the playground. Late afternoon, low eighties. Perfect weather. The Knicks are playing tonight I keep fixin' to give up on them, but I'm trying to give faith and patience a chance. I got to admit, I still wish it was me balling in the Garden under the big lights, taking it up the floor. Hitting them with a sweet move, the God Shammgod reverse finish at the hoop, taking it back to the old school, when we played the game the right way. But I know it's too late for all that. What I really want you to know is that I still have the passion. The years may be creeping up on me, but I got no plans to get old. There's just too much still to do with the neighborhood, with this city I love, with this mad country I got to live in. I feel a little tired. I guess I'll sign off here as I always do with a wish: to see you again. When you next consider flying across the waters, think of coming here, think of coming back to me

Nate Archimbald

༈

Laura met him at exactly nine o'clock on the street outside El Vasco. Jonah suggested they go for a walk, a proposition she accepted without comment. But their mutual pained attentiveness only prolonged the unbearable and she stopped him short at one of the wide corners where they had been waiting for the light.

"Why don't you get to whatever it is you want from me? I'm not in the mood for romance today."

"Well, I have to give you something that won't make sense at first, but I know that it was meant to be this way, maybe not the way I've gone about it, but I know that you need to read this, and when you do I hope you'll do the right thing and leave Salvador. Not just Salvador but Montevideo."

"What do you mean?" asked Laura, suddenly stiff.

"Trust me, promise me, no matter what—that you will at least get away from Salvador."

Before she could react, he pulled out Nathaniel's letter.

"This is from Nathaniel. Nathaniel Archimbald. I met him in New York, and he gave me this letter because I think he knew somehow that I would meet you. It's crazy, I know, but here we are. You should have this."

Laura didn't move. She seemed paralyzed. They were silent for a time, and then she spoke.

"You need to leave."

"Okay."

"Now. Please leave."

He could see anger and confusion cloud her face. He thought to kiss her on the cheek, but she motioned him away, so he murmured an apology and left her there clutching Nathaniel's letter in her hand.

All the way to the ferry terminal in Colonia, Jonah could feel his face burning. When he got on board and took to the rail to look back at the receding shore, he finally felt a terrible weight begin to lift. He was running on his own now. But the new lightness in his chest wasn't better. It was worse. He told himself that he was seasick.

22

With the letter in Laura's hands, Jonah took the ferry across the Río de la Plata. The great avenues of Buenos Aires looked like nothing so much as Paris. Proud, lively, officiously pretentious. From a cheap hostel in San Telmo he went searching for good bookstores in Recoleta. Everyone claimed there were excellent bookstores there. But it wasn't true. Not on the calle Borges and not anywhere else. Palermo Hollywood was teeming with young Americans. He got roped into a conversation with some earnest, bright-eyed banker types. They demanded he talk sports. Then proceeded to enlighten him about the terrific opportunities of sovereign debt. There was no place they could fail to presume they should get what they wanted.

He ditched them and plunged onward, losing his way in the labyrinth of the city. Groaning buses filled the air with diesel fumes. Women with tinted shades pranced through the soot clutching monogrammed bags. Finally, he found a bookstore in the city center. The cool air-conditioning and the quiet were a relief and he idled in the aisles. The shopkeeper, a potbellied man in a gray sweater, came over twice to ask him if he needed help before huffing off again. Jonah decided on a copy of *Los poemas de Sidney West* by Juan Gelman. The bookseller practically snatched the money from him while muttering something he assumed the gringo wouldn't understand. But Jonah did understand. There was no such thing as a good black person in Buenos Aires.

Large demonstrations against the government were taking place on the Plaza de Mayo. Mothers with gray hair tucked into their scarves carried signs demanding knowledge of the fate of their children. They were the mothers of the "disappeared." Over coffee, Jonah deciphered the headlines in the leading daily. The generals said they were sorry, but that they had done nothing wrong. They were following orders. What was done had been necessary to rid the nation of Marxist terrorists.

Back at the hostel, the lady who did the housekeeping and tended the entryway noticed Jonah's book of poetry while he was reading it alone in the common room. She asked him if he liked poetry very much. Yes, he said. She asked if he knew what they had done to Juan Gelman's son. No, he said. They impaled him, she said. Impale meant to stick a rod up through the anus into the stomach so you bleed to death very slowly. They sent his pregnant girlfriend to a detention center in Uruguay. No one ever saw her again. He was twenty-four. She was twenty-three. So many young people, she said. All of us will take this stain with us to our graves. Every day, I ask myself, how could this have happened? Where are you from? America, he said. Why didn't anyone in your country speak out and try to stop it? Because we supported it, he said. I know, she said, I know, but *why*? He tried to think of an answer. He thought of Katrina. He thought of how many images of disaster, torture, and death he had consumed in the relatively few years of his conscious life. I suppose it's because we don't care, he said. No, I mean, we do care, but only about money. Yes, she said, it's the same here. Well, in a way, we are everywhere, he said. It was Burson-Marsteller that made so much money by lying about it. Who are they? She wanted to know. Advertisers, Jonah said. The best in the world. Then advertisers are the greatest criminals of our age, she said. How could they? Our mothers only ask for justice, peace, answers! And they get silence, threats, and lies. All of Argentina is built on unspeakable crimes and indifference. And nothing changes. The people are still in poverty. The same forty families own all the land. The Yankees, the military men, the bureaucrats, they are still our masters. My country is built on lies too, Jonah said. Terrible crimes, even worse. Yes, she said. Yes, of course, it's very true. I suppose that's what we have in common. It was impossible to sleep in Buenos Aíres.

Without a plan, Jonah went to Constitución Station and studied the timetables. Finally, he settled on a late departure, a night train heading south to Bahía Blanca. The train went over the sweetgrasses of the Pampas in total darkness under the stars. The conductor wore a green bow tie and drank yerba maté to keep himself awake. Jonah tried to write, but the janky tracks made it impossible and he gave up. In the morning they passed an overturned Range Rover at a rail crossing. The conductor clicked his pen and made a note. At Bahía Blanca Jonah bought a sandwich then boarded the connecting bus for Viedma. As the landmass of the continent narrowed so did his options. At Viedma he saw nothing worth the price of staying a night, so he waited for another bus, this one nearly empty, that took him farther south again to Puerto Madryn, a town that promised whale-watching tours. The town turned out to be only a Potemkin village set up by the tour operators to greet visitors and ferry them out to the whales. After the hours on the road, he gulped in the oceanic air. It tasted like release.

He found himself heading out on a skiff with a young German couple from Würzburg. They spoke excellent English and insisted Jonah must visit their town. The most authentically German town, with the nicest people, the man said. Despite what happened during the war, and the heavy price they paid, the woman said. Jonah was relieved that the ocean was relatively calm. They bobbed about in the hot sun. When the breach came it was so sudden they almost missed it. A terrific snort followed by a slapping slurp in the marbled froth. Then another smaller hump just behind, a hillock soon dissolved. The boatman said it was a female, probably with a young one in tow. The Bavarians shared laconic exclamations as they watched the trail of spume unspool. They all waited, scanning the rolling swells intently in the hopes of another salutation. None came. Still. He had seen it. The Leviathan. Her lungs the size of Volkswagens, hot blood coursing through arteries thick as his thorax, perhaps dim awareness of her fingerbones. The biggest mother out there. Concentrating in her body the inspired will to dive, to undertake those long hours of nightwork in the deep trenches, bathed in sound, seeking out that nourishment so needful for ascension. Why should her mere proximity cause such emotion? Was it a sign? A hopeful nod that he was on the right path? Or a signal that he was deceived? In Milton's poem, mistaking the whale for an island got one dragged down to hell. Was that his trouble? That he could not tell the difference between signs of hope and signs of hopelessness? Or was it that all along he had assumed there *was* a problem? Believed, even before Phineas had made him self-conscious of a desire to pursue it, that he had some mission to fulfill, some heroic effort to discover, when the truth of his condition was that he was the lucky survivor of a wreck, an Ishmael, whose isolated life was defined by the privilege of floating safely shoreward on the tides, a blessing of the gods, a stroke of dumb luck, a fortune inherited precisely because the defining moments of death and destruction had already taken place. What if there was nothing left to do other than tell the story? Nothing to accomplish other than continued survival and a contemplative retelling of the ruinous past? Had he come to the far end of the world in order to learn something that was the biggest nothing of all? These black thoughts? Convinced he was going one way, was he, all along, going the other? It would be in keeping with everything else. The rotten purposelessness of the age. The mindlessness swallowing everything into itself without any possibility of resistance, only horrific jests. Neither progress, nor regression. Only this holding pattern, this undertow of disorientation. The fear of revisiting the past and the fear of the annihilating future holding everything and everyone in a nihilistic torpor, sending out fluxing lines that sparked all manner of derangement and decadence. Including his own. Yet was this anything the old folks didn't already know? Wasn't this what, in their own way, they had always tried to tell him? That it would come down to making a way out of no way, creating a future over and against its absence? Wasn't it ingrained in his impulses, this reflex to run away in order to live? But the North Star in the age of the satellite is everywhere and nowhere. There would be no outrunning in this brave new world; whatever you had, whatever you could hold onto, you would have to make into a home. And he understood that he was looking at what he could not see before. The circumference of his errant life, his ceaseless fugitivity. A line without relief.

At Puerto Madryn, he boarded a bus that cut straight west across the continent to Bariloche. They drove on unpaved roads through the desert. Late in the night, the roar came to a stop in the garish light of a service station outside a Mapuche settlement. The Indians of Argentina. Same story as far as he knew. An ancient people decimated. No one seemed to be present other than a lone attendant at the pumps who laughed with the bus driver as they waited under the glare of the Chevron ensign. In Bariloche the lakes were sparkling. Jonah stayed at a tiny hostel run by a Chilean mother and her daughter who showed up in the evening to help. They insisted he must see their country before he left, and they suggested the island of Chiloé, easily reachable across the border.

The next morning, he was on a bus crossing the Andes along the snow line. On the way down out of the mountains and into Chile, the snow gave way to green pastures, farms, and rows of poplars lining glittering streams. On the outskirts of Puerto Montt new housing developments, still wrapped in Tyvek, were marooned in barren lots. Volcanoes towered in distant other-worldliness. At the ferry dock, he decided to drink to take the edge off. This was a mistake. Later, on the crossing, he thought he saw the Devil or a troll-like person watching him. And he remembered what Orígenes had said, that even the Devil would be saved.

The island of Chiloé was on the Pacific. In Ancud penguin tours were heavily advertised. But when he inquired at the tourist office, Jonah was told the seas were too rough that day to see any penguins unless he were willing to pay a good deal more for a bigger boat. The hills around Ancud were the color of avocados. Large black birds sailed overhead, great black crosses. He was informed that they were condors, a type of vulture. The tourist office turned out to have a selection of books by and about Chileans, their culture and history. He bought a copy of Vicente Huidobro's *Altazor*. He left Ancud penguinless, but on his way found a newly opened sushi restaurant. No one there was Japanese. But they had chopsticks and the fish was fine. Jonah read from *Altazor* and took comfort in its charm. "I love the night," sang the poet, "the hat of every day."

From Chiloé he traveled again, this time straight north up the spine of Chile to Santiago. In the capital he checked into the Villa Gramaldi, the American youth hostel. There was a terrible smell in the bathrooms. Someone said it was something in the drains, an ineradicable stench. Jonah quickly headed out to explore the city but there was very little to see in terms of sights, and he ended up drifting through residential neighborhoods with no distinctive character. He thought of Salvador Aussaresses. He could have lived comfortably on any of these neat tree-lined blocks. In the roundabouts there were bustling traffic and signs for an upcoming concert by Shakira. She was performing at the Estadio Nacional, the stadium where Pinochet had set up his open-air detention center and tortured people in the locker rooms. As far as he could see, there were no black people anywhere at all.

He would later reflect that the end decisively came into view in the cubicles of that sad locutorio in Santiago. He had joined the others plugged in at the long bank of numbered computers with their telemarketer headsets. He gazed into the screen with placid relief, allowing random media to wash over him as he clicked. He had no real desire to check his email. What he wanted was the feeling of being online itself, the narcotic, effortless involvement in the hive mind. Soon enough, however, he had scrolled through all of the homepages for websites that he could think of. He ran a search for massages in Santiago. That led to more links for sensual massages. Cascades of glossy thumbnails, unlikely names, and numbers. He stared at them quizzically, then abjectly. He jotted a few down in his notebook. Downstairs, he used a phone booth to make the calls. The first one was so confusing and aggressive that he hung up right away. The second was a soothing, laughing voice. He asked for directions. He went back upstairs to check the address. It was in a suburb to the north of the city. He went back down and hailed a taxi that took off speeding along curvilinear avenues leading out to the north of the city. They pulled up to a corner in what appeared to be an affluent neighborhood. He rang the intercom in the entry hall of a residential tower. A young woman's voice buzzed him in. It was not the voice he had heard on the phone. A dark-skinned woman opened the door. Venezuelan, maybe. She was in her underwear, a green G-string and a black padded bra. She had a sweet smile and very distant eyes. Her thighs were striated in cream-colored marks. She took Jonah by the hand and led him into a living room. A large black leather couch dominated the room. Facing it was a coffee table with a shallow dish full of candies and a large flat-screen television. An episode of *The Cosby Show* dubbed in Spanish was playing at very low volume. She sat him down on the couch and asked how long he wanted to stay. He said he wanted whatever the usual was. She chuckled and put her hand on his groin. She told him to relax. She kissed him on the cheek and told him to put the money on the coffee table. She was going to freshen up and would be back in a moment. He heard her go upstairs and close a door. The Huxtables were revolving around the studio set warbling in Spanish. He looked around the room. There was a faint breeze coming through the bars of a window full of boxed begonias. He looked at the pile of bills on the table. He heard a sink faucet running upstairs. Then he was up and making his way to the door, to the hall, down a flight of stairs. Outside, he started flat-out running. He ran as fast as he could, until he got back to the large avenue where the taxi had dropped him off. Across the avenue, there was a park with a large public fountain. He stood at the edge of the fountain facing the water. The jet of water clapped and splattered in his ears. The spray beaded in the sun and he put his hands into the fuming iridescence.

The ATM never lies. This one informed Jonah that his money was almost out. All those savings from Uncle Vernon's years of patient, steadfast labor. God only knows what he had sacrificed to get those funds and keep them in his account for his family. What he refused himself. What daily humiliations he put up with. And Jonah had spent it carelessly, without anything to show for it. His head wasn't right. Or was there still time to get it together, to do something righteous? To do justice to Nate's vision. To connect with Isaac again. To make a work of art, to make something for Phineas. To make use of the impasse he had driven himself into. If he could just get around to really sitting down and sticking to it. If he could reach understanding of self.

If it wasn't too late. At Santiago Central Terminal he boarded the international overnight route on the intercity bus. Destination: Buenos Aires. He felt hopeful. Rising and falling, up and over the Andes, the bus lurched and groaned along perilous roads. Jonah thought he heard each soul among them praying for the driver to stay awake, to see them through their voyage to the end of the night.

Somewhere in that night, as he lay balled up and shivering, the feverish questions came circling, wheeling shadows like the condors. What a random place to perish! And if it did happen, what could anyone say? What account could he give for his brief season on Earth? With everything given him, every chance and opportunity, every gift, what did he have to show for it? Nothing.

But it wasn't true. There was one person who could say more than a good word and say it true. Arna, of course. And he could see her in a flash, waving to him in the rain on the rue des Écoles. Taking off her wet shoes, one foot undressing the other, and humming along to the score as Ingrid Bergman wandered through the ruins of Pompeii. Reading on the green bench with a piece of hair in her mouth. The loveliness of her forearms in the scattering sunlight at the café with the terrible omelets. Those moments and others recombine as they ride the Métro together, always to stations near the end of the line. Visit the palm trees in the greenhouses at Auteuil. The book market at the Parc Georges-Brassens. It's summer and they walk together in the dusk as the great murmuring of the city surrounds them. They argue about poetry, about the poem of the future. He says it must be made of the best of the new and the best of the old. Arna says it will be what it always was, a form of music. And he knows she is right. That it could start right here, at a moment like this, in the thick of the midsummer's night when the scent of hidden blossoms pulls an arrow through the spirit and all the songs of the human past seem close, as closely held as a letter in the hand. And set deep in the grain of this poem, she says, is the map of a feeling waiting to be discovered, the keys to our own language, which are always in reality just out of reach, like the lamps of the Luxembourg Gardens after dark. And he knows then, he is certain, that Arna will write it. Her whole life she's been wanting to write songs, not one or two, but whole albums full, with words that will catch all the music she's always carried in her head. They go along together, passing beside an old stone wall covered in ivy. Arna fingers the leaves and they clatter softly. He remembers then that this is the wall of the cemetery, one full of the illustrious dead, where Richard Wright is buried, and one branch of Arna's ancestors shares a dilapidated crypt. They say nothing more until they reach the halo of a subway entrance at a little tree-ringed roundabout. They stay there a moment, inhaling the rank blossoms of the giant horse chestnuts, pulping their flowery, clotted droppings underfoot. The dry five-fingered chestnut leaves form a papery darkness, a ladder of shadows leading up into the unfathomable blackness beyond reach. Let's go home, Arna says. Yes, he says. And they drop down below, waltzing into the Metropolitan's musty electric air.

It was dawn and the bus thrummed along, following a small stream and a rail line that ran beside it. Jonah shook himself awake. He was cold and there were specks of crystallization in the windows. Every five miles or so they passed small clusters of abandoned buildings, sheds, faint chalk marks in the wilderness. The cordillera was long behind them and they had started coming out of the ravines and into the rolling foothills. The bus continued to descend on a long sloping turn into the vineyards of Mendoza. Jonah looked back. The distant rose-tinted peaks of the Andes were glowing in the clear morning air. Then the mountains disappeared, and they followed a river that wound through the plains and larger roads that passed through vineyards and cattle ranches before merging onto the highways where they joined the dusty big rigs and the commuter traffic roaring onward toward the capital.

The first thing Jonah did when he arrived in Buenos Aires was to email Octavio to tell him that he was going back to Paris. To his surprise, Octavio responded immediately, telling him to wait, insisting he needed to come down to BA anyway and that he would arrive in time to see him off. Jonah agreed to the plan and booked a plane ticket for the coming weekend. There were even more tourists than he remembered in San Telmo. He watched tango dancers performing to the music from *The Godfather*. He found a low-key bar where he could drink and generally keep to himself. He was done. He was ready to be home, to get back on his feet, to start over.

But then it was all undone. It was terribly wrong. The day before he was to leave, he learned that something had happened to Arna. He was getting a flood of emails about it now. The actual accident had happened several days before. He had sets of forwarded emails, and updated notes from his mother. Basically, they all told the same story. A bad collision, heavy impact and trauma. She had been stabilized but they needed to operate again. Her parents were insisting they bring her to the American Hospital in Neuilly where they had specialists.

Jonah tried to find out something more. But naturally there was nothing really to be gained by it. He circled the block. All day he was in and out of the cybercafé checking the emails again. Updates. No updates. The time he had paid for was up. He felt drained and consumed with rage all at once. The faces of perfectly ordinary people looked hideous, detestable. He tried to gather his thoughts rationally and calm himself. Of course, she would pull through this. But constantly the awful sense of falling backward returned. Arna dying was impossible. The universe would never allow something so grotesquely unfair to happen. For some inexplicable reason it seemed to him important to think it aloud. So, he said it, even as he grasped feverishly at images, memories, words.

Octavio showed up the next day as he had promised. They met in a café in San Telmo. There was just enough time to have a coffee before Jonah had to head out to the airport. Octavio was looking great. He was animated as usual, and he had a healthy glow about him. Immediately, he was catching Jonah up about his time with Francesca. They were really clicking, it seemed. And Jonah asked him if he thought it would last. Octavio shrugged it off. Who knows? Probably not, in the long run, he said. But this was about the present, the extraordinary intensity of all that he had been learning from her about how to be a dad. Not for real, of course. But it was wonderful in ways he hadn't thought of, and Jonah could see that he really meant it. If they could figure out the visas, Francesca might try to bring Paolina to visit him in New York one day. Jonah was overjoyed to see Octavio. But he was embarrassed at how hard it was for him to make that even somewhat apparent to his friend. He found it hard to talk. He kept trying to think of a way to tell him everything about Arna, but for some reason he couldn't bring myself to. "What's next for you, caballero?" Octavio wanted to know. He evaded the question.

Now he suddenly wished that he hadn't waited for Octavio. It was so good to see him, but it also felt like somehow his being there was making things worse. He had botched everything, even his own departure. They tried a neutral gear, talking sports, and Octavio noted that his beloved Vasco was performing horribly this year and was in danger of being knocked out of the Brazilian Série A altogether. They tried to talk about New York, but the news about the aftermath of the riots there really didn't help. Actually, it made things worse and Jonah started to feel slightly ill. He had to get to his flight. Octavio helped carry his bags up the Avenida 9 de Julio. There was sadness in his eyes. Jonah felt stupid for not thinking of something better to have done with their brief time together. But then a cab pulled up and

Octavio was yelling at the driver in Spanish, beaming with his usual fire. Jonah got in and Octavio came over to the window and they clasped hands. Jonah was mumbling something about seeing him around, but Octavio with great dignity and noblesse, cut him off. *"Avant tout, la liberté!"* He was still shouting in his awkward French and making grandiloquent waves as the taxi pulled out into the main lanes and Jonah lost sight of him in the heavy traffic.

23

While he had been away nothing had changed, but now everything was different. The first decade of the new millennium was winding down and headed into troubled waters. The television screens in the waiting area of the baggage claim oscillated between coverage of a potentially historic American election and an economic crisis of devastating proportions. But the anxious hope and breathless panic saturating the airwaves went beyond the question of financial catastrophe or politics. It seemed to encompass a whole new way of being in the world, as if everyone had stopped to peer collectively over a cliff, allowing the new normal to momentarily come into view, or at least the outlines of its major patterns, which promised to be glittering, swift, and cruel. The France Jonah had left behind was doing its best to keep apace of the times. At the airport all the business-class types were following the bad news on their new portable screens.

What chance did Nate's injunction to do good, or the work of a few teachers at a high school, or Uncle Vernon's hope for him to do something righteous have against all that?

His mother was waiting for him under the gray high arches of the terminal at Charles de Gaulle. She looked older, more delicate and frail than he had remembered. But the deepest lines in her face hadn't changed. Not a drop of clarity was missing in her eyes. She wanted to help with the bags but he insisted he was fine. As they weaved their way through the terminal, he struggled to hear her voice over the clamor of announcements. On the RER train the fatigue caught up with him in heavy waves. They passed the suburban stations in procession. The housing projects loomed on the horizon. His mother was happy because he was home. She was talking about things that he had missed while he was away. His father's health was worsening, she warned, worsening every day. He leaned against the window. He couldn't stand it anymore.

"Mama, I'm no good . . ."

"What do you mean no good, sweetie? You're tired, you're jet-lagged . . ."

"No, no. You're not *listening*. I'm no good at anything. My life hasn't worked at all. I feel like . . . like all I've ever done is waste time."

"You've been out in the world, exploring, learning, teaching. Right now, you're hungry, you're pooped! Look at you! You probably haven't eaten a proper meal in days!"

"No. No, that's not it. I feel empty inside. About everything. I hate everything, and nothing even makes sense anymore. I'm nothing. I'm nowhere."

"Jonah, listen to me. I'm your mother, I know what I'm talking about. What happened to Arna isn't your fault. These things just happen . . . they just do, and you can't take it all upon yourself, it doesn't mean the world is against you or hates you, it's just that, I don't know, it's the way things *are*. But it's going to be okay again, I promise it will."

"Mama."

"I'm so sorry about Arna, Jonah. I'm so sorry."

He waved her away. He didn't want to talk about it. The train plunged underground, racing to the platform at Gare du Nord.

"You know she sent you all these letters. Your friend Isaac forwarded them all from New York. I've been keeping them for you in your room. I brought them with me. I thought you might want them right away."

The stack of envelopes was addressed in Arna's unmistakable hand. His mother had tied the packet together carefully with string. He thumbed through them, checking the postage stamps. Arna had sent him letters from every corner of the new Europe. He took them and closed his eyes and waited for the pain to pass. It did not.

His room hadn't changed. He put the letters on the bed, walked to the window, and opened the shutters. The accordion wings swung open with a dull thud. There was a gray, empty sky over Paris. The motor of a moped went snarling by. A car was honking. Downstairs on the corner of the rue de Tocqueville, traffic was piling up. Two black men were operating a municipal truck as it lifted a green apple full of jingling recycled glass to be towed away. Jonah went back to the bed and sat down by the pile of letters. He looked up at the big map of the world on the wall. Rio de Janeiro, Montevideo, Porto Alegre, Santiago, Buenos Aires, New York. Places and people went spooling through the projector, their memories played to the inner eye. The distance between life and inner life, as between life and its sudden evaporation, a leap incalculable. Inside the names and the abstract points was a tangle of stories, and more than that, a string of choices that led right to his very last footsteps, to sitting on the bed, to his room with the window open onto the gray afternoon. If he were a wandering poet, perhaps he would have known to make something of it. But he had always been a terrible poet, a wannabe poet, worse than corny, a phony. He felt very small. He thought of what Isaac had said, and Nathaniel, and Uncle Vernon. And he wondered if he had done the wrong thing.

He also knew it was a stupid thought. For him everything was still possible. His privileged path and all that he might do with it was just beginning another cycle full of abundant second chances. His life was not the one that hung in the balance.

Tomorrow, he knew, would be an important day. They would move Arna into an operating room sometime after noon and then she would go into surgery. In the morning he would have breakfast, then go out to Neuilly to meet her parents who were staying overnight in the neurology unit of the American Hospital. If all went well, by midnight they would know.

He heard the muffled sound of his mother coughing in a far room. He cut the string, and Arna's letters fanned out on the bed. He ran a thumb over the stamps, over his name in her writing. Her handwriting. Her hands. His mother was calling from the kitchen. He could hear her opening cupboards, pulling down pots and pans. She was making something to eat. He looked at the letters. *No*, he thought. *No. Not now, not like this.* It was impossible. But he didn't know. He heard his mother coughing again, coughing, coughing. He opened the first letter and began to read.

ACKNOWLEDGMENTS

This book would never have seen the light of day without the belief, courage, and brilliance of my editors Michael Barron, Julia Ringo, and Alyea Canada. A shoutout to Anitra Budd, who saw what I was trying to do and encouraged me at a crucial time. I could not write without the love of my entire family, my dear friends, and fellow travelers along the road, who inspire me always. The earliest draft of this novel was completed during an extended stay with Ingrid Formanek and Brian Puchaty in Villanueva Mesía in the spring of 2008 and I thank them for their hospitality. Special thanks to Namwali Serpell for reading the manuscript with such care and providing invaluable suggestions, to Joshua Cohen for his encouragement, support, and advice, and to Jamaica Kincaid and Teju Cole for their example and camaraderie.

ABOUT THE AUTHOR

Jesse McCarthy is assistant professor in the departments of English and of African and African American Studies at Harvard University. His first book, *Who Will Pay Reparations on My Soul?*, a collection of essays, was published W.W. Norton & Co. in 2021. This is his first novel.

ACCLAIM FOR THE SEAFORT SAGA
BY DAVID FEINTUCH
FINALIST FOR THE JOHN W. CAMPBELL AWARD
FOR BEST NEW WRITER

"COMPELLING READING THAT WORKS."
—*Locus*

"SIMPLY GREAT. A fresh, visionary genius with exceptional talent."
—*Lansing State Journal*

"EXCELLENT ENTERTAINMENT."
—*Analog*

"This series is probably the best military SF of the last twenty years, and among the best SF of any kind for that same period."
—*Science Fiction Chronicle*

"IMPOSSIBLE TO PUT DOWN."
—*Philadelphia Weekly Press*

"FEINTUCH IS THE REAL DEAL AS A STORYTELLER."
—*Internet Book Information Center*

"For fans of space opera as well as high seas adventure, this series offers A PERFECT BLEND."
—*Kliatt*

more . . .

VOICES OF HOPE

ALSO BY DAVID FEINTUCH

Midshipman's Hope
Challenger's Hope
Prisoner's Hope
Fisherman's Hope

Published by
WARNER BOOKS

VOICES OF HOPE

DAVID FEINTUCH

ASPECT®

WARNER BOOKS

A Time Warner Company

WARNER BOOKS EDITION

Copyright © 1996 by David Feintuch
All rights reserved.

Aspect® is a registered trademark of Warner Books, Inc.

Cover design by Don Puckey
Hand lettering by Ron Zinn

Warner Books, Inc.
1271 Avenue of the Americas
New York, NY 10020

Visit our web site at
http://pathfinder.com/twep

 A Time Warner Company

Printed in the United States of America

First Printing: October, 1996

10 9 8 7 6 5 4 3 2 1

DEDICATION

To Betsy Mitchell

VOICES OF HOPE

Part I

July 19, in the Year of our Lord 2229

Chapter 1

PHILIP

In the soft summer evening, Senator Richard Boland paced the den of our Washington compound. "That's not just my view, Nick. The puters say—"

Stretched comfortably on the couch, Father stirred. "Let the puters tell us what water is available. How to use it is *our* problem." He brooded. "SecGen Kahn's, these days."

I glanced up at Mom, worried the discussion would upset Fath. Absently, she stroked my neck. I leaned back against the leg of the settee. If she wasn't alarmed, I need not be.

"In technical matters the SecGen relies on his staff," said Mr. Boland. "Kahn's no engineer. I'm sure Philip could absorb the data as well as he."

"And faster," said Mom loyally. Across the room, Mr. Tenere, Dad's aide and friend, nodded agreement.

I wondered if I should look into it. Even at twelve, there were few math and engineering problems I couldn't tackle.

"The real issue is whether the new towers will be occupied before—"

Fath said, "No, it's that you let puters decide matters that should be in human hands."

Senator Boland gave way with grace. "You set us a better example in your Administration."

Mom shot him a warning look. She hated to see Fath reminded of the no-confidence vote that had ended his tenure as U.N. Secretary-General five years before.

Adam Tenere smiled easily. "It did make for some long meetings, sir."

Fath grunted. "I suppose it comes from my Naval background: you don't trust the machinery. Recheck everything."

None of the adults spoke, so I jumped in. "But you were proven right. When you were Captain of *Hibernia*, the day they were about to Fuse with the wrong coordinates—"

"Oh, that was just luck." But Fath's eyes didn't leave me, and I basked in the glow of his approval. "Still, I've seen some amazing behavior from puters. Heroic as well as incredibly stupid."

Mr. Tenere said, "Did you hear they trapped an Arfie in Euronet last week?"

Father frowned, and I realized he was having trouble with the jargon. My psych texts said adults were slower to adapt than the young, and objectively speaking, I had to agree. "Artificial free intelligence," I blurted, to save him embarrassment. "They're AI constructs that expand beyond the originating programs and cyber into—"

"Yes, I saw the article in Holoworld," Fath grumbled. "Sooner or later if we keep letting those things loose, there'll be hell to pay."

"They're bound by the limits of the ori prog," I told him. "Unless the programmer inserted a—"

Senator Boland said, "Robbie's sponsoring a bill on that." He seemed proud of his son, now a U.N. Assemblyman. "The nets are too complex to control, but we're going to require delimiters in all new AI programs. Then if an AI breaks loose, it can't . . . "

A Hacker would schuss past their legislative roadblocks with a gleeful wave. Whatever ice a puter could build, another puter could eventually crack. And some of Jared Tenere's e-friends might try. I wasn't sure they had the skill to succeed, but they seemed a malevolent bunch of joeys. Perhaps that's why Jar liked them so; they rebelled in ways he only dreamed of. I thought of saying as much, but it was past my bedtime, and adults tended to blame the messenger for what they didn't care to hear. Any annoyance, and Mom would glance at her watch and hustle me out.

"P.T.?" It was as if she'd read my mind.

"Aw, Mom." She'd gone parental, just as the conversation was getting technical. My eyes appealed to Fath, across the room, but he only nodded his agreement.

Reluctantly, I said goodnight, gave the expected hugs, and made my way upstairs.

Across the compound, Jared would be deep into his nightly vigil at his puter. At fifteen, he got to stay up later. He got to do a lot of things, most of them self-destructive. From time to time I thought of alerting Mr. Tenere, but I gathered there was a code of behavior involved. Certain things adults were supposed to find out by themselves.

I sighed. I didn't have friends my own age, and learning the proper behaviors was complicated.

My psych, Mr. Skeer, said I shouldn't worry about my emotional difficulties and should try to act as normally as I could, but I didn't know what twelve-year-old norm was. I'd never been there before.

I hoped the other twelves I'd run across weren't normal; that would be very depressing.

Once, Mr. Skeer said that despite my intelligence, I had the emotions of a nine-year-old. At the time, I was nine. I supposed my emotions were twelve now.

I'd be getting hair soon. I checked when I sat on the toilet, but there was none yet. Once I thought I saw some coming, but it didn't grow in. Adolescent Psychology Monthly said puberty was confusing. It'd be nice to talk to Father about it, but I had to be careful not to upset him. He loved me very much. He said so a lot.

In bed, the lights off, I worked on irrational numbers. After a time, I drifted into sleep.

Chapter 2

JARED

"Get *away* from my puter!" Dad spun my chair, his eyes blazing. "How many times have I told you?"

I grabbed his arm to keep from falling. "Don't sneak up on me."

"Your puter's in there!" He stabbed a thumb at my room. "This is mine."

"You hiding something?" My tone was sullen.

The console chimed. "Mr. Tenere?"

Dad keyed the caller. "Just a moment, sir." He regarded me, his anger slowly fading to distaste. "I have a right to privacy, Jared."

I snorted. "Now you sound like the Old Man."

Dad glanced at the speaker. "Don't call Mr. Seafort that. He might hear."

"The Old Man?" I shrugged. "He *is* one."

He turned to his desk, rummaged for a set of chips. "Come along."

Drooping red maples swayed in Washington's muggy August breeze, offering welcome shade as we strolled through the high-walled compound to the Old Man's home and office. Across the river from Old Washington, nestled in the Virginia hills incorporated into the broadened District, the compound was a public gift to the Old Man after his forced retirement. P.T. told me the Old Man would have refused it, had Arlene not insisted for their son's sake. The Seaforts lived in the main house; our bungalow was on the periphery, not far from the surrounding wall.

Dad said, "Show him more respect."

What would I care about a disgraced politician, no matter how famous he'd been in his day? I said as much.

"Oh, Jared." A sigh. I knew Dad was hung up on respect. Centuries out of date, but U.N. Naval Academy had brainwashed him for life.

Dad smoothed his hair as we reached the patio doors. Within was a hall, and to the right, a sunlit outer office where

Dad worked answering mail and handling the Old Man's stream of inquiries and responses. Beyond Dad's office were the doors to the Old Man's sanctum, which had its own entrance to the patio, seldom used.

I asked scornfully, "What are you, his trained rabbit?"

"That's it. No nets for a month!" He stalked through his anteroom office.

"Rolf and I are linking tonight! We're schussing through—"

"Too bad."

I tugged at his arm. "If you think I'm . . . " I shrugged, pretended I'd thought of something more important.

Dad's face had that look.

I'd first seen it last month. I'd told Dad it was goddamn nonsense to haul myself out of bed for school when Philip could sleep as long—and his expression had gone tight as he'd moved toward me. I'd jumped back, not quite sure why.

Normally I did as I pleased, and told Dad what he wanted to hear. After all, at fifteen I was practically grown.

"Adam?" The double doors to the Old Man's study swung open. "What is this nonsense?" He gestured with his holovid. "I had a few questions about the Freshwater Project, and they sent us three gig of—oh. Jared." His tone was neutral, but just barely.

There'd been a time when the Old Man's manner to me was cordial, even friendly. Somehow, that tone had dissipated as I grew older. What goofjuice, for me to care what an adult thought, yet there were moments—only a few—when his delight in his son drove me to rage. Why couldn't Dad treat me likewise? Why couldn't the Old Man see I was every bit as good as Philip?

Dad gathered his gear. "I'll write Richard Boland directly. He'll cut through—"

"When you do, decline his invitation to the Franjee groundbreaking. Other commitments prevent, etc." The Old Man stood aside as Dad passed. "I won't have the media gawking at me just so Franjee can pretend I endorse his . . . " The doors closed.

I slouched in Dad's console chair. When I heard the scrape of a chair in the study I switched on Dad's puter.

I'd broken about half his passwords, but a few were still beyond me. My e-friend Rolf built a zarky password-cracker, but wouldn't give me the code. He lived in Alberta, so I couldn't pound on his door and talk him out of it. On the other hand, I hadn't told him the idea I was working on, after reading about the latest Arfie.

Idly, as if paying no attention, I tapped at Dad's keyboard, one eye on the screen.

The Old Man had made my challenge more interesting: he wouldn't allow an intelligent puter in his home, not even personality overlays or voicerec. "For years they harassed me. No more." There was no use arguing: he was stubborn enough to drive anyone to a rebalancing ward, as he'd done to his second wife. Naturally he never spoke of it; hormone treatment was certainly nothing to brag about.

I stuck out my tongue at Dad's silent screen. After the netlocks on a superbox, his passwords should be a zark. If only I could hammer his ice with a CLIP. Central linked processors sliced through the hardest glacier, if you knew how to couple them and had the nerve.

Luckily, in our cottage, at least I had access to my nets. Each night, I would don my mask and gloves and schuss the white powder hills of access.

Tonight, after Dad went to bed, I'd link with a few e-friends and slalom the gates. He'd never know, and by tomorrow, I'd talk him out of his punishment.

It always worked.

I opened some of his directories I'd already crashed. A letter to Senator Boland, Uncle Robbie's father. Why did the Old Man bother with that old stuffed shirt? All Boland did was make speeches. He wanted to rebuild the Navy, bulldoze the crumbling cities to make a clean beginning, that sort of goofjuice.

Yet everyone knew we had no money for the cities; defense came first. Only a few years before I was born, an alien armada had rained terror from the skies. We lost cities, and suffered untold casualties. At last, now, the menace seemed abated, but thanks to the attacks, and the Old Man's stupidity in letting two of our colonies go free, my generation would be dead and gone before good times came again.

"Hi."

I whirled, but it was only Philip. "Prong yourself, P.T." I

had to keep him in his place; he was only twelve. I tried to break another code, failed.

"Try the base eleven algorithms; your Dad likes weird numbers." P.T. flopped into a seat. "Careful he doesn't catch you."

"He's with your Old Man."

Glancing at the door, Philip frowned. "Fath's in one of his moods. Someone told him the Senate wants to reorganize Devon Academy."

"God forbid."

"Fath has a thing for tradition." P.T. rested his chin on his hands, looking glum. "He and Mom are fighting."

"Again?"

"They try to hide it." His face twisted. "I'm just a kit."

Dad's birthday in base eleven cracked another file. It was only next year's budget; nothing of interest. The Senators merely kept the Old Man informed as a courtesy.

"Need help with homework?" Philip sounded hopeful. He studied with private tutors, and was dumb enough to miss the drudgery of the common school Dad made me attend.

"I never *need* help." Not true, but no reason to tell him. Better if he thought I was doing him a favor by letting him write some of my essays. How unzark, his being ahead of me. Had to be his mother's genes; couldn't be the Old Man's. I hesitated. "I gotta write a history report by Wednesday. Anything government-related in the last hundred years."

"Zarks." He brightened. "Your room?"

I said sourly, "If your Mom won't have a kitten—"

"Bail out!"

I slapped the screenblank just as the office door opened. Dad shot me a skeptical glance. "What are you up to?"

I put on my most sullen look. "P.T. was in the other chair, so I used yours. *So* sorry." I got to my feet.

"Hi, Philip." As I hoped, Dad chose to ignore me.

"Good afternoon, sir." P.T. stood. The sodding joeykit was always polite, except with me, because he knew I'd wipe his face in the grass if he tried it.

Not that he had much choice, with adults. His Mom and the Old Man buzzed him like flies on a trannie. I couldn't figure why he didn't seem to mind.

Dad said, "Sorry, P.T., I forgot your holochips. Why don't you come over tonight and—"

Footsteps, along the tiled hall. A light voice. "Kidnapping my son again?"

As Arlene Seafort appeared Dad's face lit with a smile he rarely offered me. But I wasn't jealous. Soon I'd surprise them all.

"Not exactly. It's just . . . I mean, I—" Dad swallowed, shut his eyes. Silently, I counted off five seconds with him. When his eyes opened they held a mischievous glint. "Yes, I am. You won't see Philip again until he finishes my son's homework."

I stared stonily at the window. Damn him; why cut me in front of the queen bitch, just to tell me he knew about P.T.?

Her voice dropped. "How is he today?"

Dad glanced at the closed door. "Well . . . moody."

Arlene grimaced. "Tell me what I *don't* know." Her hand fell on Dad's arm. "Sorry, Adam." She sounded weary.

"Trouble?" It was as if they had forgotten we were in the room.

"No more than usual. It's just . . . " Her gaze lit on P.T., then on me. "We'll talk later, perhaps." She bestowed a pretended frown on her son, though her tone held no rebuke. "Philip, do your own work before you, ah, watch Jared do his."

"Yes, ma'am."

She ruffled P.T.'s hair as she left. "Adam, join me for a drink after dinner."

"I'd like that."

I caught P.T.'s eye and grimaced. Granted, his Mom wasn't as bad as most seniorcits, though she had a mania for physical fitness, a carryover from her military days. But hearing her with Dad was like a holodrama from the Romantic Ages.

"The Vegan resettlement?"

"Who cares." I rolled over on the bed. P.T. sat at my puter, ready to translate my ideas into respectable prose. The arrangement suited us both; it wasn't my fault Philip was far ahead of his tutors, while I got nothing but drudge work. What good was general ed? Puters were useful, and a zark. Dull useless facts weren't.

Dad knew school didn't suit me, but paid no attention. It wasn't as if he *had* to send me; education was optional, and had been for a century. Hell, even the Old Man said he'd been taught at home. Try convincing Dad, though. He shrugged and changed the subject.

"Well?" P.T. prodded my bed with his foot.

"The founding of Lunapolis? Nah, I did that last time and she'll remember. The response to the fish armada?"

He snorted. "That's current events, not history."

"It's been eleven years since the last—"

"Trust me."

"Think of something."

"Social effects of the Augmented Fusion Drive? Too easy, I could quote it right out of D'Aubison's book. Let's do the Planters' Rebellion. Hope Nation."

"It was your Old Man who put down the revolt. How can you call that history?"

P.T.'s eyes widened. "Jar, that was before I was *born*."

The Old Man's three trips to Hope System were the stuff of holodramas, but I was thoroughly sick of it. Growing up with a living legend was no fun, especially given his attitude toward P.T. and Dad's toward me. "It's boring," I said, mostly for spite.

As I hoped, Philip was outraged. "Putting down the rebellion? Blowing the Station? How can you call—"

"He did it just for the fireworks." My tone was sour. Everyone applauded the Old Man because he nuked Hope Nation's station to destroy a flotilla of attacking fish. But did he stop to think who'd pay to replace it? Even Dad claims taxes are too high to raise my allowance.

P.T. was indignant. "That's not fair. Fath hated what he did."

Yeah, sure. The Old Man gathered guilt like some joeys collect butterflies. After Hope Nation they called him a hero and made him Commandant of Naval Academy. "The Fisherman," he was called, though never to his face. But when he got all those cadets killed, he cowered in a monastery for ten years, gnawing the marrow of his remorse.

I had a hunch the published reports left out part of the story. Someday I'd get Dad to tell me. After all, he was there, a middy aboard the mothership *Trafalgar*. Whenever I asked, he would only look grim and shake his head. Maybe the truth was in a file I hadn't broken. If so, I could sell it to Holoworld for a fortune. Retired or not, the Old Man was still choice meat for the mediamen. Perhaps that was why he hated publicity.

I debated. Hope Nation had plenty of juicy incidents to hang a paper on, but my goal in life was to escape Nick Seafort's frazzing compound, and I'd be damned if I'd glorify him. "Nah. Let's do . . . " I thought furiously. "The Hacker Revolt."

"Revolt? They crashed the Treasury, but that was—"

"A zark." I knew I was safe with P.T.; he'd never repeat what I'd said. In school or elsewhere, I had to keep my mouth shut. As our teachers loved to remind us, the Rebellious Ages were long past. The Reunification Church and its U. N. Government wouldn't tolerate anarchy.

"I suppose," P.T. said doubtfully, "we could write about the safeguards put in place since—"

"Sure. You write the intro." I lay back.

A moment later, I came awake with a start. "Don't shake me."

"It's done. All of it."

"Already? Let's see." I scanned the printout, yawning.

The Hackers' invasion of the U.N. Treasury in June 2129 was, like the barbarians' sack of Rome, a decisive turning point in social relations. The chaos resulting from loss of half a year's taxes shattered a growing nostalgia for the Rebellious Ages, and thenceforward most societal institutions were united behind the Rule of Law, as our era is now known.

Though stringent security safeguards have since been put in place, continued reliance on puters means that danger remains—

I grunted. "I'll have to change some words."

"My grammar's fine. Run your spellcheck, you won't find—"

"Oh, cork it." That was the trouble. If I turned in a report using terms like "thenceforward" and free of grammatical errors, our frazzing teacher would guess I hadn't written it. After P.T. left, I would throw in a few typos to look like I'd been too lazy to run the speller, and string a couple of sentences together. For Philip's benefit I said grudgingly, "It's all right. I'll fix it up."

"Fine. Do your own work!" He snatched the printout from my hand, turned back to the puter. "I'll erase it and—"

"Don't even think about it, joey." I tried to make my voice cold, like once I'd heard the Old Man's, when he was still SecGen.

Philip's finger hovered over the wipe. "Or you'll stuff more grass in my mouth?" His tone was acid. "I don't mind helping, you frazzing grode, but don't *ever* treat me like your personal trannie!"

He sounded like . . . I wasn't sure what, or whom. "Cool jets. It's a good essay." He didn't seem mollified. "Better than I'd have written," I added with gritted teeth. Soon, I'd be out of here. If all went as planned I'd savor my revenge.

His thumb left the keyboard. I let out my breath. Tomorrow, I'd reenable the unwipe in case he pulled that again.

P.T. sulked.

Despite my efforts, my anger dissipated. With Philip, it was hard to stay mad. He had a quality that made me yearn to stroke him. I'd never tried.

"Gotta go."

Curfews. I snorted. Dad thought I had one, too, but he didn't know I used the hall window. "I'll walk you back."

It was nearly ten; the floods were turned off for the night. We crossed the darkened lawn in silence.

Our bungalow was at the far end of the drive, between the compound gates and the helipad. Not much of a home for a retired Captain, or me.

Dad had made Captain shortly after the Old Man became SecGen, and had commanded U.N.S. *Vesta* before Admiralty sent him to act as Naval Liaison to Seafort. When the Old Man lost his vote of confidence and resigned, Dad had volunteered to stay with him rather than return to the Navy. I don't know why. Maybe the shuttle crash that killed Mom had something to do with it; Dad said only that an interstellar liner was no place to raise a child.

Selfish of him; it'd be a zark to have the run of a starship instead of being stuck in common school. Nobody would give me trouble as the Captain's son.

Instead, when the Old Man retreated to Washington, Dad followed.

As we neared the main house I said, "Thanks for the paper."

P.T. shrugged.

"I mean it." A little butter wouldn't hurt, for next time. "They loaded me with math and—"

"Shh!" He grabbed my arm, tugged me back.

The soft sound of voices overrode my annoyance. I strained to hear.

"No more than usual." Arlene. "It's that damned *hadj* he takes next week."

I knelt below the dim glow of the patio light, motioned to P.T. to follow. After a moment I crawled closer.

"Hadj?" Dad's laugh sounded nervous.

Arlene said crossly, "Whenever he comes home from that bloody monastery he's sick from the memories, and from shame at all the parishioners crowding for a glimpse of him."

"It's only once a year. He needs the retreat."

"I know!"

P.T. stirred uneasily at the anguish in her tone. I put a hand on his shoulder; he shook it off, speared me with a laser glare that warned against touching him again.

A long pause. She added, "Perhaps more than he needs me."

Dad sighed.

"But he *does* need me. When he resigned he was so . . . hurt."

Dad said, "He didn't deserve their contempt. I know how he felt."

"I wonder." She hesitated. "Adam, keep this between us, but part of his hurt was his suspicion that he did deserve it."

Dad sounded tired. "I thought he was past that."

"He doesn't have much confidence. His self-respect is . . . fragile."

I glanced at P.T., but his face was in the shadows.

"That's hard on you."

Her laugh was brittle. "I manage. For weeks after Lancaster, I look at him with adoring eyes, and bite my tongue when I want to criticize. Well, it's not as bad as all that. But for Christ's bloody sake, I wish he wouldn't keep going to that place!"

Dad cleared his throat.

"Sorry," she said presently. "No blasphemy meant."

She didn't have to worry in Dad's company, but in public a remark like that could have her up for sacrilege. One had to be careful; though public piety might be fading, the elders of the Reunification Church were still immensely powerful. Last year I'd told my teacher what I thought of our stupid canon law, and got hauled into the principal's office for a whipping. Worse, Dad hadn't shown much sympathy.

Maybe I should report Arlene anonymously. That'd show them.

"I wish I could help," Dad told her.

"An evening chat with you is enough." Her tone lightened. "Let's round up our offspring."

I scuttled away from the house, tugging at Philip. When he was clear, I leaped to my feet, ran toward the veranda, spoke as if breathless. "There you are! We were coming to find you." I addressed Dad. "Isn't it your bedtime, young man?"

"Very funny." He caressed the back of my neck; I refrained from flinching at his touch.

Arlene put her hands on her hips, her tone mocking. "Philip, what mischief have you been into?"

P.T. fell into her hug. "Nothing, Mom. Jared was showing me his puter."

Dad and I said good night, strolled back to the bungalow. At the outer door he paused. "How long were you listening?"

"Huh? I don't know—"

He shook his head.

I followed him inside. "All I said—"

Dad spoke softly, as if resigned. "I hate lies, Jared."

"That's right, accuse me again. All you do is find fault. We were only—"

He turned away. "Go to bed."

"Yeah, don't listen. You never—"

"Now!" It brooked no argument.

I retreated, slammed my door in futile protest.

I'd show them, someday. Dad, Arlene, all of them. Someday.

Chapter 3

POOK

Fat man sigh soft, grab at my wrist. I holdafort, proud.

He slide down da wall, like his legs tire. I reach down, pull shiv from his stomach, watch blood spurt 'til it stop. I wipe my blade on his coat, stick it in belt.

Nobody mess wid a Mid.

I look roun', don' see no one inna dark. Gotta grit teeth checkin' out his pockets. Make me feel all glitch, him still warm.

Can' fin' nothin'. But ya never know; he mighta had coin.

For a min I think 'bout making Mid mark wid blood onna wall. Dis be Mid turf, even if alla Rocks not know it yet.

Nah. Smarter ta leave it for Midboss, 'less Karlo think Pookboy tryin' ta crash. Ain' had my upbringin' yet, but it gonna come any time now. Den I be reg Mid. Old neut Changman say I be fourteen, moreless, but he so glitch wid old, I dunno.

Sometimes Chang make me drink his tea while he rememba how Fisherman come see him, 'fore I born. Boolsheet. Ain' no Fisherman; he jus' scaretale fo' joeykits.

Still, better I hang roun' Chang's place than onna street, special nighttime. Now dat Mids be pushin' out Broads an' Rocks, lotsa rumb nighttime, an' Karlo say joeykits spose ta stay outa. I tellim I big enough, but he jus' laugh, whop me on side a head.

Someday I show him. Alladem. Like fat ol' Rock tonigh', think he c'n cross Mid turf. "Fadeout," he say, hopeful. Ri'. I fade him out bigtime.

I look aroun', don' see no Rocks. Back ta lair, I spose ta, but too wired try ta sleep. Careful, crouchin' in shadows, I duck 'cross street, run roun' corner.

Knock three time.

Nothin'.

Knock again, three time.

Voice growl, "Go away. Close."

"It be me."

"Dunno any 'Me'."

I sigh. Stupid ol' man. "I be Pook. Lemme in 'fore Rocks gemme."

Bolts slide open. Time be passin'. I peer inta dark, my back itchin'. Be a soun', in build 'cross street? Dunno.

Door open. Scrunchy ol' man in robe look down his nose, suspicious. "Watcha done, Midboy?"

"Nothin'." I close door quick.

"Pah." He shuffle ta table, take his cuppa, sip loud. "Joeykit thinks he's talkin' to dumbass Mid. Try ta swind Pedro Telamon Chang, hah?"

I sniff at pot. "Whazzat, tea? Feh." Coffee better, when he give, even if he think tea be only fo' special fren.

"Tea, yah." He padded 'cross room. "Allri', I giveya. Trayfo?"

"Ain' got." Anyway, I be glitch ta tray somethin' I wan' fo' tea I don' like.

"Lemme see." He stick his han' in my pocket. I make face, but lettim. Coupla times he catch me holdin' out, and whop me good. I old enough now he can' do it, 'less I let him. Dunno why I do; I almos' big as he.

He pat me down. "Whazzis?" 'Fore I c'n stop him, he yank out my shiv. He lean ta Valdez perma, ta see it better inna ligh'.

"Gimme!" My voice jump too high. It do a lot, nowtime.

He inspec' shiv. "Blood? Cut?" His voice worry.

"Naw."

He try ta hide his relieve. "Who?"

"Fat ol' Rock joey." I shrug.

"Why?"

I surprise at dumb question. " 'Cause he Rock."

"Thassall?" His eyes anger.

"A Rock on Thirty Seven! Mid turf."

"But what'd he do?"

"He be dere, what he do!"

Stupid ol' man slap me hard, an' it hurt.

I let out yelp. "Nobody whomp on Pook no mo'!" I snatch shiv.

Ol' Changman bristle like cat some buncha scroungers figga for stewpot. "Midboy gonna diss Chang, hah?" He shuffle close, pull open his robe. "Right here, ya want to stick it. G'wan! Chang go down fas'."

"I din say no—"

He grab holda my ear an' twis'. I squawk. He yell, "This Chang house! No snotty Midboy tells Chang what he look at. Put dat back where I lef' it! An' stop cryin'!"

"I ain' cryin', ya ol'— all ri'!" I drop shiv on table. He leggo ear. Ain' no talkin' ta Chang sometime; gotta do what he say. But inside, he ain' so fierce as he think. An' he take me in, afta I pissoff Karlo.

He trot ta back room, drag out 'notha chair. "Sit. Drink tea, feel better."

"Don' wan' none." I sit.

"Wipe ya eyes an' sip. Ain' too hot." He wait.

"Why ya comedown on Pook? Rocks ain' nothin' ta Neut." I sniff. Can' help it; I hate when Chang be mean.

"Tea don' stay hot fo'eva." He slurp his cup.

I sip tea, keep 'im happy. Ain' too bad.

Outside, streets quiet fo' night. I look roun' shop, see what Chang got new.

On chair, usual piles a clothes, all wash an' fold. Jumpsuits, like Uppies got. Broads like 'em, but won' catch Pook in a jumpsuit 'less he bareass widout. Frazzin' Uppies think they own N'Yawk. Don' wan' look like 'em.

Buncha boxes inna corner. "Whazzat, Chang?" His eyes go narrow. "Mista Chang," I fix quick, 'fore he grab my ear.

He grunt, like he satisfy. "Permas."

Valdez permas. Batries we use fo' light, fo' cook. Uppies use fo' 'lectricars an' helis. "Why so lot?"

"So many." He wait 'til I say it his way, which I gotta do if I wan' him ta tell. Else, he too stubborn. "Savin' fo' tray-fo," he growl.

Dat don' 'xplain nothin'. Changman save *everythin'* fa trayfo. He be a traytaman. He trayfo permas or threads or cansa fo' trannie scrounge. He trays wid alla tribes. Even wid Subs, once in while. Not much, cause no one mess wid Subs, even fo' tray. Usetabe, they dissya soon as ya go on they turf. Now they jus' take yo' trayfo, whomp on ya har'.

Inna day, even Rocks an' Broads c'n come ta Chang's door. One time he make me hide behin' curtain 'cause two big ol' Easters come. Argue some, trayfo lotsa. After, he jus' smile 'cause I mad he make me hide. "Easters don' wan' tribes know what they trayfo. See ya here, they give Pookboy 'nother mouth." He make sign cross throat.

I finish my tea. "Gotta be makin' big trayfo, so lot— so many permas."

"Min' ya own biz," Chang grumble. He fill his cup. Afta while, he shake his head. "Two month I work buildin' truce, an' stupid Midboy mess it up dissin' Rock."

"He be on—"

"Yah, yah, Mid turf." Chang sip tea. "Turf fallin' down, an' govermen takin' what ain't. Still tribes rumb, fo' nothin'."

"Turf ain' nothin'!"

"Hah." He rock hisself, breathin' hot tea. Eyes go faraway. "Cross street, down Thirty Six, big store usetabe. Mace turf."

Never been no Mace, since 'fore I born. Jus' ol' man's dream. Still, he act like they real tribe. Sighin' inside, I nod.

"Giant store, took up whole block. They lived in. Little Mace boy came knockin' on Chang door once, like you. Scared, mad, needed help."

When ol' man look otha way, I stick out tongue. I ain' little, an' ain' scared.

"Eddie Maceboy wasn't like Pook. He listened, when Chang tol' him smarts. He learned. Ol' Eddie knew better manners than stick tongue at Pedro Telamon Chang."

Damn; he not spose ta see. I get up, stand by his chair. "Din' mean nothin'." He no answer. I pat his shoulder, feel funny inside, like bad. " 'Pologize." One a big words Chang try ta teach.

Make him smile, anyway. He sigh. "Maces died to keep their turf. Couldn' keep. Where Mace now? Turf ain' worth dyin' for. Or killin'."

"You don' unnerstan', Mista Chang. You ain' tribe."

"Afta govermen done, tribes'll be gone." His blue eyes squint at mine. "Joeykit can' imagine, but that day comin'."

"No one pushout Mids." I go proud.

"Midboys can' stop Unies."

"Unies?" I laugh scorn. "They sick ol' tribe, by riva. Can' even get pas' Sixth."

"Bah." He push me 'way. "Not Unie tribe; real Unies! Governmen!" He search my face, don' fin' what he wan'.

"When Goverman Bolan' get his way, Unies 'll tear down city, put Uppie tower where Chang shop be."

"How you know—"

"It's inna holozines, stupid Midboy. Filmatleven. If you let Chang teach read—"

"Don' wanna read," I grumble. "Ain' no Uppie."

"Ya never gonna be, not know nothin'!"

That stop our talk a while. He go wash cups, I pace shop, nervous, pickin' up stuff, puttin' down. Maybe Rocks fin' ol' fat man, an' come fo' venge when Pook run ta lair.

Chang peer from behin' curtain. "Okay okay, Midboy c'n stay night. Get hisself killed 'nother day."

"I ain' 'fraid a no—"

"Yah, yah, Chang heard it before. Wash."

Chang be glitch 'bout allatime wash. It ain' trannie way. Howya gonna wash threads, onna street? He think everyone got Valdez permas ta dry wid? Think alla tribe got good runnin' water, like Broads 'n few Mid lairs, or live near seawall?

Chang ruffle my hair as I pass. Stupid ol' man think he my motha.

Nex' day, sun shine warm. Wind blow dus' around rubbly lot ol' Chang call Mace.

Daytime, streets ain' like night. Tribes go about, sometimes even innifo passby each otha turf. Still, I gotta watch out, case someone knows I diss Rock.

Mids live in lairs. Always secret place. Mids don' like uppa flo'; mos'ly stay on groun' or basemen'. I look roun' 'fore goin' in. No one see.

Karlo be boss our lair. I wait fo' him to look at me. He ain' so pissoff since I brung innifo, but sometime he have a bad day. He nod, don' say nothin'. I figga it be all ri'.

Longtime back, my motha go ta 'nother lair, leave me behin'. Don' matta; Bigsis look afta me 'til I growed. I be reg Mid joeykit, waitin' fo' upbringin'. But Karlo gotta say okay firs', an' he make me wait extra, causa pissoff. Rab an' Swee had they upbringin', an' I bigger 'n Rab. I ain' gonna cry like Swee, neitha, when they cut Mid mark. I ready.

I peek in stewpot. Bigsis gimme look like jus' ya try. I know stew be fo' later, when alla tribe home in lair. Daytime eat, my biz. Tribe don' care if joeykit go hungry inna day.

"Whereya been?"

I shrug. "Changman."

Bigsis give me checkout look. "Why spen' allya time wid Neut?"

"Dunno. Somethin' ta do."

"How ya gonna learn, hangaroun' allatime wid glitch ol' man? Gonna be half Uppie like him?"

I laugh. Chang no Uppie.

"He shaggin' ya?" She soun' curious.

"Nah." Gimme idea, though. I gotta see if he inerest. Gemme buncha trayfo, if he do.

She don' much care. "He gon' die soon, anyway."

My heart go pump, but I say casual, "We gonna dissim?" Maybe I warn 'im, if.

"Diss a Neut?" She look at me like I glitch. "Naw. I sayin' he ol'." She frown at stew, stir. "Been ol' since I was joeykit."

I can' imagine street widout Chang. Gotta ask 'im if he think he die soon.

Ol' Chang spose ta be bes' traytaman eva. Mids say, one time he even trayfo laser, back when Rock try takeova. If ya need cansa, Chang always got, long as ya bring trayfo. He got shivs, threads, even window glass. Dunno where he get.

"Yo! Pook!" Bigsis squint at stewpot. "Gimme help."

"Innifo?" She gotta give me somethin', jus' little, else why I do fo' her? Wha's inni fo' *me*?

Her face get ugly. "I'll innifo ya, dreckface joeykit! Wan' eat tonigh', or no?"

"Watchew wan?" My voice what Changman call sullen.

"Who got cansa veg? Tomatoes or somethin'?"

"Dunno."

She scrounge unner table, pull up boots, good all roun', jus' little hole one side. "Go find trayfo."

"Me?" My voice come in squeak. I bring it low, redface. "I mean, sho', Bigsis."

I grab boots 'fore she change min'. Trayfo be job fo' grown Mids, an' she askin' me do it. I go proud.

"Can' giveaway boots," she warn. "Not fo' two, three cansa."

"Don' tell Pook howta trayfo," I say, scorny. Already I

thinkin', checkout street, fin' someone wid lotsa cansa. Don' even talk ta trannie wid jus' a couple.

If I can' fin' enough cansa, I go ta Changman. He help. On otha han', maybe he skin me on trayfo. Chang worse 'n trannies onna street.

Chapter 4

ROBERT

"What do you think, Robbie?"

I snapped off the holovid, squinted into the glare of reflected sunlight on Dad's worn cluttered desk. "You're really pushing the upside."

"Bah." He waved it away. "After thirty years of politics I know to come out swinging. Besides, what I say in the speech is true. The increase in land values alone will justify—"

I jumped in before he found his full voice. "Not the whole spiel, Dad."

"Wouldn't hurt for you to hear it again," Dad grumbled. "So, how do I handle the launch?"

"Prep the party faithful, so they follow with their own speeches in support."

"Of course. I don't want to be hung out to dry on this one." He brooded. "Could we get Nick on the bandwagon? I've tried, but he keeps asking for more data."

"The Captain won't even consider a public stand."

"Letters, to some of our friends?"

"Possibly."

"Ask him." He shoved his caller across the desk.

"Why not you?"

"He has a soft spot for you, Robbie. I'm just another pro."

I sighed. After knowing him twenty years or more, I still felt uneasy pressuring the retired SecGen. The man was an enigma.

Seafort had joined the U.N. Navy at thirteen, and sailed as a middy to Hope Nation. After a series of tragedies, he brought his ship home as Captain. More important, he brought news of the first aliens mankind had ever encountered, the fish that nearly destroyed us.

Captain Seafort's second voyage ended in disaster when a fool of an admiral abandoned him on the disabled *Challenger* with transpop passengers the commander disliked. With courage and tenacity, Seafort fought off the aliens and returned home with his crippled ship.

He sailed again to Hope Nation, but became entangled in a seething planter rebellion. Desperately ill, left in charge after the fleet's recall, Seafort managed to put down the revolt. Then, he went aloft in a shuttle and blew up Hope Nation's orbiting station to destroy hundreds of marauding fish, believing that his act was treason and he would be hanged. Had not the law been overturned during his absence, he'd have been tried rather than feted.

After, Dad and the Admiral of the Fleet wouldn't let him retire. The Captain was made Commandant of Naval Academy, where'd I'd been sent as a green young cadet. A few months after, I'd been allowed to accompany him on his fateful cruise on *Trafalgar*.

Dad moved restlessly.

I asked, "Couldn't it wait?"

"Rob, I need to know."

Reluctantly I dialed, waited for the connection to Washington. "Adam? Rob Boland here. The Senator's fine, thanks. I'm going to send you a speech Dad's planning. We'd like Mr. Seafort to look it over. I could call, um, tomorrow."

I ignored Dad's frown. It was he who'd taught me patience. If we rushed the Captain, he'd just say no.

Adam's voice was warm. "Why don't you catch the sub-orbital and join us for dinner? I know he'd love to see you."

"I don't want to impose—"

"Don't be ridiculous."

I gulped, a carryover from the days when he'd been a lofty midshipman, and I a mere cadet. "If you're sure, sir."

"See you at seven. Bring the speech along; he'll read it if I tell him I gave his promise."

"Thanks, Adam."

"Looking forward to it. We'll have drinks after, you and I."

"Zarky." I rang off.

Dad looked smug. "See? I've always known what lever to push."

"Is that what I am to you?" I smiled to remove the sting from my tone.

Dad's grin turned the lines around his eyes to crinkles. "That, and much more. Besides, you love to visit them."

"Of course." I gathered my things. "On the other hand, Adam's son will be there."

Dad's mouth tightened. "Your . . . nephew?"

"I wish I'd never agreed to that 'Uncle' business. He's a distasteful young joey."

A few minutes later I went home to pack; the Captain would no doubt invite me to stay the night. If he didn't, Adam would.

While selecting a change of clothing, I mused on my friend Tenere. He had made his own bed; he'd failed to put Jared over his knee when the boy had been small enough. Instead, Adam let the boy walk over him, until it was all but too late. Still, even at this late date, firm discipline such as the Captain had given me might yet save him.

On the other hand, who was I to know? I'd not yet married. Perhaps raising a child was more difficult than it seemed. I glanced at my watch. Time to leave for the shuttleport.

"What, Mother?" I tried to concentrate through the static of the caller, and the engine's drone.

"I saw you on the news the other night."

"The Freshwater Station? I had no choice but to go." As General Assemblyman for Seaboard Cities, I'd had to be seen at the ribbon-cutting, though the Hudson Station was another of SecGen Kahn's infamous boondoggles. I beckoned the steward to refresh my gin.

"Richard looked grim," said Mother. "How is he?"

"He's fine." Since their divorce, my parents tended to use me as a conduit for news about one another. I didn't mind; their mutual interest was benign, perhaps even amicable. Mother gave Dad curt advice about his public image, and he'd helped her through the dreary weeks following her transplant.

"He'd better do more than show up, or that prick Kahn will preempt the water issue." Mother was forthright, as always.

"Dad knows." We'd had no choice but to support Kahn's Freshwater Project. Our New York tower constituents were squeezed for clean water, and the upcoming Delaware diversion wouldn't help.

"You'd think we'd have more drinking water, with the ice caps melting. When I was young . . . " She sighed. "It was ages ago, and you're too busy to listen."

"I'm free 'til we land." I checked my watch. "Nineteen minutes."

"I was eleven when your grandfather took me to watch them build the seawall."

Slow but persistent global warming caused more snow, but the evaporation was also greater. The seven-foot rise in sea level obliterated Bangladesh, menaced Holland and other low-lying countries, and forced the hasty construction of the New York Seawall just below Wall Street. New York was threatened at high tides, but even more so by the furious summer storms that swept northward with ever greater frequency.

"When will your father take his stand?"

My eyes strayed to Dad's speech, in my holovid. Not for the first time, I wondered whether Mother could read minds. Or perhaps she knew Dad too well to think he'd stay politically quiescent.

I said, "It's, ah, an insecure line."

"Bullshit. The Territorials know he's ready to make a move."

"Mother, *please*."

Caller to my ear, I flicked on my screen, perused Dad's speech. The Cities Redevelopment Project was the key to his political future. He'd been Senator from the Northeastern Quadrant for longer than I could remember, but our Supranationalist Party was out of power, and had been ever since the Seafort Administration's fall.

"I'll let you go, dear. Back to my roses."

"Sorry, Mother. Should I stop by the house?"

"Only if you can stay a while. I hate those flying visits of yours. You flit through the parlor like a bat and disappear."

"Perhaps next week. I love you."

"Take care, Robbie." A click.

Really, I ought to see her more often. Despite her heart replacement, she wouldn't be around forever, and I cherished her blunt advice.

I finished my gin and leaned back, musing on the collapse of Seafort's government. The crowning irony was that the March 2224 vote of confidence was unnecessary. The Captain himself demanded it, against Dad's advice, after the Territorials had worried at his heels for months over the Wade affair. He had known nothing of Senator Wade's corrupt dealings, but the opposition had made that innocence itself sound like criminal negligence.

If Seafort had sidestepped rather than admitting his fault at every opportunity, we might still hold office, and could deal directly with the towers' water problems.

Well, no matter. The Captain was out of political life, retired in his prime. Now, Dad was staking his claim to the SecGen's red leather chair. Reconstruction was the issue that had catapulted him to party leadership, and hopefully would lead to the Rotunda itself.

"Care for a refill, Assemblyman?"

I glanced up, annoyed at the steward's interruption, but careful to hide it. "No, thanks."

Too bad the Hudson Station wasn't large enough to solve the city's water shortage. Regardless of the potential unrest, we would have to rechannel the old city mains. After all, the burgeoning towers were bulwarks of civilization, and the source of many steadfast Supranationalist votes. They had to be supplied.

If Dad eventually won the Rotunda, I'd try for his seat, and thanks to our name, I'd likely win. A big step for me; the U.N. Senate was far more powerful than the overcrowded General Assembly, with its thousand and fifty-five assemblymen.

If.

As my heli set down on the well-lit pad I tried to swallow my unease, knowing the warm welcome that awaited me. But, as usual in the Seaforts' presence, I felt myself the fumbling youngster Dad had brought to Academy gates.

Years later, as an Assemblyman, I wasn't often received at the Rotunda during the Captain's Administration. At our meetings he'd seemed cold and distant. Though it hurt, I did my best to conceal it. Perhaps my abandoning a Naval career had disappointed him. At least I'd made lieutenant, and I don't believe my father had a hand in it. I was vastly proud of the achievement.

One day, in the midst of a stiff discussion about colonial tariffs, the Captain had stopped short, spun his chair to the wall. When again he spoke, his voice was halting and pained.

"Robert, forgive my rudeness."

"I didn't notice—"

"Of course you did." He rose, stood at the tall, velvet-draped window, hands clasped behind him, and looked down to the filthy river.

"I don't—"

"You see, you make me remember." He turned, with a deprecating smile. "Some memories are . . . difficult."

I got to my feet. "I'm truly sorry, sir. It's not necessary that we meet in person. I didn't mean to cause—"

"Oh, stop. Please." The force of his entreaty left me bereft of words. "Something I must tell you."

"Yes, sir?"

His eyes met mine. "I was proud of you as a boy, and I am still."

I gulped.

Damn it, I was *not* a cadet. I was grown. Why the lump in my throat?

He'd come around his massive desk, touched my shoulder lightly. "I'll bear my discomfort without inflicting it on you." His eyes focused with determination on mine. "You're welcome in my office, and in my home." Shyly, as if fearing rejection, he embraced me. For a moment, I let my head rest on his shoulder.

It was as if I had two fathers.

I strove to please them both.

Arlene curled on the couch, her head on her husband's shoulder. I sat opposite; Adam sprawled in an easy chair.

"I won't stand in his way," Captain Seafort said.

I said, "I was hoping for more, sir."

"I know." He perused the printout, biting his lip.

I studied my mentor. Lean, prominent cheekbones, sunken eyes through which one occasionally glimpsed private pain. The Captain was trim and fit, and though he was of average height, one came away with the impression of great stature, a cold strength that was more than muscular.

I prompted, "Perhaps a speech to the Naval Veterans . . . "

"No speeches. I'm done with that, thank Lord God."

As usual, his candor was disconcerting. How had such a man been elected SecGen? He was an elk among wolves. Well, eventually they'd brought him down.

I'd known he'd reject a speech out of hand, and retreated

to a fallback position, my real goal. "We're fifteen votes short in the Senate, sir. If you wrote to a few friends . . ."

"They'd ignore me, or would if they deserved to hold office." He shook his head. "Besides, I'm not sure I like Richard's approach. Aside from the enormous cost, he's trying to rebuild the cities from the top down. You really think more towers are the answer?"

"Sir, I know that we're pouring Unibucks into vast new buildings. But that's what hooks the construction interests, and without them we won't have the votes for renewal."

The Captain fixed me with a disapproving eye. "You'll be displacing a lot of people for your . . . steel elephants."

"Yes, streeters." No point in denying it, with him. "But Dad's a realist. The choice is that or nothing. Which do you prefer?" He was silent. I added, "The cities are falling apart, sir. London, Denver, New York; in a few years they'll all be too far gone to save. Is that what you want?"

Arlene and Adam spoke at once.

"Don't lay it at his—"

"You're pressing, Robert." Adam looked abashed. "Sorry. Go on, Arlene."

Arlene's head moved slightly, as if to shield her husband's from my gaze. "It's not Nick's doing, and he no longer has a say in politics."

I chuckled, to ease the tension. "He'd still be the most quotable man on the planet, if he cared to be quoted."

"But he doesn't." Adam's tone was sharp.

"All right," I said agreeably.

Undisturbed by the silence, I gazed at the couple on the overstuffed couch. Absently, the Captain's hand curled around Arlene's shoulder. Still a lovely woman was Arlene Sanders Seafort.

Their marriage in the Rotunda during the first year of his Secretariat had made worldwide headlines. As Terran First Lady, Arlene had chosen to remain in the background, helping her husband manage political chores rather than adopt public causes.

Now, they made a devoted couple. I'd heard persistent rumors of discord, but found them hardly credible. They respected each other, a more vital ingredient to marriage than mere love. And they treasured their boy.

A half hour before, Philip had padded into the den in his pajamas to bid us good night. As the youngster made his rounds his father watched with fondness so unrestrained I felt an intruder.

"Good night, Mr. Boland." P.T. embraced me.

"You're getting big, joey." My voice was gruff. How does one talk to a lad almost a teener?

"Yes, sir. Thanks again for the model."

I'd brought a 1:100 replica kit of U.N.S. *Challenger*, his father's old ship. P.T. would probably complete it in a day or so; he had deft, fast hands and a breathtaking intelligence that left one slightly uneasy. Where I'd have pored over blueprints, he memorized the schematics with a quick glance.

I'd given him a hug, not only because I liked him, but also because it would please his father and make him more amenable to my request. Such was politics.

Now, I smiled at Adam. Since the Captain had retreated from public view, Tenere had become fiercely protective. My task would be difficult enough with his support; without it, I couldn't win over the Captain. I wasn't sure I'd want to try.

Lord God, how I'd revered Adam.

My first year as a cadet had been utter misery. Sergeant Ibarez was especially hard on me, perhaps to prove that my family connections carried no clout with him. My bunkies were uniformly hostile; they were certain Dad had arranged easy passage through Academy, and found constant proof where none existed.

When Mr. Seafort had summoned me to his Commandant's office and caned me without mercy for my misdeeds, I was undone. For weeks, sick with guilt and shame, I couldn't find myself.

It was Midshipman Adam Tenere who had succored me. Sarge had been decent; the Obutu woman was kind, but only Adam was close enough to my age to know what I'd felt. On long walks through the compound I'd blurted out my woes to him. He was tongue-tied and awkward, but nonetheless, he was there. Once, when he was sure no one saw, he'd actually hugged me. I cherished boyish fantasies about him, never expressed, which later I outgrew.

I was best man at his wedding. Elena was lovely; she made me regret bachelorhood. I still missed her.

Elena's death had sobered Adam; after, he comprehended that life bore pain that couldn't be eased. Some youthful quality left him, but he embraced solemn adulthood willingly enough. It was at my suggestion that he'd gone to the SecGen's office as liaison. I'd no idea he and the Captain would become so attached that Adam would gladly follow him into obscurity.

Looking at me across the Captain's living room, Adam's expression softened.

"I didn't mean to push," I said humbly.

The Captain frowned. "Pushing isn't the issue. You know I won't take offense, though I may refuse. But I have misgivings about your policy, and the sixty billion cost will come in part from the Navy's budget." He forestalled my reply. "It has to; we're the—that is, the Navy is the U.N.'s single biggest military expense."

Most of the ships lost to the alien armada had been replaced. Of course, compromises were made. Many of the new ships were smaller, and therefore carried fewer passengers. Our colonial expansion was slowed, even if the Caterwaul Stations had abated the menace of the fish.

The Seafort Administration had been steadfast in its support of the Navy, a factor which had eventually benefited our opponents in the Territorial Party. Many old-line industries that didn't profit from the shipbuilding had gone over to them.

That made Dad's plan all the more important; if we could recapture the housing lobby, our campaign war chest would be fully funded. Multinational campaigns were damnably expensive.

It wasn't much past eleven when Adam glanced at his watch. I took the cue, and we bade good-night to the SecGen and his wife. I walked Adam back to his bungalow, chatting amiably.

"Watch," he said as we neared. "Jared's light." Through a curtained window, a glow lit the wall.

"What about it?"

His voice rose. "We'll send Bennett a tightbeam in the morning. I think he'll come around."

The light flicked off. Adam lowered his voice, his smile grim. "They tell me he falls asleep in class. He thinks I don't know he's up half the night wargaming his puter."

I hesitated, unsure if my opinion was wanted. Then, "Take it away."

"The one thing he's passionate about?" He shook his head. "No, he's smarter than he acts, Rob. Puters are the only arena in which he proves it."

"Set his hours."

"Why attempt what I can't enforce?" He waved it away with a sigh. "Join me for a drink."

"A light one."

We settled on the patio outside Adam's bedroom, on the far side of the cottage.

Adam brought me a gin, uncapped an ale. "God, I miss her."

I didn't need to ask. "So do I."

He gestured to the house. "She'd have prevented—that."

"Jared? He'll come around."

He snapped, "Don't bullshit me. You never have before."

"Aye aye, sir." It was only half in jest.

"Well, that put me in my place." Now his smile was genuine. "Sorry, Rob."

I shrugged. "Jared's what, sixteen? This is the worst of it."

"Fifteen, barely. I look at him and see . . . you." He added, "And others, from Academy days. The contrast is obscene."

"Adam, why don't you rein him in?"

A long silence. "I . . . can't." Perhaps Adam saw too much of Elena in the boy's finely chiseled face, the long dark lashes.

Sensing his discomfort, I changed the subject. After a time we spoke of the Captain.

"It's painful to be near him," Adam said. "He's so determinedly . . . sincere." He studied my face. "You didn't really know him when you were a cadet; he resigned after the, um, *Trafalgar* incident. I had the fortune to know him before." He looked beyond me, to another time. "He took me to the Training Station, just the two of us. Lord God, what a privilege. You should have seen him then, Rob. Bold, decisive, determined to do right by us all."

I stirred, restless.

"Now, he's . . . tentative. Yes, that's the word. He's mislaid his moral beacon. I think he was glad his Administration lost the vote of confidence." He saw me fidget and grimaced. "Well, I can see you're tired. Sorry to—"

I blurted, "It's not that. I need to use the head." My bladder was ready to explode from the drinks I'd sipped all evening. I stood, feeling a foolish boy once more. "Back in a minute."

I'd been in Adam's home often enough. I opened the screen door, headed down the darkened hall toward the bath.

Under the boy's door, a gleam of light.

Perhaps it was the ale, perhaps the shuttle-lag. Emboldened, I knocked once, flung open the door.

Jared, still dressed, glanced up from his puter. "Hello, Uncle Rob."

"Turn that off and get into bed, before I do what your father won't."

He gaped. "You can't make—"

"Try me, joeyboy!"

He hesitated, thought better of it. With a contemptuous flick he snapped off the puter, sat on his bed, slipped off his shoes.

I shut the door, continued down the hall.

By the time I got to the patio I'd realized what a mistake I'd made. I was "Uncle" only by courtesy, and had no rights with this wayward joeykid. Best not to tell Adam; it would make things worse between us, and not only did I like him, I needed his support to persuade the Captain.

While Tenere led the conversation back to our youth at Academy, then to Elena, I sat wondering what had come over me, ordering his son about as if he were my own.

"Remember when we couldn't find her room at the Lunapolis Sheraton, and hollered at that fuddled old lady to open the bloody door?"

I nodded. I had either to tell Adam or make it right with the boy; I couldn't leave things as they were. I waited for my opportunity, excused myself once more.

I knocked. "Jared?"

No answer.

"This is Uncle Rob." I tried to quell my distaste at the title. "May I come in?"

He must be asleep. I turned the knob, peered inside.

The room was empty.

Chapter 5

PEDRO

It almost time, but Frad not quite ready. "Ain' even a holochip," I grumbled. "Jus' papah book."

Frad breathed hard, annoyed. "Gonna trayfo', Neut? I ain' got all nigh'."

I shrugged. "I already offa two cansa fo' fallin' apart book. Wan' mo', bring mo' book." If he had one. Dunno. Filmatleven.

"Got three, maybe four mo'."

I looked at teapot, decided couldn' warm my cuppa 'less I gave him some. Better I waited. "Silly Broadboy think he swind Pedro Telamon Chang, hah? If he got four book, he'd brung widim. He got jus' one."

"Four, tolya!" He glowered. "C'n bring lata."

"Hah." I trotted across shop, messed with box like I lookin' for trayfo. "Two cansa. One small veg, one big chicken, like I tolya."

His eyes flickered, and I knew I gottim. Before, I'd said two veg, one big, one little. Now he thought Chang be glitch.

"How much fo' otha papah?"

"Don' need no mo'." Hurt tongue to say it, but hadda, if I wanted to get 'em. "I'll trayfo the one you brung, look at others 'nother day."

"I c'n run get, they ain' so far—"

"Nah." I pulled out cansa, put on table. "Chang got five book already, why he nee' three mo'?"

"Four mo'." Now he committed. Good.

"Okay okay, three, four, no diff. Take cansa 'n gwan; Chang don' allow more'n one trayfo in shop atta time. Ya messin' wid Chang biz."

Frad grinned, showin' no teeth. Been in rumb. Allatime trannies fight each otha. Stupid tribes. Sad.

I managed to wait 'til he gone 'fore I picked up book. Stranger Inna Strange Lan'. Two hunner' year old. Mine. I clutched to chest like joeykit. Book go in backroom, Chang's room. Book not trayfo, anymore.

From back, a snicker.

I raised voice. "Stupid Midboy laughin' at Chang, hah?"

Pook poked out his head. "When Chang run outa cansa, he gonna eat papah?"

I growled, "Run outa cansa, eat Midboy."

He snickered again, pushing aside the curtain. "You funny, Changman." He thought about it as I headed towar' him with look in my eye. "Cool jets," he said quick. "*Mista* Chang."

Hadda be careful with Pookboy. He might be socio. Wasn' sure, but didn' think so.

He seemed to like me, mosta time. Wanted me take care him, but would he shiv me someday, like poor Rock beggin' for passby? Did Pook know diff, right an' wrong?

I went in backroom, to shelf. Put book under H, real gentle. Read later, when boy wouldn' interrupt.

Pook was stayin' my house for while.

The girl Mids called Bigsis sent him to trayfo boots for cansa. Joeykit wandered round, finally wen' back with seven cansa. She shout at him some. Pook don't got no control, mouthed her back, she told Karlo not enough cansa.

Karlo got pissoff again. Pook came knockin' at Chang house, needin' bed. I asked him if he tryin' to join Neut tribe stead of Mids, but he didn' think was funny.

What I spose to do? Send him back inna streets, he wouldn' make it to initiation. Upbringin', as Mids called it, where they cut Mid mark on chest.

After while Karlo would cool jets. He was like that, hoppin' mad, then forget.

Wasn't Chang's fault. How was joeyboy gonna learn not giveaway his trayfo, unless hard way? No good tellin' him, gotta show.

Anyway, boots weren't so good, hadda hole. Chang wasn' traytaman for joke; it his biz. And Pook coulda said no.

Pook shoved a book deeper on shelf. "What they say?"

"Say, a Midboy don' touch, or he fin' hisself on street fas'."

He grinned. I hated when he did that. Traytamen couldn't afford seniment.

"Ain' 'fraid a you, Mista Chang." He looked up. "Books say, 'Looka me? Coulda had two cansa steada me?'"

"Hah." I patted him on back. "They tellya 'bout worl'. Everyt'ing in books. Read, ya fin' out."

I waited, with hope.

It was like tray with Frad I just finished. Hadda ease him along, wait 'til he ready. If I tol' Pook the world of books open his eyes, let him see how insignificant was trannie life, he'd scare, wouldn't read. Prolly was best not to push. Tell Pook books ain't for him. Tell him keep away. Then maybe he'd want.

I warmed my cuppa tea, sat by Valdez perma, sipping. Wasn't easy bein' traytaman. Hadda weave my way 'tween tribes, takin' sides with none. An' always remember use right talk.

Trannietalk, for tribes. Natural; I trannie born. Don' use big words, keep tenses simple, like before I found firs' cob-webby books and sat to read by light from gaping hole in roof. Never make mistake talkin', or tribes'll hear an' think I got high pretenses. Won't trust.

Book talk for books. When author friend speaks, answer him same way. What you referring to, Ayn Rand, when you say selfish? What was so terrible about London, Charles Dickens? I'd tray it for Lower New York in a minute. How Chang would talk, he be Uppie.

An', Changtalk for inside Chang. Prolly closer to Uppie talk now, with alla books. But not quite. More easy in it than book talk.

Made head spin, sometimes, but used to it now.

Pook stirred. "Don' need nothin' in book. Wan' know, ask Karlo."

"Yah, ask Karlo. He know lot more'n Chang." Joeykit hopeless. Why I bother with him? Dunno.

In morning I got out wheelcart, made boy loadup permas in outer room. Eat Chang's food, gotta work. Fair, but he didn' like. Went sullen for while.

Hot summer, but I put on coat so have pockets for innifo.

"Whereya go, Mista Chang?"

"We, Pookboy. You be comealong."

He made face. "Naw. Stay."

Maybe lose him, but time to settle; he old enough now. I went to him, touched his face, gentle. "Lissenup, little Midboy." He waited. My throat went dry; longtime I lived alone. I liked havin' someone talk to. Even Midboy, who wouldn' look at book.

I said stern, "Wasn' me, asked Midboy come knockin' at Chang door. Boy still wanna stay, okay okay. Or he c'n ask Rocks fo' place to sleep."

Vein in his forehead throbbed.

Couldn' stop now. Too late. "Midboy almos' growed, gotta decide for hisself. Onna street, tell Chang go prong hisself. But in Chang's house, yes Mista Chang, I do whatchew say, I help. Midboy got choice."

Boy's eyes sliced through Chang like shiv.

I shrugged, like didn' matter. "Midboy think Chang's life be all sippin' cuppa? Trayfo be har' work. You help, or get los'."

He said shrill, "Don' need glitch ol' Neut! Keep ya cansa! I take care a self!" In rage, he kicked over table. Teapot and cups went flyin'. Steam rose from wet floor.

I didn' move.

"Lucky I don' dissya, Changman!" His face red, he clawed at locks. "Maybe will, nextime!" Got door open. Out. Slam.

I sighed, muttering to self as I cleaned up mess. Chance I hadda take, but sorry I lost.

Put table back in place. Midboy gonna be allri', I tol' self. He has shiv, he plenny rowd.

I washed cup, refilled pot. Water ran rust today, an' real low. Usetabe, have a problem, soonalate, govermen fix. Now they didn' care. More water for Uppies.

At last, I ready. Wheeled cart to door. Draped it with cloth coverup.

Bright day, hot and sunny, an' everyone knew Chang be Neut. Still, I opened door careful. A few people aroun', none too close.

Went out, locked three locks. Took chalk from pocket, drew eye on steel panel. Didn' mean nothin', but tribes weren' sure.

My shop on Thirty Five. Mid turf, now. Rock, usetabe. Rocks got pushout down to Thirty Three. Secon' time; 'fore that they was Americas an' Fifty Four in Rockcenta. I pushed cart to corner. Heavy.

"Watcha got, traytaman?" Ravan, a boss Mid, come alongside.

"Got enough sense to min' my own biz." My voice gruff. Ravan grinned. Everyone used to my talk.

He walked with me. "Any good trayfo?"

"Usual." Wondered what he want.

"Whatcha lookin' fo' special?"

"Don' make no diff. Bring it, Chang trayfo." I turned corner, started uptown. 'Nother block, would reach Broad turf.

Ravan asked, casual, "Chang got new water pipe?"

No, didn' have, but knew where to get. Not copper, like old, but heavy plastic snapons, like in towers. Careful, Pedro. I stopped, looked him over. "Whaffo Mids wan' water pipe, hah?"

Smile went from his mouth. "Fin' water main, maybe. Run to lair for new."

Heart wen' thump. Lotsa pipe, big trayfo. I'd make Mids find me jumpsuits 'n stuff I could tray uptown for cansa, coin, anything. Then tray that to other tribes . . .

Big tray.

"Pipe never been used cos' a lot," I said, cautious.

"How much?"

"Lot." I met his eye. "But I maybe c'n get. Firs', tell me how much. Then we have tea—coffee, I mean, 'n decide."

Ravan was stupe in trayfo. Bit right away. "Mids c'n pay if Chang don' tryta skin us." His look held warning.

I had him, for anything I wan'. I started thinkin', tray up, tray up more, back an' forth, maybe even to new roof fo' shop. Who know?

I hesitated.

Chang could tray lotta pipe. On other han', Mids be pissoff, if they pay for new pipe an still find they had prollem.

Like I told Midboy, growed man gotta decide for hisself.

I was trannie too.

I sighed, roof fadin' in my mind. My voice curt. "It ain' the pipes, Ravan."

He went cold. "Whatcha mean?"

I hoped he remember I be Neut. "I mean, Mids see water stoppin' in lair. Can't cook, can't drink, it be so muddy. Ya try changin' lair, but no good. Mids gotta find water quick."

His eyes dangerous. "Who tolya? Pookboy? I dissim!"

I talked quick, 'fore he blew. "Think a Mid c'n swind Pedro Telamon Chang, hah? I know. Alla lair, same t'ing. Ain' pipes."

"What it be, Neut?"

"Water. Govermen lettin' it go off. Ain' enough for trannies 'n Uppies both."

"Off?" He spat. "Now I know ya glitched. Water can't be off. Water is always, 'less pipe fill up wid goo."

"Time is new. Govermen don' care. Won' fix old pipe."

"Govermen neva go inna street." His voice all scorn.

I said, quiet, "Not for longtime. Did, once." Before Chang.

His look unsure. "Changman, what we gonna do?"

"Mids, all by self? Nothin'." I peered into face. Couldn' lose this chance; time runnin' out. "Maybe, wid' alla tribes, think of somethin'."

"Alla tribes? Think Broads gonna run wid Rocks? Mid with Unies? You glitch."

"Won' be easy, naw. No trus'. But if everyone losin' water, we c'n—"

"You glitch." He strode away.

Ah, Pedro. Who asked you to be charga savin' trannies? I rolled cart toward corner, where Broad tribesmen waited.

Neuts had it too easy, some ways. Free of tribe, free to live alone, do what they want. Read books no one else care 'bout. No upbringing, no scars.

Not a lotta trannies went Neut. Too alone for most. Those that did learned to stay clear of tribe feuds, keep mind on trayfo. But couldn' forget, bein' Neut was responsibility too. Others, they jus' Mids or Broads, Subs or Easters.

Us Neuts, we be the true trannies.

"Whoa, traytaman." Broad put out big hand.

I acted annoyed. "Ya wan' innifo? I ain' no dumbass Mid, askin' passby. I Neut."

He shrugged. "Don' matter. Broad turf, Neut or no."

Was worth a try. I dug can outa pocket.

"Thasall?"

"Neut shouldn't haveta pay innifo, nohow," I grumbled. "How else gonna get trayfo, hah? Broads come ta Chang store, wanna see empty?"

He scowled. "Might as well, Chang trayfo so high." I got ready ta move on, done with small talk. He say, "Two cansa, man."

I reared back, anger real now. "Since when two cansa fo' passby, hah? No Broad gonna swind—"

"One fo' each." He pointed to cart.

I looked. Pook was at handles, waitin' to push. I swallowed, wantin' to hold cart for steady. My tone went hard. "Gwan home, joeykit! Don' need no snotnose won' do what he tol'!"

Boy looked at sidewalk, like tryin' to read cracks. His voice small. "Please." He studied my face, added reluctant, "I do whatchew say, Mista Chang. I help."

"Fo' how long?"

He sighed. "Long I stay in Chang house."

I cuffed him, light, so no hurt. "Push, den. Think I got all day? Work to do!"

Chapter 6

PHILIP

Mom was waiting at the chem lab at three. I climbed into the front seat, glad she'd come herself. When she was busy she might ask Mr. Tenere to pick me up, or a guard. Or send a helicab.

"How was your lesson, hon?" She waited for an opening, pulled out into traffic.

"Fine." I watched her feet work the pedals. If anything happened to her, some sudden illness, I might have to drive her to a hospital. Unlikely, objectively speaking, but I liked to be prepared.

"Homework?"

"The usual." Mr. Bates had thrown me an entire chapter of college text, but if I concentrated, I could sail through it in an hour or two. I was fast. It was one of my problems.

I asked, "Are we going anywhere special?"

Mom squeezed my hand. "What would you like?"

That was another of my problems. Take me to the Jefferson Memorial, and I would read the documents in a few minutes, memorize the statue and want to be gone. At the Museum of Science, I could visualize better exhibits than they'd constructed, and it made me restless.

I said hopefully, "The National Gallery?" Rodin was onto something; his sculptures had a hidden message. Each time I studied them, I came closer to understanding. But I wasn't there yet.

"Oh, hon."

I pouted. Eleven visits weren't so many. I'd asked Mr. Skeer if Mom had attention deficit syndrome, but he said he doubted it.

"Maybe another day, P.T."

"Sure." I tried not to sound disconsolate.

We drove past the city center to the compound. To amuse myself, I kept tally of cars and trees.

We came to the gates.

Thirty-seven distinct species, a hundred four models. Did

that prove anything? I'd count again next week. The trees wouldn't change much, but I'd get a better average on the cars.

The guards recognized Mom, but didn't wave us through. They hadn't since the day she'd swarmed out of the car and shouted at them for five minutes straight. She was serious about Father's safety. And his privacy.

Jared wasn't home from school. I went to my room and flopped on the floor. Perhaps I should take up yoga; it was said to be calming. I did breathing exercises whenever I felt my nerves frazzle.

I wasn't supposed to know I was genius level, but one drawback was you figured those things out. I didn't want to trouble Fath by asking him how to handle it, because I once heard Mom tell Mr. Tenere that Father got upset easily.

On January 12, 2223, he and I were looking at holos. I was five then, sitting in his lap, and was used to calling him Daddy, even though he was still SecGen.

We studied the solemn picture of Grandfather, who was dead. Daddy said his father was a good man and had loved him, but didn't know how to express affection. I asked what Daddy called him. He said, Father. I asked if he'd like me to call him that.

If I wanted to, he said.

It took me a week to get my mind straightened so I didn't forget and call him Daddy. He was Father now, Fath for short. These days I didn't sit on his lap much.

The closest adolescent in my daily life was Jared Tenere. He was a year and eight months past puberty. He was much bigger than I. I had to be careful not to hurt him.

Jared thought I didn't know he went out at night. Hadn't he heard of infrared scopes? I wouldn't mention it, or he'd think I was spying, which I was, but just from my bedroom. My window faced his bungalow. With my lights out, he'd need an infrared himself to spot me.

Jared tried so hard to break Mr. Tenere's passwords. Often he succeeded; I had to admit he had a knack. But he was so good with puters that failure maddened him and made him impossible to live with. Unless I was to avoid him entirely, I had to drop him a hint now and then, but I had to take care not to let him realize. Crashing Mr. Tenere's icewall took me fifteen minutes. There was nothing in his puter worth Jared's trouble.

I think Jared felt a need to dominate me. One day I called up the Library of Congress and downloaded a gigameg on adolescent sexuality, to learn why. Tentatively, I concluded that he was attracted to me but didn't know it, and repressed it into hurting me. I didn't really mind; it was stuff like making me eat grass, and he didn't get in that mood often. I just disconnected my mind until he was done. Irrational numbers helped.

I decided that if Jared asked, I wouldn't let him do sex things with me. I was saving myself, in case I wanted to marry. Girls were becoming interesting, in an abstract way. I was also starting to be able to get a hard-on, if I tried. I was too young to make babies, so I didn't worry about it. To see his reaction, I asked Jared about his sex habits, but he got all red and changed the subject. I gather he found adolescence confusing. I hoped I wouldn't.

A knock. "Want a snack?"

I jumped up as Mom came in. "Sure."

"Join me in the kitchen." Her smile made me warm all over.

"Yes, ma'am." Father said I had to be respectful, so I was. It didn't bother me, like it did Jared. It was just words, and getting up when adults came in the room. Easy stuff.

I had to calm myself, thinking about discipline. Mr. Skeer said my emotions were fragile, and there was a lot I didn't yet understand. It didn't take a psych to see that. When I got agitated Father said I was revving too hard.

The last time Father spanked me was two years ago. I'd decided not to do my math homework three days in a row. I was percolating, but Father didn't realize that. He sat me down in his study, gave me a lecture on responsibilities.

When he was done I said, "Lectures don't help children understand adult rationales. We tune them out."

"You tuned me out, just now?"

"Of course." How could he not understand? "We need direction, not debate." I was hoping he'd order me to my room, to do my math. It was what I felt I needed. I would refuse, and then the issue would be clear.

"Very well." He took my arm. "I'll try a more direct approach." He thrust me across his lap.

I knew he wasn't going to hurt me, and he didn't. But what I couldn't anticipate was that each slap would proclaim, I don't like you, *I don't like you, I DON'T LIKE YOU!* I wailed and kicked in escalating desperation under the sting of his disapproval.

When he was done I lay on the carpet, sobbing uncontrollably. He waited a moment for me to stop, picked me up when I didn't. I wrapped my arms around his neck, buried my face in his shoulder, but not before I glimpsed the worry in his eyes.

"P.T.?"

I held tight, let him calm me.

He asked, "What was it I did?" He meant, what did it mean to me.

I told him.

Later, when he put me to bed, he sat close to the sheets, spoke soberly. "Philip, listen carefully." I concentrated. "With you, force isn't the answer, so I won't use it. Instead, I'll tell you a truth. I'm the father. I'm in charge. You'll do as I say from now on. Whatever strange and wonderful thoughts evolve on in that little head of yours, be aware that you're not ready to defy me, and I won't let you do it."

His hand crept across the blanket, squeezed my shoulder with welcome reassurance. "P.T., you heard the wrong message, in my study. I love you, and like you. I always will. You're my son."

I smothered a sob. My hand caught his.

"Good night, son."

"Good night, sir."

He left.

I'm not his firstborn. My brother Nate died years before I was born. The fish got him. Father doesn't mention him often. I'm named after a wonderful hero who served with Father in the fleet. I wish I'd known him. Father says I should be proud to carry his name.

I hope I grow up like you, Philip Tyre.

Jared bit at his thumbnail. "Prong yourself," he told me again.

I gave up. "I'll be in the house if you change your mind." Unless he was willing to roam the puter nets with me, I'd have to finish my homework before dinner, out of sheer boredom.

"Prong yourself." He lay across the bed, his eyes half closed.

Obsessive repetitive behavior is a disorder. Mentally, I summoned the data I'd downloaded from the Library of Congress. "Sometimes anger is misdirected at members of the peer group instead of—"

"Oh, Christ." He buried his head under the pillow.

I'd done my best. On the way out I met Mr. Tenere. He seemed preoccupied.

"Hi, P.T." He gave me a friendly pat.

"Afternoon, sir." I stood aside to let him pass, but instead of going into the house, he stopped, studied my face.

"Did I do something, sir?"

"Huh? Oh, not you." He hesitated. "Come with me." He led me away from the cottage. "P.T., do you know what's wrong with Jared?"

I wasn't sure how to answer. Many things were wrong with Jared. Did he mean generally?

As if reading my mind, he said, "Is something bothering him more than usual?"

"Yes, sir."

His relief was evident. "What?"

"I have no idea."

"Philip!"

I hadn't meant to make him angry. I replayed the conversation, thought I saw where we'd gone wrong. "Something's obviously on his mind. He won't talk to me, except to tell me to prong myself. He seems obsessed with the idea. I don't think that's what's bothering him, though."

I didn't think I'd said anything funny, but Mr. Tenere smiled. "Keep your ears open. Let me know if you figure it out. I'd like to help him."

I liked the idea of being a co-conspirator. "Yes, sir. What has he told you?"

"Hardly a word, but he's slamming a lot of doors and he skipped five classes this week."

I caught my breath. Jared was a throwback to the Rebellious Ages of the twentieth. Today, no self-respecting school would put up with that behavior. If Jared were expelled, his Dad would have his hands full trying to place him elsewhere.

I told him I'd do my best, and ran back to the house.

Chapter 7

JARED

Dad had been giving me strange looks ever since Uncle Robbie left. At first I thought he discovered I was skipping school, but after a while I stopped worrying.

Most of Dad's attention was on a series of meetings he was arranging for his lord and master, the Old Man. Politicians set their helis down in the courtyard; Seafort emerged from the house to escort the old frazzes into his study. They all wanted the ex-SecGen on their side, though he'd resigned in disgrace 'cause he couldn't keep his own joeys from robbing the till.

I avoided the lot of them, making sure I was just civil enough not to attract notice.

At night, I took my revenge.

The main house had been part of an old Virginia estate. White columns, ivy. Visitors stayed in the upstairs bedrooms on the east side. A second-story veranda crossed the rear of the mansion, over the Old Man's office and study.

The guest bedrooms had fancy doors with diamond shape panels; you could throw them open to sit on the portico overlooking the compound, enjoying the breeze. Guests did that in the fall, but in summer, people stayed inside with the air turned high.

Thanks to my friendship with P.T. I had the run of the main house. So, from time to time I'd wander into empty guest bedrooms and set the curtains open just a crack.

After dark, when the house quieted, I would shinny up the pipe and climb over the rail onto the portico. I'd walk on tiptoe, in case the Old Man was working late in his office. I didn't bother with a fancy pickup. Just an old-fashioned mini laser-mike aimed at the glass.

Once I got to watch Senator Reevis pronging his admin aide. Her nails scratched his back, her voice was hoarse as he sawed away at her. Enough to make you puke.

The next night I had my holocamera ready, but they didn't do it again. Just my luck. One call, and I'd have had a dozen mediamen waving Unibucks to get me out of this place.

That'd show Dad, with his frazzing, "Make dinner tonight; you have nothing better to do." Did he think I'd be his trannie for a lousy ten Unibucks a week?

Too bad the veranda didn't run past P.T.'s room. I'd have loved to see what he did in bed at night. The way he sidled up to me sometimes, it's like he was asking for it. I should have taught him a lesson.

Today Old Richard Boland flew in for dinner with Uncle Rob, another one I could do without. The nerve of Mister Assemblyman Boland, bursting into my room like he owned it. Luckily, I was still at my puter. If I'd already climbed out the window . . .

Tonight, it would just be Senator Boland and Robbie, a pair of gasbags, but it was worth a try. I might pick up something useful. Late in the evening I circled the house. The first floor was dark except for the Old Man's study. Upstairs, lights shone in both guest rooms.

I tried the Senator's bedroom first but heard nothing. I crossed the veranda, detoured past the deck chairs, pressed my scope to the glass.

Voices. I peered through the opening I'd left in the curtains.

Old Richard Boland sat in an easy chair, swirling a drink. He'd thrown his coat on the bed, unlaced his shoes. Uncle Rob was in the chair opposite.

" . . . warned you not to push him," the son was saying. "He hates that."

The Senator made a face. "We could use his help."

"You've narrowed the gap to, what, five votes? It's not worth antagonizing—"

"Rob, the tower people *need* the water that's pouring through those broken mains. They can't wait any longer now the Delaware's lost to the New England reclamation—"

"Dad, I know—"

"As a stopgap we're diverting more from the old system, but Franjee's told everyone we'll get them more. They're primed to jump on our bandwagon, and if we don't get in front and lead, we'll lose them. Reconstruction's the way to frame the issue, but the damn bill has to clear the Senate!"

"We'll pick up our extra votes without the Captain." Robbie sounded confident.

"You think so?" The Senator studied his drink. "Rob, I don't have a good feeling about this. Bad enough if he keeps quiet. What if he comes out against us?"

"The Captain wouldn't do that. You've been friends for twenty-five years."

I grinned. The Old Man would do any damn thing he wanted. He always had.

Old Boland shook his head, agreeing with me. "Don't you know him, Rob? If he decides it's a moral issue, friendships mean nothing. Take the North American hulls question, when he was SecGen. He—"

"That was years ago, and his Navy was involved. Don't tell me you still hold a grudge!"

"Eh? Don't be silly. He's like a force of nature; he does what he must. I might as well resent a hurricane."

For a few moments they were quiet. I shifted, easing a knot in my leg. If all I'd hear tonight was this blather—

Old Boland spoke abruptly. "Son, this is . . . " He hesitated, began again. "I know how much you think of him."

The Assemblyman snorted. "I doubt it."

"I do. He was a sort of God to you when you were a boy."

"Sort of?" Uncle Rob waved his hand helplessly. "Dad, when he took me on *Trafalgar* to get at the fish, I was . . . " A long silence. " . . . ready to die for him. I was almost sorry I hadn't."

I rubbed my aching leg. What goofjuice. Nothing's worth dying for. I stood, backed away from the door. My leg would cramp if I didn't—

I blundered into the deck chair, fell with a thud.

Christ damn it! I rolled to my feet. Had anyone heard me? I checked the curtain; the two men hadn't moved. I ran to the rail, stood poised to swarm down the drainpipe if a door opened.

Nothing. I waited a moment longer, decided it was safe to stay. I carefully set the deck chair out of the way. Again I focused the mike.

"Rob, let me handle this one. I won't make you take sides."

"What's that supposed to mean?"

Senator Boland hesitated. "Understand, we've waited years for our chance. It won't come again. With the tower interests supporting us we'll sweep the party caucuses next spring, and I'll have a full year to gear up for the general election."

A SecGen was elected by popular vote every six years, but could be tossed out of office earlier by a vote of no-confidence, as they'd done to the Old Man. I controlled my impatience, hoping to hear something worth my trouble.

"Rob, if your Captain gets in our way, I can't let him stop us. We . . . I've got to discount his influence."

Robert Boland stared at the unlit fireplace, his tone somber. "How?"

"You know how it's done. Plant stories in the holos reminding folks how moody he gets. How he dropped from public affairs to devote himself to his family. How he's aged."

"Dad, I—"

"How his closest aides worry privately about his emotional health. We'd have to feed rumors—"

"Dad!"

The old Senator was silent. Then he shrugged. "I always said politics was a dirty game."

Uncle Rob muttered, "He's our friend, and I don't want him savaged. Let me have another try in the morning."

"Fine. I truly don't want to destroy him. If you can't bring him aboard, get a promise that he'll stand aside."

"I'll see what Adam says."

I snorted. Dad's advice was glitched; it was an endless loop. Do your homework, make something of yourself, do your home—

Robbie was getting up. "Night, Dad."

Time to go, before one of them stepped out for a breath of air. Not as good as old Reevis and his aide, but a few juicy tidbits.

I stuffed the mike in my pocket, scampered to the rail. Would the Bolands pay me to keep quiet? Might be worth a try. Let them think I'd bugged their bedroom. I leaned across to the drainpipe, found my footing on the brick facing of the wall.

Better yet, I could do it anonymously, through the puter. They'd never know who'd caught them. It was time I made my move, and the Bolands were a good place to start.

On the other hand, the Old Man was our meal ticket. What

if I alerted him to what the Bolands planned? I reached down with my foot, found the brick foothold. Another step, to the brace. One more. Then, the four-foot jump, down to the dark behind the bushes. I turned.

A hand shot out of the dark, clamped my shoulder. "Hold it."

I screeched, backpedaling into the wall. My heart slammed as if it would burst through my chest.

The Old Man yanked me into the light. I stood trembling, waiting for the rush of fear to subside.

"What's that?" He pulled the lasermike from my bulging pocket.

My voice wouldn't come. I clawed at his restraining hand.

"You spy on my guests?" His voice held an edge I'd never heard. "In *my* house?"

I couldn't free myself from his iron grip.

He propelled me toward his office. "Inside, boy."

"I didn't mean—" I dug in, resisting.

"Move!" The word cracked like a whip. Like an automaton, I tottered into his office. He pulled out a chair, deposited me in it, crossed to his end of the desk.

"Mr. Seafort—I—"

"Shut your mouth."

I did. I wasn't sure why.

He keyed his caller. A pause. "Adam? Get to my office, flank."

I hunched in the chair, willing my heart to slow. My chest ached. For an endless minute we sat in silence.

Footsteps, pounding. The door flung open. "Sir, are you all ri—" Dad's eyes widened as he saw me.

"I caught your boy on the portico, spying on Rob and Richard. He had this." The Old Man tossed my mike onto his desk.

Dad picked it up, puzzled at it as if he couldn't fathom its purpose. "Lord God in heaven." He flayed me with a look of contempt, swung back to the Old Man. "I'm terribly sorry. I don't know what to—We'll go, of course. My God, how could you, Jared! Sir, we can be packed as soon as—"

"Adam." The Old Man sounded tired. "Don't be ridiculous; you're not leaving. But we can't have Jared skulking outside our windows. I called you because I've no right to discipline him myself, though I had a mind to. Spying on a guest is despicable."

I couldn't stand their talking like I weren't present. "Wait a minute. All I did was—"

Dad crossed the room in three strides. He hauled me out of my chair, bunched my shirt with both fists. I expected him to shout, but his voice was strangely quiet. "Shut up, Jared."

"I—"

He shook me like a puppy. Astonished, I fell silent. This wasn't at all like Dad.

"Adam, we ought to tell—"

"Wait a moment, sir." Dad stared through my eyes, into the back of my skull. "You." A shake, that rattled my teeth. "To your room! Don't even dream of disobeying me!" He let me loose.

I smoothed my shirt, backed toward the door. "Hey, don't jump your jets over—"

Dad roared, "Yes, SIR! Say it *RIGHT NOW!*" He took a step closer.

It was horrid, with the Old Man watching, but Dad seemed to have lost his mind. *"Yes, sir!"*

I fled to my room.

Chapter 8

POOK

I sit aroun' ol' Changman's shop, gettin' bore. Wanna go back ta lair, but can' jus' yet. Bigsis say she tell me when Karlo stop bein' pissoff. Think she feel bad, gettin' me kicked out. Meantime, I gotta do like Changman tell. Hate havin' allatime say yes, Mista Chang, but 'less I decide ta dissim, I gotta.

Ain' so bad 'xcept at nigh', when he say turn off Valdez perma an' sleep. Nigh' be time ta prowl, but he warn if I go out, he no lemme in again.

Otha times, he make me bring stuff upstair, or carry down. Say he gettin' too ol' fo' lift. I grit teeth, say, yes Mista Chang, an' carry. Upstair, he got lotsa trayfo I neva seen befo'. Boxes a cansa, but otha stuff too. Wires an' ol' puters 'n nice plasticmold chairs all cover up wid tarp.

Coupla time, I tryta see if he inerest shaggin' me. Allatime he tellin' me wash befo' bed, so when he come inna room I peel off alla threads an' stan' bareass, preten' wash, see if he look.

He no interes. Stupid ol' man.

Dis nigh', I walk aroun' lookin' at stuff while he sit wid book in fronta perma ligh'. He growl, Pook gotta piss or somethin'? No, I tellim, an' he say siddown an' fin' somethin' ta do steada botherin' joey jus' wanna read in peace.

I yes Mista Chang, an' siddown in corna wonderin' what I c'n take back ta lair fo' innifo, so Karlo stop be pissoff. All Chang's fault, was him skinned me on boots Bigsis give me ta trayfo.

Too quiet; I be bore. My min' go empty, an' I think 'bout few day back when I pushin' cart while Changman go trayfo.

Ol'man and me, we brung cart pas' Broad turf, to othaside. I don' like places I neva been. "Where we goin'?"

Chang shrug, but his eyes look round allatime, for safe. "Be 'nother Mid lair, den square."

"Be Mids othaside Broads?"

"Yah." He point to corner.

I walk proud. "Won' need innifo for me, Mista Chang. Not fo' Mids."

He chuckle. "We see."

Three Mid joeys come out, stop us. It daytime, so they ain' come on fo' rumb. "Whatchew wan'?"

Chang say, "Passby."

"Innifo?"

Chang pull out cansa. I say, "Not fo' me. I be Mid Three Five."

Mid joey turn, looka me sharp. Move like cat. Befo' I stop, he grab my shirt, pullup high.

"Leggo!"

"You no Mid." He push, an' I fall in street.

I jump up mad. "So I ain' had upbringin'! I Mid as you!"

He turn his back, say ta Chang, "Got innifo fo' joeykit?"

My hand feel for shiv, but Changman's eyes lock on mine. No, they warn, so I don'. Three Mids a lot ta takedown, anyhow.

"Yah," he grumble, pull out 'notha can. His coat gotta be all pockets, hide so much innifo.

We go on. I try ta tell Chang he shouldn't a paid, an' he cuff me easy, like pay no 'tention. I wan' tell him, keep ya hands ta yaself, but I figga better not. He be mean ol' man; maybe change min' 'bout lettin' me sleep in shop.

Afta Mid turf, we fin' open place. In middle be a tall build, all broke. "Whazzis?"

He start walkin' ta big hole in groun'. No choice; I follow wid cart. I don' wan' be lef' alone inna bad place.

He reach stair; I stop. "I ain' goin' down."

"All ri'." He push cart ta wall, leave it. "Wai' here, Pook, look afta cart. I be back."

"Where ya goin'?" My voice be alarm.

"Jus' wait." He start down.

I watch 'im go, six, seven step, inna dark. "Mista Chang?" I look roun'. Broke builds all quiet. Prolly be eyes in windows, wonnerin' Pookboy taste good.

Pook don' got upbringin', but he ain' dumbass. "Wait fo' me!" Run down stair, catch up wid Changman. Dark place. His hand be on rail. I take it, hol' onta, tight case he fall or somethin'.

Chang make soun'; I look his face, suspicious, maybe he laugh. Don' see it.

Ol' man slap at my han', fussin' 'til I leggo. Still goin' down stair, he put han' in pocket, take out, put to mouth. He whistle, two time. Soun' real loud inna hole, I put hans to ear. He wait.

"Watchadoon?" I tug at arm, he pat my head, absent min', blow whistle two time mo', put back in pocket, wait real patient.

We in lotta dark, can' see. "Changman, why we—"

"All ri', we here!" Close behin'.

I yelp.

Hans grab. I twis' free, stumble back inta Chang. His arm go roun my shoulder, hol' me. I wan' pull out shiv, but don' do it. Legs all tremble.

"Who ya brung, traytaman?"

"My helpa."

"Tribe?"

"Trannie. Neut. Whassit matta?" Chang soun' tired. I worry he pick nowtime ta die, leave me wid dark voices.

"Whass name?"

Gotta be proud. "Pook," I say, but it comeout squeak. Feel face go red inna dark.

Chang say, "I gotta cart wid trayfo, up."

"Bring inna Sub, traytaman."

Ol' man gimme nudge, like, go get, Pookboy. Ri'. Noway. He sigh. "Subs help?"

"Innifo?"

"Cansa. One."

A snicker. " 'Nuf, 'cause we knowya. Chaco, Kard, go get!" Feet scampa, up.

A click, an' ligh' come. Flashligh', wid Valdez perma. I hang onta Chang.

Dark was betta.

We be in tunnel place, real wide. Six trannie be near, lotsa otha eyes behin', watchin'.

They threads all glitch. Too lotta colors. Hair too long; joey could grab it inna rumb. Hair tie with bands. Some got chains roun' neck. Lotsa earring.

I looka Chang. "Wha' tribe?"

Han' squeeze my mouth, turn it sharp, make me look. "Talka me, joeykit. Halber, be I. Tribe be mine."

He big; I look up. Funny bands on his arm, threads way too color, more'n resta joes. Pook try ta be proud. "Wha' tribe," I say again.

Halber answer, "We be Sub."

I 'fraida dat.

They take us deep inna tunnel. Afta while, don' need perma, cause ligh' hangin' on string high up. Lotsa joeys. Chairs, some broke, an' tables. Stewpot. Sub lair, I guess.

Chang put me sit inna corna 'gainst wall, an' tell me wait while he talk.

"Noway, not widout ya!"

His eye go up. "Yes, Mista Chang, I do whatchew say. Forget so fas'?"

"But noway I—"

"Pook."

He say real sof', but I go a little scare. Dunno why. "I do whatchew say, Mista Chang!"

He pat me. "Chaco watchin' ya for safe. I be ri' ovadere, where silly Midboy c'n see me. Need ta fin' out what Subs wan'. Filmatleven."

I curl up, preten' buncha Sub joes ain' starin'. See Changman in corna eye. He sit in ol' chair, real wood one; I wunner why Sub don' burn it for cook. Halber Sub sit widim.

If real quiet, I c'n hear some a talk.

"How many c'n ya get?"

Changman shrug. "Brung twenny. How many Subs wan'?"

"Dunno." Halber look away. "All ya c'n get."

Chang lean forward, pat Halber knee like big Sub be scare joeykit. "Okay ta tell, I ain' gonna skinya. How many permas ya need?" I tense, figga Sub 'bout ta smash Chang fo' put han' on leg.

Halber voice go low; I can' hear all. " . . . diff it make? Tolya we wan'. Yo' jus' . . . "

Chang shake his head. "Subs can' trus' ol' Chang, okay okay, fin' 'notha traytaman. Mids an' Broads bring enough trayfo so Chang c'n eat." He stan'. Now I sure da ol' man be glitch. Hope I don' get diss widim. "Loadup cart," he say. "We goin' home."

"Don' go pissoff," Halber grumble, crossin' legs an' uncross like nervous. He beck Chang siddown. "Don' wan' otha tribes fin' out."

Chang sit, don' say nothin'.

"Two hunner'," Halber say, real low. He whisper somethin' else.

Chang don' look suprise. He nod. I wunner, where he gonna fin' couple hunner permas? I been ova shop; he don' got.

"Neva min' jumpsuits," he say. He stop, consider. "Okay okay, a few jumpsuits. But Chang mos'ly trayfo help instead."

Halber roll his eyes. "Still same ol' idea? Already tolya, won' work, Changman."

Chang look sad. "Gotta try. Water goin'."

"Too late. Our way bes'. Govermen won' know whatta do, afta—" he look roun', drop voice.

Han' shake me. I jump. Joeygirl be real close, grinnin'. "Tribe?" She keep voice low, so not bother growed Subs.

"G'way!" I pushback her han'; don' wan' be touch by Sub. My motha use Subs for scaretale, longtime back.

"Wha' tribe, joey?" Her red jumpsuit not hardly tore. Yellow ban' round' head.

I thinkin', middle a chest be ri' place fo' shiv if she come any closa. But she won' go 'way 'less I tell. "Mid Three Five." I make voice proud.

"Dunno no Three Five," she say. Her face go frown. "Mids Four One, allasame?"

"Naw!" Three Five lair bes' in worl'. Stupe Sub.

"I be Allie." She hol' up han', like showin' me fingas. Dunno wha' she wan'. "Who be Midboy?"

I wan' lissen ta Chang, so don' ansa.

Afta a minute, her han' come down. "Asshole Midboy," she say scorny. "Can' rememba name. Glitch." She turn, call ta otha joey. "Looka glitchy Midboy! Don' got name!"

I go anger, say, "Outaheah, bitchgirl, befo' Pook go pissoff."

"Yah, ri'. Think us gonna—"

A clap. Growed Sub standin' close. Scrawny, long hair wid curl. He look at Halber, back ta us, put finger ta lip. Allie nod, sit back. " 'Kay, Chaco," she say quiet.

Otha joeyboy wait 'til Chaco go 'way. He lean close ta whispa. "Pook? Dat be name?"

"Yah." Sorry I let slip.

"Talk shush. Chaco cool, don' pissim off." He hol' up han' five fingers, close. "Krand."

I looka han'. No ring. Wha' he showin' me?

Allie whispa, "Frazzin' Mids."

I go hot. "Why ya comedown on Pook, huh? Din' do nothin'!"

"Midboy think he too good ta touch wid Sub!"

I swallow. Din' know. Put up han', real careful, case maybe a swind.

Allie put hand next, touch palm an' fingas. "Cool meet."

She wait, poke me in rib. "Say cool!"

"Cool meet," I mumble, feelin' glitch.

Krand put up hand. We touch. "Cool."

He be small, maybe 'leven. But Allie's tits be growed. I look wid admire.

Once, Bigsis lemme do it her, fo' try. I held onta tits all while, an' she laugh. I din' like laugh, but glad she lemme, so din' say nothin'. Gotta know how, now I growed.

I turn sideway, an' quick think a somethin' else, 'less Allie see fronta my pants.

Chang still talkin' ta Halber.

She whisper, "Why ya wid traytaman?"

"Help wid cart." Less'n she think I be jus' joeykit, I add, "He give me lotsa innifo, he say, please, Pook, Chang can' do it hisself."

Her turn ta look admire. "Lessee innifo."

"I, um . . . It's inna lair," I say jus' in time. "Think Pookboy bring stuff down ta Sub, maybe lose?"

She look awe.

Krand say, all scorny, "He swind ya, Allie."

She bite her lip, lookin' at Krand, at me. "Swind?"

"Fo' sure. Looka him." He point me. "Shirt tore, full a dirt. No ring, no chain. Look like he collec' lotsa innifo? Whatcha think, Allie?"

I think Krand look good wid second mouth gapin' unnerneath.

Hand fall on shoulder. Changman. "Time ta go, joey."

I real glad ta see; it mean I don' have ta ansa Krand. "Yes, Mista Chang." I get up, all dignify. "We be go."

Allie get up widme. "C'mon, Krand. Les' goalong ta stair."

Chang an' Halber walk firs'. 'Fore we get ta dark place, Allie poke my arm. "Good ta meetcha," she say.

I go proud.

Chapter 9

ROBERT

At breakfast, I refilled my juice. "When will he decide?"

Adam Tenere tore his gaze from the sunlit, close-cropped lawn. "Perhaps—the Commandant isn't . . . you might—I don't know." He rubbed his eyes.

I pursed my lips, unsure how hard to press.

Adam's breakfast lay untouched. He poured himself a second cup of coffee. "Sorry. I didn't get much sleep, Robbie."

I said nothing. He had power to transport me back to my youth with but a single word. Robbie.

"Aah." Adam waved away his distraction. "I gather you need a commitment?"

I nodded.

"At heart, he's no politician," said Adam.

He certainly wasn't, not in Dad's sense. Where Dad thrived in the social interchange of politics, the Captain was an intensely personal, private man. My father loved finding common ground among parties preoccupied with their self-interest. Captain Seafort searched for moral truth and viewed anything less as failure. Dad was genuinely liked by politicians of both parties. The Captain was respected, and in some circles, revered. That was all.

When at last I looked up, he said, "Long ago, when we were midship—when you were a cadet. Remember the Senators' inspection visit?"

I had to grin. "No, but Dad told me often enough."

"We middies figured the Commandant had lost his mind. He hated letting a gaggle of politicians overrun Farside. So he threw them all in barracks like a bunch of plebes, regardless of the political fallout. Some of them were mad as hell."

"Dad said he had to stroke a lot of feathers that week."

"Mr. Keene had us doing what we could to soothe them, lest they call for Marines to storm the base." Adam's smile faded. "You see, the Commandant doesn't understand trade-offs and alliances. The more you push, the more he gets his back up. And Rob, he feels you're pushing."

I knew to take Adam's warning seriously.

After defeating the savage alien attack on home system, Nick Seafort had fled to a Neo-Benedictine monastery, lost in the darkness of his soul.

Ten years had passed.

Perhaps he'd be there still, if not for a visit from Eddie Boss, the transpop seaman who'd been his valet. Eddie had sought his help to protest the Territorial Party's renewal scheme for the cities.

The Captain sent them away with sharp words, but within a month, he'd emerged to bear the relentless glare of the holo-cameras. He'd proclaimed his candidacy for the Senate, denouncing in the harshest terms SecGen Anjour's cleanup of the slums surrounding the U.N. compound.

Thanks to Seafort's stand, the Territorials were forced to withdraw U.N.A.F. troops from the streets. Trannie life resumed as it had been; that is, in filth, squalor and misery. Seafort's term for it was "independence."

No matter. The Captain had ridden the issue to a Senate seat for Northern England. Dad insisted the issue had ridden Seafort, but the effect was the same.

For a while, the Captain had flouted political rules with impunity, setting an example of harsh truthfulness and unyielding honesty. A doting electorate propelled him into the Secretariat, and with him, our Supranationalist party took power.

Once in office, Seafort's refusal to be pushed turned out to be more a nuisance than a virtue. Time and again, his intransigence unraveled a bargain Dad had labored to forge.

Perhaps, in the Port of London scandal, if Dad and his colleagues had been less forceful in urging the Captain to hedge his acceptance of blame, the SecGen would have heeded their advice and their administration wouldn't have collapsed.

I sighed. Seafort's career was no longer of concern. Dad's was.

"I'll see what I can do." Adam's gaze fell again to his half-empty cup. "Rob . . ."

"Yes, sir?"

"Oh, for God's sake, stop. You're an Assemblyman, not a cadet. And I'm just a retired lieutenant."

"It's a mark of respect, Adam, and I'm comfortable with it."

His smile softened the lines around his eyes. "Now you sound like P.T."

"I'll take that as a compliment. He's a good boy."

"Yes." But Adam's visage darkened, as if a cloud had passed across the sun. A moment's silence, then, "Did you discuss anything important with your father last night?"

What an odd question. "Why do you ask?"

Adam colored. "Forgive me, that was rude. And it's not my place to . . ." He stood, abruptly. "Lord Christ, I can't just sit here and pretend . . ." He turned away.

I crossed to his side. "What's wrong, sir?"

For a moment I thought he was about to put me in my place, like a middy would an obnoxious cadet. Then he sagged. "It's Jared. I don't know what to do. I'm no good as a father."

My mouth tightened. "What's he done?"

"I'm not free to tell you." He thrust his hands in his pockets, studied the elegant facade of Seafort's house. "Anyway, it's just one more incident. God, I wish Elena was here."

"He's at a rough age."

"That's an excuse I won't use any longer." His tone was bitter. "I've made a mess of things, Rob. I'm . . . ashamed."

My hand drifted to his shoulder, rested there a moment before dropping. I owed him that, from years before. "You still have time."

"He's past fifteen."

I said, "When I went off to Academy, I expected an easy time of it, because of Dad. From the start, the Captain was so . . . cold, I guess. It shocked me. My connections meant nothing to him. When he called me to his office and whaled me, it was a terrible shock."

"I know." How could he not? He'd helped me through it.

"It helped me grow up, Adam."

He met my eye, nodded. After a while he turned his face. "I can't, Rob. I just . . . can't." His tone was husky.

I felt miserably inadequate. "Lord God knows I'm no expert, but you might be stricter. Even if you won't strike him."

A brief grin. "I was, last night. I think I startled him."

"Good."

"But today I relapsed, and did nothing. It's hard to change."

"You'll work it out." How fatuous could I get? I glanced surreptitiously at my watch. To my annoyance, Adam noticed.

He stood immediately. "I'll walk you to your heli."

"Thanks." Dad had left before breakfast, for a fund-raiser at the Sheraton Skytel.

"Robbie . . . " He sounded hesitant. "Why is it you never married?"

My tone was light. "I haven't *yet*. The time will come." If someday I overcome the fear of sharing my life and intimate thoughts with another. One who might judge me and disapprove.

I smiled. "Besides, all the good ones are taken." Arlene Sanders, for example. Arlene Seafort, these thirteen years.

Arlene Sanders had fought in the alien war, both in *Wellington* and after, on U.N.S. *Brentley* at Caltech Planet. Those who'd known her said she'd been a tough, no-nonsense officer. Once, in the worst of the anti-Naval riots after the war, she'd led a detail guarding the new Naval wing on Earthport Station, and was rumored to have killed several marauders by her own hand.

I'd never known her during our days in the Naval Service. But earlier, as a cadet in Academy, she'd been Captain Seafort's bunkie.

Years later, when the Captain emerged from his monastery, solitary and brooding, he'd entered politics without a helpmeet.

His first wife had died aboard ship; his second, Annie Wells, divorced him during his long seclusion at Lancaster.

At receptions and diplomatic gatherings he would stand alone, nursing the one drink he allowed himself of an evening, enduring the sycophants who surrounded him. His discomfort was so apparent my heart went out to him. When his eye caught mine his expression would lighten, and the corners of his mouth would twitch as if to say, "Duty."

I don't know at what event he met Arlene. Shortly after, she became a fixture at his side, interposing herself between him and the worst of his tormentors.

Ever since, she'd protected him with fierce vigilance. I

suspected it was more her influence than the Captain's that kept P.T. at heel, though to tell the truth, the boy didn't seem to mind the discipline. Though I was fond of him, I understood him not a bit. He was phenomenally intelligent, and as unnervingly forthright as his father.

I blinked away my reverie as Adam and I crossed the lawn to the house. I picked up my bag. At the helipad I took his arm. "Dad's really anxious about the Cities Redevelopment bill. We need to know what the Captain says as soon as possible." Before Dad burns his bridges and destroys an old friend.

"I'll mention it again. Let me pick my time."

"Hurry," I said. I boarded.

Chapter 10

PEDRO

Pookboy came, Pookboy went. Maybe he made up wid Karlo, maybe didn't. Every day or so he came by. I asked if he be back wid Mids, but he only shrugged. Maybe foun' himself 'nother place to stay, but that wouldn' be Mid way. They be lair folk.

I took long trip uptown, to get rest of permas that Halber Boss Sub asked for. I worried 'bout what he'd do after he had enough, but figured it was worse not to give.

Nex' day I loaded cart, started haulin' permas to Sub. Pookboy came runnin', to ask if I wanted help. Silly Midboy, tryta swind Pedro Telamon Chang. Naw, I said, do fine myself. He ended helpin' for free, 'steada for trayfo. Dunno why he wanted to comealong, but was in his eyes; he couldn' hide it yet. He never make a traytaman. After, I gave him cansa anyway, jus' because.

Leas' I could read in peace an' quiet, with no Pookboy prowlin' shop like nervous cat. Didn' know whassa matta that joeykit; he couldn' sit still a min. I read through three books Frad brought back to trayfo. Dunno why Lenin try to write philosophy; his politics was bad enough. A waste of my cansa.

Everyday, I read holozine, but didn' need daily newschip to watch pipe water go browner. Meantime, ol' Sen Boland gettin' his bill pass. He wouldn' need to send govermen to pushout trannies like SecGen Anjour, years back. Tribes'll jus' dry up an' blow way.

Not yet a problem for Chang; I had big catchbasin on roof, filtered, 'lectric fence round it with lotsa permas for charge. For years tribes knew not to mess wid Pedro Chang. Even Neut could diss tribeman, if catch him takin' his stuff. Hard, but gotta be. Else, they steal all I got.

I checked drainpipes that ran from roof to big cistern in cellar. No breaks. Enough water for two, three month, long as I boiled. An' long as desperate trannies didn' learn about it when they went dry. Maybe, if lucky, tribes could last 'til summer end. Winter bring lotsa rain. Maybe get through 'til next summer.

Nighttime I sat in chair by Valdez perma. Tea was hot, shop quiet.

Marx an' Lenin right 'bout one thing: organize. Trannies of world, unite. Only way, but I couldn' get them listen. Ravan thought I glitched, tellin' him water stop. Halber listened, maybe believed. He didn' say what Subs do.

Subs were my bes' chance. Sub tunnels went throughout, unner. All tribes respected Subs. No one ever went unner, even if stairhole sat unguard. Invader skinned alive, for warn. Like Halber said, no one mess with Subs.

They could lead tribes. United, trannies might make govermen listen.

Knock on door.

I never opened at night. Tribes respected Neut, usual. But nighttime, maybe some lonah come see what traytaman hide 'bove shop. Ol' traytaman ain' gonna object, lyin' on floor with shiv in chest.

Knock again, loud.

They knew I inside, no point sayin' nothin. I went to door. "Go 'way, we close."

"It be Pook."

"Don' care ya Arthur King of England, we close."

"Lemme in, Changman."

I bristled. "Pah. Coulda come in day, 'fore dark. Too stupid ta know Chang' don' open inna nigh'? Go way!" I wen' back to chair.

Voice come from door, subdued. "Please, Mista Chang. Pookboy do whatcha say." Pause. "Please."

Hair on neck rose. Somethin' wrong. I hurried to back room, opened hide place, took out special item I saved years back. Trotted to door. "Whoeva be wid Pookboy, don' mess wid ol' Chang! He showya!" I unbolted latch, then 'nother.

Finally, had door unlocked. Opened last bolt, swung door open, ready.

Jus' Pookboy, by hisself.

I grabbed his arm, pulled him in, slammed door. "Whatcha messin' roun' in middle of nigh'?" I took his ear, twis'. Only way make him listen, sometime. "Wanna stay Chang shop, I work ya! Work all nigh', work all day!"

"Yes, Mista Chang." He didn' pull 'way like usual.

I let go, worried. "Whassamatta, Pook?"

He turned sideway. I took in breath real fast. "Lor' God King of Universe, savanprotec' him!"

I hauled him to table with teapot, grabbed cloth I use for wipe, mopped at bloody mess underneath arm. "How bad it be? Siddown, Pook. We gotta take off shirt."

He saw what I put down on table; eyes went wide. "Chang got laser? Howya fin'?"

Shouldn't of let him see. Meant trouble, later. "Sit. Get you fix 'fore you go faint."

He siddown, obedient. That worried me more; meant he hurtin' bad.

I fumbled at shirt with old man's fingers, gave up. I patted him down, found his shiv, used it to cut away shirt. Found myself babbling. "Don' worry 'bout thread, Pookboy. We getcha 'notha." His side looked tore. "Gonna be allri'. Chang fix ya up." I poured hot water onna cloth, dabbed. Boy hissed, stiffened, sat quiet. Blood oozed.

I took his bare shoulders in hands, squeezed gentle. "I go get meds ta fix. Stay still, okay okay?"

He nodded. He shivered, winced with pain it brought.

I ran to back room, grabbed perma for light, hurried up stair.

Trannies don' use meds, usual. No point my keepin' them fo trayfo; tribes can' afford, an' they figure if it their time to die, they go. Usetabe, hospitals in city took trannies, Uppies, anyone.

Usetabe.

By time I got to thir' floor, heart goin' slam. Couldn't help Pookboy if I dead upstair. But couldn't lettim bleed out. Medkits. Had two cases, where they be? Think, Pedro. Don' go senile jus' yet.

Inna corner. I trotted across dark creaky room, detourin' rotted places. Fumbled for box, pulled out medkit with trembling hands.

Stopped to take two breath, top of stair. Can' fall down stair now, no time. I came down, careful. Pook sat in chair, looking at light. Eyes wet.

Workin', I fussed at him, to sound normal. "Stupid Midboy get hisself cut. Learn ta stay in lair at night, don' get inna rumb." I swabbed wound, gentle as I could. "Joeykit can't roam roun' nights, or he get diss. Stay in lair."

"Been."

I glanced up. "Cut in lair?"

He nod. "Karlo."

"Aiee. Joeykit gotta min' manners, he wanna be growed Mid." Skin sliced, but didn' see nothin' go through ribs. Maybe not so bad. Time would tell; filmatleven. "Pook can' mouth off allatime."

"Yes, Mista Chang." Docile.

As I worked I thought with hate about frazzin' system. Coulda been pretty Uppie boy, this trannie joeykit. Slim, nice face 'xcept for old scar over eye. If life been different, coulda gone to fancy Uppie school, live in tower. Or, born outa city, coulda growed to do honest work for Uppies. But he'll be nothin', maybe die 'fore he ever shave.

I washed his side again, this time with disinfectant from kit. Boy whimpered.

"Easy, Pook. Almos' done."

"Cold."

"Shock, maybe." Dunno; I ain' medtech. Was wonderin' why bother to clean wound; germs prolly already inside. Boy was filthy, as usual. Gotta 'xpect, livin' inna street. Trannies can' help it, don' even notice smell no more.

In Uppie clinic, he'd get skintouch cloth, and heal fast. I didn' have, couldn' keep it. It spoil fast. Thought of sewin', old fashion way, but figured tape'll hold, an' sewin' would hurt boy too much.

From kit, I took broadspec antibi. "Swallow."

"Whazzit?" He wrinkled face, looked at it suspicious.

My hand went up to cuff him, stopped. Not this night. "Make ya feel better." Obedient, he took. I poured tea, dumped in lotsa sugar. Nevamind cost. Made him drink. Maybe it help shock.

I wrapped him with gauze. "I gotta pull tape tight, Pook." I tugged. He yelped, push my hand away.

"Hol' still!"

"Leave it 'lone; I be okay!"

Enough was enough. I rapped him onna side of head. "Yes, Mista Chang!"

Boy looked up, eyes wide like puppy. I turned away quick.

Traytaman can' afford seniment. I made tape tight as I could without hurt too much. Fussin', I put rest of meds back in kit.

" 'Pologize." Pook sniffled, his eyes liquid. " 'Din' mean nothin'."

No fair. Ol' man could only stan' so much. I gathered his head against my chest, rocked, holdin' tight. "Pookboy gonna be allri.' Stay wid Chang long as he need. Be allri.'"

Boy healed slowly, but broadspec antibi did its work. I didn' tell how much I hadda trayfo, each box of medkits. Didn' matta.

Nex' day I asked him, what he do, Karlo so pissoff.

Pook gave sheepish look. "Tol' him Ravan don' know sheet."

"What wid you an' Ravan?"

"Pipes. Ravan tellin' Karlo, Mids gotta fin' new pipe or move lair." He turned over on cot, wincing.

"Bah." I wagged finger. "Joeykit stay outa."

"Don' know sheet." Voice was stubborn. "He be saying Changman gone glitch. Say—" Pookboy broke off.

"G'wan."

"Naw." Shook head.

I got up, went into shop, wonderin'. Knock on door came few min later. I got busy, trayfo jumpsuits an' cansa.

Evening, things quiet again. I fed Pookboy can a chicken. Only second day since cutup, didn' wan' let him walk 'xcept to johnny. Fed him in cot. He devour chicken, looked round like hopin' 'nother can.

Food done, I got up. He put hand on arm, pulled me back. I slapped at hand; didn' need no Midboy holdin' like baby.

"Stay a min." His voice shy.

Okay okay, I sat back. Wait 'n see.

"Dunno whassa matta, Mids argue 'bout water allatime." He checked my eyes, decided safe to go on. "Ravan be glitched, not Chang."

"What he say?"

"Dat Changman be glitch, sayin' water be stop. If pipes no good, Mids gotta move, or fix. Betta ta fix, he say. He means if . . . " Boy trailed off.

Couldn't ask. Pookboy tell or not, when he was ready.

Ran my hand through his hair, squeezed neck gentle. Got up, fussed with can, cleanin' out, savin' metal parts.

Pookboy spoke to wall. "If Chang don' trayfo pipe, Mids take. Bust inta Chang shop."

My breath hissed. It comin' to that, a Neut not safe? Times bad.

"So I tol' Karlo dat Ravan mus' be stupe from sun. If Changman say water be off, Mids oughta lissen."

I growled, "Stupid Midboy, think Chang can't take care a self, hah?" I flattened can, put with rest.

"Ravan wanna dissme. Karlo say no, but no upbringin' for joeykit wanna be Neut steada Mid. Tell me ta get out, stay out. I say ta prong hisself steada Bigsis allatime. He go for shiv. I din' move fas' enough."

"It'll be okay, Midboy. You wait a while, bring innifo like las' time."

"Maybe. Dunno if I wan'."

"Course Pook wan'. Mid gotta live with Mids, no?"

He didn' answer. Later, 'fore I turned off light, he asked, "How a trannie get ta be traytaman?"

Chapter 11

PHILIP

I wasn't supposed to know Jared got caught. I wouldn't have, except for Mom. The night the Bolands came to visit, I stayed awake a long time in the dark, playing with base eight conversions.

When I heard our guests on the stairs I knew Mom would check on me soon. I turned on my side so she'd see my eyes were still open; then she'd come in. A Pavlovian response; parents worry when their children can't sleep.

After a while she looked in, sat on the edge of my bed. "What's the matter, love child?"

I smiled. It makes me feel wiggly when she calls me that. "Nothing, Mom."

"Need to talk?"

"Depends. How tired are you?"

She tousled my hair. "I'm awake." She lay down on top of the cover. "Coin for your thoughts?"

I could talk to Mom in a way I never dared with Fath. Not that he'd object, but I had to be careful not to worry him.

I told her about my day, and listened to hers. After a while, she yawned, glanced at her watch, went into her calming routine.

I don't know why I loved her stories about the old days when she met Fath, but they helped me relax for sleep. I let her tell me about the Governors' Cotillion, and their courtship.

I'd long since figured out the dates. "That was two years after the monastery."

"Yes, he was Senator, and we—"

"Mom, has he changed much, now that he's old?"

"Old?" She giggled. "Well, now that he's ancient, almost senile, wheezing and tottering to the grave—"

"Mom! Remember he's four point four times my age. From my perspective—"

"I know, love." She giggled. "And I'm so old, too. Sagging, wrinkled, wheelchair bound—"

I hugged her, knowing it would make her stop. "What was he like?"

She fell silent. Then, "I've known him in three stages of his life. As a boy, he . . . "

I waited.

"He wasn't one I thought I'd fall in love with. So reserved, and painfully shy. So earnest. We were bunkies."

"Krane barracks."

"On Farside," she agreed. "He helped me when I panicked on a suit drill. He risked a caning for me, without a moment's thought."

"Sarge was mean to you."

"No, she was right. Someday you'll understand. When we graduated, Nick and I took our first leave together, before reporting for duty. We . . . got to know each other."

I might have translated, but it would spoil her mood.

"Years later I was on *Wellington* when the fish attacked. We didn't get along that time." She stirred, glanced again at her watch.

"And after?"

"He'd changed. What happened on *Trafalgar*, between him and the cadets . . . or perhaps it was before; I've no way to know. He's seen so much tragedy."

A silence. "Go on."

"He's . . . vulnerable. He's as sure of moral issues as he ever was. But he's lost the assurance he has a right to act on them. He sometimes says he makes things worse every time he intervenes."

"That's not true!"

"Of course not, P.T." She was quiet so long I thought she'd drifted to sleep. Then, "Politics was hard on him, especially the way his career ended. He's very fragile. We have to protect him."

"What's worrying him?"

Her voice grew hesitant. "Can I tell you these things, without your passing them on?"

I was scornful. "To whom? Jared?" I propped myself up on an elbow, spoke in a solemn tone. "You have my oath."

"Lord, you sound like your father. Actually, he's not worried, just under pressure. They won't leave him alone."

"Who?"

"The bloody politicians." She shook her head in exasperation. "They stripped him of office, packed him off in disgrace, but now they want his benediction. You'd think it wouldn't matter."

"Why does it?"

"Because, beneath it all, they respect him as much as ever." She gestured toward the window, and the gates. "Every day, those crowds outside. Why do you think they gather, though they know he won't acknowledge them? He stands for something. Integrity, or honor, or . . ."

I might have heard a sob.

She clutched my arm. "P.T., it's not just the Bolands and his old friends in the Navy. We have to protect him from the joeys outside. He mustn't listen to their pleas. They'll consume him. He's too fragile to step back into that—lion's den!"

"Don't worry, Mom, he won't."

A while later she kissed me, and left.

After a time I heard Father's footsteps, heading back down to his study.

I lay awake. Irrational numbers didn't seem to help.

The Bolands were visiting. Maybe they'd try to pressure Fath again. Mom was asleep by now, and couldn't protect him. I put on my slippers, padded downstairs, crossed the soft carpet to Father's study.

Inside, all was quiet. I wanted to knock, to ask what he could do to heal his fragility.

Better to keep silent; asking might worry him. Maybe in the morning I could download some data that would help me understand.

I curled up outside his door. I'd sit for a while to make sure no one bothered him.

Voices. I snapped awake.

"You can't imagine how sorry I am." Mr. Tenere. He must have entered by Fath's patio door, else he would have had to step over me.

"For God's sake, Adam!" Father was testy.

"I didn't mean—I'm sor—" A pause, for several seconds. "Well. I guess I don't know what to say, sir."

"Very good, Midshipman." I could hear the tired smile in

Father's voice. "But stammering isn't the issue. You have to learn you can't apologize for another's actions."

I shouldn't listen. It was dishonorable. Nonetheless, I pressed closer to the door.

"I was apologizing for making Jared what he is."

"Goofjuice. The boy's responsible for his own acts."

"Despicable, you called it. I agree."

"Adam, you've got to get him under control. No, not for my sake, for yours. And his own."

"Yes." A pause. "I just don't know how."

"Tonight was a start."

"Shouting at him? How should I follow up?"

Father's tone was bleak. "I'm the last one to ask. I destroyed the children in my care."

He couldn't mean me. My brother Nate? Someone else?

"Don't, sir. Please."

Father sighed. "He's your son. Do as you see fit. About Richard; I suppose we should tell him?"

"That Jared was skulking outside his window? To what purpose?"

I hunched closer. Why was Jared spying on bedrooms? Objectively speaking, he must have some kind of glitch.

"Richard had a right to privacy." Father.

"They're under a lot of strain, he and Rob both." Mr. Tenere hesitated. "I'd let it be. They've enough on their minds."

"If you say so." Father sounded dubious. "I almost forgot myself, outside. Jared doesn't know how close he came."

"To?"

"If he were my son . . . " I could hear his steps, as he paced.

"He'd have been better off." Mr. Tenere was bitter. "Sir, next time—I mean, if you catch him again . . . " A pause, as if he were steeling himself. "Please, treat him as you would your own."

"Are you sure?"

"Quite."

"Very well." Father's tone was flinty. "Jared won't like it."

Their conversation drifted. I lay outside the door for a long while.

I woke to Father's hand on my shoulder. For an eternity, he looked into my eyes. "What were you doing, P.T.?"

"I don't know, sir." It was the truth. My eyes teared. "I'm worried."

His expression softened. "About what, joeykit?" He helped me to my feet, guided me to the stairs. I knew he'd have carried me, if I hadn't grown so big.

About you, sir. But I couldn't say that. "I don't know, Fath."

Gently, he tucked me into bed.

Three days later Father packed his bag, said his good-byes, gave me a brusque hug, and left for his annual stay at the Lancaster monastery. Mom and I saw him off at the helipad. We walked back to the house in the muggy afternoon shimmer. Feeling self-conscious as I held her hand, I tried to ignore the gawkers peering through the gate.

"It's not for long, love. Three weeks and he'll be home."

"I know, Mom." We paused at the porch steps.

Her eye narrowed. "If you imagine his trip is an excuse to slack off on schoolwork, guess again."

"No, ma'am." Once a lieutenant, always a looey. "I asked for extra engineering yesterday. I'll finish it this afternoon, I think."

"Very well. Need a hug?"

I nodded. I usually do.

As days passed I grew increasingly restless. If I were adult I could leave whenever I wanted, but as a child I was dependent on Mom for transportation. The first week, I could only get her to take me to Rodin twice.

It was too muggy to play outside, and Jared wouldn't answer the caller or come to the house. Mom told me to stay away from his bungalow. Never mind why, young man, do as you're told.

To spite my tutors, I asked for extra assignments, finished them an hour after I brought them home, and sent them back on the nets with time and date stamp.

Mr. Skeer said my frustration arose from boredom, and I told him rather sharply that I didn't see him three hours a week to hear what I already knew. Then I apologized; he really was trying to help me, and occasionally succeeded.

I got anxious, at times. What Dad called "revving." I didn't know why thoughts flashed past at a million miles an hour. I felt out of control, and it scared me. Sometimes good ideas came, but I usually sat biting my nails and picking at my shirt. If Father saw, he'd hold me until I quieted, but then I worried at adding to his burdens, and that made it worse.

About one thing, Mr. Skeer was wrong: I didn't need more friends my own age. What counted was getting along with adults. What good was it to understand the social mores of "normal" twelve-year-olds? I wasn't "normal," thank Lord God, and I wouldn't be twelve for long.

Though I wasn't all that eager to go through adolescence, if Jared was any guide.

The fourth day Fath was gone I wandered to the bungalow, figuring Mom's admonition had probably expired. The door was open; I went to Jared's room.

He lay on his bed.

"Hi." I pulled a chair to his puter.

"Get lost, grode."

I looked over my shoulder. "You mean it?"

"You're not supposed to be here."

"Is this a privacy thing? Did you want me to knock?"

"No!" He rolled over, eyed me sullenly.

I headed for the door. "Let me know when you're human."

"I can't, you frazzing asshole!" He banged the pillow with his fist. "He won't let me!"

Many adolescents had problems with coherence, according to my downloads. "You're making no sense."

He sprang up, pushed me to the door. "You jerk! Out, before I—get out!"

I let Jared push me into the hall, slam the door. I shrugged. He was in one of his moods. I started back to the house, but hadn't gotten halfway when his window slid open.

"P.T, wait."

I sighed, turned. "Yes?"

He beckoned me. "Come on back." The window shut.

I trudged back to his room. "Well?"

"Don't give me that look; it isn't my fault." He sat back on his bed, put his head in his hands. "It's not fair. Dad's gone crazy."

I waited.

"All he did was yell. I figured that was the end of it."

"What happened?"

"He caught—found me where I wasn't supposed to be." Jared's expression was glum. "He shouted like he'd gone round the bend. I went to my room and waited all night for him to come in and settle things. By morning, it was like he'd forgotten all about it. I went to school like usual."

"You aggravate him."

"I don't need that from you, frazball."

"Take that back." My voice was very quiet.

"Go prong—"

"Take it back, joey. I mean it." I stood, trying not to tremble. He was a lot bigger.

His eyes fell away from mine. "All right, cool jets." He added, "Sorry."

I sat again, glad to end the confrontation. "Go on."

"For two days Dad said nothing. Couple of nights ago, he went berserk. Came into my room, said he'd had enough. More words, I figured. He's just your father's rabbit."

I wanted to leave, but made myself sit still.

Jared's face darkened. "I told him to let me alone, and he laughed. Said he was pulling me out of school 'cause it was doing me no good. Told me I was grounded, couldn't even leave my room except for bathroom or eating. 'Til my behavior improves,' whatever that's supposed to mean. I can't call you, or have you over. He even canceled my nets! Look!" He flipped on his puter, punched into the networks. Nothing but a blank. "You wouldn't believe the goofjuice he spouted. God-given talents wasted, why can't I use my puter skills constructively, yap yap yap."

Jar made a face and flopped back onto the bed. "He can't enforce it, that's what's so insane. I can go out whenever I want."

"Why don't you, then?"

"I will."

"But you haven't."

"It's only been a couple nights, for Christ's sake!"

I fell silent at the blasphemy. I'm not sure what else I believe, but I know Lord God doesn't care for that.

"P.T.?"

I stared at the blank screen.

"Philip!"

"What?"

His voice was uneven. "I'm scared."

I crossed to the bed. "Of what?"

"I don't know. Dad. The way he's acting. He shouldn't have gotten that mad. School's a waste, but it's something to do. I want to go back."

If he saw I felt sorry for him, it would only make him feel worse. "Straighten out for a while. That's all he wants." I punched his arm. I knew Jared liked contact games.

He wasn't listening. "I'll show 'em. Both of them."

I tweaked his ribs, got his attention. "Hey, ease up. Just do what he asks for a time."

"Hands off, grode." He flipped a pillow at me. Better. More like the old Jared. I flipped it back.

"Arm wrestle?" He always beat me, and I knew he'd enjoy that.

"Two Unibucks a throw?"

"Not a chance." I hadn't made that mistake since I was seven. I rolled onto my stomach, put up my hand.

Jared, fifteen, had weight and size on me. I tried three times, let him believe I thought I could win.

The third time, he rammed my arm down, flipped me over. It hurt a bit. "Thought you were man enough to take me on, P.T.?"

I said, "Maybe not today. Soon."

"Right." He poked me in the ribs. I yelped, pushed him away, but he wrestled me down, held my arms still. The dominance thing; Jared constantly sought reassurance that he was the stronger.

"Let me go!"

"Maybe." He held both my hands in one of his, tickled me in the ribs with the other.

"Cut it out!" I yanked loose a hand, grabbed his hair. "Let me up, or—"

He swarmed on top of me, pushed me down on my back, sat on my hips. I wasn't sure if we were playing or fighting.

He held my wrists tight, forced my arms over my head. I kicked and bucked, almost succeeded in throwing him off.

"No you don't." He pressed my wrists against the bed with all his strength. His head dipped forward, pushed my shoulder down. "Gotcha, grode."

"Jared, don't. Let go of—"

With a quick shift, he lay on top of me.

I stiffened. "Jared—" His legs held me tight.

He shut his eyes, rested his head on my shoulder. As if by accident, his lips brushed my neck.

I sagged, willing my muscles to relax. An instant later I rammed my knee into his crotch.

He shrieked, bounced off, spun to the wall clutching his testicles. He rolled from side to side, his face purple.

I flew off the bed, backpedaled to the window, wiped the tingle of his lips from my skin.

A sob.

My eye fell on his puter screen. I lunged to the keyboard, keyed his drives, called up a wipe, slammed the return. I whirled back to the bed on which he thrashed in torment. My voice was shrill. "You're a joke! We laugh at you, all of us! Father and I, even your Dad! You fail at everything, and we all know!"

"P.T.!" A croak, that could have been an entreaty.

My voice grew harsh. "I'm glad it hurts! That time you beat me at chess, I let you win! Look up the Lopez variations if you're not too lazy. Your Dad's last password is your birthday in base twelve, but you were too stupid to see it even when I told you!"

"Please . . . "

I ran to the door. "Everyone knows you go out at night; you're the only one thinks it's a secret! By the way, the school *asked* your Dad to withdraw you! You're the saddest grode in the compound!"

"Wait!" Anguish.

"I'm done wasting time with you!" I ran into the yard, almost cannoned into Mr. Tenere.

"P.T.? Where are you—what's wrong?"

"Nothing. Bye." I dashed to the house, tore up the stairs to my room, slammed the door.

I sat in the corner, hugging myself, picking at my shirt.

Again I wiped at my neck. Calm, Philip. Seventy-six times thirteen hundred ninety-four . . . I was revving, but there was nothing I could do about it. My fingers scrabbled at my clothes.

Chapter 12

JARED

Whenever Dad called me to eat, I went without protest. He told me to clean my room, so I did. I even made dinner, on his instructions. Now that the Old Man was gone to his brown-robe voodoo, Dad spent most of his time catching up on work at his desk in the main house. Alone in my room, I bided my time.

I couldn't understand why Dad had turned so vicious, especially over something so insignificant as wandering on the veranda. Each evening when he trudged up the path to our bungalow, my stomach tightened. I knew Dad hated me, and I decided the feeling was mutual.

From time to time P.T. flitted about the lawn, but I didn't wave from my window. Given Dad's manner, using the caller was out of the question, and I didn't know what I might have said to the little snark, anyway. We'd only been wrestling, for God's sake. He went berserk and hurt me, and said some things I couldn't really remember.

I didn't want to see him. I watched him through the curtains, running back and forth on the lawn with his football. He was thin and lithe. He never looked my way or smiled, though he knew I was lonely.

For three more days I moped in my room.

Finally I finished reloading my puter.

I had to escape from the compound; that much was certain. Quietly I tied back into the nets, set up base camp with Rolf, revealed the idea I'd been working on. He was properly impressed, but it took him two endless days to decide if he wanted to help.

Meanwhile, I scanned the latest issue of Holoworld. Old Boland's speech was spread over the front screens. Good. That meant they'd be interested in my story about his plans to discount the Old Man's influence. But I had to be careful.

I set it up through Interlodge. Three layers of false signons, and a quick schuss through anon valley. Then a backtrack, scattering fresh snow across my trail.

I'd written down everything I remembered of what the Bolands had said. Through Interlodge I sent Holoworld a few tidbits to whet their interest. Would they be interested in a meeting?

If we met anywhere near the Old Man's compound, someone might guess the source, so I needed a public place. I picked the Sheraton Skytel in New York; Dad had taken me there once and I could find my way around.

I figured I could pass for seventeen at least, but even so, old joeybats like the mediamen might not be impressed. I told the Holoworld people I didn't want my ID revealed and would send a messenger with the data I wanted to sell. They could give their answer to him.

I wasn't sure what they'd pay, but that didn't matter. What counted was showing the lot of them. Getting even with Dad for his nastiness, and with the Old Man for being so frazzing sanctimonious. Let him fly back from his stupid monastery to a Holoworld exclusive on how he spied on his guests, and filed his notes in his personal puter. I'd decided the story would be hotter if I tied it to him.

I wished I had something on P.T. too, but I wasn't sure how I'd use it. P.T. wasn't news; Arlene Bitch Seafort was determined to keep his name off the viewscreens, though once in a while, when her guard was down, they caught a few distant shots.

They'd stopped sending mediamen over the compound after she knocked the tail rudder off a heli with nothing but a well-aimed hand laser. No one dared prosecute, and I think the other politicians were secretly glad a victim had finally struck back.

I languished in the frazzing bungalow for days, before Holoworld bit.

The meet was set for Wednesday at five. I'd leave Tuesday, stay overnight in the Sheraton, and have plenty of time to prepare.

Over the weekend I worked so hard at browning Dad that he even complimented me on my attitude. It was all I could do not to laugh. At night, while he slept, I made a reservation on the Monday suborbital, billing it to the Terrex account I'd found in his puter. P.T. was right; it was my birthday he'd used. Dumb.

Getting the card itself was the hardest part. I had to wait until Monday night; if I snatched it earlier, he might notice, though he used it only when he left the compound.

I waited until Monday night, when he was in the shower. It took only a minute to dash into his room, fish in his pants, grab the card.

I'd show them.

Tuesday morning Dad woke me, as he had every day since our quarrel.

"Time to get up, boy."

"Okay." I forced open my eyes. I'd tossed and turned far into the night.

"Now, please."

I sighed. In a few more hours it would be over. Why not let him think he was winning? "Yes, sir." I sat.

He threw his arm around my shoulder. I tried not to cringe. His voice was hesitant. "I've been thinking . . . remember our trip to Quebec?"

"With Mom? A long time ago."

"Would you like to go again?"

"Why?"

"Just . . . for us. I could take a few days."

Three or four days tied to him like a joeykit, with no way to escape? I wanted to vomit. "Zarky, Dad. We could do lots of things."

A hug. "Dinner's in the freezer. Burgers and mixed vegetables."

"Okay." I waited for him to leave.

He paused by the door. "Keep up the good behavior, and I'll let you back onto the nets."

I turned away quickly, before he saw my lip curl. "Thanks."

He left.

The morning passed in an agony of anticipation. I couldn't leave; if Dad didn't lunch with Arlene, he might eat at home. In that case I'd better be around. He mustn't learn I'd left until I'd been gone several hours. By then would it be too late.

Of course, there was the one chance in a thousand that he'd pick today to dine out, and try to pay with his Terrex. That's what made life interesting, though I wasn't too worried. I could always ditch the card and claim I knew nothing about it.

My shuttle would leave at two.

Noon. Luck ran against me. Dad and Arlene took their sandwiches to the veranda and sat forever. I paced my room, rucksack hidden under my bed. I could slip out Dad's window on the far side of the house, but what good would that do? I still had to go through the gate, and the gatepath was visible from the veranda. All hell would break loose if Dad saw me outside when I was supposed to be grounded.

If it weren't for the gate-gawkers, I could shinny over the wall and be gone, but if I tried it, alarms would go berserk. I had to use the gate, where the guards' job was to keep people out, not hold us in. It didn't matter to them whether I went through to the street.

Once I got past Dad, my way would be clear. The gawkers had no interest in me; their focus was on the Old Man and his family.

At last, Dad gathered his plate and cup and went back to the main house. Arlene stretched and did likewise. Good; all I needed was for her to take one of her frazzing outdoor naps.

When the coast was clear I snatched up my rucksack, loped to the gate, slowed to a walk as I reached the guardhouse. I opened the iron gate from the inside, nodded to the nearest guard as I strolled through. A few rubberneckers gaped as I went past; I restrained myself from giving them the finger. Idiots, hanging around the Old Man as if he were a saint. Seafort was a pompous ass who'd failed at politics like everything else.

I managed to hold myself to a walk until I turned the corner. Then I sprinted to the end of the block.

Sometimes tourists came in taxis, gawked through their windows and drove on, but others left their cabs to wander around the compound. During the day, ground cabs were always cruising our street to pick up yokels who finally realized there was nothing to see except the guardhouse and the shrubs.

I stepped off the curb, hailed a cab. "Potomac Shuttleport, and hurry."

The driver looked me over. "Coin, joey?"

"Sure. What do you think I am, a trannie?" I slammed the door.

I had enough for the cab, but not a lot to spare. I'd intended to stop at a Terrex booth in the shuttleport and use Dad's card to get some spending money. I figured after a few days he'd find it was missing and cancel it, so I'd better be prepared until the Unibucks from Holoworld came through.

Thanks to Dad's damn picnic with Arlene, I barely made it to the shuttleport in time. I raced to the gate, boarded just as the ramplights began to flash. I tucked my rucksack under my seat, buckled in, caught my breath as the ramp wheeled away.

I debated trying for a drink. My fake ID looked good—hell, I'd paid enough for it at school—but if it didn't work, a shuttle in flight was a bad place to get caught. I'd have no chance to run, and even a first offense could land me in Federal Juv. Anyway, the drinking age was twenty-one, and I wasn't quite sure I looked it, even though I occasionally shaved.

I settled for a softie.

In New York I went to the nearest Terrex machine, keyed myself a wad of cash. I hadn't had time to withdraw it in Washington before my flight. The transaction would eventually show on Dad's statement; sooner or later he'd see I'd been to New York. Too bad I hadn't thought of scrambling his financial passwords before I left, to gain more time.

No matter. Once Holoworld paid off I'd head somewhere really zarky.

Chapter 13

POOK

Bad time for Pook, afta Karlo cut me. I go sullen, can' help it. What kinda Mid be Pookboy, widout upbringin'? An' my side hurt. Can' cry when Changman aroun'; gotta wait 'til he out.

Every day ol' man go wid cart, trayfo back 'n forth wid tribes. 'Fore he go, he sit by cot, ruffle my hair, ask how I feel. Allri', I tellim. Don' go pokin' roun' where ya don' belong, he say. Res' an' get well. Yes, Mista Chang. I do whatchew say. He smile.

I don' feel so good. It too much trouble ta go up stair, poke roun', even if my best chance ta see what Changman hide. 'Notha time. I get up slow, look aroun' shop. Usual trayfo. If I take any, he know fas', an' whop me. Or maybe he jus' looka me, make me feel bad. So I leave boxes 'lone.

Shelves in back room fulla book. Could take lotsa; ol' man got so many he never know, but whuffo? Who wan' book 'xcept glitched ol' Changman?

Afta coupla days, I start feel betta. Nighttime, I sit wid Chang by perma, he in his rickety chair, me on low stool. He tell stories from book 'bout wayback time, when tribe called knigh' rumb wid tribe in lair called cassel. Stupid scaretale. Wha' kinda tribe wins rumb, an' lettem go afta? I askim, why don' knigh's diss whole bunch a 'em afta they knock down cassel? Otha wise, cassel tribe go fo' venge.

He say, civil lashon, Pook. Whole worl' don' ack like trannie tribes. Dumbasses, I say; why I wanna hear 'bout glitched tribes who dunno howta ack? Dey bad as Subs, touchin' fingas, sayin' cool meet. Glitch stuff.

Ol' man sigh a lot. I sit still, lissen ta 'notha bookstory ta make 'im feel betta.

Coupla mo' days, I wantin' go out. Changman say no. I go proud, say, Pook go where he wan', no ol' man gonna stop 'im. Okay okay, he say, an' open door. Out, an' don' come back. Stupid ol' man. I gotta do his way. Please, Mista Chang, lemme go out fo' while. Jus' ta walk roun'.

He grumble lot, give me lotsa warn, don' run, case ya fall, stay way from Karlo, stuff like dat. He think I stupe? Finally, he goin' trayfo wid cart, an' let me out.

He tell me, "Okay okay, silly Midboy, be here when I get back, if ya wan' place ta sleep fo' nigh'."

"Yo." I shrug, go out in sun, blinkin'. He lock door, careful. Beck me over, I gotta stan' still while he fuss wid tape aroun' my cut, fin' 'xcuse ta hug me. "G'wan, Mista Chang, I be allri'."

He disappear down block wid rattly cart. I look roun', see nothin' new 'xept dead dog someone miss fo' stewpot, but now he be too bloat. I kick stones. I walk ta near lair, side hurtin' some, but not too bad. Hope Bigsis come out, but don' go too close ta lair case see Karlo.

No Bigsis. No Karlo, eitha, so okay."

I walk roun', gettin' bore. Gotta wait 'til Changman come back ta get in. Soon, now.

Noise. Motor.

Heli.

Mid joeys run pas', headin' ta lair fo' safe. I don' worry. Daytime, an' plenny places fo' hide. Heli usual means jerries, but could also be Uppies. Once in while, touris' set down, looka roun', guards showin' lasers. Mos'ly touris' come in Graybus, winnows all bar. Dey only stop at Four Two, usual.

Whomp of engine get loud. Lotsa dus'. Heli sets down mid of street near Chang house.

Motor stop.

Not jerries. Jus' helicab wid coupla frazzin' Uppies.

Afta while, Mids come outa lair 'gain ta watch touris'.

At nigh', no Uppie lan' his heli inna street. We dissim, if he do. Day, even trannies walk in sun, long as stay on own turf. Uppies ain' welc, but too stupe ta know, sometime.

Heli door open, two joes come out. One be real big, an' kinda wide. He look roun' careful, den help otha one jump down. Secon' man all starve, threads tore like trannie. But dat couldn' be; no trannie eva got coin fo' helicab.

Cabbie wait inna heli. I don' see no guard.

Big man bang har' on Chang door. "Yo! Changman! Openup!"

Don' like. How Chang gonna keep respec' of tribes, Uppies botha him?

"Yo! Chang!"

I go bristle. "Get los', Uppie!"

He ignore, bang again. "Wake up, ol' man!"

Mids be watchin'. I go proud, pull out shiv. "G'wan, outa heah!" I stan' front a door. "Leavim be!"

Bigman eyes go narrow, seein' shiv. "Watchit, joeykit."

He won' step back, so I come closa, holdin' shiv low like Karlo teach. "Fly ya mothafuckin' heli back ta towah! You too, scrawny gayfag!" They ignore, so I lunge. "Who ya think ya—"

Bigman han' dart out, catch my wris', snatch shiv an' toss it inna street.

"Leggo me, ya frazzin'—"

He whop me 'cross face, openhan'. Make soun' like stick crack. I yelp.

His mouth fulla contemp, he shove me. "Go play 'fore ya get hurt, joeykit."

I catch myself fo' I fall. "Prong—" He step closer; I shut fas'. Watchin' Mids start ta snicker.

Dunno whatta do. Wanna go proud, but he don' ack like Uppie; too rowd. I run ta street, grab shiv. Wonnerin', can I take 'im? Gotta try, 'cause too many Mids watchin'. I circle, careful.

He ask, "Where be Changman?"

"Prong yaself!" I c'n say it now; got shiv for safe.

Otha joe, skinny, shrug. He say, "Leavim be, kit ain' gonna tellya noth—"

I lunge, catchem both offgar. Stick shiv inna bigjoe's ribs.

'Xcept, I don', cause he move too fas'. Bigman catch arm, twis'. My shiv go fly. He shove me up 'gainst wall, whop me a couple, kinda easy, like he bore. "Where Changman? He still live here?"

Squealin', I tryta get loose. Can't.

Whop. "Where he be, joey?" Whop. "Ansa me!" Whop.

I cryin' like joeykit, can' help it, clawin' at his big han' slappin' me, when familia voice come at las'. "Okay okay, whatchadoon to my Pookboy? Wha's up?"

Bigman growl, "Ask 'im where ya be, is all." Whop me one mo'.

"Lettim go, he jus' joeykit." Mista Chang trot ova, paw at Bigman han' like he ain' 'fraid. "Leggo, said!"

Bigman drop me, wait impatient while Chang open lock wid one hand, his otha holdin' me tigh'. I embarrass, seen cry. Ain' fair. Uppie too big.

Changman fuss. "Don' whomp my Pook. Kit jus' tryin' protec' me." I waitin' fo' Chang ta yank out laser from coat, fry big joey. Stead, he go in, leave door open fo' Bigman. I watch, amaze.

Bigman come in, look roun'. "Ain' change none."

"Why change?" Ol' man give me teapot, push me to back like I spose ta fill wid water. He go glitch, or somethin'? More like I piss in it, fo' Uppie drink. I shake no.

"G'wan, Pook. Wan' my tea." He shove gentle.

Stupid ol' man, no care what badass Bigman do ta Pook. I snuffle, fill pot. Rub face. All bruise now, prolly.

When I come back, dey sittin' in shoproom like natral fo' Uppies visit trannie. I put pot on hotpad an' glare.

"Pook." Chang beck me. "Come meet frien' from long-time back."

"Don' wanna." I turn my back on Changman.

Bigman grin. "When I tried dat, ya grab ear an twis'. Seem like I was 'bout his age."

How he know 'bout Chang grabbin' ear? I stop sniffle, lissen.

"C'mere, joey," say Bigman. I look ta curtain, wantin' slip behin', but big joey close, an' he cruel. And Chang jus' gonna sit 'n watch. "C'mere," Bigman say again.

I go close, watchin' careful.

He hol' out han'. "Usetabe, I lived wid Changman."

I go all scorny. "Now I know ya be glitch. Ain' no Uppie live—"

"I be Eddie."

I rememba name from Chang's tale. An' I realize his talk ain' fulla snot like Uppies. I look at Chang, wish he weren' smile like I some kinda stupe.

Eddie rumble, "Sorry I whomped ya. Don' like joey comin' on wid shiv."

I go proud. "Din' hurt none."

"Course not." He keep hand out, 'til I gotta take. He shake careful, like tryin' not ta squeeze. I glad ta get my han' back. He say, "Boney an' I came allaway in heli, lookin' fo' Changman."

Ol' man go huff. "Changman, is it? How I spose ta teach Midboy respec', ya talk like—"

"Okay, okay. Mista Chang, meant ta say." Bigman roll his eyes. "Din' mean nothin'."

Chang grumble. He wait fo' tea ta hot.

"Siddown." Eddie haul on my collar an' I sit fas'. "Don' give Mista Chang no trouble, joeykit. He be okay Neut."

I lookim ova. "Who ya be? Why botha Mista Chang?"

Eddie grin 'gain at ol' Chang. "He got spirit, anyway." Look ta me, serious like. "I'm Eddie Boss. Dis my frien' Boney."

"Tribe?"

He go proud. "I be Mace." Den he look sad. "Long time back."

"Ain' no Mace. Jus' Mista Chang scaretale."

"Was Mace, once. I Boss, four flo'." He stare at pot, sigh deep. "Thas why we came to Changma—Mista Chang. Figga what to do."

Chang pour tea, han' it roun'. Now I sure Eddieboss be Chang frien'; he get tea steada coffee. I drink, pretendin' I like.

Dey talk like I wasn' dere. I don' mind; it give me time ta figga.

"You gotta help, Mista Chang."

"How? What'm I suppose to do?"

They words all differen', when dey don' talk ta me. More like Uppie, but I c'n unnerstan'.

"I losin' my Mace!"

Boney stir. "Already los', mos' of us."

"Unies are pushin' Easters; Easters push Mace. I went to visit, found Sam diss, an' Armon and' Bally and Kit . . . " Eddie look up. "They my tribe."

Chang get up, shuffle ta Eddie, pat gentle. "Not anymore. You gotta remember."

"Was, willbe!"

"No." Chang word have final. "Now ya be tribe with Annie."

"Girl can't be place of tribe." Eddieboss look up, smile shy. "She my wife, now. Uppie way."

"I know." Chang wait.

"Still, I gotta visit Mace, once in while. She don'—doesn't want to come, but she understand." He slurp at tea. "This time, I went to U.N. Square, took helicab, land in usual place south a Easters."

Boney shake head. "He din' know 'bout pushout."

"My Mace ain't—weren't there. Place all tore up, worse than before."

"You found him." Chang point at Boney.

Eddie's mouth go snarl. "Hadda whomp a buncha Easters, make 'em explain I hadda look more south. Five blocks, Mace was push." He brood. "Frazzin' Easters. Never cared fo' none of them."

We wait, 'til bigman Eddie look up. "I went south, couldn' believe what I found. Mister Chang, they be drinkin' river! No wonder they dyin'!"

Boney shrug, helpless. "No water inna pipe. Thas why we pushout. No point hangin' onta turf, can' live in it."

Chang sigh, rockin'.

Eddieboss voice go strain. "Mister Chang, tell me what to do. They can't drink river, get sick like dog. Why ain' water in pipes? What's Mace spose ta do?"

Chang's hand make fis'. "What's alla trannies spose ta do?" he whisper.

My healin' cut itch an' I wan' scratch, but sit still ta lissen.

"Should we pushback Easters? Maybe if I helped . . . "

Chang look up, eyes glisten. "Eddie, ain' Easters that pushback Mace."

"Sure, it is. Boney, tellaman. Few month back, started with—"

"Not Easters. Was Unie govermen pushout Mace."

I get all tingle. Somethin' in ol' man voice.

Chang say, "They want us gone, Eddie Boss. Alla tribes. Mids, Ports, Easters, Subs, Neuts. Gonna push us out."

Eddie study Mista Chang face. He ask, cautious, "You gone glitch?"

Ol' man don' get mad, jus' shake his head. "Tellin' ya true." He get up, fuss wid pot, pourin' fo' all. Again he sit. "Like when SecGen Anjour tried, back when."

Eddie hunch forward. "No Unie troops onna street this time, ol' man."

Chang sip tea, make face, like too hot. "Okay okay, teachya history." He glance at me. "Lissen, little Midboy, maybe learn somethin'. Time back, SecGen Anjour—ya know he was Territorial?"

Eddie rumble, "Party don' matta. All govermen be Uppies."

"Oh, it matter. SecGen Anjour wanted to pushout tribes near river, build more towers. Sent lotsa jerries, with their U.N.A.F. troop carriers rumblin' behin'."

"Course I know. They was pushin' on Mace. That's when—"

"You came ta ol' Chang, wan' miracle, jus' like now."

"Las' time, ya helped!"

"Too hard for trannies ta fight govermen." Chang look up. "Mace should know that. Didn' take a lotta jerries to push Mace outa store, back when."

Eddie go anger. "They had laser, stunner—"

"I know. But Anjour time, they wanted to push ya out, jus' like before with store. I couldn' think no way to stop 'em, but knew who would."

Eddie look down. "Hated that part."

"What part?" I jump, at sound a my own voice.

Eddie say, "Changman and me went to see Fisherman."

"Ain' no Fisherman. Jus' scaretale fo'—"

Eddie grab holt my collar, like sayin', shut up ri' *now*, Pookboy. I go quiet quick. He growl, "Went to see Fisherman. Mister Chang an' me. In monastery, where he lived."

I look up. Chang nod.

"Din' wanna go. Chang made me." Eddie's eyes soft, like rememer ol' hurt.

Chang say, "He needed to see you. Else, wouldn't help."

"But I din' need see him. Not afta Annie."

I look confuse.

"Was his wife firs', then I took. Secon' time I betray. I wouldn't a gone to Lancaster, if tribe weren' be extinguish."

Chang nod approve, like he thinkin', good word, Eddieboss.

"Lancaster. Monastery. Big ol' place, stone. Monks wid—with robes. Chang an' I wait. Go in with others for pray. Finally, he come. We kneel fronta bench, with alla touris'. Wait for him to see us, but he won' look at joes come to catch his sight, some holdin' sick joeykits, like if he touch, they heal."

I dunno if Eddie know his eyes wet.

"Fisherman kneel on flo', gaunt, prayin'. Once I catch glimpse of his eyes, an' they sick inside. Monks chantin' foreign. Changman holdin' my arm, like, is all right, Eddie, you strong enough. I sit on hard bench an' wait for Hell, when he look at my face and remember what I done."

Chang get up quiet, trot to Eddie, pat big shoulder.

I 'fraid ta move, less'n Eddie squash me.

"Service finish, time fo' public to leave. We all wait for monks to file out. Now, Eddie, Chang says. I can't make sound if it means Fisherman'll see me."

Eddie's han' wipe his eye, absentmind. "He almost outa hall. I get up, cry out, Cap'n! Looka me! Monk comes runnin', I shrug him off. Cap'n! He keep walkin'. For sake a Lord God, Cap'n, looka Eddie! At last he turn, an look. Inta me. Through me." Bigman stop.

Real slow, I get up. Heart pound. Careful, I touch his cheek, wipe gentle with sleeve. Eddieboss grab my hand, don' let go.

"Guards pushin', tellin' us gotta leave now. Fisherman comes over. I stand there like stupe ox, hopin' he'll remin' me 'bout Annie, hit me, anythin'. How are you, Eddie, he says. I look at Chang. He jus' nod. Cap'n, I say, I need ya help."

Eddie break off, squeeze my wris' 'til I can hardly keep from yell. His voice catch.

"Finish," ol' Chang say quiet. "Get it out."

"Took balls ta ask his help, afta what I did ta betray. Can't figger how I could ask. It's all right, Eddie, he says like it don' matter. That's all past. Old monk come over, want ta know what's goin' on, an' Cap'n says, please Abbot, let us talk. He was my ship—"

Eddie wrench away, go to door.

I watch. His big fist bang his leg like ta punish. Afta while he whispa ta door, "Shipmate. So Abbot let us talk. I tol' Cap'n what Unies doin' ta my Mace. I say, don' know who c'n help 'xcept you.

"He say, I'm nobody. I can't help anymore. This be my place. An' I say, no! You Cap'n, now an' always! You be

Fisherman! He shake head, sad. He say, anything I do will make it worse, Eddie. That's my curse.

"No, I tell him. My people gon' die. Unies'll listen ta you. Tell 'em stop."

Eddie stare at glowing perma. "I know what I gotta do. Like circle comin' round. I stan'. My people dyin', Cap'n. I beg you. An' I get down on knees, like he done once ta me. I'm beggin' you, for my Mace. Oh Jesus Lord, he says, don't. Please. But I say, I'm begging you. Please, sir. Begging you."

All quiet.

I let out breath, didn' realize I'd been holdin'. "An'?"

"He come. Not that day. But soon, he come. He denounce Anjour an' his Unies, and say he go inta politics if that what it take. And he do."

I look ta Chang, is true?

He nod.

Boney say, like comfort, "He stop 'em in time. We no pushout. Good years afta, tribe hol' onta turf. 'Til now."

Eddie sigh, rub arm 'cross face. "Thas how we beat ol' SecGen Anjour. Time back." He look up. "But now it's startin' again. I seen 'bout a dozen Mace sick inna cellar after drinkin' river. No meds. We ain' got much time."

"I can' do nothin," Changman say again, louder. "What ya think I be, miracle worka? Jus' ol' Neut, tryin' to get by."

"What we do? Wait 'til all be dead?"

"I dunno!"

Boney say anger, "Mace goin' down, Mista Chang. You gotta help."

Chang look real ol'. I watchim wid worry. He say, "Can't get Uppies to listen. I'm just trannie, like you."

Knock on door.

Chang get up, pad 'cross room. "We close!"

Voice I don' know. "It's gettin' dark. I gotta be off."

Eddie get up. "Cabbie." He open door. "All right you go. We stayin'." Pulls out wad of Unibucks. I watch wid amaze. Eddie give some ta joe. "Thanks."

"Sure you want to stay? Hell, it's your life, not mine." Heliman touch his cap, turn. Eddie close door, come sit. For a min, roar of engine shake shop.

When heli gone, Eddie say, "Okay, you ain't miracle

worka. But years back you gave me advice whether I want it or not. Now I'm askin'. What should we do, ol' man?"

Chang go bristle. "Ol' man, now? Was 'ol' man' when Mace kit knock at door needin' place ta stay, or was it Mista Chang, hah?"

Eddie look at me, wink. "Cool jets. Din' mean nothin'. You be Mister Chang, if that what you want. But if you ain't glitch with old, show us answer."

"Think I can' see ya manipulate? Silly Maceboy still thinks he c'n swind Pedro Telamon Chang, hah?" Ol' man fuss wid tea.

We wait.

Changman turn back, seem like he anger for true. "I tolya, don' know. Ya wan' answer, go ta Fisherman! Maybe he help. Leave ol' man be!"

Eddie sag. "Can't. Not no more."

"Sure ya can. Jus—"

Eddie grab his arm; ol' man wince. "No. Not for Mace, not for anything! Never 'gain. Not even for Annie. Cap'n be in my dreams, ever since. See his face, his horror when I kneel. Can't do it, even if Maces all die." He look to his frien'. "Sorry, Boney."

"But—"

Eddie shake his head, whisper, "Can't look at his hurt again."

We all quiet as night' fallin'.

Outside, a shriek. Someone get diss.

Chapter 14

ROBERT

I dictated another memo to my puter Eleen. While I was aloft, she'd send chipnotes based on my instructions, sign my letters, and deliver them. By now she knew my style better than I did.

Van, my admin aide, looked in. "Your Dad said to pick him up at seven."

"What'd you tell him?"

His eyes lit in a brief smile. "That you'd be twenty minutes late, but not to worry. You'd make the shuttle."

I turned back to the keyboard, flashing a rude finger but smiling nonetheless. Once, long ago, I'd missed a shuttle to Earthport Station, and ever since, Dad assumed I'd be hopelessly late for appointments. An undeserved reputation.

Today, I had plenty of time. I would leave my Washington office by two, though the shuttle didn't lift from New York until seven-thirty. Time for a leisurely shower in my tower apartment, a drink before dinner. I'd have to eat lightly, or I'd suffer during the acceleration.

My caller buzzed, but I ignored it. Van would field my calls. He'd been with me for seven years, and I could trust him to brush off constituents without offense.

A last glance at my desk; I hated coming back to a mess.

"Rob, you'd better take this one." Van indicated the caller.

I sighed. "Who?"

"Tenere."

I could call Adam from my heli, or even from my shower; I'd set callers in every nook and cranny of my apartment. But Adam didn't duck my calls, and I rarely avoided his, though I was a rising young Assemblyman from Seaboard Cities, and he was just aide to a retired politician of no further consequence.

I took the caller. "Boland."

Adam's voice was strained. "Could you swing by for a few minutes?"

"I was just—"

"Please?"

I switched gears. "—just leaving. Be there shortly."

In the heli, I wondered what had prompted his summons. The Captain was at his annual retreat, so it couldn't be the Redevelopment bill. Unless Dad had started his subtle campaign to neutralize the Captain's influence, and Adam had caught wind.

But Dad had promised to wait, though the Captain's last comments hadn't been encouraging. Seafort suggested more money be diverted to the lower cities. Politically impossible, especially given the current austere climate. Anyone but the Captain would realize that.

I peered down at Washington as we glided toward the suburbs. Despite efforts to reverse the decay, there were still places you wouldn't want to set down with an overheated rotor.

Though Seafort's idealism was admirable, our economy hadn't yet recovered from the disaster of the aliens' attack. Bombay, Marseilles, Melbourne were gone, numerous other cities still scarred by the bombs. Worse, our fleet had been ravaged. Funding wasn't as plentiful as once it had been.

Every Unibuck diverted to desolate city streets meant less spent on towers or other worthwhile projects. Only by nurturing our financial base could we provide economic growth for our whole society.

Still, I assumed the Seafort matter was under control. Adam had reminded the Captain that Dad's and my political future hung on the bill, and we knew our success mattered personally to Seafort. Mine, more than Dad's, I suspected; after all, I was one of the Captain's protégés.

I squinted into the sun, spotted the compound. My pilot homed in on the helipad.

Lord God only knew where, left to his own devices, the Captain might have settled when his administration collapsed. Dad had been one of those who'd promoted the Secretarial Foundation, which raised funds for the Captain's retirement.

From a grateful populace, the prospectus had read, and to a large degree it was true. Whatever his shortcomings as political leader, by repelling the fish Nick Seafort had preserved ‑ur civilization, and deserved comfortable retirement. Many still revered him. As always, he responded to their adulation with aloof disregard.

We flew across the compound walls. Built atop an old Fairfax estate, the compound melded high security with the most treasured commodity in a crowded world: privacy. Its ten-foot walls permitted the Captain and Arlene to raise their boy free from the glare of the media lights.

Except, of course, for the constant stream of helis bringing guests such as myself. We'd given the Captain his walls, then breached them as a matter of course.

I jumped out while the blades still spun. P.T. ducked under the arm of the guard who'd held him clear. "Hi, Mr. Boland. Mom's inside. Mr. Tenere's in his bungalow, but I'm sure he'll be coming. He's checked the pad each time a heli flew over."

"Hello, Philip." Awkwardly, I gave the boy a hug. Soon, he'd be a lanky teener. Even now, his voice was beginning to deepen.

"I finished the model you gave me. I wrote the manufacturer about the errors. *Challenger* had three laser turrets aft, not two. With two the model looks more symmetrical, which I suppose is why they misdesigned it." He stopped for breath. "Here's Mr. Tenere. Are you staying for dinner?"

"I don't think so."

"Aw." His face fell. "I hoped—I've been . . . " He fell silent. Then, in his best child-to-adult voice, "Good to see you again, sir."

"Hi, Rob." Adam offered his hand. "Ready for a drink?" Absently, he caressed P.T.'s neck.

"A light one." Tenere led me toward his bungalow, the boy trailing. In a few minutes we were seated on his patio.

"Rob, I need . . . " Adam swallowed. "If you could—I mean, I—" I waited, while he counted silently. Then, "Jared's gone."

I blurted, "Dead?" Across the patio, P.T.'s eyes widened.

"Christ, no." Adam's expression was bleak. "At least, I hope not. He took off yesterday afternoon."

"You called the police?"

"This morning, when he didn't come back." Adam stood to pace. "I kept hoping he'd crawl in through his window, and I'd find him asleep. The jerries have his holopic on their nets, but they're not releasing it to the public. I don't want to bring the Commandant's name into this. In fact, I hope he'll never hear about it. You know what Lancaster does to his mood. To burden him now . . ." He looked away, reddening. "I thought perhaps, with your connections . . ."

"Of course." My tone was gruff. "Let me use your caller." Between Dad's clout and my own, we'd galvanize every jerryhouse on the Eastern Seaboard. The boy would be found, hauled home in disgrace. No more than he deserved; Adam was gray with worry.

I called Van, explained what I wanted, knowing the moment we rang off he'd start private numbers ringing in city halls throughout our district.

When I returned from the house, P.T. was gone. Adam muttered, "I'm grateful."

"It's nothing," I said, and meant it. "What else can I do?"

"I've no idea. How do we search for a missing teen?"

"We let professionals do it." I drained my cold drink, dragged my chair out of the hot sun. "On the other hand, didn't the Captain go chasing after his first wife?"

"That was different; Annie took to the streets, fuddled by her meds. Even Jared knows enough to avoid tranni—transpop zones." Again, he paced. "There must be something I could do."

Yes, disinherit the whelp. I kept the thought to myself. "Does P.T. know anything?"

"He said if he'd known Jared was running away, he'd have considered telling me." The wry grin of old. "That's his word: considered. Ah, well. He's a good joey."

Perhaps the drink had emboldened me. "You deserve a son like him. Not Jared." I held my breath, waiting for the explosion.

It never came. "Sometimes I wish . . ." Whatever his desire, I never heard it. He sighed, got to his feet. "Thanks for the help. Can you stay?"

"Not really. Dad and I lift for Earthport Station tonight. Party business." It was ironic that with all the ballrooms and convention centers scattered among the city towers, the Builders' Association held its annual convention aloft at the Earthport Hilton. I glanced at my watch. "I'd better not be late to the shuttleport."

Adam walked me to my waiting heli. "If I—when I get him back, I'll treat him differently. I've watched the Commandant with Philip. As much as the boy means to him, he's done what he thought best, not merely what his son wanted. I was never able to follow his example."

"And now?"

His face hardened. "I'll do what I must."

A moment later, the compound shrank under our skids. Adam's form faded to insignificance. Would he carry through with his resolve? Unlikely; people don't change that easily.

A shame, for Adam. It wasn't as if he were on his own; society's institutions stood ready to help him deal with the boy. If it came to it, Adam could have Jared petitioned to state custody as a wayward juvenile. The Rebellious Ages of a couple of centuries past were recognized as an aberration. Until his majority at twenty-two, the boy was legally in the charge of his parent.

My visit to the compound cost me no more than an hour, so I had time to spare. I had no idea why I was ten minutes late meeting Dad, and pointedly ignored his frequent glances at his watch.

At the shuttleport our VIP status wafted us through departure formalities. Dad stowed his chipcase and holovid, strapped in for acceleration, his manner irritable.

Conversation was impossible in the roar of the engines while the shuttle rolled down the runway. After we were airborne, our seats in the required lean-back position, I turned to him in the moments before the main engines ignited. "What's bothering you?"

He grunted. "I hate these damned fund-raisers."

I watched the cabin light panel. "Dad, you scheduled this yourself."

"Don't remind me. Just because we need the money doesn't mean I like doing it."

The light flashed red, saving me from a reply. I braced against my seat.

After the acceleration eased I busied myself rechecking my chipnotes. There was little our wealthy supporters appreciated more than being recognized by the politicians they courted. My notes detailed each entrepreneur's business, location, and family members, displayed on my holovid alongside his face. A nearly foolproof system, though twice I'd been brought to a standstill by an unnoted beard.

Dad tapped my wrist. "I intend to tell them New York will be the pilot project."

"That'll be tricky, with half of the guests from Boston-New Hampshire. I'll try to finesse—"

"Let's not weasel this one." For all his skills as a politician, Dad sometimes spoke bluntly to his constituents, and could get away with it. "Hell, it's already begun, all but the ground-clearing. The other towers will follow. And don't forget that two-thirds of our campaign fund comes from New York."

My stomach gave a small flip. "Why we book our conventions halfway across the solar system," I grumbled, "I'll never know."

"It's only Earthport Station. And the Hilton is next door to the new Naval wing, so the Navy brass are invited to the buffet. The last thing we want is our two prime constituencies fighting each other."

I pretended innocence. "I thought your constituency was the Northeastern Quadrant."

"And these are some of its foremost citizens." Dad peered at me. "Son, do you have a quarrel with what we're doing?"

I dropped my bantering tone. "No. Sorry." I brooded. "Though I'd rather we didn't part with old friends."

"Your Captain, again." Dad made a helpless gesture. "What's his last word?"

"That he's done with politics forever, we should stop pestering him to take a stand he disapproves of, and he hopes you'll be elected, for old times' sake."

"I . . . see."

I waited while Dad evaluated what he'd heard. His lips twitched with a smile. "Forthright, as always. Remind me to call Jim Wiler of Holoworld in the morning."

His eyes revealed little. Had he already set in motion the concerted belittling of his old ally? I couldn't tell.

"To Franjee Towers, Phase Two. Soon may they be built."
We lifted our glasses.

Admiral Jeffrey Thorne, CincHomeFleet, was genial. "And to the North American hull foundries."

Dad's eye met mine without expression, but I caught his inner amusement. He said, "Four new ships scheduled in the next three years. They'll put you almost back to prewar strength."

The Admiral didn't bat an eye. "Yes, about half what we need today." Arvil Peabody, a member of the builders' group, snorted in derision. Around us, the Hilton's waiters roamed with trays of hors d'oeuvres.

Admiral Thorne fixed Peabody with a disapproving glare. "The Caterwaul Stations freed our fleet to resume provisioning the colonies, but we've lost years of work. New exploration is at a standstill. We've had to postpone opening Casablanca Colony another two years."

Suliman Franjee, the distinguished former Deputy SecGen, patted the shoulder of Thorne's dress whites. "Come, now, Jeff. The Navy will be amply funded."

I said, "With our firm support." Nods, all around. Dad had won his spurs as head of the Naval Affairs Committee, over which he still presided.

Franjee said, "And mine. By the way, we've set our groundbreaking for October. That'll give us a month or so to clear the site."

A portly fellow from Hartford looked impressed. "That fast? Isn't it twenty square blocks?"

Franjee smiled. "No voters onsite. The area has no towers."

It was as it had always been. Politicians, by necessity, counted voting cards before taking a stand. New York had cut off virtually all services to the Bronx when the Holdouts finally lost their grip. For a long while, Holdout votes had stopped us, but now, block by block, the old Bronx was being leveled and reclaimed, its savage trannie gangs swept aside and dissipated. As would be the core city, at last.

Franjee deserved stroking, both as a builder and a party functionary. I said, "We appreciate your work for the cities, sir. Let's hope next year you'll be breaking ground on Phase Three."

"Good Lord." He seemed abashed. "No, eleven towers will keep us busy a while." He corralled a waiter, took another glass.

Jeff Thorne held his peace, but when he saw his chance, he stepped aside with Dad. Curious, I followed.

" . . . as fast as they can be built. To carry out tasks we can't put off, we've had to send nearly the entire fleet Outward. Do you realize—" The Admiral gestured east, toward the Naval bays—"that the Home Fleet hardly exists anymore? We rely almost entirely on Nick Seafort's Caterwaul Stations. If a threat occurred in home system, we'd be hard-pressed to find a ship capable of responding."

"Threat?" Dad's eyebrow lifted. "Hardly likely, in this day and age. Besides, the fish are no longer a factor, and as for rebellion—" He waved toward the bulkhead, beyond which lay the spacious new Naval headquarters, replacing those the fish had destroyed in Lunapolis on the lunar surface. "Should a domestic problem occur, your laser emplacements are surely adequate to quell it. At least, that's what your designers assured us."

Thorne assumed the defensive. "Of course. Earthport's in geosynch orbit. New York and Washington are always in range, and we can set four lasers to continuous fire. No enemy could survive such a bombardment. As for Europe, we could accelerate Earthport's orbit, if necessary. Though it would be hell reestablishing geosynch, after." He paused. "If it came to it, we could pinpoint virtually any spot within forty degrees of the equator. Have you toured the laser installation? The press office will schedule ceremonies in a month or so, but we're already on-line, and I'd be happy to show you through."

I groaned. Dad never missed the opportunity to visit a Naval facility.

Perhaps he heard my groan. Dad's smile was sweet. "Rob and I would be delighted. After dinner, perhaps."

I moved away, my lips fixed in a smile. I, too, loved the Navy, my first home. But I'd been looking forward to an early night's rest, not another hour trudging through the mazes of Earthport Station.

Earthport was our oldest and largest orbiting station. Through its many gates flowed a constant stream of passengers and cargoes destined for our expanding colonies. Earthport received, in return, the crops and manufactured goods that ameliorated life on the home planet.

Scores of personnel worked and lived on the station. The

Hilton, in whose banquet room we stood, was one of four luxurious hotels the station boasted. The "A" Concourse was dotted with restaurants of every description.

I stopped, chatted with a clutch of builders from a Carolinas cooperative, assuring them they'd get their share of commitments under the Redevelopment Act.

I knew Admiral Thorne's concern for the Navy was valid. Earth's prosperity depended in large degree on imports from her far-flung colonies. For that, Naval transport was essential, and the Navy had been hard-pressed ever since the invasion.

Trade continued, but at escalating prices. Derek Carr's troublesome Hope Nation government, for example, had doubled the duties on imports from Earth, to retaliate for what he considered exorbitant shipping costs imposed by the Navy.

Such matters made the Secretariat of Colonial Affairs the second most important position in the government, more powerful even than Chief Deputy SecGen.

Even Dad didn't know that I'd had my eye on it for years. First, the Senate. Then my day would come.

Chapter 15

PEDRO

I fussed at Pook 'til he helped me load cart. Time for 'nother trip to Subs. This time, boy didn' complain about havin' to go. Seemed eager.

'Til we got to Sub stairs, that was. He got real quiet, hung onto my arm as we went down. I slapped at his hand. "Prollem, Pookboy? Stair all slip wid ice?" This, in mid of hot summer.

"Dark." He took 'nother step, hand go back round my arm. "Don' fall, ol' man."

I smiled. Boy was thirteen, maybe fourteen, but had six-year joeykit in him too. I fished out my whistle, waited for Subs to come up behind, as they liked to. They entitled to their fun, long as didn't stick a shiv in us like old.

Prancing tribesmen led us along tunnel to lair, where Halber waited. Pookboy stuck close 'til he saw couple of Sub joeykits he recognize. He sat in corner, talkin' quiet, lookin' my way every so often as if askin', you here, Mista Chang?

"How many more c'n ya get?" Halber's face gleamed yellow in light of permas.

"Many as ya wan'," I assured him. Added quick, "If ya got enough trayfo."

He grinned. Teeth bad, some gone. "Course. Chang be traytaman."

I waited.

"Maybe seventy, eighty mo'."

My eye went up. "What you up to, Halber Sub? Gon' restart whole sub line?"

He looked dark. "How you know 'bout startin' sub?"

I was smug. "Wanna swind Pedro Telamon Chang, hah?" Maybe no one tol' Halber the Maceboy who rode sub with Fisherman long time past was my Eddie.

"Chang . . ." He looked pensive. "What you said, callin' alla trannies fo' meet. How we get tribe bossjoes ta join?"

I concealed my joy. "Dunno for sure. Why care alla sudden now?"

He brooded. "Lotsa tribe be pushout, late. Dunno why, but soon we won' know who 'bove us." He spat. "Bronx, nothin' but Crypsnbloods. Blue bandannas, tattoos, is all. No brains, no tribe. Jus' hate. Don' wan' see 'Hattan go same."

In corner, commotion. Sub joeykits fussed. Sounded like mini rumb buildin'. Halber got up. "Chaco, whomp doze kits! Keepem shush!" Sub tribesman hurried. Halber held out hand, tellin' him wait. He asked me, "Wanna shush ya kit separate?"

"Nah." Pookboy gotta learn, 'fore he push someone too far.

Yelps, then silence. Halber sat. "How many Neuts ya know?"

I raised eye. "Some." Why he ask?

"Can ya Neuts get word ta tribes we guarantee bosses be safe if dey come down inna Sub? Alla tribes listen?"

Careful, Pedro. Wanted Halber's cooperate for plan. "Need guarantee Subs can' break."

He thought it over, cautious. "How?"

Time to stroke. "Course, Sub word good enough fo' Chang. But unnerstan', otha tribes 'fraid a Sub. They won' go in tunnel 'less . . . " I waited, 'til he got impatient. " 'Less ya put Sub joes fo' guarantee."

He looked shocked. "Subs on street? Outside?"

I nodded.

"Boolsheet."

Time to push. "Your joeys 'fraid?" His hand went to shiv, like I 'xpected. I sat still. " 'Cause, 'fraid is only reason not ta offa tribe joes as hostage."

If he was Karlo of Mids, I never would of tried, but knew Halber had some sense. His anger abated slow. "Hold 'em where?"

"Dunno. Don' matta, actual. Let tribes decide. When bosses safe home, Subs go free."

"How many?" He was tastin' idea. Good.

"Bunch." Enough so Subs didn' get idea of doublecross.

"No Sub joeykits go," he warned. "An' not too many."

"Can work out." I patted his knee. "Leave to ol' Chang. When?"

On way back, Pookboy was pouty. I fussed at him, to keep him alert. An' maybe take his mind offa.

"Lemme be, Mista Chang."

"Don' see no blood," I teased. "He jus' whomp you some. No worse'n Midboss."

"Ain' dat." He pulled cart over curb. "Din' hurt none." Went shy. "Allie said she gonna show me tunnel, but couldn', wid Sub bosses watchin'."

"Whas so special 'bout tunnel? Alla Sub be tunnels. One like 'notha. Hey! Spill cart an' I whop ya good!"

"Ain spill," he grumbled. "Dunno whas' so special inna cart." Waited, while we pass through to Broad turf. Two cansa, like always. Damn innifo. We walked on.

"Allie say—" He lowered voice. "Sub gettin' ready to open Parka tunnel, fo' sprise. I ain' spose ta tell."

Had to know more. Only one way, with Pook. "Don' talk nonsense, joeykit. Subs ain' gonna trayfo wid Parkas."

"Almos' ready ta unlock stair, she say. Edge a Park. Lotsa Subs moved near ta live, unner. Be ready when."

What was Halber up to? The Subs were feared 'cross city, as should be. Very rowd tribe. But Parkas . . . animals, they were. Like Crypsnbloods in Bronx. No one went near park, didn' matter day or night. Centrapark was all overgrown high trees and bush. Trannie go in, don' come out. Uppie neither.

If Halber planned to open tunnel entrance, edge of Park, he had somethin' in mind. Dunno what. Filmatleven.

Best I find out, though, 'fore setup meeting alla bosses.

Came night, I sat and rocked in the light of my perma. Sittin' quiet made Pook nervous. All action, that joeykit.

He didn' understand.

Not sure I did, neither. I needed to stop thinkin' 'bout it, for while, 'til it came clearer in my mind.

Meanwhile, water problem was gettin' worse for alla tribes.

I'd tried hard to talk Eddie into visitin' his Cap'n one more time. He said no, and meant. I couldn't push; jus' lose ol' friend. Still, Captain only Uppie we knew who gave shit 'bout trannies. Even him, not enough.

I sat, rocked.

Pookboy pestered, lemme go out, please. Can' stan' no mo' dark room. Please, Mista Chang. I moved boxes like you say.

I let him go, for peace an' quiet. Sat with tea.

Halber wantin' trannie meet was long past time. Maybe someday we weld trannies into real tribe, stead of warring pieces. But, I doubted had time enough to stop Uppies 'fore tribes all gone. Soon or late, they send govermen to tear down, like with Mace. Then, more towers, high with hubris.

Knockin' down rotted builds not so bad. Problem was, what they do with trannies inside? No plans. Push 'em out, kill if they give trouble. Didn' matter. No one cared. If they killed hundreds, maybe more, no one see story in holozines.

How to stop?

Pookboy came back, tired, happy. Ran around like joeykit he was. Why we lived in world he had to carry shiv to stay 'live?

Trannie world. The way it is, Chang. Don' fuss about it. Have more tea.

Still.

I couldn't sip tea forever, 'til dozers push down shop. Meeting in Sub was good start, but needed another card. Jusincase.

Pookboy perched on stool. "Think Bigman Eddie get home safe?"

I laughed. "Don' worry 'bout ol' Eddie. Who gonna stop 'im?"

He rested chin on my chair arm. "Why he so sad 'bout Fisherman?"

I patted his head. "He took Captain's woman, twice."

"Naw. Couldn' be, or Fisherman dissim."

"Fisherman be . . . different." I went quiet, thinkin' 'bout how twice I met Captain, once in shop, once in monastery.

Do it again?

Long way to travel for ol' man used to city. But not first time outa New York. Once before, had to grit teeth, go into lifetime hoard of coin, use almost half, to pay ticket on suborbital. Made Eddie pay his own. No matter, Eddie had pension. Chang didn'.

Mace problems had been Eddie's, not mine. But he couldn't face his Cap'n without Chang at his side, like he was still joeykit. So ol'Chang dressed in jumpsuit, cut hair like suburb, went along.

It worked. Could work again, if Eddie would try, but he too afraid. Of own guilt he saw in Cap'n's face.

Pook stirred. "Fisherman jus' 'fraid of Eddieboss, cause Eddie too big."

"Fisherman ain' 'fraid a nothin'. Dat's his strength."

I sat, musing about what I'd said.

And then I knew.

Prolly never get to see him, but I hadda try. I looked at Pook. "Maybe I take you on 'nother trip."

Face lit up. "Sub? Okay, Mista Chang. I do whatchew say."

"Naw." I chuckled. "More far."

Took me day or so, get ready. Firs', find good threads for Pookboy. That be easy. Had lotsa, upstair.

Next part harder. Hadda make Pookboy look like someone Hitrans would let on train. Trannies got stopped at gate. Tribes carried too many weapons. Wouldn't let on.

First, his hair. When I tried to cut, he carried on like Samson. Finally ran me out of patient; I whopped him couple, to calm. He felt better, knowin' who boss, but Jesuchris', he hated haircut. Kep' lookin' in mirror, stuck tongue out every time he saw self.

Saved washing for last. Not pretend washing, like he tried few times. Made him clean hisself good, use lotsa soap. Lotsa Chang's precious water, too, but no matter.

Thought I'd lose him over that. Finally got desperate, kicked him outa shop, locked door. Only way to keep him. When finally I let him in, he settled down. Face grim, but held still mostly, while I help scrub. Time to time, when his curses got too violent, cuffed him a couple. Made both us feel better.

At last, we ready. I closed shop, turned off permas, huffed an' puffed to roof, checked security wires. All okay. Climbed back down, unlocked front door. "Come on, time wastin'."

"Ain' goin'." Pook sullen.

"Okay okay, I be allri' widout ya." Took bag. Heavy. Knew I needed Pook to carry, and help other ways.

"Ain' goin', said!"

"Okay okay, I tolya. Watchew wan' now?" Boy was impossible.

"Won' wear no jumpsuit. Look like stupid Broad." He pawed at new threads.

I crossed room, glimmer in eye. "Chang patient man.

Gotta be; allatime dealin' wid tribes. C'n even deal wid Pook, mosl'y. Very patient man. 'Xcept now. Pick up frazzin' bag! Getcha ass onna street, 'fore Chang kick it out. We late. Move!" I shoved. "Stupid Midboy c'n make a statue weep! Out!"

He went, mostly from surprise. Forgot he had on jumpsuit 'til door locked, and then too late.

Mid joeykits didn' help none, whistlin' at Pook, laughin' 'bout haircut. Boy gave me look, like, pay ya back someday, ol' man.

But he decided to ignore Midboys. Took bag, walked proud like always wore shiny new jumpsuit in street. After while, could see him relax. Think maybe he liked it.

Towers always closed, at bottom. Steel alloy doors locked shut; Uppies and freight came by heli. If Uppies went touris, they used Graybus. So no way we could get in, take heli to train.

Only couple of places, could mix with Uppies.

We headed for one of them. My heavy bag had lots of inni-fo, for passby now and later, back in. Negotiated past Broads and Mids to Four Two, started east. More Mids, then Easters. Bag got lighter. Pook got quieter, in strange turf. Good. Why I be cursed with Pook, stead of Eddie? Course, Eddie wasn' easy neither, when he young. Lotsa headache for ol' Pedro. My fate in life: trannie headaches.

"Where we goin, ol' man?"

I watched shops. Couple were open on Four Two, but no time to trayfo.

"Tell me!"

Puter stuff in one. Already had lotsa. Trannies got no use for.

Boy sigh. "Please, Mista Chang. Tell me where we goin'. I ask nice."

Better. I pointed. "Unie."

"Huh? Tribe?"

"Build."

Long time back, govermen decided, matter of principle, anyone allowed in public parts of U.N. build, even trannies. Last I knew, still did. Uppies didn' like it much. Few trannies wanted to go, anyway, even if brung innifo for passby. Jerries at gate make 'em feel unwelc.

"Whyfo?"

I shrugged. "Pook don' wan' see where govermen be? Learn somethin'?"

For once, boy use his head. "Din' make me mess wid hair, wear frazzin' jumpsuit jus' fo' dat. If ya don' wan' tell, okay wid me." Lip go out, pouting. "No need ta swind."

Proud a him. Seem he learning at last. "Okay okay, we goin' on Hitrans."

Boy's voice dripped with scorn. "No Hitrans heah, Changman. Wish I know ya be glitch 'fore I come widya."

"Where be Hitrans, hah?"

"Suburb turf. Seen holo, once."

"That's where we go."

He considered it as we walked. Cautious. "How?"

"Visit Unie. Then heli, ta Hitrans."

He relaxed, full of unconcern. "Ain' gonna happen. I protec' ya, if ya get too glitch."

Long walk, crosstown over. Maybe shoulda talked to Halber, got him ta ride me in undercar. But he don' know I knew 'bout, and would make trouble.

Hadda pass through nomanslan' every coupla block. More innifo. Talk. Kept eye on Pook, case he decide to pull shiv. Never know with that boy.

Finally, afta couple hours, we passed last nomanslan'. Up ahead, tall steel Unie builds, surround by big fence, guards. Govermen offices, Rotunda, Senate, Assembly, all there. Flags waved colorful.

I took Pook's arm tight, told him what I'd do if he didn' follow where I walked an' keep hands to self. Made sure he looked me in eye an' believed. I took his shiv, which he didn' like at all. I waited til Graybus parked 'longside gate, mixed best we could at end of line goin' through.

Metal detector lit, like I 'xpect. Guards looked bored, but careful. "Open the bag, please."

I took from Pook. Man looked at cansa, snorted with contempt. "Trannies." Closed bag. Patted down Pook, whose teeth bared like trapped wolf. I caught eye, shook no, extra stern. Boy transferred his mad to me, which I didn' mind.

Finally we in. Soon as I could, found quiet place, opened bag, found shiv in hiding place under cansa, gave back to Pook. He'd need it more 'n me.

Made boy feel better, but he hung close without my asking. Too many Uppies, in their own place. Pook was outsider, and knew. I waited in line at elevate. Watched door close on full car going up. While later, door opened, car empty. Pook grabbed my hand. "Ain' goin' in, Mista Chang!"

"Jus' elevate, Pook. You seen lotsa."

"Not wid door open by itself, eatin' joeys what in!"

"Jus' gave 'em ride. Showya. This how elevate spose ta work." I shuffled in with others. Boy had to follow, or be left alone. Almos' felt sorry for him, but I recalled fuss over wash and dress.

On roof, we waited for helicab. Pook shifted back an' forth, like wanted to say somethin', but didn'. Cab came, I shoved him in. "Hitrans Term."

Driver hit autolock. "Okay." He liftoff. I watched meter, make sure driver didn' swind. I had enough coin for trip, but wanted to bring some home, at end.

Cabbie looked back in mirror. "Whassamatter with boy?"

Pook hangin' to strap, face green. I tapped his knee; he didn' move. Below, roofs flashed past. "Gets nervous," I grumbled, Uppieing my talk. "Was in crash, once. He'll be allri' . . . all right."

"Better be." Driver's tone was sour. "Don't need no joeykit upchuckin' here."

Pook shot me look of despair, groaned. "Wan' go home."

"Soon." I pointed. "There, look quick! Centralpark."

He looked down, shuddered. "Jus' buncha trees."

"Jus'?" My voice low, so driver wouldn' hear. "How many you seen 'fore, joey, hah?" Inna street, tree good for burn, nothin' else.

Boy swallowed, still pale. Clutched strap. "Mista Chang, back in Unie . . . why elevate, steada stair?"

"Unie build is too big for use stair. Joeykit, maybe could. Not ol' man."

"Mid lair got elevate." He contemplated. "Not like Unie. Stay still. It go upandown, once?"

"All elevate wen' upandown, usetabe."

"Naw. Builds broke. How could—" His eyes widened with awe. "Ain' always broke?"

I held breath. High concept, for ignorant trannieboy.

"If elevate worked, usetabe Uppie build? Ligh' work too? Pipes good?"

"Once," I said soft. "Longtime back."

He think a while. Put his hand on my leg for steady, look careful outa window. Watch builds go past. Roofs, many rotted, falling in.

We veered around a skytel, huge against backdrop of shattered city. He hugged self, waited til we flew straight, looked down again. Looked back at skytel.

"Was big ol' city, Mista Chang." Again, he looked at skytel. "Towahs musta ate it."

No point describin' HiTrans ride with Pookboy. Enough to say, don't try widout patience of Job, maybe also leg cuffs. Dunno who was gladder to get off when bullet train pulled into Washington; me, Pook, or other passengers.

I looked for groundtrans signs while Pook danced round, excited, still a bit pissoff 'bout how I stop his idea of fun, in train. Old man's burden.

We were safe, long as stay in terminal. Lots of security joes in uniform an' without. But we had to go outside, take taxi or bus to Seafort compound. I'd studied maps before startin'; knew where we needed to go. Gettin' there was the prollem.

I had Unibucks for taxi, but couldn't see reason to waste, if bus drop me there only couple hours later. I took Pook outside Station, looked for bus sign. Around us, groundcars picked up families, taxis waited in line. Bunch of joes slouched 'gainst wall, predatory eyes watchin' bag I clutched tight. Watchin' Pook. Sizin' us up. Pook glared at all, me included.

Found busline. Headed for it.

"Hey ol' man, want help wid bag?" Joey had buddy who hung back. Could be tribe, but I didn' know for sure, outa my own turf.

I ignored, not lookin' for trouble. Pook kept step with me, quiet.

"Watcha got, ol' man?"

I said to Pook, loud an' clear, "Dissim, he come one step closa."

Pook yanked out his shiv. "Yes, Mista Chang. I do whatchew say." Never heard him say with so much enthuse.

Joeys backed off quick. I signed Pook put away shiv, 'fore jerry come by.

Was reason I brought Pook. Usetabe, I use shiv, machete, whateva it take. Neut gotta earn respect, or can' survive. Now, I was gettin' old. One day I'd climb stair over shop, fall down, not get up. Soon, prolly. Filmatleven.

On bus I paid whole Unibuck for each of us, but still a lot less than taxi or heli. Maybe shoulda taken taxi. Dunno. Bus smelled like build Mids was done with. Bugs crawled outa holes in seats. Driver in bulletproof cage, passengers on their own.

I almost got off, but instead, had Pook hold shiv in lap, kept tellin' him loud, try not to get excited, I'd give him his medicine soon as we got home. Musta worked; no one bothered us.

Bus let us off near compound; I made Pook put away shiv. Walked together to compound gate.

Big trouble.

Guards said Fisherman gone.

Chapter 16

PHILIP

I told myself I was fine. Almost, I believed it.

Lying awake at night I knew better. Walter Cranston, in Abnormal Psychology, Vol 3, Prentice Hall, 2134, says guilt is a consuming force. Unwarranted guilt is a disorder, he says in another chapter. But mine was deserved.

Mr. Skeer, my psych, said he'd have to call Mom. I explained that he had that choice—I was only a child, and powerless to stop him—but if he did, I'd never trust him with a confidence again, as Lord God was my witness.

We practiced my calming exercises for nearly the whole hour. At the end, he agreed not to tell Mom, but made me promise I wouldn't do anything rash until I talked to him again.

I promised. I wasn't rash.

It was all my fault. I'd panicked when Jared wrestled with me, and I did bad things to his mind. He ran away because of me. Father said a man is responsible for what he does. An attempt to evade blame is an affront to Lord God, and to truth.

Father had wisdom. I'd have liked to knock at his study, talk to him about my dilemma, but I couldn't. He wouldn't be back from the monastery for days, and even then, he had too much on his mind, and I mustn't add to his burden. As Mom said, he'd been through Hell and found his way back to us, but the memories lingered.

Poor Jared. For a brief moment he let his urges get the better of him, and I savaged him because I couldn't deal with it. Kicking him in the balls wasn't the problem; he'd probably experienced it before, in school. But I'd let him see my contempt.

Jared couldn't handle my contempt. He had too much of his own.

Perhaps I'd even exaggerated a bit. I wasn't thinking clearly. I didn't know why. Mr. Skeer said I was in sexual panic, but I doubted it. I was too young for sexual feelings. But when Jared touched me . . . it was good to sit in the corner, my back to the wall, knees up. If I stayed quiet, breathed slowly, I knew that nothing in my comfortable room could hurt me.

Mr. Tenere had been fretting since Jar disappeared. Still, he went to work in the outer office, and sometimes Mom sat with him.

Jared had been missing two days. The police hadn't found him. They didn't know where to look.

The jerries came the first night, while Mom and I were at dinner. They went to Mr. Tenere's bungalow. I assume they looked around; they're supposed to do things like that.

After Mom brought me back from the Rodin exhibit, I walked the compound alone. The walls had familiar spots, thinking places where I could run my hands along the whitewash, perhaps pick a few small leaves off the azaleas.

The bungalow seemed very quiet.

Mr. Tenere was at the house, but I knew he wouldn't mind when I went to Jared's room, closed the door. I sat on the bed, pushed down a sharp unpleasant memory. I was beyond that.

I hoped the jerries would find him. Jar wasn't old enough to be on his own, and he was too impetuous, objectively speaking.

I opened his closet door. The floor was littered with the usual mess; dirty clothes, parts from abandoned games, old shoes. I really should respect Jar's privacy. Father said respect for oneself begins with respect for others. He was usually right.

I pawed through a shelf. If I saw enough of Jared's clothes, by process of elimination I could figure what he was wearing. That might indicate where he'd gone.

The door opened. "Jared?" Mr. Tenere, his voice eager.

I turned.

"Oh." So sad, the one word by itself. I had an urge to hug him.

"I was looking for clues, Mr. Tenere."

A fleeting smile. "Do that. Let me know what you deduce."

"Yes, sir."

He left me.

I felt better, with Mr. Tenere's permission. I turned on the puter, accessed Jared's nets.

A cluster of coded files that I didn't have time to break. Not much else.

Disconsolate, I wandered back outside, followed the wall around the compound to the gatepath.

Every week hundreds of people came to the compound hoping to see Fath. Some were deranged. Some of them brought letters, others tried to leave gifts. Most were just gawkers. Mom said I should keep away from the entrance; it was dangerous. When I argued she got her drill sergeant voice, and I knew she meant it.

At times I still went to the gates, but not often, because people pointed or turned on their holorecorders. Jared said I should moon them and they'd stop, but I told him to try it first. As far as I knew, he hadn't.

The guards were former Navy men, and I felt safe in their presence.

Today, there was the usual crowd. Hands in pockets, I wandered to the guardhouse. "Hi, Mr. Vishinsky."

"Hello, lad." His tone was agreeable, but his eyes never ceased roving the sidewalk.

"Like me to get you coffee?"

"We have a fresh pot." He glanced at his watch. The evening shift would relieve his crew at five.

I ducked into the guardhouse while a fat tourist posed her daughters in front of the gates, snapped her holos. When they were gone, I peered out.

Mr. Vish rested his hand on my shoulder. "Five years, and they're as thick as ever. It's like they're on pilgrimage."

"They just stare," I said. "What do they want?"

He was silent a while. "Fulfillment." Before I could ask what he meant, he was gone. "Stand back, please. Not so close to the gate." One old man ignored him, holding tightly to his grandson's arm.

"Back away, sir. Stay behind the yellow—"

"I wanta see the Captain." He spoke with exaggerated care.

"Mr. Seafort's left town. Sorry."

"When he come back?"

Mr. Vish's eyes narrowed. "That's not for me to say."

"I wait, if need."

"The SecGen doesn't see visitors. He's retir—"

"He might see me. I knew him."

"Many did." The guard's tone was civil, but I knew his patience was wearing thin. "He won't see you, granther, no matter—"

"Important." The old man fished in a pocket. "I have letter."

"He's in Lancaster. We'd prefer you sent mail to—"

The boy stirred, reached into his pocket. His eyes held menace. I ducked back into the shadows.

The old man waved a warning finger; the boy subsided. "Please. Take."

Mr. Vish sighed, took the crumpled paper. "All right. I'll send it up to the house."

"Please."

"When my shift's over, it'll go with all the rest. Anyway, he won't get it for days, 'til he's home. On your way, please."

The old man peered with myopic eyes, past the guardhouse, to the drive. He sighed, turned away.

A few moments later Mr. Vish ducked into the shade of the guardhouse. "People." He tossed the crumpled note into a half-filled basket. "Best be on your way, lad, before the Mizz sees you."

"Yes, sir." I ran my fingers along his fat, shiny truncheon. I'd seen him use it only once, when a pair of drunken joes ignored his warning and tried to scale the wall. After, he and Mr. Tzee had hosed the bloodstains from the sidewalk.

I wandered back to the house. Mom was dictating to her puter; she offered a friendly wave without stopping.

I started to my room, halted. Adam Tenere's puter sat silent in the outer office. A few days ago, Jared had been trying to break into his Dad's files.

Had he succeeded? I'd given enough hints. I glanced around, sat at the console. If Mom caught me, I'd be sent to my room with a lecture that would make me feel worse. If Mr. Tenere saw, he might never trust me again.

On the other hand, Jared might have left clues. And Mr. Tenere had given permission, sort of.

I unlocked his passwords, skimmed through his files. Letters, and memoranda. Nothing Jared would care about. I blanked the screen, sat thinking. Idly, I checked the remote access log, knowing that Jared couldn't have been so stupid as to leave a trail.

But he had.

Three accesses, from his own puter. I began to open newly altered files.

The shuttle schedules. Interesting. Jared could have made connections to anywhere in the world by now.

Intercontinental Sheraton reservations. That must have been his Dad; Jared didn't have the money for a skytel.

The only other file was Mr. Tenere's Terrex account. Absolutely none of my business. My hand went to the screen-blanker, hesitated.

Surely Jared wouldn't hack the Terrex account; that went beyond disobedience to a criminal act. But if we didn't find Jared soon, Father would have to be told, and we couldn't upset him further, especially after Lancaster.

I opened the file, dialed the worldwide Terrex puter.

"Password?"

I tried their birthdays.

"Access denied."

Mr. Tenere's birthday, in base twelve.

"Access denied."

I heard a sound, spun to the door. If they caught me, my honor was forfeit. No, Philip, it was already forfeit; they would merely learn of it.

My ears burning, I tried other combinations.

It was Mr. Tenere's birthday, backward. The screen flickered.

A reservation at the New York Sheraton Skytel had been charged to his account. I closed the file, heart thumping, and opened Mr. Tenere's calendar. He had no trip scheduled. Father was 'n Lancaster, so the reservation couldn't be for him.

Back to the Terrex account.

I skimmed past the monthly statements, ordered daily account review. Jared had been gone two days; I needed to see yesterday and—

Four hundred Unibucks, withdrawn at New York Shuttleport.

Jared was in New York.

A thump; an outside door closing. I flicked off the puter,

scrambled upstairs to my room. I sat in the corner, head against my knees, picking at my shirt.

All my fault. Because of my vicious attack Jared was a criminal, perhaps even in danger. I tried the calming mantras, drew my knees up closer. My fault.

Mom came at eleven to kiss me good night. I gave her an extra-special hug.

By eleven-thirty all was quiet. I got out of bed, knowing exactly what I'd do. I'd planned it all evening, instead of tackling another chapter of math.

Clothes. I'd need two changes; I'd be back before I used more. In the dark, I opened my small suitcase, the one with my initials on the edge. Genuine leather, one of the few still made. Expensive. Father had given it to me for a birthday present before our trip to Lunapolis. I stacked my clothes neatly, the way Mom liked.

Money. I dragged my stool to the closet, climbed to reach the top shelf.

I knew I'd walk to New York before I'd steal money as Jared had. Once, when I was five, I'd stolen a toy from a friend's house. Father and I had a serious talk about it, and I was never going to steal again. Nothing was worth feeling that bad.

Anyway, I didn't need to steal. I opened my toy safe, took out three hundred Unibucks, closed it again carefully. I was supposed to tell Mom or Father before taking more than ten dollars, and I was disobeying. Later, I'd make sure they punished me; I needed their control. But not now.

The money was mine. Four years ago, when I'd proposed my idea to Father, he'd been incredulous. An eight-year-old playing the stock market with lawn money? He gave his assent, warning it was illegal since I wasn't of age, and if I were caught he'd tell them I was some miner's son he'd picked up on Callisto. I didn't think he meant it, but I'd never been caught. I didn't trade too often; once a week or so, over Jared's puter nets.

I folded the money in the platinum clip Mom had given me for my last birthday. I'd seen Senator Raines with a similar one, and mentioned how much I liked it.

I glanced at my notes. I'd forgotten to pack a caller. I

reopened my suitcase, tucked in my personal caller, red and yellow. Adults think children like bright colors. Perhaps some do.

The next item added to my guilt. I reminded myself I was doing it for Jared. For Mr. Tenere, actually. That should make it all right, especially if I didn't think about it. I'd talk it over with Mr. Skeer on our next appointment.

Still in the dark, I tiptoed to my puter, dialed to Mom's, in her office. She didn't often change her passwords, and I knew her mind fairly well. I typed out the note I'd composed.

"TO WHOM IT MAY CONCERN: My son Philip is on route to the Sanders family reunion in New York. Please give him every assistance, should he need it. He is to call home every day. Arlene Sanders Seafort." I sent the note from her puter to mine, so it would arrive stamped with her personal code. I pushed the eprom, waited for the chip to pop into the bin.

Perhaps an unneeded precaution, but anyone validating my note through Mom's puter would have it confirmed automatically. There was a chance the skytel's reservation desk would inquire.

Before flicking off my puter, I sat thinking.

I'd promised to let Mr. Tenere know what I learned, but I was about to go after Jared without leaving a clue. On the other hand, I was reluctant to admit I'd been reviewing his Terrex account.

I posted a note to his office puter. "Suggestion from P.T.: check to see what money Jared could have taken with him." I hoped that would do it.

Clothes, money, caller, note. I opened my door cautiously, tiptoed down the stairs, left a scribbled note in the kitchen for the morning, telling Mom I'd had a guard drive me to my history tutor, and that I'd go directly to Mr. Skeer by cab. I selected two old pans, took them along.

Outside, all was still. I trudged down the path toward the gate, my suitcase light against my side. I was looking forward to the adventure, objectively speaking, though I was a bit concerned Father might find out, if all didn't go well. I hoped it wouldn't provoke him into breaking his promise and giving me a licking. That would upset him.

Chapter 17

JARED

My flight landed at Von Walther Shuttleport exactly on time. I retrieved my carry-on, followed the herd to the baggage and transport gates. I had ample funds for a helicab. I'd have to remember to draw more against Dad's Terrex in a day or two. I gave the cabbie a ten Unibuck tip, which caused him to grin and touch his cap.

Checking in at the Sheraton was a zark. I'd made the reservation as Jer Adamson; no harm in a small joke.

I paid cash. Unusual these days, but still legal. My biggest worry was that some officious joey would question my age, but no one seemed to care, thanks to my foresight in making a reservation from home.

As soon as the bellhop left I dropped my bag, threw myself on the huge, luxurious bed.

My meeting was set for tomorrow afternoon; today, I had only to enjoy myself. I decided on the penthouse restaurant under the skytop lobby. Then a good night's sleep. I bounced again on the bed. This was the life.

I put on my good jacket over my favorite green shirt, smoothed my hair, rode upstairs.

I frowned at the first table the maitre d' offered, slipped him a twenty just as I'd seen done in the holos. In moments I was at a zarky fountainside table, an obsequious waiter sliding my chair under me. I glanced about; decided the jacket was just formal enough so I wasn't out of place. Regretfully, I passed up the wine list. A silly mistake could destroy everything.

I opened the menu, gulped at the prices before I realized they didn't matter; I had ample cash, and Dad's Terrex besides. For an appetizer I ordered genuine shrimp, not syntho; Dad was always too cheap to get it.

The waiter helped me pick out interesting dishes from the jumble of foreign names. If they were awful I could send them back.

The waiter closed his menu. "And to drink, sir? May I suggest a bottle of Pinot Noir?"

I glanced at his eyes, saw nothing that roused my suspicion. Well, what the hell; it was his idea, not mine. "Sure." If someone asked for ID, I could claim I'd left my wallet in the room, and cancel the liquor.

I went over my notes one more time. I hadn't slept well, and my head hurt. Still an hour until my meeting. I rinsed my face yet again, sat in the easy chair.

Last night's dinner had left me in a fine frame of mind. When the bill came I'd decided against squandering the remainder of my cash. Instead, I charged it on Dad's Terrex. Though the debit would show up immediately, Dad didn't pay bills until the end of the month, and by then I'd be long gone.

Now, in my hotel room, I hoped he wouldn't find occasion to use his card; the last thing I needed was to have it canceled because he thought he'd lost it. I made a mental note to get some more cash before dinner, just in case.

I hadn't felt much like breakfast or lunch, though I usually had a great appetite. Even now, my stomach was still queasy. I visited the bathroom one more time, went up to the lobby, where we were to meet.

I waited for the desk clerk to look up from his console. "Has a Mr. Echart shown up? I was supposed to meet—"

"Over there." He stuck out a thumb, went back to his work.

I glared, to no effect. For what I was paying, I was entitled—later, Jar. I'd complain to the manager when my business was done.

I smoothed my jacket, reviewed my mental script, strode over to the waiting area, with its coffee table and chairs. "Mr. Echart?"

A heavyset joe, older even than Dad, sitting with a woman whose gaunt face seemed hard. "Yeah?"

"I'm the one who—a messenger. I was supposed to meet—"

"You?" He looked me up and down, exchanged a glance with his companion. Both remained seated.

I felt my face go red. "I'm just a messenger. I was told to find out if—"

"Who you working for?"

I wanted to turn on my heel, stalk off. Instead, I started over. "Look, I was supposed to meet two joes from Holoworld. I guess that's you, but how do I know for sure?"

The woman reached into her jumpsuit pocket, pulled out a wallet, flipped it over to show her press card. I'd seen lots of them. An advantage of living with the Old Man.

I peered. "Ms. Granyon? Good to meet you."

"Sure." She snapped her wallet closed. "What do you have?"

"The man I work for is staying in—near the hotel," I said. "He told me you'd make an offer for his story."

Echart shook his head. "Why would we? He already gave it to us."

"Not the best parts. If you—"

"How do you know what's in it?"

The conversation was going all wrong. In my plan, I was the one in charge. "He told me. Why did you waste my—our time if you weren't interested? Do you want the scoop on Boland or not?"

Again they exchanged glances. Ms. Granyon said, "Sure, joeyboy. Just—"

"Don't call me that!" I fumed. "I'll bet World Newsnet will listen, even if you won't. Let's forget the whole damn thing!"

The man grinned. "I thought you were just the messenger." I stumbled to a halt. His foot pushed out a seat. "Don't con us, joeyb—joey. We'll deal with a teener if we have to. Hell, I'd deal with Satan if he could get me a lock on the front screen. Level with us."

I sat, my legs trembling. "I want money."

"How much, and for what?"

"For a near transcript of Senator Boland and his son the Assemblyman plotting how to prong their old friend, SecGen Seafort."

"Near transcript? Have any proof?"

Damn. I should have used a recorder. "I was a witness. I wrote it all down, and my memory is good."

"Who are you?"

I said, "Why do you need to know?"

His tone was reasonable. "What's to stop anyone from

claiming they overheard a conversation, and making one up? Prove you had opportunity."

I bit my lip. "Will I stay confidential?"

"It isn't much of a story if we can't quote the source."

"No." I stood. I wasn't sure why, but I knew I couldn't have P.T. learn what I'd done. Or even the Old Man. "Sorry, it didn't work out." I backed away. "Forget I—"

"All right, you stay confidential." He sounded disgusted. "Who are you, and what do you have for us?"

"I live in the Old—SecGen Seafort's compound, and I heard them talking. You'll get my name later. I have what I told you, plus some crap about the tower people lining up behind the Reconstruction bill, and Boland's plans to run next year."

"Hell, everybody knows he's up for reelec—"

"For SecGen." That stopped him. I rubbed my fingers together. "Unibucks."

"How much?"

I'd reached the end of my script. I wasn't sure how much to ask for. "Five thousand."

"Oh, come on!"

I shook my head. "Five thousand. Take it or leave it. And don't try to chisel me. I'll walk."

Echart turned to his companion. She was silent a moment. Then, "Go."

I'd won. I restrained an urge to jump up on the chair and whoop. "Where's the bucks?"

"Not so fast. We record your story, and pay after."

"I get a written promise that you'll pay me, before I speak."

"Fair. We don't cheat sources, joeyboy. They'd go elsewhere. You have a deal."

"Zark!" I cleared my throat. "Good, I mean. When do we start?"

"We'll be back with a cameraman at nine. One hour. You have a room?"

"3023. I mean—" Too late. I blushed. Now they'd know my name. Oh, well. Like they said, a deal was a deal.

"You here alone?"

I bristled. "What's it to you?"

"Just wondering. You a runaway?" He squinted. "You're not the SecGen's—? Nah, he's younger."

"Twelve."

"Yeah. Don't tell me if you're a runaway, joeyboy, or I'll report you. Law's the law. See you at eight?" He stuck out his hand.

We shook, and I watched them go.

Five thousand Unibucks. Enough to get me out of the city, out of the continent. Hell, off the planet, if I could figure how to forge the papers.

I jostled my way onto the elevator, waited while it dropped. Five thou. Not a bad start. Maybe, after, I should hide my money, go back to the compound like a penitent son, and set up a few recorders in the guest room. Easy money.

The elevator stopped frequently; it was near the dinner hour, and people were heading to their rooms to change. Finally I reached my floor, trudged down the corridor, fishing for my key.

I glanced at a door, stopped. Damn. I'd gotten off at Thirty-one instead of Thirty. I started back for the bank of elevators, decided the stairs would be faster. Taking them two at a time, I flung open the door, darted into the corridor.

Two men, at the door to my room. I froze. They knocked again.

The fat one wore a hotel uniform. Was the other a jerry? No way to be sure.

Mystery man glanced my way; smoothly, I turned, sauntered toward the elevator bank, dropping my key in my back pocket, hoping they saw.

I rang for the elevator, listening.

"He's not in." The hotel man.

"Use a passkey."

"Left it at the desk. Besides, I got to get the manager's okay." Where was the frazzing elevator?

"For a runaway?"

"For any guest, joey." Come *on*, elevator! " 'Sides, this one's got connections. The home office called, said to be extra care—"

"Go on up. I'll wait here, case he shows."

Trouble. Big trouble.

"Right. Lemme see the holo again. Ya never know." The fat man peered. "Say . . . " He glanced at me.

I sprinted down the corridor, accelerating like a suborbital. How the hell did they *know*?

At the end of the corridor, another staircase. Up or down? No time to think.

The lobby was upstairs. Best go the other way, then. I could catch an elevator from a couple floors down. I raced down the stairwell, trying not to stumble. Twenty-eight.

How could they know? My reservation was in the name of Adamson. I'd paid cash when I checked in. I'd used Dad's card, but that was at the shuttleport. Twenty-seven.

Damn. I'd charged last night's dinner with Dad's card. But how could they connect—Christ, I'd made the dinner reservation with my room number.

I tore around the stairwell, peered down at the endless flights. I'd be wheezing when I reached the bottom. I swung open the corridor door, peered out. Twenty-six. Steady, Jar. You have time. I trotted to the elevator bank, jabbed the buzzer.

An endless wait, while I caught my breath.

The bell chimed. A car, going up. No. I waited.

Damn. At this rate even the stairs would be better. How could elevators keep going up without one ever coming—

At last. I managed to walk rather than dive aboard. I punched One, waited through interminable stops.

I glanced about. No one paid me any attention. Passengers stood in elevator silence, eyes front, except for a woman adjusting her collar in the mirrored sidewall. Fancy elevator, this. Mirrors on all sides, sleek alumalloy door, brass controls, even the security camera had brass—

Oh, God. "Hold it!" I thrust my way past an annoyed matron. Where the hell was I? Five. The lowest floor with bedrooms.

I hesitated, wondered whether to go upstairs. Had they noticed? Just how good was Sheraton security?

A stairwell door swung open. Two guards. "There he is!"

Too damn good. I raced to the stairwell at the far end of the corridor. A guard rasped instructions into his caller.

Five flights were below me. I dashed down, tripped, ricocheted off a wall. Easy, joey. Above, footsteps thundered.

Four. Hurry, but stay on your feet. The guard hurtled after. Three.

"Hey, you! Hold on!"

Sure. I'll wait here, officer, while you cuff me. Well, maybe not. I knew Dad wouldn't press charges. Even if he had a mind to, I'd talk him out of it. But, damn it, I wouldn't let my plans be ruined. All I had to do was call Holoworld and reschedule my interview at their offices.

The doorway to Two loomed. One more flight, and—

They'd be waiting below. I flung open the second floor door. There was another stairwell at the far end of the corridor, and I could run faster than they.

"Outa my way!" Baring my teeth, I lunged past an elderly man struggling with an armload of packages. Behind me, relentless footfalls. Were the guards armed? My back itched. No, they wouldn't shoot. I had connections.

I flung open the far door, raced down the last flight, emerged on the first floor.

Dusty, ill lit. A dirty tile floor. Stained carpet. Which way should I—

A guard thudded around the corner, making my decision. I sprinted the other way.

"Wait, joey. We ain't gonna hurt—"

I tore into a side corridor, slammed into a stack of chairs. Christ. I rolled to my feet.

A door, chained shut. I ran past, looking for escape.

The corridor came to a corner. A dead end ahead. No, damn it! I whirled, caromed off the guard's shoulder. I ducked past him, back the way I came. Cursing, he followed.

"We got him!" The guards from floor Two, waiting at the end of the corridor.

At the chained door, I glanced both ways. They weren't going to drag me back to Dad like some young—

The guards rushed in concert. I reared back, gave the padlock a mighty kick. The chain snapped. I tore at the links. A hand fell on my shoulder. "Easy, boy. You can't go—"

I rammed the bar. With a squeal, the heavy alloy door fell open. I tore myself loose from the clutching hand, dashed into the street. The guards hesitated. Before they made up their minds to follow, I raced around the corner and out of sight.

I was safe.

A hot summer evening. Stores were closed, though it was

still light. I slowed to a walk, trying to catch my breath. I needed to find a caller and contact Echart or his girlfriend.

The street was filthy. I stepped around the worst of the rubbish. Four or five joeys watched from a doorway. I glanced around. Others loitered further down the street, but these were the closest.

"Excuse me, where can I find a caller?"

The one in front spat, just missing my boot. Well, I'd heard the street people were glitched. Once, the Old Man had told a wild tale—

A teener pranced, circling me. "Watchadoon onna street, Uppie?"

I wrinkled my brow, puzzling out his gibberish. "Me? Looking for a caller."

He guffawed. "Ain' no callers in trannietown."

I flinched from a rank smell and hurried away, uneasy. I couldn't return to the hotel, but I ought to get back to civilization.

Two teeners followed. I spun. "Jet off!" I thrust my hand in my pocket, made a fist. "You're asking for trouble!"

One of them snickered. I hurried on, trying to increase the distance between us without breaking into a run.

No use. They kept pace. "Frazzin' Uppies think ya own da worl'! Ya onna street now, joey!"

The other grinned. "An' nigh' be soon! Betta run ta mama!"

One, the more daring, pawed at my jacket. I lunged, shoved him. He sprawled in the gutter. He leaped to his feet, his eyes blazing. "Dissya, mess wid Broad!"

I made my voice cold. "Prong yourself!" He hesitated at my assurance, and I strode away.

I breathed easier. All it took was confidence.

People in threadbare clothing stared as I passed. I searched for a street sign, couldn't find one. I had to find another tower, bang on the door until they let me in. Or a helicab stand. I had enough money for that, though not much more.

Someone jostled; I staggered, resumed my pace.

A snicker. I looked over my shoulder; the trannie teeners were back. "Help fin' ya way, Uppie?" A gap-toothed grin.

"Prong yourself." This time it didn't have the same effect.

I hurried on in the fading light. At the corner, I'd be able to spot the nearest tower above the nearby buildings.

A hand grasped at my jacket. I whirled, struck at the nearest trannie, and ran.

Shouts, clawing fingers. I slapped them away, dashed to the corner and beyond. Across the street lounged a group of ragged trannies. In the road I risked a glance back. My pursuers had given up.

I loped to the sidewalk. One of several unkempt men stepped into my path. "Ain' day, Uppieboy. Streets be ourn."

"Prong yourself." It was becoming a litany. I sidestepped him, strode on. There'd be a frazzing caller *somewhere*.

"Karlo take dat from a Uppie joeykit?"

"Naw!" Footsteps thudded after me.

I ran.

I was faster than most of them, but one was gaining on me. His grunts echoed in the humid silence. A hand clawed at my back. I shook it off, but a moment later I felt it again. The trannie grabbed my collar, nearly threw me to the ground. His gangmates were only steps behind. I cursed, squirmed out of my jacket, ran on. A frazzing coat wasn't worth getting killed for. Holoworld would buy me another.

The trannie followed.

I made it to the corner, dashed across the street. I glanced back, breathed easier. The bastard had stopped.

This block seemed deserted. No, not quite. Ahead, a well-dressed youngster. Thank Lord God, another Upper New Yorker. I ran toward him. "Hey! Where's the nearest tower?"

He smiled.

Chapter 18

POOK

Day afta we get back from Washinton, ol' man quiet, like too tire'. Sit in shop all day, rockin' wid his tea. Don' even wan' open door ta trayfo, when Mid or Broad knock. Ova an' ova I tellim, come on, Mista Chang, ya be traytaman, so trayfo. Trannies be waitin'.

Naw, he say. Leave me 'lone, Pook.

Please, Mista Chang, ya can' let shop go. Where ya respec'? He smile, pat me. Okay okay he say, an' open door. Tire' an' ol', maybe, but not so tire' he can' skin a trannie come fo' tray. C'n do dat in his sleep, prolly.

Stupid ol' man laugh when I tellim I wanna keep jumpsuit. Couldn't getcha put it on, Pook, can' getcha take it off. Who care, I say. I wear what I wan'. Mid joeys laugh, I diss 'em all.

Don' talk like dat, he say. I shrug.

Nex' day he sit an' rock, same as 'fore.

"Ya sick, Mista Chang?"

"Nah. Depress."

I dunno. He glitch. I wan' go out, but he won't answer yes or no, so I run roun' asking questions, pickin' up stuff, 'til he sigh, open door. "Okay okay, ya drive me craze. Nex' creature I raise be a stuff owl. G'wan."

"Yes, Mista Chang. I do whatchew say." I gone.

I check out street. Watch for Karlo, ta hide from, but he ain' out. Other Mids nod, talk ta me civil. A snot joeykit try joke 'bout my jumpsuit, so I stomp him. Den he shush. I feel good. Nothin ta do, so I go in ol' build 'cross from lair, look roun'.

I seen build otha times, but look different now, afta governmen place. In hall elevate, I wham on buttons, but nothin'. Broke. Be a zark make it work, but dunno how. Upstair, door hang open ta hole where elevate was. I look down. Jus' coupla feet below, be big box wid small trap in top. Climb down, checkitout. Inside awful dark, but look like elevate, buttons an' all. I figga usetabe go upandown.

Build all bust, windows broke. Wonder if Changman know what he talkinabout, tellin' me it once be like Unie build.

I bore. I go back ta shop, bang 'til Changman let me in.

"Why ya keep permaligh' so low, Mista Chang? Like nigh' in here."

He fuss with pile a Unibucks. "Midboy go back outside, he don' like Chang shop."

I go sullen. "Ain' no ansa." I turn up ligh'. He glare, but leave it be. In back, I look in mirror. My hair still glitch. Stupid ol' man, makin' me cut. If hair spose ta be shor', why it grow, hah?

Chang get up. "I don' see any otha way," he say.

"Whatcha talkinabout, Mista Chang?"

"Gotta go, 'gain."

"Noway!" He ain' takin' me on Hitrans no more. I dissim firs'.

"Din' mean you, Pookboy. Jus' Chang this time."

I go bristle. "Where ya go Pook ain' good enough ta come 'long?"

"Lancaster."

"Whazzat?"

"Cross ocean. Suborbital." He pour tea. "Can' bring ya. They search fo' shiv, an' fin'. Anyway, I be too ol', take ya so far. Don' got patient like I used."

"Why go?"

"Fisherman." He sit. "Gotta talk ta him, Pook. 'Fore it too late." Look at watch. "Tonigh'. Go crosstown ta Unie, take helicab ta Von Walther. Got just enough coin."

I go anxious. "Some trannie try grab ya bag, whatchew gon' do widout Pook?"

"No problem once I get outa N'Yawk. I go Uppie places." He sigh. "Use my last Unibuck, jusabout. No matta. Get more, soonalate."

"I wan' go!"

"No. Can' pay for both." He finish tea, stand. "Gotta pack. Go fin' Karlo; see out how much innifo ya need ta go home. I give."

"Prong yaself!" I go growly. "Don' need no ol' man ta—"

He raise eyebrow. "No joeykit talk ta Chang in his shop like—"

"Prong yaself! Prong yaself! I wan' go wid!"

He move fas', fo' ol' man. Trot 'cross room, grab my arm when I reach automatic fo' shiv. Whop me inna mouth. I go teary. "Ain' fair!"

He whop me again, take shiv from pocket, put in his.

"Leame 'lone, Changman! Leggo!"

Whop. I settle, cryin'. Can' help.

"Tolya, no joeykit gon' curse Pedro Telamon Chang in own house!" Ol' man mad like I neva seen. "Siddown!" I sit. "Shut face 'til I say!"

I be sulk, but he don' pay 'tention. Fuss at packin' his bag, grumblin' ya give Midboy nice jumpsuit, he start talkin' like Uppie, ackin' like one. No respec'. No wunner Karlo decide no upbringin'. I sniffle.

He pack. He go up stair, come back afta while, hard breathe.

I glare. "Wanna go out!"

"Did I say okay ya talk, hah?" He come close, but I c'n see he done wid mad.

"Lemme go."

"Back ta Mid lair?"

I go proud. "Don' need no lair. Be all ri'. Gimme shiv, I be gone."

He sigh. "I back tomorra. Or nex' day for sure."

"Don' care." I hol' out hand.

He jus' stare.

Always gotta do his way. "Please, Mista Chang. Gimme shiv." He give, like he ain' afraid I stick it in. I be tempt. Stupid ol' man. I hate.

He open door. "Wan' innifo for Karlo?"

"Naw."

He shrug. "Midboy ain' gonna starve in day or two." We go out, he lock door. "Come knock, when I'm back." Afta ol' man whop me, think I be back? Ri'.

I cross street, fo' safe. He walk away, carryin' bag.

"Prong yaself!"

He preten' don' hear.

"Neva talk ta ya 'gain, Changman! Hope ya die!"

I watch him go. Ain' fair, he don' take Pook. Las' time, I help when he say.

I wait 'cross from lair, til Bigsis come out. No Karlo, so I run 'longside. "Hi."

She smile, but look roun' fo' safe. "G'wan, 'fore Karlo seeya."

"Still pissoff?"

"Yeah. Prolly fo' longtime, now." She shrug. "Shouldn't a pissoff Ravan an' Karlo same time."

"Whazzat?" I checkout laserpen in her han'.

"Trayfo. Need cansa."

"Lemme help?"

"Naw. Can', wid Karlo out." She stop. "Bes' be gone, joeykit."

"Yeah." I kick sidewalk. "See ya roun'."

Rest a day, I wander, careful ta stay inside Mid turf, but not too near tribe. Bore.

Dark comin'. I no worry, figga I c'n sleep in ol' build cross from lair. Hid there once, Karlo be pissoff.

Go ta corna, checkout Broad turf. Some kinda fuss. Boy runnin', Broads chasin'.

Come closer.

Uppie.

I watch wid ineres'. Dey catchim, be fun.

Almos', dey gottim. Grab his jacket, but he twist outa. He run cross street, ta Mid turf. I look roun'. No one. I hope Broads follow. Good chance ta end Karlo's pissoff, if I yell warn.

Broads stop 'fore cross to Mid. They don' wanna start rumb.

Uppie hurry down sidewalk. He see me, slow a bit. "Hey, where's nearest towah?" Bigger 'n me.

I grin, beck him inna storefron'. Casual, I stand in fronta.

Behin', feet runnin'. I whirl.

Jus' Jag an' Swee. Mid teeners, but Karlo already give 'em upbringin'. No fair. Dey allowed ta sit wid growed, yet I jus' as big.

"Who ya got, Pook?"

"Uppie!"

"Outaway!" Swee push me 'side.

I protes', "He mine!"

"Outahere, joeykit!" Jag spit.

When dey do upbringin', Jag wail an' cry. Yet Karlo do him, an' not me. Thinkin' of it, I go a little craze, an' pull shiv. "Outaheah, Jag! He mine!" Crouch. "Dissya if I gotta!"

"Easy!" Jag back way, scare.

Uppie boy edgin' outa doorway. "I thought you were—I have to go—" I shove 'im back. He jump fas' ta stay way from shiv. "Hey—"

"He mine!" Wolfy, I bare teeth at Swee an' Jag.

Swee step back. "Fadeout."

"Botha?"

Swee an' Jag glance each otha. "Fadeout."

I turn ta Uppie. "Lessee watcha got!" I go close.

His voice drip snot. "Get away, trannie!"

Behind, hear Jag breath hiss. I snarl, "Whatcha call?"

"Frazzing trannie! Get lost or I'll call the jerries."

I smile, nice. " 'S okay, Uppie. We friens'." I take step, crouch head down, butt him har' in stomach.

He oof, bend over holdin' self. Look up, cheeks wet. "Why'd ya—"

My foot swing up. Broken ol' shoe kick him inna chin. His eyes roll up in head. He fall an' lie still.

Jag an' Swee watch, eyes wide.

I go proud. Don' need no upbringin' ta be growed. I kneel, roll Uppie ova, empty pockets. Coin. Unibucks, buncha. Neva had none, til now. I stick 'em in my jumpsuit, 'fore Jag see.

Swee come closa. "Gonna dissim?" Respec' in voice like din' usta.

I swell. "Prolly." I prod wid foot. "Frazzin' Uppie, talk ta Mids like we sheet."

"Dey allasame." Jag nod wise.

In shirt, fin' laserpen like Bigsis got. I c'n tray fo' cansa. Won' be hunger when ol' man come back. I show 'im.

Jag say, "Karlo say longtime back Rocks took a Uppie, tried ta trayfo. Uppie fo' Unibucks."

Nothin' else in pockets. "So? Wha happen?"

"Jerries kept lookin'. Hadda dissim, fo' safe. Karlo say if he get chance, he hannel it righ', not like dumb Rock."

"Maybe should take 'im back ta Karlo." Swee.

"Naw." Allatime joeys tellin Pook whatta do. Changman, Karlo, Bigsis. Like Pook can' decide fo' hisself. I stand. "I keep 'im."

Jag laugh. "Inna doorway?"

"I gotta place."

"Howya gettim dere?"

Prollem. Dunno. I stop, think. "Ya gonna help. We carry, 'fore he wake."

Jag say, "Innifo?"

Glad he din' see Unibucks. "Laserpen?" Hate ta give up, but fair be fair. Why dey help, widout innifo?

"Naw." Jag kick Uppie boy leg. "Boots."

"G'wan!" I sneer. "Noway!"

"Carry 'im yaself!" He fold arms.

I sigh. Jag be a stupe, but stubborn. "Okay okay," I say, 'fore I realize I soun' like Changman. "Not boots. Shirt." I finga Uppie thread. "Nice 'n new."

"Not enough."

"Belt."

Jag glance at Swee. Nod. "Where ya take?"

"Place." I look at both. "Secret, like lair. Pook place. No tell."

Dey excite. "Where?"

"I showya. But Pook diss ya if ya tell. Swear. Don' mess wid!"

"Fadeout." Jag make frien' sign. "Cool."

I grab Uppie's head an' arms, Jag take middle. Swee hold legs. Dark now. Nervous time.

I lead 'em down street ta build cross from Mid lair. Up stair in dark. Roof full a holes, so moon give ligh'. We stop fo' breath, go 'notha stair.

"Ya gonna stay widim allatime, he don' run way?" Swee voice sneer.

Wished I had Changman fo' ansa; he know ways do things. Meantime, I gotta figga out fo' self. But gotta hurry ta keep Jag respec'.

"I got place." Try ta soun' like I knew all along. "Up nex' stair." Dey bitchanmoan, but comealong. Curious, now.

We lug Uppie up ta four' flo'. I lead Jag an' Swee along hall. "Here." I jump down on toppa elevate. "Gimme Uppie."

"Where ya puttin' 'im?"

"In." I drag joey's legs 'til he fall on toppa elevate. I push him to trap, pull it open. "Hang onta his arm, so he don' fall har'." We push his legs in, hold arms 'til his legs near flo'. When we leggo, he go thump.

Swee all scorny. "Ya be glitch, Pookboy. He jus' jump up, climb out."

"Naw. I showya." I run up ta four' flo', ta room I been 'fore. Inna min I come back, an' go down inna elevate.

"Whatcha got?"

I show 'em rope. Firs', I take off Uppie's green shirt, careful not rip. It ain' mine now. Give it ta Swee like I promise. Jag pulls off joey's belt, puts roun' his own wais'. I rub Uppie boy's face. Smooth, like mine. Ain' ol' enough fo' shave. His ches' white, smooth; little tufs a hair startin' unner his arms. A smell like flower.

I roll Uppie on stomach, pull han's behin' back, tie tigh'.

"C'mon." I climb up. Jag an' Swee follow. We look down. "Now tell me he jump out." My voice scorny.

Jag shake head. "Noway, Pook." 'Gain, his voice got respec'.

I yank out shiv, hold near face. "I diss ya if ya tell! He mine!"

"Fadeout, Pook. He your." Swee nod too.

Too late inna nigh' ta trayfo cansa; gotta go hunger. Don' matta. Been hunger 'fore. Think 'bout sleep in elevate, watch Uppiekit wake, but naw. I wan' be by self, think a lotsa ways ta diss frazzin' Changman. Go down two flo', otha end buildin'.

Hard ta sleep, outa lair. No blanket, no mat. Wake up in morn feelin' grunge, pissoff. Day rainy, but I go out anyway ta trayfo, come back wid three cansa veg. I gettin' betta; don' get skin. Put cups out window ledge, get lotsa water drip.

I count my Unibucks. Think 'bout givin' 'em ta Karlo as innifo, but naw.

Pookboy don' need Mids what don' need Pook.

Open can, eat vegs cold. Feel betta. Time ta decide 'bout Uppie. Maybe bes' ta dissim. I go up stair, cross hall.

He yellin'. "Someone help! Please! Help me!"

I jump to top of elevate, crouch. Uppie look up. We watch each otha face. He don' say nothin' fo' a min. Den, "It hurts." Wiggle his hans behin' back.

Could tray pants fo' five, six cansa. Boots, I dunno. Lots. Two, three cases cansa, at leas'. Pook don' have ta worry eat 'til winta. I jump inta elevate.

"Don't just stare! Help, for God's sake! My name is Jared Tenere, and I . . . I'm lost. There's a reward."

Dunno who ta tray boots wid. Could try Changman, but might skin me 'gain. I gotta be careful.

I run my hand ova his boot, admirin'. Jag crazy, thinkin' I innifo him anythin' so good.

Uppie yank 'way his foot, but I drop on his legs, sit tight ta hold. Slow, not sure how, I unlace.

"Get your hands off!" He kick and rage.

I yank off boots, shout wid glad.

"Damn you! Give those back!" Boy face all red.

"Frazzin' Uppie." I spit; he duck 'way. Funny. I spit 'gain.

He shriek, dodgin' spit. "Goddamn mothafuckin' trannie scum!"

Don' like. "Shut mouth, Uppie."

"Let me go!" He try kick me.

I go pissoff, but remember he my trayfo. Lotsa Unibucks, maybe. "Brung cansa. Veg." I show.

"Jesus, where am I? Let me go!" He try ta twis' hans loose, but can'. "Who are you?"

"Capture. I ya capture." Chang word. Ol' man be proud, if he knew. I go closa, try ta pull 'im sit. Gotta feed 'im.

"Don' touch me!" Kick me har' in shin. I hop. "Get away, you filthy—"

I go rage. Grab his leg, push his ches'. Down he go. "Think ya betta den trannie? Think ya own da worl'? I show ya!"

"Scum! Garbage! Don't touch—"

I pushim lyin' back, sit on stomach. Yank out shiv.

"Jesus, don't hurt—" He thrash', but can' get his hans loose from behin'.

"Ya ain' Uppie no mo'! Jus' trannie like res' a us! Now ya be Mid!" Wid sharp point a shiv, I slice Mid mark cross his ches', deep so scar stay. "M", wid Mid tail at end.

He holler God oh God please no Jesus God. Kick and scream worse'n Jag when Karlo done his upbringin'. I climb up trap, look down ta watch. He curled in corna, sobbin' like joeykit, blood drippin' on stomach. On pants too, but I c'n wash 'fore I tray.

Oh God save me, he shriek, someone help me. He wail like niño. I watch, wunner whether ta eat his can a veg, or save.

Stupid bigmouth Uppies. Think they own da worl'.

Chapter 19

ROBERT

Snug in my Washington apartment, I'd just hung up from a long evening chat with Mother when the caller rang again. I eyed it with distaste.

Like anyone in public life I had a list of friends and associates whose calls I took at home. Like anyone in elected office, my list grew to unmanageable proportions, lest I offend some supporter who wanted the cachet of direct access to his Assemblyman.

The caller rang again, and I was tempted to ignore it. I sighed, picked it up. "Boland."

"Rob? Thank God."

"Arlene? You sound—what's wrong?"

"Can you come? I can't—Adam's in no condition—"

A stab of fear. "Is the Captain all right? Is Adam?"

"Yes, we—". Muffled voices in the background; her tone sharpened. "Then look again! No, leave the yard lights on all night, and keep the gate open."

I'd never heard Arlene sound anything but calm and collected, even while she was blasting away at the idiot from Worldnet in his low-flying heli. "I'll be right over. Turn on your landing lights."

"Thanks, Rob. I really appreciate—"

"See you." I slipped into my shoes. If Arlene was distraught, it was serious. Regardless of our political differences, I had to go.

At this hour my driver was at home with his family. No need to disturb him; I had my own keys. I rode the elevator to the roof, waited impatiently while they brought round my heli. Moments later, I was aloft.

The compound was a mere thirty miles from my tower. Night driving was somewhat more annoying than day, if you flew by sight, but I locked onto the traffic beacons at two thousand feet. Below, a steady stream of lights surged along the Beltway's twelve lanes.

As I neared the compound I keyed my transponder. The

guardhouse puter would flash my ID. Something had gone wrong, and someone might be trigger happy. I didn't want an accident.

I landed in the center of the helipad, guided by the waving lights of a guard. I switched off the motor, jumped out while the blades slowed to a halt.

"Hello, sir. Mrs. Seafort's in—"

"Mr. Vishinsky, isn't it? Shall I park to the side?"

"No need, we're not expecting anyone." His expression was taut. "But you might leave your keys."

"Of course."

"Rob?" A woman's voice, across the pad.

"Hello, Arlene." She hurried to meet me halfway. I said, "I take it they found Adam's boy? Is he—"

"Philip disappeared." Her face was haggard.

"Lord God. When?"

"We learned of it this afternoon. I'm half out of my mind." She clutched my arm. "Nick's at his retreat. I could call him home early, but . . . is it really neces—" Her voice broke.

I guided her toward the house. "It'll be all right." I was the perfect politician; a soothing inanity for every crisis. "Did you eat? I thought not. We'll sit in the kitchen, and you'll tell me all about it." We were at her door; I guided her through.

She braced her hand against the doorframe, as if to resist. "Rob, don't condescend. I'm in no mood for it."

"I—but—" I swallowed.

"If I eat I'll throw up. I'm frightened for my brainless genius son. If—when I find him I'll paddle his scrawny behind, but for now I'm worried sick."

"Of course. I would be too."

"How could you know? You never had a child." Her hand darted to her mouth. "Oh, Rob, forgive me. Didn't I tell you I'm out of my mind?"

"I understand." I tried to keep my voice flat.

She buried her face in my shoulder. "I'm so sorry. You're the last joey I'd want to hurt."

My resistance melted. "Of course, Arlene." I glanced about with vague unease. If some twit captured the scene with a holocamera, he'd cause us no end of embarrassment.

She led me inside, to the kitchen. "A drink? A sandwich?"

"Whatever you'll have." While she set teacups in the micro I loosened my tie. "What do we know?"

"P.T. never showed up at his tutor. Or his psych." She slid a note across the table. I perused the boyish script.

"You've questioned the guards?"

"The note was a lie. He never asked the guards to drive him."

"How'd he get through the gate?"

"They're not sure. Probably during the night. They heard a crash and clatter. The guard went out to check, but found no one. I assume that's when P.T. slipped through. The alarms don't sound if the guardhouse door's opened from within."

"What was the noise?"

"A pair of frying pans. Mine." Her lips twitched in a reluctant smile. "I'd guess he threw them over the wall to distract Mr. Tzee. When I get hold of him . . . " She poured our tea, sat again.

"Why did he run away?"

"Who knows?" Her eyes teared. "Don't we treat him well?"

"What does Adam say?"

"He's not sure what to think. The state he's been in, since Jared left . . . " She sipped. "Jared is truly awful; he stole his father's Terrex card. If it weren't for Philip . . . " She explained P.T.'s suggestion that they search Adam's accounts.

"Is there a connection?"

"With P.T. disappearing? Christ, I hope not."

"Do you have a Terrex?"

Her mouth tightened. "Yes, and it's still in my wallet. There are no charges. Philip wouldn't steal, unless I truly don't know him." She swirled her tea. "Adam told the police about his missing card. They put an alert on the credit nets."

"Any luck?"

"They traced the card to Von Walther Shuttleport. Nothing since."

"So that means he's in New—"

"No, it means the card is. Jared may be in a ditch with his throat slit." She covered her face. "So may P.T."

I was careful with my words. I'd been slapped down once for being inane. No need to be brutal, but Arlene wanted truth. "It's possible." Her eyes shot up. "But highly unlikely," I said quickly. "Philip will be back. Is he old enough for a girl-friend?"

"A platonic one, at most." She smiled. "Truth is, he has almost no friends near his own age." Her smile faded. "Except Jared."

"Could Jar have set this up? Or called him?"

"We've had no calls. I haven't checked the nets for mail."

Footsteps; a knock. "May I join you?" Adam.

Arlene rose. "Of course. Any word?"

"Nothing." Adam turned to me. "Rob."

"Good to see you, sir." I clasped his hand. "The jerries called me twice on the search for Jared. There's no sign of him. They're concentrating on New York."

He sat wearily. "What should we do?"

"Wait," I said. "There's nothing else." I looked to Arlene. "Did you notify the police about Philip?"

"No." She knotted her fist.

Adam said, "I urged her to. She won't listen."

She said, "Tomorrow, whenever, P.T. may come back on his own. If we call for help, they'll splash Nick's face across every holozine in home system, and that will mortify him."

I said, "The Captain would want—"

"Furthermore, an announcement will set every loonie on the continent looking for Philip. It could put him in danger."

I cleared my throat. "Wait a day, see what happens."

Adam said, "At least we know Jared went to New York. Without P.T.'s advice we'd be in the dark."

I asked, "Did you cancel your card?"

"No." He blushed.

"Adam!"

"Two reasons. If he's in trouble, he might need—"

"The hell with that. He deserves—"

"And it might help track him."

I hadn't thought that far. "But he could bankrupt you."

"He's my son." Adam's voice was tired. "Yes, I know. At times I despise myself."

Arlene snapped, "Belay that. I hear it enough from Nick!" A gentle squeeze of her hand softened her words. "Adam, you're doing your best."

Two boys disappearing within days was no coincidence. I

couldn't see how a bright joey like Philip had much respect for a fraz like Jared, but one never knew.

Had they gone off together? In that case, why leave separately? Why would he alert Jared's father about the Terrex card, unless . . .

"It's connected." I looked up, interrupting their soft conversation. "P.T. disappeared because Jared did. I'd stake my career on it. And that credit card . . . show me P.T.'s note."

Adam retrieved it.

I read aloud. "'See what money Jared could have taken with him.' He already knew, Adam. He practically rubbed your nose in it."

"Why couldn't he tell me outright?"

"A remnant of loyalty, perhaps. Who knows? The point is, I know what's happened to P.T." The two of them watched me as if expecting an oracular pronouncement. "He went looking for Jared."

It got their attention, though they weren't ready to believe me. The more we argued, the surer I became, and the more distraught I made Arlene. She paced the kitchen, mouth set in a tight line, while Adam and I reviewed and discarded all other possibilities.

At length she held up a hand. "It's all speculation. Let's wait until morning, when we may know more. Then you'll help me decide whether to call Nicky home." She eyed us both. "You know what his annual retreat means to him. The Benedictines won't allow calls, but I presume I could get through. On the other hand . . . " She crossed the room, stopped to stare into my eyes. "Rob, this goes no further, regardless of politics. Agreed?"

I didn't hesitate. "You have my oath."

"I'm . . . afraid for Nicky. If anything happ—if P.T. has an . . . " Her voice grew determined. "If P.T. dies, Nicky might suicide."

"Good lord."

"He's fragile. You can't imagine what his son means to him. He's already lost two families. I don't think he could stand losing anyone else." Her lip quivered for the slightest instant. "If I call, he'll be in an agony of worry, whether or not he leaves Lancaster. I'd spare him that, if I knew P.T. would come trooping home with his silly grin. But if I don't reach Nick, and something happens . . . "

She didn't finish.

By unspoken agreement, I spent the night in the compound. Luckily, the General Assembly wasn't in session, so my time was my own. Before turning off my light I called Dad, told him I'd have to skip the Hudson Freshwater expansion hearings because of an urgent personal commitment. He wasn't happy, but didn't ask the particulars. Dad gave me credit for common sense, if not punctuality.

I tossed and turned, grimly aware that only a week ago, in this same bedroom, Dad and I had calmly plotted the discredit of our host.

Politics.

In the morning we breakfasted on the terrace. Still no word from P.T., but Adam fielded a call from the Police Commissioner of New York District. He listened, grunted, asked a few sharp questions.

When he rang off, he shrugged. "I suppose its good news, in a way. Jared was spotted yesterday in the New York Sheraton Skytel."

"They're sure it was he?"

"He matched the holopic we sent out, and he used my Terrex."

"Great!"

"But he disappeared from the hotel. No one knows where."

I threw down my napkin. "How could they let—Half the metro jerries should have responded to that call. I pulled so God-damned many strings—"

"Easy, Rob."

Cut short, I almost blurted, "Aye aye, sir." After two decades, Adam still had that power over me. "Sorry."

Arlene chewed slowly on a roll. After a long while she sighed. "I'll call Nick."

I said, "Why?"

"We have to assume you're right, that P.T.'s gone after Jared."

She took the caller. "Best get started. Those monks are stubborn, and I may not get through."

I held up a hand. "If this hits him hard, someone should be there. London is only three hours."

She nodded. "You're right." Her expression lightened. "I'll get ready. Adam, if you'll make my reservation . . ."

I grimaced. My role was to propose all the unpopular moves. "Arlene, stay here in case your son calls. Or in case you need to, ah, get to him quickly." Lord God forbid the visions that had flashed across my mind: a deathbed, or worse, a morgue.

"Nick needs me."

"So does Philip." My voice was firm. "I'll go." It was the least I could do. I hadn't slept all that well, remembering my conversations with Dad.

"If you—I suppose—damn that boy!" She made a visible effort to relax. "All right. But if Nick gets—" She studied my face. "Rob, you'll know what to do?"

Adam said, "It's all right. I'll be with him."

"No," I said. "If Jared calls, you'd better be here to—"

He slammed his fist on the table; the glasses jumped. "Arlene will take a message. I want Jared alive, but beyond that I don't much care about his feelings." Abruptly, he stood. "Let's go."

"Are you sure—"

"It'll do me good to think about someone else. Arlene, would you stand by the caller?"

"I'm not happy about it." With a sigh, she got to her feet. "But if Philip shows up, at least I'll be here to deal with him." Seeing her grim expression, I almost hoped P.T. had the sense to stay clear.

On the way to the shuttleport I'd boasted to Adam, "Now you'll really see the perks of office." I rang my office, had Van set up VIP connections to London and Lancaster. Adam had made no reply, and a few moments later I'd blushed scarlet, remembering he'd been personal aide to the SecGen himself, while I was a mere Assemblyman. I fumbled for an apology, but he patted my knee, smiling.

At least, I made good on my promise. Airport personnel whisked us from parking to the President's Lounge, where a terminal cart came to carry us, drinks in hand, directly to the gate. We had a first-class section all to ourselves, and an attentive steward.

At London a jet heli and pilot waited on the tarmac. I wondered whose budget would bear the cost. The builders' organization, most probably, or the water recyclers. Sometimes it was better not to ask.

We'd each brought an overnight bag, just in case. A polite young man from the airline carried them to our heli, wished us a good flight, and disappeared. Moments later, we were airborne.

We arrived in Lancaster at five P.M., local time.

The Benedictine complex was surrounded by an ancient fieldstone wall similar to the one surrounding the Captain's compound. Perhaps Mr. Seafort had never truly left his cloister.

The monastery was on hilly ground, on which unruly clumps of grass sprouted amid a myriad of rocks. A spacious parking lot was nearly full. A trail led uphill from the lot to the gate, and the well-worn path to the buildings. There was no helipad inside the walls, so I had the pilot put us down in the lot. We asked him to wait until we emerged, however long it took.

More cars pulled in to park as we spoke. Adam and I strolled up the hill toward the wrought-iron gates.

No caller, no bell. A sign, that read, "Absolutely no recording devices permitted."

My tone was dubious. "Should we go in?"

"I don't—"

"Excuse me." A heavyset, sloppy fellow pushed past. "You joes better hurry, you want to see Vespers." He stopped at a ramshackle shelter a few strides up the hill, spoke into the window, nodded, pulled out his wallet, dropped a bill on the rail, hurried on.

We followed.

Before we reached the shelter a brown-robed old fellow emerged. "Sorry, hall's full." He headed toward us, and the gate. "Just sold the last seat."

"We're here to see—"

"Try Matins. Seven of the morning." He cackled through missing teeth. "Or if that's too early for you, Novenas."

"But we have to—"

"Chapel only holds seventy-five, besides us." He shooed

us toward the gate. "You'll make me late. The Abbot doesn't like that. Outside, please."

I said firmly, "We're here to see Captain Seafort."

"Of course. They all are, save the Martins and the De Lange family, who come regular. That's why the hall's full." We found ourselves in retreat from his insistent fuss. "It isn't every week that you can't wedge an electricar into the lot. Forty-nine weeks a year, two pews of visitors, then comes this!"

"Sir—"

"You think to enhance your status by gawking at him. Vanity. The Lord is hardly impressed, if Brother Timothy might say so on His behalf. Will you *please* go?"

Adam said, "Brother, may we make a donation?" He held out a banknote.

"Of course, but don't think that absolves you from another in the morning. Five Unies each, voluntary tithe."

"I—"

"Every day. You are on the *wrong* side of the gate, which I must lock, and I *will* insist that you leave now so my heart doesn't stop in my haste to struggle up the hill. You may stare at our distinguished Brother Nicholas another—"

I snapped, "Look here, old fellow—" Adam laid his hand on my arm, waggled a warning finger.

My friend's tone was conciliatory. "Brother, we're not gawkers. I'm Commandant Seafort's personal aide, and we have urgent—"

Brother Timothy drew himself up, his voice stiff. "You're on consecrated land of the Neo-Benedictine Order of the Catholic Synod of the Reunified Church. You may see a foolish old man in a wrinkled robe, but this old man represents the spiritual and temporal authority of the one true Church. The Lancaster District Police honor that authority, even if you don't. When I use the caller in my shed they arrive in minutes, and they rarely leave without making an arrest."

He paused for much-needed breath. "Out, I say!" He shooed us once more, flapping the hem of his robe at our knees. "Out!"

The corners of Adam's mouth twitched. "Sir, my employer is Mr. Seafort. We've come to tell him of a family emergency. We didn't want to break the news over the caller—"

"As if you'd have had a cherub's chance in brimstone of getting through!" The monk snorted, then his head cocked to one side. "What emergency?"

"A private matter," said Adam, stressing the second word. "But urgent. I have identification, if you—"

"Pah!" Brother Timothy brushed past us, locked the gates together. "Papers prove nothing. Seven years ago, a demon from Holoworld had a doctor's certificate saying he was deaf and needed to sit in the front row!"

I thought he was immovable, but finally he gestured to the path.

"These rules apply, or you'll have to walk over me to get in. You let him be until the service is done. You say nothing until he chooses to notice you. If the Abbot won't allow him to speak, then it's settled; you try again tomorrow. Agreed? If not, I'll call two novices who enjoy assertive physical labor." He perched his gnarled hands on his hips. "Well?"

"You have my oath." Adam.

"Hurry, then. The Abbot waits." Brother Timothy turned on his heel, scuttled up the hill. I had to lengthen my stride to keep pace. At the chapel entrance the old man darted to the side entrance, leaving us to go in through the weathered oak high doors.

The chapel was indeed full. Adam squeezed into a pew in the last row; I managed to make a place on the bench opposite, ignoring angry glances. In front of the rail, the nave was empty.

Above, a great bell began to chime.

Five times it rang, breaking the hushed silence of the hall.

At the side of the chapel, two scarred wooden doors opened. A line of brown-robed monks filed past, their faces concealed by the hoods of their garments. As they reached the altar each stopped, made obeisance, and continued to his place at one of the benches between the rail and the altar.

A hiss. "That's him!"

"Shhh."

"No it ain't."

"He's—"

I searched for the Captain among the voluminous robes, couldn't be sure which was he.

The Abbot, a wasted old soul whose robe bore a red sash, opened the Bible, began to read in a gravelly voice.

At thirteen, I'd idolized the Naval Service, as exemplified by Captain Nicholas Ewing Seafort. When, toward the end of my first year at Academy, he'd turned his back on duty and career and plunged into a monastic life, my interest in matters religious had been aroused.

For a time, with the zeal of an adolescent, I'd imagined throwing off my own Naval servitude with some dramatic gesture, and presenting myself to a monastery as a novice. Presumably, one in Lancaster, though I couldn't picture the actual haven to which the Captain had retreated.

Adam Tenere had helped steady me, for which I was eternally grateful. Nonetheless, I couldn't approach a religious service without painful awareness that my faith could not possibly match that of my adopted father.

As a result, I rarely attended services, except when political considerations made it expedient.

Somewhere, among the bent backs, amid those robed figures who chanted responses and from time to time knelt in obeisance, was the man we'd come to see. Though I'd visited his home not two weeks past, here he seemed somehow transformed, the more so in that I couldn't pick him out from his brethren.

A few in the visitors' pews seemed absorbed in the ritual. Others fidgeted. One old man, seated ahead of us on the aisle, looked not at all at his Bible; he rocked back and forth as if the pew were a favorite seat. His jumpsuit had an odd cut, as if years out of date.

What must the Captain feel, returning to his former home under such intense scrutiny? Surely he must be used to it; he'd been subject to the same mistreatment during the years he dwelled here.

A few rows ahead two women had given up all pretense of interest in the service. Nudging each other, they pointed openly. The old Abbot's glare did little good; at length, he beckoned to two tall figures, indicated the offenders. The two hooded men crossed the rail, stood at either end of the pew where the women sat, arms folded.

Silence prevailed.

At last, the service was done.

Again, the bell tolled. The monks stood, knelt in turn before the cross, filed out.

This time they passed the rail, moved toward the rear of the chapel. Their faces were visible.

I caught Adam's eye. He nodded.

"There he is!" One of the women thrust out a paper and pen. "SecGen, would you—"

Another monk, without haste, interposed himself between the Captain and the woman. His shoulder brushed aside the outstretched paper.

"Look at his eyes!"

I wanted to smother the murmurers. Did they imagine he couldn't hear?

The old man I'd seen rocking hauled himself to his feet, leaned into the aisle, said clearly, "In name of your people, stop!"

The Captain's gaze flickered to his face. Recognition. Stonily, he turned his head away. A novice pushed past the onlookers, grasped the old man's shoulder, thrust him down. "Quiet, please. The monks are not to be disturbed."

The old man's voice was hoarse. "In name of Eddie Boss, and Mace. And Subs! For them, not me! I ask!"

The Captain took two more steps, until he was nearly at Adam's row. His eyes were pained. He turned. "Please, leave me alone."

"Cannot. A few words. Must!"

"No, I—" The Captain bowed his head. His hands became fists. Other monks filed past.

The old Abbott neared. "Come along, Brother Nicholas."

"Yes, Father. This man, he's . . . from a long time ago. He wouldn't be here unless—may I be permitted?"

"Are you sure it's what you want?"

"No, sir. I'm only sure I must."

The Abbott grunted. "In the garden." He continued on his way. Behind him, so did the Captain. He passed within a foot of Adam, who said nothing.

The old man shook off the novice's restraining hand, pushed to his feet, followed.

I shoved past the parishioners to the aisle, called out, "Sir, I—"

Fingers closed on my arm, with a grip of steel. Adam Tenere. "No."

"But, why? He's—"

"My oath. He chose not to notice me."

My tone was bitter. "That foolish old man didn't bind himself by a vow. Who in God's name is he—"

"I've no idea."

"Well, I gave no oath. Come, I'll catch his eye."

"Rob." Stern, as a midshipman to a cadet.

I fell silent.

"After he's done with the seniorcit, he may see us. If not, tomorrow."

A vein in my temple throbbed. Who was Adam to reprove my conduct? I was Assemblyman from Seaboard Cities, and he was but an aide to a failed politician who—

I sighed. "I'm sorry, sir." I couldn't help it. Anyway, he was right.

We waited in the chapel doorway while the other visitors drifted toward their cars. The Captain, perched on a stone bench some twenty yards from us, listened intently, asked a question or two. The old man spoke at length.

The Captain stood and paced. He said something to the oldster, shook his head.

"Please." The one word carried in the hot summer breeze.

Again the Captain shook his head. He rested his hand on the old man's shoulder, as if in apology, shook his head once more. "No. It would mean—No. Never again." Without a glance back, he walked through the archway, into the priory.

Dejected, the old man hobbled down the hill to the gate.

"That tears it," I muttered. "We'll have to raise all sorts of ruckus to see him now."

"We'll wait, as we promised."

"Jared and P.T. are—"

"Think of the time. It would be after midnight when we got home. What could we do?"

I kicked at a pew. "What was the point of coming, if we have to wait until—"

"Excuse me." The young monk, his hands folded as if in humility. "Services are over. Visitors are requested to leave."

My impatience grew too great to bear. "We need to see the Capt—"

"We were on our way." Adam's fingers closed around my arm. "When is the gate opened in the morning?"

"At dawn."

"We'll be there, with a message for the Abbot."

The monk bowed slightly. Adam led me, still protesting, from the chapel.

Outside, my wrath exploded. He heard me out, shrugged. "So P.T. has another night to come home on his own. Maybe we won't need to bother the Commandant."

"And Jared?"

"There's nothing I can do that we haven't set in motion."

Calling ahead, we found rooms at a passable hotel. From my room I called Arlene. She'd heard nothing about either joey.

My next call was to Dad. He gave a low whistle when he heard why we'd gone to Lancaster. "A pity for Seafort. The boy means a lot to him."

"Yes."

Dad hesitated. "Rob, you're best out of this. Either way, there could be repercussions."

"What kind?"

"I'm not sure. If Philip is dead, there'll be a backlash against the trannies. Do we want to be associated with it?"

"They're blocking our towers."

"Of course, but let the Territorials take the blame. And if P.T. is found, who knows what the SecGen's reaction will be."

I said, "All the more reason to stay close. I might be able to affect the outcome. Besides . . . "

He waited, but I didn't finish. "Yes?"

"They need me, Dad. He and Adam both."

I knew what thoughts permeated his silence. I still hadn't learned to separate politics from emotion; we'd had that argument before. On the other hand, years ago, Dad had alienated a powerful Senator to save the Captain from blackmail. What political benefit had he seen in that?

We talked a while longer, and I rang off. Jet-lagged, I set the alarm for four in the morning, and drifted to sleep.

The eastern sky held a hint of light; unseen birds called briskly to one another. I yawned. "I thought he said dawn."

"Patience." Adam looked haggard. The long wait for his son must be taking a fearsome toll.

"If we can get through to Nick, we could be in Washington by noon."

"I hope so. Arlene was beside herself this morning."

"Any news?"

"Nothing. And my Terrex hasn't been used again."

I wasn't sure that was good. While I thought it over I spotted a brown-robed figure trudging to the gatehouse. "There!" I pointed.

Adam was out of the heli, striding to the gate. "Good morning, brother. We'd like to see the Abbot."

The florid monk shook his head. "Write for an appointment."

"Reverend brother, that's not possible. Kindly tell your Abbot that Mr. Tenere requests his permission to see Brother Nicholas, on a mission that ought not wait."

"You'll have to—"

"Ask." Adam spoke with quiet assurance. He folded his arms, leaned back against the fieldstone wall.

The monk hesitated. "Wait outside, along the path."

A few minutes later he returned, escorted us up the hill, to an ivy-strewn edifice adjoining the chapel.

"I'm Father Ryson. Why do you disturb us?"

"My name is Adam Tenere. This is Mr. Boland, a friend. Brother—Captain Seafort's son has run off. We've come to tell him."

"We do not allow concerns of the world to intrude."

Adam leaned over the Abbot's desk. "His son."

"What would you have him do?"

Adam said, "As he wishes."

"What man is so free as that?" The Abbot shrugged. "I'll consider it. Please wait in the anteroom."

Outside, I paced in mounting anger. "That was goofjuice. I'll mount a speaker on the heli and shout the news to the whole priory! Sit there, don't bother us, wait until he sees you—"

"Be patient." Adam sat with head down.

I flared, "What about P.T.?"

"And Jared."

I gulped. For a moment, I'd actually forgotten about his

son. "Forgive me." Yes, Adam made me feel inadequate, but only because I *was* inadequate.

A sound. I looked up. Captain Nicholas Seafort stood framed in the oaken doorway, the hood of his brown robe thrown back, his fists knotted. "Is Arlene all right?"

"Yes, sir." Adam stood. "We thought you—" He pursed his lips, began again. "P.T.'s run away and can't be found. Arlene and I thought you should know."

Seafort leaned against the doorframe, closed his eyes. A long, slow breath. Slowly, his hands unknotted. "When?"

"Two days ago."

His lips moved in silent prayer. After a moment, his eyes opened. His expression was so bleak my breath caught. "Why?"

I said, "We're not sure, sir. Probably because of Jared. He's gone too."

"Tell me all you know." He crossed to a bench, listened intently.

When we were done, he sighed. "I'll need the Abbot's leave."

He was gone a long while. When at last he returned, it was through a different door. He wore street clothes and carried a bag. "I presume you have a heli?"

"Yes, sir." Adam took the valise from his grip.

In the heli, the Captain turned his face to the window. Adam, sharing the back seat, chose not to disturb him. In front with the pilot, I busied myself arranging our return flight.

In London we had a brief wait while they made ready our suborbital. I came back from the caller booths, caught Adam's eye, shook my head.

The Captain faced the terminal's bulkhead, hands in his pockets. I said, "Sir, Philip will come home. I'm sorry we had to break your retreat."

He sounded sad. "Don't apologize. It was . . . ordained."

"Sir?"

"I was beginning to feel almost . . . ah, well." He peered out the window. "Is this flight to New York?"

"Washington. I thought—"

"Very well." He turned. In his eyes, an unbearable sadness. At last, he looked away.

While I searched for something to say, Adam nudged me, put a finger to his lips.

Hours later, we set down on the sunlit compound pad. I woke Adam, stretched. The Captain ducked through the doorway, reached for his bag.

Arlene Seafort strode across the helipad. "Nick!" Her welcoming arms enveloped his lean frame. I cleared my throat, looked away.

The Captain asked, "Any news?"

"Still nothing. He'll be all right. Don't worry."

"And Jared?"

She shook her head. Adam's mouth tightened.

We settled in the kitchen, nibbled at cheese and crackers while coffee brewed. Over the spartan meal we explained to the Captain why we assumed P.T. had followed Jared.

When we'd finished, Seafort said, "There's no other explanation, unless he's lost his mind. What else do we know?"

Arlene said, "I searched P.T.'s room. He was using his puter, but that's our only clue."

"Clue? Between his fractals and his stock speculation, he's glued to the bloody thing. I ought to take it away."

I yawned.

The Captain patted my hand. "Thanks for everything, Rob. Get some sleep. Adam, will you go with me?"

"Where, sir?"

"New York, of course." He stood. "Jared's hotel. In fact, we'll stay the night, if we don't find him."

Adam got to his feet. "I'll—whatever you—I mean—"

"If we hurry, we'll still have much of the afternoon." He bent over his wife, planted a kiss, picked up his bag. Arlene said not a word.

I said reluctantly, "I could be of help."

"You're exhausted, and you have work to—"

"No more tired than you, and New York's my district. My black book may come in handy."

His expression brightened, but he said, "Rob, it's possible Jared was kidnapped. Or worse, he could be on the streets, though I'd think even he has more sense." He paused. "It could be dangerous. Sure you want to come?"

I hadn't been. "Yes, sir. If you'll let me."

"I'm grateful."

Outside, we strode across the lawn to the heli. The Captain slowed, turned to his wife. "Arlene, keep in touch in case—"

"Of course, Nick. From wherever I decide to stay."

"—because if he calls . . . what?"

Her eyes blazed. "You hypocritical son of a *bitch!*" With each word, she stalked closer. "Think I'll be waiting here when you get back? Prong yourself! Who in God's own Hell do you think I am, some helpless female to shut in the cave when danger looms?"

Gaping, I backed out of the way.

"Arlene—"

She shoved him so hard he nearly fell. "Don't 'Arlene' me, you frazball, you insect, you—" She paused to regroup.

"What did I—"

"Didn't I make it clear? Leave me behind, come back to an empty house. P.T.'s my son. I've waited three days; when I find him I'll hug him tight and then kill him. If you search, I go along. You might even need me!"

He stammered. "Hon, I—we don't know where Philip is, or Jared. A city like New York is brutal. You've no idea how vicious—"

"Nick, I scored higher than you in every frazzing combat class. Marksmanship too, for that matter. Or don't you remember the time I pinned you three times out of three, and Sarge said—"

"That was thirty years ago! We're no longer cad—"

She shouted, "My child is out there!" Her voice dropped. "Once, you called on my courage, and I failed. Never again!"

"I don't think for a minute—"

"I love you dearly, you stupid man, but shall I pack to go with you, or to leave? Your call!" Her eyes shone with anguished resolve.

Nick Seafort regarded each of us in turn, his expression bewildered. I essayed a small smile, but his glance flicked past. "Please, Arlene, wait. He might contact us."

"No. It's been too long." She waited for his response, heard none. "I'll pack my gear. If you're gone when I come back, you've made your choice." She turned on her heel and left.

I studied the engine cowling.

Adam coughed. "Sir . . . "

"We'll wait." Nick Seafort smiled weakly. "She's had to bottle her feelings until I came home."

Adam said, "She's half out of her mind with worry. Not the least of—" He stopped short. "I shouldn't—" He hesitated. "It's not my business to—"

"Go on." It was an order.

"She's been worried how you'll take it," Adam blurted. "So have we. Are you all right, sir?"

"Of course." The Captain thrust his hands into his pockets. "I'm concerned for my son; he's too young to be wandering a big city. Too naive." He let out a long, slow breath. "Adam, I'm terribly sorry about Jared."

"I—thank you."

"We won't stop until we find them both. I promise."

"Sir, that's not necessary. Jared could be anywhere, and he's my responsibility. Don't commit yourself to—"

"Until we find both boys. Adam, you stood by me through disaster and disgrace. I know three Senators made you offers when our Administration collapsed."

Five, actually. Dad among them.

"I don't know why you stayed with me, but I'm grateful. Finding your son is as—almost as important to me as my own."

"Thank you." It was a whisper.

A beam of light, as the front door opened. Arlene Sanders Seafort, dressed in a utility jumpsuit, carrying a duffel.

She strode toward the heli.

Chapter 20

PEDRO

I came back home, fast as old body let me.

What else could I do?

No help from Fisherman. Said he burned out. No ambition left. Done too much harm already.

Bullsheet, that. Meant he didn' care about my trannies.

But why should he? Uppie he was, Uppie will be. So what if he wasn't born in tower? Cardiff, Wales, Sheraton Skytel didn' make no diff. Not city, not trannie streets.

I sat and rocked alone in shop, sipping tea that cooled unnoticed.

What to do? No one swind Pedro Telamon Chang, hah. 'Xcept time.

No one swind my trannies. 'Xcept life.

Soon, I die, troubles over.

Soon Trannies die too. Nothin' be left downtown but cold towers, an' maybe Crypsnbloods in Bronx. Animals, they, feral eyes reflectin' the high lights of towers from grassy streets below.

With Pook gone, shop was too quiet. I hadn't seen Midboy since day I left, him dancin' across street shoutin' curses at my back.

Maybe I shouldn' a whopped him. Still, couldn' let Midboy tell me prong myself in my own shop, or next he hurl shiv stead of insult. Hadda stay ahead of that joeykit.

Ah, Fisherman, I thought you'd help once more, for old time sake. For wife Annie, for old friend Eddie. For Sub tribe you once said you joined.

Foolish old Chang.

Water in pipes down to trickle. It rained hard, so my cistern was near full. Onna street, tribes restless. Heat hung over city like dark brooding spirit. Tides lapped round stumps of old Trade Center. What we done to our planet, hah? Ozone layer fragmented, poles half melt. Bowery near disappeared under filthy riv. Wall Street dike still held good, though.

Only two days I be gone. Seemed like year.

I opened shop, did few trays with Mids. Coupla Easters came through with innifo for passby. Wanted to trayfo water jugs.

Time, Pedro, to make choice. You could stay ol' Neut, by yoself, or throw in lot with Sub. Halber wasn't great leader-boss, not like some, but he what you got.

So, go along, I would. Halb already agreed to Sub meet with tribe bosses, even to sending Sub joeys to tribes as hostages for safe conduct. I passed word to Easters, Rocks, Unies that meet was comin' soon. Courtlands agreed to come down, an' Washhites too. I'd ask Halber if he'd set meet for tomorrow. Do it fast, I'd say, so ornery tribes didn' have time to plan trouble.

Evening, I locked shop, scrawled eye with chalk on door, tramped through trannietown to Sub.

Halber crossed his arms, stubborn look on face. "Nex' week." We sat across fro' each other, two old chairs, in smoky Sub lair.

I fussed, for his benefit. "Dunno wha's so importan', ya gotta put off meet afta I sen' word ta alla tribe."

"Ya don', hah?" He regard me with skepticism. "Changman knows more 'bout Sub business 'n Subs?"

I put on innocent look. "Halber be Boss Sub, and Sub is mos' important tribe. Who don' know dat?"

"Now who try ta swind, hah?" But he mollify, I could tell. "Whuffo alla hurry?"

"Causa water," I said.

"That, again?" He shrug. "Always less water in summer. It vaporate from hot."

"Hah. Tell me Sub pipes don' run brown wid sludge. Tell me Sub joeykits don' complain."

Halber's mood changed, abrupt. He leaned close, eyes full of menace. "Whatcha know 'bout it, ol' man? Pay innifo ta some bigmouth Subboy?"

Life in balance, here. Din' know if could pull off. I said easy, "Don' need no Sub spy tell me obvious. Ya ain' got good water same reason no trannies got. Govermen turn off, like I tolya. Summer, winter, don' matta. Clean water be gone fo' always."

"Bah." He waved away. "Water fine." But too late. By

askin' if I pay innifo to learn about, he already told me opposite. In a min he realized.

I sat very still, hopin' he din' decide best way to keep secret was diss Chang.

"Anyway, what c'n a tribe meet do 'bout water? We gonna trayfo water togetha?" He laughed harsh.

My bones relaxed at his laugh. "What c'n any tribe, even Sub, do by itself? Maybe, togetha, thinka somethin'." Then what, Pedro Chang? Tribe gonna negotiate with govermen? Without Fisherman to help, who gonna listen?

Nevermin'. Worry 'bout that later. First step was get tribes talkin'. Had to hurry, before water critical. Time to bribe. I said, cautious, "I foun' a hundred permas, if ya still need."

His breath hissed. "When?"

A hundred permas be heavy load. Pook woulda been useful, but he gone. Inside, I sighed. "Day afta morra, if I get help movin'."

"That soon?"

I wondered why he so anxious, and suddenly knew his plan.

Clever, he. Good general, would make.

His ambition was pushout Parkas, take Park an' middle of city for Sub. He thought Chang didn' know, but why else open tunnels near Park side, and get sub cars rollin' again?

Halber didn't understand was no point to it. If I tol' him, anger would be at me.

I went proud. "Ya gonna get permas. Set meet, sameday."

He shook his head. "Can't, so soon. Ya don' unnastan'. Once we got permas . . . " He pressed shut his mouth, to say no more.

Once Halber got permas, he'd rumb. Then Mids and Parkas and Broads be upheave, and what chance would an old Neut have pullin' tribes togetha?

My mouth suddenly dry. Big risk, but I hadda take. I leaned forward. "Halber, lissen. You want permas bad. Chang want meet, even more. No meet, no permas."

"But, soon as we got—"

I struggled outa chair, steelin' self fo' maybe his shiv, but desperate. "Tribe meet first. Then permas. Else none."

"Sumbitch! Frazball!" His chair went flyin'. "I skin ya,

like ol' days!" At his shoutin', tribe gathered quick, joeykits too. "Chaco! Raulie! Call Sub, fo' watch! Grabbim!"

"I be Neut!"

It didn' help.

As they came at me, time for only one more say. I hollered, "G'wan, diss Sub dream! No permas! I be only Neut in trannie worl' who c'n get so many! Take ya twenny years fin' a hunner' permas widout me!" Was even true, mostly.

Hands grab. I went down. Couldn't breathe, from press.

"Hol' it!"

Shiv was sharp at my throat.

Harsh steps. Boot prodded my side. Arms hauled me up. Halber's eyes full of hate. "Worth dyin' fo', this meet?"

I panted. "Prolly." We was all dyin', without.

"Worth makin' enemy of Sub?"

"Prolly not." I shrugged again, trembling with tired. With Subs as enemy, no way to join tribes together. "What choice I got? Gotta meet 'fore ya pushout Parkas an'—"

Halber made sound deep in throat.

I stopped, too late. Oh, dumb, foolish Neut. Ya haddim. Now ya be walkin' dead.

His voice was hoarse. "Howya know? Who tell?" He whirled. "Mer, be it you? Chaco?" They shrank from his fury.

"No one." I groped for chair, 'fore legs gave way.

"Den how?"

With an effort, I reached for bluster. "Think ya c'n swind Pedro Telamon Chang, hah? Was obvious. Why else ya wan' permas?"

His face ugly. "G'wan."

I try to look smug. They was gonna diss me anyways, so might as well impress. "Halber Boss Sub, maybe he don' read, don' know history, but he be great general noneless. Sub turf go allaroun' Park; what more natural 'n Subs want to take midcity too? But too many Parkas inna bush for Subs to root out. An Park too big. Sub tribe not so large it c'n surround Park. Unless . . ."

My heart pounded; I had to stop for breath.

" . . . Unless Halber c'n outflank Parkas. But he gotta move Subs fast, side to side, top to bottom, cause Parkas hold middle. Ya can't run back an' forth around Park an' still have energy to rumb. But ya could, if Subs been fixin' unnercars. Ridin' in unnercars, ya come up to fight where ain' expected."

All silence.

"Howya know?"

I squinted eyes, made signs at Halber, same hex that I used ta make Mids 'n Broads uneasy 'bout breakin' into shop.

He flinched. "Don' witch me, Neut."

I spat. "I witch who I choose. My sign jus' made ya war harder. Thirty mo' Sub gonna die, tryin'."

He growled. No matta, if I already dead.

I said louder, "Dat ain' nothin', compare ta sign I made fo' afta ya diss me. G'wan, do it, an' see. Jus' remember ol' Chang, afta tribe rot and Sub tunnels crumble. When Sub babies born widout fingers, and Easters walk Sub turf. Remember it was dead Chang did it!" My voice gathered strong. "Ya won' have no permas, so can't take Park. But all that be forget, in general weep."

Chest tight with pain, I managed somehow to get on feet, my voice risin' to a howl. "When Sub is flood and unnercars smash, when joeykits blind and Mids eat Halber's bones—"

"*STOPPIT!*"

I gazed unflinch at his horror.

"Chang, don' . . . " A croak. "Please."

I blinked. So they gonna let me live. What good it do, with my chest all constrict?

Heart pills in medkit back at shop, if I could get to.

"Take me home," I said, with dignity. "Chang too old fo' manhandle. Can't walk."

"What 'bout witchsign?"

"If I live 'til morra, sign be off. Too late fo' today. Can't do nothin' about."

Halber's face was pasty. He made a speeding gesture. "Chaco, Mer, Barth! Allayas goin' Up! Take Changman home fas'. Bring innifo fo' passby."

Pantin', I made voice steady. "What 'bout meet?"

"Ya gon' trayfo permas?"

"Afta." I nodded.

He shrugged, a tired motion of defeat. "When ya want. Morra, if ya don' die on us."

Dunno how I made it back to shop. They put me in carry

chair and I sat. By time we reached Three Four, I had some breath back, enough to wave away Subs, unlock shop. I went behin' curtain, fumbled through medkit, took pill I shoulda brought. Sat an' waited while it soothed. Chest slowly came free, pain eased. Stupid ol' man, you die nex' time you try that. Always carry pills, now on.

Last thing I said to Chaco, "Tell Halber to set meet for 'morra aftanoon." Either I'd be alive, an' want meet, or dead, and no matter.

When I felt able, I got together packs of innifo, went outside, foun' Mids willin' to help pass word to all other tribes. Was still plenny of day left, so if they quick, could get word to all. Even Parkas.

Nite, I puttered around shop, wonderin' how to persuade tribes to work togetha. If I got leaders to cooperate, we could send trannie speakfo' to Unies. If govermen wouldn' listen, maybe we talk to Holoworl'. Dey wouldn' give shit about tribes, but if trannie bosses got together, some kinda story innit.

Knock on door.

Heart thudded. "We close." I shuffle to door.

"It be me."

Pook.

I leaned head 'gainst door, warnin' self. He wasn't your own joey, silly Chang, just wild kit wid no tribe. I was sorry for glad that swept through me. "So? G'way wid ya. I don' open fo' no dirtmouth joeykit."

A growl, then voice extra patient. "Please, Mista Chang."

I went worry. "Ya hurt?"

"Naw."

"Hungry, hah? Too bad. Ya can't yell Chang dead one day, come beggin' fo' help da nex'—"

"Wanna trayfo'."

"You? Whatcha got I wan', hah? Dirty jumpsuit? Scraps a ol' wires? Nah, Pook."

"Good stuff. Lemme showya."

"Daytime is fo' trayfo'. Night fo' sleep. If tribes see me open at night, soonerlata be trouble."

"Can' come in day." His voice hinted that his patience was wearing. "Mids see what I got, try ta take. You wan' Pook get diss?"

I smiled. Pook couldn' have nothin' so good he afraid to

carry in day. But he wasn' full member of Mids yet, and Karlo still pissoff, so risk could be real. "Okay okay, betta not be swind." I undid locks one at time, hopin' Pook not crazy enough to pull shiv once he got inside, finish ol' Chang once an' for all. I swung open door. "Ya comin' in, or no?"

His eyes darted roun'. He slipped in and quick I shut door.

"Well, what—where ya get *those*?" Knew I sounded like glitch trannie din' know nothin' about trayfo, but couldn' help.

Pook had beautiful pair Uppie boots. Expensive kind that last foreva.

He went swell. "Tolya Pook c'n look afta hisself."

I looked them over. Hardly wore at all. "Where ya get?"

He frown, like I go glitch. "Whassit matta?"

True. Dunno what I was thinkin'. "Okay okay, whatcha wan' trayfo?"

"Cansa. Meat an veg."

Cautious, I said, "How many?"

"Whatcha offa?"

"What I wan' with 'notha pair boots," I grumbled, startin' negotiate.

"Ain' all I got. I c'n—" He snapped shut.

"Yeah?"

His face sudden showed nothin'. I was proud that he learn afta all, but annoyed 'cause his bein' smart make trayfo harder.

After we backanforth a while, I realized Pook not too anxious, but ready to take his time, maybe even go trayfo somewhere else. Good fo' him, but not fo' Chang. I went exasperate, to push along; if I gonna meet with tribes morra, had to sleep. "How c'n I trayfo, you won' tell whatcha wan' or what else ya got?"

Pook's look uncertain. "Ya gonna swind, if ya know."

Course; that's the whole point of knowin' what they wan'. But this was Pook, and he'd never make somethin a himself 'less I gave him chance. I sighed. "Okay okay, I go easy. Tell."

He took deep breath. "Enough cansa ta get through winta."

"Whole winta, fo' one lousy pair a trayfo boots? Think ya can swin—"

"Enough cansa fo' two."

"Now who glitch, hah? Ya starting Pooktribe or somethin'? How ya 'xpect me ta give that much fo'—"

"An' I also got . . ." Grubby hand dug in jumpsuit pocket. I watched sharp, wonderin if he 'bout to pull shiv. Stead, he dumped wad of Unibucks on table.

I reached for them slow, so to not alarm Pook, an' counted. Twenty-seven. I sat, wonderin' who he diss. "Wanna tell me 'bout it?"

"Naw."

I sighed, made him offa I knew he'd refuse, just for start. Instead making offer back he got pissoff, so I hadda fuss with him to calm. Gave him good cuppa tea. Dunno why I bothered with Pookboy, sometime. Final, he said he'd be back 'notha day, tonight he'd jus' give coupla Unies fo' coupla cansa. I made good trayfo, thought about it a min, threw in couple extra cansa, so he'd wanna come back.

Before he wen', I said, "Pook, I need—maybe you inneres' help some, morra."

"Whaffo?"

"Big meet, at Sub Four Two."

"Allie be dere?"

"Who? Sub girlkit? How I know?"

He made face. "Anyway, I got stuff ta do." Pause. "What kinda meet?"

I hesitated. "Pook, lissen. Tomorra, maybe nothin' happen. Filmatleven. But jus' maybe . . . could be history. Somethin' fo' Pook ta remember, he get ol'."

His eyes lit. "Big rumb?"

"Gaah. Out." I thrust cans in his arms. "G'wan!"

"Jus' askin'." He made no move to leave. "What comin' down?"

Dunno why I wanted to tell him. "Buncha tribe leaders meet. No innifo, no passby. Gonna talk about water."

His brow wrinkled. "Buncha tribe on same turf? Naw. Never happen."

"Morra, for sure. Early aftanoon."

"You be glitch, Mista Chang. Get 'em togetha, gonna be biggest rumb eva."

"You comin' with me?"

"Ta watch ya get diss?" His face inneres'. Then, "Naw. Can't leave my—can't go." He pawed at locks. "Seeya afta, Changman, if ya live."

And he was gone.

Chapter 21

PHILIP

I knew that even with Mom's chipnote giving permission, I'd have to wait until morning to catch a flight. My voice was high and I wasn't very tall; some ticket agent might look askance at a young child traveling alone late at night. So, for that matter, might a skytel desk clerk. Anyway, I didn't intend to use the forged note wantonly; it was for emergencies.

In addition to counting tree species on my rides with Mom, I'd noted homes without fences in safe-looking neighborhoods. I spent the night on the patio of one of them. The deck chairs were comfortable. I considered leaving a note of thanks, but didn't because word might get back to Mom.

When the sun rose higher I shed my jacket, rode the bus to a cabstand a mile away, and took a ground taxi to the shuttle-port. Changing vehicles reduced the chance I'd be traced.

I paid cash for my ticket. On the suborbital shuttle a reservation wasn't really needed; seats were usually available. If Jared had realized that, he'd have been harder to track.

To allay suspicion I told an agent my mother said to ask help finding the gate. Would he please show me the way? On the shuttle I asked help with my acceleration belts, though Father had shown me often enough. A cheerful attendant strapped me in. She sat across from me for takeoff, flashing me a reassuring smile as the wings folded.

My only problem was getting a cab from Von Walther to the Sheraton. With my overnight bag I waited my turn at the helicab stand, but passengers jostled me aside as if I didn't exist. I stood back, observed the most successful technique, and practiced on a sweet elderly lady whose mass wasn't as intimidating as some others. I tried to ignore her look of shock as I rammed past her into the cab.

"Sheraton Skytel, please." According to the posted rates the fare should be a little over ten Unibucks, so I made sure the driver saw a twenty clutched tight in my hand. He lifted off without objection.

At the hotel I held on to my bag, to save another tip. I

wasn't quite sure how Mom would react to my escapade; money might be tight for a while. I took the elevator down to the lobby, waited my turn at the desk.

"Yes, sonny?"

I kept a polite smile plastered on my face, ignoring his condescension. "A room for two nights."

"Are your paren—"

"My Mom says not by the elevators or the linen closets. And not too near street level." I counted off the bills. "She'll be here after dinner, if the Trans-Siberian isn't delayed."

He pursed his lips, still unsure. "Is there a reservation?"

"No, she called ahead and told me you had plenty of rooms."

"Your name?"

"Philip Tyre. Is the restaurant open? Mom wants me to have a proper lunch. Do you have snack machines? Is there a softie dispenser on my floor? Does it make change?" I kept at it until he thrust me a registration form, took my payment.

Lying is so often unnecessary. You just make adults want you to disappear.

I tipped the bellhop two Unibucks and thanked him politely.

As I'd expected, the room had a generic puter terminal. I dialed into the nets, entered Adam Tenere's password.

It took me only three minutes to call up his Terrex account.

I was impressed.

Mr. Tenere had deciphered my hint almost immediately, and had set a daily review of his card. I hoped he wouldn't check again soon; he could spot my access just as easily as I could his.

Jared had withdrawn three hundred from his father's account. Mr. Tenere must have seen it, but to my astonishment he hadn't blocked further access.

I spotted a charge at the skytel dining room, two nights ago.

I left my console, called the desk, asked if a Mr. Tenere were registered.

No.

Naturally, Jared would have used another name. But there were too many possibilities; I needed a look at the registry.

I doubted the desk would cooperate, and my asking might raise suspicion.

I took off my jacket, folded it over the chair, got to work.

I dialed up Standard and Poor's, checked corporate owner-ship of the Sheraton chain, copied down the owners' published access numbers.

Next, I windowed out, netted to the multiframe at Georgetown University where I had a standing account, wrote a quick password query loop with a notify alarm, and cracked a few dozen random user accounts.

I loaded my password query into each user's workspace with a ten hour self-erase, set each user to high-speed dialing into corporate Sheraton's main puter. Soon I had ninety-six copies of my password query running, courtesy of Georgetown University.

I lay on the plush bed, hands behind my head. Unless I were lucky, it would still take an hour or two.

Lunchtime came and went, but I wasn't really hungry, and there were snack machines in the hall. Mom said sugar aggra-vated my energy excess, so at home I didn't get quickfoods too often. As I saw it, Mom's perception was skewed; she suffered from energy deficit rather than I from an excess. Snacks would do just fine.

The alarm beeped just before two.

An access code flashed, for Sheraton Corporate HQ. I wiped the Georgetown users' workspaces. Next I netted to the Sheraton corporate puter, entered the code I'd deciphered, fol-lowed a maze of menus into accounting.

A few minutes later, slightly annoyed, I perused a list of the week's registrations in the New York Skytel. I could have saved so much effort if the desk would show people their reg-istration book. It wasn't really a secret. Any intelligent twelve-year-old could get access, if he tried.

No guest named Tenere, or anything close.

I had to put myself in Jared's shoes, but I was much brighter. If I overestimated him, I could end up outsmarting myself.

My eye skimmed the list.

Well, I hadn't overestimated him. Adamson, Jer. I'll bet he thought it funny.

I examined the skytel's ledger, found no checkout logged. Was he still in the hotel? Room 3023. The easiest way to find out was to dial.

"Yes?" A woman.

"Mr. Adamson, please."

"Wrong room, joey." She hung up.

I checked the screen. Every other occupied room showed a checkout payment for the day, or a carryover.

Odd.

I windowed back to Mr. Tenere's Terrex account. Hadn't Jared realized his card could be traced, or didn't he care? I worked my way backward from his most recent use. An asterisk, that I hadn't noticed before. I called up the help menu.

Police notify, priority one.

Whenever Mr. Tenere's card was used, the New York District police puter was notified. Why, then, hadn't they been called to the Sheraton restaurant?

I checked the date; the notify had been placed after Jared paid for his dinner.

Well. I had proof Jared had been in the skytel, and I knew he hadn't used the Terrex card after. He hadn't checked out, but the room was reoccupied. Where was Jared? I lay down to think it through.

An hour later I slipped on my shoes, put on my jacket. At the puter, I studied a city directory. Then I locked my room, rode the elevator up to the lobby.

"May I see the manager, please?"

"Who shall I say . . . "

"Philip Tyre."

"He's with someone. I'll tell him."

"I'll wait in the lounge."

Half an hour passed. I found it hard to sit still, and began to pick at my jacket. Perhaps I would go back to my room, curl up against the wall. Base seven was interesting, because of the irregularities. I solved random equations in my head, feet kicking underneath the chair.

After a full hour I went back to the desk. "Could the manager see me now?" I tried not to sound belligerent. "I've been waiting since two-thirty."

"I'll let him know."

If I made a scene, I'd call attention to myself.

I skimmed every holozine in the lobby.

At four, the desk began to get busy with the evening's arrivals. I stood in line, waited for the clerk to notice me.

"Excuse me, son." An expensively suited joey brushed past to the check-in desk.

"Can't you play somewhere else?" A middle-aged woman, lugging three bags.

I retreated. How would Father handle it? I mean, if everyone didn't recognize him as they did?

I'd missed lunch, and was irritable. With a deep breath, I walked back to the counter, where the woman with three bags argued with a receptionist about her room. Several clerks were on duty, all busy, and travelers waited for the next free space.

"Excuse me, I want—"

I stopped, pitched my voice louder. It was at an annoying stage and could be shrill, which usually I found exasperating. Today it would be useful. "Excuse me, I've been waiting to see the manager."

"Please, joey, we're busy. Check back in—"

I sang out, "I thought he'd like to know one of his security guards exposed himself in the hallway."

The woman gasped.

"Three times. I found it quite upsetting, objectively speaking. Mom will no doubt want the jerries called, and—"

Thirty seconds later, I was in the manager's office.

I sat on a straight-backed chair, swinging my legs while a narrow-faced man with a pencil moustache made soothing noises.

" . . . terrible occurrence. Can you describe—"

I read the nameplate on his desk. "Mr. Fenner, you have worse problems than a guard with an open fly."

"—or catch the name on his jacket—what?"

I was committed; nothing to do but forge ahead. "Forget the guard. I made him up."

"You little—" He rang the lobby. "Get this brat out of—"

I recalled Father, the time Senator Wade tried to get him to intervene with the investigators. I made my voice cold as ice. "You made me waste an afternoon in your bloody lobby, while I had work to do. How do you think Mr. Credwin will like that?"

Fenner gaped. "You know him?"

Only from the Standard and Poor's report, which listed him as CEO of the Sheraton chain. I tried to avoid a lie. "And my family knows Senator Boland, and his son Robert, the Assemblyman. I could mention Joseph Martins, the city Building Inspector, but that's not necessary, is it, sir?"

The manager studied me, saying nothing.

I flared, "Just because I'm young doesn't mean you should treat me like dirt!"

Perhaps it was my self-assurance. His manner changed at once. "Look, Mr., ah—"

"Tyre."

"There must be a misunderstanding. What can I do for—"

I leaned forward. "Jer Adamson."

His eyes changed just for a moment, but long enough for me to know I'd scored. Jared had that same look the time he denied he had any pornographic chips. I'd only asked to observe his reaction.

"How does that name concern you, Mr., ah, Tyre?"

Father, I know you won't approve of my rudeness. But I'm committed. For Jared's sake, I have to go through with this.

"Why the cover-up, Mr. Fenner? Why didn't Jared—Mr. Adamson—check out in the normal manner? What about his Terrex card?"

He blurted, "You know about that?"

Inside, I relaxed. Now it would be easy. I kept my voice cold. "Tell me the truth, all of it. Or would you rather deal with the police?"

He blustered. "We have nothing to hide, young man. Feel free to—"

"May I use your caller, or should I call Commissioner Johanson from the lobby?" I reached across his desk.

All along, I'd made a point of using names rather than just titles; Building Inspector Martins, Commissioner Johanson. A shallow trick, but as I'd suspected, it worked. The manager snatched away the caller. "Easy, joey. No need. Tell me what you want, and why."

"Every jerry east of Kansas is looking for Adamson under his real name. I think you know that."

"Go on."

"His name is Jared Tenere. His father is aide to—has connections. He checked into Room 3023, had a meal in your revolving restaurant. Then what?"

"How are you involved, Mr. Tyre?"

"Jared Tenere is sick, in need of hormone rebalancing. His father is a family friend, and is very upset. I'm helping him find his son." No outright lies, as far as I knew.

"The boy may have stayed here, but he checked out on—"

I stood. "Thank you for seeing me, sir. Obviously the jerries can—"

His voice caught me halfway through the door. "All right, damn it!"

I turned.

"We didn't do anything wrong."

I tried to sound accommodating. "You didn't check him out, and you didn't confiscate his card after the 'notify' was placed. You didn't contact the authorities. I'm sure the police would like to know why. But my only interest is to find my frie—Jared. I'm too young to have any interest in hotel business."

"Is that a promise?"

I felt dirty, and old. "If you level with me, sir."

He shook his head in wonder. "What are you joeykits coming to?"

I waited.

"All right, he checked in four days ago. Paid cash, under the name Adamson. That's not illegal, even if he's a minor."

"No, sir. I'm a minor myself, and I know that."

"He used the card to pay for dinner. The night auditor spotted the alert when he ran it through his puter. I sent our security chief to his room."

My heart pounded. "And?"

"The boy spotted us, and took off. We chased him through the corridors."

Jared was wiry, and when we played football I could never lay hands on him.

"He . . . disappeared."

"Please, sir. Tell me the truth." I tried not to let my voice tremble.

"That *IS* the—ahh." He waved his disgust, and his surrender. "All right. He made it to street level. Kicked open a door and ran out. I have no idea where he went."

Elation. Fear. Relief.

I looked up. "Why didn't you call the jerryhouse?"

"I don't know." Fenner's eyes were evasive.

"For Lord God's sake, I can't find him until I get inside his head. Tell me what you know."

For some reason, he looked perplexed. Then he sighed. "You're one strange joey. The reason was . . . do I have your promise?"

"More than that. My oath. I won't tell a soul."

It seemed to reassure him. "Sometimes, mistakes are made, son. The maitre d' . . . I wasn't there, you understand. It happens. Our policy is—we don't normally—"

I waited until he ran down. He blurted, "They served him drinks. A bottle of wine."

"Ah." No wonder Fenner was frightened. The waiter, the maitre d', possibly even the manager, risked a penal colony. As did Jared.

"So you hid the whole affair."

"Not exactly."

"He's on the streets? Where the transpops live?"

"The trannies, yes."

"I've got to find him."

He let out a long breath. "That's not our concern, is it?"

"No, sir. But I'll need a way back in at night."

He stared. "You'd go—don't be ridiculous. They'd eat you alive. Literally."

"I have to find him." It was my fault Jared had left. The vile things I'd shouted at him, when I wasn't thinking clearly. I still wasn't sure why I'd done it.

"The jerries have his picture. Let them do their job."

"Show me the door he went out. I'll call someone to unlock so I can get back in, when I'm ready."

"Boy, you can't—"

"Sir, I have to." My voice quavered. I tried desperately not to rev. "I'm going to my room. I'll be back in a while. You'll have someone let me out at ground level. Please." I stood, headed for the lobby.

"Your parents—"

I faced him, my hand on the doorknob. "The truth is, they don't know I'm here. But I wasn't lying when I said they know the Senator. And a lot of other important people. You keep my secret, and I'll keep yours. I've *got* to find Jared before he's hurt."

His tone was uneasy. "Son, I can't let you go out there. I have a youngster about your—"

"It's not your decision, sir." I peered into his eyes. "I've done a—a very bad thing. He ran away because of me, and now it's my job to find him. I'll be all right." I had to get back to my room.

"If necessary I'll hold you, call your parents—"

"You don't know who they are, and you won't find out from me. And your secret would come out. Please, don't interfere." I opened the door. "I'll call you when I'm ready." I dashed through the lobby, to the elevator.

When at last it reached my floor I hurried along the corridor, let myself in, sealed my door. I threw myself on the floor, sat hunched, rocking, hugging myself.

Jared was outside. Ten thousand sixty, in base twelve, was . . . Think. Numbers are impersonal. He'll be all right. So will you.

Relax. Stop whimpering.

Calm.

It took an hour.

When I felt better, I called room service, asked them to rush me a meal. Munching on the first of my sandwiches, I rethought my situation.

Could I count on the manager's cooperation? Would I come back to find my room locked? Would his security guards haul me to his office while they called the jerries? Why had I admitted I was a minor who'd left home without permission?

What was my obsession to tell the truth?

I know, Father, it's what you do. But look where it got you. Thrown out of office, blamed for Senator Wade's mess. There's nothing left of your career, your reputation. Nothing but your honor.

You said you'd punish me, if I told you that again. I was only eight, and didn't understand why.

Don't you have honor?

Did Philip Tyre have honor? You told me I should be proud of him.

Would he lie to a skytel manager?

Mr. Fenner was a strange man. We'd begun as adversaries, yet before long he was worrying I'd be hurt.

I piled clothes in a backpack. At the snack machines I filled my pockets with items that might be useful. I glanced at my watch, hurried to the desk.

This time, I reached the manager without delay. I said, "I'm ready, Mr. Fenner."

"It's late in the day to go streetside."

"Yes, sir. We'd better hurry."

He stood from behind his desk. "Is Philip Tyre your real name?"

"Yes, sir." Most of it.

"Odd. There's no one by that name in citizen registry. The only one listed died years ago. A sailor."

"My, ah, godfather." Close enough. "I'd like to go now."

"You brought your personal caller? I've instructed the night manager to open when you call. You're aware the public callers outside are all broken?" We headed for the elevators. "I don't know why I'm doing this."

We rode down to street level. A guard accompanied us to the heavily reinforced door. They unchained it, the guard's pistol ready, and I slipped out.

"Thank you."

The guard pointed. "He ran that way." The door shut.

The sun still shone, but dusk would soon be upon us.

People were on the street. Their clothes were wrinkled, some of them dirty and ragged.

They stared.

I stood still. Jared had run onto this street, would have continued running until his adrenaline stopped pulsing.

Let's see, now. I was fifteen. I'd just dashed out the door and made my escape. I didn't have a lot of sense, but thought a lot of my abilities. Where would I go?

Out of sight.

They said Jared had fled south, downtown. My guess was that he turned the corner. But which way?

To turn right, he'd have to cross the avenue. Left, he could disappear around the base of the hotel.

I turned left.

"Watchew wan', Uppie?"

A scruffy man, older than Father. I took a step back. "I'm looking for someone."

"Who?"

"A boy came out of the skytel, two days ago. He—"

"Bes' getcha self outa heah, joeykit. Night comin'."

"I need to find—"

"Doncha lissen? Uppies can' be on streets afta dark." He spat. "Don' know why I botha, 'xcept you so little. G'wan, go back home!" He shambled off.

"Mister—"

He didn't stop.

I chewed my lip. This might be harder than I thought. I walked on to the next corner. Half a dozen odd-looking men and women lounged against a pole. I started past them.

One put himself in my way. "Where ya goin', joey?"

"I'm looking for a boy who came this way two days ago."

The leader glanced upward, as if checking the sky. "Dark soon."

I said, "It's still daytime." I made as if to pass.

"Stay offa Broad turf, Uppie."

I wasn't sure what he meant.

"Can' go here."

"I have to."

He considered that. "Innifo?"

"What's that mean, sir?"

He spoke as if to a small child. "Innifo me, joey. Wha's innifo me?"

I repeated the words, until a glimmer of understanding came. I thrust my hand into a pocket, pulled out a chocolate bar. "This is for you."

He gaped. "Mira! Uppie payin' innifo!" They guffawed. "G'wan, den!" He stood aside.

I stood my ground, thrusting away my fear. "A boy, two days ago. From the tower. Had on a blue jacket."

"Yeah?"

I pulled out two more bars. "Where?"

"Gimme."

I yanked back my hand. "When you tell me."

"C'n take." One of his companions drifted out of my sight, behind me.

"Yes, but it's daytime." I don't know why I said it, but

uncertainty flickered in his eyes. I said firmly, "It's the rule." Steady now, Philip. You have no idea what you're saying.

The streeter shook his head. I glanced behind me; the joey who'd moved close took a step back.

"Not enough, Uppie."

I turned to the wall, shielded myself as best I could from their inquisitive eyes, and reached into my shirt pocket. I counted out two fives, put back the rest. "Money, then." I held out my hand.

His eyes widened. A pause. "Mo'."

"Who's Moe?"

"Mo'. Ain' enough."

I tried to avoid a lie, couldn't think of a way. "It's all I brought. Take it or leave it." Sorry, Fath.

"Don' try swind a trannie, joeykit. Give all, 'fore we—"

Mom wouldn't have taken that. She'd have said . . .

"Just who the hell do you think you are?" I thrust the bills in my pocket. "Do you have a name?" I poked him in the chest. "Well?"

He goggled, looking down at my finger. Someone snickered.

"Well?" I stamped my foot.

"Arrie."

I pulled out the bills. "Here's what's innifo you. You want it, Arrie? If not, I'm in a hurry."

Arrie turned to his friend. "Dissim?"

"Naw. Joeykit got rocks fo' balls. Tellim."

I had no idea what they were talking about.

"All ri'." Arrie held out his hand. "Uppie kit, two day back. Bigger 'n you."

I nodded.

"Try Mids."

"Excuse me?"

"Hah?"

"What did you tell me?"

"Mids. Nex' block. He ran pas' Riff an' Billo." He indicated two of his group, who looked sheepish. "Dey lettim cross ta Mid."

"Which way, please?"

Arrie pointed down the block. "Gimme innifo."

"Thanks a lot, sir." I handed him the two fives. "If you see him again, please ask him to wait here." I hurried to the next corner.

I didn't like the look of the joeys congregating across the street, so I circled the block to avoid them. I headed downtown, looking for someone less threatening to ask. I passed gutted buildings, their windows bare. The block I was on seemed deserted.

Abruptly a door opened, and two ragged teeners barred my way. "Hol' it!"

I stopped. "Hello. I'm looking for—"

One shoved me. I sprawled against the building. "What do you think you're—"

"Watcha got?" His hand fumbled at my jacket pocket.

I tried to twist loose. "I have innifo for you."

"Don' nee'. Got chew instead."

I tried to think, but the reek of his breath made me desperate. I snapped the fingers of my left hand. "Here. Look." Again I snapped.

He stared.

My right fist slammed into his eye. He bellowed, let go my jacket. "Ow! Ow! Swee, dissim!"

The second boy snatched out a knife. "Byebye, Uppiekit!" He lunged.

Without thinking I caught his wrist, flipped him over my shoulder. He slammed into the wall.

I'd always hated Mom's lessons. How embarrassing to have to admit they were useful.

I twisted the knife free of his grip. My foot went up to deliver the arm-smashing kick.

I hesitated.

"Dissim, Swee!" The first boy, bent over in pain, wasn't aware that their situation was changed.

I let go his arm. "What does 'dissim' mean?"

"Means I gonna diss ya!" The enraged boy leaped to his feet, snatched at the knife I held.

Mr. Fenner was right. The streets were too dangerous for me. I backed away, holding the knife low, as Mom had taught. "Easy, joey. I don't want to fight."

The boy lunged. I barely got his knife out of the way. It

grazed his wrist. He'd have to be more careful, with a sharp weapon.

"I'm sorry, I didn't mean to—"

He stared at the nick in his skin, already welling blood. "Aiee! Jag!" He cowered in the doorway. "Lookit wha' he do!"

Jag pulled his hands away from his streaming eye long enough to peer with the good one. "Dissim, Swee."

"Can'! He cut me!"

Jag gaped, one-eyed. He fished in a back pocket, pulled out a broken old kitchen knife with a jagged point. "Get 'way f'm Swee! Don' mess wid 'im!"

"Oh, for God's sake." I backed away once more. "I'll be on my way. Leave me—"

He rushed me, knife arm extended. Before I had time to think, I shifted my weight to my left leg. My right foot arced high. His knife went flying. It worked, Mom. Did Academy really teach you that?

"Hey!" Jag stumbled to a halt.

I snatched up the scarred rusty knife, before he could.

My only choice was to run back to the skytel, but first I had to get free of these two savages. We needed a truce. "Look." I walked toward Jag, extending the knife to return it. "All I want—"

"Don' hurt! Please, Uppie. Fadeout cool!" He staggered away, tripped on a chunk of concrete, fell heavily onto his back. "Aiee!"

"I have no idea what you're talking—"

The other boy intervened. "Let us fadeout, joey. Please?" He clutched his wrist.

Had I hurt him? "Let me see." I reached out.

He squawked. "No!"

There wasn't all that much blood, but it ought to be looked at. "Where's the hospital? Did you nick an artery?" I grabbed his hand, wondering what to do with the knife I still held.

"Oh God no!" He fell to his knees, sobbing. "Din' mean nothin', Uppie. Don' hurt Swee." He covered his eyes with his free arm.

I examined his wrist. Little more than a scratch, thank heaven. I fished in a pocket, wrapped my handkerchief around the cut. "You're all right, joey. Your friend can take you to the hospital." I turned. Jag was blue in the face, the breath knocked out of him from his fall.

Swee stared, openmouthed. His eyes darted to the bandage and back.

"I'm sorry, I didn't mean to . . . " I helped Jag to sit. He gasped and wheezed. I knelt, between him and Swee. "You'll be all right. Let's call it even, shall we? Here." I pulled out his knife.

Jag's eyes bulged with horror. He fainted.

Behind me, Swee cried out in dismay. "Why'd ya diss 'im, Uppie? He was down, wanted fadeout! Why?"

I stood. Too much, too fast. It didn't help that I could barely understand a word. I tried not to rev. My legs grew weak. With care, I crossed to the doorway, leaned against a smashed window. "What's the matter with you? I didn't want trouble."

Swee cowered, made as if to dash past me to the street. He clawed at the ancient, sealed door. "No trouble. Lemme go? Swee be outa heah. Cool?" He inched along the opposite wall.

Thank Lord God. I nodded, before I remembered. "No. Wait."

Swee leaped back. " 'Kay! Cool!"

"I'm looking for someone. A friend."

Swee said nothing.

Streeters were quite eccentric. Father had told me as much, long ago. I'd have to put the joey at his ease, somehow.

"What's your name?"

He hesitated. "Swee. Mid."

"Sweemid?"

"I be Swee." He pointed. "Jag. We be Mid."

"What's Mid?"

"Tribe. Trannie tribe."

"You shouldn't use that word. It's not polite." Father had made that very clear. On the other hand, this boy was older than I, and I had no business giving him lectures. "Sorry. My name is Philip." I held out my hand.

"Don' diss me!"

"Philip Tyre. Philip Tyre Seafort, actually." I crossed to him, hand extended, hoping he wasn't so angry he'd slap it away.

Swee stared at my hand as if it were a snake. With great caution, he touched it.

Much better.

"My friend's name is Jared. He had on a blue jacket, matching pants. Do you know where he is?"

Behind us, a groan. Jag's eyes opened.

"He live?" Swee sounded amazed.

"Yes. You both should see a doctor. Come on, let's help him up." Swee hesitated; I pulled his arm. He lurched after me. We helped Jag sit, and a moment later, assisted him to his feet.

"Maybe you know," I said to Jag. "A boy ran out here two nights ago, and I'm looking for him."

"Dunno." Jag shuffled his feet, eyes fixed on the broken pavement. "Wanna go."

Swee blurted, "Tellim boudit, maybe? Pookboy an' joeykit? Rememer, Uppie's got our shivs!"

"Shivs? What are—"

Jag's eyes widened in comprehension. "You afta an Uppiekit? Bigga 'n you, talk snot?"

That would be Jared. "Blond, about this high . . ."

Swee exchanged a glance with Jag. "Can' tellim 'bout lair. We promise Pook."

Their jabber was driving me to distraction. "*STOP THAT!*" I bunched my fists.

"Okay, Uppie." He edged toward the door.

"Where's Jared?"

Swee mumbled, "Pook."

"What's a Pook?"

"Pookboy. Mid, was. Prolly wid old Changman, now. Gotchur Uppie frien'."

"Pook is a Mid and has Jared?"

"Ya."

Progress. My tension eased. "Where do I find him?"

They exchanged glances. "Nex' block. Dunno where. Inna build, maybe. Dunno."

"All right. Sorry I yelled." I pulled out the second knife. "Can we call a truce, if I give these back?"

Swee blinked. "Whazzat?"

"Truce." He didn't seem to want the knife, so I laid it cautiously on the curb.

He darted toward it, hesitated. "Innifo?"

"No, I won't give you any. If you don't want the knife, I'll keep it. Someone might get hurt."

His face fell. "Swee don' got none. Guess Uppie keep shiv." He sighed.

These people were too much to understand. "Good-bye." I started toward the far corner.

"Hey Uppie!" Swee.

I stopped. "What?"

"You gonna stay out inna nigh'?" He seemed awed.

"No, of course not. It's too dangerous." I went on my way.

Dusk was upon us. Unfortunately, I was too far from the Sheraton to be sure I'd make it back safely. But I'd planned for the eventuality. Jared could wait until morning.

From my skytel window I'd seen a number of abandoned electricars. Now, I spotted one, on a side street. Good.

I crouched in a doorway, waiting for the light to fade. When I judged it dark enough, I dashed to the car. Like most models, it was low-slung.

I hadn't filled out yet, and was thin enough. I took off my jacket, slid underneath the car.

I lay on my back, my jacket a serviceable pillow. I munched on a candy bar, waiting for day.

Chapter 22

JARED

Save me, Lord God. Please. I'm sorry. If you really exist—no, I didn't mean that, honest. Help me.

Muddled bits of prayers flashed through my mind.

Behind my back, I twisted my hands in a desperate effort to free my swollen wrists. Pain lanced through my chest, making me dizzier.

The rope held.

I had to get loose before the savage trannie came back to kill me.

I tucked down my chin, trying to assess my damage. The blood had stopped oozing at last. Christ, it hurt.

Drops of sweat rolled down my temple. I licked my parched lips.

Why had he slashed me? It hurt so. Would he hear me, come punish me if I screamed again?

The only dim light was through the open trapdoor in the ceiling. Not much, but enough to show I was in a filthy elevator. If I could free my hands, I might be able to climb out the escape hatch, as he had.

On the other hand, my chest was cut to ribbons, and any acrobatics would reopen my wound.

This wasn't supposed to happen. Please, Lord God, have Dad shake me awake, tell me to get my butt out of bed for school.

I was scared.

Why had the trannie done it?

He'd looked like a civilized joey, at first. A year or so younger than me. Jumpsuit a bit dirty, but new. His hair cut not too long in back. Only when I got closer did I see the grime on his hands, smell his fetid breath.

I tugged furiously at the cord. What had I done to him? I'd only asked for directions. Was that reason to beat me, kick me in the head? To knife me?

Didn't trannies have *any* decency?

Why had he taken my jacket, my shirt? Why had he left

me overnight in a broken elevator, then slashed me and disappeared? Would he leave me to die of thirst and infection?

Why was I here?

I whimpered. My frantic activity had reopened a gouge,
and fresh blood oozed. I curled in the corner, let myself cry.

A noise.

Oh, Christ. I huddled in the corner, staring at the ceiling.

A thud. Steps. A rescuer? I didn't dare call out.

A face peered. The trannie was back.

He crouched over the hatch, stared down.

I hunched in the corner, very still.

He jumped down; the elevator shook on its cable. I drew
my knees up closer to protect my mutilated chest.

"Gotcha fix." The boy held out a dirty rag, a bottle.

I tore at my ropes, desperate. "Get away!"

"Naw. Fix." Without warning he bent, yanked my ankles.
On my back, I slid across the floor. He dropped lightly onto
my waist, pinning me defenseless.

"Oh God, not again! Please!"

"Stop ya yell." He opened the bottle, poured liquid onto
the rag.

I struggled, without effect. "What are—don't!"

He laid the sopping rag on my mangled chest. It blazed
like the fires of hell. Screaming, I tried to heave off his
weight.

Please, God, don't let this be happening.

"Shut, Uppie!" With one hand he tried to cover my mouth.
The other pressed the foul rag onto my smarting cuts.

"Oh, God, stop! Stop! I'll do anything! Please!"

"Shut, Uppie! Ya worse 'n joeykit!" He splashed from the
bottle onto the cloth.

I howled; I couldn't help it.

The trannie capped the bottle. "Shut, when Pook say!" He
grabbed a handful of my hair, pulled my head up. With measured strokes he began to slap my face, each time harder.
"Don' yell or I whop ya! Shut!"

I squealed, kicked, wept. If only my hands weren't lashed
behind my back—

Desperate, I managed to stifle my cries. I squirmed under
his cruel ministrations.

The streeter soaked my chest in dirty stinging liquid. I

cringed every time he pawed me. God knew what diseases he carried.

Eventually, from exhaustion, I quieted.

He pulled away the rag with care. I peered to see what harm he'd done.

"Alcol," he said. "Fix."

"Huh?"

"Like upbringin'." He grinned. "Ya Pooktribe, now." He waved the bottle in my face. "Alcol."

"Lord God. You poured alcohol into my cuts?" I rolled my eyes, trying to see below my chin.

"Fo' fix." He got to his feet. "An' I brung ya drink."

"Let me go. Please, I—"

A leap, a kick, and he was gone.

I hauled myself up to a sitting position, leaned wearily against the side of the car. Slowly, the sting in my chest subsided to a dull ache.

Scurrying feet. The boy landed a foot away, and my body flew off the floor in recoil. I cried out in pain.

"Water." He held out a jug. "Wan' drink?"

"Let me go!"

"Naw." He squatted by my side. "I be ya capture. Gon' keep ya 'til I trayfo."

Gibberish.

He shoved the jug at my mouth. I twisted my face away. "Let me hold it."

"Think Pook be stupe?" He grasped my hair, poured warm water over my mouth. I gagged.

"Drink!"

I had to remember he was a lunatic and had a knife. To humor him, I put my lips to the jug, swallowed rancid water. In a moment, ashamed, I greedily sought more, amazed at how I relished it.

The boy let me have my fill.

At last, satiated, I leaned back. "Thank you." My voice was small.

He crouched. "I Pook. Watcha call, Uppie?"

I watched his hands, afraid he'd pull out the knife. "I'm sorry, I don't know what you want." I inched away.

His fist lashed out, slammed into my temple. I shrieked

with new agony. I tried to roll away, could not. "Please! Don't!"

"Tell!" His fist reared again.

"Get your frazzin' hands off me!" I aimed a kick that caught his shin; he winced. "Touch me again and I'll kill you!" Ludicrous to say that, trussed as I was, but I was too mad to care.

His fists uncoiled. "Gon' diss Pookboy, hah?" He let loose a slap that rocked my head. "Don' yell at Pook. I be ya capture."

"*Don't. Touch. Me.*" My voice was low, hard. I memorized his features, so I could pick them out anywhere when I had the chance to kill him.

He nodded, as if with respect. "Uppie ain' scare now?" he settled down on his haunches. "Why? Ya scare when I cut Mid mark." He pointed to my chest.

I flinched. "I couldn't help it."

"Cut ya 'gain. If I wan'." He pulled out the knife.

Oh God. I scrunched shut my eyes, waited, determined not to give him the satisfaction of my tears.

A sharp prick, in my shoulder. I jerked away; my eyes flew open. He grinned.

My voice quavered. "So what? I could do that to you, trannieboy. The only difference is who has the knife."

"Who you callin' trannie?" His mouth turned ugly.

"Isn't that what you are?"

He considered it. "I be Mid," he said at last.

I had to keep him talking, lest he hurt me again. He seemed to respect my standing up to him, so I said, "What's your name, Mid?"

"Pook, tolya. Watcha call your name?"

"I'm Jared."

"Jared." He mouthed the unfamiliar word. "Tribe?"

"I don't know what you're—I'm from Washington."

"I been!" He jabbed excitedly, with his finger. "Changman took!"

"Whatever you say." I shifted. "My arms hurt. Untie me."

"Naw." He looked up through the hatch, gauging the daylight. "Gotta get trayfo."

I couldn't let him leave, if at last he was rational. "Pook, my father will give you a reward, if you let me go."

"What's rewar'?"

"Money."

"Already took." He scrounged in his pocket, pulled out a few wrinkled bills. He patted my pants. "From here."

"Frazzing thief!" Again I tried to twist loose.

"Mine now." He stood.

I controlled myself. "Think of all the money you could have when I'm free!"

"Naw. Gonna sell ya."

I shuddered; only Lord God knew what that entailed.

He fingered my socks, as if wondering what they were worth. For the first time, I realized my boots were gone. "Back lata, Uppie." He jumped to the hatch and was gone.

Again I huddled in the corner. Who was this creature? Why did he torment me? He'd taken half my clothes. Would he steal the rest too? Then what? A nameless dread, and thoughts I did my best to banish. Perspiration ran down my spine.

I crossed my legs, quelling a pressing need to urinate. I hoped the trannie would be back soon. Surely he'd have to let me go for that.

Hours passed. I tried to hold still, for the sake of both my chest and my raw wrists. I wondered what kind of building my jail had once been. The elevator was trimmed with brass, and the rotten carpeting had once been plush.

Restless, I called out for help, shouting ever louder until my throat was raw. No one responded.

I squeezed my legs together, hoping to see Pook before I wet my pants. That humiliation would be unbearable.

The light was fading; I'd heard streets were dangerous after dark. What if he never came back? I shivered, despite the miserable heat. Helpless, my hands lashed behind me, I'd starve without Pook, or die of thirst. The elevator would become my coffin; Dad would never learn what happened to me. I yearned for my familiar room in our cottage.

A creak.

"Pook?" It was growing too dark to see. "Mid?"

No reply.

I grew restless, then frantic. If I spent the night tied alone in an abandoned elevator, I would not be sane when morning came.

"POOK!" The scream tore at my throat.

At first, nothing. Then another creak.

I waited for the boy to appear, strained to hear any faint sound. Was it wind, or voices I imagined?

I recalled the ugly, leering savages who'd chased me.

What if it weren't Pook above, but others? Visions of torture flashed through my mind.

Very quiet now, I curled in the corner.

I waited.

Something woke me from a doze. I blinked, could see nothing.

A sound, then a light, swinging eerily. I whispered, "Pook?"

"Yo!" He jumped down at my feet. I squawked, trembling from fear.

"Scare ya, Uppie?"

I nodded, too shaken to pretend.

He giggled. "Brung ya cansa." He hauled two dented cans out of a sack. "Lotsa trayfo. No one skin Pook dis time." He set down a Valdez permabattery, with a light attached.

He unzipped a can, dug something out with a grimy spoon. "Open ya mouth, I feed."

"Please." I wiggled my hands. "Untie me."

"Naw." He shoved food at my face.

"I can't eat like this!"

"Gotta."

"Anyway, I have to go to the bathroom." I reddened.

"Wha?" His stare was vacant.

"Toilet," I said. "Soon, Pook."

He shrugged. "Dunno." Again he proffered the spoon, laden with pungent stew.

Though my mouth watered, I shook my head. "Please, Pook. Take me somewhere I can go." My need was urgent.

A long stare, then comprehension. "Piss?"

I nodded.

He helped me up. "Inna corna."

I recoiled. "That's disgusting."

"Gotta stay heah. Can' let you get 'way."

"My chest is cut up so bad I can hardly walk! You took my boots and you've got a knife. How could I get away?"

He sighed, put down the can. "Uppie be too trouble," he grumbled. "Waitasec." He grabbed the light, reached for the hatch.

"Don't leave me in the dark!"

He paid no attention.

By now night had fallen; the elevator was pitch-black. My breath came loud, from fear. I waited for the sound of his return step.

"Pook?" I gritted my teeth. I'd always hated the dark.

The building creaked.

"Is that you?"

Silence. I squeezed my legs tight, trying to control my sphincter. I had to have light. I'd ask him—

The elevator bounced. A crash, a fierce roar, inches from my face. A cold groping hand.

Screeching, I cannoned back to the wall, tugging at the rope eating my wrists. *"Oh God oh God no please someone no!"* I hardly recognized my voice.

A cackle. The light sprang to life.

Pook sagged against the wall, weak with laughter. "Gotcha, Uppie!" He pointed at my crotch, roared with delight.

I looked down at my soaked pants and wished I were dead. A whimper, that I realized must be my own.

"Brung stool ta help ya climb out, but now ya don' need." Grinning, he groped above the hatch, brought down an old bucket.

I began to cry.

He giggled. "Uppie niño." He turned over the bucket, sat. "Teach ya holler at Pook."

I hunched in the corner, tears and mucus running unchecked down my cheeks. Please, Lord, let me die.

"Awri, Uppie. Weren't so bad. Jus' scare." His voice softened. "Sit." He brought me the stool.

"No, I—" He made me sit. My legs chafed. The acrid smell rising from my pants made me gag.

"Eat. Feel betta." He picked up the can. "Jus' funnin'."

I tried to control my sobs. "Untie me for a minute. Please!"

"Naw." He patted my shoulder. "Brung cansa special fa you. Eat." He filled the spoon.

I took a bite of cold stew. Spicy, but I was starved. I sat on the stool, utterly humiliated, and let him feed me like a baby. I wolfed it down as fast as he could spoon it.

"Could I have water?"

He held the jug.

"Thank you." My tone was humble. I squirmed. "I've got to change my pants."

He snickered. "Where ya think ya be, Chang shop?"

"I don't—"

"Ain' no pant. Anyway, Swee an' I gon' take yours, 'morra. Trayfo."

"You what?" I was indignant.

"Won' need, in elevate."

Suddenly it didn't seem important to get out of my wet pants. I sighed, leaned back against the wall. "When will you let me go, Pook?"

"Gotta figga how ta sellya. Maybe ask Karlo, if he quit pissoff."

I didn't like the sound of that. "Sell?"

"Sho. Think I gonna feed ya all winta?"

It was all beyond understanding. "Sell me to my father. It's what I've been trying to—"

Pook spat. "Why he pay fo' Uppie kit so glitch he run in trannie streets?"

I flushed. "Our families care about each other. We're not like you filth—" I swallowed the rest; it was the wrong tack. "Besides, I'm smart and he knows it."

"Hah. What c'n ya do worth a shit?"

I'd have sat stiffly, but for my bound hands and the ache of my chest. "Lots of things. I can—" I groped for examples. "—program puters better than anyone. How do you think I got the money to fly here? I can schuss through any system, no matter how hard the ice." Well, a slight exaggeration, but not by much. And when I got out of here, I'd prove it. After this, I owed it to myself, and Rolf would help. Together, we had access enough to—

"Puters." The trannie spat again. "Ain' got none."

Exhausted, I closed my eyes.

"Don' sleep yet. Gotta alcol ya."

I blanched.

"Fo' heal, Uppie." He tapped his chest. "What Karlo do, in upbringin'."

"Please!"

"Fo' heal. Won' hurt as much, sec time." He got out the cloth and bottle. "Hol' still."

I clenched my teeth as he came near. It was useless to argue.

When he was done with his torture I lay against the wall, only an occasional moan escaping my lips. Pook snorted with contempt, patted his chest. "Bad as Jag. Oooh! Ow! Wah!"

I snarled, "Let me do it to you, trannie!"

His eyebrows raised, as if he was considering it. "Naw. Karlo gotta, or it ain' righ'." He sighed. "I be ta bed. Feed ya in morn." He took the light.

My tone was urgent. "I can't stay in the dark. Leave the light."

He shook his head. "Ain' give ligh' to no Uppie snot. Cos' too damn much."

"DON'T LEAVE ME TIED IN THE DARK!"

Surely he sensed my panic. But he said, "Wan' me fall downstair cause I lef' ligh' wid Jared Washinton Uppie?" His voice was indignant.

"Pook, for God's sake!"

He sighed. "Awri', awri', I stay wid ya."

It wasn't what I'd had in mind. I watched with consternation, but he settled on his back, fully dressed. He dialed the light low. "Sleep, Uppie."

I lay on my side, my body aching. My pants were soggy; I tried not to remember why. I licked my lips, wishing he'd given me more stew. Had I seen him bring two cans?

"What was that we ate, Pook?"

"Cansa."

"It was good." I hoped he'd take the hint.

Silence.

"Where'd you get it?"

"Trayfo. Got whole buncha, now."

"Can I have more?"

Again, he sighed. "You be pain inna ass, Uppieboy." After a moment he sat. "Awri'." He took another can from the bag he'd brought. "Here." He zipped it open.

My eyes widened. "Hold still!"

"Wha?"

"Hold it where I can read it!" I squinted. "Oh, Christ!" I gagged. "You frazzing bastard!"

"Whassamatta!"

"Prong yourself!" I twisted, managed to aim my feet at his stomach, kicked hard. He oofed and fell.

I gagged again, tried to vomit.

"Stop dat!" He scrambled across the car, shook me. "Whassamatta?"

"You fed me dog food!"

His brow wrinkled. "Whas' wrong wid? Eat allatime!"

I gave my ropes a desperate tug. "Ow!" I recoiled from the pain, felt something part in my chest. I looked down; blood oozed. "Oh, no!" I collapsed in helpless tears.

Pook watched, crouching alongside. His expression slowly turned to concern. "Din' mean nothin'," he mumbled. "Food, is all. Wha' diff, eat dog food, or eat dog?"

I wailed.

Pook's eyes glistened. "Don', Uppie," he pled. "Din' mean hurt." He tried to stroke my head. I pulled free.

He sat next to me, hauled me down so I lay on my back, his lap a pillow. He dialed low the light. I struggled to free myself, to no avail.

Forlorn, I lay sobbing. A long while passed before my breathing calmed.

After a time I slept, his hand gentle on my head.

Chapter 23

POOK

When Changman tell me 'bout ol' cassel an' knigh's it soun' zarky; burn cassel, diss enemy sojers. But Pook learn bein' a capture is harder 'n he figga.

Chang's book don' say capture can' go onna street widout he worry his booty gonna 'scape. Don' mention haulin' jugs a water upstair, feedin' Uppie every bite, lissen' him complain 'bout food an' cry hisself ta sleep.

Fah. I ready ta diss 'im, sell resta his threads.

Inna morn, I catch Chang an' trayfo Uppie's boots fo' so many cansa Pook don' worry 'bout eat all winta. Bes' boots Pook ever got; not a single hole. Think Uppie 'preciate trayfo? Naw. Bitchanmoan cause cansa say dog instead a people.

Uppiekit be some kinda stupe. Can' unnerstan' simplest stuff Pook say, even when talk loud. Allatime he whine rope too tigh', please, Pook, loosen jus' a little, I be good. Please Pook, I gotta go bathroom, not in here for God's sake don' ya unnerstan', I don' jus' mean piss, *PLEASE*.

I wave shiv in face, show 'im how I cut 'im good if he run, untie hans, help 'im outa elevate. His wrists swole; maybe rope too tigh' afta all. He walk along hall clutchin' ches' like he 'fraid it gonna flop open from tiny Mid cuts. Den, more whine. Oh God not in here what is this place, doncha have a real bathroom? I can't do it here. I say, aw ri', don', but he go sniffle. I 'xplain we wen' allaway otha side a buildin', not near elevate, in room hardly eva be use for shithouse.

He whine, can't while ya watchin', Pook. Ya gotta wait outside.

No way. I ain' glitch. If I leave him, he go rabbit. I fol' arms, shake head, tap foot, say coupla min I take ya back, letcha do it in elevate. So he crouch in corna, cryin' while.

Uppieboy could neva make it onna street. Too weak. Anyway, what kinda name be 'Jared'? He keep addin' 'ten air', but I ain' stupe enough ta lissen. Air be free, an be only one. Not two, or nine, or ten.

I gotta figga how sell him 'fore he drive me craze. Maybe

I ask Chang, but firs' he'll wanna know all boudit. Hard enough trayfo Uppie boots widout Changman skin me like las' time. Where ya get, why dey so good, whatcha been up to, Pookboy?

Fah.

An' somethin' glitch with Jag an' Swee. Dey look at me funny, turn away fas'. I figga dey tell Karlo 'bout my booty and Midboss gonna take. Dat be end of Pook, or Karlo. I won' give up my Jared Uppie.

Nex' time I take Jared ta shithouse, he go on knees beggin' an' cryin', please Pook no more rope, it hurts so bad, I do watcha say. I knock him down, sit on him ta tie him, fin' his wrists all swole an' oozin'. Can't sell no booty if he cripple. 'Sides, I like what he tell me; makes me rememba Changman. I make him say ova an' ova, please, Pook, I do watcha say.

Fo' safe, I put Uppie back in elevate, close trap, pile lotsa bricks on top. Inside, he cry an' carry on, but I don' pay no 'tention; I gotta get away from his yellin'. Ain' my fault he scare widout light. Anyway, I be back in a while, or morra.

I go lookin' fo' Swee an' Jag ta see why dey fadeout so fas' with funny look. Can't fin' em. Maybe Bigsis could tell, but can' ask 'less I see her on street. I wander, careful ta stay clear of lair. Ain' fair, Karlo won' give me upbringin'. I more ready 'n Swee or Jag, who promise Pook ta not say a word, but run some kinda swind. I know 'em both since joeykits; somethin' dey don' wanna tell me. It gotta be 'bout Jared frazzin' Uppie.

Plenny a food fo' give my booty, but not lotta water. Pipes in my private lair fulla rust an' junk. Outside, puddles so buggy I can' stan' 'em. Could walk ta riva, but what good dat? Riva stink; trannies who drink it soonerlata die. Don' know what ta do.

Hate it, but gotta ask Changman. I knock on door. No ansa. I curse some, kick door hard, only hurt my foot. Cross street, Mid joeykit name Sall laugh. I grab rock, throw at his head. I miss; only smack his shoulda, but it enough ta yelp 'im. I catch 'im in doorway a dead store.

"Fadeout, Pook, fadeout!" Younga 'n me, he go cringy.

"Ya laugh now, shitface?" I finga my shiv.

Sall wait ta cry or get diss. "Din' mean nothin', Pook!"

Be fun ta dissim, specially now Karlo say I can' have

upbringin'. But if otha Mids see, Karlo call out his milisha afta me. I sigh. "Innifo?"

He turn out pockets. "Ain' got, Pook."

I din' expect none. "Ya fin' Swee 'n Jag, be my innifo. Bring 'em 'mediate fas'." Sall run off, surprise I lettim go.

I sit in doorway, waitin'. I suspec' Swee won' hide, if he know I look fo'. He know I be good wid shiv.

Twenny min lata, who come slouchin' by but Jag, peerin' otha side a street like some Uppie touris.

"Ova heah, Jagboy." I beck him inta doorway. "Whatcha upta, hah?"

"Nothin, Pook." Innocent, like joeykit.

I get between him an' street. Whatta stupe, ta let me. An' ta think Karlo gave him upbringin', steada me. "Try ta swind ol' Pook, hah? Ya tell Karlo 'bout my Uppie."

"Din'!"

"Gonna cuttem off, makeya a squeaker!" I work on pissoff. Need a real mad, ta hurt Jag.

"He din' tell nothin!" Voice behin' me.

I whirl roun'. Swee, but no shiv. Cloth wrap roun' his wris'.

I considera. " 'Kay. What ain' ya tellin'?"

Swee look away, say nothin'.

I point at wris', scorny. "Whazzat, new kinda thread, go wid ya Uppie shirt?"

He go blush. Now I real inerest. I finga shiv, say quiet, "Thought Jag and Swee be Pook's frens. Don' I trus' ya wid my Uppie lair? Whas so bad ya can' tell Pook?"

Look at each otha. Jag shrug, say ta Swee, "He c'n help us dissim."

"Stoppit! Diss who? Don' make me confuse!" Now I don' have ta work up a pissoff; gettin' good one.

Swee wriggle like embarrass. Slow, he take off cloth from wris'. I mira scab. "Rumb? So?"

He look down. "Uppie done it."

"Frazzin' Uppies, swoopin' down in helis. Think they own worl'! Ain' your faul' coupla Uppies shiv ya."

"Jus' one."

"Jerry?" Hadda be, if Jag 'n Swee lettim cut.

Swee shake head.

I figga, mus' be one helluva Uppie. "Ya chase him offa turf?"

"Well . . ."

Jag blurt, "He stay all nigh'."

Now they actin' goof. "How?"

"Hide." Jag look roun', drop voice. "We follow 'im. he sleep unner car."

"Why din' ya dissim nighttime?"

Dey don' say. Won' look my eye, neitha.

Couldn' be real Uppie. I deman', "Where he be?"

Swee point ta roof. I look suspicious. "Swind?"

"Naw. Been onna roof all day, hidin'."

I go proud. "I dissim fo' ya." I hesitate. "But afta, gimme innifo'."

"What kine? How much?"

I think. "Water. From Mid pipes. Lotsa."

"We ain' got lotsa, Pook. Real bad."

I go chill. Water gone all ova. Somethin' wrong. Gotta ask ol' Changman, when he back. "Some, den. Much as ya can."

Dey agree fas'.

I climb up through ol' store, skippin' bad places in stair. Mids know alla roofs in Mid turf, in case a rumb. Where we walkin' be fulla hole, so gotta go careful. I look roun'. No Uppie.

"Not here, Pook. 'Cross." Swee, nervous.

Sighin', I slide cross board ova edge, skip ta otha side. "C'mon."

"Shh!" They peer roun' like 'xpectin' Broads or Subs.

I go quiet ta corna, look roun'.

Joey sit at edge a roof, lookin' ova. At his side, bag fulla stuff. Shiny red caller in joey's back pocket. Once I saw Karlo wid caller he snatch from Uppie touris in bus. Karlo pushed numbas ova an ova. Wheneva someone ansa, he scream 'n curse. Lotsa fun for coupla days. Then stopped workin'. Nothin' but voice sayin' "disconnec'."

"Him?" I point.

Jag nod.

I pull out shiv, put behin' my back, walk proud. "Hey, Uppieshit!"

He whirl.

"Gonna dissya fo' cut Jag!" I come close.

"Hello." He stan'.

I gawk. Dis be Uppie cut Jag? Smalla 'n me, or even Sall. My nervous be gone. He only joeykit. I go guffaw.

"Glad to meet you. Hello, Mr. Jag."

I turn ta Swee, scorny, "Needs ten of us, take dis babykit. Poor ol' Swee—" Forgot I had shiv behin' back, where Uppie could see.

Joey's breath hiss. He back up, too close ta edge a roof. Stupe. Don' he know *nothin'* 'bout rumb?

I leave off Swee, hol' shiv low like Karlo showed. "Whatcha doin', Uppie?"

"Looking for a friend. Please put away the knife. Someone might get hurt."

I snicker. "Damnri'." I wunner: bes' if I shiv 'im, or push him off an' watch him splat?

His eyes slide past me ta Swee, and go narrow. "Where'd you get that shirt?"

Swee say, "Mine. Innifo."

"You weren't wearing it yesterday."

"Savin'."

Uppie face red wid anger. "It's not yours!" He think I made a stone, ta ignore?

Swee back away, like Uppie gonna steal his green shirt. "Lemme be!"

Uppie follow. I step between, lunge wid shiv. "Gonna dissya, Uppie. Eat ya guts—"

Sky go lurch, roof come at me hard. I throw han' in fronna face as I slam down. My arm fulla gravel. "Oww!"

For min, I can' breathe good. When I scramb to knees, shiv gone. Swee runnin' fa his life 'cross otha roof, Uppie joeykit close behin'. Jag hidin' roun' corna.

Swee an Uppie disappear inta build.

I stagga ta feet. "Frazzin' Uppie!" Whole body hurt; I hol' arm where scrapes startin' ta bleed. Jag duck away. I go rage. "Hide when I wantcha, hah?" I go afta him, kick 'im tween legs. "Soma kine fren!" I whomp 'im harda an' harda. He wail please no, Pook, and cower 'gainst wall. I don' lissen.

Frazzin' Uppies.

When I done wid Jag, can' fin' Swee or craze Uppiekit.

My arm scrape, so I don' wan' Jared Washinton Uppie ta see, 'less he laugh an' I gotta dissim. Can' go near Mid lair in case a Karlo, and Chang shop be close.

Grody day.

Afta while, I notice odd feelin' 'bout street. Broads ain' standin' at edge a turf waitin fo' innifo. Mids neitha. I wonnerin' why everyone so lazy, when I 'member ol' Changman's meet.

I think aboud it. Wunner what faraway tribes look like, if dey dress all glitch like Subs.

Sheet, why not? Jared ain' goin' nowhere, an' Pook got nothin' betta ta do. I run back to lair an bringalong buncha cansa, in case someone sudden ask fo' innifo. Start nor', towar' stair at Four Two.

Still, Pook ain' no stupe; he don' march through Broad turf like he own. Dat askin' fo' troub. Stead, go careful, watchin' both sides. Afta Broad turf, come to Mid Four Two. In doorway, sharp whistle. I freeze, thinkin' run fo' ya life, Pookboy.

"Whatchadoon, joeykit?" Big Midboy, one who push Pook down when walkin' wid Chang.

Instant, I go swell. So what I don' got upbringin'? I got my capture, my Pooklair, enough cansa fo' winta; I ain' no joeykit. "Goin' ta meet." My voice fulla defy.

He scowl. "Innifo?"

"Don' need none. Special day." So Changman say. Hope ol' glitch Neut know what he talkinabout.

"Meet is fo' bosses."

"Fa anyone who want!" Ain' sure, but I hide anxious.

He wave like he anger. "Well, g'wan, joey. Meet be ova fo' ya get ta!"

Wanna run, but I walk fo' proud.

Outside Sub lair, Four Two Square ain' empty like usual. Buncha joes stand roun' broke stores lookin' nervous. All diff tribes.

A Three Five Mid like me don' see much trannies 'xcept nearby Mids 'n Broads, maybe Rocks. But when ya live wid ol' Chang, lotsa tribe come ta door. And sometime ya go out wid', wait while he grumble an' pay innifo ta otha tribe dat usual ya never meet.

So Pook not too surprise at threads an' tribe marks.

Easters, Washhites, Unies, Harls, more. But I notice each be standin' wid his own, tense like storm 'fore light go bang.

What I see is rumb waitin' ta roll. I drift from nearest bunch, fin' self near Sub stair.

"Whatcha wan', joey?"

I whirl. Scrawny Subboy look up from halfway.

"Here fo' meet."

"You jus' a kit. G'wan home."

I go bristle. "Fo' alla trannies wanna come!"

"Dunno 'bout joeykits. Hey, Kard! We spose ta let kits inta meet?"

From unner, a voice. "No one say ta, Chaco."

I ask, "Where be meet?"

"Big hall, downunner." He point. "Whas' in bag?"

"Min' ya bidness!"

"Cmon down, I teach ya ta mouth Subs like—"

Sudden, Pook tire bein' treat like kit. I swing bag ova shoulda, stalk downstair, maybe ta get diss, but don' care. History be make, Chang say; I gonna watch. "Where ol' Changman?"

"What diff—"

"I got bag he ask me bring." Subgirl look suspicious, so I add, "Got his meds, jus' in case."

"I dunno, joey." He scratch. "He busy wid—"

"Pook!"

I look roun', see Allie. "Yo!"

"Watchadoon?"

"Tell dis stupe I come fa Changman, like—hey!" I duck jus' in time. "Tell 'im!" I hold bag 'tween me an' enrage Subboy.

"Lastime Pookboy came wid Chang," Allie admit. "Lettim go, Chaco. I'll take 'im ta meet."

"Halber said we gotta lettim in," Subboy growl. "Don' mean I gonna take sheet from a—"

"I bring 'im." Allie grab my hand, yank me downstair.

'Fore I know, I be in long dark tunnel, nothin' but Allie hand ta hang onta. "Hey, whereya—"

"Cool jets. We turn off lights so tribes won' see parts a Sub we don' wan'. Almos' dere."

Please, Mista Chang, gemme outa dis. I do whatcha say.

How I know Alliegirl ain' gonna diss me here in dark? My skin prickle as I think sharp shiv in rib.

In min, see light ahead. Big room, low ceil but real long. Lotsa joeys mill roun' in every tribe threads ya c'n 'magine.

Voices fulla anger.

"Stupid Neut, who care if Washhites go thirst? Easters tryin' ta pushout—"

"Lettim talk!"

"Rocks don' take boolsheet from no frazzin' Harl—"

Allie nudge me. "Been like dat all day."

"Getcha hansoff," I growl, tryin' ta push forward widout actual touchin' no one; too many tribes in strange place an' everyone be bristle.

Bes' I figga, be thirty diff tribes in cave, ten or twenny joes from each. Musta take some trayfo, givin' Sub hostages ta each tribe what come down unner fo' meet.

Ol' Changman sit next ta Halber, lookin' wore. His eyes resign, like he waitin' fo' shout ta stop.

Allie nudge me 'gain. "There he be. Give 'im ya bag."

I hiss ta warn backoff, an' watch.

Easters 'n Rocks screamin' at each otha, like ready fo' rumb. Joes near be eggin' 'em on.

Chang lean closer ta Halber. I can' hear, but see his mouth move. "Can ya stop it 'fore everythin' fall apart?"

Halber grimace, lunge ta his feet. Automatic, joeys in front pull back. A space open, an' I dart through, duck unner Halber's arm, drop on flo' at Chang's feet.

Ol' man look at me with surprise. His mouth twitch, but he say nothin'.

"DIS BE SUB AND I BE HALBER!" Boss Sub's voice shake with mad. "Stop ya yammer or I diss yas all!" He wave fist, an' Easters scatter. "Ol' man gonna talk, so lissen!"

Onna street, it wouldn' a work. But no one 'xcept Subs feel home down unner; angry tribe joeys wanna rumb, but what if Subs turnoff rest a lights? Lotsa grumble, but soon quiet.

Chang stand. "Melio of Easters, ya righ' 'bout Rocks tryin' ta push ya out. Sho, it be yo' turf. But think why Rocks wanna move. Prollem wid water."

"Dat don't give em—"

Chang spoke quiet, but somehow it cut across indignant Easter boss. "Same prollem alla yas got." He look roun'.

Uneasy silence, joeys shiftin' foot ta foot.

"C'mon, who be first ta admit pipes go rust, and can' find water?" Again he look roun'. "Shez, tell 'em 'bout Harl. Rangie? Lotsa good water in Washhite, hah?" Changman stamp foot; I snatch away hand, try not ta yelp. "Okay okay, I go firs'. In Chang's shop, water all rust, usually not enough. Who next?"

Long quiet. Den, from somewhere in crowd, "Won' last. Water always come back."

"Not this time." Chang raised hands. "Befo', govermen come ta fix. Now be govermen takin' it 'way."

Shez say, "Boolsheet. Think we don' guard turf? No Unies been on Washhite street since—"

Mista Chang bang his chair, in frustrate. "Doncha unnerstan'? Water doesn' start in pipe. Gotta come from somewhere, yah? Govermen shut off main pipes for all time."

"Why?"

Changman spoke wid care. "Hudson Freshwater Project, dey call it. Means city gave up water from faraway riva called Delaware. But towahs keep buildin'. Need lotsa water for Uppies in towahs. So they take."

Angry growls. "Frazzin' Uppies think—"

"Yah, yah. Think they own the worl'. Well, maybe dey do. 'Less we stop 'em."

"We get tourbus every week. Could trap bus, open like cansa, diss alla Uppies—"

"Nah. Jus' bring down Unie troops. Then they clear out Washhites, put up more towahs."

Rangie from Harls say, "Whatcha wan' us do?"

Chang get look I know from shop, when he finally get angry joe ready ta trayfo. "I ain' sure, exact. Firs', talk ta Holoworl' or otha zines. Tellem be trouble 'less we got water. But whateva we decide, gotta be togetha. Alla tribe."

"Thassit?" Scorny. "Uppie zines don' giva shit 'bout trannie—"

Ol' man shout, "What else we got, hah? Doncha unnerstan', tribes goin' *down!*"

From back, 'notha voice. "I be Lach, of Morninghites."

Chang nod, like, goahead.

"Killin' bus fulla Uppies won' fix water. If ya say true, prollem ain' touriss. Prollem is towahs."

Way Lach said it run chill down my back.

"I saw towah be build, long back, when we pushout. Start wid big hole way deep."

"So?"

"Deep like Sub." Lach pause, like tryin' a think. "C'n we get inta towah from unner? 'Xplode the poles holdin' it up, or burn? We get ridda towahs, dey won' need our water."

Silence all roun'. Can see trannies lookin each otha like never befo'.

Chang was righ'. History.

But ol' man shook his head. "Maybe, all else fail, we try."

"Do it now!"

Chang say, "Soon as we attack towah, streets fulla Unie troops, more 'n ya eva seen. An' they won' stop 'til trannies gone."

Someone spit. Othas laugh. "Can' pushout alla tribes at once. Too many lair, too many tunnel—"

Big dark joey say, "We kill jerries fas' as dey land."

Chang shift in chair. His face gray, but he make voice strong. "Armor troop carriers. Robotanks and helis. We ain' talkin' jerries, we talkin' Unie troops what defeat fish, back when. Now they even got lasers high on Earthport. Could blast trannie streets an' never touch a towah."

"We could—"

" 'Sides, soon as we knock down one or two towahs, they make othas harda ta hurt. And they jus' rebuild."

"What then?"

"Dunno. Way ta get at Uppies ain' through towahs. It's puters that keep Uppies on toppa worl'. If we could disrup' nets, threaten ta bring down finance, crash taxes like Hacker League did, longtime back . . ."

Ol' man so intent, he don' realize he lose 'em. Can' talk puters ta trannie tribes; we got none. Finance means bank, but trannies don' trayfo wid banks, nohow. Banks wan' coin, not cansa. Anyway, banks too strong ta break inta, too high in towahs.

Halber shrug. "I'd like ta take down towah or two." He wave away Chang protes'. "I know whatcha say 'bout puters. Alla Uppies use 'em. Even jerry helis got puter maps.

Holoworl' an' otha newschips be made for Uppie puters. If we was educate' like Uppie, maybe chance. But looka us! Hardes' job in worl' jus' gettin' us togetha fo' meet."

Chang ask as if defeat, "Whatcha wanna do?"

Halber's ansa surprise. "Think. And 'notha' meet, three days."

Tribes don' like. "What good be comin—"

"Took four hour, hadda passby alla turf—"

Halber's voice ride ova. "But leas' we know we all got same prollem. Afta three days, maybe new ideas. Maybe somethin' change."

Chang look up sharp, but he stay quiet. Face sad.

More bitchanmoan, of course. Can' even get coupla joeys passby corna widout argue. But afta while, meetin' ova.

Alla time, I sit thinkin'. No water, end a trannie worl? Can' be. And what dis mean fo' Pook? Got his lair, got his—

Back go cold.

Pook got his capture.

What was it Jared Uppie Washinton say? If I tell, could lose chance ta sell 'im. On otha hand, gotta be lotsa innifo if Pook solve trannie water prollem.

I tug at sleeve. "Mista Chang—"

He shook off. "Not now, Pookboy. Come see me in shop, afta I rest."

"Stupit ol' man!" Couldn' help myself, when he go scorny in fronta all.

Steada growlin' at me, he look pain, an' call ta coupla Subs; they help him stand.

Tribe joeys stream out to Up, with Subs showin' way. No one pay no tention ta Pook 'xcept Allie. I stan' up, look roun', see Halber. Wait for sec when he ain' talkin.

"Halber Sub Boss—"

Widout even lookin' his han' go whop, practical knock me down. "Allie, getcha scrawny joeykit 'way from—"

Dunno wha come ova Pook. Come down unner in Sub like he his own tribe. Sit in meet with bosses. Could get hisself diss, 'specially now.

I say loud, "Ya talk 'bout puters. Think I know way."

His head come roun' real slow, and corna of eye go up. Pook maybe dead. But can' stop now. "Gotta talk private," I say. "I know joey c'n work putahs, do anythin' he wan'. Bring down alla towahs inna minute."

Hold breath.

Halber point 'cross hall ta empty room. Den his finga swing back ta me. An' beckon.

Chapter 24

ROBERT

I sat between Adam and the pilot, glad to be clear of the crackling tension of the back seat. Arlene seethed, while the Captain brooded, unable or unwilling to calm her.

I called ahead to the New York Sheraton Skytel, booked rooms for our party. After, I made desultory conversation with Adam, and was thoroughly glad when at last the rooftop heliport floated into view. I jumped out while the blades still spun, held the door for the others.

A smoothly dressed joey with a thin moustache ducked under the slowing blades. "Assemblyman, it's a pleasure to meet you. I'm Arwin Fenner, the Sheraton manager. Mr. SecGen, we're honored. My staff will do their best to—"

"Is our room ready?" The Captain made no effort to hide his impatience.

"Yes, sir. We've put you and Ms. Seafort in the Presi—"

"Where?"

"This way, sir." A snap of his fingers. "Their bags!" He led us to our penthouse suites.

The Captain waited, hands in pockets, while manager and bellman fussed with lamps, bedcovers, and a huge complimentary basket of fruit. When it was done, Seafort waved the bellman out, nodded to me, glanced at Fenner.

I recognized my cue. "We'd appreciate your help finding a young man."

Fenner nodded. "Anything we can do . . . "

"This is Mr. Tenere, of the SecGen's staff. We're looking for his son."

Perhaps Fenner's eyelid flickered. Nothing more.

"We traced Jared to this skytel."

"He had a room?"

"We're not sure," I admitted. "Three days ago he ate in your restaurant—"

Fenner's voice was smooth. "Sir, ours is a large establishment. I have no knowledge of the joey, but we'll search our records. If there's any trace . . . "

Arlene said, "Another boy was with him, or looking for him."

"I really don't know—"

"It's quite important. Could you check—"

Adam Tenere stirred. "Fenner." His eyes held an expression I'd seen only once, when he'd found a cadet cheating on an exam.

"—we'll be happy to—yes, sir?"

"I want my son. So if you withhold information . . . " He drifted closer. "I have influential friends. Mr. Boland, and his father the Senator. I work for SecGen Seafort, who isn't without influence."

The manager licked his lips. The Captain watched, expressionless.

Adam said, "I knew a hotel in Washington. The health, fire, and building inspectors came through. It closed. Then tax auditors looked at their employment records. The owners found a new manager before trying to reopen. By the way, your regional Unemployment Payments Trustee is a Seafort appointee. Consider the difficulties a lost file would cause should you apply for unemployment—"

"Sir, I assure you—"

"And if a crime were involved . . . " Adam's feral grin raised my hackles. "The Regional Prosecutor is a Seafort nominee. My ship docked at a penal colony once. Not a pleasant sight."

"Please!" Fenner's handkerchief dabbed at his forehead.

"The truth."

"All right!" A cry of surrender. "We had no idea he was ill when he checked in. Though in retrospect, his use of a false name, the concealment of his age—"

Adam growled, "Ill?"

"The rebalancing problem. I assure you it wasn't evident. He merely—"

"What are you saying?"

The manager glanced to Captain Seafort as if for comfort, found none. He addressed his plea to me. "The boy checked in as Jer Adamson. He only used the card later, in the restaurant."

"Go on."

"Mr. Boland, is your purpose to find the lad, or to investigate—"

"Tell them, man!" I fought disgust. "They want the boy, not revenge."

Adam listened stone-faced as the story of Jared's escapade emerged. The night auditor caught an alert on the Terrex card; hotel security visited the boy's room. A chase through the corridors ensued. The boy escaped to the street.

Adam and the Captain exchanged glances before Seafort turned to the window. I recalled how, years ago, Adam helped him search New York for Annie Wells, who in her illness had reverted to her trannie past.

The manager blurted, "If we'd had any idea he wasn't in his right mind, we'd have taken immediate custody and—"

"You're saying my son is glitched?" Adam's tone was acid.

"I understood from the other joeykid that rebalancing was sched—"

"Who?" Seafort swung to face him.

"The youngster who came searching—"

"Philip!" Arlene's eyes lit.

"Yes. Mr. Tyre, a very self-assured young man. He said—"

"Where is he?"

"Ma'am, I had no idea he knew you when—"

With a guttural sound, Arlene sprang across the room, shoved Fenner against a wall. "God damn you, where?" Her forearm pressed against his carotid.

"Out!" It was a squawk.

Momentarily, her pressure eased.

He babbled, "Tyre insisted on following his friend. I begged him to call the jerries, but he insisted on looking in the streets. He was to call me at dusk to open—"

"When!"

I could barely hear his answer. "Two days ago."

"ARLENE, NO!" The Captain's tone was a lash.

Slowly, she relaxed the rigid fingers that hovered over Fenner's neck. "He sent Philip onto the street!"

"Not sent. Allowed." The Captain's tone was mild. "P.T. can be . . . persuasive."

The manager rubbed his throat. "Who is the Tyre boy?"

"Our son."

Fenner went pale. "Oh, my God."

Arlene said, "Pray we find him, or . . . "

I coughed diplomatically. "Easy, now. Mr. Fenner, we'll call when we need you. Ms. Seafort is overwrought. I mean, ah, in a high state of tension. You've cooperated, so we'll disregard your liquor violation; fair is fair. Thank you." I held the door; he dived through it.

Arlene growled, "Overwrought?" She strode to the window.

The Captain muttered, "Let it pass."

She stared at the devastation below. "Philip's out there, utterly helpless." She chewed her lip. "Rob, call the Police Commissioner. We'll need every jerry he can put on the streets."

Seafort shook his head. "The streets aren't in their hands."

"You told me in daytime—"

"Armored tour buses, an occasional heli. From above, the jerries wouldn't spot P.T. unless he were standing in plain sight, and in that case the transpops would have him first."

Adam nodded.

I knew Seafort was right, but the glimmerings of an idea stirred. What a coup, if I could bring it off. I said cautiously, "Captain, you intend to go after him?"

"Of course."

"How?"

"I'll ask the streeters. Adam, remember how Eddie brought a sack of trading goods, when we went after Annie? We'll want—"

"Listen," I said. My knees were shaky. "You're right about the jerries, they've lost the streets." A dramatic pause. "But it's time we took them back." And cleared the way for the towers, and Dad's hopes.

"How?"

"Granted, SecGen Kahn is your political opponent, but if you ask his help as a former SecGen . . . " I waited for him to see.

"Get on with it." The Captain's voice was testy.

"He'd send in the Unies. Regiments, if need be. We'd take back our city once and for all. Within a day or so you'd be free to search all of midtown. And every trooper could carry a holo of P.T. to compare—"

"To the other corpses?" His voice was acid. "You'd start a war, and hope to find Philip in the rubble?"

I said quickly, "Not a war, a police action. After all, we already intend to move in. Next month we'll be ground-clearing a few blocks south. There'll be riots, if not worse."

I glowed in the genius of my plan. If the Captain himself called in the Unies, he'd be committed to the Supranationalist water project. No need for Dad to discredit him; I'd spare the SecGen that humiliation. And with the Captain on board, our bills would sail through the Senate with votes to spare.

Arlene said, "Make your call, Rob. Set up a meeting, or whatever it takes."

I nodded.

"Arlene—"

"He's our son, Nick!"

I reached for the caller. Seafort turned away, as if in pain.

Though the U.N. was but a few blocks distant, my best entry was through Van and our network of contacts. I placed the call. The Captain paced in agitation. Adam watched us both, saying nothing.

"Van, this is Rob." I turned to the window. "I need SecGen Kahn, flank. Try Marion Leeson, she'll know how to find him."

Waiting for Van's callback, I chafed.

The Captain caressed Arlene's shoulder. "Hon, have you ever been on the streets? Do you know how dangerous they are? The transpops are desperate. Sending troops will start a war, and make it worse for Philip."

"It can't get worse!" Her eyes filled with tears. "He may already be dead. Without help, we'll never find him."

Van came back on the line. SecGen Kahn was at his residence in the U.N. compound, enjoying a working rest day.

I said, "Make the call. Patch me through as soon as—"

"No." From behind, a firm hand took the caller from my grasp, switched it off. I looked with astonishment at the Captain's grim resolve. "Rob, I entered politics to stop SecGen Anjour from sending troops onto the streets. You'd have me come full circle and demand them. Well, I won't."

"Nick." Arlene's voice was ominous. "Think of P.T., not your transpops."

"We can't wipe out a culture to save Philip."

"I can, if that's what it takes. He's our son."

Seafort sat heavily. "Wait a moment." He stared at the thick luxuriant brocade of the carpet.

She said, "Nick—"

"Wait, Arlene."

We waited endless, agonizing minutes.

At last he looked up, his eyes bleak. "I won't destroy a people. Not even for Philip."

"I will." Arlene. She grabbed the caller.

"Arlene, we came here to look for him. Give me time."

"How long? A day? Two? What hope for P.T. then?" She knelt by his side. "We didn't know Philip was in trannietown. He's twelve, Nick. He has no time. We're calling Kahn."

Seafort's eyes met his wife's. "I can't stop you?"

"No. Rob, make the call. I'll talk to Kahn myself."

The Captain sighed. "So be it." He stripped off his tie. Then his jacket. I thought he was changing to more comfortable clothes until he went to a planter, wrenched out the shrub, plunged his hands into the pot. He rubbed dank earth on his face and shirt.

"What in God's name—"

"I don't want to look Uppie when I go out. I'll stay the night. Tell your Unie troops I'll be with the transpops."

"Nicky!"

"I'll try to find Philip." He looked to Adam. "Jared too, as I promised."

She said, "Adam, talk sense into him. Once it's dark they'll knife him as sure as—"

Adam cleared his throat. "Sorry, I'm going with him." He blushed at her mute reproach. "Arlene, a search will be hard enough without adding riot and war. The sooner we're started—we'll bring our pocket callers, of course. If we find the boys . . ."

"Have you lost your mind?" Arlene's face twisted.

Seafort regarded his wife gravely. "Possibly. If you want to help—"

"Oh, Nick." She flew across the room, buried herself in his arms.

"—drop this talk of Unies. Give us a few hours, then rent a heli, join us below. We'll stay in touch. Don't try to ring us; I don't want the caller beeping at the wrong moment."

"I can't risk losing you too. You win. We'll go together."

"No, an Uppie woman will be too distracting for them. Anyway, I can't sleep in a soft bed tonight while he's . . . Lord God knows where." He turned to Tenere. "You're still licensed?"

"Yes, sir. And I brought my pistol." Adam sounded grim.

A laser pistol would offer protection against the menace of the night. Few civilians had license to carry one, and fewer risked the mandatory death penalty for illicit possession.

"I'll be ready in a moment, sir. Rob, outside." Adam's tone brooked no argument. Reluctantly, I followed him into the corridor. The door shut on the Captain and Arlene in heated conversation.

Adam backed me against the wall, eyed me with disdain. "I never imagined how low a politician could stoop."

I blushed. "I don't know what you—"

"I thought I knew you, Robbie."

I took refuge in silence. His eyes bored deeper.

What he said about my maneuver was . . . searing. I felt the most devious, unscrupulous cadet in Academy. Twice, I tried to interrupt, and each time he silenced me with a word.

When he was done I felt more humbled than ever I had as an adult. Perhaps as a boy, too. I tried to kindle my anger, but the suspicion he was right doused my ire before it could ignite. Had it been anyone but Adam, the words wouldn't have mattered.

But I loved him still.

Humiliated, chastened, I wanted only to escape to my room. Instead, gritting my teeth, I offered to go along, to make amends however I could.

Adam refused.

I insisted on helping find a heli; perhaps my connections would save time. A call to the manager brought an immediate offer of one of the skytel's craft. My task completed, I waited in awkward silence with Adam outside the Seaforts' suite.

After a time Nick Seafort emerged, rubbing his eyes. Under his arm was a valise. "She demands we take her with us, but I insisted she wait until tomorrow. At night, the streets are . . . " He sighed. "And we need someone to stand by, in case . . . " He left the rest unfinished.

Adam said, "Sir, is it necessary to spend the night outside?"

Seafort's voice dropped. "The truth is, I can't be sure Arlene won't ask Kahn for troops unless I'm on the street. She thinks it's the best chance to save Philip, and she's one determined joeygirl." He shrugged. "We'd better go. Rob, what are your plans?"

"I'll wait with the heli for your call. In the morning, I'll bring Arlene to meet you."

"We've imposed far more than we could ask. Haven't you work to do?"

I tried not to look at Adam. "Van will clear my schedule. In a few days I'll join U.N.S. *Galactic* for the blue-ribbon Jovian cruise, but until then, my time is yours."

For answer, the Captain pressed my arm. "We'd best go." As we headed to the elevator he shot a glance back to their suite. "I'm not sure she'll come home when this is over." His face held something beyond sadness.

From the helipad we flew to a rooftop Blue and White. The convenience store, named for its summoning nightly beacon, was open twenty-four hours. Nick opened his bag on the checkout counter and strode the aisles, tossing in foodstuffs, pocket lights, medkits, and baubles as fast as the autoclerk could scan them. Even a small Valdez perma. He tossed a handful of Unibucks at the receiving arm. "Let's go."

I asked, "Where shall I set down, sir?"

"A block or two south of the Sheraton."

"Do you know P.T. went south?"

"No, but we want to go that way." He consulted a wafer-thin electrimap, punched in a query. "Our skytel's on Forty-seventh. Thirteen blocks . . . "

"To where, sir?"

"An old friend I snubbed."

"What for?"

No answer.

Before we set down, Adam and I went over our arrangements. I was hesitant at first, smarting from his reprimand, but I needn't have fretted. As at Academy, once he'd delivered a rebuke, the issue was closed, his manner infused with his usual warmth. My hands on the collective, I swallowed a lump. How had I lost the eager boy I'd been?

I focused on the street below, checked the infrared sensors. "Captain, they're all around us. In doorways, on the roofs . . ."

"I know. Lift off the moment we're out the hatch."

I had no intention of becoming prey to whatever creatures lurked. "Aye aye, sir." We dropped.

Seafort grinned without mirth. "So it's back to that, Middy?"

"For now." As we settled to the broken asphalt I groped for words. "Sir, about the Unies, I'm sorry if—"

"No time. Adam, the pistol is a last resort. Stay with me." Shouldering his valise he slid back the door, jumped. Adam followed. They sprinted south into the crumbling city.

Chapter 25

PEDRO

Again Sub joeyboys perched me in chair, carried me along dimly lit tunnels to far stair. Then, up to day. I blinked in unexpect light. Hang on, Pedro Telamon. Home soon.

At shop, I unlocked steel door, tottered in, fussed while they loaded carts fulla Valdez permas for return to Sub. After, I lay on cot in back of store, surprise I was alive. I'd used all the pills I'd brung, and medkits were stored upstair, but no way could I have nosy trannies carry me to third floor, where I kept my stock. Crawl, first. An' I woulda had to, 'xcept at last min I remembered medkit I brought down for Pook's cut. Was still near bed. I rummaged through box, tore open sealed pills.

Angina, I had. I knew from books, and the way it hurt. Pills worked before. If I were Uppie, I'd go for heart transplant or plastic boomer implant, solve problem. But for trannie, alla coin I had, or could raise resta my life, wouldn't be enough.

I sighed. You gone old, Pedro, an' wearin' out. Gonna die soon, alone in shop. Then tribes come, knock for trayfo, an' wonder why ya don' open door, 'til 'ventual they break in and scavenge all what was yours.

I lay musing, sippin' tea, while ache faded. Time passed. I woke to rapping at door.

Felt well enough to get up, but not in mood for trayfo. Still, might be Pookboy rappin'. I padded to door. "Chang close. Comeback morra."

"Mr. Chang?" Strange voice. Like Uppie, but too polite.

"Why ya botha ol' man, hah? Back to tower!"

"Let us in, please."

My knees suddenly weak. Couldn't be him; not here. I pawed at bolt. "Lemme hear ya 'gain." I hadda be sure.

"A crowd's gathering. You'd better hurry."

"Lor' God." I clawed at lock with fingers useless from haste. At last, got it open. "You came!"

Fisherman stood framed against last of sunset. Pistol dan-

gled from one hand; other supported a dazed-eyed joey with
blood-caked face. "Can we get him inside?" He crossed to
my favorite chair, eased down his frien' with care.

Frien' stirred. "I'm all right."

"You lost blood, Adam." To me, "He needs a drink, and a
place to sit. Someone hit him with a rock. I was afraid if he
went down . . . "

"Water. Tea." In own shop, I felt helpless. I prodded mind
goin', found medkit, handed to him.

Fisherman took it from my hand. His eyes met mine.

Moment without words.

"I'm sorry," he said. "For not coming."

"That why you're here?"

He didn't flinch. "No." My heart plunged to toes.

I poured water, dampened cloth from medkit.

He busied himself with gash in friend's scalp. Joey stirred,
reached in pocket for holo. Fisherman snapped, "Keep still."

Friend's voice was rusty. "Have you seen this boy?"

I hissed, like stiff-back cat. "Fisherman, I know. Twenny
year back he knock on Chang's door with Eddie Maceboy.
You, joey, be jus' some bigmouth Uppie. Think ya come ta
Chang's shop, ask questions widout innifo, hah?"

Uppie looked perplexed to Fisherman, who shrugged as if
to suggest, cool jets.

I grumbled, put pot on warmer, went in back room for best
tea I hoard. When I came out, I still mutterin'. "Frazzin'
Uppies think they own the worl'."

"I'm sorry." Uppie pointed to joeykit in holo. "I'm his
father. He's missing."

"Fah." I set down cups. Too bad 'bout joeykit, but principle be involve. What kinda traytaman Chang be, without
demand innifo?

Uppie Adam went to pocket, came out with wallet.
Handed it to me.

I looked in. Unibucks, plenny. "So?"

"Take what you want." Sounded tired.

"All?"

He shrugged. "The Commandant—Mr. Seafort said to
trust you."

Clever, but I learned that trick as a kit. "Try to swind Pedro
Telamon Chang, hah?" I helped myself to mosta wad. Teach

him to play games wid Neut. I tossed wallet in his lap, took holopic.

"Would you help find him?"

I debated self, sat with sigh. "Where he went?"

"On the street."

"Why did joeykit run off?"

Adam Uppie's tone bleak. "He needed a father, and didn't have one."

I shrugged. "On street overnight, he dead."

"Possibly." A grimace. "But I have to know."

Won' ever know, if some tribes caught him. Cryps eatim. Subs, maybe skin, even nowdays.

I said, cautious, "C'n ask. May need innifo, fo' tribes."

His eyes closed, tired. "Whatever you want."

Fah. Too easy. I turned to Fisherman, careful to make my talk Uppie. "Why'd you come too?"

His face grim. "To find my son Philip."

I squinted, to remember. "Joeykit, 'bout this tall?" I showed. "Brown hair, thin?"

He straighten. In his eyes, fierce joy. "You saw him?"

I nodded. "Week ago."

Light faded from face. "Couldn't be. He wasn't here then."

"Not here. Compound."

He searched my face. "You? My home?"

I shrugged. "Hadda try, but you gone." He looked so forlorn, I had to help him past moment. "Why Philip here?"

Fisherman's shoulders drooped. "He followed Jared to bring him home."

Pity. Joeykit his size had no chance at all. I poured hot water.

Fisherman would pay whatever innifo I ask. Anythin'. So I hadda be careful, not to even suggest. Fisherman's help with water pipes was worth more 'n I could name. But according to Eddie Maceboy, his help wasn't thing I could trayfo.

I asked, "Got holos of your kit?"

Fisherman reached into his pack. "The hotel ran copies."

Small lithe body, hopeful face.

"Can you show his picture to the—your friends?"

I shook my head. "Righ' now, everything be unsettle." And would be even more unsettle tomorra, if Halber Boss Sub had his way. I hadda start now. I took coupla deep breaths, testin' chest. Seemed okay. I carefully opened door, peered out. Still day. Few inquisitive Mids hung aroun' across street. No matta. I put on long coat, slipped Philip's holo in pocket, took a few cansa fo' innifo.

"I'd like to go with you, Mr. Chang." Fisherman's voice was quiet.

Shook my head. "Better without ya." But my chest swelled with foolish pride. "Mista Chang," from him? I lived long time, neva heard from any otha Uppie. He jus' strokin, of course. "Ya come with me, too many questions. Trannies be interest' in you, steada joeykit."

He considered it. Treated me serious, like colleague. Maybe wasn't strokin'. "Are you sure?"

"How much help did they give, 'fore ya came to shop?" His face told me answer. "Wait here, take care of Adam Uppie. Plenny a—" I hated to say it, but had pocket fulla his innifo. "—Plenny a tea in jar. Take what you wan'."

"Thank you."

Outside, I went direct to waitin' Mids. "Whassamatta, nevah seen Uppie come shoppin'?" I took out holo Fisherman gave. "Lookin' for dis joeykit. Plenny innifo if ya know where ta fin'. Or lotsa trayfo for give him me. But no swind." I pass around holo. "An' only if he safe."

I could see from faces, not much chance anyone seen him. But they look, some debatin' if could swind Pedro Telamon Chang, despite what I say. I frowned, to discourage.

Afta the growed Mids looked, joeykits wanted ta see too. Could brush 'em away, but why bother? Easier to let 'em.

One young joey's face was puff, like in rumb. He stood on toes to see over 'nother's shoulder. Eyes went wide; maybe he never seen holo before. He turned away like din't wan' me to know his interest.

"No one? Okay, okay, how 'bout this joey?" I took out other holo.

"Innifo?" Voice in back.

Hadda be careful. Too much, an' they wouldn' believe. "Twenny cansa. More if ya bring him." Was enough to get their attention. All of them crowded round to look again at holo, even joeykits. 'Xcept kit with puffy face. He was gone.

I walked to second corner, edge of Broad turf. Showed

holos to Broads, same message. Hadda pay innifo to get to Mid Four Two. Same again with Easters. I spread word far as I could without clutchin' heart and pawin' for meds. Then I went home.

Was dark when I got there. Longer walk than I realized.

Door barely closed before Fisherman was at my side. "Well?"

I shrugged off coat; he took from my shoulders as if to hang. I snatched it back. "Think Chang too old ta take care a self, hah?"

"I'm sorry."

I grimaced, ashamed of self. Afta all, it was Fisherman hisself in Chang's shop, and I talkin' to him like Pookboy. Gruff, I said, "Uppie frien' seein' straight now?"

Adam stirred. "I'm fine."

I sat, tapped teapot to see if was warm. "Trannies watchin' for 'em now. But nobody seen—saw joeykits." I set pot back on heater, fussed with cup.

Fisherman asked, "Is that possible?"

"Lotsa streets, lotsa trannies. All we c'n do is spread word." I gestured to door. "Dark now. You go out, won't see mornin'. Gotta stay."

Adam said, "We're armed." He touched his pistol.

I snorted. "Ya weren' armed when they bashed ya with rock?"

"I'll be ready this time." His eyes were cold.

"Ready to diss trannies? Easy thing, for Uppie!"

Fisherman patted his friend's knee, to quiet. "Mr. Chang, Philip's been on the street two days, and Jared longer. We must go. There's no time left." He fished in a pocket. "Before we leave, I need to call Arlene. Excuse me a moment." He tapped a code into his caller, waited.

I felt eyes boring, looked down to meet Adam Uppie's. "Yes?"

He asked, "You're a—a transpop yourself?"

"What else?" It came out a challenge.

He looked about. "You've lived here . . . long?"

Fisherman said into caller, "Of course I'm all right. We're at Pedro Chang's. Remember I told you . . . " He turned to corner, stood facing wall as if private.

Chang's story too complicate to tell Uppie. Besides, I wanted to hear Fisherman. "Yah. Long."

Adam touched sore spot on head, winced. "How do you survive?"

I shrugged. "Trayfo."

" . . . we're leaving now. If he's out there, I can't—"

"Where do you get your goods?"

What was I, some kinda cyclopedia? If Uppie curious, why don' he ask his terminal? "Here 'n there."

Too late, though. Fisherman lowered voice, and I couldn' hear rest. I glowered at Adam Uppie. "Don' go burnin' my trannies wid laser. Unnerstan', in nighttime, no rules on streets. Any Uppie stupe enough to go out, okay to diss. Same everywhere."

Fisherman's friend pointed to door. "My boy Jared is out there. Would you let some trannie's life stand between you and your son?"

Couldn't know for sure. Never had son, 'xcept maybe Eddie. Wife, once, but she died too young.

"Warn 'em first," I said gruff, fussin' with tea. "Show 'em laser, they prolly scatter."

Adam's voice surprisingly gentle. "I won't kill for pleasure, Mr. Chang. But I'll protect the Commandant with my life. Certainly with theirs."

Not sure who Commandant was, 'til I realized he meant Fisherman. Strange folk, Uppies. Diff name for everything.

Chapter 26

PHILIP

Swee winced, his face jammed against the fetid wall. "Doncha unnerstan'? I can' tell ya!"

I'd never really hurt anyone on purpose. Well, only Jared, and thanks to my cruelty he'd fled to the streets. I hoisted Swee's wrist higher along his shoulder blade. Torture conferred a sense of power I wasn't sure I disliked.

"Ow! Please, Uppie! Hurts!"

It was Jared's shirt the boy wore. I steeled myself. "Where's Jared?"

Wailing, Swee stretched himself taller. "Pook gonna diss me if I tell! Oh God, please! Stop!"

I let go, struggling not to retch. "I'm sorry."

Swee leaned sobbing against the wall.

He'd led me on a mad chase. Across two rooftops, through sagging buildings, up rotting stairs dimly lit by gaping holes in the roof. After a time my quarry was reduced to a green shirt flitting through the shadows. When at last I'd caught him I had no idea where we were; luckily, the dank hallway seemed deserted.

Swee was bigger than I; he should have been able to defend himself. Yet my newfound rage had prevailed. I wondered if it would come on me often, now it had been wakened. Not a pleasant thought.

If I hurt him any more I'd become a savage myself, and I couldn't have that. But I doubted this was a good time to tell him so. Now that my fury was fading, he might remember how much stronger he was.

Would it help if I acted like the streeters I'd seen? I gathered a wad of saliva and spat, narrowly missing his foot. Sorry, Mom; I know you'd go ballistic.

Swee didn't seem impressed. Perhaps, crying and hugging his arm, he hadn't noticed. How to persuade him? Dominance was beyond my experience.

What would Fath do? I thought back to the tales he'd told of his shipboard days.

I snarled, "Turn around!"

"Wha'?"

As if I were unafraid, I spun him to the wall. "You heard me!" I needed a weapon. Anything. Swee glanced over his shoulder; I gave his ear a sharp cuff. He yelped. I forced down a surge of guilt, reminding myself I'd done him no real harm. Acting like a bully would keep him from realizing how helpless I was.

I remembered the caller buried in my pocket, reached for it. Gone; it must have slipped out in the chase. No time to worry about it now. What else could I use? I dug into my jacket, found the money clip I'd brought from home. I stuffed the few Unibucks into my jacket, pressed the corner of the clip to Swee's back. He squirmed.

"You asked for it." I kept my voice low; it gave me more control over pitch. The last thing I needed was my voice shooting an octave in mid-word.

What was the term they used? Diss. I still wasn't sure what it meant, but . . . "I'm your problem, not Pook. I'm going—" No. It had to be more crude. I growled, "—I'm gonna count to five. Tell me about Jared, or I diss you right here and now." I pressed harder. "It'll hurt a hell of a lot." Sorry, Lord, about the language. But a life is at stake. "Four. Three."

"You don' unnerstan, Uppie! Pook gets . . . grody!"

"Two!"

"All righ'!" A squeal. "Pookboy has 'im!"

"Jared's alive?"

"Yeah."

The wave of relief was almost dizzying. "Where?"

"In Pook lair!"

Only Lord God knew what that meant. I slipped the clip into my pocket. "Turn around."

I made sure to stand very close. In the psychology texts I'd downloaded to study Jared, I'd found an intriguing dissertation on personal space. When one invades personal space, the subject becomes nervous. I experimented with Jared, and he'd abruptly shoved me away.

Swee wiped his face. "Yah?"

"We're going to Pook's lair. Lead me astray—I mean, to

the wrong place—or try to run, and I'll . . . " Deliberately, I left it unfinished. It sounded more menacing.

"Cool jets, Uppie." He raised a hand, as if to ward off a blow. "Won' run. Swear."

"Take me to Jared."

"Pook gonna diss me fa tellin'!"

I said authoritatively, "I'll handle him."

Still, he hesitated. "Gotta go on street."

"So?"

He stared at me, amazed. "Uppie ain' 'fraid?"

Of course I was. Only yesterday I'd learned how danger-ous the streets were; that's why I'd been hiding on the roof when Swee appeared with Jared's shirt. But I shook my head. "Take me by the back ways, if you'd like. And stop calling me 'Uppie.'"

"Why? It what you be."

"Don't be silly; Uppies are from the towers. I live in Washington, in a—" I sighed, doubting he'd understand. "Call me P.T.," I said.

Snuffling, he wiped the last of his tears with a grimy sleeve. " 'Kay, Peetee."

"Remember, I'll diss you if you run." Wondering what that meant, I kept a firm grip on his arm as we walked. Mom held me that way when she was really irked, or when she insisted on a time-out in my room. Objectively speaking, I found it rather intimidating.

Swee led me through a courtyard half-filled with rubble, then to another building. To my surprise, he took care to avoid our being seen, as if protecting me. We worked our way down the block. Eventually he pointed to a sagging apartment across the street. "Gotta run har', case Mids see ya."

I didn't like that idea. I looked around, saw a jagged bar protruding through the dusty brick at waist level. Perhaps it once helped support a wall. For a moment I released Swee. Catching my jacket on it, I pulled hard. A loud rip, and my jacket was torn down the middle.

"Stop!"

I bared my teeth in warning; Swee drew back.

"Coulda trayfo a zillion cansa," he said plaintively.

I shrugged, wishing he spoke English. As he watched,

openmouthed, I carefully worked the point of the bar through the knee of my pants and let myself fall. Now my pants were torn too.

Overcoming my disgust I rubbed some grime into my hair, and, gritting my teeth, gave myself a streak on the face for good measure. "We don't have to run."

Swee's brow wrinkled. "Think ya make yaself trannie?" He studied me, broke into a slow grin. "Not too bad, actual. Could pass, from far. Walk close wid me."

My spine prickled as we strolled across the lonely street. At the far corner, a group of transients lounged against a rusting pole. They regarded us with indifference. Swee headed to a boarded door. In the recessed doorway he stuck his hands in his pockets, glanced out casually. His eyes flicked left and right. " 'Kay, no one lookin'."

"What now?"

"Uppie stupe." Scornfully he pushed me aside, shouldered open the door. It gave way with a loud creak. "C'mon." After closing the door, he led me upstairs.

I followed, my eyes still accustomed to daylight. In the gloom I was almost blind. Was Swee leading me into a trap? He was several steps ahead of me, and gaining. In panic, I scrambled up the stairs, yanked on his arm. "Not so bloody fast!"

Swee squealed. Frantically, he tried to free himself. "Fahgadsake! Don' grab me in dark!" For a moment I thought he was going to cry again, but he pointed upward. "Two more stair." His voice dropped. "If Pookboy in lair, we be diss."

I was disgusted with my cowardice. At home I slept in the dark, didn't I? "Go on." I made my voice rough.

We tiptoed down a dim hall. Open doors to abandoned offices provided the only reflected daylight. Midway along the hall was an elevator shaft, the safety doors ajar. Swee whispered, "In dere."

It was a trap. "You think I'm glitched?"

"Look down, see a li'l room."

Look down and he'd shove me into the shaft. I pictured myself windmilling to my death. "I told you not to fuck with me!"

I couldn't believe I'd said it. Mom would wash out my

mouth. She had, the last time, and I'd promised her—no time for that.

"I didn', hones—"

My fist shot out. I caught him in the eye.

Swee howled.

From the elevator shaft, a screech.

I nearly jumped out of my pants. "Jesus, Lord Christ!" Amen. Sorry, Lord, but it scared me out of my wits.

Hands to his face, Swee stamped away his pain, crying and snorting.

Downstairs the door creaked loudly.

Swee gasped, shot me a look of terror. "Run hide!" He raced down the hall. I dashed after, no more anxious than he to meet whatever was coming upstairs.

Swee dodged into an open doorway. I skidded after. He pressed himself against the wall.

"What are you—"

"Shh!" He made a frantic gesture of silence. "If it's Pook . . . "

Footsteps. Dim voices. I strained to hear. Swee dabbed helplessly at his tearing eye. The footsteps stopped.

Standing in utter silence, I was aware of a horrid stench. "I whispered, "What's that smell?"

He waved to the corner. "Shithouse."

Oh, great. Cautiously, I edged my head through the doorway. In the hall was a teener a bit older than I, and with him, a brawny joey with a menacing air.

With great care Swee knelt and peered down the hall. "God, it's Pook!"

I stared at the figure hunched over the shaft. No wonder Swee feared him; the big joey could tear us in half. My whisper was barely audible. "Who's the joeykid with him?"

A snort. "Joeykit *is* Pook."

I squinted, as the teener straightened and came into the light. I bit back an exclamation; he was the one from the roof, who'd tried to stop me from catching Swee. He'd walked into a simple armlock and shoulder-toss. If I'd done anything so stupid, Mom would have had me doing push-ups for a week.

I whispered, "Who's the big one?"

"Dunno."

"Where's Jared?"

"Tolya. Inna hole."

I watched with foreboding. Abruptly the two of them disappeared into the elevator shaft. A clatter. I waited. From within, a cry of protest. Should I tiptoe down the hall to look? From the shaft a hand appeared, then a head.

Pook. Then the big joey.

And Jared.

He emerged from the shaft, clutching his chest. The big joey pointed toward the stairs. Jared shook his head. The man slapped him hard.

I was surging into the hall when a hand closed around my collar and hauled me back.

Swee hissed, "Ya crazy, Uppie? Wanna get us diss?" In the hall, Jared wailed.

"He hurt Jar!"

"Jus' whomp him a bit."

"What's 'diss'? You keep saying—"

Swee drew his finger across his throat in an unmistakable gesture.

"Oh." I could think of nothing else to say. I peered around the door. Barefoot, Jared shuffled toward the stairs, his captors close behind. He sniffled. I eased back into the debris-strewn office.

Swee kept his voice low. "Bigman ain' no Mid. Threads like Sub." Whatever that meant, it seemed to frighten him. "Dunno why he here. Must be Pook brung 'im. Guess he pay innifo." The boy's brow knotted, as if puzzling through a problem in advanced trig. "No one 'xcept Pook knows 'bout hole. So maybe he sell Uppie ta Subman."

I glanced out. The hall was deserted. "Where are they going?"

Swee shrugged.

I said, "We have to follow. Don't give me that look; I came here for Jared. Move!" Reluctantly, he came along.

We were halfway to the stairwell when footsteps thudded up the stairs.

"Sheet!" Swee spun on his heel and dashed to safety. His foot caught on a loose board; he went down with a thump. In an instant he was on his feet. Together we dived into the nearest office. We cowered against the wall on opposite sides of the door.

"Who dere?" The voice was too high to be the big joey; it

must be Pook. I looked across the doorway to Swee, who emphatically shook his head.

In the hall, silence.

A creak. Another. Swee's eyes darted, as if searching for escape. I hardly dared breathe.

The crash of a door, somewhere down the hall. A muttered curse. Swee flitted past the doorway, put his mouth to my ear. "Gotta get out!" Before I could reply he tiptoed to the rotting window, pulled loose a splintered chunk of wood. It gave way with a loud protest. The noise didn't much matter; my heart pounded loud enough for all to hear.

Swee tiptoed back to the door, raised his club as he pressed back against the wall.

A thunderous kick. The door flew open, narrowly missing my ear. Pook lunged into the room. "Gotchas!"

Swee smashed his club down on the teener's head. It drove Pook to his knees even as the rotten board crumbled to pieces. Swee tossed the remains aside. "C'mon!" We collided in the doorway, and my breath was knocked out of me. Sucking for air, I dashed to the stairs. Behind us, a roar of anger.

I tore down the steps three at a time and wrenched open the stubborn street door. Above, a despairing cry. I raced out to daylight. Jared and his captor were nowhere to be seen. I waited in a frenzy for Swee to join me.

Nothing.

Ignoring a pair of curious transpops I dashed to the corner, peered down the street, whirled around to look the other way.

No one.

Come *on*, Swee!

What chance would I have finding them if they disappeared in some hovel among the thousands of the city? Swee could take care of himself. It wasn't my fault he chose not to follow.

My reluctant feet took me back to the door. I peered into the gloom. Odd sounds. Grunts. Perhaps a whimper. The hair on my neck rose.

Every lost moment made finding Jared less likely. As quickly as I dared, I forced myself up the stairs.

In the hall, a pair of feet faced the stairwell. Sitting atop the prone form, a hunched figure. Occasionally the feet kicked, to no avail.

I inched forward. The grunts were Pook's, as he savagely pounded Swee's bloody head and chest. With a cry I sprang on the maddened Mid, hauled him kicking off the prostrate Swee.

"Leggo! I diss ya!"

"Leave him alone! Run, Swee!"

Swee groaned, rolled onto his side.

Pook shook himself loose, sprang to his feet. A knife flashed. He lunged.

I leaped aside, but the point caught in my torn jacket. I stumbled. The knife came up, ready to plunge.

For an instant Pook froze. His eyes narrowed. "You!"

I whipped off my jacket, rolled it around my arm. Any port in a storm, Mom had taught. I aimed a kick at his wrist, but it missed. I shouted, "C'mon, frazball! Take me!" Part of me knew it was glitched to say such things, but part of me didn't care.

Pook stood his ground. Unexpectedly, I lunged at him, stamped loudly. He careened backward, into the wall. Could it be he was afraid of me? Press your advantage, Mom said. But how?

Grinning now, Pook worked his way closer. "Gonna eatcha livah, Uppie."

To regain the initiative I spat at his face. He flinched. As if I knew what I was doing, I knocked on the wall three times. The teener whirled, searching the empty doorways. I sprang toward the knife, stamped my foot as hard as I could, let out a dreadful shriek.

Pook bolted toward the stairs.

No! That's the way *I* need to go!

At the stairwell he turned, waiting.

I bent to Swee. "Get up."

He retched, brought up nothing. "Can't. He hurt me, Uppie."

I caught Swee's arm, tried to heave him up. "Do you want Pook to get you?" Moaning, he staggered to his feet.

Pook charged. So did I. As our paths converged I dived at his legs, slid clear of the knife. I grasped his ankle. My inertia carried me past him, breaking my grip, but not before he fell with a thud. Now he was between me and Swee. Not what I wanted.

Pook wasn't happy either. He leaped to his feet, pivoting between us as if expecting a concerted attack. Not likely, with Swee lurching to the rear of the hallway, clutching his stomach.

Pook sized us up, made his choice. He turned his back on me, dashed after Swee, knife raised to strike.

No time to think. I raced after. Lighter on my feet, I swarmed onto his back. He tumbled, just missing Swee's calf with his jagged blade. I clawed at the knife. Pook was bigger and heavier; suddenly, he twisted loose.

In an instant he was on top of me. He tore his wrist free, raised the knife to plunge it into my chest. I squealed in panic.

Swee's foot shot upward, caught Pook in the side of the head, slammed him into the wall. The knife clattered to the floor. In a frenzy borne of desperation I squirmed from underneath, scampered across the hall. I grabbed the knife just as a hand latched onto my ankle.

I whirled, leading with the knife.

Pook was on his knees. My blade hovered a millimeter from his throat.

He froze.

After a moment he began to cry.

Chapter 27

JARED

What good had it been for Pook to untie me, leaving me trapped in that dark elevator?

If only I could have reached the hatch. But even if I could jump so high, my swollen hands couldn't hold on to the edges. And I had no way to pull myself up without ripping open the wounds on my chest.

So I'd waited endlessly in the pitch black, every creak above a new terror.

Sitting in the dark, I'd tried to be brave. Dad was a selfish grode, but on *Trafalgar*, he'd faced the alien fish. Perhaps, if I got out of this, I could tell him how I—

A shriek, outside the shaft.

I'd screamed; I couldn't help myself. I cowered in the corner.

The elevator bounced; someone had jumped on top. Pook? Could he be bringing real food? I licked my lips. Please, God. Not dog food. Anything. If I lived to a hundred, I'd never outgrow that shame.

The hatch opened. Pook jumped down, with a metal bucket. "Stan' on this, Uppie. Takin' ya out."

Eagerly I complied. As I reached for the hatch, other hands helped pull me up, while Pook hoisted my waist.

In a moment we were in the hall. I blinked at the light.

With Pook was a big joey in a ragged jumpsuit streaked with garish colors. He shot me a dubious glance. "This him?"

"Ya."

"Don' look like Dosman. Jus' a joeykit. Ya know puters, Uppie?"

"What?"

Pook said, "Tolya, Halber, he c'n do anythin' ya wan'. Bring down towah. Anythin'."

Halber pushed me toward the stairs. When I refused, he beat me.

I found myself on the street, barefoot, my chest aching. My face stung miserably where the big trannie had slapped me. I stepped on a stone and yelped. The trannie's answer was to plant his palms in the small of my back and shove me onward.

At least I'd managed to convince them I needed water. Pook ran back upstairs to get it, but Halber wouldn't wait. Three trannies marched me down the center of the street.

I hoped Pook would be back soon.

In a few blocks I was hopping from foot to foot, trying to ease the pain in my soles. If only they'd give me back my boots.

The trannies all wore shoes or sandals. It did no good to explain I was barefoot; all Halber did was push me forward. "Move, Uppie! Gotta be unner 'fore dark."

We stopped twice at corners, while one of Halber's men negotiated with other trannies. Before I could rest, we moved on.

I peered backward. Pook was nowhere in sight.

The avenue opened onto a wide square. The jagged remains of a building dominated the center. An open stairway descended into a tunnel. Halber steered me to the steps.

Below, all was dark.

I balked. "Let's wait for Pook."

"Down."

"No!" A wave of fear added emphasis to my words.

A growl. He caught my arm, jammed my wrist up between my shoulder blades.

I squealed.

The trannie bent my fingers, all the while heaving my arm upward.

"STOP!" It hurt beyond bearing.

"Down frazzin' stair, Uppie!" He trotted me, wailing and protesting, into the cavern.

Halber bellowed, "Chaco!"

"Yo!"

"Ligh'."

Abruptly, a light switched on. As it swung, shadows danced along the walls.

A dozen trannies in gaudy dress, all with clubs or knives. One joey held a Valdez permalight.

Halber shoved me down a corridor that reeked of sweat and Lord God knew what else. It opened into a smoky chamber strewn with mattresses and broken furniture. In the center, a fire flickered. Above it bubbled a stewpot. Despite myself, I licked my lips.

Halber beckoned a tribesman. "Five Nines be ready?"

"Waitin' at unnercar."

"Lexunners?"

"Whole clan onna track, near stair."

"Allie! Krand!" Halber waited, hands on hips.

A girl darted forward. "Krandboy went piss. I tellim afta."

Halber jerked a thumb in my direction. "Watch Uppie kit. Take couple otha joeys for safe. If he run, ya be diss. Unnerstan'?"

"Awri, Halb." As he turned away, she tugged at my arm. "C'mon."

I tried to pry her fingers loose. "Let go."

She dug her nails into the flesh of my upper arm. "C'mon, Uppiekit. Yo! Krand!" Excitedly she beckoned to an approaching teen. "Halber says ta watch Uppie from run."

Krand's tone was jeering. "Uppie? He be Mid."

"I am not!"

"Yeah." He jabbed at the mark on my chest. Frightened he might open my cuts, I lashed out, straight-armed him into the wall.

"Chaco, help wid Uppie!" In a moment I was surrounded by jabbering trannies. I was taller than any of them, and heavier. But against them all, I hadn't a chance. A melee would open my scabs, and worse, I couldn't run on my bruised bare feet.

Krand grimaced, rubbing his elbow. "Frazzin' Uppie!"

Allie giggled.

At her scorn, the boy bristled. "Barth, Chaco, holdim!" They seized my arms. Krand's foot swung back, slammed into my crotch.

I convulsed. Curled into a ball, I thrashed on the floor.

"Now look whatcha done!" Allie was frantic. "Halber said ta keep safe. He see, he skin ya! Gettim outa!" Unknown hands dragged me to an alcove.

"OhGodohGod!" My knees were drawn up to my chest, my hands cupped around the dreadful pain in my groin.

Allie knelt. "Shhh. Sorry 'bout Krand. He stupe." Her fingers flitted across my brow.

"Fucking trannie bitch! Oh, God!" I rolled from side to side.

"Shush, ya wan' Halber hearya?" She shook me. "Lie onya back, Uppie, bring legs up."

Despite my agony I managed, "What would *you* know about it?"

She grinned. "Think I ain' never kneed a joeykit? Even Krand, one time." The boy reddened, looked away.

After a while my torment eased to misery, then to a persistent ache. Surreptitiously, I wiped my face.

"It all righ', Uppie." Again her fingers touched my forehead.

I gritted my teeth. "My name's Jared."

"Cool meet." She held out a hand, palm and fingers raised.

I groaned, sat cautiously.

"You bad as Pook." Her tone dripped scorn. She grabbed my hand, pressed it to hers. "Say cool, Jared!"

"I don't—" I gave up. "Cool meet."

She rounded on Krand. "G'wan."

"Wid Uppie? Naw."

" 'Kay. I tell Halber watcha done." Without another look she started off.

"Wait, Allie!" Krand's hand shot out.

I slapped away his hand. "Prong yourself."

"See? He don' wanna—"

"Say again, Krand," she growled. I didn't like the look in her eye.

"Cool meet." A mumble.

I swallowed my pride. "Cool."

" 'Kay." She squatted between us. "Why Halber brung ya, Uppie?"

"How in hell would I know?" And where was Pook, when I needed him?

"Why ya got Mid mark?" She pointed to my chest.

"Pook did it. Is he here? He was supposed to—"

Her eyes widened. "Pook be growed enough ta give upbringin'?" She turned to Krand. "Tolya he wasn' no joeykit."

"Hah, don' mean nothin'. Watch me give him Easter mark!" He pulled out a knife.

She punched him, not that hard, the way I poked P.T. sometimes, as a warning. "Ya be Mid now, Jared?"

What was the safest answer? "Yes." Maybe it would impress them.

She nodded. "Chaco, when Halber ain' talkin', ask him where he wan' Uppie kept in rumb wid Parkas."

"Noway. He too pissoff today."

" 'Kay. I ask. Leavimalone, bothayas." She disappeared into the main corridor.

In no shape for a confrontation, I sat quietly. After a moment Allie was back, her eyes dancing. "We ride in unnercar wid Halber! He say bringalong Uppie."

"Awrigh!" The boys slapped hands.

"C'mon. We wait unner." Chaco and Barth hauled me to my feet as she trotted away.

I hobbled as fast as I could without boots. The corridor gave way to another, dimly lit, even danker than the last. Stairs, down, to a crumbling station.

On a track, a bright-lit car, the size of a bus. Around it was a crowd of trannies.

Allie said with dignity, "Halber tol' us come widya." We found a place near the wall. I huddled between Allie and Chaco, yearning for my stolen shirt. The tunnel was cold, and Allie kept glancing at my bare chest. I wished I had hair, like Dad. It wouldn't be long now.

Halber shouted, "C'mon! All in!" I jerked awake.

With whoops and boisterous yells the streeters swarmed into the car. I wrinkled my nose at the reek of their bodies. From the opposite seat Krand giggled. "Uppie too good fo' us!" He hawked, and a gob of spittle landed on my bare foot.

With a scream of rage I launched myself, but a hand shot out, tightened on a shock of my hair, hauled me unceremoniously back to my seat.

I swung, protesting to Allie, "Did you see what he—"

Not Allie, but Halber. A growl. "Put ya ass on bench, Uppie."

"Yessir." Part of me marveled that I'd said it. Even at his most furious, Dad hadn't elicited such quick obedience, or so meek a tone.

"All on? Lesgo!" Halber shouldered his way to a compartment in the front of the car. A lurch, a painful squeal, and the car was in motion. Its lights dimmed.

The trannie jabber fell to near silence, as joeys looked about with awe at the crumbling concrete walls that slid past.

Allie leaned close, said loudly into my ear, "Uppies got unnercars?"

"Huh?"

"Unnercars, like dis? You ride in?"

"Are you glitched? Think I'd be caught dead—" It was the wrong tack. "Buses," I told her. "Helis, sometimes. Or a Hitrans, if time doesn't matter."

She looked smug. "Even Uppies ain't got Sub car. Hah."

I looked around. "Did the city restart the transport grid? I thought it was abandoned."

She snorted. "No powah unner since Halber's mama was joeykit. Maybe 'fore dat, even." She leaned close, as if imparting a secret. "Valdez permas."

"It would take a carload to . . ." I tried to calculate, but I was too weary. "Where'd he get them?"

"Trayfo wid Changman."

With that gibberish she lapsed silent.

A few moments later the din eased. The car ground to a halt, and exuberant trannies crowded at the doors.

Halber emerged from his cubicle. "Lissen, allyas!" He clapped his hands, sharply. "Don' want no stupe pokin' head outa stair, or makin' noise ta wake Parkas. Any fuckaroun', I dissim fast. Cool?"

"Gotcha, Halber." A general murmur of assent.

He opened the doors. "Wait in tunnel 'til signal. I be up inna min. Krand, you ain' goin' up. Get back wid Uppie!"

The boy scuttled to obey. I smirked, knowing it would irritate him.

Halber slid onto my bench. I cringed, awaiting the inevitable blow. Instead, he scrutinized my face. "Pook say you smart wid puters. Wyorenn?"

"Excuse me?"

In an instant Halber had me up against the side wall, fingers wrapped around my throat. His other hand drew back.

With great daring, Allie tapped his forearm. " 'Xcuse, Halber. Uppie don' unnerstan' ya."

"Why? He glitch?"

"Naw. But if dey gave 'im Mid mark, he mus' be stupe like resta Mids. Gotta talk slow."

Halber put his bristly face in front of mine. His eyes were bloodshot, and held a mean look that chilled me to the bone. "Pook say—" He spoke with exaggerated care. "—ya talk good wid puters. Wyorenn?"

I shot a helpless glance at Allie. She blurted, "Yes or no, Uppie?"

"Oh! Y! I mean, yessir!"

From a trannie perspective, I was an absolute genius. And with my friends, and their hackcode . . . I had a hunch my status was about to shoot upward.

"Ya unnerstan' towah puters?"

"Of course." I tried to sound just short of contemptuous; that ought to impress him.

"C'n ya bring down a towah?"

Again I gaped. He frowned, and I said quickly, "Bring it down how, sir?"

His brow furrowed. "Stop elec. Turn off powah. Stop banks an' chips 'n all."

"God Almighty. You mean—"

"C'n ya crash it, so they ain' no better 'n us?" His voice was savage.

"Destroy my whole world?" Despite myself, my lip curled. "Do you think for a minute I'd—"

"No, Halb!" Allie's voice was shrill, but too late.

Halber's fist slammed into my eye, smashed my head into the window behind. I ricocheted into his arms. "Oh, God! Christ Jesus!" Blood dripped down my split cheek. I stamped on the cold floor, trying to hold on to consciousness. I probed my eye, wondering if he'd knocked it out of my head.

"Canya, Uppie? No more frazzin' shit!"

"Yes! No! I don't know!" I lapsed into sobs.

"Hang onta him, Allie; I goin' up. Nex' time, Uppie, I wan' ansa!" He stomped out.

Chapter 28

POOK

Never in million years Pook so pissoff. Frazzin' Uppie put my own shiv ta my throat 'n make me cry.

Afta, I didn' care what he do; I so mad I grab a bucket an smash it 'gainst wall 'gain an 'gain till handle come loose an' bucket fly back an' hit me in face. I don' 'member what happen next, 'xcept coupla minutes later I crouch inna corna, Uppieboy pattin' my shoulda sayin' easy Pook, don' rev, don' rev.

Can' figga out how it all happen. Everythin' seemed ta go so good: Pook fin' Uppie Jared, make him capture, trayfo his boots 'n shirt for buncha cansa. But Peetee come an' ruin everythin'. He throw poor Pook down on roof wid Jag an' Swee watchin'. How Midboys respec' Pook afta? Okay okay, Pookboy pick hisself up, get Halber agree ta borrow Jared fo' while steada buy; means when he finish Pook c'n sell Jared back ta Uppies fo' even more 'n Halber gonna pay.

But Peetee back, like itch in hot summa. Can' he find someone else ta beat on 'sides Pookboy? Ain' Pook's fault Halber say ta fetch water fo' Jared. Go up, hear noise. Maybe could ignore, but what if Mids find Pook lair an his cansa?

Ain' righ' dat Uppiekit smalla 'n Pook know magic rumb tricks. Pook figh' like tiga. But jus' as I go ta pick up shiv, Swee smash me, an' Uppie grab it firs'.

Now, in upstair hall, Peetee askin' where Subs take Jared. If I don' tell him, dunno what he do. But if I say, Halber be royal pissoff.

Worse, I migh' lose Jared, 'cause Peetee say he take his Uppie fren' back ta towah.

I stall, thinkin' a Changman. He c'n handle any tribe, even Uppies. Meantime, wheneva Peetee look away, I glance Swee sayin' don' botha askin' forgive; ya gonna pay.

Peetee sigh. He hold shiv, wid look like his dinna don' taste good. I tense, but he got me in corna, no place ta run.

"Look, Pook; I've really got to find Jar. So I'll ask you where they took him. Each time you don't answer, I'll cut you. I'll try not to hurt you too much, especially at first. But I'm going to keep doing it, until you tell me, or—" He swallow, an' his voice go hard. "—until you can't. I'm sorry. Really."

Sometimes a joey hate himself fo' what he can' help. Pook wanna be brave, but noway wid Uppiekit wavin' shiv pas' face. I start ta sniffle. Before I c'n stoppit, turn inta wail. I sound jus' like Jared in elevate.

Peetee mumble, "Lord God, I'll do penance after, I swear. This is for Jared. Please understand." His eyes meet mine.

As shiv come up I squeal, "Don', Peetee. Pookboy show ya! Swear!"

He shout, "Where's Jared?"

"Changman know! Gotta ask!" My mind marvel I come up wid great idea, jus' as Uppie shiv ready ta slice. Changman'll fix Peetee.

"Who? Where is he?"

"Changman ol' trayta Neut. Cross block, up one!" I point, tryin' not ta whimper.

Peetee frown. "Swee, is he zarking me?"

Midboy know he gotta take Uppie's side, 'cause I dissim soon as I getta chance. "Dunno. Pook couldn' tray Jared ta Subs by hisself widout help. Maybe Changman involve."

I go indignant. 'Notha reason ta diss Swee.

I sigh. Not all his fault. If Peetee didn' whomp on me two separate time in fronta, Swee unnerstand Pook all growed now. I wipe eyes on sleeve. "Changman tellya 'bout it in shop."

So, das how Pook fin' himself walkin' casual down street, Swee on left, Uppie wid shiv on righ'. But before he lemme down stair, Peetee give so many warnin's he soun' like Chang. Don' do dis, don' do dat, you hear me Pook?

Could run, but two prollems. One, he got shiv, and migh' catch me. Two, if Mids see I 'fraid a scrawny Uppie joeykit, dey laugh me outa Mid turf.

Minute lata, we knockin' at Chang door. Peetee stand close, point a shiv makin' Pook's back squirm.

Chang do his usual grumble. "Who dere? Watcha wan'?"

"It be me. Pook."

Pause. His voice change. "I dunno any Pook. Usetabe joeykit dat name, but he wen' off by hisself."

I grit my teeth, say real nice, "Please, Mista Chang. Lemme in."

"Can' be same Pook I knew. That joeykit called Chang stupid ol' man. Wouldn' come ta shop for tea or visit."

Peetee stir, restless. "I thought you said—"

I try again, "Mista Chang—"

'Notha pause. Then, "Go 'way. We close."

Peetee's eyes go fire. "I warned you, didn't I?" Shiv poke me tight ta door.

I squeal, "Mista Chang, help me! Ohgod no, Peetee!" I tryta push away his shiv hand widout getting cut.

Inside, chains rattle. Sudden, door fall open. Chang loom ova, fierce. "Leggo my Pook! Now!"

Peetee lick his lips, uncertain. "Sir, I'm Philip Seaf—"

I see chance, an' dart unner Chang's arm, safe in shop. Wid howl, Peetee plunge pas' Changman ta follow.

Uppie get between me an stair; we dance round Chang's table. I try fo' door, but he too fast, an' I end up in corna, my han's tryin' ta protec' alla me at once.

"What the fuck did you pull, you little trannie fraz—"

From door, Chang's voice surprising quiet, considerin' his shop invade. "What Fisherman gonna say, his joeykit talk like dat?"

Peetee almos' past listenin'.

"Philip . . . Tyre . . . Seafort!" Chang use name like magic. Maybe it a real hex. Uppieboy straighten, but hold tigh' ta shiv. "I don't mean trouble, sir, but this joey—"

Chang relock door. "'Little trannie fraz?' Dat what he taught ya 'bout us?"

Peetee shake his head, his rage fadin'. "How do you know my name?"

"He tol' me."

"Who?"

"Fisherman. Your father."

Peetee stamp flo'. "Can't any of you tell the truth? You're as bad as this—"

"He sat right there, las' nigh', in chair you knock ova." Chang point. "Where you gonna sit, while tell me what goin' on."

"Here? Really?" He study Chang's face. "Oh, God. Why—"

"Came ta ask my help findin' ya. To beg." In Chang voice, no gloat. Sadness.

Tentative, I edge away, but Peetee grab my collar. "I've had it with you, joeyboy!" His voice ain' quite broke, but scare me, like Karlo at his wors'. "If you run . . . " He shove me inta chair. "If I go to Hell for it, I'll slice your throat!"

"Cool jets, Uppie." I slink small in chair. "I do whatcha say." Chang smile.

"Where's Swee?" Peetee.

"Outside," say Chang. "I c'n only deal wid one rampage at a time."

"Please let him in, Mr. Chang. I won' make trouble."

"Slicin' Pook ain' trouble?"

"I didn't hurt him. Yet." Peetee glower at me. I try to look 'greeable.

Crazy half hour. I can' unnerstan' why Chang don' diss Uppie fo' mess wid me. Chang start water boilin' fo' tea. He ask Peetee why he got me hostage. Peetee keep askin' Changman where be his frien' Jared. Chang say he dunno. And Swee, mos'ly quiet inna corna, figgerin' how ta make me fadeout from dissin' him afta.

An' mosta all, Peetee ask ova an' ova if Fisherman really came ta Chang shop.

"Las' nigh', I tolya," ol' man say. "With frien'." I lissen, tryin' ta figga Changman's swind. Fisherman, inna street? Hah. Wouldn' make it two blocks, specially at nigh'. On otha han', they both say Peetee be his joeykit. And Peetee toughest Uppie I eva seen.

Teapot on Valdez perma boil and boil, 'til Chang finally notice. He hurry ova, turn it off. "Ain' enough water ta waste," he mutta.

Philip Uppie think a while. "Lord God knows what Fath will do when he sees me." A grimace. "But I think it'll hurt." He knot his fists. "When he finds me I'll have to go with him, so I've absolutely *got* to find Jared first. Mr. Chang, please help—"

"Ain't seen him. How many times I gotta tell ya?" Chang sound annoy as he pour tea.

"But Pook said you . . . " Slowly, Peetee's eyes turn to me. Chang's too. I sit real still.

Chang stand, hold table for min 'til his dizzy pass. I go worry; bad time for him to die, leave me 'lone wid Uppie. "Pook and I have ta talk," he say. "Private."

"I'm not letting him out of—"

"He won' go nowhere, Philip Tyre. My word. Sit an' drink tea."

Peetee study him. Finally, he nod.

I get up, cautious cause a shiv. 'Fore I c'n take two steps, Chang grab ear, haul me protestin' ta back room, an' out side passage. I hope he show me secret door an' lemme 'scape, but no; he plant hisself in fronta me. "Bran' new Uppie boots ta trayfo, hah?" Stern. "Watcha done, Pook? Ya dissim?"

"Please, Mista Chang, lemme go quick, 'fore he—"

Holdin' my ear, Chang slap me. My han' dart ta shiv, but it ain' in usual place. Uppie got it. Chang whomp 'gain, harder. "Ya dissim, Pook?"

"Please, I—ow! He ain' diss!"

Slap. "Where, then?"

I try ta break free, but can' widout leave ear behin'. In coupla min, Chang got me blubberin' like joeykit. "Stop, Mista Chang! Ayie! Don'!" Face stingin', I claw at his han'. "Halber got him! No swind!"

"Howya know?"

"Was my capture." Snivelin' an' cryin', I tell 'im how I take Jared, and what I do afta.

His look show admire, but mix wid disgus'. "Ya got yaself a Pooklair afta all, hah? Okay okay, couldn' stay wid Karlo's Mids. But what did Jared joeyboy do, make ya hurt him, cut Mid mark, treat him like animal? Ya socio, Pook? Ya be sociopath?"

"He jus' Uppie, Mista Chang!"

"So what if—"

"In Mid turf. Doncha unnerstan?" I cradle my achin' ear, tryin' ta stop cry. "Joey wanda out of own turf, he belong ta whoeva catch."

"Fah." He shove me towar' shop.

"Hide me, Mista Chang. Tell Uppiekit I run 'way. Or lemme go."

"Nah. I gave word."

"So? You no Uppie."

"And so did you, joeykit. 'Pook showya. Swear.' Ain' that what you said?"

"How c'n I take Peetee ta Halber? Boss Sub'll diss us both."

Chang cuff me hard, when I don' expec'; I blink, hold sob in back a throat. "Shoulda thought of that 'fore ya swore!"

"Mista Chang . . . " I make nice face, ta show him I ain' lookin' fo' rumb. "Swearin' be Uppie thing, not trannie. Whassit mattah what I tol' Peetee?"

He look at me long time. 'Ventual, I realize he lookin' through me ta somethin' else.

Final, he say, "Uppies gotta unnerstan' trannies have own ways. We ain' animals to capture inna street an' send to far planet, like they did to Eddieboss. We ain' prey to hunt, like Unies do. We be people."

I wait.

"An' trannie joeys gotta learn Uppie ways ain' all wrong. If Uppie give his word, everyone know he'll do what he say. Allatime. Even if no shiv pokin' his back."

I go red.

"Long time, Pook, I thought trannies couldn' afford honor; too hard jus' tryin' ta survive. Well, in months, year maybe, we be gone. So nothin' in our way; now we afford honor." His eyes wet. "I gave word to Philip not to let you escape. So I won'. And you gave word to show him where Jared gone. So you take him to Sub. Why in name a God you give Uppiekit to Halber, anyhow?"

I start to answer, but he wave it away. "No time. Gotta bring Peetee back here 'fore nigh', Pook. Halber startin' rumb wid Parkas. No time fo' Uppiekit to be in way. Take Philip to Sub quick."

Chang be glitch fo' sure. But 'fore I say so, I stop ta think. Why I botha swind Peetee take me ta Chang, if I won' follow ol' man's advice? Beside, if I tell Chang he glitch, he jus' whomp me mo'. Between Swee, Uppie, and Changman, Pook be whomp enough fo' rest a life.

"What about Fisherman, Mista Chang?"

Chang frown. "I could keep Philip in shop, hopin' Fisherman will come back like he promised. But his joeyboy got shiv; dunno if I could hold him without hurtin' him. Anyway, Fisherman may be dead. He spent night onna street."

My brain whirl wid too many ideas. First Chang slappin' me, now explainin' hisself like nevah did 'fore. Fisherman, Halber, Rumb. Peetee. Jared Washinton Uppie.

I take in long shudderin' breath. "Pook do whatcha say, Mista Chang. I take Peetee ta Subs."

He nod approval, but I ain' done. I rememba knigh's an' cassels.

"I take 'im. I swear."

Chapter 29

ROBERT

Arlene paced my bedroom in the Sheraton Skytel. "I'm sorry I woke you," she said again. "But Nick's so obstinate I could—" She muttered something I didn't quite catch.

"What?"

"Nothing. What can anyone do when he—" Abruptly she loosed a string of oaths that would make a sailor's hair curl. I listened with interest. I hadn't heard the like since my middy days, when *Sarnia*'s Captain tripped over Seaman Ead's smuggled cat.

"Sorry," she said.

Stifling a yawn, I glanced at the clock. Six in the morning. I'd have liked another hour, but . . . "It's getting light. We'll go after them."

She brushed aside the curtain, peered at the dawn. "Do you have any idea where this Chang joey lives?"

"No. Did you call Nick?"

"His caller's off."

"Then wait."

"How long?" A pause, before she added, "He may be dead too—er, I mean . . . dead." She bit her lip. "I've had it with waiting, Rob. We have to call the SecGen."

"You heard how the Captain feels about—"

"Do you know how *I* feel? P.T. is my child. I can't abandon him. Do it. Make the call."

My heart leaped. "If you'd like." Retaking the streets would clear the way for Dad's bid for office, and my own campaign to follow. But at what cost to Arlene, when the Captain learned?

Worse, at what cost to me? It would cast away Nick Seafort's friendship.

Perhaps, as Arlene feared, the Captain was already killed. The thought made it easier not to think of betrayal. "Let me get dressed and we'll go to breakfast. It's too early to reach anyone who counts."

"I can't eat."

"You have to." Like a benevolent uncle, I shepherded her to the door.

It would have been useless to call the SecGen without laying the proper groundwork; he'd have been cordial and carefully noncommittal. One doesn't pluck the strings of power; they must be coaxed to resonate to the frequency of the instrument.

With Van's concerted assistance, we began calling in favors, reaching ever deeper into the Rotunda to attune the SecGen's advisors to the personal appeal Arlene was to deliver.

It was a game I knew well, and one I played to perfection.

Political opponents though we were, at times the Supranationalists and the Territorials who controlled the General Assembly needed the other's favors. And I also knew that if we could prompt the SecGen to act, clearing the streets would benefit us all. And trannies didn't vote.

By midmorning all was ready; it was time to seek the SecGen's direct approval. Arlene made the call, while I listened from the couch in her suite. I'd coached her as thoroughly as I could. She managed to convey her urgency without seeming obsequious.

"If he's alive, Mr. Kahn, we have to find him . . . find them both." She listened. "I don't know. He stopped at the shop of an old trader, but I doubt he's still there. Robert, where did you set them down?"

"Two blocks south of the Sheraton."

She told Kahn, "They covered that area, so you ought to start elsewhere . . . If you send in the police while you're mobilizing troops . . . " A pause. "No, my first worry is Philip. He's only twelve, and the boy he followed is fifteen. When Nick went out he took Adam Tenere—his adjutant. Adam has a laser." She frowned. "Of course he's licensed!" She covered the caller. "What a question!"

A pause. "No, I'm not asking you to clear the whole district . . . "

I flinched.

" . . . just find the former Secretary-General and his son. Certainly that's a reasonable request, regardless of party."

Again she listened. "Mr. Kahn, it's been three days; they *have* to move sooner! Damn it, have you any children?"

I stood, waving a warning finger, but she paid no heed.

"Two days is ridiculous." From the caller, a tinny protest, but she shook her head. "Now. Today." Her voice hardened. "As much as I appreciate Robbie Boland's efforts to reach you, he isn't my only resource. If I tell Holoworld you refused . . . well, that's a matter of opinion; I consider two days a refusal. Tomorrow? You're saying you want them dead? Put me in widow's weeds, and so help me, I'll crucify you in the press!"

I groaned.

"Mr. Kahn, when my husband sat in the Rotunda we had control of the apparatus; are you saying you don't? If Nicky ordered the police onto the streets—any streets—they'd have been on the move in hours, if not minutes."

Weakly, I said, "Arlene . . ." She was trampling my carefully laid plans.

She waved me aside. "In return? You'd have me make promises for Nick Seafort? Don't you understand him in the least? In return you get my public gratitude. No, I have no idea who he'll endorse for the nomination."

She listened, her foot tapping impatiently. "Yes, I've heard that drivel before. I thought better of you. You have—what time is it?—until noon to decide. Then I call Holoworld. Very well. Good-bye."

She rang off.

"Jesus, Arlene."

She stood quiet a moment, before flinging the caller across the room. "The devious son of a bitch. He was expressing his sympathy, and suddenly we were discussing the election."

"That's politics."

Her lip curled. "I know. I've lived politics." She pointed vaguely at the corner in which the caller lay. "That's why Nicky wouldn't dream again of seeking office. He told me he couldn't imagine what had come over him, wading deliberately into that cesspool."

I said carefully, "I wish you hadn't antagonized Kahn . . ."

"Faugh. Did you know him as Senator from Greater Austria? He fawned over Nicky, and SecGen Anjour and De Vala . . . If he has any principles, I've yet to see them. All he respects is power."

I sighed. Her way might be best after all, and ultimately,

SecGen Kahn's ire didn't affect me, or Dad. We were his opponents, and he knew it. I knew Dad would agree.

Her shoulders slumped. "If only Nicky would let us know . . ."

I blinked. "Arlene, did P.T. by any chance take along his caller?"

For a moment she only stared. Then her face went gray.

I leaped to her side and eased her to a chair. "I'm sorry; I only meant—"

"How could I be so stupid? Oh, God! Where's the caller?" Frantically, she looked about.

I retrieved the machine from the corner, where she'd hurled it. "What's his personal—"

She punched in a code. "I never thought to ring him! Robbie, I'm glitched. I'm an idiot."

"Easy, Arlene."

I leaned close, while it rang.

A click, and the circuit light went green. Her eyes widened, and she clutched my wrist. She said eagerly, "Philip, it's Mom. Where are you?"

A giggle, and random tones, as if someone were dialing.

"Answer me, P.T."

"Heya, Uppie bitch. Comin' outa ya towah?"

"Oh, Lord God!"

I pried the caller from her frozen fingers. "Who are you? Where's the boy who had this—"

Another click.

Silence, and the light blinked red.

The two hours that followed were grim. Arlene paced, as years ago I'd seen her husband pace, on *Trafalgar*'s bridge in the time of the fish armada.

I thought I knew her well, but never had I seen such emotion. Between bouts of silence or tears she berated herself with savage scorn for failing to remember P.T.'s caller.

"I could have saved him." She thrust her hands into her pockets, strode back to the window before turning anew. "He wanted to be rescued; I'm sure of it."

"You can't know—"

"Why else did he take along his caller? He wanted us to stop him. Are you as stupid as I? Christ." She opened the

door, peered for a moment into the hall, for what purpose I
didn't know. "Sorry, Robbie, I don't mean that. But how
could I be so foolish as to forget . . . "

"Sit down."

"Don't be ridiculous, I can't—"

"Now." My voice held a note that surprised even me.

Startled, she sank slowly into a chair.

"Arlene, get control of yourself, or I'll call a doctor and
have you sedated."

She gaped.

"I mean it. You do neither yourself nor P.T. any good in
this state. I knew he had a caller. So did the Captain and
Adam, and none of us thought to ring his number. Why are
you alone responsible?"

"I'm his mother!"

"But you're not Lord God." I stood. "We'll get something
to eat. You didn't touch your breakfast, and—"

The caller rang.

She dived for it, listened, covered the speaker. "It's Kahn.
Talk to him. I'm in no mood for diplomacy."

I took the caller, listened. "No earlier? Very well. Yes, we
agree. And I give my word the Supras won't sandbag you on
this. Oh, one other thing." I glided toward my own suite, shut
the interconnecting door. "It would be best for all concerned
if this . . . affair appeared to have nothing to do with the
Seaforts. Announce it as a general crackdown."

From the SecGen, silence.

I said, "As you heard, Arlene Seafort is . . . volatile. And
the Captain is a wild card I think neither of us cares to play.
Do you agree?"

He did. I worked out a few of the pressing details, and rang
off, well satisfied. After, I went back to her quarters.

"Well?"

"At seven this evening every jerry in the city moves in. We
have until then to search."

"Just the police?"

"I imagine they'll have troops as backup," I said smoothly,
knowing better than to reveal the deal I'd struck with Kahn.

Unie troops would assemble this afternoon, and go in at
dawn, after the jerries. In force. I knew that for the sake of
the tower projects, it was necessary. I'd guaranteed Kahn no

criticism from the Supranationalists, and promised help with the Vegan resettlement bill.

Arlene strode to the closet. "Will you drop me off in the heli?" She thrust on her jacket.

"Where?"

"To search for my son, of course."

"Last night you promised—"

"To wait until morning. And Nick didn't call. If there's a chance I can spot P.T. before any disruption . . ."

I couldn't let Arlene risk herself on the streets. She had no idea of the turmoil our conversation had set in motion. There'd likely be house-to-house fighting, and scores of ruined buildings. If she were caught in it, or worse, killed . . . political repercussions would be dreadful.

Aghast, I realized I'd considered Arlene's death from a partisan perspective. She was my friend. Her loss would be a personal tragedy. And it would utterly destroy the Captain. I swallowed. "I doubt I can hire one at such short—"

"Bullshit. You rented your heli for two days, and it's waiting for Nicky's call. If you're afraid, I'll have a joey from the hotel run me down to street level."

I sighed. My ambition had gotten me into this; if we succeeded, my ambition would be well served. And if Arlene died, I'd rather be with her than face the Captain's rage. "We'll go on foot; I'll have someone pick us up before seven. By then, we must be off the streets."

"On foot? How far can we—"

"It's the way P.T. went. And Jared."

That silenced her.

Every U.N. legislator was licensed to carry a laser. I rarely wore mine, but always had it near. Today, but for its reassuring presence in my jacket holster, I don't think I'd have had the courage to walk out the streetside door. Arlene brought little but her caller and her son's holo.

I pointed south.

"Why?"

"That's where I took Adam and the Captain."

"So we'll go north. No point in covering the same ground." Without waiting for an answer, she strode on her way.

I scurried to keep up. "Slow down. See those joeys at the corner? And across the street, they're moving—"

She cupped her hands. "P.T.!" Her shout echoed. "Philip!"

"For God's sake, Arlene."

"How can we find him if he can't hear us? Philip, come out where we can see you!"

At the corner, transients gawked.

Arlene strode on. I kept a hand near my laser.

"Hey, Uppie!"

I whirled.

A gap-toothed streeter grinned. "Watcha doin' onna street? Lost?"

I saw no weapon, but nonetheless I backed away uneasily.

"Getcha bitchgirl back inna towah!" The trannie bent for a rock.

"Arlene . . ."

"I see him." As if unafraid, she walked up to him, fished the holo out of her pocket. "Have you seen this boy?"

He snickered. "Mama los' her babykit?" He beckoned to a companion. "Look, Uppie bitchgirl got holo!" He snatched it from Arlene's hand. "Make me good trayfo. Betcha joeykit be—aiyee!" He clutched his arm. Arlene wrested away her holopic, turned to the second trannie. "Have you seen him? There's a reward."

"Frazzin' Uppies think ya own the worl'. Don' mess wid us Broads!" The streeter emitted a piercing whistle. "Yo! Look what Uppie did ta Pol!"

They gathered, all eyes on mine. It wasn't me, I wanted to cry. Her. She did it.

Arlene gripped my arm, led me across the street. "Philip," she shouted. "Come out!"

A trannie youth, more daring than the rest, ran up behind us. Before I could pull out my laser, he shoved me so hard I went down. "Teach ya ta mess wid—"

Arlene stepped over me, grabbed the boy's grimy jumpsuit, punched him in the stomach. His hands flew to protect himself, but not before she hit him again, harder. "Run, boy, before you get hurt. Rob, get up." The young joey stood slack-jawed.

It was a side to her I'd never seen. Had the Commandant known he'd wed a tigress? I scrambled to my feet.

"Have you seen this boy?" She thrust the holo in his face. "Look at him!"

"Naw!"

Angry murmurs. Running feet. Before I could warn her, we were surrounded by a dozen trannies, with more on the way. One bore a club, another a rock. I slid the laser from my holster.

"Whatcha done ta Skat?"

"Say goo'bye ta towah, frazzin'—"

"Jumpsuit be mine, afta!"

"No one mess wid—"

"Listen." Arlene's thin, hard voice cut through the din. Then, lower, "Rob, don't shoot unless we've no choice." To the crowd, "You know what a reward is? There's a reward for this boy." She held up her holo.

Skat rubbed his stomach. "Bitchgirl whomp me!"

"You started it." Her tone was curt. "We didn't come for trouble. Just to find him." Again, she fished in her pocket, came out with Jared's picture. "And him."

A woman's voice. "Diss 'em!"

My hand tightened on the trigger.

"Hol' on, Chassie. Lessee what dey brung."

"Diss 'em, an' take rewar' afta."

Arlene shouted, "Why're you so frazzin' ready to diss? Don't any of you have joeykids? Wouldn't you search if they were lost?"

A pause. The woman said, "Not outa our turf."

"Why?"

"Leave Broad turf, dey dead. An' joeykit who wanda outa turf be too glitch ta worry 'bout."

Arlene brandished Jared's picture. "This boy came here first. This one came after, to look for him. Someone's seen them, somewhere."

A lean joey with a scarred face pushed through the crowd. "Lemme see." He peered at the holos. "Innifo?"

Arlene glanced at me. "What's he saying?"

"I'm not sure."

"Innifo me, bitchgirl. Ya wan' data, gimme."

"You've seen them?" Her tone was eager.

"One."

"Who?"

"Innifo firs'."

She dug into her pocket, brought out bills, handed him one. "More when we find him."

"Ya don' got cansa?" The streeter grimaced. "Hard ta spen' Unibucks. Gotta take ta ol Chang, an he skinya."

Arlene waved a twenty. "Which boy?"

He jabbed the holo. "Him." Jared.

Her face fell. "When?"

"Dunno." He shrugged. "Mornin'."

"Rob, is he making it up?"

The holo only showed Jared's face. I said to the trannie, "Describe him."

"Huh?"

"Tell me about him. How big was he? What was he wearing?"

The transpop looked smug. "Innifo."

Arlene peeled off another bill. He reached for it, but she balled it in her fist. "After."

The trannie scowled. "Size a Skat. Brown hair, light like blondie. No shirt, no boot, blue pant. Gimme innifo."

Arlene handed him the bill, and another as well. "Take me to him."

"Haw, no way, Uppie."

I could see Arlene's patience wear thin. She grated, "Where was he going?"

"Sub Four Two."

"Where is Sub?"

The streeter pointed north. "Five, six block."

She looked around. "Who'll take us?"

Guffaws from several of the trannies. "Can' go near Sub, Uppie. Subs'll diss ya. Us too."

I asked, "Arlene, what in hell are they talking—"

"Sub, for subway. The old train system. Years ago Nick went down there, to look for Annie."

"Good Lord." Then the rumors I'd heard as a cadet were true; the Commandant was capable of anything.

She asked, "Why would Jared go to the Subs?"

The boy Arlene had slapped began to caper. "Oh please, lemme be, mista. Where ya takin me?" Giggling, he clutched his chest, pretended to limp. "Not so fas', rocks be sharp! Please, lemme go!"

Arlene stood very still. Then, quietly, "Rob, give me your laser."

I hesitated. I'd intended to be her protector. On the other hand, I was beginning to realize we were safer with the pistol in Arlene's hand than mine. I handed it over.

She flicked off the safety. "Skat, they call you? Ever seen a laser? Watch." She set it to high, aimed at a flaking light-post. The metal glowed white, began to drip.

From the trannies, awed murmurs.

Her hand went to her pocket, emerged with a wad of bills which she dropped in front of the boy. "Here." She extended the pistol, aimed at Skat. "Lead us to the Sub, or by Lord God, I'll fry the eyes from your face!"

He whimpered, "Uppie, if I do they gonna diss—"

She shouted, "You think some trannie in a tunnel will stop me from finding my son?"

In seconds the crowd melted away. The boy Skat backed toward a building, but I caught his arm as he slipped past. "She means it, joey."

He quailed. "Ya gotta pay innifo fo' passby. I take ya ta Sub stair, is all. Ain' goin down. Even laser bettah 'n skin alive."

"Let's go."

We hadn't taken five steps when Arlene's caller buzzed.

Chapter 30

Pedro

Whole day had passed, an' not a single trannie came to trayfo. It was as if all trannietown caught in tension of Pook and Fisherman and Subs. I sat alone, chest achin', welcoming silence of dark shop.

Tap on door. "Mr. Chang? It's Adam Tenere, with the Commandant. Could you let us in?"

Not sure I wanted to, with what I had to tell them. But, weary, I shuffled to door, unlocked.

Tenere came in first, hand on laser. I scowled. "How many you execute, Uppie?"

He shook his head. "None, but it was close." Without invite, he slumped into chair. "I told you I wouldn't kill for pleasure. But their hostility is incredible. It was a near thing."

Fisherman looked tired, despondent. "Nothing. Not a clue." He sighed. "No one spoke to him; no sign of his body." A glance at Adam. "Or of Jared." His hand flitted to Uppie friend's shoulder. "Sorry."

I spoke, voice hoarse, had to try again. "Peetee was here."

For a moment, no understanding. Then Fisherman's eyes locked on mine, like twin lasers.

I said, gruff, "This afternoon. Left coupla hours back."

He cried, "You let him go!"

"He had shiv. Knife."

"P.T.? You're glitched. He wouldn't dream of—"

"You don' know him, seems. He was ready to use." But not on me. I'd been worried for Pook; couldn't stand seein' him diss. But for self, never a second's fear. Knew from first look at joeykit, I coulda talked him outa harm.

"Why the knife? Why didn't you stop him? For Lord God's sake, was he hurt?" Fisherman's voice broke.

"Easy, sir." Tenere.

"Don' 'easy' me, it's not your son—Lord, I'm sorry." Fisherman sank into chair, buried head in hands.

"He didn' have a mark on him." I fussed with teapot, pouring water, setting cups, babbling all the while. Big news, big innfo; I coulda made Fisherman pay lotsa for tell. But words come tumblin' out like I a joeykit needin' his respec'. Dunno why; maybe I gettin' too old.

When I done, he absently took tea, blew over rim of cup. "How did P.T. learn Pook had Jared in his lair?"

"Not sure. All happen too fast."

"Is Jared all right?"

I shrugged. "Right enough to walk, this mornin'." From Tenere, a soft sound. Without thinkin' I trot over, pat shoulder. "You be findin' him. Drink tea. Help ya think." Obediently, he took his cup. I marveled he hadn' slapped away my hand.

Fisherman rubbed his eyes. "Your Pook traded Jared to the Subs. You made Pook admit it to Philip, so my son went after them. Is that it?"

I din' blame him for being confuse. "Best I can figga."

"Why would Pook help P.T.?"

I hadn't tol' him that part. "Cause he swore it, when Peetee held shiv to his throat."

Tenere stirred. "What's an oath to a goddamn trann—"

"Adam!" Fisherman's voice was like a whip.

Tenere recoiled. After a moment, his face lifted. "I haven't slept in a week. I know my son's cut, hurt, frightened, and I can't find him. Please forgive me."

I waved it away, along with my own pissoff. Didn' matter now. "Words can' hurt. 'Bout oath, you be right." I forced self to meet his eyes. "Maybe we learn in time. Not sure. Filmatleven."

Fisherman ask, "Will Pook hurt my son?"

Couldn't help smile. "Don' think so. He pretty scare. An' was Peetee carried shiv, not Pook."

Fisherman shook his head in wonder.

I had pang of worry. "Danger isn't so much Pook, as Subs."

"Do they still kill intruders?"

I'd heard of promise he extracted, years past. "Not usual."

"We'd better get help. I'll call Arlene and Robert; they'll round up a few jerries."

I hated to tell. "May not have time. Big Sub rumb comin', prolly tonight."

Fisherman's voice sharp. "You didn't warn the boys?"

I said, with dignity, "A man choose his way. Your joeykit

growin' to man. Anyway, he wouldn' care. Jared only thing on his mind. When I tol' him 'bout you, just made him hurry."

"Christ." His tone was so forlorn I couldn't stand.

"He wants ta see you," I assured. "Aches for it. But afraid you'll stop his search. So he gotta find Jared first."

Fisherman stood. "They headed for the Sub entrance at Four Two?"

I nodded.

Adam stirred. "Sir, we'd better hurry."

I looked out keyhole, sighed. "Not good to go in Sub."

"We're armed, Mr. Chang."

I hit table with fist; tea jumped. "Doncha know nothin' 'bout Subs? Think ya gonna fin' joeykits alive, afta you diss a Sub? Can' go down alone. Ya need vouch for."

"Jared and P.T. are so near, and you say a tribe war is brewing. There's no time—"

I yelled, "Frazzin' Uppies think ya own the worl'! I'm tellin' ya I go along, take ya to Subs." I fished in pocket case, gulped pill, stopped for calm, hopin' chest wouldn' explode.

Fisherman studied my face, as if memorizing for always. "You'd do that for us?"

I shrugged. "Tribes wouldn' listen when I warn they're dyin' for good water. Halber dreams of takin' Park. Every tribe ready to fight for their piece a turf. Can't help my people, so help you. Do some good 'fore I die." I managed to get to feet. "Better we hurry. Ol' man can' walk too fas'."

Tenere said, "You won't have to, sir." He took out a caller, looked to Fisherman. "May I?"

In a moment he made a connection, spoke urgently, waited. "Out? What the hell do you—He said he'd—taking his calls? Who?" he covered the mouthpiece. "Robert left the hotel. Some joey is standing by at—hello? Where's Robbie Boland? Who are you? What happened to the frazzing heli he—"

"Adam." Just one word, in the Fisherman's quiet tone.

A long pause. Was almost like Tenere was counting under breath. Then, "All right, go ahead." He listened. "The heli's fueled and ready? Can you meet us at—sir, where are we?"

Fisherman told him.

"Yes. A small shop in an old brown building that looks ready to crumble. We'll be outside. Three of us."

I waved finger in his face. "I ain't gettin' inta Uppie copter, hellor hiwater."

Fisherman said, "You've taken longer trips, Mr. Chang. There's no danger—"

Was so mad I spat on own floor. "Danger? Think I some silly joeykit? This be my shop, Uppie! I got reputation. What kinda trayfo I make with trannies afta they see me climbin' into heli, hah? Put me right outa biz, it would." I dug into pocket, pulled out Unibucks Adam Tenere gave, yesterday. "Think Pedro Telamon Chang c'n live on this innifo rest a his days? Bah!"

Tenere's hand over caller, he an' Fisherman exchanged look that made me even more infuriate.

"All right, Mr. Chang. We'll manage." Fisherman.

Adam said to caller, "Two of us, then. But hurry!" He rang off.

I wandered shop, mutterin' to self, regrettin' waste of good tea.

Soon, the whap of blades. Without askin', Tenere went to door, fiddled with chains. I trotted ova, pushed him aside. "Let Chang do it 'fore ya break." I fussed with locks, as heli settled on broken street.

The two men went out into brooding cloud-struck afternoon, ducked under whirling blades. Pilot watched from side to side, ready to lift in an instant, but hardly any trannies were about, and those stayed well back. Weather, maybe. Somethin' electric in air. Or perhaps all in foolish ol' man's head.

While I watched, Fisherman got in rear seat, then Tenere climbed in front. Adam buckled belt, looked up startled at insistent knock on window.

I scowled. "Gonna help me in, or no?"

Door opened; hands reached down to haul me up.

"Welcome aboard, Mr. Chang." Fisherman's voice was dry.

"Bah." I gripped seat of unfamiliar machine, shook finger at pilot. "You lurch, tell me firs'. Too ol' ta be breakin' bones."

"Head north, please." Tenere. "Four Two Square."

Pilot lifted off with evident relief.

Tenere demanded, "Where the hell is Rob? He agreed to stand by."

Pilot said, "He told me to wait in his place, sir. He and Ms. Seafort went streetside."

From rear seat, a strangled sound. I looked to Fisherman. His face was red. His fist slammed into chair.

Adam asked, "Where?"

"Don't know, sir. Assemblyman Boland said they'd go on foot."

Fisherman began to curse, in low steady monotone that didn't cease. It frightened me more than a laser.

It didn' seem to worry Adam Tenere. Instead, he took out caller, punched in numbers. He waited for ring, handed it to Fisherman. "Perhaps, sir, you'd like to speak with her?"

Heli landed on Three Eight. On street, crowd of trannies scattered, 'xcept one kneeling docile by wall. Near him, two Uppies stared upward with impatience.

Fisherman swung open door, jumped out, strode to woman.

"Where the hell have you been?" they shouted, simultaneous.

Engine noise covered rest of what they said. Lots of hands wavin'. For min, looked like she gonna hit him. Other Uppie with her tried to interrupt. Seafort turned on him with snarl, backed him 'gainst wall an' chewed him good. Joey's face got grimmer as Fisherman went on.

I asked Tenere, "Who's Uppie joeygirl?"

"Ms. Seafort." His eyes roved back and forth across street.

I muttered, "Whole family glitched, runnin' around streets like buncha trannies."

He ignored me, but his mouth tightened.

While they argued, joeykit who was kneelin' looked round, careful. He glanced across street to safety, tentatively got off one knee. Uppie woman spun on him, kicked his leg out from unner, in an instant had his head 'gainst wall, his hands laced behind neck.

Interestin', though; she didn' hurt him doin' it. One hand holdin' him in place, she turned anger back to Fisherman. Other Uppie joey jus' stood an' watched.

'Ventually, commotion subsided. Red-faced an' angry, Fisherman and Uppie joey stalked to heli. Seafort wife hauled the Broad joeykit to his feet, shoved him to door.

Space was tight when all crowded in. I took a look at

joeykit. Wild dirty hair, faint start of moustache. Sixteen, maybe. Scared more of heli than Uppies.

As he recognized me, eyes lit with hope. "Changman? They gonna diss us?"

"Naw."

His voice dropped. "That Uppie be one mean bitchgirl. Whomp me fronta alla Broads!"

I shrugged. "I be Neut." Tribe should know better 'n bring complaints 'bout rumb. I hadda stay outa, not take sides. On other hand, wasn't tribe he bitchanmoan about, but Uppie. On other hand, was Fisherman's wife he talkinabout. On other hand, I on Uppie side now. Way too many hands. I shrugged.

Fisherman said to Adam, "This joey saw them bring Jared to the Sub."

Tenere took long, slow breath. "Was he hurt?"

"Whas' innifo—"

I growled, "Tellim, 'fore Uppie diss ya." Wasn't true, but this no time for trayfo.

Joeykit said, "Was cryin' an' beggin' a lot." He giggled. "But no shiv stick outa him."

Tenere gave Broad same slow warnin' look I saw Pook give Swee in shop. I didn' blame him.

"Where to, sir?" Pilot.

Fisherman said, "Four Two Square. We've wasted enough time."

Seafort wife said sweetly, "Picking us up was a waste of time?"

"Arlene, please—"

"You're an insufferable bastard."

Dunno why I expected bolt of lightning, or worse. This was *Fisherman*!

Whateva else Arlene had to say was lost in engine roar. I held strap as we lifted, wishin' I was back in shop. They didn' need me now, with Broad joeykit for guide. 'Course, even if he got them to stair, down below would be 'nother matter.

Once more we landed. Four Two seemed deserted, though still daylight. I licked lips, glad I brought heart pills. "Lesgo." I pushed open door. "Leggo Broad kit. Don' need him, now you got me."

Seafort wife looked me over.

Fisherman said hastily, "Arlene, this is Pedro Chang. Remember my telling you——"

For a moment her gaze remained stony. Then it melted. "Of course. You were my husband's friend, and Eddie's. Nick says you saw Philip. Our son's all right?"

"Was." Wondered why I sounded gruff.

Her hand darted out, touched mine. "You gave him tea. Thank you." For a moment, she thought. "Mr. Chang, what will P.T. do next?"

I made face. "He ain' my joeykit. No way to——"

"You saw him last. What was his mood? Tell me about this Pook."

I found myself babbling private thoughts. Tol' her how Pook almost like son. How he scared under his bravado. How he amazed at steel under P.T. soft exterior. How I figured P.T. wouldn' stop short of bringin' home his Jared.

Nothing I said surprised her. At end, she nodded, pressed my hand again. "Thank you, Mr. Chang. Thank you."

Felt lump in throat I didn' understan'.

Broad joeykit said, hopeful, "Lemme go, Uppiegirl?"

I thought she gonna agree, but she said, "Sorry, Skat. Mr. Chang may know the Sub, but you'll recognize the joeys who took Jared. When we find him, you're free to go."

"Tolya I ain' goin' unner!" He scrambled toward the door.

She caught his hand, did something with his fingers that brought a sharp yelp. "Going somewhere?"

Skat muttered, "Frazzin' bitchgirl." He cuddled his fingers under his arm.

Pilot cleared his throat. "Sir, we're in hostile territory. I'll stay parked if you insist, but I'd prefer to circle——"

Fisherman said, "By all means. Arlene, let's go before they heave rocks through the windshield or dent the blades. Rob, wait in the heli while——"

"I'll go with you." Uppie's tone was curt. He jumped out.

In min, we crossed square to under stairs. Heli threw wind and sand in our eyes as it rose.

Two lasers among us: Adam Tenere carried one, an' Uppie Rob 'nother. I didn' feel safer; if Subs rushed and Uppie went down, we could all find shiv in ribs.

"Arlene, would you rather . . . " Rob blushed, offerin' laser.

"Keep it for now." She pulled stunner from her pouch, set to high. With other han' she kept a firm grip on Skat.

I raised voice as we started down stair. "Yo, Sub! Chang comin' down, wid friens! Got innifo fo' passby. Cool jets, no one diss!"

Skat snorted, shook his head. "Soon as they shiv ya, I gone," he told Fisherman wife.

Long time back, was lights unnergroun'. Anyone looked up, could still see wires from where they torn down. But today, dark as tomb. Took several breaths, knowin' Subs liked to jump out an' scare. Hoped my heart wouldn't stop when they did.

We got to bottom, peered into black. No sound.

"Yo, Sub!" My voice echoed. We all stood waiting at bottom stair, reluctant to move into dark.

With muttered curse Fisherman's friend Tenere dug in pocket, brought out battery light, switched it on. He aimed bright beam to one side. Nothin' but wall, leading to empty corridor.

Light swung other direction, in dizzy arc.

Three Sub joeys raced our way brandishin' shivs an' clubs. Arlene hissed. Lasers came up, red aim-lights flickering.

"Stop!" I jumped 'tween Uppies 'n Subs.

Lasers wavered.

Two Subs skidded to halt few feet away. Third knocked me aside as he flew past. I fell hard. Couldn' breathe.

Fisherman shouted, "No!" He shoved Rob's laser aside jus' as Uppie fired.

Scuffle sounds. Sub joey flew outa Uppie ring, bounced on hard floor. The other Subs circled, waitin' for chance to rush. "Outa Sub! No one comes unner today!"

Somehow, managed to get to my feet. "Fa Godsake, stoppit, allayas!" I panted fo' breath. "Got plenny innifo. Show 'em."

Angry Sub snarled, "Don' matta, Changman! Halber say no one! Gettem out!"

I pulled out Unibucks I got from Tenere, waved in face. "Innifo! Halber be royal pissoff if ya don' take."

He shook head. "He skin me if I let ya in."

I stamp. "Halber didn' mean *me*, stupit Subboy! I be Chang. Dincha come ta shop few days back, for carry Valdez permas?" Showin' contempt, I threw Unibucks on filthy floor. "Pick 'em up. Halber want' em all." Without waitin' for answer I waved to Uppies. "C'mon. We'll fin' Halber, straighten out."

Arlene reacted fastest; strode 'cross corridor, draggin' Skat. Others followed.

As she caught up to me I took her arm, rested some of my weight on her. Tried not to pant. My side hurt. Chest ached, leg too. Too damn ol' fo' rumb.

As if she understood, she slowed to pace I could manage.

Subboys came racin' afta. One held fistful of Unibucks. "Changman, stop. Ya get me skin fa real!"

I said with authority. "No way. Halber unnerstan'." Hoped it was true.

To Uppies, I pointed down corridor. "Main meet room there. An whatever ya do, don' turn off light." In dark, Subs the dread a N'Yawk.

Chapter 31

PHILIP

When we left Mr. Chang's shop I assumed Pook would run for safety or turn on me. If he fled, I'd make Swee show me the way to the Sub. But if Pook came at me, I doubted I could beat him off yet again. He was bigger, stronger, older. My only advantage was from Mom's lessons, and my luck was bound to run out.

Pook insisted on bringing along cans of vegetables as gifts for his associates. Mr. Chang grumbled before giving them to him, but at the last moment, when we were at the door, he added more.

Swee tagged along, very careful to keep my body between Pook and himself.

" 'Notha coupla blocks, Uppie. We go Sub Three Six steada Square. Fasta." Pook was resolutely cordial, in marked contrast to the ominous look he shot from time to time at Swee. He seemed quite keyed up, a feeling I completely shared.

For several blocks Pook chattered away, a demented transpop tour guide. I could understand only a fraction of what he said, and a persistent throb beat against my temple.

"Mid turf ends here. Waitasec, Peetee. I give innifo ta Broads." He strode off. Automatically I followed; with too much head start I'd never catch him.

Pook jabbered at a tribesman, handed him a couple of cans as a present. Swee stayed well clear of the corner, as if afraid of both Pook and his new companions.

Two of the transpops stared at me, asked Pook something incomprehensible.

"He wid me. We wan' passby both ways fo' us two." He waved a thumb at Swee. "Okay ta diss shithead Midboy on way back."

Their appraising eyes flickered from me to Swee.

Pook seemed more cheerful as we moved on, perhaps because he no longer had to lug a sack of cans. "Sub stair jus' past Mid turf," he told me. "Ya gonna need lotsa innifo. Whatcha brung?"

I shrugged. "I don't understand. It's an interesting dialect you speak. Has anyone done a dictionary? I'll suggest it to Mr. Frowles for a term project."

He stared at me as if I'd spoken gibberish.

Pook led me to an open square, with stairs to a subterranean tunnel. He paused, licked his lips. "Sure ya wanna, Uppie? Wait here fo' Jared, 'stead?"

"Is he down those stairs?"

Reluctantly, he nodded. "Halber gottim."

"Come on, then." I started down.

Pook nerved himself and rushed down the steps. At the bottom of the stairwell, he emitted a piercing whistle. "Yo! Sub!" He seemed poised to flee to safety.

I peered into the dark.

Above, Swee said uncertainly, "Don' wanna go down."

I said, "Wait outside. I'm sure you'll find joeys to talk to."

His eyes flicked back and forth among the crumbling buildings. With a whimper he ran downstairs, and stayed close to me as we groped our way onward.

"Hello?" I could see little more than shadows.

"Far enough!" A voice in the dark. Swee grabbed my hand.

"Who dere?" Pook's voice quavered.

"Raulie, Sub."

"Pook be I, what trayfo Jared Uppie ta Halber. Halber tol' me ta comealong wid."

"Why dincha, joeykit?"

"Couldn'." Pook's tone was aggrieved. "Hadda go back ta lair, and I got . . . " He groped for a word. "Anyway, we here now."

"We, Midboy?"

"My . . . frien', Peetee."

"An' me." Swee, nervous.

"Nah." Pook. "Dunno 'im. Skin 'im, okay wid us."

A squawk. "Pook!"

"Dunno 'im," Pook insisted. "Midboy, looks like. An' he ain' brung no innifo."

Abruptly, Swee let go my hand. Footsteps raced toward the stairs. A thud, a squeal of protest. "Gottim!"

"PEETEE!" Swee's voice was desperate.

"Hold it!" My voice shot into embarrassing upper registers. With an effort, I brought it down. Summoning an image of Father, I tried to sound authoritative. "Enough! Let him go."

A snicker from Raulie, who appeared to be the leader. "Who say?"

"I do. Didn't Pook tell you we're guests of Halber?"

"You what?"

Had I gotten the name wrong? "Pook, did Halber ask you to come here?"

"Ya." The transient seemed glad to follow my lead. "Tol' me hisself."

A pause. Suddenly a light flicked on.

We were in a rubbish-strewn corridor, surrounded by some half dozen colorfully dressed tribesmen. Halfway to the stairs, Swee stood, eyes scrunched shut, gripped from behind by a Sub, a knife pressed to his carotid artery.

What would Fath do?

I strode across the hall. "Put that down! Let him go, he's with me!" I prayed for Swee's sake that my voice wouldn't squeak.

Raulie nudged Pook. "Who he be?"

"My frien' Peetee. Uppie, like Jared."

I stamped my foot. "Put that knife away!"

For a moment, they considered. Raulie said, "Take Pook ta lair; Halber'll skin 'im if he boolsheet us. Bring Midboy too."

"What 'bout Uppie?"

Raulie hissed, "Dissim."

"But he—"

Raulie spat. "Frazzin' Uppies think dey own da worl'! Teach 'em ta come down in Sub an'—"

Hands clawed at my shirt. I batted them away. Swee's captor shoved him clear to focus on me; Swee stumbled, caught himself.

Three Sub joeys came at me. What now, Mom? How do I fight if I'm scared out of my wits? Another step back. I bumped into a wall.

"He mine!" A wicked knife glinted. One joey was between me and the stairs; two others circled behind.

With a sharp cry I lunged at the knife, halted my charge an

inch short of impalement, spun, and dived between the two startled transpops behind me. I rolled to my feet. Only one direction was open to me: deeper into the tunnel.

"Gettim!"

I took off, leaving the dim light behind.

"Run, Peetee!" The cry might have been Pook's.

Footsteps thudded.

The corridor widened. I careened through a fetid chamber full of shabby furniture and strewn mattresses. Transpop joeys milled about. Behind me, the footsteps neared.

I tore through the cavern, leaped over a broken chair, narrowly avoided a steaming stewpot. Behind me, angry shouts. I slapped at a grasping hand, catapulted over a couple entwined on a mat, dashed down a dim corridor at the far end of the room.

The light from the common hall faded. As the dark became more intense I let my fingers skim the wall, holding one arm in front of my face for protection.

My pursuers knew the corridors better than I; even in the dark, they gained on me.

Desperately, I increased my pace. I felt cold air. Suddenly the floor disappeared. Flailing, I fell into a hole, lost my balance. I fetched up against a cold iron rail. I wondered if I'd cracked my ribs.

Still, the voices pursued. Shadows flashed against the ceiling; my trackers had brought a light.

With a silent curse I hauled myself to my feet. I stumbled over a rail. I was on some sort of sunken railbed. Could I climb up to corridor level? No time; the tribesmen were almost upon me.

Groping in the dark, holding my aching side, I staggered along the trackway.

Calls, voices, footsteps.

"There he be!"

"Where?"

"Shadow in tunnel!"

"Don' see nothin'."

"He runnin' track."

Behind me, half a dozen pursuers jumped down to track level. Their light sent crazed shadows spinning.

I spurred myself into the dark. Behind me, voices encouraged the chase.

I ran until my chest heaved. With luck I'd outrun my pursuers.

I stumbled over a rail and lost my balance. My head crashed into something hard. I fell on my back in a blaze of light and pain that faded to black.

Was it time to get up? Mom was annoyed when I got a late start. I strained to see the bedroom clock, and failed. I was in absolute dark. Someone moaned.

Disoriented, I peered the other way, realized the moan of anguish was my own. I clutched my head; gasped with pain, let go immediately. With great care, I brought my fingers up to my scalp, probed gently over an oozing clot.

Where was I?

It took me a while to remember.

I was underground, in what they called the Sub. I stopped moaning, held my breath, terrified I'd hear my pursuers.

Nothing.

Slowly, my head throbbing, I sat up, leaned back against cold concrete.

I couldn't stay here. Not in the dark. Not with enraged tribesmen combing the tunnels.

I struggled to my feet, but a spasm of dizziness left me sagging against a cold steel pole.

I was lost in the dark beneath New York. I yearned to sink to the ground, rocking, crooning to myself. My fingers picked at my shirt. *Not here, not now.* I wrapped my arms around the pole and pretended it was Mom. I gritted my teeth. My forehead pulsed anew.

I couldn't help it. I began to cry.

When I was done I wiped my nose. What would Mom think if she heard me sniveling like a baby?

In any event I was in trouble. I had to find my way out of the tunnel before my nerves gave way, and I abandoned all rational thought.

In the process, I had to avoid the Subs. It seemed they wanted to kill me, though I'd given no provocation. Was that why they'd marched Jared belowground, to sacrifice him to their hate?

Well, Jared was on his own. I wanted nothing more than to make my way back to our Washington compound, to face Mom's wrath and Father's injured reproach.

How shameful. Hopefully, daylight would renew my courage.

The transpops weren't at my heels; I had no need to run. Gratefully, I tottered along the track, carefully feeling my way. Another blow on the head and I'd be completely undone.

I wasn't even sure which direction I was headed. I recalled reading about New York's underground railway. It evolved during the Civil War, to help escaped slaves. Or was that in another city? I was confused, and my head ached too much to sort it out. In any event, a tunnel this large would certainly have other exits; sooner or later I'd find daylight. If I found my way blocked, I had only to turn around. Eventually I'd reach my starting point.

My watch was luminous and spoke the time as well; it told me it was eight in the evening. It seemed like I'd been walking for hours, but I wasn't quite sure when I'd started.

Voices.

I tensed, poised to run even if it meant bashing my brains on a rock.

In the distance, confused calls. Shouts. A piercing scream.

I backpedaled down the track until I fetched up against a pillar. My heart thumped. My fingers tore at the snaps on my shirt.

I found myself crouched against a wall, rocking, keening, sobbing under my breath. Frantically I worked at base twelve divisions, at cube roots, at anything that would slow the racing of my thoughts.

Mr. Skeer had given me exercises to use when I revved; dutifully, I went through the lot of them. A hug from Mom would have helped, but she was hundreds of miles away, and in no mood to hug me.

On my own, I forced myself to calm, reassembly my protective shell until my pretense became real.

Again, I got to my feet, moved resolutely toward the distant voices.

Dark gave way to shadows.

A light flickered.

A voice rasped, "Turn it off, ya frazzin' asshole!" Immediately the light was extinguished, but not before I made out a corridor floor, several feet above me. "Wan' 'em ta seeyas?"

"Cool jets, Fro!"

"Parkas righ' above us, fa' Chrissake. Chaco an rest a Subs nevah came back unner!"

"Shush, the lotta yas!" Another voice, with authority.

I hoisted myself over the trackbed wall to the station level, straining to see past dim forms huddled in the tunnel. One end of the corridor was definitely lighter.

"Where's the frazzin' unnercar?"

"Be here when Halber decide. Jus' guar' the staysh."

Somehow, I forced myself forward. Anything was better than the madness of the dark tunnel.

An unseen figure stumbled into me, shoved me aside with a curse.

I groped toward the light, found myself at the foot of a stair. Above, firelight cast its dancing shadows on the stairwell walls.

"Watchit, joeykit!" Someone elbowed me aside.

My hand tightened on the rail. I would climb that staircase no matter what the cost. Not for life itself would I return to the black of the tunnel.

A hand clasped my forearm. I squealed. My captor spun me around.

A woman of the Sub tribe, her clothes a swirl of colors. "Whatchadoon here, joey? Halber said no kits near stair!"

"I—I just—" I broke free, dashed up the stairs, thrusting through a crush of joeys gathered near the exit.

I burst into cool night air. Outside, near the stair, a fire flickered. I tripped over something soft. A Sub tribesman, his throat cut from ear to ear.

Across the street, a scream of torment. I peered into the night, unable to see the danger. Nonetheless, I had to move on. I walked cautiously down the sidewalk.

A Sub sat against the ruins of a building, drenched in more blood than I'd ever seen in my life.

"Jesus God!" The ragged voice was mine.

His hands rested in his lap, atop his severed head.

I backed away, spun and vomited.

Across the street, howls and catcalls.

Desperately I fought not to rev, knowing I had to flee this spot regardless of the consequences. I bolted into the night.

To my right, buildings. Behind me were the stairs. Across the street, a chest-high wall ran the length of the road. Heavy brush lined the far side.

"Here's anotha! Gettim!" Hands loomed in the night. I swerved toward the wall. My two pursuers were dressed in rags; one brandished a rusty pole sharpened to a spear.

I reached the sidewalk, vaulted the wall into the brambles beyond. Thorns ripped at my clothes. I tore free.

After a time I stopped to take my bearings. I stared at the wall, hoping the tribesmen hadn't followed.

No one moved.

A wild howl raised the hair on my neck. It was near.

To my side, a soft voice. "Help me. Jeezgod, help . . . "

I put my hands over my ears to block the sound.

From another direction, panting breaths. "Friggin' Subs everywheah! Hit us on Fifth, bunch more at Columbcirc!"

I dropped to the ground, curled in a ball, hoping my dark clothes would shroud me in the night.

"We diss alladem what cross street. Couple ran back ta sub."

"Gonna eat their livah, come mornin'! C'mon."

The voices faded.

"Chris' it hurt . . . " A moan. "Help."

I scrambled to my feet, raced through the grass. When I was free of the voice, I slowed, looked about.

I was in a clearing surrounded by brush and scrub trees. Beyond, to the south and east, tower lights outshone the dim stars. Northward, few lights glowed.

For a long time I was still.

What should I do?

Jared was beyond my reach, at least for now. In the morning I'd find a way to get back to the Sheraton Skytel and call Mom. Meanwhile, I had to stay clear of the madness of the night. That meant finding a place of shelter. The moans I'd heard were none of my concern.

Nonetheless, my feet led me, slowly at first, then faster,

back toward the moans. When I neared the wall I stopped, listening.

Another groan. I trotted toward the sound.

Bodies, in the grass. Blood. I grimaced, looked for one that moved.

I passed a joeykid not much older than myself. Dead, beyond doubt. His left arm was gone. Beyond him two men, draped one across the other, knives still in their hands.

Another corpse, entrails falling from his stomach. Gagging, I moved past.

A hand snagged my ankle. I stifled a scream, fought not to pass out from sheer terror.

"Help me, joey. Fa' Godsake." The corpse.

I licked my lips, crouched by his side. "What should I do, sir? You're badly hurt."

A snicker, that ended in a gasp of agony. "Chris', don' I know it?"

"Is there a hospital near?"

"Oh God, you ain' Sub!" His hands scrabbled at the grass, as if to drag himself away. "Don' hurt me worse, joey!"

"I won't. I came to help. What can I do?"

"Whassa use? Chaco gonna die anyhow. Take along buncha Parkas, maybe. Gotta tell Halber they gatherin' Hunner' Ten wall."

"I'm afraid I don't understand."

"You sound like—" A spasm hit him. His hand groped for mine. "—like Uppie, fa Godsake."

No use explaining the difference. "I am, sir." I looked around. "Is there anyone who can help you?"

"Not no more." A long pause. "Alla Subs I brung out be dead. Halber gotta sen' reinforce. Gahh, it hurts . . . " He squeezed my wrist with desperate strength.

I swallowed.

"You really Uppie?" He panted, before he could say more. "Watchadoon in Park?"

"I'm . . . not sure." I groped for a simple explanation. "I came to see Halber."

"Alla nigh's, ya pick dis one . . . " His grip relaxed. I thought he was dead. Then, under his breath, "See Halber, hah? Tell him fo' me 'bout Parkas."

The soft pat of running feet, in grass. Instinctively, I leaned over the fallen Sub. When the sound faded, I came away with blood on my tunic.

"I can't tell him, sir. I—"

"Gotta! Chaco ain' gonna."

"Sir—Chaco—I'm not part of your war. Maybe I could get your friends to—"

A cough, that ended in a wail. "Ohgod ohgod ohgod . . ."

"Oh, please, don't die!"

His breathing slackened. A long pause. "Bettah hurry, Uppie. Tell Halber. I can't."

"They'll kill me if—I mustn't—what do you want me to say?"

"Tellim . . . Chaco scouted Park . . . like he say." The voice grew weaker. "Mosta Parkas . . . live roun' ol' lake bed."

Silence.

"Is that it, sir?"

Nothing.

"Sir? Chaco?"

"Cold." A sigh, that might have been a sob. "Chris'! It mean I'm goin'."

I could think of nothing to say.

"Lissen, Uppie . . . Halber in Sub, unnerstan'? . . . Tellim when . . . Sub attack at Five Nine . . . *ahrr!*" He convulsed, panting. Sweat beaded his brow, and his voice came with desperate hurry. "We only got a few a 'em. Mosta Parkas run ta trees at nor'side. I heard 'em talkin' rumb at Seven Nine Sub, early morn."

"Chaco, your speech—I can't understa—"

"Tellim my words like I say, joey! Rememba 'em; Halber'll understan' what he hear. Parkas bunchin' at Hunnert Ten wall! Hunnert Ten wall. Hunnerten ohgod I can't . . . Hunnert . . . *Chris' God in heaven!*"

It was a plea, unanswered in the dark of the night.

I lifted Chaco's blood-caked hand, nuzzled it with my cheek. For a reason I couldn't understand, I kissed his fingers, dampening them with tears. "I'll tell him."

"Uppie, 'fore you go . . ."

I made my voice steady. "Yes, Chaco?"

"Can' . . . leave me here like this . . . Parkas fin' me, cut out my livah while I watch."

"I'm not strong enough to drag—"

"Do me, Uppie."

Appalled, I opened and closed my mouth. No words would come.

"Gotta finish me."

"No!"

"See what . . . Parkas done ta othas? Mercy a God, Uppie. I beggin' ya."

"I'll climb over the wall, run to the stairs, and bring your friends. They'll carry . . . "

"In rumbtime no Sub leave lair 'xcept ta figh'. Gotta do it yaself."

"I can't. Not for anything."

"Lissen, joeykit . . . hurts godawful . . . All I c'n do not ta scream . . . My guts rolled in dirt; I diss fa sure. Ya gotta help me 'long."

My voice caught. "It's a sin! Please, don't—"

"Always I hate frazzin' Uppies . . . 'cause think ya own da worl' . . . well . . . joey . . . tha's what come wid it. Respons . . . " He panted. "Responsa . . . bily. Ya wouldn' even leave a dog ta die wid guts hangin' out. End it, fa Chrissake!"

I lurched to my feet, staggered away. Lord God, help me. Stop me from doing what he asked.

I walked off.

"*Don' leave, Uppie!*" Terror.

It's remarkable, objectively speaking, what one can accomplish if one closes off a compartment of one's mind.

One can stand, and stretch in the sultry evening breeze to flex the aching muscles of one's back.

One can close his ears to the ebbing pleas of a gutted tribesman, while searching aimlessly for a rock or stick.

One can find a thick broken branch that would accomplish the unspeakable, and saunter back to a bloodstained stretch of grass.

One can stoop to kiss a sweaty forehead, hear impassively a final plea. "Rememba my . . . face . . . Uppie . . . an' carry Chaco inside . . . ."

One can raise a branch over one's head, bring it downward with all one's strength in a whistling arc that ends at the terrified eyes, and squeeze the shoulder while the blood of the shattered skull seeps under the soles of one's brown leather boots.

One can amble away without a care in the world, push through the thorns, slip over a cold stone wall.

One can stroll across the firelit street as if unafraid of anything on Lord God's earth, to stand over the dark recess of the Sub.

"I have—" My voice wasn't quite right; I tried again. "My name is Philip Tyre Seafort. I have a message for Mr. Halber." My voice echoed from the crumbling brick of the darkened edifices above.

Behind me, muffled sounds. I turned. A shaggy head peered over the park wall. I turned back. "Do you hear me?"

From the stairs, a growl. "Sho', Parka. Jus' come on down."

A hiss. "Shh. Don' talk ta him!"

"I'm not a Parka. I need to see Halber."

I glanced over my shoulder, watched a Parka leap over the wall. "I'm coming down."

"Dissya if ya do."

"All right." It didn't matter. I hoped they'd let me deliver my message first. Chaco would want that.

Behind me, running footsteps. I paused at the top step. Below, dim faces glowed in the reflected light. Gripping the rail, I started down.

A cry of rage. Behind me, a figure loomed. He thrust a pike down the steps. An instant before it impaled me I was snatched aside, slammed into the stairwell wall to tumble unnoticed to the landing.

Half a dozen wild-haired Parkas threw themselves into the chasm, knives and clubs flailing.

A frenzied melee. Someone trod on my arm. My cry was lost in the roar of a mass of Subs charging upstairs in a mad counterattack.

The battle grew desperate. The stairs grew slippery with blood, most of it from the attacking Parkas.

In a few moments silence reigned anew, except for the gasping breaths of the defenders.

Someone hauled me to my feet. "Tribe, joey?"

"My name's—"

A cuff, that rattled my teeth. "Tribe?"

"—Philip. I'm an Uppie, from Washington."

"Dissim!"

Blood dripped into my eyes from my reopened gash. I made no move to wipe it, or to free myself. After Chaco, I knew there was worse than death. "Do it, then. But I have a message for Halber."

"Boolsheet!"

"From Chaco."

"Where he be?"

"Dead."

"Parkas dissim?"

I took a deep breath. "I did."

Someone seized my chin, hauled it back, catching my head against his chest. A knife glinted. Its sharp edge nicked the skin of my throat. I closed my eyes.

"STOP!"

A frozen moment, in which the only movement was the slamming of my heart.

"Let joeykit tell Halber what he wan'. Dissim afta."

"Halber ain'—"

"Be here in a min. Lissen!"

From under the earth, a screeching rumble that increased in strength. After a moment, it came to a stop. Chattering, exuberant voices came near.

"See? Halber brung help."

"He royal pissoff if he see ya let Uppie come unner."

"Don' matta. Gonna dissim inna min."

In seconds we were surrounded by jabbering tribesmen dressed in lurid, discordant colors.

A hand seized the nape of my neck and guided me firmly through the throng. We strode down a dark corridor, down another set of stairs.

Light. The hum of a motor.

I saw the sunken track I'd stumbled along in the dark. Now it was lit by a humming car nearly the size of a Hitrans train, waiting with open doors. Transpop joeys milled about a burly figure. He moved slowly through the throng, issuing directions, pointing from time to time down the track.

My captor propelled me forward, threw me at the man's feet. "Gotcha a frazzin' Uppie."

"In Sub?" The joey's voice held disbelief.

"Came down stair like he own it. I want 'im, afta, fo' skin. He diss Chaco."

From deep in the leader's chest, a growl.

"Said he hadda talk ta ya firs'."

"Pickim up." Someone hauled me to my feet. "Allri', joeykit. Watcha wan'?"

I said shakily, "I have a message for Mr. Halber."

"Halber be I, Boss Sub."

I shook myself free from my captor, planted myself before him as if reporting some misdeed to Fath in his study. "I met one of your joeys, outside. He was wounded, and wanted help."

"So ya dissim!" The Sub who'd hauled me down the steps.

"That was after. Chaco made me promise to tell you the Parkas—"

"Why din' he—"

Halber stirred. "Shut face, Krall!" To me, "G'wan."

"I was in the park when Chaco grabbed me. His stomach was . . . " I swallowed. "He couldn't move. I could barely understand him. He said to repeat his sounds, and you'd know what he meant. The Parkas who lived around the old lake moved to nor'side when you attacked. They're gathered someplace that . . . " I wrinkled my brow. "At Hunnert Ten wall. That's what he kept saying."

Halber frowned. "Were movin' to ColumbCirc, last dayligh'."

"Yes, sir. Hunner' Ten wall is where they are now. Massing for a big rumb at Seven Nine Sub."

Halber's eyes were like twin lasers. "Tell me all, 'gain."

I did.

"An' about dissin' Chaco."

I licked my lips. As the words poured out, a fragment of my mind marveled at my dispassionate tone, my clarity of speech, the remorse I neither showed nor felt.

Chapter 32

JARED

The boy Krand curled up against the wall throwing pebbles.

I slumped on the chilled bench of the understation, nursing my throbbing cheek.

I tried to blink, but one eye was swelled shut by the force of Halber's blow. I whimpered. Allie shot me a sympathetic look. Only she, of all the trannies, understood I couldn't make out Halber's jabber, and had persuaded him to slow his speech.

Everyone hated me, even Dad. He'd all but turned me in to the jerries by putting an alert on his Terrex; if he'd cared a whit for my survival, he'd have let me use his card until I got on my feet.

It was how the world always treated me. In school the teachers paid me no mind, shoving their assignments under my nose as if that was all that mattered. Holoworld had tricked me. Even the skytel had betrayed my trust: I was a guest, not some filthy trannie to be chased into the street. Old Man Seafort despised me, and that hurt even though I knew he was only a pompous old has-been. Hell, even P.T. looked down on me, though I ran rings around him with my puter nets.

Now I was robbed of clothes, lost deep in trannie tunnels.

The greatest adventure of my life had turned to shit.

As to Pook . . . my lip curled. To him I wasn't even human, just booty whose clothes were to be parceled out to the highest bidder. His 'capture,' he called me. He'd sliced my chest, fed me dog food from a can. True, he'd made a pillow out of his lap, calmed me in the elevator with a desperately needed touch.

But just as I was getting used to his ways, he'd given me to Halber and his vicious Subs, with their mad idea of bringing down the towers.

Who did Halber think I was, a Hacker? For a hundred years, since they'd wiped the accounts at U.N. Revenue, Hackers had been despised and hunted.

Because they'd had the right idea. Bring it all down.

The social order Dad and the Old Man supported was beyond contempt. In the Old Man's very guest room, Uncle Robbie and his precious father plotted their political schemes. They would sacrifice the Old Man in a minute if he stood in their way.

Halber was right; let the U.N. die in revolution and fire; if the process destroyed him and his trannie scum, so much the better.

I wondered how much trouble I could make, if I really tried. Alone, not all that much, but the trick was in having the right e-friends. If they could do half what they bragged . . .

When the Unies caught me, it would be the prison ship at Callisto, or a penal colony.

Not that I cared.

With no more than a dumbterminal I'd cracked Dad's Terrex account. If the trannies could access the nets, I'd have access to Rolf's password breaker and Fiona's ID simulator. I'd met them on separate slopes, and neither knew about the other. I'd seen instantly how powerful they'd be together, but kept the information to myself.

In tandem, we could wreak havoc on Terrex Ltd.

But the trannies couldn't find me a ski lift. They barely knew what a puter was. Besides, they wanted more than a few days annoyance for Terrex. Bring down the towers, Halber said.

Now that would be something.

If I could crack a tower access . . .

Arno lived in a tower; in fact his father was a member of its owning syndicate. He'd shown me the puter rooms. In the towers, *everything* was on-line. Power, water consumption, locks, financial accounts . . .

I wondered what kind of power surge it would take to blow the generators.

Could it be done?

And did I want to?

I must have dozed. When I woke, Allie was swinging her feet restlessly, and I felt oddly alive, as if in my mind some switch had clicked open.

"Allie."

"Hah." She yawned.

"Find Halber."

She snickered. "Halber callya when *he* ready, Uppie."

"I can do what he wants. Bring it all down."

She appraised me, her look curious. "Cool. But gotta wait 'til Parka rumb finish."

I searched my new vocabulary. Pook had spoken of a rumb, a fight. Why was Halber picking a fight now, and what were Parkas?

"Your rumb doesn't matter," I told her, but she wouldn't see the point.

I tried to contain my frustration. Whatever his motive, Halber had offered me a chance to *count*, to make a difference. If I succeeded, I'd be famous forever.

I paced the station, hardly aware of the cold concrete under my bare feet. Allie was a just dumb trannie bitch, and Krand was half asleep. I wondered if I could slip out and find Halber on my own.

Not without shoes.

I padded over to Krand. "Where am I supposed to piss?"

He yawned. "Roun' corna."

Obediently, I went. As I assumed, he followed to keep an eye on me. I fumbled with my pants, stepped back. Suddenly I whirled and swung with all my might. I caught him in the throat.

His eyes bulged; his mouth flew open but no sound came. He clawed at his neck. His face grew red, then purple.

I eased him back, slammed his head against the wall. Something gave, and he slid to the ground.

Frazzin' trannies. That'll teach them to treat me like dirt. I slipped his sandals onto my feet. A far cry from my boots, but they'd do.

Now, to find Halber.

Chapter 33

POOK

Ain' my faul' Subs decide ta diss Peetee. In tunnel, when Uppiekit run fo' his life, I stay real still, skin pricklin', 'til cries of hunt fade distant. Nobody lef' 'xcept me, Swee, an Sub Raulie.

"C'mon, Pookboy. Halber bettah be 'xpectin' ya." Raulie shove me through long tunnel to distant staysh.

Ordinary, I bristle an' go proud. But we be in dark Sub place, an' today everyone's nerves be spook. Even walkin' ta Sub stair, somethin' wrong wid way Mids an' Broads trayfo passby, like they heart ain' in it. Like lissenin'. Make me chill.

So I go quiet, an' don' even care when Swee stay real close. Latah be time ta settle us. Now, we two Midboys togetha in dark.

"Where dey takin' us, Pook?"

I go scorny. "Ta Halber, stupe." Or maybe ta quiet corna, ta cut new mouth 'cross neck. I try not ta think 'bout.

Subboy lead us offa track ta open staysh. Big place, wid lotsa ligh'. Immediate, I feel reassure.

Long time pass while we wait. Prolly nigh' by now, but can' tell, unnergroun'.

Afta hearin' Changman talk, I ain' too surprise when grumblin' inna tunnel grow loud like ta shake down walls. Figga, gotta be unnercar like allatime dey whispa 'bout.

Swee look fo' place ta run. So of course I go proud. I stan' roun' nonchalant, like unnercar hissin' along track be most ornary thing in worl'.

Wid shudder, car stop. Subs pour out. Halber catch my eye. "Wonnered if ya'd comealong."

I go red. "Prollem. Okay now." I look pas' him. "Where my Jared Uppie?"

"Took m uppa wes'side, fo' safe. Got coupla joeykits watchin'."

I nod, like we be two growed Mids talkin' biz.

"Whomped him some, 'til he 'greed ta help."

I go indignan'; Jared mine ta whomp. 'Sides, afta help him sleep in elevate, I don' wanna whomp him much as I use ta. But I don' let thought show on face.

As Swee watch us talk, his eyes grow roun'. 'Bout time he realize Pook ain' one ta fuckroun' wid. Too late fo' him, though, 'less I decide go easy.

"Well?"

I yank mind back to what Halber jus' say. Somethin' 'bout Jared need lotsa persuade, an' keep eye on.

"No prollem," I say. "Jared Washinton Uppie don' give no trouble ta Pook."

Halber grimace, like Changman when tea too hot. "Joeykit say he need nets. Even when I whomp him, kep' repeatin' it." He fix me wid warnin' eye. "Ya tol' me he do anythin' wid' puters."

"Course," I say positive, tryin' hard ta believe.

"Din' say nothin 'bout no nets. Whassit mean?"

"Special kinda puter," I guess. "Don' rev jets, Halber. When I haddim inna elevate, all Jared do is complain. Don' mean nothin'. When ya wan' him ta start?"

" 'Morra, day afta, maybe. Gotta finish settle wid Parkas."

I say, casual, "Lemme talk ta him tonigh'."

"'Kay. But now I busy wid unnercar." He point ta Swee. "Who ya brung?"

I 'ready ta tell 'im Swee be nobody, allri' ta dissim, but realize I look real stupe ta bring Midboy unner, who I don' even know. "Frien'," I say, reluctant. "Help me wid Jared Uppie." I ignore Swee's grateful look.

"Raulie'll take ya ta wait fa unnercar. You kits stay outa way 'til afta rumb." He tell joey where we spose ta go, an' stalk off.

We walk long way in dark tunnel, wid nothin' but Valdez perma fo' light. Afta while shadows make me dizzy. Finally, we come out inta 'notha' staysh. Sub guides tell us sit onna bench 'til one a' unnercars free ta take us. An' we betta shaddup, cause Subs sleepin' alla roun' us.

Swee twis' roun'. "Where dey got us?"

I shrug. "Safe place. Dunno."

"Why special place, Pook? Ain' whole Sub safe? Who go down inna Sub ta rumb?"

I glower in dim ligh'. "Who ask you ta comealong? Think I don' 'member who bonk me on head wid board, in Pook lair?"

He blush. "I hadda, Pook. Peetee made me."

"Ri', some Uppie joeykit scare ya enough ta bash frien'. Think I so stupe . . . " My voice fadeout, 'cause I remember how yestaday Peetee whomp me on roof, an' do it 'gain today outside elevate. Still dunno how it happen. But when his eyes go fury, I wanna promise anythin' ta make it stop.

"Ya shouldn'a took him ta lair." I make my voice accuse.

"I hadda," Swee say again. Inside, I believe. But I still try ta look pissoff.

Few min later, unnercar come 'long wid usual screech. I relieve ta see Halber ain't on it. Don' wan questions 'bout Jared 'til I kick sense in him. Uppie gotta realize Halber ain' one ta fool wid; could get diss.

Fac' is, Pookboy feelin' bit nervous hisself. Maybe promise Halber bit too quick 'bout Jared an' puters. Dunno what Uppie means 'bout nets; one time Karlo use net on toppa roof ta catch birds fo' stewpot, but can't figga how Jared use one in puter.

"Comin', Midboy?" Sub driver only one in unnercar.

I go proud, jump in car like 'luminum beast in scary tunnel is mos' natural thing in worl'. "C'mon, Swee," I say, scorny. "Won' hurt ya."

Couple min later, unnercar screech ta stop. Staysh got Valdez light hangin' from roof. "G'wan," driver say. "Out."

I ask, "Where be Jared?"

"Sittin' wid Allie 'n Krand."

"Dey comin' wid us?"

"Naw. Ya wait wid em, 'til Halber say."

Gettin' use ta Sub, little bit, but don' like way dey ride us roun' one staysh ta 'notha, so Pook got no idea where he be if wanna go outside.

I get out, Swee stayin' close like usual. Make me laugh; first' Midboy 'fraid I diss 'im, den he 'fraid ta leave me.

Unnercar rush off wid screech. I look roun'.

No Allie.

"Yo! Jared!" My voice echo louder 'n I 'xpect, an' Swee flinch. "Allie!"

Nothin'. Then, cautious, head peer roun' corna, see her, duck back.

Time fo' fun. I wait a sec, shout "AARRGGHH!"

Allie shriek.

I duck roun corna, grinnin'.

Subgirl ain' laughin'. Her eyes frantic. "Halber be wid ya?"

"Nah."

"Crise onna crutch!" Her han's clutch at jumpsuit, twistin' an' scrabblin'. "Ohgod ohgod!"

I snicka; she sound like Jared wailin' inna elevate. "Whassamatta, seen a ghos'?"

Her lip curl like cry, but 'stead, she leap at me, claw my face good 'fore I grab han'. "Don' fun me, Midboy asshole! I gonna get diss, soon as Halber see!"

Should knock out her frazzin' teeth fo' claw me, but she so scare I go pity. "Why?"

"Jared gone!"

I go cold, can' breathe. "Jesus, whatcha done?"

"Look!" She pull me roun' corna. "He diss Krand!"

Subboy lay on flo', head all bus'.

Swee say, "Jeez, he ack like Peetee!" Tug at my sleeve. "See, Pook? Dat's why I hadda tell."

My mad come out all at once. I whomp Swee ova an' ova 'til he hunch down cryin'. "Shut frazzin' face 'til I tell ya!"

Allie pull at my arm. "What'll I do, Pook? Halber diss me fa sure when he fin' out!"

I growl, "I be one gonna diss ya, stupid bitchgirl!" 'Cause alla sudden I realize, not only I lose what Halber promise me in trayfo, but lucky if Sub Boss don' start blood rumb 'til he venge on me. "Stop bawlin! Where he go?"

"Krand took him here ta piss."

"Jared run upstair ta outside?"

"Nah, I was 'tween him an' stair. Couldn't."

"Fo' sure?"

She flare, "Tolya, I sittin' 'tween! He musta run in tunnel. Took Krand's shoes."

I rub scratches on face, thinkin' furious. "Which way?"

"How I know, Pook? Din' see him."

"Obvious, he tryin' ta escape. Which way closest?"

She go calm unner my questions. Feels good, be in charge. Swee quiet an' respec'ful. Allie look ta Pook like he growed.

Now all we gotta do is fin' Jared.

She say, "Next staysh eight block north. Got stair up, but—"

"Les' go, den!"

"I don't think he tryin' ta escape, Pook!" Dat got my full 'tention. "He wanted me call Halber, like Halb come runnin' when joeykit call."

"Why?"

"Said he could do what Halb want wid puter. Hadda tell Halb rightaway."

Made no sense. "Fo' dat, he diss Krand? What he think Halber do when he fin' out?"

"He gotta be glitch, Pook."

I sigh. "Don' matta. We still gotta fin' him. Okay, which way he go ta look fo' Halber?"

She say tentative, "Unnercar brung him from south."

Guess right, Pook, cause else ya get shiv stuck in ya.

"South. Hurry."

"Neva catch him in dark," Allie say. "Pull down light an' take. Halber already pissoff as he can get."

We all three dash down tunnel, light swayin' wild, throwin' shadows every way.

I pant, "Jared got light?"

"Naw."

Good. Mean he go slower.

We don' go fas', 'cause we gotta look in every alcove, case Jared hidin'. But all of us realize how 'portant it is ta catch 'im, and by spreadin' out we cover ground.

I ask Allie, "What if unnercar come? Smash us flat?"

She go scorny. "We see lights an' hear far away. Get off track is all."

Make me feel stupe, and I go red. Too dark for her ta see, so I don' gotta whomp her for respec'.

But already I plannin' how I gonna stomp Uppie. Ol' Jared Washinton gonna see lights, even in dark. Spit a few teeth 'fore I done. Yes, Pook, he gonna whimpa. I do watcha say.

If I don' fin' him, I head for stair and run nor'. Take my chances in Harl turf 'fore I face Halber widout my Jared.

Ahead, tunnel wall get wider.

Allie pant, "Staysh."

"Stair ta outside?"

"Yeah, but Subs guard it good, cause a Parka rumb."

"What dey think, see us runnin' through?"

She shrug. "Whassit matta? I diss widout Jared." Den, "Turn off permalight."

We run through staysh, stayin' low in tunnel.

No Subs down unner. We safe.

I glad when safe to turn light on 'gain. Not *sure* somethin' mean lickin' its lips in dark, breathin' down Pookboy's neck, but not sure it ain't, neitha.

Swee grab my arm tigh', and I squawk. "Don' *do* dat!"

"Saw somethin move." He point ahead.

I swallow, not sure I wanna know. "What it be?"

"Joey. Maybe Jared."

I go relieve. "Gettim!"

Chapter 34

ROBERT

The Sub cavern stank of smoke and bodies and Lord God knew what else. Chang, the old trannie, sat unmoving in a rickety chair they'd provided. Behind him, the Captain waited against the grimy wall, arms folded. Adam and Arlene stood together, as if for mutual protection. From time to time I glanced at Arlene. Her mouth was set in a grim line.

Halber, the tribal leader, hadn't yet made an appearance. Our chamber looked to be a gathering place, but was virtually deserted except for the nervous trannie who'd followed Chang here, and who remained with us, half guide, half guard. I waited with mounting impatience. We had little enough time to find Philip before the Unies began sweeping the streets.

I caught my breath. Did the Captain know they were coming? Arlene had taken him aside and spoken privately when he'd swooped down on us in his heli. But would he wait with such stolid patience, if he realized war was about to erupt?

Someone should tell him, if Arlene hadn't. I considered it, but put aside the thought. An hour ago, the Captain's temper had ignited when he learned I'd helped Arlene wander the streets. He'd rebuked me as I hadn't been since I was a cadet, and I didn't care to undergo the experience again. Uneasily, I wondered if Arlene would take responsibility for calling in the Unies, or tell him of my prompting. It was I, after all, who'd had the connections to contact the SecGen.

No, better I said nothing. An inner voice chided my cowardice. I sighed; I'd been too long a politician, far removed from the ideals of Nick Seafort's beloved Navy. I was out of my element.

Unies aside, it was pointless to wait in this fetid cave hoping to bargain with a savage, if indeed he ever appeared. Philip was nowhere to be seen; if he'd ventured underground, he was long gone, or dead.

I said tentatively, "Arlene?"

"I know." She turned to her husband. "Nick, why wait?"

Unexpectedly, it was Chang who answered. "Without they cooperate, ya won't find joeykit."

"We can search on our—"

"Won't fin' nothin' they don' let ya fin'." Chang spoke softly. "This their turf. Go in with force, you'll have to kill 'em by dozens. That what you want?"

"I want my son," she said.

"Our son." The Captain cleared his throat. "Mr. Chang's right, hon."

Despite myself I said, "Perhaps we should go home to the hotel, and try again later." I risked a glance at my watch. "It's already dark."

Adam said, "Jared's been gone for days, and this is as close as we've gotten to either boy."

"All right." Almost, I added, "sir."

By the time fifteen minutes dragged past, I could barely contain my impatience. What if our heli was damaged? What if the Unie troops didn't recognize us as civilized folk? What—

At the far end of the hall, a commotion. Subs poured into the tunnel, carrying injured comrades.

"Set 'im down gentle, Kass!"

"Don' make no diff, he be dead inna min."

"Bring in othas. Look wha frazzin Parkas done ta—"

"GODINHEAVEN, LOOK! UPPIES!"

In an instant, all eyes were upon us.

"Cool, joeys." Our guide's tone was cautious. "Changman brung 'em. Waitin' ta see Halber."

"Inna Sub? Raulie, ya let Uppies *inna Sub*?"

"Hadda, or dissem. Dey wouldn' stop. An' dey got stunners an' lasers."

An iron bar whistled across the room, clanged against the wall inches from the Captain's head. "Get 'em!"

Arlene snapped, "Nick, stay down. Adam, in front with me. Aim to kill, but don't fire until—"

In response, the Subs spread to all sides. Clubs appeared, and knives, and spears. Word spread to the end of the tunnel, where ever more tribesmen crowded in.

The one called Kass growled. "Get outa Sub!" His eyes blazed. "Ain' fo' Uppies!"

Chang said, "We here to see Halber."

"Shaddup, ol' man! No one lissen afta ya bring Uppies unner."

Raulie glanced between us, as if to placate both sides. "Subs rumb wid Parkas. Bad day. Winnin', finally, but lotsa hurt."

Arlene's voice was flint. "Damn your hurt. I want my son."

A spear flew. Adam ducked, stumbled on a mattress, fell with a crash.

"Gettem!" The mob surged.

"NO!" Shouldering us aside, the Captain strode through our ranks. "Subs, looka me."

"Nick, get back!" Arlene's cry was urgent.

"We won't do murder here." He turned back to the Subs, set hands on hips. "I be Fisherman Cap'n. Come unnergroun' wayback ta see Alwyn. Frien's we was, willbe."

A Sub turned to Raulie. "Who Alwyn?"

"Boss Sub, long time back. 'Fore Halber, 'fore Josip even." Raulie spat. "Fisherman jus' a scaretale fo' joeykits."

"Naw." The Captain stepped forward. "Looka my face. I the one. Come back now ta see Halber. Where he be?"

His accent sounded amazingly like theirs; I wondered where he'd learned the dialect. Then I remembered his trans-pop wife.

"Dissim?" Raulie's voice sounded unsure.

"Nah, Halber decide, like wid Uppiekit."

The Captain jerked as if galvanized. "Uppiekit? Was he small, about this size?" In his excitement, the Captain forgot to speak their jargon. "Light brown hair?"

"Ain'chur bidness, Uppie." Murmurs of agreement.

The Captain looked around. "Was it in this room? Yes." He pointed to a post. "Alwyn stood dere, shiv in hand. Behin', Subs was holdin' Eddieboss 'gainst wall. Gonna diss me, cause I come down unner. Sub law, den." He drew a hand through his wavy hair.

"Alwyn held shiv like dis, han' unner." He demonstrated. "Circle roun' me. 'I call ya out,' I tellim. 'Rumb fo' boss, by Sub law.'"

An old woman's shrill cackle broke the silence. "An' Alwyn say, 'A Cap'n talk trannie?' He couldn' believe. He ask Fisherman, 'Ya win, ya stay Sub?'"

The Captain's voice was a whisper. "Long as I wan'. Same as you."

The wrinkled old crone nodded. "It be him, joeys."

Raulie asked cautiously, "One Alwyn chased outa Sub?"

"Naw." The old woman shook her head vigorously. "Alwyn made that up, long afta when Josip think 'bout callin' him out. Alwyn din' chase. Stopped rumb, helped Fisherman fin' his girl."

Raulie snorted his contempt. "Helped an Uppie?"

"Took me crosstown ta Easters," the Captain said.

"Noway."

"In unnercar. All lit up wid—"

"WHO TOL' FRAZZIN' UPPIE 'BOUT UNNERCAR?"

The room was electric with tension. I gripped my laser.

"I rode it," the Captain said patiently. Calmly, he walked up to Raulie. "I joinup wid Subs wayback. Be Sub now too." He pulled open his jacket. "Gon' diss a Sub? G'wan, den. Do it."

Arlene bristled. "Nick . . . "

"Do it!" After a tense moment the Captain pried the knife from Raulie's nerveless hand.

My finger relaxed on the trigger. It was as if a ghost had risen.

"Where is Halber?"

Adam glanced at me, and at Arlene.

The apparition in the Sub cavern was the Nicholas Seafort of old, the Captain who would not be denied. Gone was his mild mien, the apology in his bearing that bespoke his years of anguish.

"Halber be here."

"All right, then. Where's Halber?"

At the deep rumble, the mass of Subs began to part, like a wave in slow motion.

Bearded, stocky, muscles bulging from within the multicolored tatters of his clothes, Halber thrust his way through the hushed crowd.

They halted face-to-face.

"Fisherman be I. Capt—"

"I know. Been lissenin'." Halber's mouth flickered with distaste. "What you wan'?"

"Two boys—joeykits—went underground. One is Jared Tenere, this man's son. The other, Philip, is mine."

Halber said nothing.

"Take me to them."

Halber regarded him a moment. "No." He turned to a Sub. "Loadup unnercar at Seven Nine wes', bring joeys ta Hunnert Ten stair. Come back here fo' more. Fas'!"

The trannie bolted from the room.

"Halber—"

"Dis *my* turf!" The Sub Boss's muscles rippled. "Who ask ya bust inta rumb? Busy. Talk afta." His eyes fastened on Pedro Chang. "Wasn't righ', Neut, bring Uppies unner."

Chang's voice was brittle. "Hadda."

"Can't trus' no more."

"Maybe not me. But him."

"Got no time fo' fooltalk, ol' man. Whatcha sayin'?"

Chang tottered to his feet. "Fo'get ya frazzin' Parkas, I brung the *Fisherman*! Pipes go muddy: tellim 'bout it! Alla tribes restless fa pushout: tellim! Trannie life collapsin': TEL-LIM fa Chrissake! I brung only Uppie in worl' who lissen!" He panted. I slipped behind him, eased his chair forward.

Halber's face was cold. "No time."

The Captain snapped, *"Make* time."

Chang said, "Halber, ya gotta lissen!"

With a roar, the Sub Boss snatched a chair, swung it over his head, smashed it down on the grimy concrete. He grabbed the splintered remains, flung them past his tribesmen to the far wall. "Gonna call out Halber, ol' man? You want run Sub?"

Arlene's eyes darted to mine. Slowly, she raised the tip of her stunner.

But Halber's storm passed as quickly as it had arisen. He jabbed the Captain's chest. "Alrigh', Fisherman. Trayfo."

"I've got coin, I can get cansa. Or Valdez permas—"

Halber spun to Adam Tenere. "Jared Washinton Uppie. Wanna see 'im?"

"Yes." Adam's voice was hoarse.

He leered at Arlene. "An' ya wan' Peetee?"

"Where is he?"

"Where ya won' find. We trayfo. Subs c'n take Parkas. We gottem corner at Hunnert Ten wall. Dey stay in Park no matta what; outside wouldn' survive a min. So we c'n take 'em 'ventual. But too many Subs already diss. You got lasers, stunners. Help us wid Parkas, an' I take ya ta joeykits."

"No!"

Halber breathed hard, staring through the Captain. After a moment his voice was quieter. "Fisherman, Parkas be trash. Even eat they dead, sometimes. Can't walk in street near wall widout fear Parkas grab 'em."

"I won't kill for you."

"Dey no better 'n Crypsnbloods. Ask Chang!"

The old man's voice was subdued. "He right in that, Fisherman. Parkas be outcasts, prey on trannies. Can' talk wid 'em, can' trayfo. Even Neut ain' safe."

Nick Seafort's fists knotted, and he cried, "What do you want of me?" Whether his plea was to Halber or Lord God, I wasn't sure.

Halber licked his lips. On one hand he faced a war, on the other, an Uppie invasion of his tunnels. And his former ally Chang had brought us underground . . . For a moment I saw the loneliness of the power I myself sought.

Halber's face raised. "Be Sub, ya tol' us wayback." For a moment he smiled, and his eyes were cruel. "Fisherman, I call ya inta tribe. Our Sub dyin' at han's of Parkas. You c'n save. Watcha do, Sub? Ignore, or help?"

"Don't ask it!"

"I ask."

For a moment the cavern was still as a grave.

Nick Seafort sagged in defeat. "All right."

Halber waited.

The Captain turned to us, his stream of orders as natural as if he were on his cherished bridge. "We have two pistols, two stunners. Arlene, Adam, Robbie, one for each of us. We'll do what's necessary, no more. Halber, take us north to a Hundred Ten in your subcar; it's faster than anything but our heli. Mr. Chang, you'll wait here. Halber, Chang is ill. Detail two of your men to help. See he has water, and anything else he needs."

"Alrigh'."

Seafort's voice sharpened. "They're his helpers, not guards. Mr. Chang is free to go where he wants."

Raulie took in a hissing breath, but Halber merely nodded. "You heard 'im."

"One last thing." The Captain faced his wife. "If I don't survive, see that Halber takes you to P.T. If he refuses, kill him and search on your own."

An hour later, we lurched down a dark tunnel in a rusting yellow-lit car, surrounded by an uneasy throng of unwashed trannies gripping homemade weapons of every description.

Arlene's mouth was set in a grim line. When I made to speak to her, she merely shook her head. Adam seemed dull and drained. I myself wanted nothing more than to be rid of our new allies. The Captain might cherish the ludicrous pretense he was a trannie Sub, but not I. Lord knew how I'd let myself be drawn into such folly; if Dad heard, he'd be outraged that I would risk our future. Would the headlines read, "Assemblyman Boland Risks All For SecGen's Son," or "Boland Joins Trannie War In Senseless Quest"? Or, even, "Boland Killed In Trannie Fray"?

I owed Adam much. But Dad's forthcoming campaign was the culmination of his dreams, and my own. I'd maneuvered SecGen Kahn into clearing the streets, which could only rebound to our interest; he would suffer whatever backlash ensued, while the trannie hovels would be cleared for new tower construction.

The subway lurched; I grabbed a bar. Time later for the political repercussions. My goal was to stay alive, and of course find P.T. and Jared. I had no doubt Arlene would kill Halber without hesitation if he failed to honor his promise. I brushed the barrel of my laser. Three recharge packs would surely be enough. I had only to keep my head.

I staggered, as an inexperienced driver applied the brakes. Steel shrieked against steel. I marveled that trannies as ignorant as the Subs managed to restart cars in the abandoned tunnels, without a power grid.

In moments we found ourselves in a filth-strewn station.

"Hunnert Ten," Raulie told us. "End of Park."

"Halber, where are your joeys?" The Captain.

"Got some outside wall, case Parkas try goaround. Don' think dey will. Otha Subs pushin' north through Park, pas' lake."

We headed up the stairs.

"The Park's surrounded by walls?"

"Both side, an' end too. Not enough Subs ta guard all, but Parkas be glitch if try ta break out sides. Easters gather, an' High Mids, waitin' fo' venge."

"They're fighting with you?"

"Trannies togetha? Nah, you mus' be glitch as ol' Changman. What we did, tol' 'em Parkas migh' try pushout. Too many Mids was Parka dinna, over years. So tribes be waitin'."

I felt a chill.

"We go in at Hunnert Three, maybe. Subs in Park got Parkas pushed pas' dat."

We emerged in fading light, joined a troop of about fifty Subs, among them children no older than Philip. I grimaced, sickened that the savages would risk their young in a greedy war for territory.

We strode down the center of the street alongside the park. Raulie danced at my side. "Usual, no Sub eva go abovegroun', 'less he give innifo passby. Tonigh', diff."

I paid little attention to his babble.

"Mira, joey! Subs walkin' down Cenparkwes' like we own!" His eyes glowed. "Park be Sub turf, now on!" He giggled. "Ya Uppie Subs c'n visit us wheneva ya wan'!"

I snapped, "I'm no Sub."

"Nah, ya be Uppie piece a shit think ya own da worl'. But looka Fisherman, walkin' wid Halber!"

Ahead a cluster of Subs guarded an opening in the wall. About them lay a handful of dead and hideously wounded.

Halber's voice boomed. "Lissenup, joeys!" My mouth twitched in a hint of a smile. For a moment, he was a drill sergeant at Academy, calling the attention of his cadets. "We goin' in. Know ya be hurtin'. But I tolya we pushout Parkas. Tolya we'd use unnercar for special surprise, din' I? It worked; by movin' fas', we got Parkas run allaway to Hunnert Ten wall. Now we show 'em otha surprise."

"These Uppies,"—his wave encompassed us all, except the Captain—"got lasers an' stunners."

"Uppies?" A murmur of surprise.

"Dis be Fisherman." He stood next to the Captain. "Sub Fisherman from long back, come ta help his tribe. No time ta 'xplain. He figh' fo' Sub. Do as he an' I say. Lesgo!"

The Captain slowed Halber with a touch. "Have you a plan?"

"Yeah, diss 'em all."

He turned to me. "Rob, how wide is the Park?"

It was in my district; I ought to know. I concentrated. "Perhaps half a mile."

"Halber, how many Parkas are left in the north end of the park?"

"Four, five hunnert, prolly."

"How many Subs inside the Park?"

"Two hunnert, no more. 'Bout as many dead."

I caught my breath. It had been a costly war.

The Captain said, "Have your joeys guard the northwest corner against a breakout. We'll push straight north to the wall, then swing west."

Halber frowned. "We can' let Parkas in east corna break south. Nevah fin' 'em in trees an' ruins."

"That's right. So you'll also have to reinforce your line at a Hundred Three."

Glowering, Halber folded his arms. "Who said you in charga?"

The Captain waited, saying nothing.

A sigh. "Alrigh', do as he say. Raulie, send half the joeys to hold line. Rest, go wid Fisherman and me." He crossed to the wall, hoisted himself over, looked coolly at the Captain. "You comin'?"

We boosted ourselves over the low wall, struggled through yards of brambles and bushes.

Arlene said, "Rob, stay close. I know you're not a street fighter."

My pride was wounded. "We went through the same training. I'll take care of myself."

The Captain said, "We use stunners first. Lasers are a last resort. Shoot to make them run. Kill only when you must."

Adam cleared his throat. "I doubt the Subs will show as much mercy."

"That's their doing, not ours. Understood?"

We murmured assent. I marveled at how the battle had become his to command. For years Arlene and Adam shielded the Captain from stress. We'd all cooperated, knowing his fragility.

"Switch weapons with me, Rob." He held out his hand for my laser.

I gaped.

"Give it here, and use the stunner."

Dumbly, I complied. "Sir, why . . . ?"

"I've killed, and I don't wish the memory on you." His face closed to a mask.

A long trek through bushes and brambles, to the remains of a road. Our breath came harsh in the moonlight. After a time, we turned northward.

The Subs made no effort to hide behind us; they spread into a line some three deep, perhaps twenty men wide. We moved forward, weapons brandished.

Arlene Seafort was at her husband's right. Where he moved, so did she.

We met resistance at about a hundred yards. A cry cut short; a Sub pitched backward, a spear through his throat.

The snap of a laser; a dreadful shriek from the dark. Subs cheered.

The Captain's harsh voice split the night. "Run, Parkas. Here be death."

I strained to sense the whisper of a spear.

Ahead, through the brush, torches flickered. Guttural cries pierced the gloom.

Nearby bushes parted with a crackle. Someone shouted a curse. Screams. Clubs whirled, spears flew. A lithe Parka catapulted onto a Sub's back. In an instant the Sub's head was jerked back; a knife glinted. The splash of blood. Together they went down. The Parka rolled off, launched himself at me. I had barely time to bring up my stunner. I fired; he grunted, sagged atop me. Pressed into the cold earth, I struggled to free myself.

Adam thrust aside the limp form of my attacker. "Up, Rob!" A Parka woman sent him sprawling, raised her club. He rolled aside, kicked her in the stomach. Again she charged. He fired into her face.

Her hair crackled, burst into flame. Her features hissed and sizzled, too quickly for her even to scream. She dropped like a stone.

I vomited on my boots.

"No time!" Adam hauled me along. "Keep up with the others. Where's your stunner?"

"Lost it." It was all I could manage.

"Christ, Robbie."

"I'm sorry, I—"

Halber shoved him forward. "Parkas runnin! Get 'em!" He put fingers to mouth, emitted a shrill whistle. "Now, Subs! Pushem ta wall!" Feet pounded, and our escort surged to a run.

Above, lights circled. They veered to the north.

Halber tugged at the Captain's arm. "If you be Sub, time is *NOW!* Park gonna be ours!"

Arlene's eyes met mine, with grim realization of the work ahead. "We'd better hurry, Nick." She urged him forward, and he complied.

I leaned retching against the northern wall, my hands sticky with blood.

As we'd thrust northward the Parkas grew ever more desperate in their sallies. I'd snatched up a fallen club and swung it with bloodthirsty determination. I knew how it felt to split a warrior's skull to fragments, to stave in the ribs of an armed and frothing child.

Somewhere, I'd lost Adam. The Captain had hurried east, trying to stop the relentless slaughter of cornered Parkas. Arlene was with him.

It was over, and I wanted nothing more than to return to our hotel and wash the death from my body. Searching for P.T. and Jared no longer seemed of consequence.

Halber's Subs had held Hundred Tenth north of the wall; they milled jubilantly in the roadway amid the disfigured corpses of Parkas and their own.

Overhead, lights loomed. The whap of heli blades. In the dark fields of the Park, screams.

On the road beyond the Park wall, the Sub trannies, used to impotent heli patrols, ignored the sound of motors.

Suddenly, death swept the street.

The snap of lasers was lost amid the helis' drone, but the bolts cut a deadly swath through the Sub ranks. At first, consternation. Then terror. A band of trannies raced for the shelter of the Sub stairs. Few reached it.

Sickened, I looked away.

Feet pounded. A mighty hand seized my arm, hurled me against the wall. Halber's eyes blazed. "Whatcha done, Uppie?"

I strove to keep my voice calm. "We fought on your side, remember? I have no idea why the jerries—"

In the bloodied street, a heli landed, its blades slowing. Unie troops poured out.

"Dey govermen, not jerries! Whatcha done?"

"I told you, I don't—"

He clubbed the side of my head. I reeled. With one hand he held me fast against the wall. His fist flew back for another blow. "Tell!"

My words tumbled. "The Captain's wife . . . desperate to find her son. They called in the Unies. They're—"

"Why?" He shook me like a rat.

"To clear the streets."

His eyes showed no comprehension. Mechanically, he pounded me against the wall until I feared my spine would snap. "Clear how?" Smash. "What governmen doin'?" Slam.

With the last of my breath I wheezed, "Clearing the streets—of trannies. Tearing down trannietown once and for all."

It was his iron arm that held me, not my legs. "Dey can't. Too many of us. Too many ratholes, builds, lairs!"

"Unie troops. Block at a time, if they have to. They'll tear down everythi—"

He let me fall. His fist reared to club me to eternity. Slowly, it fell. "Frazzin' Fisherman calls hisself Sub! Tellim—" He raised me off the dirt, spoke almost into my mouth. "He ain' no Sub. Neva was, neva willbe. Tellim rememba dat, while I eat his joeykit fo' venge!"

He let me sag, turned, bolted south along the wall. He ran low, almost in a crouch. In a moment he was gone.

Adam found me, minutes later.

"Christ, Rob, what have they done to you?"

My hands and face were caked with blood. "I'm all right. Help me sit."

"Medic!" Adam's voice was lost in the idling engines. "I'll call help."

I clawed at his leg. "Get the Captain."

"You need—"

"Goddamn it, Adam, NOW!" Only my blasphemy convinced him.

It couldn't have been two minutes. My ribs ached. I practiced breathing. Perhaps I was less injured than I felt. Footsteps, through the bushes at the perimeter of the park.

A familiar voice. "Are you all right, Rob? Who called in the jerries?"

"Sir, I—" My voice faltered. "Arlene, tell him . . ."

He knelt. "What is it?"

I took a careful breath. "Look in the street."

"*DOWN!*" Adam bowled him to the ground, as laser bolts snapped branches inches from his head. "Christ, they don't know who we are!"

The Captain peered over the wall, at the carnage. "Lord God in heaven!" He dropped back to his knees, his face level with mine. "Rob, what haven't you told me?" His voice held anguish.

I said nothing.

He swiveled. "Arlene?"

Haltingly, as if sharing the burden, we confessed what we'd done.

Chapter 35

PEDRO

For long time after Fisherman left I sat in Sub cavern, massaging chest, yearnin' for hot cuppa tea. I wasn't sure what I'd started, bringin' Fisherman down to Sub, and didn' know if I'd live to fin' out. My heart felt ready to stop from tired, and I clutched pills, ready to gulp if felt worse.

Maybe Halber would win his Parka war, maybe not. Filmatleven. I knew it didn' matter, but he couldn't understan'. After, maybe I make him see reason.

My mouth curled in sour smile of irony. I brung Fisherman himself, former SecGen, but in process I lost Halber's trust, and he prolly never listen no matter what I say.

"Sit here wid ol' man!" Harsh voice. I looked up. Raulie Sub flung joeykit at my feet.

Fisherman's son Peetee picked himself up, dusted his pants.

My heart gave flip. He alive, afta all. "Cool jets, Raulie. He only a kit." I patted my bench. "Sit, joey."

Obedient, he slid next to me. Lookin' off into distance, he shivered, wrapped his hands round chest.

"You all righ'?"

Slowly his eyes turned ta meet mine. "No." They held somethin' so cold an' bleak, made me want to cringe. He took long breath, like pullin' himself togetha. "Have you seen Jared?"

I shook head. Opened mouth to tell him 'bout Fisherman and mizz come to fin' him, but shut without sayin'. Not sure what Peetee would do, if he knew. Was awful determine to fin' his friend.

I think hard. To help tribes with water, I needed Fisherman grateful. No better way than give him his son. So all I hadda do was keep Peetee 'til Fisherman come back.

I shook my head, exasperate. Was SecGen Seafort glitched, involvin' himself in tribe rumb? Didn' he know it made no diff? Halber 'bout to make himself king of anthill, but whole hill dry up and blow away without water in pipes. River water was salty like ocean, an' too pollute to think about.

For now, no prollem keepin' Peetee with me. He sat quiet, head in hands.

I asked, "Why you here?"

"Halber sent me. He said he'd take me to Jared, after. I'm not sure he will. They're very angry."

"Why?"

"Because I—" Again he shivered, clutched self. He shut his eyes, and his mouth formed silent numbers.

I asked Raulie. "Whas happenin' in Park?"

"Dunno." Sub grimaced. "Halb took unnercar to Hunnert Ten, all I know. Parkas can' last much longer." He tapped his foot, said sullen to Peetee, "But ya din' have ta diss 'im!"

"Who?" I swiveled.

"Chaco." Peetee turned away.

Cavern erupted with shouts of hate an' alarm. Buncha Subs came runnin' from Four Two stair. One skidded to stop. "Where's Halber?"

Raulie. "Park."

"Gettim, fas! Govermen onna streets. Startin' ta pushout Mids, shootin' everyone what fight. Frazzin' helis landin' in Broad turf, Easter, Rock, everywhere!"

I found myself on feet, heart poundin' so hard room spin. I clutched Peetee's shoulder for support.

"Easy, sir. Sit."

I ignored. "Gotta see." Was this end of all? Too late for even Fisherman to help? "Goin' to stair."

Raulie said, "You supposed ta wait—"

"Fisherman said I guest, free to go, and Halber agree." Painfully, I shuffled to exit corridor.

Peetee walked by my side, allowing his shoulder to be crutch. "What's happening, sir?"

"Unie raid, big one." Or worse.

"Why?"

"Dunno. They do, every few year." I saved my breath.

After while, could see foot of stairs. I dreaded long slow climb. Outside, whine of helis, occasional cry of pain.

Behind, cavern was fillin' with agitated Subs.

Peetee roused himself from his lethargy. "Sir, is it safe to go out? Shouldn't you wait—"

Shoutin' in cavern got louder. "Outa my way!" Halber, mad like I never heard. "WHERE'S FRAZZIN' PEETEE UPPIE?"

Voice said timid, "Helpin' Changman ta stair."

Somethin' gone bad wrong; I didn' know what. I gave Peetee shove. "Run! Right this sec!"

He gaped.

A roar. "GETTIM! BRING'IM ME!"

"Run!"

Boy gave me wild look, pounded up the stairs into night.

I leaned tired against wall, waitin' the inevitable.

Hour later, I still alive. Mighta helped that I looked boss Sub in eye and tol' him Peetee bolted when he heard Halber's voice, and I was too old to hang on to him.

Lyin' ain't moral, but sometimes necessary.

Halber so anger at losin' Peetee he could hardly speak. He sent three Subs upstair chasin' after. None came back. But Halber held his rage, steada lashin' out at me or Subs tiptoein' round careful not to rouse him.

Hour by hour, cavern filled with frightened Subs. I did best to stay outa way, hopin' Fisherman be back. If he was diss in Park, no help fo' any of us.

Halber spat wild tale that Fisherman hisself called in Unies, but I dismissed that outa hand. Couldn't be. Then Halber claim it was Fisherman's wife. I still doubted, but too smart to say aloud.

With confusion of Unies roamin' above, Parkas beaten, Fisherman gone, so many Sub dead, I found myself in mid of Sub counsels. Alla talk about lost trust forgotten.

I advised Halber to forget about Park for now, an' keep Subs completely unner.

Halber said, plaintive, "But Parkas 'll retake turf. Subs get diss for nothin'?"

I snorted. "Govermen shootin' Subs with laser, righ'? Think they gonna ignore Parkas?"

"No, they shoot Parkas too." Halber bit his knuckle. "Ain' right, even fo' Parkas or Crypsnbloods. Unies diss 'em wid no more worry than dogs inna road."

"Stay unner," I said again. No one argue; unner be natural haven for Subs.

* * *

I learned more 'bout Sub tribe in next few hours than in years of trayfo. Only two, three unnercars they fixup, but lotsa track clean of rubble, south almos' to Wall where sea lappin'.

Usetabe car was power by track, but Subs change that. Now car bringalong its own power; track jus' place it go. My Valdez permas did all that. I proud a my Subs.

Halber tried to explain tracks didn' all go same place, lotsa lines, hadda connec' wid special unnercar at Four Two. Okay by me.

Reports came to Halber from all over city. Course they didn' have callers, but flashin' lights in dark tunnels could spread news far and fast.

Word was, there weren't too many Unies at Hunnert Ten; apparently they only came 'cause rumb brought out so many trannies. Streets roun' Four Two Square were anotha matter. Dozens of helis, troop cars. Unies shouted into callers, squads moved out south.

Fourteen east was anotha landin' point. Unies there were movin' north toward Four Two. I chewed at lip, worryin' for trannies in between. None gonna agree to be pushout. Lotsa lives would end tonight.

Over and over I tried to figure what cause commotion. Obvious, this bigger 'n Unie raid. Some 'portant goverman get hisself killed? I hadn' heard nothin'.

Only thing could stir up Unies so was Fisherman's son bein' on street. But Fisherman hadn't mentioned Unies, and he went with Halber's troop to fight Parkas. Meant he didn' know Unies were about to attack.

I couldn't figure.

Chapter 36

PHILIP

"Run," Mr. Chang said, and I did, up the stairs and into a battalion of troops.

Normally, I weigh the evidence before acting on advice, but, objectively speaking, Halber's roar held a menace I hadn't heard even when I'd told him how Chaco died.

I couldn't imagine what had enraged him so.

At the top of the stair I found myself in night lit almost to day by floodlights and the beams of vehicles. Bodies of Subs lay about. I considered turning myself in and asking the soldiers to take me home. Instead, I dashed around the corner and cannoned into a trooper who bristled with armaments. My impact sent his rifle flying.

"Stop, you!"

I picked myself up and raced north. I'd rather have headed south toward the Sheraton; it was time I took a break to think matters through, but the roads south from the square were too brightly lit to risk crossing.

I was small, my clothes were dark. The combination helped me lose myself in the night.

Ahead, buildings were burning. Not many, but enough to light my way.

If I couldn't reach my skytel, I wasn't sure where I ought to go. North lay the Hundred Ten wall that seemed so important to Chaco and the Subs. Could I cross it? I knew little of the geography of Old New York.

Surely, given Halber's battle plans, the wall would be swarming with Subs. If the Sub Boss had ordered his joeys to capture me, that was not a good place to go. Anyway, I had little idea what lay beyond the wall.

Why were troops swarming about the square? I'd heard the government and the transpops lived in uneasy truce, neither provoking the other. What had provoked the raid? In the square I noticed insignia from the Sixth Airborne, the Twenty-Fifth Armored Cavalry, and elements of the old national guard.

The uniforms matched those in my battalions of toy soldiers. It seemed more than a casual raid, especially given the hour.

It seemed the Unies intended to take control of the streets, at least temporarily. But why?

After a time I had to slow my pace. I leaned against a broken window, panting.

"Dey movin up, Midboy?"

I whirled, stifling a scream. "What?"

"Unies. Buncha trucks come through, few hours back. Ain't seen none since. You?"

I could barely make out three figures huddled in the doorway. "Saw them in the square." I pointed.

"Where ya goin'?"

I tensed, remembering their strong sense of territoriality. "North."

"G'wan, den. No sense rumb now."

"Thanks." I moved off.

"Watchout roun' Five Nine," he called. "Parkas go craze. Subs came out."

"I know." I squinted, trying to make out their clothing. "What tribe are you?"

A snort. "Nor' Broads, stupe."

"Thank you." I hurried on.

I trudged northward, block after endless block. Ahead I heard the drone of heavy transport. Afraid I'd stumble into soldiers in the dark, I veered east through pitch-black streets strewn with rubble. Above me loomed rows of sagging apartments. I finally came on a wide avenue, then a low wall, realized I was just outside the park.

I wasn't thinking too clearly. The Hundred Ten wall had become fixed in my mind. I didn't know what that was, but it was a defined place, and I had no other. Perhaps I could inquire of some Sub tribesman why Halber was so angry. Perhaps I could see what was taking place. Perhaps . . . I didn't know. It was a goal, and I fastened my sights on it.

Chapter 37

JARED

After I put out the trannieboy's lights I ran like the very devil. At last I had shoes again, even if only filthy sandals that barely stayed on my feet. Without shoes I'd been helpless in the rock-strewn streets, but I'd been patient and crafty, and had finally outwitted my captors. Not that it was so hard; after all, they were just a bunch of trannies.

It would have been easier if I'd had a light, but I knew that Halber's car ran on tracks in a tunnel, and that the tunnel had many "stayshes," as the trannies called them. I had only to locate one, find a Sub whose manner was anywhere near reasonable, and demand he take me to Halber so I could explain my plan.

If all went really well, I might even escape to the streets, though that might not do me much good; the trannies there were unaccountably hostile and avaricious.

My eye throbbed brutally from Halber's blow, but at least, in the dark, my lost vision was no problem. I loped down the dark tunnel, one arm stretched in front for obstacles, the other pressed to my chest lest the exertion reopen my cuts.

Finally, I reached a station. Above, a dim light hung from a Valdez perma. I saw half a dozen Subs, drew breath to call out to them, but changed my mind.

They were armed with spears, knives, an axe. Scant feet ahead of me, a red puddle dripped onto the track. Two bodies lay dismembered on the platform.

I ducked low, scuttled past as quietly as I could. All trannies were savage animals, but these were worse than most.

I risked a last peek. A grimy sign hung on the wall: "Ninety Sixth." There seemed but one stairwell up to street level.

I wasn't happy running again into the dark. As the light receded, I cast a wistful look backward.

A shadow moved. I hesitated.

Yes, I was sure of it.

The light was on the track, not above on the platform.

Someone was following me.
I tore into the black tunnel.

It wasn't fair, their having the light. As fast as I ran, they'd make better time; they could see where they were going.

Who was chasing me, the girl Allie? I doubted it; she was small, and even a trannie would have more sense than to chase me alone in the dark. I squinted. It seemed like there were several figures. Three at least, perhaps as many as five.

I pulled the jackknife from my pocket, the blade I'd taken from the trannie boy Krand. Too small to do much good, but I could threaten them, give them pause, keep them from worrying at my heels.

I wished I knew how many they were. How could I ambush them, to lower the odds?

I looked for a place to hide. Unseen, I could count them as they passed, perhaps double back the way we'd come. I might even fall on the slowest of them, disable one or two of my pursuers before fleeing again.

I paused for breath.

The tunnel was supported in its center by steel posts, and by concrete beams wide enough to hide me. I was nerving myself to duck behind one when I spotted a doorway. Only the dimmest light escaped it.

The opening was built into the crumbling concrete wall. If the Subs saw me in the doorway, I'd be trapped. I swallowed my fear. No point in running further; sooner or later they'd catch me. Already they were so near I might not reach the doorway unseen.

I took a breath and lunged.

Now my problem was to control my panting, else they'd hear me. I forced myself to breathe more slowly, felt myself growing red in the face.

I crept backward.

Abruptly I struck cold iron, and it was all I could do not to yelp. I felt about. A ladder?

More light. I looked up, disoriented, realized I was peering through a distant grating.

I swarmed up the ladder, my sandals flapping on the treads.

The grating was stuck. I put my shoulder to it and heaved.

"Lissen! C'mere widda light, Allie!"

I slammed my shoulder into the grating. With a squeal, it gave way.

"C'mon! He here!"

The grating was impossibly heavy. I thrust it aside.

Fingers closed on my ankle. "Hol' it, Jared!"

Pook? Impossible. Besides, he was my enemy now. I kicked free, struggled out of the hole.

Behind me, a hand reached the pavement. Then a head.

I lashed out with my jackknife; the hand shot back into the hole.

I ran as fast as I could.

No use. They were better armed, could run faster. I'd been mistreated for days, cut to ribbons, beaten by Halber. And all I had on were these damn sandals. Sure, Allie could run in them; she was probably born in them. But I was used to civilized boots; how could I be expected to sprint in beachware?

They caught me at the corner.

Allie. Pook. Another trannie, the one they called Swee.

Pook seemed as winded as I. "Whereya goin', Jared?"

I brandished my knife. "Get away! I'll kill you!"

Pook snorted. "Look at 'im, Swee. Thinks he c'n hold us widda frazzin' toy."

My breath came in a sob. "Goddamn you!"

Pook licked his lips and edged closer. Despite my race through the humid night, I felt a chill.

Allie pushed Pook aside. "He diss Krand. He mine."

I wasn't going to be a prisoner. I wouldn't be tied, carved upon, fed scraps, thrown into a reeking elevator.

"Kill me, bitch? Go ahead and try!" I spat. "Lose the best chance you'll ever fucking have!"

"Wha?"

I pounded my chest; flinched at the pain. "You trannie bitch, I can bring down a tower. Can this asshole Pook?" I aimed a kick at his kneecap, but missed. "But we need Halber's help. Fifty men, maybe less. Enough to buy time!"

If they wouldn't listen I would die here on the street, with no chance to exact my revenge. In a moment of clarity I realized I hated them all equally: Pook, Allie, Halber, Dad, the frazzing Old Man and his bitch wife Arlene. And P.T., worst of all. Somehow, he was involved in my fall. If ever I had time, I'd think it through, but for now I had a job to do.

Allie's knife slashed; the blade caught my pants pocket. I leaped clear in the nick of time, lunged at her anew. "C'mon bitchgirl! I don't fucking *care* anymore!"

Pook caught her arm. "Hol' it." In his eyes, a wary respect.

Allie said, "Gotta bring Uppie back, Pook. Else can't face Halber."

Pook made a sign. "Wait." Back to me. " 'Kay, Uppie. Whazzis 'bout tower? Halber say you babble 'bout needin' nets."

I hammered on the rotting doorframe. "Of course. A decent puter with access. But that's the point! I can get that in the tower!"

Pook's face fell. "Ya 'xpect us ta letcha walk off ta ya frazzin' towah? No fuckin' way—"

I shrieked, "Listen, you stupid trannie!" Pook tensed himself, knife poised. Again I pounded the doorframe. "I'm not going to the tower. *We* are!"

Slowly, as I spoke with ever-increasing urgency, his knife dropped to his side. The boy Swee looked from one to the other of us with wonder, and even Allie drew close.

Chapter 38

POOK

Who c'n figga Uppies? In my elevate, Jared cry an' wail like babykit. "Lemme go, Pook. Please, Pook!" Now, even afta Halber whomp him good, he diss Krandboy Sub by hisself. Take Krand's shiv, take shoes, run through tunnel like ta 'scape sure.

We lucky ta corna him in store, where nobody but a real stupe would cringe, but he taunt us ta dissim like he don' care.

Seems all he really want is bring down towah full a his Uppie frens.

Go figga.

Helis roar ovahead, lights probin', but I pay no 'tention, tryin' ta think. Allie an' Swee wait nervous, while Jared glare at alla us.

He demand ta see Halber, but Halber put him in staysh he 'scape from. He demand chance ta bring down towah, when dat's what Halber tellim ta do in firs' place.

Course, by dissin' Krand he make everythin' complicate. Allie take me aside ta whispa Jared be hers afta, fo' venge. He pay fo' Subboy, even if Halber decide ta lettim get 'way wid. I nod, payin' no 'tention.

An' Halber gonna be royal pissoff when he hear 'bout Krand. At leas', Allie say, she c'n go back under, long as Jared come wid. So togetha, we 'xplain ta Uppie only choice be comealong.

He look at me accusin'. "Why ya leave me, Pook? The Subs took me away and you didn't come."

I go red. "Couldn'," I say. "Prollems." How c'n I 'fess Uppiekit small as Peetee whomp me? "When I come lookin', ya gone wid Halber. Anyway, he an' I got deal. Gotta bring ya back."

"Fine," he say, wid Uppie pride. He add, "But tell him I'm his only chance. Make sure he knows if he hurts me again, I won' work for him. I want respect!"

It time fo' test. "Think I'll cut ya mouth, Uppie, fo' makin' us run afta." I pull out shiv. Maybe I do it, too. His attitude got me pissoff.

He grin, wait til I get close. Then he spit full in my face. "C'mon, trannie! See if ya c'n cut me, 'fore I rip your fuckin' head off!"

Can' help it. I go chill. Finally, I say, "You change, Uppie."

He giggle. "Yeah. Once you lose everything, it don' matter no more."

"Don' care if I cut?"

"Sure I care. What the fuck can I do about it?"

We look at each otha. Helis drone low ova us. I know something wrong wid night. We in Broad turf, an' no one challenge. Sounds ain' right, neitha.

Jared point high at towah. "Look at those smug bastards. I'll bet the Sheraton tower holds two thousand, maybe more. And that one." He swivel, pointin'. "The Holoworld offices. How'd you like to see that mother *burn*?"

For min, I imagine zarky flames flickerin' roun' spire. I lick lips. "Allie, how c'n we bring Jared ta Halber, not gettim diss?"

She bite knuckle. "Firs', we go back unna, 'fore Broads get us. Halb be eitha at Hunnert Ten or Four Two Square. I talk ta him. He likes me sometime."

So dat's what we do.

Only, Pookboy nevah been nor' past Four Two, so don' realize how far we gotta walk. Feet hurtin' bad when finally we climb up ta Four Two staysh.

I wipe forehead, still dizzy from watchin' Allie's light swing on tracks.

Big room was crowded wid Subs. I amaze ta fin' ol' Changman sittin' wid Raulie. At firs' I try ta hide, but afta min I go proud; I ain' done nothin' wrong. I brung Peetee ta Sub jus' like I promise. Ain' my fault he runaway.

"Stay outa," Allie warn me, an' tug at Raulie's arm. "Where Halber?"

He point. "Decidin' what ta do wid wound joeys."

Allie's eyes go wide. 'Cross room, Halber kneelin'. Laid out like dead, maybe fifty Sub, some drippin' blood, othas awful burn. "Jesusgod," she say ta joey. "Parkas did that?"

"Naw. Unies."

Halber's eyes come up, fix on us. My stomach lurch. Boss Sub stare us, one at time. He look long an' har' at Jared.

Allie go to him. "Please, Halber. Lemme 'xplain." She talk sof'. Point at Jared. Halber crouch near wound Subs, lissenin'.

Afta time, he walk towar' us, slow. Casual, I look roun', decidin' where ta run.

But he got 'tention only fo' Jared Washinton Uppie. "Ya diss Krandboy."

"Don' touch me!" Jared's voice be shrill. "Not if you want towers!" His eyes lock on Halber's. "I swear to Lord God, lay a hand on me and it's over!" Tremblin', he face Boss Sub. "Did she tell you my plan?"

Long silence. Den, "Some."

"Want to hear the rest?"

'Notha silence, while I watch amaze. "Yah."

Togetha dey walk off.

I whispa ta Allie. "We safe?"

"Prolly. Shush."

Dey gone long while. Nothin' betta ta do, so I wanda ta Chang an' wait fo' his scold.

He ack like don' see me.

"Watcha doin', Mista Chang?"

"Waitin'." He look up. "Stay off street, Pook."

"Yeah, Unies. I hear 'bout." I jerk thumb at Sub dead. "Wha happen wid Parkas?"

"Subs won." His voice flat. "Don' matta."

"I brung Peetee unner," I said, cautious.

"I know. Was here wid me."

"No swind?" Couldn' help myself. Last I saw, Peetee runnin' towar' track wid pissoff Subs afta him.

"What happened to him, Pook?"

"Ain' sure." Hated ta admit.

"He changed."

"Not jus' him." Words came 'fore I could stop.

Chang's ol' eyes watch me, shrewd. "G'wan."

"Jared Uppie. He mouth Halber like he ain' scare." I shake head. "Worl' upside down, Mista Chang."

Sudden, Changman sob. "Pookboy . . . "

Dunno why, but I rush close, put han' on his shoulda.

He rest his han' on mine, wipe eyes. "Bah. Gettin' glitch wid old."

Silent, I agree. But not right ta tellim jus' now. "Upside down," I say again.

Allie come runnin', tug my arm. "Halber wantcha *now*!"

I follow.

Sub Boss look like he been in month a rumbs. Hair matt, eyes wild, he pace backanforth like can' keep still. "Show 'em good," he growl. "Subs won' go widda whimpa. Gonna shake worl'!"

I nod, like I know what he mean.

He whirl, grab my shirt, haul me close. Reek of nervous sweat. "Ya Uppie ran off!"

I squeak, "We gottim back, Halber. I tolya ta, lemme stay wid—"

"Ya bring him back, or he come hisself?"

"We brung!"

He shake me har', make my teeth rattle. "Truth!"

I swallow. "He run lookin' fo' you, ta ask 'bout towahs."

"He get his chance." Halber spun me round, put han's unna my arms, lifted me high, wid bellow. "Mira, Subs! Looka Pook Midboy! Rememba his face!" He drop me down, twis' me ta face him. "If Jared Uppie runs away, bring back dis Pook so I c'n skin him inch by shriekin' inch!"

I shudder. "Cool jets, Halb—"

He shove damp face close. "Stick ta him like adhese, joeykit. Make sure he do what he promise, or I getcha if it last thing I do!"

"Cool, Halber! I do watcha say! Cool." I try to stop from gabble. "Hones'!"

"Raulie and you gonna take fifty Subs south. Carry as many Valdez permas as Jared say. Help him."

I recoil. "Jared in charge? Ya lettin' Uppie lead trannies?"

He snarl, "Raulie in charge a Subs. Uppie in charge a frazzin' puter an' equip, an' bustin' inta towah. You in charge a Jared Uppie." With effort, he make hisself calmer. "Look, Pook." He shove me inna chair, pull one close for hisself. "It comin' ta arma geddin upabove. You been up, musta see."

"Yeah," I say, doubtful. All I rememba is coupla helis buzzin' roun'. Wonder why Halber so shakeup.

"Sub ways won' be safe, long as Unies onna street. Govermen gonna squish us 'less alla tribes rumb togetha." His brow go knit. "Runners gone ta every tribe we c'n reach, tellin' 'em big meet this aft, unner. Not ta worry 'bout passby or innifo. I called everyone what can come. Changman was right. Gotta ack like one tribe."

I feel skin prickle. Makin' history, ol' Chang say.

"Hope Jared c'n distrac' 'em some, give us a chance."

"Don' matta he diss Krand Subboy?"

"Later, time ta think about. Now, so many more been diss . . ." He rub han' ova face. "Pook, help wid our venge much as ya can. Do it, ya got Sub frien' fo' life." His voice hard, but his eyes pleadin'.

I go swell. "Jared an' me Simese glitchkits join at hip. I stay wid him, swear. Help him bring down towah!"

"Good." He clap my shoulder, like I tribe.

I ask, "Wha' happen wid Peetee? He run all ova lookin' fo' Jared, an'—"

Halber bare his teeth. "Peetee mine, if I catch. Goes in stewpot fo' what Fisherman did."

I try ta unnerstan'. Las' I hear was Fisherman visit Chang in shop.

"Frazzin' Uppie!" Halber pace. "Came unner, stood righ' here, coupla feet from ya chair. Swore he Sub now, was, willbe. Then he 'n his bitchgirl call down Unies."

I nod. "Frazzin' Uppies think dey own da worl'." Only surprise is why Changman think otha.

Halber beckon. "Get along."

"Righ'. C'n Allie come wid?"

"Don' matta." He scrunch face at new arrivals from tunnel. "More? Livin,' or dead? Put em near res'. Lor' Chris'!"

I much happier trampin' tunnel wid buncha Sub joes than chasin' Jared Uppie in scary dark. We walk fas', everyone carryin' load.

Like I promise, I stick close ta Jared like adhese. But I don' worry 'bout Jared run, 'cause he gettin' 'xactly what he ask.

Raulie 'xplain plan. Usin' Valdez permas fo' torch, we gonna force streetside door of towah. Meantime, Jared and resta Subs break in 'notha towah, head fo' puter room.

Don' make sense ta me, but I jus' along fo' watch.

Afta while, we reach Three Fo' staysh. Few Subs still guardin' stair.

Raulie ask, "Unies upabove?"

"Buncha truck on Three Six," joey say. "Lots roun' Two Eight. Only few sojers 'tween."

"Lesgo." Raulie beckon us up.

I warn, "Sojers see us."

"Ain' dawn yet, joey. We got time ta get ready."

I shake my head, confuse. Livin' unner, howya suppose ta know diff night 'n day? I wunner how Subs stan' it.

We creep out on street. Raulie's scouts peek roun' cornas, beckon safe. Few at a time, our trannies dash 'cross streets. Final, we huddle roun' base a office towah, Subs grippin' axes, spears, torches.

Jared go bossy, order us roun' wid equip in his snot Uppie way. Subs do as he say, more nervous 'bout sojers comin' roun' corna dan mad 'bout his Uppie contemp'.

"Hook your Valdez together, like this. Then the others on separate line. Now 'cross. Haven' ya heard of series/parallel connect, fa Chrissake?" He look roun'. "Who knows how to cut?"

"Me. Sollie." Older Sub joe. He grin, showin' hardly no teeth.

"You're sure?"

Sollie grunt. "I worked on unnercars. When we ain' got acetylene we hook permas fo' torch, so we din' need ya tellin' us." Two glare at each otha. "Whatcha wan' torched?"

"Hinges."

Sollie slip mask ova face. "Don' look at," he warn. "Too bright."

I watch, mouth open. Allasudden, can' see nothin'. I curse, rubbin' eyes. Allie snicker. I swing blind, but miss.

"He tolya," she say.

"Stupe Sub!"

"Shush, joeykits!" Someone shove.

I blink spots. "Where ya get cutters? How ya learn ta torch?"

Allie shrug. "Trayfo from Chang, mos'ly. We figga how long time back, when Alwyn fix firs' unnercar."

"Wha's light doin'?"

"Burnin' door." She glance roun'. "Jeez. Mira shadows on buildin' 'cross street. Unies gonna see." Glare from Sollie's torch got whole street lit, justabout.

"One more!"

Soon, door sag. Inside, loud bell is bongin'. Subs pour inta build. Raulie light first torches at doorway, den Subs light res' from each otha.

I grab joey's arm. "Watcha gonna do?"

Fierce grin. "Run upstair, burn frazzin' towah!"

My eyes light. "I go witcha!"

Jared an' Sollie finish pack up equip. "C'mon!" Dey hurry 'cross street.

"Gimme torch!" I c'n hardly stan' still.

Allie poke my arm. "You spose ta stick wid Jared."

"Naw, I gonn . . ." I stop dead, cursin' Halber, Subs, Changman, God hisself. Ain' fair. C'n Pook walk away from torchin' towah? Impossible. Even Halber unnerstan'.

Long moment I stop, poundin' my side wid fist.

Wid sob, I run afta Jared.

Ain' frazzin' fair.

Chapter 39

ROBERT

"I'm sorry, sir, we have our orders." Colonel Wirtz was in full battle dress.

The Captain was beside himself. "Orders to kill everyone in sight?"

"No, but—"

"Stand down! I'll take responsibility." He ran his fingers through his hair, shot Arlene a look of reproach. "Lord God, how could you?"

Colonel Wirtz said, "Mr. SecGen, the best I can do is put you through to headquarters."

"Do that!" The Captain paced back and forth.

Dizzy, I leaned against the troop carrier. Halber's fist had been like a club. I took a deep breath, and my ribs gave sharp warning.

Within the Park, the distant snap of lasers.

I groaned, laid a hand on Adam Tenere's shoulder as I took a tentative step.

Tenere's face was a mask.

I said tentatively, "This time it was Arlene's idea. The boys had been gone so long . . ."

His voice was flat. "Robbie, I won't pretend I care that much about the trannies. But what you did to *him* . . ."

"I know." Yet Dad and I had gotten what we wanted; the streets would be cleared.

It might cost the Captain his marriage, if not his sanity.

When first we'd told him, crouched behind the wall, his eyes were glowing coals that mirrored the lights of the Unie encampment. He'd heard us out. "You did this," he finally said, "in my name?"

"The official reason is trannie unrest." I tried to look away.

He'd swung to Arlene. "You started a war to find Philip?"

If I'd expected she'd be cowed, I was mistaken. She grated, "Think how long he's been gone. What was I supposed to—"

"Wait. Search."

"We tried that!"

"Pedro Chang had Philip in his shop!"

"But I didn't know, Nick. You wouldn't call."

He'd looked to me, back again to her. "How many deaths are on our hands?"

He stood, a target for any half-witted trooper, and cupped his hands. "Hold your fire! I'm Nicholas Seafort, with Assemblyman Boland! We're coming over the wall!"

I'd expected him to be burnt to a crisp, but by some miracle he wasn't.

Now, outside the Park, safe with the Unie troops, I weighed our clearing the streets against the loss of his friendship, and decided Dad and I were still far ahead.

It gave me no joy.

Waiting for an answer at headquarters, the Captain paced anew. "P.T. is in the Sub, but Halber wouldn't say where. Now Halber wants to kill him. How large is the tunnel system?"

Wirtz shrugged. "Much of it's collapsed. At one time it honeycombed the island." A pause, while he considered. "Sir, give me a few hours and I can flood the tunnels with knockout gas. There's a good chance—"

A trooper ran up. "Sir, I have General Ruben."

The colonel spoke into his caller. "Wirtz reporting. Sir, former SecGen Seafort is here. Yes, on One Tenth, outside the park wall. I'm not quite sure, it's rather confused. He demands we call off the operation; I told him I'd put him through to HQ. Assemblyman Boland is with him."

He handed the Captain his caller.

"Hello?" Seafort faced away, a hand to his open ear. "Yes, of course I remember; a stirring occasion. General, there's been a ghastly mistake. How quickly can you call off your troops? My son's life depends on it."

He listened.

His replies were vehement, but he kept his voice low. I heard only part of what was said. After a few moments he threw down the caller, thrust his hands in his pockets.

Adam Tenere said, "Well?"

"He's sorry for my situation, but there's nothing he can do. He'll try to get through to Kahn."

I doubted Ruben would talk SecGen Kahn into calling off

the U.N.A.F. sweep. The SecGen had taken some persuading, and having moved, he wouldn't abruptly withdraw the troops. That would look indecisive, the dread of any politician.

Besides, there was no love lost between Kahn and Captain Seafort. Though only a junior Senator at the time Seafort's government fell, Kahn helped speed the process with a series of bitter attacks on the SecGen's integrity.

Arlene's hand flitted to her husband's shoulder. She seemed exhausted. "Nick, let them go in with gas. Better P.T. have some chance than none."

"The Subs aren't helpless, you know." The Captain's voice was surprisingly mild. "They'll resist. There'll be more death."

"Joeys will die regardless." Her arm spread in a sweeping gesture that took in the city. "Do you think this will stop short of pacification? But if we catch the Subs off guard, while Philip's yet alive . . . for God's sake, tell Colonel Wirtz to prepare a gas attack!"

"The decision isn't ours." Seafort frowned at the troopers. "Kahn's in charge, and Ruben." He paced alongside the troop carrier. "But calling off the assault is the only way to prove to Halber I wasn't behind it."

Arlene waited, saying nothing.

A long sigh. "No, Arlene. I can't lend my approval."

A quarter hour passed, and the first hint of morning light unwrapped the grim ruined structures of the city. I tried to focus on the wall, but it kept moving. I'd already refused one offer of transport to a hospital. Dizziness be damned; I wanted to see this through.

To my surprise, SecGen Kahn returned the Captain's call. I'd have guessed he'd choose to be conveniently absent. Seafort sat within the troop carrier; I could hear nothing of their conversation, but afterward, the Captain's face told us all.

"I'm going back to Forty-second," he said. "Colonel, could we have a lift in your heli?"

"Sir, it's a battle zone. Civilians are prohibited—"

"My son is in danger."

Wirtz shook his head stubbornly. "I'm under orders not to risk civilian casualties. That is, among, um, our own kind. I can't let you—"

The Captain's tone was savage. "I'll walk." He spun away, strode toward the street that ran the length of the park.

"Sir, it isn't safe, trannies are still about. Look!" He pointed at a shadowy figure loping north along the wall. "Every damn one of them's armed. I've lost a dozen men to rocks and spears, and the bastards swiped their lasers. Get down, ma'am. You too, Mr. SecGen."

I moved uneasily behind the shield of the troop-carrier.

"Stewart, Vesca! Pick that one off!" The Colonel pointed. "Ma'am, will you *please* get—"

Arlene screamed. "Stop!" She hurled herself at the trooper taking aim, swung to the other soldier. "Don't fire!"

The Captain stared. "Oh, my God in heaven." He broke into a run.

The loping figure slowed.

Arlene sobbed, "Don't shoot!" She ran back and forth between the soldiers, the last vestige of her composure dissolved. "He won't hurt you! Please!"

As the Captain ran, a high-pitched voice floated across the dawn, tentative. "Fath?"

Philip sat, wan and dejected, on the step of the troop-carrier.

When the paroxysms of joy at their reunion had passed, he'd separated himself from his parents' embrace. "I almost found Jared," he said. "I saw him." He looked to Adam, and his eyes fell. "I'm sorry, Mr. Tenere."

"Lord, P.T., it's not your fault."

"Yes it is," the boy said.

"Nonsense. How?"

A long pause, as if he were reflecting. "I'm not ready to tell you, sir."

Arlene knelt at her son's side, drinking in his presence in a sort of dazed bliss. "We were so frightened . . . "

He regarded her somberly.

"Philip . . . " Her hand flitted to the boy's hair, touched the laceration behind his ear. "After you left Mr. Chang, what happened?"

P.T. shivered. His eyes darted to the Park, and back. "I won't talk about it." He tugged at his father's hand. "They have Jared in the Sub. We have to go back."

Arlene's eyes met her husband's. "Let's take him home."

"Fath, Jared's not at Forty-second. I was there, but—"

The Captain nodded to Arlene. "The hotel. A meal, a warm bath, and rest. Let's go, son." As he turned, his eyes fell on Adam, and he stopped, stricken. "Lord, I'm sorry," he said.

Tenere said, "Sir, it's all right."

"I'll stay with you. Arlene, take him—"

"Commandant . . ." Adam braced himself, took a deep breath. "Jared is beyond helping. Either he lives or he doesn't. Go with Philip."

"It's not over. I swore—"

"Sir, I'll never forget your promise, but I release you. Colonel Wirtz, as Mr. Seafort's son is safe, you need not hesitate to use knockout gas. My boy Jared is somewhere in the Sub, and it's his best chance."

The colonel regarded him gravely. "It's within my authority, but are you sure?"

"Yes." To the Captain, "I'll see you later at the skytel."

P.T. dug in his heels. "Fath, help me find Jared." He gazed at his father with urgent appeal.

"Son, it's too late. The troops have to do their job. We'll wait at the hotel until we have word. Robbie, are you coming?"

I roused myself. "Yes, sir." With his boy safe, the Captain might yet be brought around, and political disaster avoided. But the less he saw of the streets, the better.

We climbed into a heli, waited while the engine revved.

From time to time during the flight P.T. shuddered, lost in some memory. Before we landed he stirred, and said a remarkable thing. "Father, when this is over I need to be punished. But not now."

"I know, son."

And it seemed he did.

We set down on the skytel roof as dawn was breaking. In a few minutes we were in our adjoining suites. I shook off my shoes, lay on the bed pressing a cold compress to my aching temple. I dialed Washington. If I closed my eyes, the room stopped spinning, and I could think. "Senator Richard Boland, please." I waited. "Dad? Listen." I brought him up to date on the latest developments.

He said "Rob, your voice is slurred. Are you all right?"

"Just a bit dizzy. Now, about Franjee. Let his syndicate know it was I who lit the fire under Kahn. And naturally, tell them you were instrumental in moving me."

"Of course." His tone was dry.

"Luckily, P.T. is no longer an issue. The Tenere boy is most likely dead."

"A tragedy." He meant it. "But it has no political effect."

"I'll need to spend time with Adam, after." It was the least I could do.

A knock. Arlene peered in, through the door between suites. "Rob?"

"I'll call you back," I told Dad, and rang off. "Yes, Arlene?"

Her expression was troubled. "It's not over, in Nick's view. He intends to go back the moment P.T.'s asleep."

"Has he lost his mind?"

"He's furious. With me, with you. At Kahn. Talk to him."

"I can't." I shook my head vehemently, and immediately regretted it. I closed my eyes. "He won't listen."

"He trusts you."

My ribs stabbed, whether from my sharp breath or her words, I couldn't tell.

She caught a sob. "I went to rest my head on his shoulder, and he pushed me away. We can wait, he said; the tribes can't. He wants to see Halber, arrange some sort of truce before they're all dead. But Halber wants to kill him. I don't want to . . . want . . . " She forced herself to finish. " . . . to lose him." I wondered if she was aware of her double meaning.

"Wait here, Arlene." I took a long breath, straightened my clothes, walked with careful steps to confront the man who, in my cadet years, had been to me as a god.

He stood at the living room window; the bedroom doors were shut. Behind one of them, P.T. would be recovering from his ordeal.

He snapped, "Don't start on me, Rob, I warn you."

I gaped.

He came close, and his eyes were pained. "You're a decent man. How could you do it?"

"Do what?" I asked, knowing full well.

"Talk her into that abomination."

"I didn't exactly—"

"Not that she needed much persuasion." He pulled me to the window, jabbed a finger at the street. "They're people down there, Rob. As Assemblyman, you even represent them!"

I said forcefully, "No I don't. I represent citizens in the towers, taxpayers, decent joeys who—"

"Oh, Rob. Did we teach you nothing?" His anger had vanished, and was replaced by a grim sadness. "*Trafalgar.* The cadets." For a moment he couldn't speak further. "Don't you remember?"

"Yessir." Suddenly I was fourteen again, and petrified.

"That day, we sacrificed forty-two cadets and nine midshipmen. You were aghast at their loss. When you testified, you never once let your eyes meet mine."

I'd worn my dress whites, and stood before the row of seated Admirals, my heart pounding so hard I thought it could be seen through my starched jacket.

He said, "In His wisdom, Lord God let me imagine their death was necessary. But you're sacrificing a hundred, a thousand times that number, for *political* ambition!" He spat the last words with venom.

I swallowed.

"Boland, look at me!" For a moment, I was before my Captain, on Farside.

"Yessir." I managed to meet his eye.

He said, "It's wrong."

Softly, barely audibly, I said, "I know." I grabbed at his arm, fighting a wave of dizziness.

I slumped on the Captain's couch, trying over and again to get through to SecGen Kahn, who had now flown to London in a gesture to downplay the gravity of the uprising. I'd had Van pull every string possible, even called Dad and asked his help. The Captain himself was on the other caller, begging old friends, cajoling, threatening, pleading. Seafort told everyone he spoke to that his son had been found; the point of the mission accomplished.

We couldn't reach the SecGen.

I'd known it would be so. From Kahn's point of view, it was understandable. We'd made a deal, he'd gone out on a limb, and we were trying to renege.

While we called, Arlene had settled herself in an oversize chair, rousing herself every so often to check on Philip. The boy wouldn't or couldn't sleep.

Abruptly she snapped awake. "What's that damned commotion? How's he supposed to settle down if—" She flung open the hallway door.

Running footsteps. Shouts of alarm.

The caller rang, and both the Captain and I dived for it.

"Attention hotel guests." A recording. "The Sheraton Skytel is under precautionary evacuation. Please move immediately to the rooftop heliport, or if access upward is blocked, to the south streetside exit."

The Captain said, "What the bloody hell—"

In the hall, a piercing alarm shrilled.

"All elevator assemblies and shafts are guaranteed fireproof for one hour after commencement of alarm. Doors will not open on floors where—"

He spun to Arlene. "Wake P.T.! Flank!"

She was already on the move, but the door to the boy's room flew open of its own. "Mom? What's the siren?" He wore only his underwear.

She snapped, "Pants and shoes! Go!"

Her tone galvanized him; he spun back into his room, reappeared a moment later, struggling into his slacks, boots in hand.

I keyed the caller, trying to reach the desk. "Why won't someone tell us—"

"Easy, Rob." In a crisis, Arlene was her steady self. "Nick, bring your laser." She fished hers out of a deep pocket.

"Where's your stunner?"

I said, "I lost it in the Park." I felt like a hapless cadet.

"Everyone bring a caller, set it to your personal code. You too, Philip." Cautiously she opened the hallway door. "Let's go. No, wait. Wet towels." She ran into the bathroom.

Within a minute she was back. She slung a sopping towel over P.T.'s neck, another over mine. "All right, we're ready." She shepherded us into the hall.

The elevator alcove was jammed with apprehensive guests. The atmosphere was quiet, but with an undercurrent of high tension.

The chime sounded. After a moment the door slid open. The elevator was already jammed full.

An instant's pause. The crowd battled to squeeze in. One joey flailed at a nearby face. A scream. Curses.

Pandemonium.

Someone hauled on my arm so hard I staggered, and a lance of pain shot through my ribs.

Arlene. "Come *ON*, Rob!"

"Where?"

"The stairs!"

Gripping P.T, she flung open the door. In the stairwell, a wisp of smoke.

The Captain looked up, "How many flights?"

I struggled to think. "We're on sixty-two."

"The heliport's at eighty-one." He grimaced. "Let's go."

I took two steps, reeled with dizziness. "I can't make it. I'll go back and wait for an elevator."

Arlene snapped, "Goofjuice. We'll carry you."

"Not nineteen flights."

"Nick?"

"I'll take his left."

My head spun, and my ribs hurt; I really should have let the Unies at a Hundred Ten send me to a hospital. Protesting, I let the Seaforts guide me.

We weren't alone in the stairwell. A nimble young man jogged upward, a sheen of sweat on his forehead. He said not a word, his eyes fastened on the tread ahead. Others shouldered past us, some with curses. From below, shouts and screams. Smoke curled lazily up the stairwell.

It was seven flights before the Captain stopped to rest.

"Nick, smoke rises." Arlene's tone was anxious. "It'll be worse at the top."

"It doesn't seem to be, so far. Maybe the outside door's propped and letting it out."

She nodded. "P.T., you all right?"

"Yes, ma'am."

"Stay with us, unless I tell you to run ahead. Rob, here we go again."

From below, pounding feet. Whoops and hollers. I peered over the rail. "What in the name of . . . ?"

"Come *ON*."

Laboriously, we toiled upward.

A clang.

Philip was half a flight ahead of us. "Mom, look!" He seemed near panic.

Above, the hallway door was wedged open. Angry black smoke billowed into the stairwell, and upward.

"Philip, down. *Now!*" Her voice was a lash, and he raced down the stairs. "Help Mr. Boland," she told him.

Cautiously, she climbed the stair, wrapping a towel over her right arm and hand.

"Arlene, what are you—" The Captain.

"Closing the door." A grunt. "Damn. It's stuck."

"Stay here." Seafort trotted up the stair. I peered up. Arlene was on her knees, the Captain crouched at her side. Together they tried to wrestle the door shut. Their faces were darkened with smoke and grease. "It won't budge."

"If we—*DOWN!*" She pulled him to the deck. A gout of flame blasted through the opening.

"Mom!" Philip careened up the stairs.

As the blaze receded Arlene got to her knees, cursed, rolled on the deck. "God damned sparks!" She slapped at her smoking jumpsuit. "Nick, are you—"

"I'm all right." He pulled her down to the landing below. "P.T., I said to wait with Rob!" The Captain turned the boy's shoulder, pushed him to the stair.

From somewhere below, a scream of pain.

I called, "Can we get past the door?"

"I'm not sure." He crawled toward the doorway, peered through. Above his head, smoke poured into the stairwell. "Even if we could, the smoke may be toxic."

"Fath, look!"

"Not now, P.T."

"Lever the door shut!" The boy jabbed at a hose compartment, and the fire axe within.

"It might work." The Captain wrenched loose the axe and wedged it between the door and the wall. Together, he and Arlene strained at the handle. As he rose to his knees, he was caught full in the face by a huge billow of smoke. He fell back, coughing as if he'd never stop.

"Fath!"

"Easy, son," he wheezed. "I'm not hurt." His eyes

streamed. He redoubled his efforts. Suddenly the door gave way with a scream of protest. Together, they pushed it shut, but it wouldn't close the last few inches.

The Captain stopped to cough anew. When he could breathe he hurried down to our flight.

Arlene took her position at my side. "Rob, this may hurt, but we'd better hurry."

I braced myself. We made it past the burning hallway, up two more flights.

Several floors below, exultant shouts. Again, feet pounded.

We managed half a flight, then they caught up with us: half a dozen trannies in wild garb, their faces streaked. "Uppies!" A fearsome whoop of joy.

Three of the streeters bore torches.

"Nick, watch Philip." Arlene planted herself, pistol extended in both hands.

A trannie boy looked past her up the stair. "Look! Da Fisherman!"

"Allrigh'! Halber want his head!"

Arlene fired. A bolt sizzled at their feet, blackening the stair. "Get away!" The trannies retreated past the bend.

"Wait, Mom." P.T. raised his voice. "You're setting the building on fire?" He sounded curious. "Why?"

"Burn out towah! Frazzin' Uppies think ya own da—"

Another voice. "C'mon, Barth. Plenny 'partments coupla flo' down. Curtains 'n beds 'n—"

Philip asked, "But why come here?"

Above, the pound of running feet. A shriek of agony. Then desperate cries. "No. Please!"

The trannie below us snickered. "Hah. Gotcha corna!" He called upward, "Yo, Sub! Fisherman inna stair 'tween us! Throw down mattress 'n stuff! Burn!"

Arlene raised her weapon.

P.T. tugged at her arm, still calling to the trannies. "Why the Sheraton?"

A giggle. "Jared picked. Said he'd show ya all fo' chasin' him out."

"Holy Jesus." I wasn't aware I spoke.

"Where is he?" P.T. took a couple of steps down, but the Captain caught his arm, hauled him back.

"Not far. Doin' office towah."

From above, a stuffed chair hurtled down the stairwell. It had only begun to burn. The Captain slapped at it with his damp towel, to little effect.

"Nick, which way?" Arlene.

"Up, I think. Most of the Subs must be below."

P.T. broke free from his father's grip, looked over the rail. "Did you joeys climb all the way?" His voice was almost affable.

"Philip, for God's—"

"Naw. Foun' elevate." A guffaw. "Upandown. Upandown. Bust fire pipes. Burn."

I coughed from the increasing smoke, and waves of pain rolled through my chest. I tried to sound calm. "Captain, we can't stand here chatting."

"I know." Reluctantly, Seafort drew his laser pistol. "Yo, Subs! Wasn't me called the Unie troops! I tried ta stop 'em! We goin' ta roof. I got laser, but don' wanna diss anyone. G'wan, outa buildin'! Back ta Sub!"

The only responses were catcalls and hoots.

Philip said, "Father, Jared's somewhere close."

"Stay behind me, is that clear? Arlene, watch downstairs. I'll clear the path." The Captain's voice receded. "G'wan, I got laser." He climbed further. "LOOK OUT!"

The Captain squeezed himself against the wall as a flaming mattress flew past. It tumbled to our feet in a shower of sparks.

"Philip?" Arlene dragged me up the stairs with manic strength. "P.T., answer me!"

"I'm all right, Mom."

A dreadful shriek echoed in the hallway for what seemed like ages. The Captain's voice. "Back, you son of a—I warned you!" Running steps. Another scream, cut short after only a second.

"Christ, we need help." Arlene pulled out her caller, keyed the emergency code. "Hello? Damn. Answer!" She shook the caller. "I'm not sure I'm getting through. All the steel—"

"Arlene, hurry!"

She tightened her grip around my waist. I thought I'd pass out. Before lunging up the stair she leaned over the rail, fired downward. From below, a howl.

"Mom, I've got to find Jared."

I pushed against the rail, did everything I could to lighten her load. Somehow, we managed another flight. I tried not to see the two charred corpses we passed. The Captain was half a flight above. "The rest are gone, I think." He rushed down, took my other arm. "Come on, Rob."

As he gripped me, I stumbled, struck my head against the rail. I cried out, and fell into blessed dark.

Fresh air. Cold. Wind. I looked down, found myself in a patio chair. "Where are we?"

"On the roof." Arlene. "Sit still."

"Fire?"

"They say eighteen floors are engulfed, and more near street level."

I looked down at my hand. It actually trembled. I tried to contain my panic.

Across the roof P.T. argued with his father, tears streaming. I couldn't hear their conversation.

Above us, a steady stream of helis hovered near from the pad. As fast as one was loaded, it lifted, and another took its place.

All sorts of craft had been pressed into service: helibusses, U.N.A.F. troop carriers, larger private vehicles.

I said, "Dunkirk."

"What, Rob?"

I shook my head.

Armed U.N.A.F. troops guarded the pad's walkway.

Below the pad, elevator doors burst open, disgorging a horde of frantic passengers. Immediately, the soldiers took them in hand, guided them to the waiting line. The doors slid shut. I watched the indicator. The elevator descended seventy floors, stopped at ten. No doubt, the lowest floor on which occupants still waited.

I tried to recall briefings from Dad's tower constituents.

These days, building height could be almost unlimited, they'd said. Stairwells and elevator alcoves were virtually fireproof. Specially shielded cables prevented the puter-controlled elevators from stopping on floors where fire raged.

The buildings were safe.

Safe from all but trannies we'd pushed too far.

"How close is the fire, Arlene?"

"Seventy-five."

Six floors below; not nearly far enough. I shuddered, watched a rescue heli fill.

Philip pounded his father's chest. Grimly, Captain Seafort shook his head.

Arlene patted my shoulder. "We'll be on the third heli. Nick won't pull rank, or let me mention his name. When I suggested it he asked if I was considering divorce."

It drew me out of my own misery. Awkwardly, I squeezed her hand. On the pad, a heli lifted. Within seconds, far more quickly than flight regs permitted, another set down.

She was silent a moment. "Did we do wrong, Rob? I'm still not sure."

"Ask Lord God." Another elevator emptied its cargo.

"He doesn't answer." She looked miserable.

In moments, another heli lifted. Arlene beckoned to a young, frightened soldier. "We're on the next bird. Mr. Boland's injured; we'll have to carry his chair."

He hesitated, but her tone of command prevailed. "Yes, ma'am." He shouldered his rifle, called a comrade.

Together, the three glided my chair across the pad.

Nick Seafort's hand lay on his son's shoulder. P.T.'s eyes were red.

Luckily, our heli was an army transport with foldable seats. Before anyone else boarded they wedged me, chair and all, into a corner behind the pilot.

A sudden gust of wind; the heli rocked. I clutched my seat, terrified for a moment that the fire was near and the floor of the pad was collapsing.

Yearning to be airborne, I watched the controlled havoc through the heli's windows. On the rooftop, elevator doors slid open, and a new throng mingled with the waiting refugees.

The Captain helped Arlene climb aboard our heli. She held out her arms for Philip.

Abruptly P.T. twisted free of his father's grip. He raced across the pad, dashed into the empty elevator. His finger stabbed at the keypad.

"STOP HIM!"

The doors slid shut.

Arlene jumped off the heli. She pulled loose her laser, sighted at the corner of the elevator door.

"NO!"

My scream was more of a croak, and came far too late, as the soldier's rifle swung in a vicious arc that knocked the laser from her hands and sent it flying over the parapet.

The next moments were a blur. Joeys crowded onto the heli, blocking my view. The Captain pounded desperately on the elevator's alloy door. Arlene screamed curses at the soldiers. The elevator indicator plummeted.

The Captain ran to a sergeant, pointed at a heli, gesticulating at the street. The sergeant shook his head in refusal.

The indicator light stopped. The elevator was deep in the bowels of the tower, one floor above street level.

Arlene caught sight of the indicator, and became still.

"Ma'am, we've got to clear the pad!"

"Go!" She waved us away. "Rob, we'll find you in hospital."

The elevator began to rise.

The soldier demanded, "Are you boarding? Is Mr. Seafort—"

"Go!"

At floor ten, it stopped.

"Next!" The soldier waved two more aboard. "Lift off!"

I shook the pilot's shoulder. "I'm U.N. Assemblyman Robert Boland." Every word hurt. "After you lift . . . clear the pad and hover for a moment."

Sixteen.

The blades spun lazily. Above the engine the pilot shouted, "Why?"

"I need to see."

"We're to proceed to the U.N. compound."

"It'll be four minutes. Three." I ground my nails into his shoulder. "Do it."

Thirty-two.

We lifted.

In a moment the elevator display was too distant to read. A minute passed. Two.

The pilot twisted. "I've got to head out, sir."

The elevator doors slid open. A score of people rushed out. P.T. wasn't among them.

Our heli veered east.

On the roof, Arlene was on her knees, hands rending her hair.

The Captain, diminished to a dot, stood motionless in front of the empty cage.

Chapter 40

PEDRO

Halber paced like tiger, unable to contain hisself. "Any othas come yet?"

Satch shook his head. "Jus' Easters 'n Mids. An' Nor' Broads."

Halber growled.

"It be early yet. Har'ly past three hour."

"Dey *wanna* come, dey'd be here."

I said tentative, so not to pissoff further, "They got Unies pushin' 'em hard. And long walk, some of them."

He waved it away. "I'll send unnercar, soon as I know dey in Sub."

I hid smile. Halber was so used to his undercar, he forgot some trannies rather walk than risk jumpin' into iron beast screamin' through dark.

Above, somewhere on street, a crash. I said, "Halber, whas happenin' over?"

He went grim. "Unies everywhere. Nevah seen so many." For a moment his mood lightened. "Some dead ones, though. Firebombs. Rocks from roof. An' Unies don' know sheet 'bout scopin' out upper flo's."

I could imagine the hand-to-hand fighting, as trannies resisted loss of every build.

I wondered how soon havoc of streets would come to Sub. Was marvel we safe so long. First time couple doz Unies with lasers crash down Four Two stair, we'd be fleein' through tunnels for life.

Halber snapped his fingers at a Sub. "Any news 'bout Raulie?"

"Poke ya head outa Three Four an' mira. Helis buzzin' like bees. Top half of towah scorch black. Windows broke, fire lickin' everywhere. Come look, Halb!"

I said hoarsely, "Whatcha done?"

Halber ignored me. "Uppies puttin' it out?"

"Don' look like." The Sub giggled. "Treyboy come out, arm burn, sayin' Fisherman try ta dissim inna stair."

"Fisherman?" Halber came to his feet. "In towah?"

"Burned him up! Jass an' Kolie was on higha floor. Threw mattress, burnin' shit down 'til he cremate!"

I recoiled. Lord, let it not be.

"Fo' sure?"

"Trey say."

A figure raced in from hall. "Halb! Washhites comin' unner, nor' end!"

"Ahh." For a min, look of satisfaction on Halber's drawn face. "Send Jubie in west car far as track is fix. Tellim go slow 'case otha trannies walkin' unner."

"Gotcha." The Sub sprinted off.

"Halber." I waited until he caught eye. "Whas up with tower?"

He spat. "Like ya said, Chang. Time ta bring tribes togetha, pushback Unies. Get ridda towahs."

"I never said—"

"Burn 'em all. We c'n do it!" His eyes like coals. "Yeah, some our trannies diss each time, but there more of us 'n be towahs! We drive frazzin' Uppies outa city!"

I shook head. "It ain' the way."

"Don' go glitch, ol' man; I need ya ta sermon trannies. Dis time they lissen. "Beside . . . " He sound like give concession in trayfo. "Was Jared Uppie's idea. No need ta throw Uppies outa towahs. Burn 'em out, dey go by selves. An' burnout ain' only way. He say he c'n knockout towah wid putah!"

"Can he?" I didn' know if I felt chill, or hope.

Halber shrugged. "Tryin'. If can't, I venge Krand. Ya know—" He jumped ta feet. "I c'n unnerstan' Uppie dissin' trannie, tryin' ta save self. But Allie said Krandboy wen' down widout a soun'. Diss wid his own shiv. Know what it mean?"

"Means he dead."

"Mean he was knockout first. Jared didn' have ta dissim." His mouth was grim.

"Ya sent him ta work fo' Sub. Gonna dissim afta?"

Long pause. "Ain' sure," he said at last. "Might. Krand was Sub."

Afternoon drew on, slower 'n I could stand. I glad of pills I brought from shop.

Shop. At thought, I rocked, moanin'. Frazzin' Unies, stay away from shop; it all Pedro got. Widout, no home, no trayfo, no food. No water. Starve.

Don' matter, old Neut. Goin' to die soon enough. Anyhow, mira the Subs. Their worl' crumblin', dead lyin' about, othas wish they dead, pleadin' for end of pain from burn. But Halber fight on.

Young joey like Sub Boss could do that, I tol' myself. Could put aside hopelessness, while Pedro Telamon Chang wanted to lay head in hands. Young joey focus on venge 'gainst Uppies.

'Xcept, venge wasn' what we needed. Okay okay, we hadda use some force. Couldn' bring govermen to negotiate without. Any traytaman could tell that.

Prollem was, kill too many Uppies, destroy too much before negotiate, an' govermen be too pissoff to care.

Beginning of plan took shape in my head. Unlikely to work. But nothin' else had better chance.

I turned to Halber. "How soon 'til meet?"

Four, five 'clock we gathered in deep unner tunnel. I surprised at how many tribes sent speakfo.

Washhites, Broads, Easters, Rocks, Mids. Even coupla Eddie's Mace. Lexes. Huds. Joeys I hardly never seen in years of trayfo. Walls. Chinas. I shook head. Once upon time I'd call it miracle. For a min, wished Pook could be here to see.

History.

Anotha miracle: no one worried 'bout push an' shove. No one demanded innifo. They was almost too subdued.

Halber led off. "Time ta put aside old tribe grieves. We fightin' fo' life."

A Lex mutter, "How this frazzin' mess start?"

"Fisherman done it. Midboy brought me his joeykit Peetee. Then Fisherman an' his bitchbroad called in Unies ta fin' boy."

Someone shouted, "Give kit back!"

"Did. He ran safe ta Unies on street. They musta took him home early this morn. You see sojers stoppin' rumb? If anythin', got worse the min Peetee outa trannietown."

A dozen trannies had dozen ideas why govermen came in such force. I watched Halber, kinda amaze at how he work crowd. Coulda made wonnerful Neut, if he tried. He lettem all talk, brung 'em slowly his way.

When talk slowed he said, "Why it happened don' matter. Point is, they won' stop. Right while we talk, sojer trucks are bringin' Unies uptown ta parkside. An' who can't figga why?"

"Dey crashin' down whole builds!" A Washhite. "Don' matta who inside."

"Trapped twenny our Huds in sewer tunnel, headin ta ol' bridge. Dissed em all."

"Dissed my bitchbroad!" An Easter, his voice hurtin'. "While she hide my kit!"

Murmurs of sympathy, outrage.

Halber saw his moment. "Time fo' rumb. All out rumb!"

"Yo!" Hoots, cheers, applause.

A Mid, cautious. "Too many Unies fo' us, Sub."

"Then we become too many fo' them."

"How?"

"Alla tribes gonna fight same place at once."

It gave them pause. "Like Uppie army?"

Halber grinned. "Since when trannies go Uppie? Rumb *our* way."

A roar of laughter, that loosened tension.

"And we got new ways. Towah burnin', that be us Subs. We got few lasers now, from they dead. That mean we c'n diss sojers an' get more."

Cheers.

A Nor' Broad said, "But they keep attackin', and when they do, we got no place ta run."

"That gonna change." Halber raised his hand 'til silence. "Dozen lifetimes ya feared Subs, an' right so. Today . . . " He paused. "We open Sub."

I felt skin prickle. Wasn't small thing he say. Was givin' Sub turf to all trannies.

An' they knew it.

They looked about, some with awe. "Unnercars too?"

"Long as Valdez permas last." Halber turned to me. "Changman, ya got more in shop?"

"Buncha. But no way to get."

"Broads, Three Four Mids, ya help Chang ta shop?"

"Yo!" A shout, unanimous.

I got to feet, heart givin' warnin' pound.

It was my time.

"Will do," I said, tryin' not to think of lost trayfo. Didn' matta, I reminded self. "Soon as ya help me south. But trannies gotta do more 'n rumb Unies an' burn towahs."

Easter said, "Can' even do that much, Chang. What else ya wan'?"

Ha. Thank you, joey.

"Negotiate," I said, knowin' word was above most of them. "Trayfo."

Mutters of discontent. Stares of confusion. "Changman wants ta give Uppies cansa!"

I join general laugh. "Naw. Negotiate, one army ta 'notha!" I explain. "Send speakfo to tell 'em us trannies actin' togetha. Say we stop rumb when they pullback. We wan' truce, decent trannie life, water flowin' proper."

Absolute silence, like they stun.

Then the babble began, and grew. For few min, couldn't hear self think. Some joeys argue so vehement I worried I started rumb in mid a Sub.

Halber cupped hand to my ear. "You ain' so glitch afta all, Chang."

"Ya approve?"

"Yo!" He clapped hands sharp, 'til got 'em listenin'. "Well, joeys?"

An Efdear, his voice drippin' scorn. "Who wanna negotiate like pussy Easters!"

In instant, half a dozen Easters clawed toward him.

Halber put stop to it. He stuck fingers in mouth, whistled shrill. "Allayas be in Sub turf," he bellowed. "Knockitoff!" I held breath, but in a min, riot was quell.

A China said, "Pussy way or no, I don' care. Fine wid us if it stop Unies. 'Notha couple days we be complete pushout!"

From those aroun' him, unease. It ran against grain of trannie culture to admit weakness. Even faced with pushout, tribe way was to bristle.

A Rock said soft, "Us too. Down ta two lair."

"An' us." Slowly, the admission of disaster ran aroun' the room.

"Well, then." Halber. "Seem ta me, we rumb an' negotiate, same time. Prollem is, who c'n we get ta negotiate?"

I watch him careful, realizin' he my match as traytaman. Not a hint of smile on his face.

I rode in undercar with dozen Mids and Broads to Three Four staysh. Subs on guard at stairs warned that Unies crawlin' all ova place. No way could I scuttle cross street under Unie fire, but didn' have to. Mid joeys conferred with each otha, 'cause was their turf.

Two joeys ran out side stair, dived into build.

Twenny min, they back, exultant.

"No Unies near wes' stair. From there, alleys an' through builds ta shop."

"Shop bust?" I couldn' keep anxiety out.

"Naw. Cross corna, they brung down ol' build, but yo' block safe still."

We all went in anxious group.

It cost me months of life, but finally we huddled round door while I unlocked shop. We all crowded inside.

More 'n anythin' I hated to lettem see upstair, but no choice. I couldn' lug down Valdez by self. Anyway, my best trayfo hid under tarps, case of wet.

While up, I rummaged through medkits. Reason to stay alive, now.

Much harder to flee back to Sub, with everyone 'xcept me loaded with heavy permas. Somehow, we managed.

Undercar waited.

Back to Four Two.

Tribe meet was long over, only few speakfos left. Rest had started home to tell tribes 'bout new world.

Halber busy takin' trannie refugees inta Sub, organizing attack on Unie base at Fourteen.

Before we left for shop, he'd told meet it was for me to decide how to arrange negotiate. He assigned twenty Sub joeys to help. They eager, like some kinda game.

"Now . . ." Wished I could fuss with tea. Easier to think. "Bes' if govermen don' know Four Two Sub be our command. Gotta sneak me up to some build so I get to them from there. 'Kay?"

"No prollem." One joey punched 'nother in arm.

"Stoppit! Upside, joeys dyin' ever min." I tried to make voice less sharp.

"Cool jets, Changman." But they subside.

I said, "Need someone 'special brave." I looked around. If was buncha Uppies, I'd prolly have dozen volunteers. But trannies fear swind.

"Need white cloth on stick, to make flag. And brave Sub out on street, to wave."

"Me!" Four hands, all at once.

Stupid Subboys thought it some kinda adventure. Inside, I sighed. "Wave at Unies. Army rule is, don' shoot no one wid flag. Hope, anyway. When they take ya, show 'em note I wrote, an' say, hol' ya fire, tribes sendin' out speakfo negotiator. When they agree, ya come to build to get me. But mustn' tell 'em where I at 'til they agree."

I hoped it wasn' too much for them to understan'.

I swallowed pill from medkit, let them help me up side stair half cover with rubble, an' scoot into bashed shop. From there, out back door to other build half a block south. I woulda preferred further from Sub, but too far for old legs, this long day.

Hid safe in my build, I sent out Sub flagman Barth, hopin' they wouldn' burn him down. Too much glee in eyes, this almos' grown joeykit.

I waited hour at leas'. Hear shootin', rumble of tanks. 'Nother hour.

I grew agitate, massaged achin' chest with stiff fingers.

'Nother hour still.

Sounds of govermen army quietin' down.

"Chang?" Barth poked in head, still wavin' flag like glitchboy. "Dey wantcha ta meet Genral."

"Who?"

"Genral. Tol' me ta say, dey'll lissen."

"Sure they won' shoot?"

"Dunno. Din' shoot *me*."

Despite feel warm, I button coat, take deep breath. "Les' go."

Proudly wavin' grimy white flag, Barth led me down Broad, back into Four Two square.

My mouth dry. Didn' know what I faced.

Filmatleven.

Part II

September 2, in the Year of our Lord 2229

Chapter 41

PHILIP

I prayed all the way down in the elevator. Please Lord, don't let the doors open to a blast of fire, don't let me watch my skin blister while I gasped one last breath of superheated toxic steam that roasted my lungs and . . . a hundred thirty-two divided by five expressed to four decimals in base twelve and concentrate on that until—

The doors slid open.

I was so paralyzed with relief I almost waited too long. I dived out just before they shut.

The hallway carpet was sopping wet. A small stream of water trickled through an open door.

I was on the floor above street level. I'd chosen it intentionally, hoping not to blunder into a hallway full of frenzied transpops. From what I'd heard on the roof, the lowest fires were above me, and anyway if they had any sense, the Subs would have left themselves an exit.

Though if they had any sense, why would they burn a tower?

I followed the stream to the same stairwell we'd helped Mr. Boland climb, so many flights above. The steps were slippery; I carefully gripped the rail, stopping every so often to listen for voices, but there were none.

Cautiously, I descended to street level.

The stairs opened on a long corridor. Emergency lights flickered, giving the passage an eerie glow that died in the distance. I prepared equations to solve, just in case.

Someday, I'd tell Mr. Skeer how they helped. I might also tell him how it felt to crush the facial bones of a dying Sub in the Park. How it felt to defy Fath and to witness Mom's anguish as the elevator doors slowly closed.

They might never understand, but Jared came first, before them, before even me. It was I who'd provoked him into leaving. I'd aroused the misery that so unhinged him he'd urged the Subs to rampage. I'd read in my downloaded psych texts that acute pain engenders rage. I could guess what Jared felt.

Luckily my own thoughts were clearer than his. I hoped someday I'd feel remorse for what I'd done, so as not to become a sociopath. If Fath punished me, it might help me deal with it.

But for now, all I felt was resolve.

Chaco would have to wait.

Ahead in the corridor, the glow of day. I hoped it indicated an open door to the street, else I'd have to backtrack.

Two sacks lay on the floor. I stepped over one, recoiled. It was a tribesman, his dead eyes staring. Near him, a guard.

I gulped, practiced equations, steeled myself not to rev.

Did something move behind me, in the dark? I walked at first, then raced to the open doorway and shot out to the street.

The light was blinding.

I rubbed my eyes. A handful of bloody dead lay about. Their clothes suggested they were hotel guests. Were the transpops killing everyone they caught?

At the far corner, a massive fire-fighting heli hovered, its vast water tanks almost too great for the rotors to lift. Below it, slow-moving vehicles of U.N.A.F. soldiers.

Across the street loomed another massive tower, and a block south, a third. I searched the facades for clues as to which building Jared's captors had attacked.

No smoke, no shattered doors. In the windows a block south, office lights flickered.

I doubted it was safe to run the length of the block; I'd try the tower across the street first. Taking a deep breath, I dashed across.

A faint cry. "There's one!"

Though I'd come out to search for Subs, I didn't care to meet them on the open street. Halber's people didn't seem to listen to reason.

To my right, a chunk of pavement smoked and cracked. Instantly I veered left, to the south.

Another bolt. Sparks flicked into my legs. I yelped, veered again. Zagging and dodging, I reached the far side of the street and pressed myself into a recessed shop doorway.

The shop was long abandoned, of course. No help there. With infinite caution, I peered out. Two troopers were approaching with weapons ready. On the road, an abandoned electricar. If I used it as a shield . . . I leaped out of the doorway, raced down the street, glancing back. I co ... soldiers past the car. That meant they couldn't se ... ld a rifle fire through a ruined car and pick me off? ... My shoulders itched.

I reached the corner, glanced both ways.

West half a block was a platoon of Unies. They strode down the center of the road, rifles across their chests.

I raced past the side street before any of them took aim. My lungs were about to burst.

No choice now. I veered right, toward the looming tower.

Like the Sheraton, the building was a fortress. Heavy steel emergency doors, no windows. I ran to the nearest door, clawed at the knob. Locked shut.

In a moment the Unie platoon would reach the corner. Following the building, I dashed around the side, found another door. Also locked.

I sucked air into my heaving chest.

At the far corner was another door. Wheezing, I no longer cared if the troopers got me. I walked.

The doorknob was missing. I put my hand into the hole, yanked hard.

Nothing. Disgusted, I turned to go.

"Yo!" Voices, inside.

I froze. Then I turned. I rapped on the door and said hoarsely, "Gotta see Jared."

"Who go?"

Unable to think of another name, I said, "Chaco."

The door swung open.

Three Subs gaped at me, and I stared back. One of them was old and toothless, and carried a cutting assembly.

"He ain' Sub."

"A frazzin' Uppie!"

"Mr. Chang sent me. Where's Jared?"

"Wha?" A suspicious look, first at me, then to each other.

"Take me to Jared!" I used Mom's tone that meant, right *now*, young man. I added, "I'm supposed to help." With what, I wasn't sure.

The leader said, "Closa frazzin' door, Poul." Suddenly we were all inside in the close confines of the corridor.

"Seen Unies, Chaco?" Poul.

"Yes, sir. I just missed a platoon coming around the cor-her. And there's soldiers at a command post on the avenue a block north. They shot at me."

It was the best thing I could have said. Their suspicions dissolved. "Frazzin' Unies pushout every tribe in trannietown," Poul growled.

"Mr. Chang wanted me to see Jared right away," I said hopefully.

"I ask Raulie. Sollie, get the frazzin' door weld shut."

The old man bobbed his head. "Long as some Uppiekit don' comealong an' pop it open while I work."

"C'mon, Chaco." Poul tramped down the corridor. He took me to a door. "Elevate. It go upandown." He stabbed the button.

"Where are you taking me?"

"Nine flo'."

"Why?"

He giggled. "You see." Then, a frown. "Thought ya was sent ta help."

At that moment the caller in my pocket buzzed. Until now, I'd forgotten I had it.

"Whazzat?"

"Nothing," I said.

It rang again.

I didn't know what to do. Tentatively, I drew it from my pocket, keyed it on. "Hello?" I found it hard to speak.

Mom's voice cracked like a whip. "Philip, where are you?"

I said nothing.

"Tell me this instant!"

With a dazzling burst of clarity I knew I was at a threshold that could never be recrossed. I said, "No, ma'am."

Her tone reeled with hurt. "Why, P.T.? What are you doing?" Almost, it made me relent.

"I've got to find Jared."

Poul stared, openmouthed.

"If he's burning towers with the trannies, he's made his own bed. You've done all you could."

I cried, "No I haven't!" Why couldn't she see? "He ran away because of what I said. I'm responsible."

"No, you're—"

"I almost had him in Pook's lair, but the Subs took him.

Then I got in the middle of . . . Mom, there's dead joeys and blood and I can't begin to sleep and I've got to find him and talk to him so somehow this will end!" My voice cracked.

A long silence. "I'll let you speak to your father."

"*NO!* He's already too hurt, and he's fragile."

She was silent.

I said, "I think Jared's upstairs. I'll try to bring him home."

"Which building are you in?"

"Ma'am, I won't tell you." I gripped the caller, wishing it would shatter in my hand. "Stop trying to find me. I'll call when I'm ready."

"P.T.!"

"I'm taking out the battery, so I can't be traced. I'm sorry." I keyed off the caller, pulled the power unit, wiped my eyes.

Poul growled, "Ya said Changman sentcha, Chaco."

The elevator bell chimed.

"He sort of did. I—"

The doors slid open, and I was face to face with Raulie.

His mouth fell open. "Peetee!" His hand whipped to the knife in his belt.

I skidded backward into Poul, inadvertently shoving him into the wall.

"Wait!" Raulie lunged.

I bolted.

I headed for the outer door; Raulie was between me and the elevator and left me no choice.

A bright light, like the sun. Sparks flew.

Raulie yelled, "Diss 'im! Halber sayta!"

The toothless old man looked up from his work. "Whazzis?"

The handle of the door glowed red, as did the steel frame.

I launched into a dropkick, hurtled feetfirst into the knob. The door crashed open. The old man cursed. I rolled to my feet, raced into the street.

The Unie patrol was nowhere to be seen, but I knew their command post was a block north. As I ran I glanced back. Raulie pounded after me.

I dashed around the corner, heading west. Across the street, a building burned.

Somehow I had to evade Raulie and try again to get into

Jared's tower. I reached the avenue, veered north. I needed to get far enough ahead to find a hiding place.

Raulie wasn't a fast runner. I did my best, ignoring the ache in my calves.

I looked back again, didn't see him. I'd go another block, no more. I didn't want to end up too far from the tower.

Again I glanced over my shoulder. No sight of him, but . . .

I cannoned into an unseen figure. The wind was knocked out of me. I lay on the ground, gasping.

A Sub. He carried a pole from which a filthy sheet hung.

"Watchit, grode!" His eyes narrowed. "An uppiekit, onna street?" Automatically his hand went to his knife. "Why?"

I couldn't move, even to save my life. My head reeled. I couldn't tell him Raulie was after me, or ask help getting home. I could barely speak. I made a sound, half laugh, half sob, and desperately invented an errand. "I was looking for Mr. Chang," I said.

"Why?" He leaned close, knife in hand.

I had to keep him off-balance. "Halber sent me. I have news."

A moment's pause. "Okay," he said, and helped me up. "He wid Unies. Our negotiate."

I gaped.

"I be Barth. C'mon." Proudly, he waved the sheet, and started north.

I had to get off the street before Raulie found me, and in my befuddlement I let Barth lead me to a Unie outpost. Several soldiers stood guard, their expressions tense. I edged behind the Sub, hoping if they were going to shoot, Barth would be hit first.

This wasn't working out well. In the hotel, Fath told me he'd given my holo to the jerries. When the troopers recognized me, they'd have me in Mom's hands in no time, and the consequences would be grim. But it was too late to run. Casually, I rubbed my face to spread the grime.

"Message fo' Mista Chang," Barth said. "Where he be?"

A soldier's rifle swung. "Who's this?" His look was one of loathing.

I said quickly, "Chaco. I got word for Mr. Chang."

"Sit there." Then, to Barth, "Get the fuck out of here."

"Flagga truce," the Sub said in an injured voice. "It's a rule."

The soldier clicked off his rifle's safety. "Disappear!"

Barth scuttled off.

I swallowed, afraid to say a word. Surreptitiously, I reached down, gathered more dirt, ran my hand across my shirt.

The trooper keyed his caller. "Lieutenant? This is Affens, on Forty-first. Some trannie joey, with a message for the negotiator." He listened. "God only knows, sir. He's too young to be more than a messenger." Again he listened. "Right, sir. Will do."

Minutes passed. A four-seater landed, its rotors twirling to a stop.

"In, trannie!"

I tried to get the accent right. "Where ya takin' me?"

With a curse, he threw me into the heli.

We lifted off.

Minutes later, we landed on a tower pad. I cringed. If Mom or Fath were here, I'd be tempted to throw myself from the parapet. I'd disobeyed them outright; only my finding Jared might justify the price.

Two troopers came for me, led me into the tower. They led me down a long corridor, opened a door, thrust me in.

Pedro Chang sat in a heavy coat with many pockets, alone, massaging his chest.

Chapter 42

JARED

Anyone can brace himself, slide into access, snowplow a clumsy turn from the crest of the nets, and schuss the scant beginner slopes with hardly a lean, on big fat beginners' skis. On these hills the ski patrol is a keystroke away, and every electronic pathway is swept clear of bugs and fluffed to perfection.

The more daring can race the multiaccess downhill where images flare, webs tingle, pages flip with dizzying speed. They whiz through password blocks and shoot over the gentle rises to the semiapproved, the no-joeykits, 'warning; heresy-ahead' mild thrills of social disapproval.

It's all legal, tested, fundamentally decent, safe.

True schussmen scorn the licit slopes.

I'd told the trannies I needed my nets. With luck, I thought I'd get uniaccess, or at best a sixteen multi.

It hadn't worked that way.

We'd sliced through the tower door like butter. The two guards met us halfway to the elevator. They'd burned four trannies before falling to the fury of the rest.

Towers have safety systems, of course. Good ones. The puters that controlled access, elevators, heat, cooling, lights, and callers, were locked deep in a fortresslike control room, supervised by the very puters themselves. The steel hatches were so strong it would take a welding torch to break through.

In addition, the towers were huge, bustling places. In office towers such as the one I chose were our huge multi-planetaries' head offices. Massive puter access was *de rigueur*. Somewhere in the world, at any hour, financial markets were open, so brokers were always present to work them. Even in these days of universal net access, the corporations that ruled the world huddled together and drew their minions close, as if for mutual protection. Twenty-four hours a day, office warrens buzzed with drones doing their masters' bidding.

A pack of intruders wasn't about to land on the roof and invade unnoticed. Someone would see, and call the jerries.

The towers were a hundred percent invulnerable.

Well, perhaps not. Let's say eighty-five point seven one percent invulnerable.

That is, six days out of seven.

Today was Sunday. The Sabbath was inviolate; the building would be virtually empty except for the few guards. No businesses were open; they couldn't be, under the azure acts.

And elsewhere in the city, the jerries were rather busy.

Once we broke into the ninth-floor puter center, the rest was easy. Raulie's Subs took two lasers from the dead guards at street level. Two of the building's security joeys had barricaded themselves in the control room, frantically calling the jerries. We killed one, forced the other to surrender.

As if in church, I drifted reverently past the banks of puters and peripherals. They were mine, if I had the passwords.

And that was easy. I asked Raulie to find them out for me. He smiled, dragged the terror-stricken guard into the hallway.

Two minutes later I had the code to the safe, and the book of passwords in hand.

The now-compliant guard called the jerries, told them the Subs had been caught and expelled.

I sealed off the lower floors, brought all elevators down to ground level.

Then I called up a list of the building's tenants.

Holoworld, of course. A couple of snowworms would give their system fits, and I knew just where to dig for them.

I slipped on my ski mask, zipped up my parka, and grabbed the chairlift to the nets. Issuing crisp orders to the voice inputs, tapping all the while, windowing half a dozen screens simultaneously, I put out a call.

Rolf? Fiona? Wanna schuss?

I doubted I'd get them both until later; Fiona didn't come out until late afternoon.

After killing the last guard my trannies were getting restless. Twice I had to tell Pook to stop yelling at the inputs.

Idly, I scanned the tenant list: dozens of corporations, large and small. Sales offices, accounting firms. The U.N.A.F.

Eastern District Base Construction Office. I raised an eyebrow. Now, *that* had possibilities.

On the thirty-ninth floor was Bank of London Shearson, the world's largest brokerage. Could I get in?

"Pook!"

He jumped. "Yo?"

"I got a job for you. Go to thirty-nine, see about breaking into the B of L office."

"I spose ta stay wid you."

"You think I'd go anywhere, dumbass? The only reason I'm sending you is so I can stay here."

"I dunno, Jared." He fretted. " 'Sides, dunno how ta read elevate numbas. Or doors."

My tone was magnanimous. "No problem, Pookboy. I'll run the elevator from here. And on thirty-nine . . . " I checked my codes, tapped a few keys. "It'll be the only office that's lit."

"How we get in?"

"Up to you. Smash the door if you like."

"All *ri'*!" He jumped up. "Allie, ya watchim' for me?"

Her teeth bared. "Absolute."

I added, "Pook, when the caller rings, answer it."

"Huh?"

I picked up my console caller. "Once you're in I'll tell you what to do."

"Bissie, wanna comealong?" He raced out with a whoop.

I studied the layout, turned to Raulie. "Your skills are wasted here. How about taking your joeys to another tower?"

"Why?"

"This will take a while," I said. "Meantime, I can't have jerries busting in. Maybe you could start a couple more fires and spread their attention."

Raulie's face went sullen. "Buncha trannies get diss each time. Ya wan' us dead so ya can play widya toys?"

"You don't realize what these toys can do." Of course not; he was a trannie. "First I'll blast Holoworld off the screens." I jumped up, paced the puter room. "If I crash the B of L nets we can break into thousands of brokerage accounts. Then—"

"Broke her what?"

"Never mind. When Fiona helps me with the links, we can go for air traffic control, tax files, databanks . . . "

Raulie's face was blank.

"Look, With enough free RAM I can build an Arfie. I've figured how." Excitedly, I paced. "After we link I'll dump a few gig of Holoworld's junk and build a mammoth icecracker, in borrowed CLIP RAM. An AI, got it? But he'll be too big for Holoworld to contain. And if we squeeze him out of Holoworld with a timed dump, he'll be floating wild, and answerable only to us! Don't you see what that means?"

I grabbed Raulie, shook his shoulders. "You want to bring down a tower? With an Arfie behind it, maybe my CLIP can bring down a hundred towers. Crash the Uppie world!"

"What's a CLIP?"

"Central linked processor. A few superboxes in tandem can—never mind, you wouldn't understand. The North American Stock Exchange reopens tomorrow. Right now the streets are in chaos. But at seven A.M. five thousand people will pour into this building to work. So the jerries will know just where to find us, if this is the only tower we've broken into."

He said slowly, "Ya wan' us ta fuddle 'em? Hit an' run?"

"Yes." I held my breath.

"Dunno."

"If Halber gave you more trannie—more joeys . . . it's not like you'd have to start fires on a bunch of floors like the Sheraton. Just break in, smash what you can, start a blaze, and get the hell out."

Finally, he shook his head. "Naw. Halb don' want us ta leave ya."

I tried to hide my dismay. My eye fell on a caller, and it inspired me. "Look! Every office has dozens of these. I'll show you how to use them. Take a sackful back for the Subs. Won't that help you fight the Unies?"

"Yeah, but . . . " He wrinkled his brow. "Usual, govermen shut off callers when we take."

"Sure, if you steal one from some lost Uppie. But we're talking dozens here, maybe hundreds. And every tower you hit will have them. It'll take the Unies weeks to figure which to shut off."

"Means leavin' ya alone?"

"Let Pook stay." It wasn't what I wanted, but if that would appease him . . . "And a few of your Subs, if you must.

Besides, I'll need someone to bring me softies and snacks from the machines. Look, I'll preset these three callers so you and Halber can reach me whenever you want."

"How get out?"

"I'll open a ground floor door."

He fretted, "Halber be pissoff."

"Raulie, look outside!" I keyed the console screen, displayed the building perimeter and the streets beyond. "This is war! Do you want to win?"

While he thought about it, I rang Pook on thirty-nine.

It was late afternoon.

I stretched, yawning. Outside my door, Allie and her trannies slept.

We were high in the electronic Alps, schussing passes that had never known a keyboard's touch.

Rolf was with me, and Fiona. They'd brought a few friends I hadn't met.

It took a while to convince them I wasn't sucking goofjuice, that my access was as hard as I claimed.

It took a longer while to set it up. Pook wasn't merely an illiterate, he was a stubborn illiterate. My voice was raw from screaming through the caller, explaining over and again how to power up and call in, what keys to hit to mini-net with my command console. When he was finally done, I sent his joeys on to Holoworld's private floor to do the same.

It took two hours to link.

Pook came downstairs sullen, looking for a fight. I recalled the slashes he'd left on my chest, and praised him lavishly until the thunder on his face cleared.

I set Rolf's codebreaker onto the brokerage accounts. It was normally a slow process, but my superbox linkups provided all the processing power we could ask.

While my joeyboys zarked through the accounts I crosswired Fiona's ID builder to the B of L database, and entered a few hundred phony accounts, to add to the confusion.

B of L wasn't without defenses. Automatically, their CLIP raised them.

A blinding sleetstorm swirled over our heads.

The electronic wind howled. I leaned hard to the right; skied away from the edge of a cliff. I gritted my teeth, bent my knees, leaned into the blizzard, straining to peer through the electronic chaff. If I crashed, I'd be buried in an avalanche. If not, I'd own the mountain.

I worked three keyboards, windowing like a madman. My throat was dry from growling constant verbals to the obedient inputs.

I crouched low, shot over a cliff, skis bent high as I plunged toward the sheet of snowcapped ice.

Slam. A moment's unbalance.

I raced downhill past useless drifts piled in flimsy defense.

Suddenly I coasted through a calm chill valley.

The Bank of London CLIP was mine.

Chapter 43

POOK

Bustin' through doors be zarky. Resta stuff, noway. Why Jared Uppie figga I know 'bout inputs an' pitchers onna screen? Only screen I know is big newscreen on side a Holoworld build.

No reason fo' him ta yell like I stupe.

I come back down from thirty-nine wonderin' whetha ta dissim an' take my chances wid Halber, but he musta realize it ain' good ta mess wid Pookboy, cause he allasudden nice.

Still, not much ta do 'xcept sit aroun' an watch, an every time I fidget he go inta orbit. Finally he say in Uppietalk, ya know I gonna stay here. Why doncha go upta eleven or twelve and smash a buncha Uppie offices?

"Smash what?" I ask.

"Anything you want," he say. "Just don't break any windows. From outside I don't want anyone to know we're here."

"Dunno," I say.

"You'll find puters, desks, chairs, water lines. You could have fun."

"Well . . . " I be godawful tempt. "Jus' fo' a while, maybe."

"Long as you want," he say. "Allie's here. The other joeys too."

So I go have fun. Afta, I so tire I couldn' smash a Unie's face if it lyin' unnerfoot. I go back ta putah room, lie quiet in corna.

When I wake up, screen show outside is dark. Jared sit at console tappin' like loonie, time ta time snickerin'.

He got two callers, one talkin' ta whole room', otha at his ear. "They *can't* trace," he say inta one. "We routed through London on a scrambler to Madrid and I rescrambled to ring you. Cool your frazzing jets, Rolf. We're just two friends talking. These airway lines have nothing to do with net fiboptics."

Allatime his hands busy.

"Tellya what," he say. "I'm wasting my time doing this by

hand. Have Arfie write a quickie that manages a couple thousand accounts and performs random trades. Huh? Yes, I have a reason. About six times during the day, program half the accounts to sell off a big chunk of some multiplanetary. Start with Holoworld. And come back to hit those fuckers twice; I owe them. Toward afternoon let's crank up the volume. If you can feed me the program by opening bell, I'll crank the customer list through and generate orders."

He lissen a long while.

"Yeah, they'll close it down when they realize, but you know what? I got the B of L CLIP in London purring like a kitten. Betcha I can get it to feed me customer accounts worldwide. Wouldn't that be a zark?"

Again he lissen. "Right. Happy schuss."

He click off caller, talk to his desk. "Sorry to keep you waitin'. What'd you say your name was again?"

A grunt. "Shooter."

"Kay, feed me your idea one more time."

"Rolf says you're friggin' around with brokerage accounts."

"So?"

"Why waste the time? Go for the gold."

Jared roll his eyes. "Kill the dramatics, it's been a long night."

"I'm talking literal. Go for the gold."

I lissen, but hard time figurin' out what he say. Somethin' about a run on the Unidolla, tradin' pounds fo' francs fo' yen. An' a frien' who once busted inta treasury central putah.

Jared's eyes go wide. I ask somethin', but he shush me fas'. He listenin' har'.

Chapter 44

ROBERT

I spent the night in the aerie of Midtown Hospital, under a fair amount of sedation.

It was a busy night for hospital emergency rooms, and it was two hours before I was seen. But when the admissions office discovered who I was, obstacles disappeared, and I found myself in a private room on a VIP floor.

Perhaps I should have pulled rank the moment they wheeled me to the clinic doors, but for once, I didn't care about the perks of office. I made sure Dad was notified and told I'd call him in the morning, and sank into much-needed sleep.

When I woke to daylight, I had an unexpected visitor: Mother. She sat placidly in the corner, scanning her holovid. "Hallo," she said, switching it off. She hitched her chair closer.

I held out my hand, squeezed hers. "How did you know?"

"Your father."

"Considerate of him. I'd have called you as soon as I woke."

"I'm sure." Perhaps she meant it. My relations with her were cordial but lacked affection, as was also the case between me and Dad. Somehow, I'd never learned the art. That didn't prevent me from calling her regularly, or working closely with Dad in party politics.

"Lie still," she said. "You're concussed. That trannie prick nearly bashed in your skull." I was careful not to show annoyance. Mother's language was uninhibited, and was one of the many causes of her breakup with Dad. Though some of his colleagues saw her candor as refreshing, others were put off. It had added to the strain of the entertaining that was a *sine qua non* of political life.

"Halber was a bit annoyed with the Captain," I said. "And with all Uppies."

She wrinkled her nose. "I wish you wouldn't say 'Uppie.' That snobbishness doesn't apply to all of us."

"I suppose." I tried carefully to sit. "Are my ribs broken?"

"Bruised. The bandages will help you breathe easier. Lie still."

"Mother, can you get me released?" I studied the door. The room no longer spun.

"Probably, but why? They say to rest three days before—"

"All hell's breaking loose. I want to be at my console, not buried in a boneyard. This trannie fracas is the break Dad needs. I want to help." Perhaps I could even moderate the war's fury, to make amends for my excess of enthusiasm.

She asked, "Will he declare?"

"Not during a police crackdown. His announcement would be buried. But soon." Sooner than planned, I realized. The upheaval would bring a spate of news stories, a mild backlash of sympathy for the oppressed, and an intense desire to forget the blood and the men who'd caused it.

"He can destroy Kahn, head to head." Her tone was casual, acknowledging what we both knew. Dad was a master debater, and his wit would shine in contrast to the stolid SecGen.

I said suddenly, "Would you have liked to be First Lady?"

"Not a whit. But see that I get an invitation for tea during his term of office."

"Done," I said, and we both smiled.

"First spouses don't often do well," she reflected. "Mrs. Kahn is bored senseless with diplomatic soirees, and your confidante Arlene's jaw was clenched through the entire Seafort administration."

I giggled, but it hurt my chest.

"I'll find a wheelchair," she said, getting to her feet. "And a stick of dynamite for the paperwork." She paused at the door. "Call Van," she said. "He must be worried sick."

I frowned, but she was gone before I could reply. Like most who knew me, she thought I concealed an amorous relationship with my long-term aide, and paid no heed to my denials. But it wasn't so. Van's regard was elsewhere, lavished on a young joey who'd been a Senate page when they'd met. And my passion was unengaged. I still hoped the right joeygirl would come along, but knew that with each passing month it grew more unlikely.

While Mother was battling the hospital administrators, the caller rang. It was Dad. "Robbie, you all right?"

"More or less. I was about to call; we need to meet. There are things you should know."

"Van filled me in on some. All in all, I approve. I'm at my office. I can be down in an hour." Dad's suite was in the legislative tower overlooking the U.N. Rotunda.

"No, I'll come to you."

He asked, "Can you walk?"

"I haven't tried yet, but I'll be there." I rang off.

When Mother came back to gloat over her success I said, "Have we heard from the Seaforts?"

"No messages. Why would they call?"

So Kahn had kept his bargain; Mother's response told me the Captain's involvement wasn't public news. Good; I owed him that much.

I wondered how the story was playing. "Can you lay hands on a Holoworld?"

"Yes, but don't bother. Abbreviated edition, compiled over the nets. Their home office is closed, along with a dozen other towers."

"Good lord. Did the Subs burn them all?"

"The Sheraton was worst hit, but there's been trashing, looting, and fire. The Mayor's advised everyone in midtown towers to work from home for the day. Ah, here's the nurse to help you dress."

Two hours later an aide was wheeling me into the Hugo Von Walther Senatorial Office Building, an address I hoped to claim after the next election. Built on the extensive grounds of the enlarged U.N. compound, it was one of the city's few towers that had entrances both above and at streetside.

Outside his private office Dad gave me a quick embrace. "You look better than I feared."

"I'm well enough. I don't need this chair."

"Stay in it for a day. Anything I should hear privately? I have Rex Fizer from the Senate U.N.A.F. Committee and Admiral Jeff Thorne from Lunapolis in the office."

"In brief, Kahn agreed to total clearance of the streets, and I promised we'd give him no flak." Quickly, I summarized our conversations. "Arlene Seafort gave me the opening, and I leaped on it. I also got Kahn to keep the Seaforts out of it. Dad, the heat will be his to bear, and we've cleared the way for our construction people."

"You did well." For a moment, his hand flitted to my shoulder. I basked in his benediction. "Confidentially, Jeff Thorne supports a change of government. Fizer is of course a Supranationalist, and with us. But don't rub their noses in the political aspects of our agreement with Kahn."

I was nettled. "Obviously not. That was for your ears."

We joined their meeting in progress. Dad said, "Kahn's people called this morning. They want a visibly bipartisan committee to consult on this one. No doubt Kahn will keep his distance and send a flunky."

Admiral Thorne nodded. "You'll include the military?"

"Yes, I'll propose you for the Navy. And Rex here, from the Supras' Senate caucus. For the Assembly, I thought perhaps Rob would be a good choice. So as not to upstage him, I'll find urgent business in Washington for the week."

I made sure my face revealed little. Dad liked to spring surprises on me. Political training, he called it. What my face would have shown, if I'd allowed it, was elation. I'd be in a position not only to inform Dad but to influence events.

I also noticed Dad had played it like the wily fox he was. The Boland name would be prominent, but not his own; he could take credit for success, and avoid the worst of the fallout if some fiasco ensued.

I asked, "Who's in charge overall?"

"General Ernst Ruben. Mildly political, but professional through and through."

"Where is he?"

"At the moment, Lord knows. He's made headquarters in Franjee Tower on Fortieth."

I said, "I'd like to watch from there. Can you swing it?"

"I imagine. Give me 'til this afternoon. Now, I don't know why you went down to the street, but don't let it happen again. That's why we train joeykids as soldiers. You served your time."

"Aye aye, sir." It was deliberate, to remind him he was issuing orders in front of our allies.

"They say it's a nightmare down there." He went to the window, but it fronted on the river, and none of the carnage was visible. "Mrs. Kahn's aunt was evacuated in the Sheraton fire. All sorts of people are inconvenienced, and many are hurt."

"I was there," I said dryly.

"Of course. Forgive me."

After our conference I borrowed a desk, netted with Van and our office puter, and delegated as much of the routine work as I could.

No word from the Captain or Arlene.

In the heli heading to Franjee Tower, I tried Seafort's personal caller code, got only his voicemail. He could be maddening. Most joeys let their puter screen incoming calls and forward those it thought important. But the Captain refused to work with intelliputers, no matter what inconvenience he caused others.

I tried Arlene's line, and she answered. "Rob?"

"Thank God! Where are you?"

"Refugees have taken every hotel room in the city. We're with the Tamarovs, Alexi and Moira. Do you know them?"

"I met Alexi once, after the war."

"They're putting us up until Philip's found. You saw what he did?"

"He headed down in the elevator."

"And he disconnected his caller; we can't trace him. In the Sheraton stairwell, a Sub told him Jared was nearby."

"Did you look?"

"Rob, we can't get near midtown. No helis are to rent, the helicabs won't consider the trip. The Unies won't take us, or the police. The Tamarovs' tower is at the foot of the island overlooking the seawall, or we'd walk. Nick is beside himself."

"Stay off the streets. The soldiers are on edge."

Her voice broke. "Rob, I need to find my son."

"I've been assigned to the oversight committee, and I'm on my way to military HQ. I'll do what I can."

"Please! And keep us informed."

"I will." I rang off.

The caller buzzed immediately.

"Rob, it's Adam Tenere."

"Wonderful. Are you all right? Have you a caller with you?"

"Programmed to my home number. We have a problem. I just got a call from the Commandant. It seems Jared escaped the Subs and is on the street."

"We'll do everything we can to—"

"Remember Colonel Wirtz, on a Hundred Tenth? He's about to gas the Sub tunnels."

"It's probably for the best. Knockout gas is humane. In the long run, it will—"

"He called off the knockout gas. Apparently the Subs counterattacked in midtown. Overran a Unie post, about seventy U.N. casualties. No wounded. The orders are now to kill on sight. Wirtz has a new plan to flush the tunnel with cyanide gas."

"Lord Jesus."

Adam's tone was urgent. "Even the trannies don't deserve that, Rob. You've *got* to help."

"I'll do what I can."

"Hurry!" He rang off.

We set down on the rooftop of Franjee Tower. As the blades slowed I ducked out, hurried to meet the officer waiting to escort me to the elevator.

"Mr. Boland? Major Groves." We shook hands. "General Ruben's headquarters is on floor ninety-three."

"What's the latest?" My ribs were still sore; I slowed my pace.

"You heard about the massacre on Fourteenth? The General's called for massive reinforcements, and meanwhile we've pulled back." Savagely, he punched an elevator button.

Ninety-three was a whirlwind of activity. Ernst Ruben had commandeered the floorwide offices of Peabody & Company, one of the larger real estate companies. Desk consoles had been cleared of civilian business, callers appropriated, detailed city maps displayed on the sales screens.

I made a mental note to see the Peabody firm was amply compensated; they were among our firmest supporters.

"General?" Major Groves snapped a salute. "Assemblyman Boland to see you."

Ernst Ruben turned from a viewscreen, pointer in hand. "Goot to meet you, Assemblyman."

"Call me Rob; everyone does," I said smoothly. Major Groves edged away, giving us privacy.

"In that case, I'm Red. I understand you were on the streets with Seafort?"

"God, yes." I grimaced. "You have no idea . . ."

"Oh, I do, believe me. They ambushed us yesterday, and . . . " His eyes searched mine. "You realize this has gone far beyond a mere riot?"

"I'd call it full-scale insurrection."

"Ja. Truth is, we can't contain it with the Seventy-fifth Regiment alone; I've called in Thirteenth Armor."

"Tanks and artillery, for an urban disturbance?"

"They'll support our troop carriers in the house-to-house assault." Ruben's gaze was steady. "We're only going to do this once. That's straight from the Rotunda."

"At what cost in lives?"

"None, if the trannies give way."

I hated to begin my liaison with an objection, but morality and Dad's upcoming campaign left me little choice. "General, for politics' sake, if nothing else, we have to give them a chance to surrender."

"I already have." He grinned. "They sent an envoy of sorts."

"You're joking."

"Not at all. A ragged old man. Came under white flag."

"What does he say?"

"He's waiting for our terms, but I'm letting him stew. The trannies must be worried; they've already sent him a messenger."

"When will your offensive push off?"

"Probably not before tomorrow. We'll give their negotiator one chance to make peace."

"Can he? The trannie tribes are scattered all over the city."

"It's a problem. I'll set him a test, I think. Later tonight."

I looked around for a place to sit. "The oversight committee . . . where will we meet?"

"By vidcon, mostly. Admiral Thorne's gone to the Earthport Naval base. Senator Fizer's still in Washington, and the SecGen flew to London."

"As far from responsibility as they can get." My tone was glum.

"Oh, there's always Timbuktu. But I doubt you'll have trouble getting them on the caller."

A window rattled, as one of the incessant military helis flew past, closer than was absolutely necessary.

Ruben snapped, "Groves!" The major left his map. "Once

was funny, twice was a nuisance. Tell the flyboys to give us two hundred damn feet clearance, and I mean it!"

"Right, sir."

"And get me another coffee. Then find Mr. Boland a console."

Groves strode off. I said, "General, I'll try to stay out of your hair, but we have problems that can't wait."

Suddenly his look was less friendly. "Such as?"

"I had a call from Adam Tenere, who works for former SecGen—"

"I know of him."

"At your outpost on a Hundred Tenth, a Colonel Wirtz is planning an attack on the Sub tunnels."

"And?"

"Have him wait until we can discuss it. He intends to use gas, and there may be civilians—"

"When Groves gets back, I'll tell him. What else?"

"SecGen Seafort's son."

"Thank God he's been found; having him off the streets makes our job less of a nightmare."

"Well, that's a problem. He went back."

"He what?"

"Ran away again. They had him at the hotel and . . . he was searching for a friend, and the trannies torched the hotel, the situation was confused . . . " I trailed off.

Ruben's eyes were ice. "Assemblyman—Rob—we've lost a hundred-twelve troops as of last count. I hope the boy's all right, but if his parents had him and let him go, I'd say we were absolved of responsibility, and I'll so advise SecGen Kahn."

Chapter 45

PEDRO

I sat in windowless room, a negotiator without negotiate. Early in day, governmen troops escorted me to tower office. Wasn't long 'til brusque Unie officer Groves came to ask what I wanted. End to fightin', I said. Have trannie rebels come out and give selves up, he replied.

I shrugged. "What else you offa?"

"Nothing. Only the chance for you to save lives."

Be patient, Pedro, I tol' self. You be a traytaman, and understand. Trannies won't give in without trayfo. But Unies don't seem to want nothin' 'xcept total surrender, which you can't give. Halber's fightin' might change that, but isolated in negotiate room, I wouldn't know what he achieve. Prollem.

Wait 'n see, I told major; maybe one of us change his min'. Without a word he got up an' left. I heard door lock from outside.

Alone, I sat. Wished I had my teapot, or old bound book for read.

After hours passed, door to my windowless prison opened. Fisherman's joeykit walked in, dirty and dishevel.

"Peetee!"

His eyes flickered to the guard. "I'm Chaco," he said casual. "I brought—brung a message. Private."

I looked at guard, then door. "If ya don' min'?"

Soldier sniffed, stalked out to the hall.

I beckoned Peetee close, whispered in his ear. "They prolly listenin'. What you doin' here?"

"I'm . . . not sure." For a moment he groped for words. "I found Father, the hotel was in flames . . . the Subs in the stairs mentioned Jared . . . " Haltingly, he told me his story, and how Barth led him to me. In return, I tol' him how I made myself negotiator for trannies.

"Do you know where Jared is, Mr. Chang? I've *got* to find him."

I shook my head, whispered, "I gotta send you back, joeykit. We need Fisherman's grateful."

"Don't you understand?" His voice trembled. "If I go back without Jared, it's all wasted. The fighting, the respect I've lost forever from my parents, even . . . Chaco."

"I dunno where he is, Peetee."

He clutched my wrist. "Don't call me that! If they find out I'm here, they'll call Fath."

I debated. Findin' Peetee cut both ways. If I sent him back to Fisherman, was likely they'd fly off to Washington compound, an' I'd never see again. On other hand, if boy went back to street and got diss, Fisherman never forgive. "All right, Chaco," I say loud, for hidden pickups. "Stay with me a while, we see what happen." I nodded to boy, put finger to lips.

I bent to joeykit's ear, tol' him what I had in mind. At last, he nodded, reluctant.

"Chaco, bang on door 'til they answer."

A sergeant appeared, then a Unie major. "What is it?"

"Can' negotiate surrender 'less I talk to tribes. Put me out on street with flag. I come back in coupla hours."

"That's up to General Ruben."

"Ask 'im."

"Fraz yourself, trannie." The door slammed.

For while, Peetee fretted with hands, like counting.

Door opened, and thickset man with carrot hair come in. Wore fatigues, with general's stripes. "Chang?"

I drew myself up. "Pedro Telamon Chang, speakfo tribes. We ain't introduce."

"Ernst Ruben. I'm in charge." He didn't offer hand. "You want to arrange a surrender?"

"Possible. Or cease-fire. Gotta talk to my joeys."

"Do you have authority? Would all the trannies listen to you?"

I said with dignity, "I have authority they choose to give."

"Here's your chance to show it. I'll give you two hours. As proof of your credentials, get me a trannie cease-fire for the rest of the evening, from Forty-third to Forty-first where we picked you up."

"I'll try."

"Do more than try, Mr. Chang, or don't come back."

I nodded and said casual, "I'll need Chaco here as messenger for after. He'll stay here while I go out. No point riskin' joeykit too."

"Whatever." He didn't spare Peetee a glance.

"See he gets food. All of us, we gotta take care of joeykits in world."

Ruben's eyes lifted to my face, with a note of reappraisal.

Two soldiers came for me, poised at either side like they ready to grab in case I go heroic. I walked with them up to roof. Wind blew my hair and billowed my coat. Was different, above. Cleaner. Wind was stronger, and without grit from streets. But no time to appreciate; they bustled me in heli and a min later we swooped down to street.

Below, Unie patrol waited with white flag. Loudspeakers already blarin' don't shoot, don't shoot, negotiator comin' out.

They escorted me to center of Broad, left me to walk down mid of street by self, feelin' like thousand eyes be watchin'. Maybe they were. I went into same build I first came out of, and wait 'til Barth march in, his flag held high.

Ten min later, I in Four Two Sub.

Halber met me few paces from stair, walked me to main cavern. "Losin' too many joeys, Chang. C'n ya negotiate meds, help for wound? Laser burns be godawful. We dissin' Trannies be hurt too bad."

"Dunno. Unies wouldn' talk all day, then allasudden their General anxious."

"Didja trayfo?"

"Nothin' yet." I saw his look of disappoint. "He sizin' me up, Halber. Be natural, if ya haven' trayfo with someone before. Ain' Chang bes' traytaman aroun'? Trus' me."

"Why'd you come unner?"

"I need info to tray. Tell me 'bout fightin', and what ya doin' next."

"How dat gonna help?" His tone was suspicious.

"Righ' now all they want is we give up. If we hurt 'em, maybe they settle for less. Don' waste time, only got coupla hour. Talk."

He sat back, thought a min, described the trannie war.

The south tip of island was beyond our savin'; too many Uppies, too few trannies. Far north, near Bronxbridge, not so many towers built yet, so Unies were givin' it less attention. Washhites holdin' on best they could.

The Hundred Ten wall at park had grown to major Unie base. Govermen pushout Nor' Broads near alla way south to Ninety Six.

Three Four was another Unie camp, 'long with Four Two at Sixth, a mere two block west of where we sat.

Halber had ferried undercars full of trannies past them all, to Fourteen Square. Bypassin' Sub stair, they'd sneaked out of ventholes, infiltrated buildings, attacked the Unie camp. Govermen were better armed, but tribes fought with savage abandon 'cause little left to lose. Halber sent his precious few lasers, and that caught Unies total surprise. Soon, tribes had more lasers. Then more yet. Trannies quick showed each other how to use.

Our raiding party burned troop trucks. Took rations, med-kits, and, in major coup, supply boxes fulla laser recharge packs. Disappeared back into Sub as first counterattack helis appeared overhead. Too late for Unies on street, though. None left alive.

I asked, "When?"

"Finish three hours back."

"Ahh. It figure." General Ruben poked head in, soon after.

Halber said, "Natch, alla tribes wanted lasers firs' thing. I warned 'em, gotta hold for rumb. So buncha joeys volunteer ta rumb wid us." He grinned. "Maybe trouble gettin' lasers back, afta. But fo' now, plenny of trannie sojers."

"Good." I smiled to encourage, but inside I knew it wasn' enough. A few untrain trannies couldn' dislodge Unie army, even on own turf.

"I sen' our laser joeys ta help Mids on Three Four. Broads and Rocks joined 'em." Halber shook head. "Your idea workin', Chang. Think we be one trannie tribe when it's ova?"

"Dunno," I said, cross. "Filmatleven. What else ya plan?"

"Sheraton still burnin'; Raulie did good job. Lotsa tribes saw scorch an' it made 'em jealous. So I sendin' ten bands, each wid coupla laser, try ta hit more towahs."

"They be ready this time," I warned. "Lotsa Unies waitin' inside, ready ta rumb."

"Sure." He shrug. "But we'll hit 'em all at once. An Sollie, he say give him few hour, he c'n make pipebombs. Ya know what dey be?"

"Dunno." In shop, I read 'bout Napoleon, Hitler, Gettysburg. Nothin' 'bout pipebombs.

"He say they bus' through door by self."

"Still, if Unies inside waitin—"

"Go back ta ya negotiate, ol' man; I already work it out wid Raulie. Start seven clock tonigh'. We'll bomb one door in towah, but burn in through 'notha, so Unies confuse. Sure, some of us diss. But some won' be."

"I thought Raulie was sent with Jared."

"Yeah, but he left." Face brightened. "Look!" He crossed cavern, led me to box of callers. "Fo' communicate, jus' like Uppies," he said proud. "Thas how Raulie's joeys know ta blow towahs, all same time. Hey!" He thrust one into my hands. "Take wid ya. Ya won' have ta come back ta Sub fo' negotiate."

I said, "Okay to use sometime, but Uppies 'll lissen."

"Don' matta if we careful."

I put it in coat pocket. "Gotta go. Govermen wan' me to prove I be speakfo, so we agree, no shootin 'tween Forty One an' Forty Three whole eve."

He glowered. "Ya helpin' 'em push us out?"

I bristled. "Ya wan' 'notha negotiate? I go home ta shop, make cuppa tea."

"Okay okay, cool jets. But tell ya Uppie frien': sojers move in durin' no-shoot, we diss 'em."

"Runnin' outa time." I started to stair.

"Dunno 'bout Jared." Halber walk 'longside. "Is he glitch, or jus' Uppie? He say don' burn Holoworl' tower cause he need it. But when I talked ta Pook onna caller, Pook say Uppie jus' playin' wid putah."

"Pook's still with him?"

"Like adhese, he say. Prolly cause I put scare in him 'fore I lettim go." He sighed. "Jared called ta complain Pook jus' a trannie stupe, don' know importance a what he doin'. Buncha bombs goin' off inna markets every coupla hour. Why can't I hear 'em, Chang? Worms inna system, he tell me. Gonna start hittin' tonight. Watch London 'xchange, he say. An N'Yawk."

Halber shook his caller. "Prollem wid callers is ya can' whomp joey on otha end when he talkin' glitch. Fah. Hate 'em." He spat. "Got any idea what he talkinabout?"

"Maybe," I say, weight in chest feelin' lighter. "Maybe."

Chapter 46

PHILIP

I dozed, my head on the table, until a trooper opened the door, carrying a hot and savory tray.

My mouth watered.

"Need to use the bathroom, joey?" His face was almost as young as Jared's, but I knew he had to be older. U.N.A.F. didn't allow enlistment until seventeen. And then there'd be training.

"Yes, please."

"Out here." He took my arm, led me to a cubicle. "You know how?" He indicated the flush mechanism.

I remembered just in time I was supposed to be a transpop, and stuck out my chest as Pook had done. "Mr. Chang show me." My dialect wouldn't fool a real tribesman, but I suspected this soldier wouldn't know the difference.

When I was done, I washed some of the grime off my hands—not too much; I didn't want to ruin my disguise—and hurried back to my tray. Objectively speaking, I was rather hungry.

Another soldier wandered in. They watched me eat. I used my fingers, in a manner that would have scandalized Mom.

"Better hope the old man comes back," said the older. "Or we toss you off the roof."

"He didn't mean it," the younger said quickly. To his mate, "Look at his eyes, for Chrissake. Don't do that."

"Fuckin' trannie scum."

"He's a joeykit. About my brother's age."

"You Dan's brother?" The older jabbed at my arm. "Are you?"

I shook my head, not trusting my accent.

"Where you live on the street?"

"Lair." I stared at my dinner.

"Why they using you for a go-between?"

I shrugged, but it didn't seem to satisfy them. "Dunno. Ask Halber."

"Who's he?"

The door opened, and Mr. Chang shuffled in. Never had I been so glad to see an adult.

His eyes flitted from me to the soldiers, and back. "Whas' up?"

"Feeding him."

"Takes two? Why Chaco look so scare?" Again he looked back and forth. "Been interrogatin', hah?"

"Nonsense. Come on, Dan."

"Bring the tray. Don't leave them with metal silverware."

Mr. Chang snorted. "Yah, an' take bootlaces too, so I can' strangle ya in sleep. This whatcha call negotiatin'? Feh!"

The two stalked to the door.

A few moments later the major looked in. "General Ruben wants to know if you brought surrender terms."

Chang swelled with pride. "Absolute. We ready to 'cept your surrender righ' now."

"Don't give me that—" With an effort, he restrained himself. "Did you bring terms?"

"Uppies gotta learn ta trayfo. Neva survive onna street for a min." He waved the soldier away. "Hey!"

In the doorway, the major turned.

"Message for ya redhair general. Tellim I don' need lotsa sleep. Tellim when price o' war get high, I be waitin'."

The moment we were alone I bent close. "Did you find out about Jared?"

He hesitated, as if making up his mind. "Yes."

"Where is he?" I couldn't keep the eagerness out of my tone. All Mr. Chang had to do was tell me where Jared hid and invent an errand to get me out of the building. Finally, I'd take my battered friend home.

"Cancha forget 'bout him, Peetee? I mean, Chaco. I gotta call ya that, else I make mistake in fronta."

"Forget Jared?" I didn't hide my indignation. "Mr. Chang, look how far I've come to rescue him."

The old transpop brooded. He sighed, patted my hand. "Ya ever wonder, joeykit, maybe he don't want rescuin'?"

I'd curled up in my chair, too angry to speak to Mr. Chang. They'd cut Jared's chest, beaten him, tied him helpless in a dank elevator, taken his clothes. Of course he wanted rescue.

After a long while, I dozed.

A commotion in the hall. The door swung open. Blearily, I checked my watch. It was two in the morning. Mr. Chang sat at the table, looking as if he hadn't moved. In front of him were papers, pens, even a small holovid.

The major strode in, his expression grim. Behind him, in the hall where the old man couldn't see, was red-haired General Ruben.

Mr. Chang stirred. "Yah. Whatcha wan'?"

"You ready to arrange terms?" The major planted his hands on his hips.

"Always have been."

"We want the riot ended, and that means now. No more attacks on towers."

In the corner, I sat up cautiously, hoping not to be seen but anxious to hear.

"An' we get what?"

"I'm not done. U.N.A.F. patrols aren't to be harmed, and we want our weapons back. All of them."

Mr. Chang sighed. "You woke me for that? Think I didn' know?"

"Well? Do you agree?"

"Wha's innifo?"

"You'll end the killing. Do you know how many of your trannie friends are dead, thanks to your rebellion?"

Mr. Chang's eyes grew cold. "Yes, do you?"

"Few enough, compared with what's to come."

"You come in wid bluster an' hate, wakin' me fo' nothin', to tell me ya wan' us to lie down an' die quiet. Fo' years we been dyin' an' you didn' notice. No more. Streets be ours, an' towahs fallin'!"

"I'm warning you."

Mr. Chang snarled, "And I warnin' you, Genral's errand boy! How long ya think it be only N'Yawk, hah? Think you can stop word gettin' out?"

"Newark's the only other—" He bit it off. "Old man, rebellion is treason against the Government of Lord God. We're under martial law; if I hear so much as one more threat, I'll have you hanged!"

Mr. Chang rose unsteadily. "I'll save you trouble! All it takes is I jump up 'n down few times and I fall dead with stop heart, 'fore you c'n call medic. Then who you gonna negotiate with, dumbass?" His face grew red. "I only one they lissen to!"

"Go ahead. If you think I give Lord God's damn whether you live—"

Mr. Chang flapped his arms, making short but energetic hops.

I lunged to my feet. "STOP, BOTH OF YOU!" I ran to the old man, tugged desperately at his coat.

The major folded his arms.

Mr. Chang thrust me aside, continued his erratic dance.

"That's enough!" From the doorway, Ernst Ruben's voice sliced through the tumult. "Mr. Chang, sit down."

The old trader glared.

"Please. I ask as a personal favor."

Panting, Mr. Chang regarded him a moment, tottered to his seat.

"That's all, Major."

"Sir, you shouldn't be alone with—"

"Dismissed."

"Yes, sir." The major stalked out, his mouth grim.

Mr. Chang's face was an unhealthy hue. I poured a cup of water. He fumbled in one of his many pockets, emerged with a pill box. He swallowed two pills, took a gulp of the water, clutched my arm.

General Ruben waited stolidly. "Let me know when you're well enough to continue."

"Few mins." Mr. Chang gasped for air. His lips moved, perhaps in prayer. After a moment he muttered under his breath. It sounded like a curse.

After a time his grip on my arm eased.

"I apologize for Major Groves," Ruben said. "A close friend was stationed at Fourteenth Street." His tone was quiet, almost companionable. "But he was wrong to provoke you."

Mr. Chang let out a sigh, gestured for me to pour more water. "Too old for this nonsense," he muttered.

"Are you recovered now, Mr. Chang? Time is short."

The trader nodded.

"Your trannies are behind the Hacker attack?"

Mr. Chang's expression went bland. "Attack?"

"What else would you call it?"

"Wha's happenin'?"

"The international markets have gone berserk, and the disruption is puter-driven. We'll have a trace soon, but do you realize the harm you're causing? The markets are so complex, if they crash they can't be rebuilt in weeks, even months. When depression hits, your people will starve."

Mr. Chang snorted. "Already do."

"Not like they will." He leaned forward. "Are you a reasonable man, Mr. Chang? Help me find a solution."

The old trader peered into his eyes. "Water pipes goin' dry all over city. Fix."

Ruben looked puzzled. "That's a municipal matter. I know nothing about it."

"For us it's life matter! Tribes be pushout all ova, an ya don' even know why they dyin'?" He grimaced. "Betcha could fin' out inna hurry if you wan'."

General Ruben nodded. "Wait here." He left.

In the stillness of the room Mr. Chang sighed, and struggled out of his heavy coat.

"Sir?" My voice was hesitant. "Why?"

"I try ta die?"

I nodded.

"Hadda, Chaco. Was all I had lef'." He saw my confusion, and added, "Either they wanted to negotiate, or not. If so, hadda force 'em; more Unie troops on street each hour. Time runnin' out fo' Halber." A pause. "And if not, no point in ol' Chang stayin' to watch."

"Please, sir. There's been enough death." My eyes stung.

"What you know 'bout death, joeykit?"

I tried to speak, but my voice failed. I shook my head.

He patted my arm. "Okay okay, Chaco. 'Nother time, you tell. Don' flare jets."

Disguised as a transpop, sitting at a Unie conference table high in a tower, I thought of the Sub who'd lain dying in the park, and tried not to rev. Instead I focused on the transpop war, on Mr. Chang's confrontation with General Ruben, on the city's slide into bedlam. I wondered why the General was concerned with hacking, at a time like this.

Some joeys couldn't get puters out of their mind. Like Jar. Patterns.

After a time I said, "Mr. Chang, where's Jared?"

"Huh?" He jerked awake. "Why allasudden you—"

"It's Jar, isn't it? He's been hack—"

Mr. Chang's hand shot out to cover my mouth. "Some things, don' say in watched room, *Chaco*."

"He *is* the one!" I jumped to my feet. "Tell me where to find him!"

"Can'. Anyway, if you—"

"Don't you know?"

He pursed his lips. "Not 'xactly."

"I need to tell him—"

The door swung open. "All right," said General Ruben.

I sat quickly.

"It's called the Hudson Freshwater Project." The General took a seat across from Mr. Chang. "The city's grown. The towers need water, and they built a new system to supply it."

"By takin' water from street pipes!"

"Only temporarily, until more desalinization plants—"

"Hah!"

"Look, Mr., uh, Chang, our urban economy is centered in the towers. Their needs must be met. In the city of New York not a single ratepayer was cut off. Not one. It's only the abandoned areas that—"

"We didn' abandon 'em!" Chang's eyes glowed like coals. "You talkin thousands of lives, hunnerts of thousands!"

"Sir, this isn't my province. If we restore peace, I'll submit your objections to the authorities. I'm sure they'll . . . "

Mr. Chang folded his arms, swung his chair to the wall.

Ruben's voice sharpened. "Damn it, we're out of time. Talk to me!"

Mr. Chang swiveled. "What you wan' me to say? What you give me, take back to my trannies?"

"The Administration will hear your protests. The SecGen would consider leniency for the ringleaders. The U.N.A.F. is ready to move in force; you'll save countless lives if you end resistance. Isn't that enough?"

Mr. Chang looked like he was searching for someplace to spit. "Not even a promise. Nothin'."

Ruben's fingers tapped the table. "If . . . we gave you a new purification plant?"

"How much water? When?"

"I don't know. As soon as possible, obviously."

"Turn pipes back on, meantime?"

"I doubt they'd do that, now the Phase One towers are occupied. You'd have to conserve as best you could. As to construction schedules, I'll check with the political committee they've assigned us." Ruben waited, but no answer came. "And we want your Hackers off-line this hour, as a demonstration of good faith."

The old man said coolly, "Annoyin' ya, are they?"

Ruben snapped, "It's no joking matter." Again he waited. "Mr. Chang, we're two hours from dawn. By first light it will be too late; I won't be able to recall the troops."

From Mr. Chang, a long silence. Then, "Gotta talk to my people."

"You have a caller. Make contact." The general stood, strode to the door, and left.

I said, "Mr. Chang, it's time I—"

"Not now, Chaco."

I leaned close, spoke softly into his ear. "Yes, now, sir. I've been through hell to find Jared, and you know the way. I'm going to him."

"Negotiate is more important than your spoiled Uppiekit frien'." Mr. Chang fingered his caller.

"Jar's part of the negotiations, if he's the Hacker." My knuckles were white against the table. "Do you know how I got to you? I ran from my father and mother. You understand? I tore loose from Father's hand and ran!"

I paused, to force my voice under control. "He'll never forgive me. I've lost my family, ruined my future, killed a man I wanted to save! You can't tell me it was all for nothing. I'll talk to Jared and try to make sense of this . . . this madness." My eyes stung. "Let me save him before hell breaks loose. Perhaps I can't, but I have to try. Tell me where he is or . . . " I found it hard to finish.

"G'wan, joey." Mr. Chang's tone was soft. His fingers no longer stroked the caller.

"If you leave me with nothing else, I'll tell them who I am, and have them call Father. I won't betray you or your Sub friends, but I'll tell them it's Jared behind the hacking, and that he's somewhere near."

It seemed like a long time passed.

Mr. Chang sighed. "Dunno where he is."

"Bullshit." Mom would have washed out my mouth.

Chang pulled me close, and for a moment I thought he meant to hit me. But he only put his lips to my ear. "Halber knows how to fin' him," he said so softly I could barely hear. "I c'n send ya to Sub. Trouble is, Halber royal pissoff at Fisherman, an' wants to diss ya for venge. Dunno if I c'n get him to lissen first. Wanna take risk?"

I nodded.

"Also . . . " For a moment, he pulled back, and his eyes met mine. "Ya gotta face up to: Jared may wanna stay. If so, you let him?"

It was beyond imagining, yet I felt a chill. "Yes, sir. If that's what he truly wants. But I have to know."

Chang regarded me sadly. "You better than he deserve." He took up the pen, wrote a long series of numbers on the pad.

I watched, trying to make sense of the figures.

He forestalled my question with another whisper. "I'll tell govermen ta send you back unner flag of truce cause you got message for Halber. But this paper don' mean nothin'; it's jus' ta give Unies somethin' to stew over. Real message is in your head; you unnerstood Ruben, yah?"

Again I nodded.

"Gotta explain choices to Halber. Trouble negotiating by caller is, Unies are sure to listen any call I make. Halber might say anything comes in head. If you're there to help, maybe he won' tell Ruben all his plans. Your job, show him how to tell me what he wants over caller, without tellin' Unies.

"Soon as you're outa buildin', I'll call Halber, warn him to hear you 'fore he go craze. An' I'll tell him if you help with negotiate, he let you have what you want. Deal?"

I demanded, "Innifo?"

Mr. Chang's eyes widened, until he saw my smile.

He growled, "You make trannie yet, joey."

I hoped so. I might have nowhere else to go.

Chapter 47

JARED

On the security screen I watched the pack of trannies race through the halls, and opened the door to the puter room before they did it more damage.

"C'mon, Jared, we gotta go." Raulie's face was matted with blood. "Halber say Unie army gather round U.N. Rotunda, looks like they gonna move anytime. Beside, buncha patrols searchin' through towers!"

"Jesus!" I jabbed at the console keys, swiveling the cameras. Outside, the lights of a lone armored carrier peered down the avenue. Beyond that, all seemed as before.

Waking from his mattress, Pook rubbed his grimy face.

"You trying to scare me?" My tone was sour. "There's no one near."

"Not dis block, stupe. How ya think we got here? But helis are droppin' from one end a Broad ta otha. Halber says everyone back ta sub fo' now."

I keyed the rooftop cameras, searching for a more distant view.

"Les' go. Halber say you valable, not ta waste."

His words gave me the confidence to lean back, clasp my fingers behind my neck. "They're nowhere in sight. Besides, we've been schussing with the London CLIP, and we're a snowdrift away from the Treasury trading accounts."

"Huh?"

"There's plenty of time," I said, wanting to believe it. I tapped the screen, and figures flashed. "Look at this. Cruncher—one of Rolf's e-friends—lives near New York Spaceport."

"So?"

"He fed his satdish harvest to a miniclip, and kept it live and decoding for weeks." I pointed. "See those codes? We could ID half the ships in the fleet, and damn near all the shuttles."

Raulie didn't understand a word, but I hardly cared. Trannies were too fucking dumb.

Still, I needed his help. I tried to make my tone patient. "Eventually Cruncher caught a bounceback of the ID from Earthport Station, and used that to ski down their recog slope. Don't you see what it means?"

"No." Raulie spat. "Stop talkin' gibber. You comin' wid us."

"I can send random orders to any Naval or U.N.A.F. unit we have codes for. We can make them—*let go of me!*—shoot at themselves!"

Raulie's eyes widened.

I freed my arm. "I already told Halber on the caller, but he doesn't get it. Damn it, Raulie, go back and make him understand."

"Can't. Halber be total pissoff if I come back widout ya."

"For God's . . . " I stifled an urge to tear out my hair. "Pookboy, go with him, help explain to Halber."

Pook shook his head. "Gotta stick widya like adhese. C'mon, Jared."

My heart was pounding. As long as the Unies didn't come in shooting, I'd be all right. When they found me I'd look like a frightened Uppie who barely escaped the trannies. But if they gave me time, I could pay back the lot of them. Kahn, Dad, the fucking righteous Old Man in his compound, the whole world.

When I turned to Pook my voice was soft. "With those codes, we'd actually have a chance to win. And you could be the one who brings the news to Halber."

The trannie grimaced. "If I don' get skin first." But his eyes were calculating.

I wasted precious time getting rid of them. Neither Raulie nor Pook dared go back to Halber alone, but as a pair they bolstered each other's nerve.

To convince them, I had to exaggerate a bit. Even with the massive computing power of the London CLIP, at best it would take our Arfie many hours to slice into fleet traffic. As to making U.N.A.F. fire on itself, well, it was theoretically possible.

Not trusting the screens, I crossed the hall and peered out a window. Now that I was alone, the tower seemed eerily quiet. The soft sigh of the air circulators failed to calm me.

Once, when I was eleven, a lunatic had jumped the compound wall, and the guard Vishinsky had burned him. It gave me nightmares for months. I'd be all right, unless the Unies came in shooting. If they did . . .

Perhaps it would be a good idea to divert them.

I pored over our available codes, wondering which units were stationed near. I sent one tendril searching the nets for the answer, sent another to retrieve a semantic compiler.

When the compiler was in my hands I linked with Cruncher's miniframe, remembering to scramble and rescramble so I'd be harder to trace. I fed the compiler a year's worth of military comsat traffic, waited while it digested grammar, spelling, and syntax. The last thing we need was to raise suspicion by my style.

Multiple connects and a couple of scrambles added security, but eventually my tracks would be found. And by now someone was certainly looking; bombs were starting to go off in the markets. London opened high, but within two hours it plunged seven hundred points, the worst slide in its history. New York night trades staggered under frantic buy and sell orders. Only a third of them were ours; panic was setting in.

By the time the ski patrol caught our tracks I hoped to be long gone, sliding through the wind into the next snow-swept valley.

Again, I swiveled the cameras, hoping to see Raulie or Pook skulking in a dim-lit alley, or slipping in through the broken door.

NYSE would soon open for day trading. Fun times ahead. But I needed cover. A distraction.

I turned to the military codes.

What I needed was an avalanche.

Chapter 48

POOK

Like ol' Changman say, we watchin' history.

Seem like history changes ya. Chang forget 'bout his frazzin' trayfo. Unie sojers drop inta streets like spiders from high, tryin' ta drive out trannies. Halber start seein' hisself leader of trannies, not jus' Sub tribe. Jared Uppie Washinton switch sides, ack like he trannie all his life. Peetee be so glitch he ain' 'fraid a nothin'.

An' Pookboy realize he never was no Mid. Ain' my fault I got no upbringin' from Karlo, but don' matta now. Got lair of my own, maybe someday even have Pooktribe. Like Chang say, filmatleven. But meantime, not bein' Mid means Pook gotta look afta his own life.

So, back in Sub, while Raulie fall behin' tryin' ta hide hisself in crowd, I walk right up ta Halber. "News fo' ya," I 'nounce, like tellin' Sub Boss ya din' do what he say be mos' natural thing in worl'.

"Yah?"

I notice how Raulie watch, ready ta push his way through if Halber don' explode. I go bristle. Pook don' risk his skin ta share applause wid Raulie Sub.

"Private," I say in important voice. "You 'n me only."

Halber stare me down, but I don' cooperate, jus' stare back. I figga he 'bout ta put his fist through my head, when he grunt and say, "Kay. C'mon." We go off ta corna room.

I tell him what Jared wanna do: drop helis flamin' from sky, send Unie troops ta Philly 'stead a N'Yawk, break open buncha banks, whole rest of it. I tell him what Jared show me in putah, alla Unibucks he takin' from frazzin' Uppies. I don' mention I take Jared word fo' what putah say, cause I can' read. Inside, icicle grab my heart; I hope whole biz ain' some crazy swind. But rememberin' Uppie's face when Allie 'n Swee 'n me catch him, I don' think so.

Halber think it ova. I figga it be time ta freeze out Raulie. "Was my idea ta come back," I say, serious. "Raulie wanna drag Jared 'way from putah, but I say betta ask ya firs'. Who know when we c'n get Jared 'notha chance in towah."

Wid dat, I shut face, knowin' I say enough.

Halber put hand ta wall, lean 'gainst it like real tired. Chew his lip, starin' at me, through me.

I wait.

"Can he do it, Pook?" One leader ta 'notha.

I go thrill, but try not ta show. "Think so, Halb. But wid Jared, never know fo' sure. He glitch."

"Course. Othawise why he help trannies?"

"Yah." I scratch behind ear. "Seem like he c'n make Uppies awful lotta trouble."

"Means we need him bad."

I gulp at bleak tone in voice. "How's rumb go, Halber?"

"Lotsa dead. Tunnels from Hunnert Sixty Nine south be full a joeys hidin', but thas only small part a tribes. Never knew was so many trannies." He shake head. "Since we stomped Unies in Fourteen Square, govermen been careful. Means they hadda pull back some, and that gave us room for while. But jus' day later, thousands a sojers are landin' in friggin' helis. Can't do much 'gainst a heli gunship, Pook. They ain't like tin cans da jerries use."

"Whatcha plan, Halber?"

"We need a distract, bigtime."

"A what?"

"Distract Unies, keep their mind offa tribes, give us time."

"Whas Changman say?"

"Jus' he sendin' messenga an I should lissen careful, then give 'im what he wan'. Dunno what Chang talkinabout. What messenga?"

"Stupe ol' man too glitch ta remember his own name."

"Yah, well, g'wan back wid Jared, case he need ya."

Noway. Ain' gonna be stuck inside boring crummy towah wid snotty Uppiekit, not when could be here wid Halber Sub Boss askin' my advice.

I think fas', wonderin' what mos' 'rageous thing we could do.

Halber start back ta main cavern.

"Halb?" I trot ta keep up. "At Fourteen Square, we capture any 'plosives?"

He stop short. "Some."

"Been thinkin . . . " Take deep breath, cause a scare.

Dunno how he reac'. "Lotsa towahs 'tween Wall and Fourteen. We—"

"So?" He make face. "We can' move enough joeys down ta make a diff in rumb. Too many Unies now."

I g'wan like he ain' interrupt. "Sea dike be at Wall."

He frown. "Watchew sayin'?"

"Blow wall. Let Hud Riv come in."

"Mid stupe, trannie tribes live south a Fourteen!" His teeth go bare. "Who ya wanna drown firs', Subs or frazzin' Uppies in towahs?" He squeeze my neck. "Or maybe Midboy don' care how Subs get diss, hah?"

I go babble. "Ya din' think it alla way, Halber. Unies won' expec' break in wall. Ow! Show 'em our rumb be serious. An trannies, well, ya gotta warn. Water won' flow in 'til high. Ya c'n 'vacuate Sub an' move nor'. Think 'bout water sloshin' through towahs!" I pry his fingas. "Please!"

He consider a min, an' leggo. I twis' neck ta see if it still work.

"We'd need time ta arrange," he say slow. "I gotta sen' unnercar south ta bring Subs back. Fourteen Square is 'bout far south it c'n go; past Fourteen, tracks be mess. When do water get high?"

I remember trouble I had wid Karlo in Mid lair, an' dis time hide my proud. Tribe bosses don' wanna be showed up.

"Dunno." One leader ta 'notha, I reach out fo' caller. "But my Jared, he c'n fin' out."

Everythin' inna hurry now. Jared's putah say highest tide in nex' several weeks come jus' afta noon, an' it already near day when I ask. Halber warn his wall Subs ta walk north fas'. Meantime he send both unnercars racin' south ta meet 'em at Fourteen Square. He put Raulie in charge a buncha Chinas an' Huds, ta hit seawall.

"Wish I could wait," he mutter. "Need time. An' I need more friggin' callers; Hunnert Tens took whole buncha. Firs' they call each otha like craze joeykits. Now they tire of playin' an won' even ansa. I need 'em get ready fo' Subs from Fourteen."

I think about wall goin' boom. "Ya got enough 'plosive?"

"Cool jets. I got what we took from Unies, an' lasers too.

'Sides, no big deal makin' 'plosives. All ya need is 'cetaline from torch."

Ta my disgus', Halber wouldn' lemme go wid Subs he sen' south ta organize. I protes', but Halber want me near, case I get more ideas. He tell me come wid him ta Hunnert Ten; he gonna knock sense in heads of stupe Subboys. Stayin' close, I walk proud.

I look round Sub, thinkin'. Sub ways run all unner N'Yawk, but Sub tribe's biggest lair be Four Two cave. Funny: ol' Changman negotiate wid general in Unie head-quarry jus two block away on Forty, yet we plan rumb unner they feet.

Lissenin' while Halb talk ta Mids an' Subs an' Easters, I learn 'bout how Sub life organize. Sub tribe got one boss, Halber, but live in buncha tunnels spread all ova. Got separate Sub leaders each place, 'xcept fo' Four Two. All gotta do what Halber say.

I can' figga. Onna street, each Mid tribe got own Boss. Mid Three Four lair ain' gonna lissen ta Boss a Mid Two Six. What Halber gonna do if Subs unner Hunnert Fifty Nine ignore 'im? Sen' unnercar ta start Sub rumb?

Dunno, but it seem ta work. Now dat Halber got buncha callers, it work even betta. He allatime call up 'n down track, askin' 'bout Unie patrols ova sub.

"Halber!" High voice callin'. Alliegirl come skiddin' ta stop. "Flagga truce!"

Halber's eyes light. "Changman back?"

"Dunno. Couldn' see."

"Send Barth ta bring 'im down."

Halber pace anxious. I smart enough ta make myself small, say nothin'. I wanna be near ta hear what history Chang make.

Inna distance, grumble sound. I been roun' sub long enough ta know it be unnercar.

Halber growl, "Lesgo downstair. Soon as Chang gets here we goin' ta Hunnert Ten." He stride down hall ta unnercar, an' I scampa afta.

Unnercar be pack full a joeykits, bitchgirls, all kinda Subs. Outside, in staysh, Halber pace like gotta piss.

Afta while, Barth 'n Allie poke head round corna. "Halber?"

I go boggle. No Changman. Can' believe who dey brung.

"You!" Halber's fists bunch.

Peetee look defiant, but his words not. "Yes, sir. Mr. Chang sent me."

Halber stride 'cross room. "Gonna skin ya fo' stewpot, ya little—"

"We've no time for that!" Uppiekit's voice curt. "Let go!" He stare at Halber like he ain' afraid. "Why do you hate me? I never hurt you. Didn't I tell you about the Parkas?"

"Ya diss Chaco," Halber say, but his heart ain' in it.

"Yes. I'll pay for that my whole life."

"Damn ri'." Halber glower. "Beside, you my venge on Fisherman."

"I don't know what you're—"

"Fisherman, what call down Unie troops! Fisherman what stood here talkin' boolsheet 'bout always bein trannie! Lyin' Fisherman who—"

"*Son of a bitch!*" Peetee claw at Sub Boss eyes. "Don't say that about my father! He didn't betray you!"

Halber's fis' rear back ta club joeykit ta flo', and I shriek, "No!" Somehow, I put myself 'tween. "Lissen him firs'. He brung info fro' Chang. Gotta be reason he come back, Halb, knowin' ya be afta!"

Fo' min, thought I watchin' end. Halber let out great howl, whirl roun' and grab chair an' smash it 'gainst wall. Trannies scatter. "Bastads! Alla yas friggin' bastads!" He kick busted chair so hard it fly. "Goddamn Unies stompin' streets, fuckin' glitched Chang, fuckin' Hunnert Tens playin' stupe wid callers! Goddamn asshole Easters, an frazzin' joeykits don' know they place! Prong the lotta yas!"

I squat low fo' safe, but Peetee jus' stand waitin', his eyes close.

Min or two pass. Halber stomp roun', mutterin' unner his breath. Then, he plant hisself fronta Peetee. "All ri', get on unnercar." His voice surprisin' calm. "Need ta take trannies north, 'fore send car back south. What Changman wan'?" He signal driva ta start.

'Xcept fo' Allie, resta Subs hang back, knowin' Halber too well ta risk near. Halber lead Uppiekit to car bench an' sid-down. I preten' it natural ta go sit nex' ta, lissenin'.

Over screech a unnercar, Peetee explain Genral Ruben's govermen ready ta dance wid trannies, if we can' stop rumb.

He say Unies offa ta build new staysh ta fix water, but not rightaway. He tell us Uppies be royal pissoff 'bout Jared's hackin', which make me go proud.

"What Chang say ta do?"

"He said it's your decision, sir. Objectively speaking, I think you ought to make peace. You can't fight the whole U.N.A.F."

At end, Halber silent. Nobody dare disturb, while car jounce through dark tunnels.

Halber say cautious, "How'm I gonna talk ta Chang, widout they hear?"

Peetee say, "I know a way. But I want innifo."

"C'n still diss ya, joey." A growl.

Peetee say slow and careful, "I'm not afraid of you."

Halber blink. After min, he ask, "Why not?"

"I've been terrified all week. It's time to stop."

Don' make no sense, but Halber nod like he unnerstan'. "What innifo?"

"Take me to Jared."

"Noway!"

"We need to talk. And you know I can't stop him if he wants to stay."

Halber make fist, open it again. He sigh. " 'Kay. Afta ya help me call Chang, Pook'll take ya. We better hurry, 'fore Raulie an Chinas blow—" He stop sudden. "Betta hurry."

In few min, Peetee connec' while Changman, Halber an' Allie an' me watch. He say, "We talked it over, Mr. Chang."

Halber hiss, "You don' sound like no trannie!"

Peetee cover his caller. "I'll try."

"Yah?" Ol' man soun' tired. "Whatcha wan' me to do?"

Halber mutter, "Tellim we accep', if dey go quick on water."

Joeykit say, "Mr. Chang, think 'bout ya shop."

"Wha'?" Halber spring ta feet.

Peetee wave him quiet. "When you go in door, you c'n turn right or left. Right is—right be yes, left be no."

I giggle. Peetee don' sound like no tribe I eva hear.

Chang's voice cautious. "G'wan."

"We wan' you ta turn towar' the table where you keep ya teapot."

Long silence. Then, "I unnerstan'."

I think. Chang's table be ta right. Peetee sayin' yes, we accep'.

"Mr. Chang?" Peetee concentrate har'. "Remember when ya were going ta serve me tea, and the water was boiling away? Ya ran to the teapot, and quick turned it off."

Halber frown. I shake head, wonderin' if Peetee go glitch.

Chang soun' like he don' unnerstan' neitha. "You want me to run to the teapot?"

"No, sir. I wancha to think about what you tol' me when it boiled."

Again, silence. Then, "Ah! Okay okay, if I can. Filmatleven."

"Ya understan'?"

"Yah. An' one more thing. Ya frien' prolly real tired. Lettim sleep a while."

"I don' follow you, sir."

Chang sound irritable. "Joeykit been workin' too hard, is all. Give 'im rest."

"Okay," Philip say doubtful. Then his face suddenly clear. "I'll tell him."

"Get back witcha soon as I can."

Halber grab caller back from Peetee. "What's his givin' ya tea gotta do wid rumb?"

"I told him you wanted them to hurry with the purification plant. When he made tea he told me there wasn't water to waste. He knew what I was—"

Unnercar slowed. Someone tug at Halber's arm. "Halb, look!"

"Glitched, both a yas." Sub boss shake his head at Peetee, punch numbas inna caller. "Need ya, Raulie." He wait, bang caller on bench. "Why doncha ansa when I need ya?"

As unnercar stop, caller light blink green. Halb growl, "Raulie? 'Bout time! Lissen, don't blow wall. Changman is workin' on trayfo an'—"

"Halber!" Allie sound urgent. She point through broke window. I look.

We at Nine Six staysh. Across track, whole buncha trannies sleepin' on far platform.

Halber snarl, "Whassamatta? Can' they hear car? Allie, wakem up."

She jump down on track. In min she at otha side. Clap her

hans. Ben' down. Jump up an' whirl. *"HALBER!"* She back away from sleepin' Sub so fas' she almos' fall off edge.

Halber bolt from car, race 'cross track. Peetee an' I trayfo worry look. "C'mon." I follow.

Halber on knees, longside sleepin' Sub bitchgirl who remin' me a Bigsis. Comin' close, I see blood roun' her mouth an' nose. Eyes wide-open.

Sub Boss lay her down gentle, run ta anotha. I could tellim no point in it, if I stupe enough ta make soun'.

All of 'em dead. C'n tell from way dey lyin' even widout blood run from nose, mouth, sometimes eyes.

"Lord Christ!" Peetee. He stumble, catch hisself. "Jesus God, no!" He clutch stomach, gag.

Halber run from one Sub ta next.

Retchin', Peetee yank my arm. "Get me out of here."

I try ta free myself, but he hold onta metoo har'.

"Inna car!" Halber. *"INNA CAR!"*

Peetee ack like he can' walk. I drag him 'cross track, help him climb in car. Sub Boss swarm afta. In car, he knock trannies aside, stomp ta motor room, haul out driva, push self in. Car start wid lurch.

Tremblin', Peetee sag ta flo', hans workin' at shirt. His mouth go fast, but I can' hear words. He hug self an' rock.

Unnercar race through dark. Trannies scare an' silent.

Screechin' an' shudderin', car grind ta stop. 'Notha staysh. I ask Allie, "Where we be?"

She mumble, "Hunnert Three." Eyes red.

Halber bound out. Cautious, I go afta.

Only two lyin' in cave. Sub Boss kneel at firs'. In his throat, odd soun', like growl.

From door Allie say timid, "Where's rest, Halb? Was coupla hunnert livin' here."

"Dunno."

Scare but tryin' not ta show, I walk roun' grim staysh, wander towar' upstair.

When I get back Halb sayin', "Dey prolly run fa safe. We'll fin' 'em at Hunnert Ten."

"No ya won'." Voice so strange, takes a min ta realize it be mine.

Halber come at me, fists bunch, but I jus' step 'side.

He stumble pas' ta stair. I don' follow; already seen what

he gonna fin'. 'Stead, I go back ta crowded unnercar, sit next ta Peetee.

Huggin' self, I stare at broke window, at dirty nervous Sub joeys packed in unnercar. Stare at boots, bes' I ever had thanks ta capture Jared.

"Hold my hand." Peetee.

Car movin' again. "Fraz yaself."

"Help me." His voice, low, urgent. I look up; his face white. "I'm revving."

I shrug, look away. When I look back, he lost in self, nails pickin' at skin of hands. I grab his fingers, hold.

He rest his forehead 'gainst my arm. Awkward, I stroke hair.

Bumps. Unnercar stop so har' trannies flung all ova.

From fronta car, yellin'.

I look up. We ain' reach staysh.

I don' wanna get up, but gotta. Like bad dream, I can' escape monstas chasin'. Peetee won' leggo, but when I get ta feet, he too.

I squeeze through trannies ta front a car. "Whassamatta?"

Halber's face pressed ta window. He don' ansa.

Lights from unnercar gleam in black tunnel like animal in nigh'. Shine on walls, on stone pillas, on dim staysh ahead.

Track full a still trannie bodies.

"Jeez." Sof' whispa. Mine.

"We been run over 'em." Halber's cheeks wet. "My Subs. Wid unnercar." His hand grip my wrist so hard I gasp.

"Couldn' help, Halb. Ya din' know."

"Ova *Subs!*" Like he don' hear, he climb down from car, pullin' me along. Peetee leggo, but follow like he walk in sleep.

Both sides a tracks cram wid a bodies. Obvious, most trannies caught runnin'. I stumble ova Easter joey. His shirt bloody where drip from chin. Eyes rolled back in head. Arm curl roun' joeykit whose mouth be wide like tryin' ta breathe. Halber look at slick wheels a unnercar, an' retch.

Slow, we step ova dead, 'alla way ta nex' staysh. Can' believe tunnel so full a bodies. Climb onta platform. I step on han'. "Sorry," I mutter, 'fore I c'n help it.

Dead joey don' min'. Won' min' much, now on.

Nobody lef'. I look roun', feelin sick. Dissin' some Broad n rumb, no prollem. But dissin' hunnerts . . .

Halber walk slow, like in dream.

At far end a staysh, a soun'. " 'Licia?"

Sub Boss whirl. "Whossat?"

"Crina be I." Ol' joey, har'ly any teeth.

"Wha happen?" Halber gesture, like need ta 'xplain his question.

"Shoey an' Dross an me wen' up Hunnert Twenny Five, lookin' fo' water cans. Too many joeys crowdin' unner, now days. Not enough water." Ol' man limp towar' us. I back away, like he carry death. "When we start unner, saw buncha trannies runnin' our way. Ya seen my 'Licia?"

"What happen ta Subs?"

"Some was coughin'. Few fell on groun' twitchin' an' shudderin' til dey still. And some escaped ta out. I saw Pango runnin' past. He live wid us on Hunnert Ten. I grabbed him ta ask where was 'Licia."

"G'wan."

"He din' know." Ol' man peer roun' at bodies. "Been lookin' fo' bitchgirl eva since. She ain' so pretty now days, but I been wid 'Licia since we was joeykits. Not righ' she die widout me."

"Crina . . . " Halber's voice surprisin' gentle.

"I know, I know, 'Licia my prollem, not you's. I asked Pango wha happen. 'Unies,' he yell, an pull free from my hold. 'Crazy Uppie tried ta warn us. Raced down stair shoutin' ta run away, Unies 'bout ta gas us. Alla joeys laugh.'"

Crina squint roun'. "Dat you, 'Licia?" He shuffle ta still form among many. "Hon?" He crouch, look ta Halber like beg help. "How'm I gonna reconize her, face all blood?"

Peetee stir. "Jesus God Jesus God Jesus God Jesus . . . " His voice tremble. I put arm roun' his shoulda, 'til he quiet.

"Naw, you ain' 'Licia; she won' wear nothin' blue. Hates blue. 'Run,' Uppie was shoutin'. 'Get outa confine space.' But Pango say by then, too late. Unie troops charge downstair, shootin', draggin' giant hose. Smoke come out. Pango said he run fas' he can, holdin' breath 'til he 'bout collapse. When he jumped down ta track, he heard screams south a Hunnert Ten staysh, like Unies stickin' hose unner grate too."

"Chris'!"

Crina shrug. "Later, coupla joeys wen' back, careful, sniffin' air for bad. I guess afta while, smoke musta wen' up stairs an' out airholes. When I saw trannies come back safe, I come home ta fin' 'Licia. I even poked head out, upstair. Dozens a trannies burn by laser, lyin' on street where dey fall. Unies musta waited toppa staysh ta shoot any tryin' ta escape. Dunno why dey wasn't at Hunnert Twenny Five too."

Ol' man move away, stoppin' time ta time at woman's body. "Really wanna fin' her, Halb. Gettin' late, an' I tire."

'Xcept fo' shuffle of Crina's feet, all was still. Halber wander, sayin' nothin'. Afta time, so do I, Peetee stayin' close. I 'fraid ta go near stair, but can' stan' still.

We go roun' corna. Here, bodies cram togetha like fo' protec'. I can' keep lookin' at agonize faces. See arms, legs, shoes, wonnerin' how ta reconize Crina's bitchgirl.

Peetee stop short, starin'.

"C'mon." 'Gain, I put arm roun' shoulda. He look down at bloodstain jumpsuit.

Behin' us, Halber make soun'. I turn. Sub boss snatch caller, stab numbas. His eyes be craze. "Raulie?" He stalk back an' for', stumblin' ova bodies. "RAULIE!"

From calla, faint soun'. "Yo, Halb?"

"Blow the wall. Hear me?" Halber's voice rise ta yell. "Frazzin' Uppies think dey own da worl'! Now we show 'em!"

I say, "High water isn't 'til—"

He slap me wid back a hand, sen' me flyin', without even look. *Blow the fuckin' wall!*

Chapter 49

It was early morning. In Washington, Dad listened patiently while I poured out my frustrations over the caller. Outside, a persistent haze drifted. Even the tower's air scrubbers couldn't remove the acrid tang. "And Fizer won't leave Washington. These damn conference calls . . . he can't see what's going on, smell the smoke in the air."

On the screen, Dad nodded. "He's playing it safe. If it all blows up in our face, Rex can say he was consulted, but wasn't on the scene."

A third caller light blinked. Resolutely, I ignored it. "Jeff Thorne's even worse, at Lunapolis. You know how hard it is to reach consensus under a time lag?"

"He's with fleet command, where he ought to be. Unless he's back to drinking. Why do you need him?"

I spluttered. "Why? We're a committee, for Christ's sake."

"Don't blaspheme. He's not a colleague, he's a sure vote. Why do you think I chose him?"

"Am I supposed to work alone, without—"

"Of *course* you are." Dad's voice sharpened. "That's what I intended. Rex Fizer may offer a few suggestions, but basically he's with us. Thorne will keep the Navy happy. The show's all yours."

"But I don't want it!" I paused to regroup. "Dad, it's getting out of hand."

"How so?"

"We're fighting a major rebellion. General Ruben is sure the market disruption is tied in, though he can't figure how the trannies accessed the puter power it would take. The U.N. Securities Board has a task force tracing—"

"I know, and they'd better hurry. Holoworld took a massive hit; Peabody and Co's almost down the tubes. If Franjee's group goes with them . . . " He shook his head.

I said, "We've had two conference calls with SecGen Kahn. The Thirteenth Armored is ready to move, and the SecGen is pushing for immediate action. Tonight, if possible."

"Good. The sooner it's over with . . . "

"Ernst Ruben argued for a delay, to give them time to surrender. You know what the trannie terms are?"

"Diversion of the Freshwater Project? Impossible, Robbie."

"I made that clear."

"We'd lose our campaign kitty." Dad sighed. "Get it over with."

"We have to offer them something, for the record. I proposed a speedup on the next purification plant, but Kahn wants agreement on both sides of the aisle."

I grimaced. "How much?"

"Over a hundred million. More than we can afford, but do we have a choice?"

"Not really. If Ruben brings in an armored division, the damage to the city will exceed that. Tell him we agree."

"Done. By the way, have you heard from Adam Tenere?"

"No, Robbie He never calls me. You're his friend."

"He's been out of touch since . . . " I couldn't remember when. A fourth light blinked on my console. Then a fifth. "Dad, I've got to go."

"Okay. Robbie, we've got the votes. We'll back you however this plays out. But be sure you leave the public statements to Kahn."

"He'll want us on the podium when he takes the heat."

"Of course. Look solemn and say nothing."

We said our good-byes and rang off. I sighed again; Dad too, was out of touch in Washington. Thank heaven, a massive show of force had prevented trouble near the old White House. But because he saw no fighting, Dad didn't realize how close the city was to a bloodbath.

Frowning, I punched the call button.

From outside, a voice raised in protest. "Hold it! You can't just barge—"

The door flew open. *Robert!* I jumped, as Captain Nicholas Seafort strode to my desk. "Where the hell are you running?"

I realized I'd retreated behind my console. "How did you get—I'm glad to see you, sir."

He spun a chair, sat backwards, rested his arms on the back. "Do you have word of Philip?"

"Robbie, we —

I swallowed. "No, sir, I —

with the SecGen would injure Dad, and — it was possible.

"Very well. Have your soldiers let me out streetside, and wait at the door for my return."

I shook my head. "They won't let you. There's full-scale war brewing."

"I'm going for my son." It was as if I hadn't spoken. His finger shot out, transfixed me with a warning. "Lord God help you or Richard if you try to stop me."

I smiled, to ease the tension. "Is that a threat?"

"Yes."

I swallowed. In his political days the Captain had led by persuasion. Rarely—never—had I heard him threaten an opponent.

Was that what I'd become: an enemy? With a pang of regret I recalled my days at Academy.

"Move it, Robbie." His fingers drummed on the chair back, as his eyes burned into mine.

"I'll see what I can do." Gladly, I left him.

We choose our paths. His might well lead to death. If so, he'd become a martyr. Well, it wasn't what I wanted, but we could live with that. As the last Supranationalist SecGen, Nick Seafort still carried weight. And, on this issue at least, he directly opposed Dad.

Ruben was gone, for some much-needed sleep. I found Major Groves, told him what the Captain demanded.

He shook his head. "Impossible."

"Then make it possible. He's a man who can do us great harm."

"Us? Are you including me in your political schemes?" The major's lip curled in disgust.

"You lost a friend in the Fourteenth Street encampment.

chai   He
sound

"I'm

"I fo   , he'll need one of us
alive. Bu   street anyway."

"Jesus.

"Don't   You men stand back, I'll laser the
bloody chain.   drew his pistol.

"The lock's frozen; it's been years since—there, sir." The
soldier stood aside, his task done. "We'll relock it the moment
you're outside. The major's ordered a squad posted here until
you return, or . . ."

"Yes, or." With a curt nod, the Captain pushed open the
door, peered in both directions, and was gone.

On the screen, Rex Fizer grimaced. "There'll be heat from
the bleeding hearts."

Fifteen seconds later Admiral Thorne said, "So be it." The
damned delays from Lunapolis were inevitable, but driving
me to distraction.

"Up to a point." Marion Leeson, SecGen Kahn's political
advisor, sat in for him while he pretended to be busy in
London. At least she was actually in the room, and not just

"No. Jared neither."

"Where's Adam?"

"I don't know. Sir, at this point it's beyond a search for the boys. They're sending in—"

"The Thirteenth Armored Cavalry, the bloody fools. You know what the SecGen's up to. Can you stop this?"

"Captain, I'm only a liaison. It's General Ruben who—"

"Robbie, we're done playing games."

I swallowed. "No, sir, I can't stop it." Breaking a bargain with the SecGen would injure Dad, and regardless, I doubted it was possible.

"Very well. Have your soldiers let me out streetside, and wait at the door for my return."

I shook my head. "They won't let you. There's full-scale war brewing."

"I'm going for my son." It was as if I hadn't spoken. His finger shot out, transfixed me with a warning. "Lord God help you or Richard if you try to stop me."

I smiled, to ease the tension. "Is that a threat?"

"Yes."

I swallowed. In his political days the Captain had led by persuasion. Rarely—never—had I heard him threaten an opponent.

Was that what I'd become: an enemy? With a pang of regret I recalled my days at Academy.

"Move it, Robbie." His fingers drummed on the chair back, as his eyes burned into mine.

"I'll see what I can do." Gladly, I left him.

We choose our paths. His might well lead to death. If so, he'd become a martyr. Well, it wasn't what I wanted, but we could live with that. As the last Supranationalist SecGen, Nick Seafort still carried weight. And, on this issue at least, he directly opposed Dad.

Ruben was gone, for some much-needed sleep. I found Major Groves, told him what the Captain demanded.

He shook his head. "Impossible."

"Then make it possible. He's a man who can do us great harm."

"Us? Are you including me in your political schemes?" The major's lip curled in disgust.

"You lost a friend in the Fourteenth Street encampment.

Don't you want him avenged? What if the Captain publicly opposes us, and Kahn pulls back the troops?"

"We're committed. There's no way Kahn would—"

"Are you certain?"

His eyes met mine a long moment. Finally they fell. "I won't spare troops for his wild goose chase. If he's hurt, it's his own doing."

"Agreed. He understands."

Minutes later, we stood at the foot of the tower. My conscience stirred; I said again to the Captain, "Are you sure, sir? There's really nothing you can do."

He shrugged. "You may be right, but P.T.'s on the street. This is my last chance; I had to bribe a helicab to get me here. Arlene and the Tamarovs are holed up in the apartment. She's . . . distraught."

"I'm sorry."

He paced impatiently while the soldiers worked at the chained door. "I don't know what will come of us, after." He sounded glum. "We're barely speaking."

"I'm surprised she isn't with you."

"I forbade it; if P.T. lives through this, he'll need one of us alive. But she may well be on the street anyway."

"Jesus."

"Don't blaspheme. You men stand back, I'll laser the bloody chain." He drew his pistol.

"The lock's frozen; it's been years since—there, sir." The soldier stood aside, his task done. "We'll relock it the moment you're outside. The major's ordered a squad posted here until you return, or . . . "

"Yes, or." With a curt nod, the Captain pushed open the door, peered in both directions, and was gone.

On the screen, Rex Fizer grimaced. "There'll be heat from the bleeding hearts."

Fifteen seconds later Admiral Thorne said, "So be it." The damned delays from Lunapolis were inevitable, but driving me to distraction.

"Up to a point." Marion Leeson, SecGen Kahn's political advisor, sat in for him while he pretended to be busy in London. At least she was actually in the room, and not just then a barrage of shouted queries and demands. An old man shuffled past their holos, his ragged coat buttoned tight as if for protection. When his eyes crossed mine he nodded shortly.

I gaped. It was the old joey who'd flown to the Square with the Captain. The one who'd escorted us below to the Sub. Mr . . . . I searched, and like a good politician, came up with the name. Chang.

After the media left, the session was brutal.

We attacked the old man with scorn, with wheedling, with passionate argument, with the cold facts of the trannies' inescapable defeat.

He sat like a stone.

Finally Marion Leeson raised a hand. She spoke slowly, with exaggerated diction. "Are we getting through? Do you understand a word of what we said?"

Chang stirred. "Yah, I unnerstan'. Ya figga ya won, so no need to talk 'bout my people dyin' from lack a water. No need to offer trayfo, like ol' red-hair suggest."

Ruben bristled. "It was your idea. I only—"

"Why bother, since ya already own the worl'?" The old streeter leaned over, spat deliberately on the floor. Marion Leeson wrinkled her nose.

On the screen Rex Fizer rapped for attention. "That's beside the point. Will you surrender now and save lives?"

"In return, water plant? Yes or no?"

All eyes turned to Marion. "The government," she said, "will consider it. After."

Chang regarded her with something like puzzlement. "Sleep at night, do ya? Feel good 'bout whatcha doin'?"

A muted buzz. I looked to the console, but the sound had come from Chang's coat. He reached in, fished out a caller, keyed it on. "Can' talk now," he told it. "Meetin'."

General Ruben held up a hand. "No, we'll give you privacy. Tell them you'll be a minute." He whispered to an aide, who escorted Chang to another room.

The moment the door closed Ruben leaped for the console. "Now!"

I asked, "What's going on?"

"We've been tracking his caller since last night. The joey

he talked to used some kind of code our people couldn't break. Listen."

He keyed the console, and static filled the speakers.

A military voice, from outside the room. "The sender's underground, that's why the static, sir. We're triangulating for a fix. You've got audio, but they can't hear you."

"All right. Quiet."

Heavy breathing, then Chang's rheumy voice. "Yah?"

"Mr. Chang, this is Philip." The boy's tone was dull.

My jaw dropped. Quickly I glanced around, to see if the others realized who was speaking.

"Chaco, ya shouldn'—"

"They're probably listening, so this is for their ears too. They gassed the sub tunnels from Ninety-sixth north. The trannies inside are dead. Thousands."

"Oh God." Chang panted for breath.

"Tell the authorities they killed Mr. Tenere. He ran downstairs trying to warn them. I saw his body."

"Chaco—"

"My name's Philip. I don't care anymore. I'm on my way to see, uh, my friend. I don't know if I'll tell him. Mr. Tenere's face was purple. I only noticed him because his clothing was so different from the tribesmen. Blood dripped from his nose and mouth and obscured his face." The boy's voice caught. "Objectively speaking, I'd say he died in agony."

In our room, utter silence.

"Halb—your leader said to tell them, no surrender. Not 'til they kill every last Sub. And to tell them we aren't done. That you'll pay. All of you."

A click. The connection was broken.

I sat staring at the console.

Devon was five hours away by suborbital. Perhaps I could excuse myself from this business, catch a heli to the shuttleport. I had an inexplicable craving to visit Academy, to stroll once more its quiet tree-lined walks.

I made a sound.

Only when Marion glanced at me with alarm did I realize that tears were streaming down my cheeks.

Chapter 50

PEDRO

Dunno how I endured endless walk back to hateful conference room. Heart pounded fierce. For once in life, wished I wasn't Neut full of words, jus' reg trannie with shiv.

Wearily, I took chair again, looked around at faces. Uppie Boland was gone, but others same as before. Outside, in the distance, an ominous boom. Prolly more trannies dyin'.

On long trek after Peetee hung caller, I concluded there was nothin' more I could do but play out game of death. Maybe, somehow, I'd earn us time.

Time was all we had left. An' not much a that. I tried not to see accusin' dead.

In conference room I grin at Uppie bitch, showin' bad teeth. "You was sayin'?"

She said sweet, "I trust all is well?"

Ruben slammed palm on table, with crack that startled all. "We'll have none of that."

She didn' blink. "You can be replaced, if you find your job distasteful."

"As can you," he snapped. "You think Mr. Kahn will sack me on your advice? Shall we see?"

Eyes met, and was hers that dropped. Holdin' back ache, I waited, lissenin' an' learnin'.

Ruben turned to me. "Is there any point in talking further?"

I said only, "You heard?"

At least he didn' try dissemble. A nod.

"Who do it?"

"A colonel at a Hundred Tenth came up with—*no*." Slow, he squared his shoulders. "Wirtz asked my approval, and I gave it. I'm responsible. Your fighters were . . . we thought they . . ."

Woman Marion rapped table, a sharp sound. "That's beside the point. What are you going to do with this old—this person?"

On screens, Fizer and Thorne watched with unwavering eyes.

Ya don't have shiv, Pedro, or ya'd plunge it in arrogant General's heart. Don't have strength ta wrap fingers round his neck 'til he look like trannies lyin' in Sub.

Don' got nothin' but words.

Think, Pedro. Anyone with buncha cansa c'n make good trayfo, but it takes a Neut ta tray with none. An' not jus' any Neut. Best traytaman that eva was, a foolish ol' man who incited trannies to fight what can't be fought.

I cleared throat. "I wonder how many towers ya gonna lose. Two already be past repairin'."

"I beg your pardon?" Woman's eyes were cold.

I took off coat, like prepared ta stay long while. "Good view here." I gestured to window. "C'n watch alla smoke driftin' past." I lean forward. "Think trannie nations gonna lie down an' do their dyin' jus' cause ya snap finger? Hundreds a thousands left, all ova city." I hoped it was true. "An' now they royal pissoff."

"Don't try to threaten—"

"Facts ain' threats." I glower. "Think they didn' tell me with code words onna caller? Better be prepare, cause ya gonna lose—" I paused, mos'ly for drama, but also to think of somethin', anythin', they might believe.

Door burst open, and scornful Major rushed in. "Sir, the trannie bastards bombed the seawall!"

"They what?" Ruben was on his feet.

"A few minutes ago. That boom we heard . . . they took out the seawall at Wall Street. The tide's rising, and water's pouring in!" He glared at me with unconcealed hate. "Two huge breaches, about fifty yards apart."

I laced fingers together, offered smug smile.

"Look at that trannie son of a bitch—"

"Groves, full report!"

The major tore his eyes from mine. "All we have is a flash from Lower Broadway. Water's gushing in, and they're evacuating north."

"Trannie soldiers in the area?"

"None seen."

On screen, Admiral asked, "What damage?"

"Water's rising, but not so fast people can't get to high ground. The Fulton Towers basements are already flooding. God knows how we'll plug the—"

Ernst Ruben snapped, "I want video from a heli, stat. No, by God, I'll go for a look. Blanket the area with gunships; the trannies are somewhere near. Shoot on sight. And get me data. Meeting adjourned for an hour. Move!"

"Yes, sir!" Groves strode out, the General close behind.

I put on smile, for benefit of Uppie woman. To the men waitin' on screen I said, "Tolya trannies were pissoff. Whatcha 'xpect?"

Fizer, the one they said was politician, shook head as if tired. "And to think I urged them to go easy."

"Hah, think ya c'n swind Pedro Telamon Chang? Feh." I restrained urge to spit. In trannie trayfo, would be good time for it, but now . . . "Make peace while ya can, Uppie. Our nex' move be worse." I forced rancor from tone. "All we want is water, fo' Lor' Chris' sake. C'n ya imagine what it's like not to know where drink comin' from, forget 'bout bathe, no clean water for cook—"

Distant Admiral in screen stirred angrily. "We've been over that. There's nothing we can do. And the seawall was the last straw. You people made your bed; now you'll lie in it."

I shrugged, wonderin' what he talkin' about.

Caller lights were flashin' on consoles. Uppie Marion frowned.

While time passed, I argued for water, jus' to keep somethin' going. Was desperate for them to make offer, any offer, that would allow end to rumb.

I didn' get nowhere, of course. Wouldn't, 'til General came back to advise.

Caller buzzed urgent. With a sigh woman answered. Joey's face appeared on screen. Plump, harried, he held caller to mouth.

She listened. A hiss of breath. "My God, when? How bad? Just a second, let me key in Rex Fizer." She searched console, stabbed at unfamiliar keys.

Man's voice gabbled in speaker. "Hello? Marion, are you there?"

Hands fluttering, she gave up search. "Rex and Admiral Thorne are standing by. Repeat for them."

"Word from London; the U.N. Treasury's been hacked. They're down and scrambled; indications are it'll be a long while before they're back on-line."

"Those Goddamn trannies." Fizer, his mouth tight.

"This morning the Treasury began selling gold at a fraction of what it's worth; but as no reports reached their screens, the keepers just learned of it. As you know, trading is automated. By the time they put a lid on, they'd already lost hundreds of millions."

Marion asked, "Can you undo—"

"Christ, let me finish. Remember reading about the Hacker raid of 'Thirty Two? Almost a hundred years of added safeguards, but they did it again. Millions of tax files are corrupted with false data."

Door opened, and General strode in. The glance he threw me wasn't friendly. "The lower city's a mess. I've called in the Corps of Engineers but—"

Marion waved him silent. "Listen."

Onscreen, pasty-face man wiped at gleaming forehead. "Do you know how to spell disaster? 'Treasury'. Lord God knows how the Hackers got through security; the OS joeys swore there was no way anyone—" His caller rang, and he held up finger for woman to wait. He listened, and shoulders sagged.

When he keyed back to us, his voice held panic, like trannie trapped in doorway on hostile turf. "New York stocks are down fifteen hundred points. Sell orders outnumber buys five to one. The SecGen ordered the market closed."

Who woulda thought silly Uppiekit have such power? Somethin' glitch with how world is organize.

No time to reflect; my moment come. I rapped table, said loud, "*Now* maybe ya lissen? How much more damage we gotta do? Negotiate. We reasonable."

Door opened. My favorite major. "Sir, a call from the Rotunda."

Ruben glanced my way, muttered a curse. "I'll take it outside."

Uppie Marion was jugglin' three lines, speaking urgent into caller. Fizer spoke to someone offscreen. Only Thorne, Navy Admiral, sat stolid, waitin' like me.

A coupla min later Ruben returned, three soldiers behind. They in full battle gear, guns ready. Behind them, a host of officers crowded in the doorway.

General snapped, "That was the SecGen." To Marion,

"You're to call him, stat." To me, "No more negotiations. No compromise."

Sent chill down spine.

"Casualties on both sides are to be, ah, disregarded. The SecGen wants the solution to the problem."

I swallowed. "Final solution, hah?"

"We believe the hacking originated here in New York. All fiber optics, all satnet connections to the city will be shut down for the duration. Groves, get on it."

"It'll take a while; I'll need the phone companies, the satel—"

"Move!"

"Right, sir." He thrust through the assembly and was gone.

Uppie woman said, "But the towers—"

"They fend for themselves. Nalor, take what men you need, reinforcements are on their way. Search every office tower, floor by floor. Start in midtown."

"Yes, sir."

"Colonel, new orders to troops. The streets are closed. If anything moves, shoot to kill."

"What about him?" Fizer, indicating me.

I stood. "Ya don' wanna negotiate, okay okay, I go back ta my trannies."

"Sir, he heard everything you said!"

"I know." General's eyes swivel to me. Now, they like ice. "Go with these men."

I swell. "Came here under flagga truce. Take me down ta street so—"

"Your trannies rebelled against the Government of Lord God. You're under arrest for treason. Take him away. Hold him incommunicado." As arms lifted me rough from chair and propelled me to door, Ruben swung back to waiting soldiers.

"Prepare a gas attack—knockout, not lethal—on the subway tunnels starting at Forty Second. Go! You, lieutenant, get on the horn to Trenton. They're to put the Eighteenth Cavalry Division on our streets in six hours. Loaded weapons, full battle gear. Don't stand gawping, move! Hawkins, you'll take the Thirteenth north. At every corner . . ."

As soldiers shoved, half dragged me down hall, Ruben's voice faded. I walked fast as I could, not wantin' to fall an' lose dignity on behalf my trannies. Wasn' easy. They moved me fas'.

Chapter 51

PHILIP

Raulie scuttled to the corner, crouched low, beckoned me close. "Be safe, Peetee, if ya hug wall an' run."

I asked, "How will I get in?"

"Secon' alley door be open. Only looks shut."

I took a deep breath, but paused before my sprint. "Raulie . . ."

"No time, Uppie. Unies see ya, dey shoot."

I faced him, looked up to his strained and haggard face. "About your people . . . I'm sorry."

"Yah, well." His hand flicked out to my shoulder, touched it the barest instant. "Ya couldn' stop it."

I cried, "I should have!" If he knew the truth, he'd despise me as I did myself. I pounded my leg, fought not to rev yet again. I was reeling with exhaustion, miserable with frustration and the bitter tang of guilt. And I was starving; it had been uncounted hours since the soldiers had brought me food in Mr. Chang's cubicle.

"Well . . . Halber said ta leave ya an' run home; got work ta do." He scuffed his feet, blurted, "For an Uppie, ya ain' so bad." He looked past me to the looming tower. "Tell Jared, Halber wants him unner where it safe. He c'n go back ta putahs afta."

"If he doesn't go home with me."

On the next block, treads rumbled. "Outaheah," Raulie said, and was gone.

I watched until he disappeared into a ruined storefront, then turned to my task.

A few moments later, I waited in the deserted office tower for the elevator, hoping Jared hadn't turned it off.

He had.

Raulie said the puter center was on the ninth floor. Laboriously, I climbed the fireproof stairwell, thinking of Mom, Fath, our skytel in flames. How many weeks had it been? Days? Hours? I'd lost track.

Doggedly, I trudged up endless steps, while outside the world staggered to an end.

In the sub, our ride south from a Hundred Tenth had been in grim silence. Halber disappeared into the tiny driver's compartment, with a look that dared us to speak.

I sat dazed from my episode of panic, Pook's arm across my shoulder, while the undercar lurched through darkened stations back to the Subs' main lair.

Two hours later, Halber left the enraged Easters, Broads, Chinas, and other tribesmen demanding revenge, long enough to give me his grudging consent to see Jared.

Raulie and I had trod crowded Sub tunnels to Thirty-eighth, where he'd poked his head out a manhole and decided we could risk the streets.

A pall of smoke hung over the city, obscuring the upper floors of the gleaming alloy towers.

More than towers burned. Unie troops were torching any building where they found resistance. And resistance was everywhere. Word of the bloodbath had spread like wildfire, in part through the Subs' network of stolen callers. I didn't know what Halber planned next. I focused on persuading Jared to come home.

Then, I would turn myself in for prosecution.

I was to blame for the bloody death of thousands of streeters. For Adam Tenere, lying still on the station floor, finally released from his agony.

I had caused a holocaust.

If I hadn't provoked Jared, he wouldn't have left the compound. If I hadn't followed, Mom would be at home, Father in his beloved monastery. It was my fault they'd called out the troops, my fault Jared's dad was dead, my fault the city burned.

My life was over. I wasn't sure I could face a penal colony; instead, I might opt for suicide. I'd have to get a message to Father, to tell him I was sorry. It was the least I could do, and it would leave him with something. Time to think about that later. For now, there was Jared; it was my job to bring him to safety.

I faced the ninth floor stairwell door, braced myself, opened the door, and strode through.

* * *

The puter center was deep within the honeycomb of tower halls and offices, but helpful signs marked the way.

To my surprise, the door was open.

Jared's back was to me. He wore a ragged shirt and pants, sandals that didn't fit. A caller was clipped to his belt. "Schuss with me, you bastard." He stabbed at the console. On his screen, program instructions scrolled.

He snapped to me over his shoulder, "What do you frazzing joeys want? I just broke into Earthport Station, I have codes, frequencies—"

I said, "I came to take you home."

"Tell Raulie I'm too—" He spun. His mouth worked, but no words came. A sheaf of notes slid from his lap to the tiled floor.

"Hi, Jar." I didn't know what else to say.

"You?" His swollen eye flicked to the door, back to the screen, to me. "What—how did you—P.T.?" Slowly, as in a dream, he got to his feet. "I saw you on the security screen, you looked like a trannie, I thought . . . what in Christ's name are you doing here?"

"Don't blaspheme," I said automatically. Then, "I've been looking for you."

"Why?"

"To bring you home."

"Are you out of your fucking mind?"

"I may be." My voice was unsteady. "The things I had to do . . ."

"How did you find me?"

"I traced you to the Sheraton through the Terrex card. The manager told me you went to the streets."

"The grodes chased me out."

"I followed, and picked up your trail. When Halber took you from Pook's lair, Swee and I were in the next room."

His tone was astonished. "You know Pook?"

"We had a . . . quarrel. I persuaded him to take me to the Sub. They were going to let me see you, but Halber turned on me and I ran out, and there was Chaco . . ." I felt my voice rising, and forced it under control. If I counted in base eleven . . . "Jared, it's time to go home."

"Goofjuice. Look what I've got here!" His hands shot out to encompass the console, the machines humming quietly as they communed with their brethren. His mouth grew ugly. "Should I trade my CLIP for a bedroom in your frigging Washington compound? Where Dad treats me like a joeykit and sucks up to the Old Man?"

I blurted, "He's dead."

"That fucking asshole takes away my nets whenever—who's dead?"

I said gently, "Your father. I'm sorry, Jar. Really."

He wrinkled his brow, as if puzzling out a particularly difficult riddle. "He can't be. He's home with the Old Man."

"They're in New York, searching for us. Were, I mean. Fath's still here, but Mr. Tenere . . . " For the first time I could remember, my thoughts and words were a jumble. "He's dead. Unies killed him this morning in a gas attack on the Sub."

"No. Why would he go there?"

"He was trying to warn them."

Jared Tenere blinked. Slowly, he settled into his chair. His vacant stare was fixed on the console.

I wanted to touch him, didn't dare.

"It's a lie."

"Jar, I saw him. It was—"

"It's a trick to make me go home!"

"No, I swear—"

"He put you up to this!"

I shouted, "Listen to me!" His eyes were wild, but I rushed on. "From a Hundred Ten to Ninety-sixth, they're all dead. The gas threw them into convulsions; they fell on the tracks, in the stations . . . I found him lying—God, what am I saying? You have to believe me, he's—you can't imagine what it was like, they . . . *Christ Jesus, son of Lord God!*" My voice had risen to a keen.

Stubbornly he shook his head.

Desperate, I pulled at my hair, trying not to rev. "I don't want to remember it! He's dead, Jar! They killed him!"

"Shut up!" He pounded the console. "Hear me? Shut up, or I'll—"

"Dead!"

He covered his ears, spun away.

I sagged into a chair, hugging myself.

Minutes passed. He sniffled.

When he spoke it was almost a whisper. "How?"

"The Subs had a battle with the Parkas, and somehow Father was involved. Mr. Tene—your dad was with him. I found them at the park wall. Fath and Mom took me home, and he stayed to look for you." It was like an accusation, stupid and cruel, and I didn't realize until I heard Jared groan. "The U.N.A.F. officer at a Hundred Tenth wanted to use knockout gas in the tunnels to find you. I guess the plan changed when the fighting got worse. I heard a Sub tell Halber that your dad tried to stop the attack."

"What did he look—I mean . . . you saw him?"

Lying was a sin, but I knew with absolute certainty I couldn't tell the truth. "It looked quick and peaceful. I'm sure he—"

"Liar! Convulsions, you said."

I wished I could sail back in time and bite off my tongue. "Maybe small ones, I don't—" I rocked, hugged myself. "Oh, God, Jared. I'm sorry. It wasn't pretty. He died hard. But he sacrificed himself, Jared. It was . . . " I searched for a word. "Noble. You should be proud of him."

He stared through me with reddened eyes.

I said softly, "Come home, Jar. There's no point anymore. No need to run—"

"Idiot!" He aimed a savage kick at my chair, but I slid out of the way. "At least I can get even with the Unies for killing Dad!"

"Pook said he held you captive and cut you, that he traded to Halber—"

"And I talked my way free! The trannies need me, P.T. Do you know how hard I hit the nets?"

"You hacked your way into U.N. Treasury. That's a terrible thing to do, objectively spea—"

"Oh, prong yourself. We're schussing with the London CLIP, and downhilling through the stock markets . . . Our Arfie broke into the Unie base construction office upstairs, and look!" He keyed his console through a series of screens, switched on a wall speaker. A constant stream of military traffic, interspersed with static. He lowered the volume.

"So?"

He didn't answer. He keyed up a city map, fiddled with magnification, drew in on a Hundred Tenth Street, marked the coordinates.

Apprehensive, I drew closer. He switched screens, entered another program.

"Jar, what are you—"

"Wait. See if this works." He held up a hand to forestall my questions.

Numbers flashed, requests for passwords. Then: "Target coordinates?"

His fingers flying, Jared clipped the coordinates from his map, entered them.

"Confirm firing coordinates?"

"Jared, no!" I lunged for the keyboard.

He shoved me hard, and I fell.

"Burn, you fuckers!" He stabbed at the keys.

I swarmed onto his back, got an arm around his neck. "Don't make it worse!"

He struggled to throw me off. He staggered to the wall, drove himself backward. My spine slammed into the doorjamb. I lost my grip. He whirled and clubbed me in the temple. He hit me again, then grabbed my shirt, hauled me forward, rammed me again into the wall. I slid down, dazed. He ran to the console.

"No!"

He didn't seem to hear. He typed, checked his figures. Then, *"Yes!"* He spun away. "Yes! Oh, yes!"

I struggled to my feet. "What did you do?"

"I'll teach those bastards to mess with us! We'll pay them for the trannies in the tunnels, for my frazzing school, for . . ." His voice quavered. "For Dad." He spun the building's cameras north in a dizzying arc. "I wonder if we can see."

I shook him. "See what?"

"I coded in a strike on the Unies!" He danced from foot to foot in a sort of ecstasy.

"Where? How?"

"The Naval base at Earthport Station has lasers trained on us groundies. I heard that old fraz Boland telling Robbie, the night the Old Man—" His lip curled, at some unpleasant memory. "I fed Earthport's lasers the coordinates for the Unie positions on a Hundred Tenth. They think I'm New York U.N.A.F. Command."

Oh Lord God, no. "Don't, Jar. There's been enough killing."

"It'll never be enough! They murdered Dad!"

"I thought you hated him."

Jared raised his fist, slowly brought it down, opened his hand. "I can say that; I'm his joeykid. You think I'll let them gas him like—like a piece of garbage? Like an animal?" His voice grated. "Oh, they'll pay. I'm just starting." He stalked to the console. "Out of my way; I've got to program laser strikes before they change the codes."

Should I launch myself at him in a desperate attack? I had more confidence in Mom's training, now that I saw its results, but a few moments ago he'd easily thrown me off. "Wait."

"No way." He screened through target lists. "Get out of here! Go!"

"Where?" I spoke softly, and he didn't hear.

His voice changed. "Don't you understand? Without our help, the Unies crush the trannies, and nothing will change."

I leaned over the console, waited until he looked up. "Jar . . . is this about the tribes, or you?"

"What are you, my psych?"

My palm struck the console with a sharp crack. "I've been through hell for you! All that time I thought you were scared, desperate for help. If it weren't for me, there'd be no trannie war! I've got to know why. Answer, or I'll—I'll . . . "

His eyes met mine, mocking. Slowly, as he gauged the expression I held, his sneer faded. "It's for them. For me. Christ, I don't know; why does it matter? I get my revenge, and they'll lose without me."

"Try to stop the war, not make it worse."

"Why?"

"Have you ever killed someone?" It wasn't a rhetorical question; if he hadn't, I would have to tell him about Chaco. Until he understood the loathing it engendered, he'd—

"Yeah, I smashed the skull of a fucking trannie who . . . " After a moment of silence his face reddened. "Drop it."

I stared into the eyes of a joey who'd been a sort of friend, companion at least, for as long as I could remember, and saw nothing I could recognize.

Jared's caller buzzed.

He frowned, keyed it on. "Yeah?"

I heard the gravelly voice through the tinny speaker. "Halber."

"Why'd you send P.T. here, you frazzing loonie?"

From the other end, a roar. Words I couldn't distinguish.

"Yeah, after what I'm doing for you? Bullshit." Jared covered the mouthpiece, stuck his tongue out.

Halber rumbled. From Jared, a sigh. "What do you want? I'm busy."

The voice snarled, "Ya goin' wid him, Uppie?"

Jared snorted in derision. "Fat chance."

A pause. "Lissen . . . don' think south tunnels safe much longer. Thinkin' a havin' Subs try fo' the Hud."

"Why? Gonna swim across?" On the console, Jared keyed his map.

"Don' fun wid me, Uppie." Halber's voice was like a knife. "Still time ta send Raulie ta diss ya."

"Cool jets; maybe I can help. Where are the Unies strongest?"

"Everywhere!"

"Halber, for Christ's sake!"

"Three Six, by Broad. Seven Two an' Columb. Fourteen Square." Halber sounded ragged. "Easters an' Mids pushed 'em back some on Lex, but helis all over the place! What we spose ta do?"

"Pull back. Lemme try something." Jared fingered the touchscreen at the locations Halber had called off.

"How long, Uppie?"

"Shit, how do I know? An hour, probably. Two. Less, if you let me be." Jared ported to the screenful of codes, began making assignments.

"How we know if it work?"

"You'll know." He keyed the caller, slipped it back on his belt.

I swallowed. Father, you taught me to do right. But what if I don't know where right lies?

"Jared . . ."

He faced me. "Do you want me to help them or not?"

I hesitated. Jared ported back and forth between screens, setting up coordinates.

A screen filled with new orders, and frantic queries.

With a curse, Jared closed his datafile, set the program to execute. "There. Now, even if they change the codes . . ."

"I'm leaving." I wasn't sure where I might go. My quest had failed, and I'd brought a city to ruin.

"Listen!" Abruptly he turned up the speaker.

"This is Wirtz at Seventy-fifth Regiment HQ calling clear on all channels, Earthport or Lunapolis stop the laser attack, repeat halt the laser attack for God's sake, you're firing on the wrong—oh my God!—"

Static.

"We got 'em!" Jared pounded the console. "Now let's knock some helis out of the air!"

Sickened, I turned away.

Minutes passed, before I roused myself. "Good-bye."

"See ya." He was engrossed in his console.

"I'm not sure I can make it back to a tower." I felt leaden. "If I don't, I'm sorry I hurt you . . ."

"Yeah, sure." Suddenly he looked up, mischief in his eyes. "Back to a tower? I can get you clear out of the city."

"How?"

"Watch." Once more he keyed the puter, netted to the Greater New York Police. *"UNAF NYCom to Greater NYPolice. Bylon Sanders, nephew of Senator Richard Boland, trapped roof on Fortescue Tower Broadway/Fortieth. Due to emergency no military craft may be diverted to civilian purposes; request immediate repeat immediate assistance."*

I asked, "Where'd you learn to talk like that?" In his school papers, Jared had been lazy and disorganized.

"By observation. Shut up." He tapped on.

"Request GNYP transport Sanders ASAP repeat ASAP to Trenton Shuttleport where home travel arranged. Confirm response c/o Captain—quick, P.T., give me a name—"

"Vishinsky." It was all I could think of. I wondered what the supervisor of our gate guards would think of my choice.

"*—Vishinsky, immediate."* He closed with a long routing. "See? Nothing to it."

My eyes flickered from the console to the banks of inputs, the multi lines, the satelnet links. "You have the power you wanted, Jar."

"Yeah."

We waited for the confirmation. Minutes passed. I wondered if they'd seen through Jared's ruse. If hostile troops were on the way, it would be just as well. I'd pay my debt.

The speaker crackled. *"Stand by for emergency transmission, Earthport Naval Command to all U.N.A.F. and Naval stations."*

"Maybe I can get visuals." Jared fiddled with the frequencies. The screen swirled.

A new voice. *"This is Admiral Jeff Thorne, CincHomeFleet, at Earthport Naval Station."* Jared found the frequency; suddenly the screen cleared. *"New York UNAF, put Ruben on the line. All other stations, now hear this!"* Thorne's face was red. *"The fucking trannies hacked into Naval comm codes. Effective forthwith all current codes are abandoned. Unseal codes slated for Tuesday next, in the pink envelopes—"*

"Jeff? Ruben, New York Command." The General sounded breathless. "What in hell's gone wrong? You blew out four of my command posts and you're knocking down Unie helis left and right! Hold your goddamn laser fire! You're killing troops!"

"It's the trannies." Thorne swelled with rage. *"Laser fire is stopped, as of two minutes ago. We—"*

A printer beeped. I glanced down. Confirmation from GNY Police: ETA fifteen minutes.

"Why the hell are you in clear? Go to scrambler!"

"Not 'til we straighten this out. You want us chasing our own tails? Listen, damn it. I shuttled up from Lunapolis to take personal charge. We're going to new codes, both groundside and the fleet, but let's not trust them; who knows how deep the trannies hacked. There's to be no laser fire from Earthport's batteries unless I personally approve each target. And I'll do so only when I have confirmation from you, with visuals and voice."

"That's cumbersome as—"

"Ernst, how many more troops must we kill before we learn?"

"Agreed, but we have a complication. SecGen Kahn's livid about the laser attack on Wirtz. He's suspended the oversight committee, and taken personal charge. He wants the old city cleared."

"I'm sure you'll do your best—"

"Of buildings," Ruben said.

A gasp. I realized it was mine.

"Their blowing the seawall was the last straw. Kahn says

it's time to renew the city, and he'll take the heat. I'm ordered to pull back our troops so we take no more casualties. He wants laser strikes from Earthport targeted on abandoned stores and apartments. We're to level anything not on our tax rolls, which includes all the trannie areas. After, they'll be redeveloped as towers and parks."

A long pause. *"I see. And the trannies?"*

"Survivors will be resettled. You'll have Kahn's confirmation through channels. In the meantime things may get a bit confused; we're shutting down satdish relays and fiber optics to the nets."

From Thorne, no answer.

Jared muttered, "Shit. I'll have to cut loose, or I'll leave tracks."

Ruben said, "Jeff, I was surprised as you, but it may be for the best."

"Yes, of course, I . . . " Thorne pulled himself together. *"I'll need target coordination from your people."*

"You'll have it. First priority is securing the midtown towers; they're vital. Then the old subways where the trannies hide their HQ."

"I . . . very well." Thorne's voice was bleak. *"I'll gear up on our end, and wait for Kahn's confirmation."*

"Very well." General Ruben sounded cross. "Now for God's sake go to scrambler. Christ alone knows who's listening."

The screen cleared.

I found myself huddled in the corner, weeping silently.

Father, I understand now. About the monastery. Why you go on retreats, why you took refuge for all those years. You'd done something unbearable.

As have I.

I doubted I could get them to listen, but I had to try. I turned to Jared, put a touch of awe in my voice. "I've never seen anyone schuss the nets so well. Ever."

Jared's chin went up. "You always thought I was stupid. No, don't deny it; it's all right. I just needed a chance to show you."

"It's . . . wonderful." I paused. "Jar, I've had a rough week. Before Fath gets hold of me, I deserve a vacation. Could you set it up?"

He shrugged. "If we hurry. The nets will be going down. Where to?"

I thought a moment. "How about the Lunapolis Hilton?"

Jared slipped on a throatmike. "Puter. Oral. Code Bossman Alpha. Travel, air. Ticket to passenger pickup, charged to Holoworld Ltd. Next departure after 2100 hours this day Trenton Shuttleport, destination Earthport / Lunapolis."

Chapter 52

JARED

P.T. always lacked true imagination. But what could he expect, burying his head in schoolbooks?

Why bother with a vacation when he could stay with me and have a ringside seat for the end of the world? Now all he'd get was acceleration ache and a room in a tourist warren.

On the other hand, a comfortable hotel bed wasn't that bad an idea. I stretched, easing my aching shoulders. I'd sat at the console for what seemed like weeks, with nothing but bathroom breaks. I needed a meal, a bed. Decent clothes to replace my trannie rags.

First, I had business to conclude. I toyed with the London CLIP, sliding in through the back door I'd installed. The CLIP's preprogrammed robins were industriously searching out my worms, so I tossed in birdseed to distract them.

It served the multinats right, the bastards. With the immense power of central linked processors, they netted every tiny detail of our lives. But the same connectivity that allowed Dad instant access to my grades also handed me his Terrex card; what goes round comes round. If you link the facets of our lives to prevent rebellions, you hand rebels the key to success.

On screen, I flicked idly through SearsNet clothes catalogs while waiting to rendezvous with my Arfie. It was high time to wield the chaincutter, and how we broke links would determine whether I could be traced.

Of course, from my standpoint it didn't matter. Even if they traced our operation to this room, I'd be long gone. I had set up a series of credit accounts that would keep me in funds regardless of whether Dad cut my allowa—.

My mouth tightened. All right, don't overreact. Yes, I supposed I'd miss him. He was the only adult I'd ever known well.

Nonetheless, he wasn't worth my regrets. He wasted his life as the Old Man's pet rabbit, ignoring me in the process. He was so selfish and conceited, he imagined he knew best for me, though it had been decades since he'd been a joeykid.

I was better off without him.

So why was I sobbing?

Bullshit; I was getting as bad as P.T. I was exhausted and overwrought. I wiped my eyes, schussed through the nets, gave myself a zarky new wardrobe, courtesy of SearsNet and Bank of London.

Still, for a moment I yearned to pick up the caller, dial a familiar voice. Arlene. Uncle Robbie. Anyone.

Instead, the caller buzzed me. I took it warily. "Yeah?"

"I sendin' Raulie ta bring ya home."

I snorted. "Learn how to start a conversation. It's 'Hello, this is Halber,' then—"

"*Shut ya face, joeykit!*"

I said coldly, "Don't talk to me that way, Halber. That time is past."

"Time be past fo' thousands a trannies! I got tunnels full a dead, hear me?" With an effort, he made his voice calmer. "Bad day. But ya done good, Uppie. Raulie saw heli fall right outa sky. An' Unies climbin' inta troop carry, ridin' 'way. Dunno they be back, but least it give us time."

"Yeah." I wondered whether to tell him he'd soon be a laser target. He'd just snarled at me worse than Dad, and treated me as a child. Besides, what was the point? His people had nowhere to run.

"I wanna meet wid Raulie an' Pook an' you. Figga out what ta do nex'. Can't get through ta Changman on frazzin' glitch caller."

I felt a peculiar pride; despite his ill temper he thought me a leader with whom to confer. But knowing what was coming, I'd be out of my mind to go down to the Sub caves. "You need me here."

"Why?"

"My nets are still up. I'll try to hit the Unies again." False, of course. A move against the alerted U.N.A.F. would be suicidal. They'd have a gunship lobbing missiles through the wall in less time than . . . I shivered.

He grumbled, "Wish I could talk ta ol' Chang." I'd never met the old man he'd sent as a negotiator, but Pook described him as senile and foolish. An apt spokesman.

Well, it didn't matter. My tower had food machines, water, and softies. While the Unies targeted the streets, I would stay right here. Then, when it was safe, I'd allow myself to be found.

I felt a pang of . . . not guilt, but mild regret. "Halber, you ever think of leaving the tunnels?"

"Tolya we was gonna run fo' the Hud, coupla hours back. But thas cause we desperate. No place fo' Sub tribe onna street. Sub be our home."

"Yeah, whatever." On my screen, a window flickered and was gone. My link to the London CLIP was no more. "Halber, I gotta go. Bye." I flicked off the caller, knowing it would enrage him. I didn't care; it was time to tighten my skis and schuss to safety. Carefully, oh, so carefully, I left intricate instructions for the Arfie. By now it was roaming the free electron slopes, well clear of New York. Then I began to extricate myself, brushing fresh snow across my trail as I backed out.

I was none too soon.

One by one the pylons snapped, and the ski lift slowly crashed into the powdery snow. Unicredit went off-line, then Citizaccess. Holoworld. I watched the last of my net connections flicker and die. When the fiber optics went, I keyed to satlinks, adjusting settings to compensate for the crawling pace. Not long after, I lost my main feed, the Geosynch Optinet. I'd barely logged through my first alternate when it too went dead. Without much hope, I tried other links, but my suspicions were confirmed. They'd shut down the nets.

My work was done. I dialed into a local news carrier to watch the fun, but halfway into connection my screen blanked.

I sighed, keyed my puter to satdish. Outgoing feeds were down. A thin blade of panic stabbed at my spine; I was isolated, lost in a deserted tower in the middle of a war. But as I flicked frequencies I found incoming links were undisturbed: Worldnewsnet, Holoworld Hourly, romances, even the mindless puter-construct soaps that livened the dreary afternoons of stay-at-homes.

I settled back in my chair, hugging myself, staring at the screen.

Chapter 53

POOK

Changman like ta complain he get ol' tryin' ta teach me patience. Always I ignore. Now, followin' Halb through sub tunnels wid Subgirl Allie trailin' behind, I gotta learn it fo' myself. Halber keep changin' his mind what he want. Firs' he say attack Unies, don' matter where, so long as trannies take venge fo' gas.

But afta Unie sojers hit trannies so bad near U.N., he talk 'bout tribe 'scapin' 'cross Hud Riv. Den he call Jared Washinton Uppie, an' now he wanna stay in Sub ta rumb.

Final, eatin' bit a stew in lair, he rub eyes like he daze. "Pook," he say, "how c'n I think if I can' keep 'wake? How long it been since I rest?"

"Dunno, Halb." I cautious eva since he swat me 'cross room, screamin' at Raulie ta blow wall. "Coupla days?" Word go roun' dat 'xplosion be zark; Uppies runnin' aroun' like pis-soff ants. But now sub tunnels south a Twenny be flood. Less 'n less our turf left.

"I'm gonna lie down."

"Chinas been waitin'. An' Faron's Easters say got nowhere ta go, tunnels full, Lexes won't move deeper 'cause—"

"Chris'!" He fling metal stew dish cross room. It roll an' clatter. "Gimme peace!"

I say real careful, "Wan' I should talk ta 'em, Halb?"

"You? He spit wid scorn. "Joeykit Mid talk ta tribes fo' Subs. Fahh!" But afta min he add, "Blowin' wall was yo' idea . . . wouldn't make no promises, wouldja?"

"Naw."

He sigh, see empty mattress, hand me caller, kinda slide down wall. " 'Kay."

Lotsa times I watch ol' Chang trayfo wid Mids an' Broads. So I know I gotta stay in charga, an' not lettem push me roun'. 'Notha thing I notice, the louder trannies get tryin' ta trayfo, the quieta go Chang, 'til dey gotta shush ta hear 'im. It work every time.

So I fin' Chinas' speakfo. Joey come roilin' in, all fury an' noise an' sputter. Unie sojers pushem outa turf, streets full a mud, where dey spose ta go? Sub flood fo' mile north a China. Wha happen Halber's promise Sub be open ta all, hah?

I sen' Allie ta ask if space in tunnels furtha north. Meantime South Harl stomp in, deman' rest a trannies help take back Amstadam; Unie patrols had streets block.

He be interrup' by pissoff Lex. His joeys can' crawl inna dark tunnel two block from stair, while frazzin' Easters what ain' lift finga ta help got turf right by staysh.

"Okay okay," I mutta low. Wish I had tea ta offa, like Chang. "We fix, make yas happy."

"How? You ain' even Sub. How ya goin—"

"We take care a. Filmatleven." Prolly what Chang 'd say. But South Harl joey scowl. "Wan' help *now*; tomorra maybe Unies be back strong wid—"

"Pook, Lexes ain' gonna let no frazzin—"

Caller buzz. Annoy, I turn it on an off quick, so it stop. "No prollem, Lex. We sen' someone talk ta Easters, soon as—" Goddamn caller buzz again.

I fling it 'gainst far wall, but somehow it ain' broke. It keep buzzin', insistent. Cursin', I go get it. "Yah?"

"Halb?"

"Naw, Pook. Who be?"

"Raulie, on Two Six near Broad. Need Halb quick."

"He sleepin'. Watcha wan'?"

"Gimme Halb NOW, ya frazzin' Mid, or I skin ya head ta toe!"

I go chill, cause ain' nothin' in worl' worse 'n a pissoff Sub. Dey grab ya inna nigh', pullya inna tunnel, throw back skun body inna morn'. Nobody mess wid Subs. Still, I wish could crawl through caller wid shiv. Raulie ack like I never help Subs, when I give em Jared, and I think up blowin' wall.

My teeth bare, but instant 'fore I speak, I feel Changman watchin' from nowhere, an' say quiet, "Halber tol' me lettim sleep. Meantime I hannel calls an' talk ta tribes."

'Steada rage, Raulie's voice go beg. "Pookboy, I never seen nothin' like this. Tellim I say jump in unnercar, meet at Two Six in few min. Hurry!"

Was Raulie blew up wall, Raulie what bust inta towahs. If *he* soundin' scare . . . I push pas' Easters an' Mids and Chinas ta where Halb lay curl. I reach ta shake him wake, but think better. I kneel, talk close ta ear til he groan, turn ova.

Allie say, "Lemme, Pook." She bend ova, prod him wake. He sit up sudden. I jump back, like he stewdog gonna snap wid fang. "Raulie want ya fas', Halb."

Halber growly wid loss sleep. He chew me fo' leavin' him a bunch hysteric trannies allatime want somethin'. Den he stomp ta unnercar, beckon me comealong. Allie come too, like invited.

Ride south quiet, tense. We race through staysh. I look away, 'fraid I see bodies lyin' stack, wid blood roun' mouth. But Subs wave as we pass, while joeys of otha tribes run fo' stair at two angry lights comin' rumble outa dark.

Car slow. I run ta driva seat. "Whassamatta?" I peer at track.

Halber bring us ta stop. "Ain' no staysh at Two Six. Jus' 'scape hole." He open door, jump down. "Wait here."

"Wanna come."

"Don' matta." He stalk inta dark. Runnin' ta keep up, I fall flat an' smack my face. I curse, jump up afta disappearin' Sub. Behin' me, Allie giggle. I think 'bout cuttin' her a nice fresh Mid mark.

Raulie be wait 'cross track, near side openin'. "Halb!"

I stumble on track, but Allie grab my arm ta steady. I push her off, proud, but afta min take her han' fo' guide.

Raulie beckon us ta grate ovahead.

We climb ladder ta ledge. Halber say, "Well? Whas so import I couldn' res'?"

"Lissen!"

Cracklin' soun'. Rumble.

Pushin' aside grate, Halber growl, "What now? Frazzin' Unies can' make up their mind, come afta us, run away—" he poke head out ta street. "Oh Jesus Lor'."

Icicle ooze down my back. Gotta look. Squeeze pas' Halber's arm, look roun'.

Crackle be from fire. Whole block burn, as far south I c'n see. Crumble brick walls fill road.

'Cross street, build slides slowly inta street. I duck from crash, get tangle in Halber's arms. He thrus' me 'way.

"How it start?" Halber's voice hoarse.

"They did it!" Raulie.

"Unies ran roun' setting fire? Get on caller, send alla trannies south. We guard streets best we can, make em pay—"

"Naw! Doin' it from up."

"Wha?"

Raulie tug Halber's arm. "No Unies. C'mon. Lesgo Two Three." He jump down ta sub tunnel.

Halber bellow, but Raulie run ahead to unnercar. Sub Boss stalk afta.

Soon as we in, Raulie jump in cab, drive car south. At Two Three staysh, Raulie dash through dim tunnel ta stair, peek careful aroun' corna. "No Unies. C'mon." He don' wait fo' us ta follow.

Breathin' his mad, Halber an' I go afta. Allie hang back.

I blink in late day's ligh'.

"Stay close ta stair," Raulie warn, searchin' ruined ol' office builds wid eyes. Good builds, wall still strong, make nice lair. Prolly already be, fo' whateva tribe live here.

Halber glance roun', wary.

"Gahh!" I seize his arm, point ta build 'cross street. Roof begin ta peel an' smoke. In a sec, wall buckle. "Wha' is it, Halb? Monstas?"

"Naw." Like he disgus', Sub Boss stroll ta mid a empty rubbly street, put hands on hips. "Gonna move now, betcha."

Sure enough, jus' as firs' build burst inta flame, monsta move south, eat anotha'.

I stare, in stun. Two mo' builds smoke.

Invis monsta cross our street slow towar' stair. Black pave go bubble an' heave. In coupla sec, monsta chew on roof prac'ly ova our head.

"Come ON!" I dart inta street, haul Halber towar' sub. "Monsta gon' getcha!"

He shake me off, walk slow an' contemptuous. "Laser. No monsta."

"Ha, think ya swind ol' Pook? Noway. Raulie use laser on towah door, couldn' barely cut."

"Not pistol. Cannon. Longtime back, saw in news holo on side a towah. They tested it on ruins." He start down stair.

I ask, "Where it be, in heli?"

"Naw."

"On toppa towah? Maybe wid enough trannies, c'd break in, run upstair—"

"Pook." His han' give warnin' squeeze, but not unkind. "We can' get to. Be up. Earthport."

"Whazzat?"

"A staysh in orbit. Navyboys." Frustrate, he shake me, point ta sky. "Doncha unnerstan'? Orbit. Go roun' worl'."

Raulie say, "What we do, Halb?"

"Dunno. Back ta Four Two. Call Jared. Call Chang." We hurry from stair towar' unnercar.

Behin' us, a rumble, a crash. Shriek, cut off.

"Who dat?" I whirl. Where was light from stair, now dark.

"Get inna car!" Halber shove me.

"Allie?" I look roun'. "Joeygirl!"

"Inna car!"

I twis' outa Halb's grip, run towar' stair.

In dim ligh', almost don' see small form lyin', head at bottom a stair. Big rocks scatter roun' where stair usetabe open. Gentle, I sit, slide knee unner head. "C'mon, Allie, gotta go." Coupla rocks clatter down blocked stair. A ragged breath lift her shirt.

Halber grunt. He pick up Alliegirl like she sack a cansa, hurry ta track.

In car he lie her on seat, head in my lap. He squeeze in cab, start us wid lurch.

Allie gasp.

"It okay, joeykit. Jus' unnercar. Don' be 'fraid." I croon like I be glitch, dunno what ta say. "Fin' safe place, take care a ya."

Raulie sit 'cross, silent.

Car rattle ova bad piece a track. I put han' on her shoulda like ta protec'. Allie cough. Her lips open. Mouthful a blood pour onta my knee. She stop breathin'.

I look ta Raulie, shakin' head a furious no.

He nod, cross arms, look at flo'.

We streak pas' Three Four staysh, Raulie los' in his own worl', Allie restin' on my lap, I stiff 'an straight, joeygirl's blood oozin' down leg an' soakin' shoe.

At Four Two staysh Raulie pry me loose from Allie. I fight him some, but he don' even whomp me. Final, I too tire ta protes'.

Daze, I wander back ta main lair. Ignorin' chairs, I sit in

corna near entrance, lookin' back ta stair. I wait fo' crash from laser, an' sudden dark. Anytime soon, I figga.

Halber shoutin' at Jared on caller. "Don' tell me ya can't; jus' stop 'em!"

Sub Boss jump on chair, peer roun'. "Sollie!" His voice loud, but ominous calm. "Take buncha trannies an' hit neares' towah. Cut inta, I don' care how many lives it cos'. Kill any Uppie ya see. Burn."

"But Halb—"

"Ya challenge?" Halber jump down from chair. "Who be Sub Boss?"

Ol' man run tongue 'cross his lips. "I too ol' fo' fight, Halb. C'n cut through doors, but—"

"Joss! Rana! You Easters, go wid! Lissen, all!" Halber begin ta frazzle. "Unies burn ol' city, entire. No place ta run. We goin' down. But if we fry a coupla towahs, could be dey stop. Maybe no. But at leas' we take 'em wid us!"

Roar of agree.

"Show 'em how we rumb!" His sweat shine.

Shadow fall 'cross my leg, 'cross my red sticky knee.

"Alla tribes became one in rumb wid Uppies!" Halber's eyes burn like towah. Subs, Easters, Chinas go frenzy, shoutin' an' yellin' approve. "If we gotta go out, go as one!"

I look up as shadow passby. I catch glimpse a face.

Slowly, I get ta feet. Hair on neck rise.

Halber yell, "Go! Les show frazzin' Uppies who own da worl'!"

Mob a trannies turn, race towar' me an stair. Toward one man standin' in way.

He snatch chair, sling it inta crowd. *"NO!"* His roar echo through cave.

Trannies in front skid ta stop, but be push from behin' just as chair fly. Go down in clumps.

"You?" Halber's mouth work wid rage. "You!"

"Me." Uppie's voice like lash.

Easter joey firs' ta scramble ta feet. "Who he be?"

Halber snarl, "Fisherman, an' he *mine*!"

A murmur, like trannies don' believe.

"Fisherman," Sub Boss repeat. Sudden, shiv gleam in han'. "Came down ta Sub, said he frien', an' fight fo' us 'gainst Parkas." Slow, he come closer.

"But was he called Unies ta diss us when we take Park. Was he sent gas ta tunnels, called lasers ta burn city. Mus' be a Lor' God afta all, send him back ta me 'fore too late."

Fisherman calm. "Is P.T. with you?"

"Dead." Halb spit da word. "Ate him yest'day. Venge."

Uppie stand froze like ice.

"In stewpot, Uppie." Halber's grin worse 'n I eva seen. "Taste good." Drift near.

Fisherman's eye fall on me. His voice harsh. "Is it so?"

Halber stupe. I too petrify ta speak, but 'steada waitin', Halb snap, "Stay shut, Pook! Or getcha self diss!"

Fisherman sigh. "Thank Lord God." For moment, he tremble. Den, as Halber close wid shiv, he pull himself togetha. "I didn't come to fight you."

"I betcha didn'!" Halber lunge. Uppie step aside fas'. His stiff hand slice down on Halb's forearm. Sub Boss grunt, clutch arm.

Uppie look roun', grab chair fa shield. "Listen."

Sollie call out, "We'll rush 'im, Halb."

"Naw! Touch, I skin ya. He mine!" Halb spit. It run down Fisherman's ches'.

Uppie say, "I didn't call the troops. I've been trying to stop this madness! Halber, why would I—"

"Don' care why! You be diss!" Halber lunge wild.

Somethin' in Uppie change. He fling down chair, stalk ta Halber. Quick like cat, he evade upper thrus' intend ta open his gut. "You trannie bastard, *listen*!" His foot swing like ta kick Halb's nuts inta throat.

Halb slice down wid shiv, but Fisherman's kick jus' fake; Uppie's han' waitin ta close roun' Halber's wrist. Locked together, two dance slow through corridor, 'til Uppie fetch Halb 'gainst wall, shiv arm pinned tight.

Boss Sub's muscles ripple as he try ta break free. Eyes bulge.

Sudden, no warn, Fisherman leggo Halb's otha han'. He whomp stupendous punches, one two three. Stomach, throat, balls.

Halb go down, but Uppie grip his shiv han' like a vise. Halber kneel, one arm raise behin', otha pressed 'tween legs.

Slow, unrelent, Fisherman pry loose shiv. At las', Halber's fingas give way.

Halb raise head, mouth grimace in agony. Shiv glint high.

Uppie's fingas spread. Shiv fall to flo'. Hand open, he slap Halber one, two. Crack like thunder. Sub Boss head rock; spit fly loose. Again, one, two.

He let go Halb's arm. Sub Boss sag.

Fisherman turn roun', glare at tribes. Take step; they fall back, stumblin' ova each otha.

He drag Halb ta sit 'gainst wall. Fisherman kneel in fronta. "I'm sorry I called you a trannie."

No ansa. Halber still clutch hisself, face red.

Uppie's voice slow an' clear, like talkin' ta glitchjoe. "I didn't call the Unies. I swear before Lord God."

Nothin.'

"You hear me?"

Daze, bleedin', Halb nod.

"Where's my son?"

Across lair, Easters, Chinas, Subs stare. No one say word. I sit very quiet, but don' matta; Fisherman see me anyway. "Answer!"

I say, reluctant, "Wen' ta fin' Jared."

"He was here?"

I nod. "Yah. Called Changman."

Halber grated, "Shut, Pook!"

Eyes wild, Fisherman dash across cave, haul Sub boss ta feet, slam him 'gainst wall. "You shut! Philip be my son, my joeykit! I gonna fin'!" I gape, at trannietalk in Uppie mouth.

Halb may be beat, but don' know quit. "Why we care? End a worl'."

"Boolsheet. Jus' gotta stop rumb. Don' shoot sojers, give back lasers—"

"My Nine Sixers gone!" Halb try feeble ta twis' free. "Doncha unnerstan? Can' give up afta dat."

Fisherman say, "Okay, ya lose some fightas. Dass way rumb go. End!"

"Frazzin' Uppie don' give shit 'bout—"

"Goofjuice. I'm tryin' ta—"

Allasudden, I unnerstan'. "Halb," I say, urgent. "He don' know. Tell 'im."

"Boolsheet! He—"

"Mira his face!" I dance wid frustrate. "He ain' hear yet!"

Fisherman look back an' forth 'tween us. "Hear what? Tell!"

"Dissed my Subs!" It be cry a pain. "All 'em." Halb try ta go on, choke.

I say quick, "Unie sojers put gas hoses in tunnels. Diss everyone 'tween Nine Two an' Hunnert Ten. Was thousans trannies refuge in tunnel. All gone."

"No." Fisherman's face white.

"Dey did it, Uppie. C'n see fo' yaself. Smell gettin' fierce, though. No place get ridda bodies."

Shaky, he sag 'gainst wall.

I say, "See, Halb? Didn' know."

Sudden, Easter joey add, "Blew up lair, Secon' Ave. We hid joeykits unner. By time we dug 'em out, none lef'. Halber sendin' us ta towah, fine wid us. Venge."

"China lairs burn." A dark tribeman, who eyes smoulder.

"Came through Lex turf like monstas inna nigh'. Shoot everyone, even tryin' ta run."

One by one, voices add woes, 'til Uppie cover face.

I ask, "Ya know 'bout lasers from up?"

Fisherman shake head. "I left Franjee Tower this morning. They wouldn't help me; I had to find—"

"We wen' down ta Two Three, me an' Halb an' Raulie. Lasers be crumblin' builds all ova. City burn. All."

"That's impossible."

Halb stir. "I called Jared Uppie. He say Earthport Staysh lasers doin' it. Unie Navy. Cantcha smell the smoke?"

Fisherman groan.

Halber eye his shiv on flo', but make no move.

Long quiet.

Fisherman say, "It's got to stop." Somethin' in his tone make me chill.

"Hah. Sojers gonna 'gree?"

"Probably not. Nor will the government. I'll need . . ." He chew lip. " . . . about fourteen hours. Don't attack any more towers until I've done what I must." His voice raise. "Hear me, tribe? Gimme time. I try ta fix."

Lexboy spit. "Why we trus' you?"

"Because . . . " Fisherman swallow. Afta min, his eyes glisten. "I love my boy so much . . . this started because of

Philip. Adam Tenere and I combed the city, and my wife was . . . for a week, I've barely slept. If he dies, my life is over."

"So?"

"I'm done looking. Your lives come first. I'll stop the lasers."

"How?"

"I'll go aloft. I think I know a way."

Halber ease himself ta chair, balls still hurtin'. "An' if ya stop laser, Uppies go back ta gas us like rats inna sewer. Take only water we got, sen' in troop carries an' Unie troops . . ."

"I know." Fisherman be deep within himself. "Yes. I've known a long while." He shudder. "Even that, I'll give you."

He haul Halb ta feet, stoop ta pick up shiv. "If I can stop the lasers, I'll stop the rest also. I know how. I just hoped . . . I'm sorry." He put shiv in Halb's han', put own arms behin' back. "Diss me now, if ya don' trust. Or lemme help yas." He close eyes, raise head like ta bare throat. "Diss, if ya wan'. Dunno if I care."

Halb glance at Easters an' Subs, back ta shiv. I c'n see flicker a venge in his min'.

Voice say sharp, "No one touch him." I in fronta Fisherman, protectin', lookin' backanforth. "No one!" My own shiv out, glintin' sharp.

Someone snicker. I spit, signalin' ready ta rumb.

Halb say soft, "How long, Fisherman?"

"Give me 'til midmorning. The lasers will stop . . . or they won't."

I look in Halb's eyes, beseech.

He nod.

Few min later Fisherman stand at stair. "Keep your joeys underground. Disperse them—you know what that means?— as far as possible from the square."

"Yah." Halber look morose.

"And remember laser fire comes from the south; the station's in equatorial orbit. Low buildings north of a tower should be safe."

"Yah."

"Keep that caller with you, the one I recoded. Don't change to another; they all have different codes. I'll call as soon as I know."

"Yah, you'll call." Halb look like he don' believe it.

"Bring Jared Tenere under, if you find him. His father is desperate."

I tug at sleeve. "Whassis name?"

"Adam Tenere."

"Mista Tenere? Peetee call him Mista?"

"Yes."

"He diss." Immediate, I regret sayin' it so bald, 'cause Fisherman go white.

He manage, "Why'd you kill him?"

"Not us. He run down ta warn Hunnert Ten Subs 'bout gas. Peetee foun' him wid othas, blood ova mouth."

Long silence. Fisherman's voice impossible weary. "How do you know?"

"Peetee tell Mista Chang onna caller."

"Why Chang?"

"He our speakfo."

Fisherman mutta somethin unda breath, cross hisself. Then he stalk 'cross Four Two Square, stride towar' towahs 'til he disappear in swirlin' smoke.

Chapter 54

ROBERT

Alone in my luxury suite at the Earthport Hilton I massaged my forehead, hoping to soothe the dull ache gripping my skull. I'd been more than foolhardy to endure liftoff after a concussion.

Still, I'd had to leave the war room, had to leave Franjee Tower. Had to leave New York.

I poured a second glass of whiskey, took another sip. It didn't seem to help.

"I only noticed him because his clothing was so different from the tribesmen."

I swirled the scotch.

"Objectively speaking, I'd say he died in agony."

Did the boy know what he'd done to me?

How could I face life without Adam?

Even when he was furious with me, in his middy days, or when he saw me manipulate Arlene and the Captain, his rebuke had an undertone of respect, his disapproval something akin to love.

I'd called Dad, and told him the news. He grunted, said he was sorry. Then he told me the situation had changed; the Navy was intervening with pinpoint laser fire. My job had been to stay with General Ruben. The least I could do, having fled to orbit, was to attach myself to Jeff Thorne.

Our public position was that we approved the Navy's pulling U.N.A.F.'s chestnuts out of the fire. Of course, it helped that Supranationalists had always supported the Navy, while the Territorials favored U.N.A.F. I should make sure I was interviewed when the dust settled.

It left a sour taste that alcohol couldn't etch clean.

I groped for the caller, punched in familiar codes. "Mother?"

"Robbie? You sound a million miles away."

"I'm at Earthport."

"Good heavens. Why?"

"I'm . . . not sure."

"Concussions are tricky. I'll call Van to get you."

"No, I feel fine." Other than a persistent headache that threatened to suck in my eyeballs, and a gentle sway to the room that I assumed was an excess of whiskey on an empty stomach.

"I was dusting the roses. The damn aphids have them again. It's time I changed the service; those lawn people don't know the slightest—"

"Mother, Adam's dead."

"About spraying—who? Someone I know?"

"Adam Tenere."

"Ah, yes. Your . . . friend from the Navy." As always, she made it sound as if we were sodomites. No matter how often I told her . . . "Had you known he was ill?"

"He wasn't." My tone was sharp. "They killed him in the insurrection. We killed him. Our side."

"Oh, dear." A pause. When she resumed, her voice was soothing and, well, more motherly. "I'm sorry, of course. Should I take you to the funeral?"

"Damn you, Mother, his body's rotting in the subway tunnels!"

"And damn you, I'm sorry that's so. What was he doing there?"

Her sharp speech was a comfort; it meant she knew I spoke from stress, that I was forgiven. With Mother, bluntness was itself a code.

"He was trying to warn the trannies. They—we—used poison gas to flush them out."

"I feel for you, Robbie. Come home today, help me with these detestable roses. We'll talk."

I swallowed a lump. "I don't think so. Thanks."

"Weren't you godfather to Adam's son?"

"An unofficial uncle."

"Really, the trannie tunnels weren't his concern. The man should have known better."

I stifled an urge to shatter the caller on the bedside stand. "Mother, did you hear? We pumped in poison gas. There's hundreds dead, maybe more." My tone was curious. "Don't you care?"

"About your friend, yes." She paused. "They're censoring news of the insurrection, but I'm old enough to read between the lines. Besides, at your hospital I had a perfectly good view of the burning buildings." Her tone sharpened. "A trannie rebellion is insufferable. You and Richard should have dealt with those joeys during Seafort's administration, when you had the SecGen's ear. Now Mr. Kahn's taking care of it. He's saving your father the trouble after the election."

"Mother, we killed innocents. Women, joeykids . . . "

"Regrettable, but not surprising. Except possibly to the trannies. That's what happens in war, Robbie. It's why we have world government, and why we've done a fairly good job of banning combat."

"You approve of the gas, then?"

"I'll ask Dr. Wilkes if I can handle liftoff. If so, I can arrange to bring you home in a few hours."

"Do you?" It was almost a shout.

"Yes. Overall, I do. It's bizarre to approve of some ways of killing your enemy, and deplore others."

"Your enemy . . . " I closed my eyes, pictured Adam sprawled in a filthy tunnel.

"Robbie, were you consulted?"

"Not about that."

"Well, then. To the extent there's blame, you're absolved. You can't bear another's guilt."

I whispered, "The Captain did."

"Who? Seafort? He revels in contrition. He's obsolete, a relic from when belief in the Reunification was dogma. Think of yourself, and Richard."

I roused myself. "You still care about him?"

"I believe we had this conversation at your bedside. Remember, I'm planning on an invitation to formal tea. I love you."

"I love you too, Mother." I keyed off the caller, set it in its cradle.

"Mr. Assemblyman, the Admiral will see you now." A lieutenant, his uniform starched and stiff, as befit a shoreside post. I followed him through bright-lit Earthport corridors to the installation I'd visited with Dad a few weeks past.

As if I were still a lieutenant reporting to a superior, I flicked my tie, adjusted my jacket. I smiled; Naval habits die hard. But now Jeff Thorne and Admiralty came hat in hand to our committees for their appropriations; I was perforce welcome whenever I chose to visit.

Nonetheless, I hoped the breath rinse I'd used was successful. I didn't want Thorne thinking I'd retreated into a bottle, even if he wasn't one to carry tales.

The Admiral grunted, his attention on the overhead screen. "Hello, Rob." He squinted at a satellite recon holo of New York. His voice rose a trifle. "Let's see the other."

A new picture flashed.

"Very good." To me, "See? You're getting your money's worth." He flicked a laser pointer at the screen. "Those blocks, from Twenty-third through Thirtieth, already cleared. Urban renewal, courtesy of your Navy."

I had a sudden suspicion, and moved close. "You're drinking."

"Nah. Martinis with lunch." He waved it away. "To settle my stomach for the grind ahead. Ernst Ruben confirms coordinates, I set them up, he confirms fire results, we proceed. In a couple of days, it'll be done."

I hesitated, drew a deep breath. "Why do you need your stomach settled?"

"What business is it of yours?"

"None, really." I took the plunge. "Except that I feel the same."

"Do you, now." An appraising glance. "How interesting." He keyed a mike. "Continuous laser fire, throughout the marked grid."

I glanced at the screen, but nothing changed. The view wasn't real-time, though it could well have been. Technically, it was no problem. I wondered if using a still photograph was Thorne's attempt to distance himself from his operations.

Morose, I took a chair. "I wish there was another way."

"Please. I've had my fling with idealism."

"When?"

"Long ago, and it almost cost me my career." I recalled that he'd been assigned to Academy when the alien armada attacked. Though I'd been a cadet, I'd had no encounters with him, and he'd requested transfer soon after Captain Seafort resigned.

The speaker came to life. "Sir, General Ruben again."

"Put him through."

"Jeff, I confirm fire on Thirty-first at East River, moving west and north on both sides of the street." Ruben sounded tired.

"Understood."

"Is there any reason to keep confirming? They haven't interfered since—"

"I won't fire without personal confirmation." Thorne's tone was sharp. "They got us once, but, by God, they won't do it again. What's next?"

"The fools are still resisting. We're about to go for their command. Nearly all caller traffic emanates from the Forty-second Street tunnels. Can you penetrate concrete that thick?"

Thorne's fingers tightened on the edge of the console. "Yes."

Ruben sighed. "Let's get it done. Forty-first through Forty-third, from Eighth through Broadway. Bypass Seventh and Forty-first, of course; Franjee Tower is just south and would block your shot. And run a line of fire down the center of Forty-Second all the way to Lexington; the crosstown tunnel runs under the road. Coordinates follow." He read off a long string of numbers.

Painstakingly, Thorne copied each, read it back, waited for verification. "Very well, Ernst."

"Confirmed. Lord, I need sleep. One more thing. Be prepared for a visitor."

"Who?"

"Believe it or not, former SecGen Seafort."

"Christ."

Ruben added, "Seafort's been wandering midtown in a hopeless search for his son. A few hours ago he came back, hopping mad. God knows how he made it through the streets. He stormed through the building, made reservations on the fly, lifted off in a taxi for the shuttleport."

I blurted, "What about Arlene?"

Thorne said, "Ernst, Rob Boland's here. He asks what you know of Ms. Seafort."

"She's on her way to see me. She heard the trannies sent a negotiator, and wants to speak with him. I have the old man in isolation, but I'll probably allow it. She won't give up hope."

I shook my head. P.T. was alive; or had been when he

called Chang. But he was beyond the reach of his parents and in mortal peril. The sheer folly of running back into the streets . . . I wondered what demon possessed the boy. I'd always seen Jared Tenere as the foolish one, Philip as more stable. Perhaps I'd been mistaken.

In the outer corridors, raised voices. A shout of frustration, the clatter of feet. Then, silence.

After his call from Ruben, Thorne sat musing. "Rob, I can't refuse to see him. Not a former SecGen. But I want you here for support."

"Are you out of your mind? Absolutely not." I got to my feet. "He's your problem, not mine."

"Together we can—"

"No!" I made for the hatch.

"Let me make it clear." Thorne's tone had a bite. "If you care about your father's campaign, you'll be here when the SecGen shows. Else I'll go over to the Territorials, and tell Richard that you're three sheets to the wind even now."

"The hell I am!" I paused. "Jeff, there are reasons I don't want to see him."

"You think I've none myself?" He laughed bitterly. "He knew me as a boy, for God's sake. And brought me back to Academy for those final days. You expect me to stand up to him unaided?"

It occurred to me that we both knew exactly what the Captain wanted of us, though neither had voiced it.

"What if you don't see him 'til it's over?"

"Then I'm a heel. It's already hard enough to look at myself in the mirror." A sour smile. "Even in politics, there are civilities. You simply don't refuse to see a SecGen, past or present."

"I know." It was the sort of affront that left one vulnerable, ever after. Even the deadly game of politics had its rules. I sighed. "Ring me; I'll be here." I left to clean up and swig another mouthful of breath freshener.

In the anteroom I asked a duty lieutenant, "What was the commotion?"

"Bloody civilians." He shook his head crossly. "There's a dozen demonstrators in the corridor. One silly joeykid tried to push past to see the Admiral. 'It's terribly important,' he shouted, as if I'd let him through. I had a middy haul him out to the main concourse; let him yell at joeys in the ticket lines. By the way, there's a side passage, if you want to bypass the picketers."

"No, that's all right." I smoothed my hair, put on a somber expression.

Chapter 55

PEDRO

A hand on shoulder shook me out of sleep I needed. "Let's go, old man. They're waiting."

I sat up in bed, groggy. "Who?"

"Move." Unie soldier, young an' arrogant.

I made face. "Wan' me to piss on floor, or in pants?"

With elaborate sigh of disgus' he led me to gleaming Uppie cubicle, all tile an' white light. When I done, I washed face to come alert, slipped on my coat. Dunno where they was takin' me; didn' want to risk losing. Only one I had, 'xcept for trayfo stock.

After General had turned his back, they'd locked me in room on next flo' lower. Had no windows. If I listened har', could hear constant drone of helis, so I knew rumb wasn't done. Now, I let them escort me back to elevate. I shuffled extra slow, for annoy.

Even with sometime dramatic stop for breath I didn' really need, wasn't long before I back to conference room I'd been in before, where P.T. called hisself Chaco. This time, two people waitin'.

One was my favorite U.N.A.F. officer. I quizzed self to recall name: Groves. "Ah," I said. "Major Groans."

"Groves." His tone icy. He turned to Uppie woman. "Are you sure—"

"That's the negotiator? Him?" Her body was tense, face haggard. I grinned inside. She in bad condition fo' trayfo.

"Unfortunately."

"I had no idea." She studied my face. "Mr. Chang?"

I too mad for polite. "Mizz Fisherman." Let her think I just a trannie stupe. Prolly true. 'Cause I worried about frazzin' water lines, I started rumb that gonna 'xterminate all my trannies. If that ain' stupe, what was?

She said to Groves, "If you don't mind?" Gesture to door.

"Alone? Impossible; I'm responsible for your safety."

Fisherman wife Arlene regarded him like roach in stewpot. "I beg your pardon? *I'm* responsible for my safety."

"Mrs. Seafort, if you object to me I'll call a trooper, but all trannies are regarded as armed and dangerous until—"

Her hand slammed on table. "Out, you bloody ass!" She stalked to door, held it open. "You think I'm in danger here? Shall I tell Ruben you countermanded his order?"

"Very well." His tone stiff, he tried to retreat dignified. "I'll post someone outside. Call if—"

"Good-bye."

I said quick, before he disappear, "Have nice day, Lieutenan' Groan."

She shut door, faced me. "They say you'll be charged with treason. Possibly, if you help me, I could testify—"

I spat big glob on table. It sat between us.

It stopped her, as I wanted.

Her fingers drummed table, her eyes bored into mine. Then, "Mr. Chang, I'm desperate for your help." Abrupt, she jumped up, paced length of room. "And I'm not sure . . . " She stopped, put hands on back of chair, leaned on it as if exhaust. Final, she faced me with resolve. "I don't think I deserve it."

Think she gonna swind Pedro Telamon Chang, appeal to his sympathy? Hah. My sympathy with my trannies, with Halber Sub, with resta tribes who die in streets.

"But P.T. deserves it." Her eyes sought mine. "Nick's gone to try to stop this horrid war, and he sounded . . . " Allasudden, her eyes filled with tears.

I sat stony.

"Like he didn't expect to come back. Nick's abandoned Philip. I'm all our son has left. Please, help me find him."

In trayfo, admission of weak was usually bad idea. Once in a while, clever move. Apparent, she thought so.

I said only, "Innifo?"

"What's in it for you? What should I give?"

Aha. She lay hand on problem. What point in making trayfo, no goal left?

I say harsh, "Bring back trannie dead."

"If only I could. And Adam. I'll miss him so." Weary, she pulled chair next to me, rested arms in lap, leaned forward, head near mine. "I need confession. Would you hear me?"

Reluctant, I muttered, "I ain' no Uppie pries'." For first'

time, felt afraid. Woman had unsettlin' way about her, like Fisherman.

"All else has failed. Even if I damn my son, it's time for truth." Eyes shot up, found mine. "You see, I started it. I called SecGen Kahn, asked his help finding Philip. My son is so young, so trusting. When Jared ran off, P.T. decided it was his fault. He followed Jared to the hotel, searched the streets . . . if he'd called, or explained . . . we were frantic, Nick and I. Adam and Robbie Boland joined us when we traced the boys to the city."

She paused, stared at table, at my glob of spit. "We were getting nowhere, and with each passing hour . . . when I wanted to ask Kahn for help, Nick had a fit. But he went out again and half a day passed. Robbie and I talked it over . . . it seemed a good idea."

Hand flitted to her hair, back to her lap where it held other tight, as if prisoner. "I admit at the time I didn't care what happened to your joeys. But I had no idea it would go so far." Again her eyes came to mine. "Evil people never do, do they?"

I shrugged.

"And it's gotten worse. How much have they told you?"

"Been locked in room. Blowin' seawall was last I heard." I cursed myself for stupe. Never tell what you don' know. You glitch with old, Pedro.

"Your trann—your Hackers played hell with the markets, and broke enough codes to make the Navy fire on U.N.A.F. troops. SecGen Kahn decided he'd had enough. This morning the Naval base on Earthport Station began targeting laser cannon on the old city. They're taking it down block by block."

"Ahhh!" Sob escaped me. Furious with self, I put up hands.

"Mr. Chang, they *want* to clear the streets. I can't get through to Kahn to stop it. I can't undo the harm I've done. Neither can Nick."

Silence, that went on long.

"You see? I'm honest with you." She sounded drained. "But my son is a twelve-year-old child. Could you find compassion, after all we've done to you? At least for him?"

I said cruel, "Innifo?"

"I won't insult you with money. There's only one thing I can think of."

I waited, hope mix with unease.

"Me." Her mouth grim, but determine. "I caused your ruin. Do your people want revenge? If they have Philip, or can find him, tell me where to go. I'll be there, unarmed, and give myself to your joeys. I only ask that I know Philip's safe first. It can be by caller; that part can be arranged."

"Subs kill you."

"I know."

I forced self to think of lasers devourin' city, an' made voice hard. "Ya think Fisherman won' come back. Who gonna raise joeykit without ya?"

Her eyes teared. "I hoped I would. He'll need . . . He'll have a hard time. But at least he'll be alive."

"Not just kill ya. Skin ya live."

"I've heard that." In her eyes, fear, but still resolve. "Can you help us? Will you? Let me send for a caller."

I fiddled in pocket, came out with pill, reached across for old water jug. Not fair. Uppiebitch shouldn' strain ol' man's heart so.

I said, "P.T. was with Sub leader when he called here."

"You'll trade, then? Me for him?" Her tone pathetic eager.

"Can't. He ain't there no more. Went to look for Jared."

She cried, "Jared isn't worth it! Why can't P.T. understand?"

I said gentle, "Cause he your son. Too much good in him."

"Oh, Philip . . ." She rocked, huggin' self. "I need you so."

"He hadda go through streets to find Jared, that much I certain. If he ain't called 'gain, maybe too late." Hated to say, but it time of truth.

Slowly, her composure dissolve. With a cry of despair, she threw herself on my shoulder.

After min, my hand stole out like got mind of its own. I stroked her hair, thinkin' of trannie woman Neut made wife, long years past.

When she calmer I said, "Prollem is, even if you get me caller, Halber won't tell me where Jared hid. Not now, when I been so many hours without callin'. He'll figga I'm capture. Which true, more or less."

She wiped eyes. "Why would Halber care? Jared's a surly

joeykid who thinks he's too smart to work. Why bother hiding him?"

I cursed self for fool, an' maybe traitor. " 'Cause trannie Hacker who givin' ya fits, joey who broke system, that be Jared."

She searched my eyes for confirm, found it. "Lord in heaven." For min she sit in silence. Then, "How can I find Jar?"

"He in a tower, but dunno which one. Halber never said, and I didn' ask."

"But if you call . . . "

I shook head. "Jared be secret weapon, best they have. If I ask, Halber hang up. No way in worl' he'd tell me."

"Is there anything you can do—anything—that will help me find P.T.? My offer still stands."

I said gruff, "I don' wan' your skin. Beside, if he alive, Peetee's prolly with Jared. Even for venge, Halber won' tell me where that is."

For long while she regarded me. "I'll do my best to have you freed. You came as a negotiator; they owe you that much. And if they try you, I'll be your witness. I'll hire lawyers, do what I can to save you."

I smiled, wan. "Save ya coin. I gone soon anyhow." Tap chest. "Too much excite nowadays. Can' last."

"I'll help you get a transplant."

"Don' wan' one." How c'n I explain? Without trannies, why live? With who I gonna trayfo? "Don' want one," I repeated.

Chapter 56

PHILIP

I'd been to Earthport twice, once with Fath, once with Mom too. The first trip aloft I barely remembered; I'd have been about three. The second time was four years ago, to attend Captain Edgar Tolliver's retirement ceremony, in the Naval wing. He and Fath had shaken hands stiffly, as if there was something between them they didn't care to speak of. Mr. Tolliver's remarks had an acid tone, but they didn't seem to bother Fath. Occasionally he smiled at hearing them.

Now, on the crowded shuttle, willing myself to relax at liftoff, I tried to deal with not seeing Fath again. It brought me too close to tears, so I let it be. I was near the end of my emotional rope, but I had only one more chore, and then nothing would matter.

Somehow, I'd have to get in to see Admiral Thorne, tell him it was all a mistake, that I'd made Jared crazy and brought the troops onto the streets by running away. Perhaps if I explained how upset I'd made Father . . . I knew Fath liked Mr. Thorne, even though he told Mom the Admiral hadn't lived up to his promise despite his career advancement.

I waited impatiently for the shuttle to dock.

In the Station's huge concourse I found a clothing shop and spent almost the last of my money on a fresh outfit. I doubted I'd get in to see the Admiral looking like a tribesman; nobody would believe I was an Uppie. After washing and changing, I looked much more presentable.

The Naval wing wasn't wholly isolated; reception areas were open to the public. To my surprise I found a small but loud demonstration in progress. The protesters didn't look much like Uppies, but they certainly weren't transpops. I doubted they'd paid their way to Earthport solely to carry pickets; they must be travelers with a conscience. Heartened, I presented myself at the desk, asked to see Admiral Thorne.

The lieutenant refused.

I demanded.

The officer raised an eyebrow, told me to lose myself. It was most likely a euphemism for what he really meant.

I'd been so sure I could make the Admiral listen, I hadn't planned how to reach him. I was intensely frustrated. Time was wasting; my transpop friends were dying.

I knew Fath had called the authorities and circulated my name. If I identified myself properly, they'd arrest me instead of letting me see the Admiral.

If during the past last week I'd had sleep, enough food, less worry, I might have thought it through. Instead, I lost my temper. Watching me, Fath would have shaken his head sadly, Mom probably promised me a licking.

It got me ejected, kicking and biting, all the way back to the main concourse.

For a time I was frantic, then I settled into lethargy. Yet if I could do nothing to help, there was still expiation. Rousing myself, I began to make plans. A quick snack in a nearby restaurant, and I emerged with a serrated table knife. I wasn't particularly brave, but it would do. A toilet cubicle would provide seclusion. I doubted they'd spot the blood until too late.

Tranquil now, I waited on a ticket line, borrowed paper and pen, thought about a note. Though contrition was between me and Lord God, He might be pleased if I made public confession. It might even ease Father's mind to know I died in a state of grace.

I sat unnoticed, composing my letter. My writing grew more agitated. Despite my resolve, I was beginning to rev. I couldn't understand why; I'd accepted responsibility for what I'd done and was ready to pay the price. It wasn't fair that my body betray me. My fingers scratched at my knee. I began to rock.

Six point five times seventeen hundred ninety-three is . . . I don't know. Well, in base thirteen it would be—

And then I saw Fath.

He strode across the concourse toward the Naval wing.

It wasn't I who lurched to his feet, legs unsteady. It was a stranger whose note fluttered to the deck. It was someone else who gave a sharp lonely cry, like a bird of despair.

I stumbled across the hallway, past vendors and stairwells, past weary travelers awaiting their shuttles. I moved slowly at first, then with desperate haste.

"Father!"

He turned. His face showed incredulity. Wonder. Joy.

I flew into his arms.

"Oh, dear God." He hugged me as if to squeeze the very life from me.

I clung to him as to a life raft, leagues from haven. "I'm so sorry, it's my fault, I can't think what to do and they're all dying, I tried so hard . . ."

He rocked me slowly, arms enfolding me in the security and protection I craved. "Steady, son. It's all right." It was as a benediction from Lord God.

But he had to know the truth. "Father, I started a war!"

"No, son." Slowly he released me, held me at arm's length. "That burden isn't yours. But you ran from me."

"Yes, sir, I—"

He slapped me, very hard. I stood blinking, and began to cry.

A firm grip on my wrist, he strode to the Naval corridor. Numb, sobbing, I trotted behind.

In the reception area, a lieutenant gaped at Father, came to his feet. "You're . . ."

"Nicholas Seafort, the former Secretary-General. Take me to Admiral Thorne." His tone brooked no refusal.

The officer's eyes flicked to my wet cheeks, runny nose. "I'll have to ask if . . . just a moment, sir."

Father planted me in a chair, his grip still locked around my wrist. "Make it fast."

The caller had a privacy hood; I couldn't hear what was said. It seemed to take a long time, and Father gave an exasperated sigh.

I squirmed. "Fath, I need to go to the toilet."

"Hold it or go in your pants." Father's tone was curt. It brought on a new spate of tears, which he ignored. "I won't let you loose."

My wrist chafed, and I yearned to ask him to ease his grip, but didn't dare. This was a Father I'd never known.

"Lieutenant, in two minutes I'm going in, with or without your permission."

"Mr. SecGen, you can't just—"

"Then call your guards. But I warn you, they'll need to use force."

"Please, sir." The lieutenant grabbed the caller. I could

imagine his quandary. Father was world famous, and still had a following. To have him arrested . . .

A hatch slid open, and a sailor saluted. "This way, Mr. SecGen."

Father pulled me from the chair.

"Sir, it's a restricted area. Sorry, but the boy can't . . . "

"He goes where I go." Father strode through the hatch, trailing me like a sagging balloon.

The sailor eyed me dubiously, then shrugged. He led us through a maze of corridors to a sealed hatch. He knocked. "Roylaff, sir, with Mr. SecGen Seafort."

The hatch slid open. Father pulled me through, into a large console room lit with simulscreens. One showed docking bays, another a large map. Only two men were present. Admiral Thorne sat at a console. I recognized him from the holoscreen in Jared's tower.

At his side was someone I never expected: Rob Boland. What was he doing here? I'd last seen him on the roof of the burning hotel with Mom and Father.

Mr. Boland looked startled. "You found Philip. Thank heaven!"

Ignoring him, Fath eyed the Admiral. "Hello, Jeff."

"Sir." Mr. Thorne looked uncomfortable. "It's really stretching a point to allow . . . they're retargeting lasers at the moment, but we're rather busy . . . "

"I can imagine." Father's tone was cold. "You don't seem surprised. General Ruben warned you I was coming?"

"Yes, sir. But not why."

"Ah." Fath turned to Mr. Boland. "But you know."

"I'm afraid so." Mr. Boland seemed to have trouble meeting Father's eye.

"I gather," said Admiral Thorne, "you have a moral objection to what we're doing. Unfortunately, our orders come directly from SecGen Kahn—"

"Fuck Kahn's orders," said Father. I gasped.

Silence.

Trying unobtrusively to slacken the pressure on my wrist, I marveled how I might live with someone so long, and not know him at all. Father was supposed to be fragile and moody; our role was to protect him. But he dominated the meeting in a manner I couldn't have imagined, using language

I couldn't believe came from his mouth. Perhaps, if I downloaded more psychology texts . . . No. When this was done, I faced a penal colony, if not worse.

The Admiral said smoothly, "That's not possible, Mr. SecGen."

"Jeff, using the lasers is absolutely, unequivocally wrong, and somewhere inside, you know it. Remember the joey you were, who wouldn't pimp for the captains? Who urged me to aim for one more level in the Arcvid of life?"

Mr. Thorne flushed. "Yes, I followed you. We all did in those days, and it damn near destroyed my career. It's taken years of hard work to recoup, to get where I am."

"Hard work." Father's voice dripped contempt. "You wouldn't want to waste it."

"No, I would not." Thorne, though red of face, met his gaze.

Mr. Boland cleared his throat. "Captain, I'd be the first to say the situation got out of hand. In fact I'll say so, as will Dad when the investigations are held. But—"

"There are no buts. Civilians are dying, and the Navy's killing them."

"Rebels, who're defying—"

"God *damn* it, Robbie!" Father's eyes blazed. "You *know* better!"

Assemblyman Boland gulped, like a small child.

Fath spun a chair, sat me in it, planted himself behind, his hands on the shoulder-rest. "The streeters live like animals, but not by choice. I met them first when I had *Challenger*. Given a chance, they'll learn, many of them. Eddie Boss. My wife, Annie . . . ."

Rubbing my wrist, I peered up. His eyes were distant.

"Annie tried so hard, came so far, before they hurt her . . . " He shook himself. "That's neither here nor there. Robbie, you've been in the sub; tell him. Ragged joeys of all ages, women, children, desperate for food and water."

"The worst stench you can imagine. Hatred. And everywhere, the dirt." Boland's voice was bleak. "The government's policy is harsh but fundamentally sound. It's a deadend culture, hopeless lives, rotting buildings collapsing into the street . . . "

Father spoke as if he hadn't heard. "Pedro Chang, with his treasure of books, his fierce dignity."

Boland's tone was placating. "Of course there are exceptions. But overall, they're not worth saving."

"That's not your decision!"

The Admiral cleared his throat. "Mr. Seafort, I'm afraid it is."

Father's hands beat a tattoo on the chair. His voice was strained. "I know you're moral people. You can't carry out cold-blooded murder."

Mr. Boland fidgeted, licked his lips.

"Robbie?"

"I'm not in charge, sir."

"And if you were?"

"That's not—I'd stop . . . perhaps more negotiation . . . I don't know." He took a deep breath. "Thank Lord God it's not mine to say."

"Jeff, I appeal to you."

Mr. Thorne looked obstinate. "I'm sorry."

"I beseech you."

"Sir, please!" The cry seemed drawn from him. "Of course I know it's wrong! But I've served the Navy thirty years, and I'll obey orders. It's not my place to usurp the authority of my lawful superiors."

"Whose place is it?" Father's gesture encompassed the console, the maps, the unseen lasers. "It's you who's making the killing possible. Stop. Give me time to save my friends."

"Friends?" Mr. Boland sounded shocked. "They kidnapped Jared Tenere, tried to kill P.T.—"

"They did not!" I surged to my feet. "I went to look for—"

Father spun me around, slapped my face, rammed me back into the chair. I cradled my cheek, willed away the sting, tried not to snuffle.

"Yes, Halber of the Subs is a friend. As they all should have been, had I not closed my eyes so many years." Fath raised his hands in a futile gesture. "At first I was ignorant, and that might be excused. But twenty years ago I searched the streets for Annie; then my eyes were opened. I still did nothing. At least I won't repeat that folly now."

Thorne sat, heavily. "Damn you."

"Jeff, act. Take responsibility."

When at last he spoke, Thorne could barely be heard. "I can't."

"Very well. Come along, son." Father prodded me from my chair.

"Yes, sir." Astounded, filled with pride, I did as bidden.

"Where will you go?" Admiral Thorne sounded reluctant.

"To find a ship."

"Homeward?"

"Something like that."

"Damn it, Nick!" Slowly, the Admiral got to his feet. "You can't fool me; this is Jeff Thorne. Midshipman Thorne."

"Yes, sir." But Father's smile was bleak. "My cadet days are long past."

"Yes, we've aged." Thorne came close, as Father waited. "I can't face the grief, Nick. They'd crucify me."

"I understand." Fath sounded sad.

"But you never flinched. Tell me."

Father paused at the door. "I don't think so."

"I could lock you in."

"But you won't."

"No," the Admiral said heavily. "I won't."

Mr. Boland stirred. "Jeff . . . "

The Admiral said, "What, Rob? You'll intervene? Take the responsibility?"

"I can't. Dad would have a . . . no, that's not the reason." Mr. Boland sounded forlorn. "I'm sorry I let you down, Mr. Seafort."

Somehow, I knew he spoke of more than the laser cannon.

Father moved to the door, but the Admiral's arm barred the way. "Tell me, Nick. I must hear it."

"Will you interfere?"

A long pause. "No."

"Swear it on your soul."

"Before Lord God in his majesty, I do."

"All I need is a shuttle, really. I'll talk my way into the cockpit. They'll be glad to show me around."

"I assumed as much. It's a capital crime."

"Yes."

"I can't let that happen."

I looked from one to the other, mystified.

"You gave your oath, Jeff."

The speaker crackled. "Sir, General Ruben, with more coordinates."

The Admiral said, "In a moment. Nick, take time to think it over."

"I have no time."

"A day or so, no more. You could stay in the hotel, walk a while . . . or why don't you take a cruise?"

"Have you lost your mind?"

"U.N.S. *Galactic* is leaving in an hour for the Jovian satellites. She'll Fuse back to disembark sightseers before she sails to Vega. She's a small ship, but quite comfortable, and it's only three days. They're booked up, but Captain Flores would be glad to have you."

"Good-bye, Jeff." Father pulled me to the door.

"Nick!" Mr. Thorne gripped his arm. "Forget who I am now. Once, as a boy, you needed me. If I ever meant anything to you, get away from this madness and go on Captain Flores's cruise. I beg you!"

Fath studied him a long while. He said quietly, "Are you sure?"

"More than I've ever been in my life!"

While Father thought, his hand tightened unbearably on my shoulder. At last, he said, "Very well."

I couldn't have so misread what I heard, but it seemed Father was serious about a Jovian cruise. Without luggage, with no money but his Terrex card and bare moments to make the gate, he hustled me toward the far bay where awaited the huge Naval starship.

Until now, Fath seemed so sure of purpose, I was reluctant to prod, but I was stunned that he'd abandoned the transpops so easily at Mr. Thorne's urging. "Fath, what about Halber and Pook? The lasers are still burning—"

"That's no longer your concern."

I stopped short. "I'm sorry, sir, but it is. I know you're about to hit me, but I've got to make you listen. Did you know Mr. Tenere is dead? And what about Chaco, all those people on the tracks—"

"I love you so."

It stopped me short.

His eyes glistened. "Hurry, or we'll miss the ship."

"But, Fath—"

"I *will* hit you if you don't start moving. Now!"

I let him guide me down the corridor. "It's so important but you're ignoring me. Worse, you're letting them down. Objectively speak—"

"I'm not ignoring you." His voice was quiet. "I intended to ship you home. But now I won't."

All I could think to say was, "Why?"

"You've earned the right to see it through, wherever it leads us. May your mother forgive my soul."

His hand moved to my shoulder, and it seemed more a gesture of love than guidance as he steered me to the waiting lock.

I peered out the porthole as Earthport Station slowly receded. "What happens now, Fath?"

Our welcome aboard *Galactic* had been perfunctory; the ship was due to cast off within minutes. Captain Flores sent his respects, and a promise to invite us to the bridge after breakaway. The purser told us cabin assignments would be rearranged to accommodate the former SecGen—the cruise had been filled for months—and settled us in the lounge with drinks and hors d'oeuvres. At last I had a chance to visit the head; it enabled me to sit more quietly.

"We'll cruise under thruster power until we reach Fusion clearance." Fath spoke with calm confidence. There was no question about a ship to which he didn't know the answer. After all, he'd captained a similar vessel for many years before my birth. Once, he'd even been on the same ship as Mom.

Across the lounge I recognized a holo star whose face adorned all the news screens. She sat with two men. They glanced our way, as if gathering the nerve to approach us.

Fervently I hoped they wouldn't bother Fath. He hated his notoriety; all he wanted was seclusion, and peace. I pressed my forehead against the transplex porthole, trying to see around the side. "Where's the Naval wing? Can you see the lasers fire?"

"You studied optics. Tell me." For a moment, we were back in his study.

"The light isn't visible of itself. But if there were dust motes . . ."

"And they have warning beacons." Father tapped his

nuckles to his lips, as if pensive. Once again he checked his watch.

"Mr. SecGen, is it really you?" A well-groomed man in an expensive suit, a heavyset woman.

I wanted to shout, "Leave him alone," but knew better. Fath would be furious.

"Yes."

"We voted for you. I'm Darwell Reins; you've heard of my books, perhaps? It's such a thrill to meet you. The Senate was so unfair, when they—" His wife's elbow jabbed his ribs. "Well, of course you already knew . . . I was wondering, if you wouldn't mind, an autograph for our daughter?"

"Very well." Father's voice was stony. He took the proffered menu, scrawled his name.

"Mr. Seafort?" A starched midshipman hovered. "An honor to meet you, sir. Captain Flores asks if you'll please come to the bridge."

Reins gabbled, "It's an honor; we'll tell all our friends, it's so wonderful to have met . . . "

In the corridor Fath growled, "Who in hell is Darwell Reins?"

"I don't know, Father."

"That's why I loathe leaving the compound."

Galactic, one of the new smaller ships, had only two Levels. Our lounge was on the second, and we trudged up the ladder to Level One, the middy politely leading the way.

He said, "It's just past the curve, sir."

"I know."

The midshipman blushed. "I'm sorry, Mr. SecGen. I forgot."

Fath grunted. "It's been a while. Before your time."

The hatch to the bridge was open, which surprised me. I'd heard it was usually kept closed.

A burly lieutenant and the Pilot flanked the Captain's chair. They seemed tense. A sallow man with receding hairline rose to greet us. His Captain's insignia was bordered by a gleaming row of length-of-service pins.

"I'm Flores. It's an honor to have you aboard, Mr. SecGen."

"I brought my son. I hope you don't mind."

"No, of course I . . . Mr. Zorn, you may go." The midshipman saluted and left.

Fath said, "Thanks for inviting us topside."

Flores looked uncomfortable. "I intended to have you visit but there's a . . . situation. Admiral Thorne, CincHomeFleet, sent us a signal demanding your presence forthwith. I'm to return his call while you're on the bridge."

"I see." Father's face showed no expression. "Are these joeys my guards?"

"Surely not—I hope it won't—" A sheen broke out on his forehead. "Please, sir, I must make my call." He keyed the console. "Comm room, go ahead."

In a moment Admiral Thorne's stolid face filled the screen. He seemed bloated, tired, and his eyes had baggy circles I hadn't really noticed when we'd seen him in person.

"Captain Flores reporting, sir."

"Is Seafort with you? Ah, I see him now. Mr. Flores, have your Log record our proceedings."

"Corwyn, record."

"Aye aye, sir." The ship's puter.

"No doubt you're aware of the civil disturbances in New York, Newark, and Greater Detroit. Mr. Seafort demanded, rather forcefully that I defy Naval policy, which I refused to do. While I didn't place him under arrest, I don't want him roaming Earthport raising tensions while we assist U.N.A.F. in the cities. I persuaded him to join your cruise. But Mr. Seafort can be, um, disruptive. We can't have that."

I was hot with indignation. I glanced at Fath, but his face showed nothing.

"Captain Flores, you are to deal with the situation as follows. Declare an emergency. Impress Mr. Seafort into the Naval Service for the duration."

"What?" The Captain was dumbfounded.

"You heard me." Thorne's voice was hard. "And make sure the entire ship knows what you've done."

"But . . . he's the SecGen! Former, I mean. I can't—sir, are you absolutely sure—" Flores sounded near panic. "Not the SecGen!"

"I've thought it out. This way, you see, Naval rules of discipline will apply."

"Let me confine him in his—I could set a guard around . . ."

Thorne's tone became icy. "Captain, I gave an order. Carry it out."

"Aye aye, sir. Mr. Seafort, I have no—" Flores glanced at is lieutenants for support. "Admiral, for how long? Surely ot the usual five-year—"

"No, of course not. For the duration of your cruise. Say . . . ntil *Galactic* docks again at Earthport Station."

"Aye aye, sir."

"I protest," said Father. "Vehemently."

"I imagine you do," Thorne said. "Proceed, Captain 'lores."

Apologetically, the Captain faced Father. "Mr. SecGen, ursuant to Article Twelve of the Naval Regulations and Code f Conduct—I believe that's the authority I need—I declare a tate of emergency. I do hereby impress you into the Naval ervice and require you to take the oath."

"NO!" I jumped in front of Fath. "Let him alone, he only ried to—"

The lieutenant seized my arm, twisted it behind my back, auled me aside. Father made no move to intervene.

On ship, a Captain's word was law, his power boundless. Ie was an acknowledged representative of Lord God's overnment, and was always obeyed. I could do nothing to revent Father's disgrace, his incarceration in the Navy, if that vas Captain Flores's will.

And it was.

Appalled, I watched them give Father the oath that bound im to the Service.

On the screen, Thorne nodded, satisfied. "Very well, Mr. ecGen. That should settle the matter."

Galactic's Captain wiped his forehead, sank into his chair. Sir, I have no idea what rank to—"

"Check Earthport's puter for Mr. Seafort's old file. As a eenlisted officer, he assumes his last-held rank and seniority, whatever that was. If you've any doubt, look to the Naval Regs of 2087. In fact, follow the regs to the letter in all things egarding Mr. Seafort; I don't want him abused. Disobey me at your peril."

"Aye aye, sir, of course. You understand that means we'll ave two Captains aboard."

"A technicality. You have the conn. Get him a uniform— something close to his size, no need to make him look ridicu-

lous—and make the announcement to your ship. That's all
Have a pleasant cruise." Abruptly the screen cleared.

The Pilot was carefully engrossed in his console.

I realized that my cheeks were wet, and the keening noise
was my own. I sniffled, wiped my face.

Father said to the lieutenant, "Let Philip go, please. He'll
give no more trouble."

The lieutenant glanced at Captain Flores. "Aye aye, sir,"
he said automatically, and let loose my arm. I massaged my
shoulder.

Fath said, "If you don't mind, I'd like a uniform. If I'm to
be an officer, I find civvies awkward."

"Of course." Flores was anxious to accommodate.
"You're a bit taller than me, so . . . Lieutenant Bjorn, would
you be so kind as to lend us a kit?"

"Of course, sir. What about insignia?"

Fath said, "Bring them, and I'll pin them on after. Just put
me in blues."

"Aye aye, sir." He excused himself, hurried to his cabin.

With a pained expression, the Captain took up the mike,
delivered a halting announcement to the ship's company. He
stressed Father's years of accomplishment, and somehow
made his impressment sound like a sort of honor. After, he
leaned back with a thankful sigh.

The speakers said, "Shall I continue to record?"

"No, Corwyn, that will do."

Flores fiddled with his console as the silence stretched.
"I'm sorry," he blurted. "I had no idea . . . As far as I'm concerned, it's an absurd formality. Feel free to go where you
wish. I certainly won't burden you with duties, or assign—"

Lieutenant Bjorn hurried in, a neatly creased uniform over
his arm. Not in the least self-conscious, Father stripped off his
outer clothing, donned the new. I swallowed. He looked so
like his old pictures. Only the gray at his temples denoted that
two decades had passed since his last command.

"Ah, that's better." Yet, Father's smile was grim.
"Insignia?"

Bjorn fished in a pocket. "I stopped at stores to get
Captain's bars."

Fath pinned them on.

"I brought a handful of L.O.S. pins; I wasn't sure how long ou'd been—"

"March 2195 through January 2202." Father selected the ppropriate length of service badges. "If you'd be so kind as o confirm my time against Earthport's records?"

"That's hardly necessary," said Flores. "I trust your recol- :ction."

"But you logged Mr. Thorne's order to follow regs to the :tter, and they require it. Please humor me, sir. The Admiral's nnoyed enough with the both of us."

"As you wish." Flores tapped in an inquiry. In a moment e said, "Confirmed."

With meticulous care, Father attached his pins in a neat ow. "Very well, sir. I hereby report for duty as a member of ie ship's company." He saluted.

"Acknowledged and confirmed. Now if you'll excuse me, Ir. Seafort, we have to ready Fusion coordinates. You've vis- ed the Jovian system? It's quite spectac—"

Fath's voice changed. "Sir, your attention, please." It ounded almost a command.

Lieutenant Bjorn gaped. The Pilot looked up, startled.

"Examining your length of service pins, Mr. Flores, it ppears I am senior."

"But that's—"

"Please tell me your dates of service."

"This is my second ship. I was promoted two years ago . . . anuary fourth."

"Am I senior, sir?"

A stab of worry flitted across the Captain's face. "Only by technicality. I still have the conn."

"Nonetheless, by a literal interpretation of regs, I have right f command." Fath's eyes bored into the Captain's.

"You've no right to take my ship! Not if you were mpressed only to—"

"Corwyn, record. Mr. Flores, being a lawfully constituted Captain U.N.N.S. and a member of this ship's company, I take command of this vessel by right of seniority."

"You can't! Bjorn, get him out of here!"

"Aye aye, sir." The lieutenant moved forward.

Fath snapped, "Think, Lieutenant! Admiralty will not tol- :rate mutiny against lawful authority. You'll be hanged."

"Hold it, Bjorn." Flores spun his chair. "I'm calling Admiral Thorne. Comm Room, priority to Admiralty!"

"Put down the caller." Father's voice was harsh.

Flores said desperately, "Let the Admiral settle this."

"We'll go by regs, as instructed. Look them up. Section ninety-seven. Point one, as I recollect. Read it aloud."

Flores muttered, "Corwyn, screen the Naval Regulations Section Ninety-seven." He peered at the display, read with obvious reluctance. "Wherever two or more members of a ship's company hold similar rank, seniority shall prevail, and the most senior shall be deemed of higher rank." He seemed to shrink in his chair. "Mr. Thorne couldn't have intended—"

"Undoubtedly. But the regs are clear. Acknowledge my assumption of command."

The speaker crackled. "Sir, comm room reporting. Earthport says Admiral Thorne is not to be disturbed."

"Well, Captain?" Father's eyes burned into his.

Flores was ashen. He stumbled to his feet. "I have no choice, Mr. Seafort. I acknowledge. The conn is yours."

"Pilot," said Father, "turn the ship about."

Chapter 57

JARED

I thought of dialing out on standard copper wire backups, but what was the point? It would be like skiing a beginner's slope at Aspen, when I'd schussed the high Alps.

I sat, dull and exhausted.

Again I keyed to the public holos, idly flicked through the news.

"*—well under control.*" The mediaman looked excited. "*Though he remains in London, Mr. Kahn has taken personal charge—*"

"Members of Richard Boland's Supranationalist Party are publicly supporting the police action that—"

Damn old fraz. I recalled peering through the window of the compound's veranda, watching him scheme to prong the Old Man.

"—markets expected to reopen soon. Secretary Tai said that through one mechanism or another, catastrophic losses will be made good or reversed."

Hah. That'll be the day. Without my codes, they'd never identify, much less recover from, the Arfie I'd sent burrowing. And I wasn't about to reveal the codes to anyone. Well, maybe if they paid me another fortune . . .

I turned off the sound, flipped to a newscreen that pictured the city. Huge billows of smoke drifted across midtown. I wondered if the idiots would manage to create a fireball. Enough separate fires could cause an updraft that would suck away the oxygen, leave us gasping our lungs out. That much I remembered from my frazzing ecology course.

It would serve the Uppies right, after their attack on the trannie tunnels. Towers wouldn't be immune to a fireball, either. Including mine. I thought about it, discovered that I didn't much care.

That disturbed me, though not greatly. I considered it. My inspired hacking had turned a police crackdown into full-scale war. The trannies were disgusting, but I supposed even they were people, after a fashion. Their deaths would be on my conscience, if in fact I had one.

The screen lurched, as the heli from which the broadcast was emanating banked sharply. The view refocused. A majestic old stone-clad building with carved and ornamental cornices broke, sagged, fell. A cloud of dust swirled.

Not all buildings burned, then. Perhaps the fires would be contained, and I'd be safe.

After a while, I tired of news. I felt grimy and stiff. No reason to stay glued to the screens; I stretched, wandered about. The guards' locker room was down the hall. I went in, used the toilet, saw the shower. A rack of towels waited.

Well, why not? I ran the water, tested the temperature. Still hot, though I hadn't monitored the automatic backups since I'd taken over the puter center. I stripped, stepped gingerly into the cubicle, luxuriated in the welcome hot spray.

After, I dried myself in front of the mirror, stared at my battered image. I was on my own, now. I wished I looked more, well, masculine; I'd only shaved a few times in my life. I ran my finger over the scabs on my chest. So recent, yet so long past. I wondered if the scar would interfere with hair. I'd have it removed, as had the Old Man his famous laser scar, a generation ago. Cosmetic repairs were routine.

I examined my chest more closely. The mark would stand out vivid and clear. I reached a sudden decision.

I'd keep it.

Pook's silly Mid tribe wasn't much, but he'd adopted me, in a sense, and he was the only relation I had. I certainly couldn't go back to the Old Man's frazzing compound and live with Philip. I had money now, lots of it. A new identity, courtesy of my nets. Everything but a life, a place I belonged.

Perhaps, if he survived, I'd take Pook under my wing, show him what life was really about. Teach him manners, of course, and how to obey an Uppie.

I doubted he'd have much choice. Trannietown was crumbling before our eyes.

Anyway, it would give me something to do. School was over forever. Dad wasn't around to nag me, to yank my nets if I disobeyed, to jump at the Old Man's whistle.

I found myself crying. My fist hammered the tile.

Frightened, I brought myself under control. I'm too tired,

I told myself. When this is over, the first thing I needed was a week's sleep. It was just exhaustion.

I wished I had fresh clothes, but all I had were the rags the trannies had left me. I dressed, combed my hair. On the counter was a box of plastic razors. I shoved one in my pocket.

I went back to the puter room.

On the silent screen, some old fraz's mouth moved. I watched without interest. The sooner this was over, the sooner I could get on with life.

Morosely, I stared at the silent console.

The caller buzzed, and I nearly jumped out of my seat.

I took it cautiously. "Hello?"

"Jared, be Pook! Stairs done crash in! I ran ta otha stair, can' go up, all fire. Sheeet! Roof crackin', can' fin' Halber, what I do?"

Frazzing Uppie bastards. They'd targeted the Forty Two station. "South in the tunnel. Run!"

On the screen, the word *BULLETIN* faded from white.

" 'Kay. Where?" Pook must be on the move; his breath rasped.

Why ask me? It was his problem, not mine. I tried to think through fog. "A few blocks. Go to one of those gratings, like I climbed through when you chased me. Watch the tunnel both ways. If you see it caving in, get out to the street and run for safety."

STAY TUNED FOR SPECIAL ANNOUNCEMENT.

"Gotcha. Christ, Halb, where ya be?" Pook sounded plaintive. "Subs runnin' every which way. No one know what ta do."

"Hurry."

"Yah." A click, and he was gone.

I stared balefully at the holoscreen. I wanted to make news, not watch it. How long would I be stuck in this dumb tower? I didn't really care who won, just so it was over. I fingered the razor.

I flicked channels, keyed on the sound. "—unlikely the unrest will spread further. Illinois officials assure tourists the Chicago area is completely quiet, that no vandalism or—"

"—stand by for an extraordinary interview with former SecGen—"

"Marnie, what's your view from the Trade Center?"

"Still hazy, Will, although authorities assure us the few remaining fires are under control. Within hours they expect—"

Goofjuice. Why did they lie? Couldn't they stomach what they were doing to the trannies?

For that matter, why conceal the truth? Nobody could interfere with the Unies. The government—Lord God's Government, as our teachers made us say—was all-powerful. The one problem with a world government is that there was nowhere to escape, no place to rally resistance. Perhaps that was why so many emigrated to the colonies.

I felt a surge of anger, and hauled out the razor. I smashed it on the edge of the console, exposing the blade. I'd shown them all. They thought I was a nobody, but I'd brought them down. I touched the razor to my forearm, pricked a drop of blood. Now I'd show them how little I cared for their lying world.

What good was my new wealth? Our Uppie life was despicable. Yet, I'd beaten them. I'd flaunt my prosperity in their faces. A month, two, no more, and it would be safe to begin cautious transfers from my accounts. In the meantime, any bank would honor one of the new Terrex cards waiting for me at General Delivery. Ah, the magic of our puter age.

Gloating, I laid my head on the console and began to weep.

An hour passed, and I couldn't stop.

Chapter 58

POOK

I run like monsta chasin', down centa a track. Okay, okay, sub tunnels ain' scare when ya used to 'em, even like now when I too stupe ta grab Valdez perma, gotta run in dark. They ain' no monsta, Pook. Cool jets.

Behin', wall collapse wid sudden boom, an' I shriek. I clutch caller tight, wonda where ta fin' grate like Jared Uppie say.

Final, I run myself outa breath, gotta stop no matta what.

I lean 'gainst wall, pantin', hopin' Unie lasers don' stomp roof where I stand.

I hear voices. While back—few days, only—if hear Sub joeys in dark, I figga I be diss, 'cause Subs gonna skin me fo' sure. Dat be when I jus' a Mid, an' Changman take me down ta tunnel.

My breath come like rasp a heli inna nigh'. I so dry I c'n hardly swallow. I rememba fuss ol' Chang make 'bout water. Somehow, pipes don' seem ta matta now. Nothin' do.

Light come on sudden. I squawk. Someone snicker. I peer through light. "Who?"

"Me, Pook."

Almos', I sob wid relief. Voice be Raulie's. I wanna jump in his arms like joeykit. I snarl, "Where ya been, ya frazzin' turd? Look all ova fo' ya."

"Yah, sure." Ligh' swing as he come near. "Who witcha?"

"No one. Who ya bring yaself?"

He shrug, like embarrass. "Happen too fas'."

"Where's Halb?" we ask each other in same sec.

"Sheet." Raulie turn away, frustrate. "Thought you was his shadow, joey."

I get sudden realize. "You wanna be dat, Raulie."

Always stupe ta goad a Sub. His han' fly ta shiv. But rage only las' a sec; he sigh, spit on track. "So? Ain' gonna challenge him, noway. But what if, someday?"

I say, meanin' it, "Ya make good Sub Boss, Raulie. Ain' 'fraid a nothin'."

" 'Xcept lasers." He shudder. "Allatime I thought, Subs get holda lasers, no one stan' in our way. Not Parkas, not Easters, not even Uppies. But I seen so many get diss, las' few days. Burnin', shriekin', rollin' in agony." He wave it away, like scaredream. "Where ya think we oughta go?"

"Jared Uppie say stay near grate, run out if we gotta."

"Fah." Again he spit. "Street ain' safe neitha."

I point out, "Unie sojers gone away. Even helis, mos'ly."

"Who say they won' be back soon as ya poke out head?"

"Watcha wanna do, den?"

He think. "Go back."

"Ta Four Two? Ya glitch?"

"Don' hear no more roof crash."

I lissen. Maybe it true, but my skin go cold thinkin' 'bout it. Was sittin in main lair, eatin' col' stew leftova, when Sub joeys race in screamin', stair walls collapse behin' 'em. I look up jus' as big crack split roof and chunks fall. I see one crunch bitchbroad's head. Nex' I know I flyin' down track.

"C'mon." Raulie start off, 'fore I ansa. Prong him, I'd say, 'xcept he take ligh' wid 'im. Allasudden bein' in dark don' feel so good.

I trot 'longside, tryin' not ta feel like baby joeykit. "Halb prolly be diss," I say gloomy.

Raulie growl, like keep ya distance, Midboy.

I wunner why he still thinka me as Mid, den realize I don' know what he think.

I ain' no Mid, thas fo' sure. Got idea a bein' Sub, kinda, but seem like ain' gonna be no Subs. Jus' refugee, hidin' in broke tunnels til Unies gas 'em.

We trudge down track, pass few Subs, coughin' from dus'. Raulie stop an' talk wid 'em 'fore goin' on.

Waitin', I think 'bout it all, kinda amaze. Coupla week back I hidin' in Chang's shop, scared a Karlo's pissoff. Den I find Jared, my capture. Get my own lair, trayfo his boots so many cansa I couldn' har'ly carry.

Raulie move on, an' I walk 'long.

Wish I could talk ta Changman.

How I know Uppie be so much trouble, Mista Chang? Don' looka me so sorrow, shakin' head. Weren' my faul'.

How I know I start a frazzin' war?

I stumble, hang on Raulie's arm. He snort a laugh, but don' make me leggo.

Dunno why I wanna cry. Subs ain' nothin' ta me, no more 'n Uppies or Washhites. Chang an' Halber wrong; trannies ain' one tribe. Dey many, each wid its own want an' demand.

Still, when I think 'bout bodies in Hunnert Ten staysh, I wanna spit up stew. Ain' right, dissin' joeys dat way. Chris', I spose it ain' so good dissin' no one, don' matta what tribe, even if I be in none.

Sheet. Be nice ta sit in warm tribe lair, lissen ta stories 'fore settlin' ta bed.

But in end, guess we all our own tribe, inside.

Anyway, how I know Uppies gonna come lookin' fo' Jared? Steada fightin' Peetee in front a Swee, what if I'd a help joeykit fin' his frien'? Maybe he give me trayfo even betta 'n I get from Chang. An' maybe his Fisherman Fath don' come down ta street like shinin' knigh' outa cassel, makin' Subs all confuse.

"Ya alrigh', Pook?"

I realize I make soun', almos' like sob. "Yah."

See, Mista Chang, one thing lead ta 'notha. I ever see ya again, I try ta 'xplain: ya can' do nothin' widout consequent. Jared lead ta Peetee. Peetee lead ta Fisherman. Fisherman lead ta Unies. An' I lead Halb ta Jared, an' his hackin' gets Uppies pissoff, which turn rumb ta war.

I plod 'long track, holdin' Raulie's arm, sick inside. Din' mean fo' worl' ta end, Mista Chang. Swear.

"Look." Raulie stop short. Somethin' move in shadows where tunnel meet staysh.

Automatic, I pull shiv. So do he. I whispa, "Why doncha use laser?"

He grimace. "Empty. Lost my recharge, runnin' from Unie patrol."

We 'pproach slow, but it only a few Subs pickin' ova rubble. Dey as scare as we, seein' us 'merge from track.

Raulie ask, "Seen Halb?"

Bitchgirl Allie's size say, "He by lair usetabe."

Raulie move eager, an' I hurry ta stay wid.

One side a cave ain' damage. Trannies from all tribes sittin' an' lyin' near. Some groanin', othas quiet. Coupla Sub joeys back slowly outa lair, carryin' injure. Blood ooze from his head, but he hold arm a helper, talkin'.

I stoop by Easter who don' look too daze. "See Halber?"

He point ta lair.

Hallway full a fallen rock; I pick my way 'cross, but I gotta crawl in. I scramble through, unease. Ain' righ' ta live unnergroun', 'gardless what Subs say. I get ta feet, cough in haze.

Halber's ghost loom outa dust. White face, white threads, red eyes.

"Jeez God!" I pedal back from ghos', slam inta wall. "Lemme 'lone!"

"Whassamatta you?" Where he wipe face wid arm, normal skin show. "Look what they done ta lair." He flick finga at bodies stickin' outa rubble.

I weak wid relief. "C'mon Halb, les' get outa."

"Gotta dig."

Togetha, we toss broken rock 'side, pullin' out dead. Eventual, Raulie roun' up more Subs ta help.

Halber stretch his back. "Looka lair, Pook." His voice forlorn. "Mira."

"Can' help it, Halb." I try ta soun' pacify.

"You couldn', maybe." Eyes glower, he stab at self wid thumb. "I could." He sit on pile a rock, rub face. "Didn' think."

I wait, wonnerin'.

He take out caller, grimace wid disgus'. "Us callin' stayshes backanforth like some kinda trannie army. Fah."

"It work for while," I remin' him. "Look whatcha done at Fourteen Square. Or blowin' wall."

He grunt. "Yah." Get up, wander ta passage, crawl through. When I catch up he bendin' near hurt Sub, tearin' dirty piece a shirt ta wrap leg. He straighten sudden. "Ya hear 'em?"

I don' hear nothin, 'xcept few groans. "Who, Halb?"

"Cancha hear joeys screamin', got hurt fightin' sojers firs' day?" 'Gain, he rub face. "Don' think they'll ever stop. Laser burns hurt so frazzin' bad . . . " His voice catch. "Never had no medcine, Pook. Coupla medkit Chang had long gone. Nothin' help, 'xcept put 'em outa misery."

I say gentle, "Ain' no screamin' now."

He thunder, "I couldn' help my Sub!" He kick broken wall. "Why I start a war, if couldn' protec' 'em?"

"Halb, wasn' you who start—"

"Mira!" He grab my neck, twis' me ta face broken lair. "See what we done?"

Raulie look apprehense, but don' interfere.

"Was me made Subs rumb wid Parkas. Was me got Fisherman involve, me what got him pissoff by threatenin' ta diss his joey." Halb glare, like darin' me ta ansa.

He add, "Was me sent Jared ta frazzin' towah, wasn' it? Cause I wanted ta pissoff Uppies. Well, I did, an' look!"

"Halb—"

"Was me tol' Raulie ta blow seawall!"

I keep shut, tryin' not make Halb anger. He drag me 'cross cave ta blocked stair. "See what they done ta Four Two lair? Time was no one dare mess wid Sub, no trannie, not even Uppie peek downstair for 'fraid a gettin' skin."

I grope fo' somethin' ta say, but no need. He lemme go. I rub neck.

"C'mon." He wanda through side tunnel 'til we reach far stair. Buncha rubble fall in, but left side a stairwell still open. Dim light show through; mus' be moon.

Halfway up, he stop, survey his cavern. His grim eyes rove from rows a wound trannies, ta broke-up lair. "Frazzin' Unies!" He pound wall. "Why'd ya bust my Sub?" He rush up stair, vanish inna nigh'.

Aghas', Raulie an' I stare at each otha, run afta.

Top a stair, I recoil.

Street like nothin I eva seen.

Usetabe, ya couldn' see Forty Street towahs from close 'cause a ol' broken builds. Now hardly nothin' lef' ta block view. Franjee Towah's harsh lights gleam, from bottom at rubble street up ta smoky sky. "Streets ours, trannie," dey say. *"Ours!"*

Beyond, otha steel towahs loom. Few blocks south, sky lit wid smoke an' fire.

Halber plant self in mid a Four Two. "See what dey did? Bust down alla builds roun' towah, but so careful dey don' even touch it." He shake fist at sliver a moon. "Frazzin' Uppies!" His roar echo off broken wall. "Think ya own da worl'!" He pull out laser, aim at towah, shoot 'til beeps ask why botha. Dunno if he hurt it any.

"Halb, get outa road!" I 'xpect Unie heli ta loom ova, lasers snappin'.

"Why?"

"Fo' safe."

He cry, "Doncha unnerstan? Ain' no safe!" He start down middle a road, like gonna stroll ta Gran'cent wid sack a innifo fo' passby.

"Halb, don'," Raulie say plaintive. "Need ya."

"Whyfo?" Halber don' stop.

Cautious, I catch upta. "Hey, Halb." I soun' like I once hear Bigsis talk ta glitchkid. "C'mon home ta Sub."

He scream, "Ain' no Sub!" He look fo' rock, haul out caller instead, fling it at my head. I flinch; it bounce off shoulda, sting hard. "Sub gone, Pookboy. Tribe gone. Trannies gone!"

"Not all. Not yet." I scramble fo' caller. "C'mon." I look past him. Dust motes glow red in beam a ligh' from high. "Oh jeez! Run!"

Slow, majestic towah of ligh' move down street, roilin' pave as it go. Behind, smoke, steam, sparks as somethin' burn.

"GODDAMN FRAZZIN' UPPIES!" Halber grab rock, throw it at beam. It pass through, bouncin'. Watchin', he stick hands on hips, spit his contempt.

"Run, both a yas!" Raulie's scream bring me ta senses. I tug at Halber, but he plant like rock. I dash ta stair, arms an' legs pumpin'. I careen inta Raulie, bounce off. Togetha, under roof, we turn ta watch.

"C'MON, HALB!" I frantic with frustrate. "Save yaself! Go!"

Halb stand brave. Towah a ligh' bear down on him like unnercar in nigh'.

Sudden, he throw up han's, sprint full speed towar' sidewalk. For a sec I think he gonna make it, but ligh' pass ova an' he go down. I flinch fo' his scream, but not a soun'. None.

Pavemen' spit up sizzlin' rock as ligh' pass stair. I hurl myself ta bottom. Raulie tumble afta. Ovahead, rumble shake sub.

When roar fade at las', we creep up broke stair.

Halber gone, no sign. Like never live.

'Xcept I rememba him. Rememba his die. Rememba his fierce.

Rememba his defy.

Chapter 59

ROBERT

"I confirm coordinates as follows." Jeff Thorne read off a series of figures.

I watched over his shoulder. "Where's that?"

He fiddled with his display. "Forty-second."

"Coordinates acknowledged." General Ruben sounded exhausted. "I need sleep. We've been at it what, eighteen hours?"

"Sign off 'til morning, Ernst."

"That's not possible. SecGen Kahn wants it done. I'll have Major Groves spell me for a while."

"For security, I'd rather—"

"For Lord's sake, I'll keep him on line with us until you're familiar with his voice."

I waited for Thorne to object, but he said only, "Very well."

The General said, "I want this over with as much as you."

"I doubt it." They rang off. Thorne immediately called below to laser control, fed them the coordinates with painstaking care. When he was done, he leaned back, eyes on the city map overhead.

"Ernst gave you an excuse to delay," I said. "Why didn't you take it?"

His eyes met mine. "Because my Commander in Chief wants us to proceed." His face showed nothing.

"I don't understand you." Wearily, I sought a seat. "Why did you betray Seafort?"

"Rob, he'd have destroyed himself. For his own good I took him out of harm's way."

"He'll never forgive you."

"I don't need his forgiveness." Thorne's tone was sharp.

"I do." I didn't know why I said it. Exhaustion, perhaps.

"It's a bloody mess. Get some sleep."

I stared dully at the map. "If I leave this God-damned place I'll never come back."

Thorne said quietly, "What is it, Rob?"

My hand took in everything, and the lasers below.

He said, "It's my doing. You're just an observer."

"Hardly." My ears still rang with the Captain's plea. *"You can't carry out cold-blooded murder. I beseech you."*

"Can't I, though?"

"What?" The Admiral looked startled, and I realized I'd spoken aloud.

"Nothing." I sat. "What happens next?"

"I assume Ruben will concentrate on midtown. As many blocks as we've blasted, there's far more still standing."

"Must it all go?"

"That's not my decision."

"As Nick said, it should be."

"Oh?" He raised an eyebrow. "Is that why Richard put you on his task force? To be his voice of conscience?"

"Dad doesn't need one. He's a just man."

"Does he have doubts?"

"I don't think so. Perhaps. He—I don't know."

A minute's silence.

I said, "Is there a caller in that alcove? I'm calling home."

"It's rather late, eastern time."

"Then I'll wake him." I stalked to the alcove.

A few moments later, Dad and I were joined on audio/video. Tousled, he sat on the edge of his bed. "Robbie, four in the morning is no time for a policy review."

"Kahn's going too far."

"You're right. What of it?"

"Lives are being lost."

"Lives are always lost, somewhere. It's tragic, but our casualties aren't a hundredth of what the fish cost us, and we didn't flinch from them."

"It's not the same, Dad. This is preventable!"

"Not anymore." He squinted into the screen. "Robbie, you look like hell. You should have stayed in the hospital anoth-er—"

"Prong the hospital!" I lowered my voice; I'd never per-suade Dad by sounding like a spoiled child, like Jared Tenere. Thinking of Adam only made me more determined. "What if there's a sympathy backlash? Shouldn't you be the Senator who—"

Dad said sharply, "I won't be the Senator who backstabbed the SecGen during a war!" He put up a hand to stay my rejoinder. "Robbie, in a crisis both parties pull together, or appear as if they do. To criticize Kahn in public, especially after promising our support . . . " He shook his head. "Since when must I teach you about appearances? Voters would remember me as a whiner, a carper who threw obstacles in the path of the noble SecGen while he—"

"But that's not reality!"

"Reality won't elect me SecGen. When the dust settles, I'll have a chance to make clear how brutal was his response. We'll call trannie survivors before the Committee, introduce a bill to recompense. You know the drill. But I will *not*, at this juncture, go public." He paused. "Besides, Ruben has agreed to target the sites we need for Franjee II. At least some good will come of this debacle."

"Dad, intervene privately. As soon as your sites are cleared, get through to Kahn, you have the clout. Tell him it's gone far enough."

"For forty years my word has been good. It's the only currency a politician has, Rob. I won't debase it."

"Dad, in Washington you don't know how bad the slaughter—"

"The hell I don't!" Only his eyes showed his fury. "How dare you lecture me on morals! Do you think I haven't seen Ruben's confidential reports? Think I don't know what orders Thorne is giving even now? What data Ernst is feeding him? How many casualties the U.N.A.F. took, and the estimates on trannie losses? This got out of hand, it's sickening, and it's without moral foundation. That's why Kahn has to be replaced. Would you like that to happen, Rob?"

"Yes, but—"

"Do you want me elected?"

I swallowed, tasting the sour flavor of defeat. The worst of it was that he was right.

"Yes, Dad. I want to see you elected."

"Then we'll do nothing to raise doubts about me in this critical moment."

I nodded.

"About your friend Adam; have they recovered his body?" Dad never ended a call on a bitter note if he could possibly help it.

"I don't think so."

"Horrid. Did Seafort ever locate the Tenere boy?"

"P.T. actually saw him, at one point, a prisoner of the trannies. He may still be alive. That's all I know."

"I wonder who'll raise him." I knew Dad was just making conversation, to let our emotions cool.

"I have no idea. I'm sorry I shouted at you. Good night."

"I love you, Robbie." It startled me.

He rang off.

I sat a long while, staring at the caller.

As a boy I'd yearned to go to Academy.

I liked Naval life; at times I even loved it. But though I'd made lieutenant, I never felt all that competent. In politics, I discovered a flair, an innate sense of what was practical, what would appeal. I'd set goals, achieved them, raised my sights.

I was a political man.

I could have been more.

Had I stayed in the Navy, I might have become Captain. Had I pursued Elena before she chose Adam, I might be raising a family.

Had I stood up to Dad tonight, I might not loathe myself so.

When history was written, who would know, save I, of my part in this dreadful fiasco? By manipulating Arlene's anxieties, I'd managed to parlay a family's search for lost children into a war of extinction. The blood of thousands of trannies was on my hands.

Adam's blood was on my hands.

I could do nothing to make amends. Meanwhile, two decks below us, the deadly lasers did their work.

Unable to sit alone any longer, I strode back to the console. "No luck. He won't—"

Thorne held up a hand. His face was apoplectic.

An anxious face filled his screen. "Sir, Lieutenant Bjorn ordered me to call without informing the bridge. SecGen—uh, *Captain* Seafort's taken over the ship and relieved Captain Flores. No one knows what to do."

I thought he was speaking directly to Thorne, but an unseen voice responded. "All right, I'll tell him. What else?"

"He's put the ship about. Mr. Bjorn says we're returning to Earthport."

"Very well, stand by. I'll page the Admiral."

The screen flickered, and a new face appeared. A portly Captain, one I didn't know. "Well, sir? Shall I connect you?"

Thorne snarled, "The devious son of a bitch! What's Seafort's length of service?"

"Wasn't it six or seven years?"

"Something like that. Look it up." The Admiral slapped the console, and swore. "I forgot Flores was junior."

"Yes, but . . ."

"There's no 'but'; the wily bastard's put us in a box. For the sake of fleet discipline, we have to uphold the regs."

"He's hijacked a warship!"

"Not yet, Ed. In fact, he seems to be returning to base. I told him his impressment was over when *Galactic* docked. I assume he merely wants off."

"What will you tell the comm tech?"

"Not a thing. I'm not involved yet, and I need maneuvering room. Stall. You can't find me. But I won't be hung out to dry on this one. Log *Galactic*'s call, and all my responses. Other than that, put a lid on it. Absolutely no one is to know."

"Aye aye, sir. What's your next move?"

"I'll call Seafort, find out what he's doing. Hopefully he just wants to go home. We'd better wait a few minutes or he'll realize someone on his ship snitched, and we can't acknowledge that; bad for discipline. How long before I can say we noticed their course is altered?"

"Station computers can notice any time, I'd imagine."

"Very well. Lord Christ Almighty."

"Amen, sir." They rang off.

Jeff Thorne cursed in a steady monotone.

The speaker crackled. "Sir, General Ruben's got more coordinates. He has a second officer on the line."

"Damn." Thorne snatched the caller. "Not now, Ernst. Something very urgent's come up. I'll get back to you in a few minutes." He set the caller down. "You know Seafort as well as I, Rob. What's he up to?"

"I'm not sure. Would he threaten to blow up the Station? Fire his lasers at Ruben's HQ? He's not exactly predictable."

"Would he go that far?"

I said, "He's savagely angry, and you betrayed him. Where sane men would rein in, he charges full speed ahead. Have you other ships you can send against him?"

The Admiral's eyes narrowed. "I don't care for the sound of that. We do *not* have a mutiny on our hands. Just an orderly and legal transfer of authority, though somewhat unexpected."

"Tell that to Flores."

"I probably will when it's over. Rob, we damned well have to treat this as routine. Imagine the holo newsleads if we admit a hijacking on top of a trannie rebellion."

I shook my head, disturbed by the threat to the world's sense of stability. Nonetheless, I had a sneaking admiration for the Captain's gall.

Traffic Control estimated *Galactic*'s return at seventy-two minutes. Thorne busied himself rechecking the regs, while I paced with growing anxiety. If the Captain's intention was to disembark, well and good. If not, Lord God knew what wrench he'd throw into the works. I was glad of Thorne's gag order; if word of a fiasco got out, Dad might be compromised.

The Admiral glanced at the time, keyed his console. "Ed, have Traffic ask *Galactic* to explain their change of course."

"Aye aye, sir." A few moments later he was back on the line. "She doesn't answer."

"Preposterous. A comm room is always manned."

"Yes, sir, unless the Captain orders otherwise."

Thorne grunted. "If they think he's lost his mind, they'll relieve him."

That was unlikely; the risk of hanging was too great. On our interstellar liners, authority must be maintained at virtually any cost. How else could ships sail for many months between stars, cut off from any communication with home?

"Keep trying, Ed." Thorne turned to me. "It's a chess game. He's forestalled communication; what's our next move?"

"I don't know. What's his?"

Thorne folded his arms, stared at the console.

Little more than an hour later, we had our answer. *Galactic* lay a few kilometers off Earthport's Naval docking bays.

She maintained radio silence on all bands.

Her two gigs sailed to the station's airlocks, braked, disgorged a handful of suited figures. *Galactic*'s officers.

Minutes later, Captain Flores and Lieutenant Bjorn were before us. Nine other officers fumed in the outer room.

Bjorn paced, unable to contain himself. "He stole our ship, sir. Refused to consult you, ordered us to disembark, refused—"

"I know." Thorne made a placating gesture. "That's not the issue. Did he say why?"

"The bastard ordered us silent when we asked. Sorry, sir." For a moment the lieutenant looked abashed. "Even Captain Flores! In front of the lot of us, he told our Captain to be still!"

Thorne asked drily, "And was he?"

Flores snapped, "Of course. It was a direct order."

"I apologize, Ramon. We'll make it up to you. Do any of your joeys know more? Are your officers all here?"

"All but Allen Zorn, the first middy. He—"

"Ahh." Thorne brightened. "Seafort kept an officer aboard?"

Bjorn snarled, "The prick broke Zorn down to crewman!"

The Admiral reared. "Sir, your language!"

"He revoked Zorn's commission, sir! Entered it in the Log, neat and proper! And with no cause; the boy's a fine young officer and did nothing to offend."

Flores said, "Sir, give me back the ship, at least long enough to rescind Zorn's—"

"Of course. That goes without saying." The Admiral exhaled slowly, and rubbed his face. "That's all. If you think of anything else, inform Captain Wilkes. I'll make sure Ed is available to you."

"Aye aye, sir." Bjorn hesitated. "If anyone asks, what should we say?"

"Nothing."

Flores sputtered.

"For the moment, Captain, this is a routine change of personnel. In fact, confine your officers to barracks; we can't have the story come out or we'll make the Navy a laughing-stock."

"But—"

"Do as I say, until I get him relieved and off ship."

"Aye aye, sir." Reluctantly, they left.

I said dryly, "So much for Nick's going home."

"The least he could have done is dock." Thorne's tone was sour.

"You know better, Jeff."

"Yes. Even if we didn't storm the ship, by my own command his impressment ends the moment *Galactic* docks. But that's disturbing: he's not done with us yet."

"Why don't you rush the ship where she lies?"

"Don't be a fool. Her lasers could pick off anything we send, and I don't want her damaged."

A comm tech came on the speaker, his voice tense. "Sir, call for you. From *Galactic*."

"At last." Thorne dived for his caller. "Seafort? You're to relinquish command forthwith and—"

"Is this Admiral Jeffrey Thorne?" An unfamiliar voice, exceedingly nervous.

"Yes."

"Seaman First Class Erin McDonald reporting. My orders are first to advise you that until further notice U.N.S. *Galactic* will not monitor or receive incoming signals. Then, to transmit the following recorded message and to remove myself from the line, or face immediate court-martial. Which I now do." A click, and he was gone.

"What the—"

Captain Nicholas Seafort's austere voice filled the room. "In ten minutes, my ship's launch will begin offloading passengers. I won't allow the launch to dock, or to receive broadcasts. However, she'll sail to within a hundred feet of the nearest open bay, and they'll put the passengers out in suits. I leave it to you to arrange their passage through the airlocks."

"You son of a bitch." Thorne spoke softly.

"Admiral, I defer to you as to how public you want this affair. If you use only Naval personnel, you might manage to avoid excess publicity. Of course, that may require a quarantine of the passengers. You might want to consider some mention of a virus. When the passengers are offloaded I'll contact you again on this frequency. I suggest you hold it open." Another click, and silence.

"Excess publicity!" Thorne's fist hit the console.

I hid a smile. The only way the matter could be kept secret was to lock up ninety outraged passengers. Even then, the Admiral would have his hands full keeping his own joeys from talking.

Thorne must have been thinking along similar lines. On the caller, his voice grew hoarse issuing a rapid stream of orders. A shuttle bay was isolated; *Galactic*'s own former officers were drafted for the delicate task of rounding up ground-siders and herding them to the bays.

The drama played out on our simulscreen, against the stunning depth of the stars. At two-thirds full magnification, *Galactic* loomed vast.

The ship's launch was completing its fourth trip to the Station.

Naval personnel swarmed about in thrustersuits, towing, pushing, propelling suited figures to the airlocks.

The Admiral summoned two of them, a husband and wife, from the first shuttle. "What is he up to?"

"I have no idea. It's insane. Will we get a refund? When will our trip be rescheduled?"

Thorne roared, "Answer me!"

The man grew red; it was the woman who responded. "He made an announcement . . . something about a virus, so we couldn't dock. It didn't sound—what were we supposed to do? The crew came for us, ordered us into suits. He seemed so nice, before. In the lounge he gave Darwell an autograph, and—"

Her husband growled, "Never mind that."

"Well, I'm just saying. Cantra Ilena, the singer, said the crewmen in her section were laughing like a bunch of joeykids on holiday, as if they enjoyed putting her friends off the ship! It's an outrage!"

"Very well. We'll look into it." Thorne herded them out with scant ceremony.

I chewed my thumbnail. "I think I'll call Dad."

"Refused. We're all under quarantine on this one."

My jaw dropped. "You can't be serious."

"Because I'm Richard's political ally? For the moment we'll keep this buttoned. The Navy comes first with me, Rob. Always has, always will."

"And if I choose to leave?" I looked at the hatch.

His smile was bland. "I could use your help. Please don't."

Fuming, I nonetheless respected his integrity. A man who didn't buckle to political pressure would be invaluable in Dad's administration. I sighed. "Then explain what's going on."

"In a moment. I can't put this off any longer." He keyed

the caller. "Ed, get me through to SecGen Kahn. Code double A priority. Tell his flunkies it can't wait, and it's person to person, no one else on the line, scramble comm. Make sure they're using the new codes, the one's the trannies haven't seen." He swung back to me. "Now, you were saying?"

"What's Nick doing?"

"You've heard everything I have."

"Yes, and I know Seafort; there's a reason for every move he's made. I don't recall the regs all that well. Help me."

On the screen, the launch expelled propellant, glided toward *Galactic.*

Thorne folded his arms. "Remember standing regs during wardroom hazing? The shipboard classes, with their constant review of regs? Nicky knows them intimately, plays them like a fiddle."

"Nicky." The name startled me, until I realized just how far back the two of them went. At one time, in Academy, Thorne had been Seafort's superior. His close friend.

"My orders to him are effective no matter how delivered. Once he hears them, he's duty-bound to obey. So he isolated his ship, or claims he did. Supposedly, orders I issue won't be heard. I can't relieve him."

"Seize his launch when it opens its locks. Or put a man on it with—"

"Rob . . . " His tone was gentle. "He'd let us have the launch, and simply eject the passengers alongside his vessel. He's cooperating as best he can."

"With what?"

"The Navy. He loves it as much as I, and he detests personal publicity." His pause seemed uncomfortable. "Unless he jettisons crew as well as passengers, he'll be done in one more trip. What a canny bastard. He ejected every officer."

"Except that Zorn joey."

"No, every officer. Zorn's now a common crewman. It offends you? It's nothing; Nick knows his demotion can be reversed in a moment. Zorn probably knows too."

"Then what's the point?"

"Under the regs, a ship's officer could relieve him. A crewman can't."

"But why didn't he offload Zorn as well?"

"That's what disturbs me. He feels he needs an officer. Or someone with an officer's skills."

I paced, battling a mounting alarm. Dad had been a key member of the Seafort Administration. If Seafort went off the deep end, it would impact on Dad's campaign. And yet . . . was I utterly against what he attempted?

The caller buzzed. Thorne took it, glanced at me, slipped on the privacy hood. He spoke urgently, for a long while. Then he slipped off the hood. "I told SecGen Kahn you were present, and he wants your input." He switched the call to the speaker.

I took a deep breath. "Mr. SecGen?"

"Is Seafort sane?" Kahn's tone was blunt.

Are any of us? I stopped myself from saying it. "I . . . think so."

"What's your father's position?"

"He doesn't know about *Galactic*. As to the insurrection, he said he'd back you publicly, and he'll honor his word."

Kahn's tone was sharp. "Why do you mention *Galactic* and the trannies in the same breath?"

"My, ah, working assumption is that Seafort's goal is to stop our pinpoint laser fire."

"Jeff told me he seemed upset." Kahn sounded pensive. "I'm not on the scene, and we have our hands full here. Chicago's on the brink; we're readying a standby force. Take back your ship, Admiral, whatever the cost. Even if it means destroying her. I will *not* have an armed vessel overhead defying our authority."

"You're telling me to fire on *Galactic*, sir?"

"Handle it as best you can. No, I'm not ordering you to open fire, but I authorize it if necessary. Certainly do so if he threatens our land forces or Earthport. And keep this quiet, for God's sake."

"Aye aye, sir." They rang off.

We were discussing our options when a new recording came from *Galactic*.

"Admiral, this is Seafort. Please inform the Secretary General that I'd prefer to avoid embarrassment to the Navy, but unless he halts laser fire on the city of New York within thirty minutes, I'll take what further action I deem necessary."

"Nick? Listen to me!"

Silence.

I said, "There's your threat. You'd better ready an assault."

"I heard no threat, but I'll tell Kahn."

The SecGen listened without comment. Then, "I want every laser cannon in your arsenal on continuous fire, carrying out Ruben's strikes. All but one. Save that for *Galactic*."

"Sir—"

"I'm in charge, not Seafort. If he fires, destroy his ship. Utterly."

"Aye aye, sir." Thorne replaced the caller.

I said, "Jesus, Jeff."

"Don't alarm yourself. I'll bet you dinner at the Lunapolis Hilton that Seafort doesn't even power his guns."

"Why not?"

"It's not his style."

"You think he's bluffing?"

"No," said Thorne. "I don't." With a grimace of disgust, he called down new instructions to the banks of lasers.

For the next half hour, I paced the Naval command center, biting my fingernails.

"Admiral, this is Nick Seafort."

We waited for the recording to continue.

Silence. Hesitantly, Thorne keyed his caller. "Nick?"

"Yes."

"You're relieved! Put yourself under arrest, open your outer locks and—"

"No, sir." The Captain's tone was firm.

I stood rooted, stunned. Now he would be hanged.

"Nick, for God's sake—"

"Your laser fire continues. It's an abomination. It will stop."

Thorne said quietly, "How?" He covered the caller, keyed another line. "Splice Mr. Kahn into this link, flank!"

From Seafort, a grim chuckle. "I've been busy. I needed *Galactic* for her comm channels; the launch's radio is much less versatile."

"What have you done?"

"*Galactic* has some competent technicians; they're to be commended. I set young Zorn to modifying comm links with the launch; it now has video as well as audio. And whatever she sends will be rebroadcast down to Earth at full power by *Galactic*. Though, really, the launch's radio would suffice, now they know where to find her."

"Down? To where?"

"Holoworld, Newsday, WBC, BBC, Satelnews, United Commlinks, a dozen others. They're standing by for a flash feed at seven AM Eastern. I'm going to make a speech, in time for the breakfast news. Our comm room is cleared of techs and sealed; the ship's puter Corwyn will control our comm circuits."

I whispered, "Oh, my God."

"I'll be sealing the bridge and leaving *Galactic* in a few moments. But don't try to board her; I've given very specific instructions to Corwyn."

"And they are?"

"I've declared a state of emergency and superseded the puter's standing instructions. Corwyn is instructed to log but otherwise ignore all signals from Earthport or Admiralty. He's to construe any approach as an attack, and open defensive fire. Our own launch excepted, of course. My instructions lapse upon my return or the destruction of the launch."

"You're forcing us to destroy you!"

"Not forcing, Jeff. Just offering the option. Excuse me a moment."

We waited.

"Kahn here. What's that bastard up to?"

Thorne told him, while we waited for Seafort.

"God damn him!"

I licked my lips, suddenly uneasy.

"Shoot him down! Destroy the launch!"

Thorne said quietly, "Sir, Captain Seafort has made no physical threat to my command, to Earth, or to any other vessel. I will obey your order when it is faxed to me in your own writing, with your thumbprint and seal."

"You goddamn sea lawyer!"

"If you wish, you may have my resignation."

I listened to Kahn's heavy breathing.

"Very well, the order is . . . suspended."

Seafort's voice suddenly resumed. "Sorry, a few last-minute details to settle. Thank you for waiting. I trust you'll listen to my interview, and notice my vessel's course."

"Seafort! Stop what you're doing!"

"Will you do likewise, Mr. SecGen?"

"You dare to threaten me?"

"Not physically. I'll give you a way out, if you listen closely. Try to control your rage. Signing off."

"Thorne! Jam every channel he uses! Close down the newsfeeds!"

"That too will require your written order, Mr. SecGen."

"When this is over . . . " Kahn's threat was implicit.

"Yes, sir. Please call back if you need me. I must devote my attention to the crisis and our laser fire." Thorne broke the connection. "Ugh."

I warned, "Kahn has a long memory."

"He'll need me, when this is done. I doubt he'll be able to afford wholesale firings."

I paced. "This is . . . astounding." Seafort had turned the tables on us utterly. From a supplicant, he had made himself the focus of events. If it hadn't been for the freak circumstance that put him senior to Flores . . .

I whirled, stared at the Admiral. Could it be? I replayed the day, and slowly, doubt melted.

I raised my hands, and began to clap.

When I didn't stop he said, "What's that for?"

"I'm applauding your performance, Jeff. Magnificent."

"What are you talking about?"

"You knew all along."

"Knew what?"

"Every Captain in the Navy is aware of his place on the seniority list; it's practically a reflex. Just because you made Admiral, you wouldn't stop noticing."

"So?"

"You gave him *Galactic*. You were so smooth I never realized, though you did it under my very nose."

Jeff Thorne's voice was like ice. "Assemblyman Boland, you accuse me of something akin to treason. Dare you suggest I subverted the war policy of my government that I am sworn to uphold?"

"Beautiful. That's the only position you can take. Brilliant."

"You will by God cease this line of accusation, or I'll have you thrown out of my office!"

"Thank Lord God you found a way to help him."

His steady blue eyes met mine, and there was not a hint of confirmation in his face.

Chapter 60

PEDRO

I dreamed of shop, an' doin' trayfo. Dreamed I'd climbed stair, long stair, to reach room where I kep' best stuff. I pawed through piles an' boxes, searchin' for what the waitin' trib joeys wanted. Meantime, trannies I left downstair in shop were gettin' impatient, stompin' round mutterin', but I was stuck upstair gropin' what to use for trayfo.

I woke in sweat. Had no idea of time; they'd taken watch along with caller.

Light flicked on. "Come with us." Voice was cold, hostile "Now where?"

But they wouldn' answer.

I followed soldiers through halls. Caught glimpse of window. Dark night, lit by eerie glow.

They took me to different room, bigger. White lights overhead, desks everywhere, most deserted. In corner, glassed office. Inside was General Ruben, caller to ear, boots on table. He waved guards to bring me in.

Coverin' caller, he told soldiers, "Leave us." They closed door behind. He asked caller, "How many? Armed? Of course they have knives, but anything else? Use the damn megaphones, instruct them to surrender." He ran fingers through his short red hair.

I pulled up chair, sat. Woulda put legs on desk like his, if coulda gottem up so high. I didn't have joeykit's body I useta.

"Promise you'll take them to safety if they——no, do *not* let them break through the lines, regardless. Hmm? Call Wirtz, I put him in charge of transport."

Ruben sighed, set down caller, raised his voice to soldier outside. "Walt, I'm available for the SecGen or Admiral Thorne, but no one else." He regarded me, face bleak. "So."

I said nothin', waitin'. Had good practice, over many years of trayfo.

Ruben put fingertips together, like spider on mirror. "We have disturbing reports." If he 'xpected me to ask, he'd be disappoint; wouldn' give him satisfaction for life itself. "So many deaths," he said. "It's over, Chang. You have no significant weapons, no way to escape. It's time to lay down your arms, what little you have."

I raised flaps of coat. "Don' got none."

"You know damn well what I mean!" Ruben dropped feet to floor. "Don't you care?"

I studied him. Why he bother arguin' with sick ol' man captive, when time for negotiate past? What I got that he want?

He sat somber, arms crossed on desk.

Long silence. Outside, callers buzzed, soldiers pored over maps.

He said slow, "It took a hundred years before the world forgave my people. Genocide is an ugly word." He hesitated. "Am I using language you understand? Words in your vocabulary?"

I moved sudden inside coat. Hands trembled with rage. I tried to speak, but figured God would curse him if He exist; what diff what I say? My chest seized with ache. Face stony, I sat.

"I'm a professional soldier." He stood, paced room as if examine walls. "We have one Government, one Church. By serving them, I serve humanity. My loyalties can't be divided; it's morally impossible. Lord God's Government has ordered me to put down this uprising." He faced me. "And I will. They've ordered me to furnish coordinates to Earthport, and I do. There is no chance I will go against my instructions."

He pulled chair around table, set it next to mine, settled self close. "Yet as a human being, I feel a certain . . . distress, given the history of my nation. The more so because I was selected to lead our forces." He leaned forward. "Help me put an end to it. If your people surrender, there's no need of lasers."

I told self to be still, but answer welled forth. "Wan' me to sell my trannies inta slavery to soothe ya conscience? Bah." I looked for place to spit.

"It's not slavery, but even if it were . . . " His gray eyes didn' flinch. "Slaves might free themselves, in this generation or the next. The dead cannot."

I shrugged. "I don' lead trannies; they jus' sent me as speakfo'."

"As one man to another, I ask: will you help end this?"

Was preposterous. What could I do? Yell out window,

"Stop"? Made me so mad I said as if meant it, "Sure. Fix water. Turn off laser. Call home Unies an' leave us 'lone."

"You fool!" He leaped from chair. "This is *not* a joke, no a contest of wills! By God, you'll—Walt!" He flung ope door. "Two guards, on the double!"

Back ta windowless prison, I thought. But no.

"Take him—not so rough, he's fragile—to the elevator Now!" They hustled me through halls, Ruben stalking ahead

Officer stuck head outa door. "Sir, where are you—"

"Downstairs. Streetside." General stabbed at button as i plungin' shiv in my heart.

"I'll have a platoon ready in about five—"

"Don't need one. Come *on*." Ruben tapped foot 'til elevate arrived, shouldered past opening door. Guards piled me in after.

We plummeted ninety floors in min, while my hear bumped hard. Who he think I was, some Uppie 'customed t droppin' outa sky?

Below, he marched down corridor, demanded guards open door. Hassle, growling, snapped orders. With drawn guns guards unlocked.

To me, "Come along. You men wait here."

"But sir, you need an escort to—"

"Who'll take a shot at me? Ghosts?" Ruben flung open door. "Let's go, Chang."

I buttoned coat against night cold an' stepped out. After min, realized coat wasn' necessary. Air sultry an' heavy, like before rain. Sky had glow, enough to see by, as eyes got used to.

I blinked, stopped to orient self. Franjee Tower was on Forty, jus' two block from Halber's lair. Did General know? Dunno; filmatleven. But somethin' was wrong, like tower was moved to smaller city. Street even shrunk. Took me min to figure why.

Most of builds 'cross street from tower had tumbled into road, so hardly any street showed under. I saw why Ruben wasn't afraid of snipers. Where they gonna hide?

I stumbled over rock, and General grab my arm gentle. "Careful, now." Like old friends we walked togetha arm in arm down avenue.

Forty One as bad as Forty. Coupla block west, builds still stood. East, I wasn' sure; too dark to see.

"We haven't targeted east from Lexington yet," Ruben said, as if read my mind. "That's scheduled for midafternoon. First priority was to prepare a killing ground outside the towers."

"Killin' ground." I pulled loose my arm.

"A military term. It means a fire zone where the enemy can't approach without—"

"I know what it mean."

We picked our way towar' Four Two. Road churned up like giant worm burrowed under. I tried to hide my sick.

Relentless, he pointed to north sky. "See the glow? It's Harl. The fires are out of control."

"Don' matter," I said, stony. "Only buncha trannies."

He spun me to face him, shook me hard. "Why would I waste my time, if I had no misgivings? Kahn wants the old city gone; very well, it will be gone. But it's my hands that bear the blood!" His voice tremble with passion. "It was I who advised the SecGen we could suppress the unrest in a few days. It was I who sent in the shock troops. I was wrong, but now we're committed. Damn it, I don't want to be a Van Rourke or a Hitler! Help me save your people."

"How?"

"We'll send them to reeducation. They say there's arable land available in North Canada. Late last night I called Senator Boland; he'd support a resettlement bill, and I hear his son Rob is on his way down from Earthport. I'll explain to him, and he'll confirm for you. But for a cease-fire I need to present Kahn with an accomplished surrender. Who are your leaders? We have to reach them *now*."

I shrugged. "I forget. Gettin' glitch with old."

He cried, "I'm trying to help!"

"No you ain'!" Like fierce sparrow I pounded on his immovable chest. "Gonna stop war an' herd trannies outa streets? Trannies *are* streets, ya Uppie stupe! No streets, no trannies! Jus' buncha los' joes wanderin' roun' widout a soul!"

"But they'd survive, build a new life—"

I thundered, "We ain' ya Apaches an' Sioux! Ain' ya Afric slaves! We N'Yawk trannies! Was, willbe, long as one of us left!"

His eyes anguished. "The laser strikes will proceed 'til there's nothing to target. They clear the streets without risking U.N. troops. I won't—can't—stop them. Tell me where to reach your ringleaders."

"Noway. Wanna know so bad, use ya frazzin' drugs an' poly. How long ya think I resis'?" How long he think I'd survive, way heart squeezin' chest righ' this min?

"I can't. You haven't denied committing a crime. You do have constitutional rights."

I stopped dead. "Ya burn babykits wid orbit lasers, break builds a hunnert years older 'n God, gas tunnels full a trannies, but worry about druggin' ol' man fo' truth?" I panted. "Ya glitch, Uppie?"

"We live under a system of laws."

"Fah." I spat. "Take me back, I sick."

Seethin' with mad, he took my arm, guided me cross rubble. Automatic, my eye swept ruins for useable trayfo, like any trannie.

Chapter 61

P HILIP

On *Galactic*'s unfamiliar and alien bridge, Father gently caressed my neck. I closed my eyes, basking in the security he offered, terrified to confess what I'd done since last we'd known each other. How he would hate me.

Allen Zorn raced back to the bridge. "Midshipm—Seaman Zorn reporting, sir. The launch is ready, I stored extra tanks of oxy as you—sir, *please* tell me why." His once-crisp shirt was damp from exertion. His blue jacket with middy's insignia lay across the chair, where Father had made him leave it.

"You're safer if I don't. I assure you again, I have no plans to harm *Galactic*. Don't try anything foolish while I'm away. They won't hold this against you."

"I'm not concerned about—aye aye, sir." The boy's eyes were troubled.

"The engine room is on standby?"

"Yes, sir."

"I logged your appointment as Engineer's Mate; that means you'll have authority to control the drives and thrusters in the absence of an officer. I repeat my orders: take *Galactic* nowhere except to avoid imminent physical danger to the ship."

"Aye aye, sir. Acknowledged and understood." Zorn chewed at his lip. "May I go with you on the launch?"

"Certainly not. Why even ask?"

"It's just—I don't what's right, don't know what to obey . . ." He seemed on the verge of tears. "Everywhere I go, there's questions from the crew . . ." He hugged himself.

Fath sighed. "I'd better speak to them." He keyed the caller. "All crew except radar and engine room watches report to the dining hall in five minutes." Then, to Zorn, "I'll try to settle them. As for you, I have a task while I'm gone."

"Yes, sir?"

"Stay with Philip, or bring him along on your rounds. He's had a rough time of it, and his nerves are frayed. Remember he's a civilian, and not yet thirteen."

Zorn's glance flickered to me, and back, with something like compassion. "Aye aye, sir."

I cleared my throat. "No." It mustn't be.

"He won't bother you, son. He'll just make sure—"

Tremulous, I came out of my seat. "Listen, Fath. Even if I start crying while I talk, hear me out!"

He checked his watch. "All right, but hurry."

"You're bigger than I, so I have to use words to persuade you. How can I make you understand you can't leave me behind?"

"It's only for a short—"

I flared, "You told me you hated a lie!"

His eyes closed briefly, as if he was in pain. "How would you know whether I lied?"

"Extra oxygen, on a launch used only as a ferry? The instructions you gave the puter, your tone of voice . . . Father, *please!*"

"If I hid the truth, it was to protect you from hurt. Don't assume from my precautions—"

"You see," I said in a conversational tone, "I've earned my place with you. By what I've done, and failed to do. You think because you're adult and I'm not, that I'm not as involved, not wholly committed. I can't tell you how I know this, because I'm not sure myself, but . . . " I fought to keep my voice steady. "If you don't take me along, you'll destroy me."

Silence.

"Sir, I *must* be part of it!"

"No."

I shrieked, "I tried to be a man, even if it wasn't my time! I took responsibility like you always taught! What more do you want of me?" I kicked the chair into the console. "So I need a psych sometimes and I'm weird. I did my best, my frazzing best!" My eyes streamed, burning my reddened cheeks. "I have to see it through, I've earned it! *I HAVE TO!*"

Thoughts whirled and swooped inside my skull, too quick to grasp. With bitter fury I wiped a sleeve across my face. Father valued self-control, and I'd just lost mine. When I wanted him most to take me seriously, I was bawling like a baby. Was it my exhausted body or my ragged emotions that betrayed me, that cost me the most important prize of my life?

The silence stretched, broken only by my sobs.

"Mr. Zorn." Father sounded forlorn. "Find a suit Philip's size and store it on the launch."

On the way to the launch berth I tried stumblingly to thank Fath for his gift. He cut short my effort. "Don't be grateful for what I'm doing to you. You asked to be treated like a man. You get a man's reward. Sometimes that's a bitter pill."

"Fath . . ." As we passed through the launch bay lock, I tried to summon the words. "Are we coming back?"

"Perhaps not, son."

I'd guessed as much.

At least Mom would know where I was. During the endless wait on *Galactic's* bridge Fath left a message for her at the Tamarovs, that I was safe on the ship. She'd be enraged at where I'd gone, cold and unforgiving until the memories faded, but I knew she'd be glad her quest was done. Perhaps, if I survived, we might someday reconcile. It crossed my mind she might be irked that Fath allowed me to follow him, but I thrust such thoughts aside. Mom was strong and could deal with problems. It was Fath who was the fragile one. No, wait. Perhaps I was wrong about that, too.

We boarded the ship's launch. I looked about. Seats for fourteen people. Only a rail separated the pilot from the main cabin. A transplex porthole stretched the width of the prow, in front of the pilot's seat. In the distance, Earthport Station's lights gleamed.

I looked for a bathroom, saw none. Aft was a hatch marked "Engine compartment." I peered through. A crawl space, no more. Machinery, tubes.

"Stay out of there." Father's voice was sharp. "Strap yourself in. Sit with me, if you'd like."

"Yes, sir." I hurried to obey.

A hiss, as the launch bay doors slid open. That meant the berth was pumped to vacuum. Ever so gently, Father nudged the side thrusters, allowed the launch to drift clear of *Galactic*. My stomach churned as we floated free of the starship's gravitrons.

Father sat back, adjusted the holocamera that was awkwardly strapped to an overhead grip. "Corwyn, comm test. How do I look?"

The puter's voice filled our speakers. "Video signal from launch received. As instructed, I'm rebroadcasting your signal groundside."

"Not yet, Corwyn. I'll tell you when."

"Aye aye, Captain. Program modified."

Fath's hands flew over the console keypad. Figures flashed on the screen.

"Sir?" I craned to see over his shoulder. "What—"

"Not now, I'm busy."

I tried to remember when last he'd snapped at me, and couldn't recall an occasion. Nor, for that matter, could I remember a time he'd slapped my face, before today. He was setting limits, drawing a line I wasn't to cross. Unconsciously, I nodded. Part of me was bitter at relinquishing my recent freedom. The remainder felt relief.

He finished his calculations. "Let's see, now." He fingered the controls. I peered out the porthole. Our position relative to *Galactic* was changing ever so slowly. His eye on the puter readouts, he tapped the thrusters to make minute corrections. At last, he grunted. "That should do it. Corwyn, a message, on all preset frequencies. 'Standby. Broadcast commences in two minutes. Please transmit live to all network feeds.'"

"Sir, will you warn them, so they can suit up?" I knew Fath's plan was necessary, but the cold-bloodedness of it troubled me.

"Who, son?"

"The men at the laser cannon, before you ram."

"Good heavens. Is that what you thought?" He tousled my hair. "Don't make a sound while I broadcast. Not even a cough."

"No, sir." I stared at the screenful of calculations, at *Galactic* receding ever so slowly, at the vast bulk of the Station. What could his plan be, if not what I'd assumed? Objectively speaking, I was the smartest joeykid I knew. Surely I could figure it out.

"How's my hair? Is my tie straight?"

I gaped. Father detested interviews, and didn't give Lord God's damn how he appeared in the media. Perhaps it was his very reluctance that made them chase him so, made the high walls of our compound necessary. Dumbly, I nodded.

"Very well, then." He took a deep breath, flicked on the holocamera.

"Good morning. I am Captain Nicholas Seafort. Some of you know me as the former Secretary-General, but by direction of Admiralty I have been restored to my Naval rank and now command U.N.S. *Galactic* in orbit over the equator."

His voice was crisp and firm, his palms steady on the flat of the console.

"From here, our planet appears blue and tranquil. But you and I know it is not. In Lower New York, citizens have rebelled against the government of Lord God. They've razed towers, attacked and overrun U.N.A.F. patrols. This is reprehensible, and a sin.

"Understand, though, that their despair was triggered by relentless and increasing thirst. You see, through the Hudson Freshwater Project we denied them the water of life. They were beginning to die."

I hardly dared breathe.

"Our response to the uprising was brutal beyond any moral justification. Thousands of refugees were deliberately gassed in the city's abandoned tunnels. Censorship has not permitted news of their extermination to reach you.

"In desperation, the transpops struck back. They breached the New York Seawall. They intensified their assault on our puter security. They even, in a stroke of genius, caused U.N. forces to fire on themselves.

"In a mad spiral, the reprisals escalate. By government order, Earthport Station's laser cannon, ostensibly installed solely to safeguard U.N. Headquarters, are roasting transpop families in their hovels, while U.N.A.F.'s pinpoint targeting spares the luxurious towers in which our Uppie culture thrives."

Slowly, my hand slipped across, below the level of the camera, to wrap itself in his.

"Even as I speak, citizens of the United Nations are dying by the thousands under the remorseless glare of the lasers. It is the Administration's avowed intention to clear the streets of transpops, their shabby buildings, and their culture.

"This is an abomination. This is genocide." Father leaned forward. "You and I, together, must intervene to restore sanity and civil order."

I stared openmouthed at a man I'd never known. No wonder that rebels at Hope Nation had quailed, a legion of brave cadets sailed to their deaths at his bidding.

"I will not under any circumstances utilize the weapons of U.N.S. *Galactic*. That leaves only the force of our moral indignation."

Silently, I began to weep. Father gave my hand a reassuring squeeze.

"*Galactic* floats some four kilometers off Earthport Station. I speak to you from the pilot's seat of her launch. Earthport is in geosynch orbit; its laser cannon have a continuous opportunity of fire upon the defenseless city. Here, less than four kilometers distant, I can see the orange glow of the lasers' warning beams, cautioning ships to avoid the deadly shafts of invisible light."

Father gazed serenely at the camera.

"I have set our fragile launch in motion. Our velocity is exactly two kilometers per hour. I shall not alter course.

"At precisely 9:47:00 A.M. eastern time—" My glanced flicked to the console: a hundred two minutes from now—"we will traverse the first of Earthport's lasers, at a distance of one hundred fifty meters. If the cannon are firing, our launch will be annihilated, and I with it."

My breath caught. The sweat of desperate fear drenched my shirt. But I felt a stir of wonder, a pride that Lord God could allow me to witness such an act.

"I can only believe that Mr. SecGen Kahn, busy in London, has not been apprised of the full situation. That it is some nameless subordinates, acting without his express authority, who have perpetrated the obscene rain of death on our principal city. I was unable to reach him when I visited the areas of destruction. Certainly as a moral man, he must be unaware of atrocities performed in his name, or he would act to stop them."

Fath cleared his throat. "In what time remains, I shall work to arrange a truce. If one is achieved, I shall return to *Galactic* and surrender my command. But if the lasers merely cease their fire when I obstruct their target, without our effecting a full military truce, I shall brake the launch so that she remains in front of the cannon until our air supplies are exhausted. Then I shall aim our vessel at Earth's atmosphere, fire our thrusters, and commence my final voyage home."

He paused. "In either event, I ask that you consider my acts a protest against the inhumanity that government—my own Administration no less than the current—has shown to its homeless masses.

"You see, we knew better. The transpop tribes are joeys who might have been you. They live in hopeless misery, and that has made them hard. It has not made them less than human.

"Now." Father straightened, and his voice became brisk. "There's little time. If you find this state of affairs abhorrent, go to your callers. Call every agency of government, local, state, national, and global. Call Mr. Kahn. Wake your friends in other time zones. Call your news providers, your local holo stations, the station that sends you this broadcast. Call your local military bases. Call Earthport. Call your family. Don't stop calling until the issue is decided.

"I will not tell you what to say. With Lord God's grace, you will perceive your moral obligation. Aboard *Galactic*'s launch, I await your decision.

"This is Nicholas Ewing Seafort, near Earthport Orbiting Station, signing off." For a lingering moment, he gazed at the holocamera, then raised his hand and flipped the switch.

I sobbed.

"Now the hard part. Steady, P.T., it's not over yet."

"Will they stop firing?"

"Possibly. More likely not."

"Do we just . . . wait?"

"No, I've work to do. Would you care to help?"

"Oh, please yes!"

"Let's get into our suits. Then I'll need help at the comm lines." He unstrapped, swung from handhold to handhold until he reached the rack. He took down my three-quarter suit, helped me climb into it. He adjusted the clamps. "See this green light? Yellow is a warning; you're down to fifteen minutes of air. Red means to change tanks immediately."

"Yes, sir. The cabin is aired; why do we need—"

"Because I said so." The edge in his voice was the only hint of the strain he must have felt. Ashamed, I helped him secure my suit. He put on his own, but left off the helmet. When he spoke, his voice was more gentle. "I don't think

Earthport will fire on us—their defensive lasers, I mean—but if I'm wrong and we decompress . . ."

"What about you?" I tried not to sound insolent.

"Don't argue, son." It avoided the issue, but I let it be. Fath was already under enough pressure.

We settled back at the console. In the porthole, *Galactic* had receded appreciably.

Briefly, Father explained the comm switches, showed me the list of frequencies, how to select, how to scan. "All right, let's listen in." He guided my hand over the keys.

"—astounding announcement by former SecGen—"

"—said he would offer himself as sacrifice should a truce not be arranged. Captain Seafort appeared calm, though his voice held a tinge of urgency which, considering the situation, was—"

"Marion Leeson, advisor to SecGen Kahn, said the Administration would not comment until Mr. Kahn studied the full text of—"

United Commlinks and WBC were rerunning Father's address. It was odd to flip frequencies back and forth, listen to different moments of his speech.

"Good." Father switched off the screen. "Let's get to work."

A comm light glowed. I stared.

"Well?" Fath sounded mildly impatient. "Aren't you my comm tech?"

"Yes, sir!" I keyed the switch.

"Seafort!" Admiral Thorne. "Have you gone glitched? Return to *Galactic* while there's still time. You made your point; Kahn must be frothing at the mouth. You've focused—"

"Sir, I'm rather busy. Please don't gabble."

"Gabble?" I could picture Thorne's face going red. "*GAB-BLE?* For Christ's—" I could almost hear what it cost to bring himself under control. "You lunatic, end this for the love of—"

"Of God. That's what it's about, Jeff. A token effort at redemption. He has much to forgive me." Father's tone turned brisk. "Will you help? Hold your fire, while we work out a truce."

"I can't." Thorne sounded agonized. "You know that."

"Yes, that's why I'm the one who must. Any new instructions? Are you in touch with the Rotunda?"

"A secure open line, manned at this end by Ed Wilkes. We've got Marion Leeson standing by. You caught Kahn's security advisors with their pants down. They're setting up a link."

"I'd deem it a favor if you'd keep me advised."

"I—" His voice softened. "Of course, Nick."

"Could I talk to Robbie?"

"He's on his way groundside to meet Senator Boland at Ruben's HQ. Rob's furious with you."

"I'd expect."

"And with himself, I'd guess." A sigh. "Keep this frequency open, if you would."

"It's yours," Fath said. "If you talk to Kahn, tell him the deal must include a full pardon for everyone involved: streeters, U.N.A.F, Hackers, civilians. All but me." He gestured, and I broke the connection. "P.T., line up our incoming calls, but don't identify yourself, no matter who asks. Voice only; I'm done with that bloody camera."

"Yes, sir."

I keyed the comm lines to my suit radio. "United Commlinks newsdesk to *Galactic* for Seafort, please respon—"

"United Commlinks, Fath?"

"No."

"*—tell him that it's Holoday Syndicate; we want an immediate interview, we'll pay—*"

"Captain Seafort, this is Edgar Tolliver, I've been asked to contact you, if you hear this, please—"

"Earthport Traffic Control to *Galactic* launch, you are in prohibited space, confirm immediately and—"

"Nick, this is Senator Richard Boland; pick up the goddamn caller! Why won't he answer? Seafort, this is—"

"Mr. Boland's father on frequency eight."

"Yes." I keyed Fath's caller.

"Seafort."

"Thank God. Who's that with you?"

"A joey from the ship. What do you want?"

"Nick, we've known each other, what, twenty-five years? Too long to play games. What will you settle for?"

While Fath spoke, I ran the gamut of frequencies, whispering at callers to wait or try later, trying to hear the conversation while I fended off his suitors.

"Just what I told you. No more, no—"

Boland said, "Ruben can't call it off without Kahn's approval, and damn it, you backed the SecGen into a corner. His dander's up. Let me find a face-saver so—"

"A cease-fire and truce. Pardon for the participants. Time's running out, Richard."

"You stubborn—that's exactly what cost you the Rotunda!"

"Call me back when you've made progress." To me, "Next?"

"Earthport Traffic Control. Senator Rex Fizer. Old Admiral Duhaney; isn't he retired? Marion Leeson. Newswo—

"Yes."

I jabbed the keypad. "Ms. Leeson, here's Captain Seafort."

"Mr. SecGen? How in hell did you reenlist? That's political, it should have gone to . . . never mind, no time. This call is strictly unofficial, you understand; the SecGen—I mean SecGen Kahn—has no personal knowledge of our—"

"Get *on* with it!" Father's tone was cold.

"Why couldn't you throw your tantrum at a reasonable—all right, don't cut me off." She paused, as if to regroup. "If I can talk him into a cease-fire, long enough to get you out of—"

"No."

"I'm not even sure he'd listen. He blistered my ear when I woke him for your broadcast. He can be obstinate when—" She broke off. "Look, I'm doing my best, we're all a bit tense. You're a professional; we want to know what deal you'll make. The trannies have to be suppressed; that's our bottom line. As to the mechanics—"

"Here's my bottom line."

"Go ahead. I'm taking notes."

"Halt the laser fire. Send the Unies back to barracks. Stop the demolition. Restore water service to the—"

"Seafort, be serious!"

"I *am* serious!" Father's voice shook with passion. "How could we build a new city on the bodies of our citizens? Have you no scruples?"

"I can't afford them, I'm in politics. One more try: in what area can we compromise?"

"You tell me."

She said, "We've got to clear the abandoned streets; it's the first chance we've had in years."

"They're not abandoned. Next?"

"The trannies have to be resettled—"

"Nonsense. The city's their home."

"If we clear the streets with troops instead of lasers—"

"No!"

Her voice was a nail scratching glass. "An hour from now you'll be dead, and it won't matter!"

"True. So?"

"You're a lunatic! You're hateful. You know what, Mr. SecGen? When it happens, I'll be glad." A click.

"Fath!"

"It's all right, son." He took a long, slow breath. "That's why it was a joy to leave office."

I knew I had to distract him. "Fath, you have calls on every channel."

"Who now?"

"Corwyn, on *Galactic*. Newsworld. Earthport Traffic. General Ruben. Someone screaming your name over and over and—"

He sighed. "Corwyn first. Yes, puter?"

"All my comm circuits are on overload. They've taken to riding over each other's signals, and it's hard to filter—"

"Do your best."

"Aye aye, sir. Engineer's Mate Zorn is pounding on the hatch. He demands that I open the bridge. He wants a line to Admiralty and insists he has the right—"

"Relay this to Zorn. Behave yourself, boy! Permission to use radio denied. Permission to enter bridge denied. Official reprimand in your file, and Captain's Mast next Sunday. Leave Corwyn alone except in emergency. End. Signal to all news carriers: requests for interviews denied, for the moment. Perhaps later, stop jamming my lines."

"Fath, look!"

"And signal to Earthport Traffic—what, P.T.?"

I pointed. A small vessel glided across the void, unmistakably heading in our direction. Puffs of exhaust, as it maneuvered.

"Is your helmet secure? More later, Corwyn, continue as before." He peered. "It's a small shuttle. Private."

I flipped through the frequencies.

"BBC Seven to *Galactic*; we'd like to schedule Mr. Seafort for the afternoon news summary—"

"Nick, this is Thorne, I have news, please—"

"Earthport Departures to Holoworld shuttle, you are in restricted space, change course immediately to—"

"*Attention* Galactic *launch, attention launch, this is Holoworld News; hold your fire, we're approaching only for pictures; please hold your fire—*"

Father muttered, "They're groundsiders, or they're not thinking. Everyone knows launches are unarmed. Hold my fire indee—"

"*Hold fire! Mr. SecGen, how does it feel to—*"

"Philip." Fath's tone was quiet. "Look down at the console. Don't let them see your face."

"Yes, sir." I stared at the blinking lights.

"Ah well. They probably can't recognize you through a helmet. It's all right."

The tiny craft, even smaller than our launch, shot alongside. Through their porthole I glimpsed two figures, holocameras aimed. The pilot tapped his thrusters and his ship drifted closer. With minute squirts of propellant, the shuttle positioned itself some two hundred feet in front of our prow. Her forward thrusters fired briefly, and she no longer seemed to approach.

"Idiots. They'll sail ahead of us into the cannon." Father threw up his hands. "Bloody civilian jetstreamers! They shouldn't be let out of the atmosphere!"

"I'm sure the Admiral will warn them." I tried to sound soothing.

"I know." He reached over, keyed the caller. "Yes, Jeff?"

"This is Captain Wilkes." A stiff voice. "Just a moment, the Admiral's speaking with—just a moment."

A click, and Thorne's voice. "Nick? Don't go away." Click. We waited.

I asked softly, "Why does he call you Nick if he hates you?"

"What makes you think that?"

"He tricked you onto *Galactic*. He forced you back into the Navy. He—"

"Oh, Philip." Fath gazed into the distance. After a time he said, "Perhaps he hates himself, a little."

"He betrayed you."

"You didn't follow the conversation. Remember our talk in his office?"

"Yes . . . " I fought to recall the words. "He said he couldn't take responsibility for shutting down the lasers."

"And I let him know I would."

"How? Without *Galactic*, what could you—"

"I as much as told him I'd seize whatever ship I boarded. He warned me it was a capital crime."

I caught my breath. "'I can't let that happen.'"

"We were very close, when we were boys."

"And so he . . . "

"Gave me *Galactic*, knowing full well I was senior to poor Flores."

"But . . . "

He leaned forward. "Poor Jeff wants to be a cynic, an opportunist, but he can't stop himself from doing the right thing. P.T., you mustn't ever tell. None of this has been spoken; it's locked within his heart and mine."

"I swear, Fath." My chest swelled.

He made as if to tousle my hair through the helmet. "You see—"

"Nick? Captain Seafort?" Thorne.

"Yes, Admiral?"

"That was the SecGen himself, demanding my assurance the lasers won't cease fire when you cross their path."

"I see."

His voice was heavy. "I gave it to him."

"I understand." It was a sort of consent.

"Along with my emphatic recommendation to stand down the damned lasers. He said quote the prestige of the entire United Nations is at stake unquote."

"I suppose it is."

"I don't want you dead!" It was a plea.

"Thank you."

"I'm your superior. I order you to turn away."

"I refuse."

"Nick, it's a hanging offense! We'll set it aside if you comply."

"No."

"I order you to surrender command."

"I will not."

Thorne's tone was bleak. "I asked Kahn to talk to you again; he refused outright. The old city is to be cleared; a pardon's out of the question; you're mentally ill and your suicide will be deemed a tragedy though unavoidable, etc. There's nothing I can do. You understand I won't hold fire unless he so orders?"

"You've made it quite clear."

Thorne's tone became more formal. "On behalf of Admiralty I order you—I plead with you—to abort your mission. You've made your point. My callers are ringing off the pad, and Ed's only passing me the priority list."

"Sorry, Jeff. Signing off now." Fath nudged me, I clicked the pad. "He makes it hard. Poor joey."

"Poor?" I jabbed a finger at the slowly nearing Station. "He'll kill you!"

"He'll allow me to be killed. That's not quite—"

Our porthole lit with a blaze of light. I flinched, waited for the sear of heat.

"It's those fool mediamen and their cameras. Look down."

My heart pounding, I panted for breath. "I thought . . . "

"Let's listen to the news." He flicked on the screen. It was a clumsy attempt to divert me, and I was grateful.

"—vote of no-confidence ended his term in the Rotunda, yet even today there are those—"

"Sharon, his words were 'commence my final voyage home.' A ship's launch has no heat shield and can't survive reentry. I don't know how you can assume he meant he'd dock at Earthport and transfer—"

"Although Mrs. Seafort cannot be reached for comment, sources close to the family said—"

"—so questions about his mental stability cannot be discounted. Back to you, Erin."

Inside my helmet, a yellow light blinked. Time for a new tank. I unbuckled my belt.

"—reporting a larger than normal volume of calls but North American Bell attributes the surge—"

Fath squinted through the blast of light, keyed the caller. "Seafort to Holoworld shuttle, do you read?"

"—calling Capt—yes, we read you clear. Sir, is it fair to say you're—"

"I want a live feed. I'll give you half a minute."

"—*making a statement—hang on, you'll have it.*" A muffled voice, a click. A long pause.

"Fath, may I open my helmet? I'm roasting."

"I suppose. Keep it near."

Gratefully, I pulled it off, reveled in the fresh cabin air.

"*Captain? Sir, we're live to our world feed. This is Holoworld Newsnet, in the vicinity of Earthport Station, Jed Stroyer reporting. We have Captain Nicholas Seafort on line. Go ahead, sir. Can you tell us who's with you?*"

"I'm approaching Earthport's laser banks. I have, let's see . . . sixty-three minutes left. I'd have liked to watch the Station, perhaps say good-bye to Earth as well. Instead, I'm about to activate solar shields and sail blind. The last view I'll have—" His voice caught. "—is of my own console."

"*Why, sir?*"

Fath's tone sharpened. "Because you're shining ten thousand candlepower directly in my face. I can't see a thing! You're distracting me when I need my judgment clear. Is that how you want the fate of New York decided? Is it?"

"*No, but—*"

"Not to mention that you're about to back tubes-first into the laser beams. This isn't a story, sir, this is a crisis of lives! Extinguish that light."

"*Sir—*"

"Now!"

The light went out.

"Thank you, Holoworld." Father keyed off his mike. "Sometimes," he drawled, enjoying my shock, "I'm shameless."

I stammered, "You—you can joke about this?"

"Would you rather I cry? At least we can see again, and if I hadn't chided them publicly . . . ." Then, after a moment, gently, "Philip . . . I haven't told them about you."

"I know."

"I . . . this is hard to say." His eyes glistened. "They mustn't know."

"Why, sir?"

"It's . . . " He laced his fingers. "I'm looking ahead, on the chance we're successful. I don't want sentiment about a child to muddy the issues. This must be about the trannies. About me."

"Why?"

"I owe it to them." Brooding, he stared at his knuckles. "I'm betraying you for it."

"What?" My voice squeaked.

"I didn't go aloft to look for you; it was for them. I won't reveal that you're with me, even to save you. If that isn't betrayal, what is?"

"It can't be betrayal if it's what I want!" I thought to say more, to persuade him I meant it with all my soul, but his look of anguish eased. I blurted, "Fath, was this how you were, in the old days? You're so good at playing the media. We all thought you were afraid of—you wrap them around your little finger. You must love it."

"I abhor it!" His vehemence set me back. "P.T., you have no idea . . . the way I worked the camera today makes me want to vomit. I didn't ask to be a 'hero' all those years. I hate politics, I only ran because . . . What I want is privacy. That's all I ever . . . "

I looked for a way to comfort him. "When this is over we'll retreat to the compound."

He looked away, saying nothing.

"You'll never have to talk to them again. Honest."

I heard what might have been a sob.

It was 9:01. Forty-six minutes remained. We were five thousand thirty-five feet from the mouth of the cannon.

Father was on the caller.

The Holoworld shuttle had moved to starboard; they'd content themselves with outside views, or glimpses through our portholes.

Groundside, the media pounded a growing cadence of anticipation. I flicked channels.

"—is asking the public to leave lines open for emergencies so that—"

"*Ms. Leeson added that regardless of his grandstanding the Administration would—*"

"—groundswell of public opinion—"

Into his caller Father snarled, "Tell Ruben only a base coward refuses to discuss—"

"—mayor says the City of Boston has no say in the decision, and to direct their calls—"

"Erin, what's the mood in Riverwatch Tower?"

"Ah, there you are. Ernst, let me speak to Mr. Chang. The transpop negotiator, that's who. Are you pretending you don't—what? Not authorized to negotiate?" Fath slammed his fist on the console. "If not with him, then who? Very well, I'll announce it immediately to Holoworld. 'General Ernst Ruben denies all knowledge of a transpop negotiator and says the government has no interest in settling—' Then get him. So, wake him! You know where to find me." He keyed off the caller, muttering under his breath.

I said, "Thorne on three."

"Admiral?"

Mr. Thorne sounded reflective. "You're astounding. You'll go down in a blaze of glory. Rex Fizer—did I tell you he called?—he's buttonholing every Senator he can find. They're calling here, the Rotunda, the newslines . . . if this keeps up they'll crowd you off the lead."

"Why are you telling me?"

"I guess . . . I thought you should know. Nick, would you do me a favor?"

"Don't ask for—"

"A personal favor. Turn on the visuals."

Father reached out, flicked the switch. "Yes, Jeff?"

Thorne looked haggard. In the few hours since we'd seen him, he'd aged years. "Nothing. I—just wanted to see you."

Father's tone was gentle. "Jeff, I absolve you. This isn't your struggle."

"Of course it is. You said as much in my office."

"I was wrong. It's too much for one man to bear."

"Fah. Who are you, that you'd take on our sins?"

"Don't blaspheme. Jeff, after it's over, help Arlene. She'll want to sell the compound. She'll need to settle my estate—"

"Stop!"

"I'm sorry." Father looked uncomfortable. "God, I didn't think. Forgive me."

"There's nothing to—what, Ed? I've got to go, Nick. It's the SecGen."

"Very well."

Thorne's face stared at us a long while. "Good-bye."

Thirty-nine minutes.

"General Ruben on two," I prompted.

"Seafort." He listened. "Yes, unofficial and all that. Just put him on."

"Allo?"

"Mr. Chang, have they told you what's going on?"

"General didn'. I heard it from yo' mizz."

"Arlene? What's she—you understand the urgency? If I work out a truce, can Halber call off his people?"

"Dunno. Ask 'im."

"I will."

"Mira, Fisherman . . . " A pause. *"Yo' Mizz be tuggin' my arm, sayin' to trust you. But General Redhair is standin' with arms fold, glarin'. He lissenin' every word. You unnerstan' everything I say go to him?"*

"Yes." Fath spoke quietly. "But it no longer matters. I'll put the question to you that I'll ask Halber. If you get water immediately—they'll send in a hundred trucks every day, while we work out the rest—will you guarantee an end to the fighting?"

"Unies stay onna street?"

"Not for now. Later, yes. It's their city too."

"An' trannies who fought? Trials? Hangin'?"

"No. A blanket pardon, to everyone involved except me."

"I ain' their speakfo'."

"Mr. Chang, I'm your only chance. Help me. Once I'm dead . . . "

A long silence, then a sigh. *"I'd tell Halber to accep'."*

"If he agrees, would all the tribes get the message?"

"Streets awful tore up. Trannies still alive be hiding."

"But you have callers."

"Some. Take few hours, maybe day. Bes' way, put Halber's voice on speakers, ride aroun' in troop carry. Helis be too loud."

"I understand. Ruben, keep him in the room with you. I'll confirm with their leader; when we have an agreement you can initial—"

The General's voice was sharp. *"Mr. SecGen, it's too late to strike a deal. The streets are to be cleared, those are my orders. I'll recommend a laser cease-fire, but only after unconditional surrender of all armed trannies. That's nonnegotiable."*

Father spoke as if he hadn't heard. "I'll see if Halber

agrees to my proposal. Please confirm what water carriers you have available. We'll—"

"Did you hear what I said?"

"Of course." Father switched channels. "Now who?"

"Everyone. Mediamen, a Captain Reynaud says it's urgent, some joey from the Security and Defense Agency—"

Father tapped a number into the pad. "Try this code. Tell Halber to wait a moment. Reynaud? Seafort here."

"Arno Reynaud, on U.N.S. *Melbourne*." His voice was stiff. "We've cast off from the Station. You'll see our lights to port."

"Yes?"

"We're cruising to coordinates one two five, three nine, oh six four; I'll begin braking maneuvers in a moment. That puts us between you and the laser fire zone. We're to remain there. Impact estimated seven minutes thereafter."

"Just a moment." Father keyed a switch. "Corwyn, copy this conversation to all news channels." To Reynaud, "You'll cause a collision."

"If that's what it takes. My orders come directly from Admiralty in London. You're to be blocked from interfering with the cannon. Please turn about."

"No, sir."

"I can calculate your trajectory to within meters. I'll position *Melbourne* so you hit our cargo holds. At two kilometers per hour you'll do us little damage."

"Good. But be aware that I'm in the cockpit of the launch, and I'm unsuited. The impact will probably crush our transplex bubble."

"That's not my doing. I'm not responsible for your insanity."

"No. Understand that if I survive, I'll reposition the launch to try again. Or failing that, I'll aim for Earth's atmosphere and begin my descent."

"Seafort—Captain Seafort." Reynaud's voice was unsteady. "Mr. SecGen, or whatever I should call you."

"'Captain.' My rank was confirmed by Admiralty just hours ago."

"Sir, I'm thirty—God, how we admired you!"

Father's eyes widened. He turned to me in bewilderment. "When I was young my friends and I . . . your face was on recruitment posters, why do you think we applied to Acad—Please, I beg you, stop this madness."

"Why, that's what I'm trying to do."

I tugged at Father's arm, whispered, "Halber doesn't answer."

"Try again."

"I *will* follow orders, Captain Seafort. I must. Else service to the Navy means nothing."

"Quite so, Mr. Reynaud."

"Please, sir, stand aside!"

"No, Mr. Reynaud. I will not." Father keyed the caller, and sat silent.

Twenty-eight minutes until we crossed the beams of hell. Three thousand sixty-four feet. And seven inches.

I set the comm screen to scan.

Reynaud's huge starship loomed in the porthole.

"—reiterated his intent to sail his launch—"

Answer, Halber. Key the caller.

"—London Admiralty confirmed U.N.S. Melbourne's mission to—"

Alongside each laser an orange beam cast its warning into the night. Dim when viewed from the side, they were growing steadily brighter.

"Damn it, Halber." I wilted at Father's frown. Intemperate language annoyed him. I'd have to watch—what was I thinking?

Earthport Station loomed.

"—flooded with calls—"

"Now what, Ms. Leeson?"

"—crowd massing outside Ottawa's Government House. Rocks have been thrown—"

"Seafort, Kahn's willing to make one concession. Listen well, this is all you get."

"Captain Seafort, Reynaud on *Melbourne*. Contact two minutes thirty-five seconds. Sir, please. For the love of God, stand aside!"

Father flicked the caller. "For the love of God I will not."

"He'll provide water trucks from now through the end of trannie relocation. That's providing there's not a single inci-dent—"

"Philip, clamp on your helmet and go to the stern. Brace yourself."

"Fath, I—"

"MOVE!"

"—*It's as good a deal as you can get. Tell me now, we're running out of*—"

I stood, bounced off the ceiling, clawed my way back to the engine compartment, clenched and unclenched my fists. I would not rev. I would not rev. *I would not rev!*

"Two minutes twenty. At least put on your suit, sir! We'll send our gig to pick you—"

"—a hastily called news conference, eleven Reconstructionist senators denounced Seafort's political ploy to aid his old crony Richard Boland in his quest—"

I pulled myself forward, stood behind Fath's shoulder gripping his chair.

"—Jed Stroyer of Holoworld News alongside the doomed *Galactic* launch where Captain Nicholas Seafort—"

"—spokesman for Senator Boland issued a statement deploring the standoff—"

"*Well, Seafort?*"

"Ms. Leeson, there will be no transpop relocation during my lifetime. Good-bye."

Melbourne's cargo lights loomed.

Father sat placidly at the console. "Admiral Thorne, please."

"—gathered in front of the U.N. complex chanting, 'Seafort, Seafort'—"

"One minute fifty-five—"

"Earthport Admiralty, Captain Wilkes here." His voice was harsh.

"Seafort. Give me Thorne."

"Sorry, he's gone to his quarters."

"Transfer the call."

"Sir, he—" Wilkes hesitated. "Fifteen minutes ago he resigned his command. I've linked with Lunapolis and London, and am following the orders of—"

"*Seafort, this is Marion Leeson, I warn you, that was our last*—"

"Thorne left word he's not to be disturbed. I advise you I will carry out whatever instruc—"

"Wilkes, find Jeff. Have someone stay with him 'til this is over."

"Captain, this is Reynaud. One minute forty."

"Sir, that's none of your—why? Is he . . ."

"He's distraught, I know him. He needs help, flank. Move!"

"Right." A click.

"One minute thirty. Captain Seafort, turn your ship. I repeat, turn your ship before it's too—"

"—on the Holoworld shuttle. It appears a collision is imminent. Stay tuned for exclusive live coverage. Notice the launch's transplex porthole. Our technical advisors say even at slow speed the fragile—"

"One minute. Captain, please! fifty-five—all engines full! Engine room, flank speed! *Melbourne* to Earthport Admiralty, I can't let—these orders make no damn sense; he's in the clear, not aimed at anyone, posing no danger to anyone but himself. I won't imperil my ship just to stop—I'll resign if that's what you want. I won't do this!"

Slowly, ponderously, the great ship began to move.

Placidly, our launch sailed on.

I moaned.

"Steady, P.T. It'll be close." Father made no move to turn us aside.

I rested my head on his shoulder. "I'm sorry. I couldn't wait in the stern."

"I understand." Like a leaf in a celestial stream we floated onward. *Melbourne*'s port side slid past. She began to turn, easing our way.

We cleared her bow by twenty feet. I pulled off my helmet, trying not to retch.

On the Station, orange warning lights loomed.

"Father." Eighteen minutes to traverse, by the console clock.

"I see. Try Halber again."

Shakily, I eased into my seat. The caller rang. And rang.

"Do you think they'll hold fire?"

"I think so," he said. Then, after a moment, "The truth?"

"Yes, sir. I'm old enough."

"It's unlikely. I'm a two-hour phenomenon. Half the world's asleep, the other half electrified. When I'm gone there'll be a memorial service, regrets, hearings that accomplish nothing. Kahn knows this. He'll wait it out. Perhaps some good will come of our stand nonetheless."

"Did you know from the start?"

"I suspected it."

"Then why . . ."

He was silent a long time. "In some things, son, it's not the succeeding. It's the trying."

"You'd give your life for trying?"

"For this, yes. Philip, I have only a few minutes, let me make this fast. Somehow we took a terribly wrong turn. I can't say when. We've divided ourselves into Uppies and trannies, and it's dead wrong. If we win, there's a chance to heal. We need that desperately."

"For the sake of the trannies."

"For the Uppies. Our brightest, best joeys isolate themselves in the clouds, forgetting the world from which they spring. Forgetting the humanity in those teeming streets. They're both dying, Philip. Uppies and trannies alike."

"*'Lo?*"

I practically leaped from my seat. Fath grabbed the caller. "Halber?"

Eighteen minutes. The orange glowed bright.

"*Naw. This be Pook.*"

"Who? Put Halber on."

A pause. "*Fisherman? Watcha wan'?*"

"I want Halber, damn it! Now!"

His voice grew sullen. "*Frazzin' Uppies think ya own da worl'!*"

"Let me, Fath."

"Shh. He's being—"

I tugged at Father's arm. "I know him!" I took the caller. "Pookboy, it's P.T. Where's Halber?"

"*Peetee? Fo' real?*"

"Please, you've got to help us. There's no time!"

"*Halb be diss. Lasers get 'im.*"

"Lord Christ." Father covered his face. "Not now. It's not fair." He said into the caller, "Can you tell the Subs to stop fighting?"

"*C'n fin' a few. But why botha? Peetee, Halb go out defy. Zarky, 'xcept fo' end. Last sec he try ta run.*"

Desperate, I tried their dialect. "Tell 'em no more rumb. Fisherman call truce."

"Hah."

Fath added, "I getcha water, make Unies pullout. Stay low, wait fo' word. Tell alladem."

"Alla Subs already diss, that was jus' fo water, an' pullback?"

"It's a start. There'll be more."

"Subs decide, not me. Raulie prolly gonna take ova Sub. Dunno."

"Who they lissen to? Chang?"

"Changman, maybe. He talk good. Filmatleven."

"I'll get back to you. Philip, Ruben's HQ!"

Sixteen minutes left. I had to piss. I keyed the caller.

"What now, Seafort?"

"Give me Chang, flank." He drummed the console. "Mr. Chang, Halber's dead, you've got to take charge. Have Ruben record your voi—who else but you, that joey Pook? Explain the situation; make the tribes listen. Tell Ruben—General, come on the line!"

"Yes?" Ruben's voice was cold.

"Mr. Chang will give you a recording. Get it out to the tribes immediately. Take him on the streets—"

"I told you, we have no deal."

"Make the bloody recording, in case somebody comes to his senses! Do you truly want more blood?"

A pause. "All right, but I'll need the SecGen's personal okay before I transmit."

"Be ready."

"And, Seafort, switch your caller channel. Captain Wilkes on Earthport is frantic to reach you. Don't you check your circuits?"

"Right." A click. "Yes?"

"Wilkes here. SecGen Kahn is standing by. We're speaking on ultrasecure scramble. I want you to change codes to—"

"No time. Use clear."

"If he agrees to demolition only from Ninety-sixth south, partial resettlement only of those trannies uprooted by—"

Fath said, "No."

"They'd stop using the cannon. But a pardon is out of the

question; treason will be punished. Martial law for the first six months, then—"

"No!" Fath jabbed the comm button, set it to scan.

"—Holoworld can't get through to U.N. Military Command; circuits are jammed. But this just in: U.N.S. *Melbourne* has—"

"—huge bonfires in Hong Kong—"

"—says he will not be swayed by momentary public frenzy. Mr. Kahn met with—"

"—outside the launch, where you'll see live transmission of the final—"

"Seafort, this is Ruben! Answer!"

"—elders of the Church met in prayer outside the cathedral—"

"Citizens of Lunapolis broadbanded the nets with an E-mail petition signed by nearly every—"

"—captured trannie rebel said his gang would fight to the finish, or in his words, "rumb 'til we diss ya all, ya motha—"

"Seafort!"

"Yes, General? What about our water trucks?"

"Prong the water trucks! Kahn will agree to stop the lasers, I told him we didn't need—but there's a condition: first he wants the Hackers. Full list of names, codes, accesses—"

"You keep setting up roadblocks!" Father's voice rose to a shout. "Chang can end hostilities, but you won't broadcast his recording. The trannies will accept water and a pullback, but you won't arrange trucks. Now you want me to stop the hacking? How in hell do I manage that in twelve minutes?"

"That's not my—"

"You bastards!" Father launched himself from his chair to the back of the cabin. I cut the comm link. Behind me, Fath pounded on the airlock hatch with a gloved fist.

"—appears to be some commotion aboard—"

"—electricars blocking the Champs de Elysees, horns blaring—"

"—SecGen will not comment publicly until after—"

"—moving in for a closer look—"

"Philip." It was a whisper.

"Yes, Fath." I worked my way out of my chair, floated from handgrip to handgrip until I hovered close.

"Sit over there, calm yourself for a moment. Make your peace with Lord God."

"Fath?"

"It'll be soon now. Pray. I find the psalms a comfort. Be quick."

I flung my arms around him. He pried me loose.

I cried, "What about you?"

"I can't imagine any prayer can expiate what I've done. But if Abbot Ryson's right, I'll know soon." He led me to a seat, strapped me in.

The tinny radio of my suit blared. The cabin speakers squawked. I clutched my helmet, fought the betrayal of my body.

"—the SecGen is strapping himself into his seat—"

I really had to piss. Why hadn't I taken the time to hook up the suit tubes? Because I didn't know how, and was too embarrassed to ask Father.

"—long delays for airtime because of the massive volume of calls—"

Our Father who art in heaven . . .

"—fires burning out of control from Seventy-Third south to—"

"—confirmed the tales of dead refugees in the tunnels—"

Why wasn't there a bathroom? I didn't think I could—

Hallowed be thy name . . .

"—town hall will fly flags at half mast in memory of—"

"—Seafort's wife is escorting the trannie delegate Pango Chang, a prosperous bookseller—"

Thy kingdom come, thy will be done . . .

"—eight minutes until—"

"—Lunapolis Admiralty confirms there will be no cease-fire regardless whose ship—"

"—moving in for a close-up of these last—"

On earth as it is in heav—

A stupendous crash. My head slammed back against the porthole. Scraping, along the far side of the hull. A hiss of air.

"P.T., YOUR HELMET!"

I popped it on my head, clawed at the clamps.

Between my legs, a pleasing warmth. Then, horrified, I realized what it was. I'd wet myself. Please God, no.

"Fath, what hap—"

"Those God damned mediamen!" His voice came through the suit radio as he sealed his own helmet.

I ran to look, bounced off the hull, scrambled as best I could to the cockpit.

Stars drifted lazily past the porthole.

Fath's fingers flew. "God knows what they did to our momentum." Figures flashed on the screen.

The shuttle drifted past, a rent in its side. Lazily, it turned on its axis. From its portside aft thruster, a spew of propellant. I watched appalled.

"Her thrusters jammed. She's got rear and side thrust both."

Ever faster, the media shuttle spun toward the Station.

"—*Association of Retired Veterans opposes any concessions to*—"

"Shuttle, this is Earthport Traffic Control, you're sailing into the laser beam, change course flank to—"

Orange light swept the Holoworld shuttle. Her stern glowed red, and seemed to sag. Sparks, a puff of air. A red tongue of fire. A split ran along her hull as she floated through the deadly laser light. Abruptly the cockpit melted and was gone.

I took a deep shuddering breath of the reeking pungent air of my suit. "Oh, God."

Six minutes.

Fath cursed. "Our propellant lines are cut. I won't attempt an adjustment; we'd only get about four seconds of burn. She knocked us askew, but we'll still get there."

"How soon?"

"I don't know; we lost about half our velocity. Nine minutes." Father reset the console clock, turned toward the camera. "I'll make one last statement, a harsh one. We'll leave them regretting the tribes, not us. Corwyn, general broadcast on my signal."

"Seafort, this is Kahn."

Father's hand froze.

Captain Wilkes's tone was urgent. "Do you read, launch? I'm relaying the SecGen."

My hand crept to the comm switch.

Fath said, "Yes, Mr. Secretary-General?"

"You're an egomaniac. We're far better without you."

"You must be busy, sir." Father's tone was cool. "No ne
for me to disturb—"

*"I'll trade you Hackers for lasers. You're down to minut
Yes or no?"*

I listened dully, my pants drenched, wanting only to cra
away in shame.

"A pullback? Restored services?"

"That's impossible and you know it."

"Sir, I'll get their agreement to a truce. You get access
the streets; they get to live. I can't help you with the Hacke
I don't know who they are. Lock them out of the nets whi
you—"

*"God damn it, we can't! We spent two days trying
rebuild the Treasury and it keeps imploding! There's som
thing wild inside and no way to trace it without further co
rupting the data. I want their balls. Public hanging, and
far as I'm concerned that's a mercy. I'd skin them alive i
had the—"*

"You'd make a good Sub."

"What?"

"Nothing, sir. I'll try to locate the Hackers, but I doubt i
possible. In any event, they're to be included in the gener
pardon."

*"You have to give me something, Seafort. Politics is the a
of the possible."*

Father gazed at the Station. "Sir, I can give you nothin
Morality is . . . the art of the absolute."

"Christ damn you."

"Good day."

I closed my eyes to the drift of the station. It made n
dizzy.

*"—Assembly meeting in emergency session, though fewe
than half—"*

Fath muttered, "The art of the possible? He knows there
no way on God's earth I can find—"

My numbed mind jerked as if galvanized. "Yes, you can.

"How? God knows where they—"

*"—at least a hundred thousand demonstrators snakin
through Lisbon streets—"*

"Not they. He. It's Jared."

"P.T., it's been a long—"

"I saw him, Fath! He's working in a tower across from ranjee. Jared's the one who broke into the London CLIP and t loose an Arfie. He's proud of it. I *told* you he knew put-rs."

"The boy's glitched." For a moment I thought he meant e. "Arrogant, self-centered, stupid—can you find him?"

"Will you hurt him?"

"—quarters of General Ruben has sealed itself off from edia—"

"Yes, if I get my hands on . . . No. Not if I can arrange a ardon." He glanced at his figures on the screen. "Hurry. Six inutes."

"Captain, Ed Wilkes. Please, I beg you, sail to safety. In oments it will be—"

"Slow us, Fath. Give us time." I keyed the caller.

"I can't; they cut our propellant lines."

"Ask them to stop firing, while we talk to Jar."

"At the moment I have a certain . . . moral authority. If I ave them hold fire, it will collapse."

I waited for my connection, sweating inside my suit.

"Pook. Watcha wan'?"

"This is Peetee. What's the code to Jared's caller?"

"Why should I tell ya?"

"Because I'm begging." I took a deep breath.

"Hah. 'Bout time, an Uppie come beggin' ta trannie. Ya oun' like Jared Washinton Uppie when I haddim—"

"Pook, please! What's his number?"

His tone turned cunning. "Innifo?"

"—An impassioned statement from Marion Leeson. She efended SecGen Kahn's refusal to bow to public hysteria hen—"

"For God's sake, Pook!"

Fath whispered, "Cansa. Lots."

"Cansa, Pook. More 'n ya c'n carry." My heart pounded.

"Laser? Boots, an' sof' new bed—"

Inspired, I blurted, "Pook, I'll take you to Washington, how you our compound. My bedroom, Jared's cottage. verything."

"Inside walls, where ol' Changman took me?" A long ause. " 'Kay, but don' forget cansa. Here be numba." Slowly, e recited a code.

"Later." I punched in the code, misdialed. Frantic, I tri
again, fingers slipping over the keypad. I flushed, tried aga

Five minutes.

"Easy son." Father tapped the caller code himself.

A buzz. No answer.

"Come on, come on, *COME ON*." I panted for breath.

Click. "Good morning. The trannie you have reached
not in service at this time." A giggle.

"Jared? This is Philip. Listen, we need you to—"

"The sky's black, to the north. What did they take out,
munitions dump? Funny I didn't hear an explosion."

"Jar!"

"Everything's dead except the newsfeeds. They took aw
my nets."

"We're trying—"

"Just like Dad when I pissed him off." A sob. "I'm sor
I need my nets. How can I . . . I *need* them, Dad! I mea
P.T."

I stole a glance at the console. Four minutes. I panted
terror.

Father pried the caller from my fingers. "Jared? Son, th
is Nick Seafort."

"I know. You're famous again." He laughed, a har
sound. "Or is it 'still'?"

"Jared, there's no time. Where did you put the puter cod
you used in the Treasury?"

"In a file. Leave me alone; I'm busy."

"Doing what?"

A long pause. "I'm playing with a razor."

"Are you at your puter? Is that where the file is?"

Jar's voice dripped contempt. "You must think I'm st
pid."

Father said, "I used to." I gasped.

"Yeah, figures. Ahh!" A sharp breath. "That hurt."

Three minutes. A hundred sixty-nine feet. The Static
drifted slowly into view. Mesmerized, I stared at the thro
bing orange beams.

"Jared, you showed us. But now it's time for an end. I
time to go home."

"—*Holoworld shuttle was apparently destroyed in a tra
ic*—"

"I have no home. Will you flare when the shuttle burns? Think you'll feel it?"

"Son, will *you*?"

A long silence.

On the caller, Jared began to weep.

The beams drifted closer. We'd rotate one more time, probably face the Station at the end. We moved at just under a kilometer an hour. Three thousand two hundred seventy-three point six feet. Fifty-six and a half feet per minute. Just under a foot per second. Twenty eight seconds, from porthole to stern. Time to know, and to scream.

"Jared, I'm sorry we hurt you. Come home."

"—*whole North American calling grid has collapsed*—"

"I'm an adult. I don't need you to raise me."

"Jared, I beg you! Help us for Halber's sake. For mine. For yours. We'll see you through this!"

Two minutes and six seconds. From Jared, silence.

"—*through the Station porthole. You can see the damaged launch slide inexorably*—"

"Oh, Jared!" Fath's tone was anguished.

"Secret Mystery Bossman Alpha Ace One."

"What?"

"Your frazzing code. It's filed in the London CLIP."

Father switched on the camera. "Public broadcast now on all channels, Corwyn! This is Nicholas Seafort. We're sailing into the laser beam. I caused my own death, and have no regrets. Forget me. Think instead of the joeys you dismiss as trannies. Their spokesman Pedro Chang has offered to tour the city and announce a peace. The U.N.A.F. has ample water trucks to supply the streeters until you work out a truce. The Hackers' puter codes are in the London CLIP under file Secret Mystery Bossman Alpha Ace One."

He paused, stared earnestly as if beseeching the camera. "You see, you have all the tools for a truce. If you must raise a memorial to me, let it be that. And the pardon of all concerned. I am a man of Wales, of Washington, of the tribe of Subs. If we cannot find peace in life, let it be in death. May Lord God bless us all." He keyed off the camera.

One minute. The Station edged into view.

He breathed, "Father, I most contritely repent my sins. Have mercy on my son Philip, on those who—"

My stomach lurched. The orange beams gaped wide.

Frozen at the console, I began to shit my pants.

"—did as they thought wise. Thou art my shepherd, my—"

"Here on the Station all is silent save the steady hum of the lasers. Every porthole is jammed with watchers. Even those who oppose him are in awe of his gallant—"

"I don't want to die." I hardly recognized my voice. "Not ever."

"I'm with you, son."

"We're too alive to die!" I clawed out of my seat, hit my head on the bulkhead. "Stop it, Fath!"

"It's too late. The feed lines—"

Forty seconds. "I want to live! Help me! Someone help! *Mom! God!*" Frantic, I clawed at my helmet. Father knocked away my hand. "Not yet, Fath! Take me home!"

"—a few seconds from destruction. Here in the Station women are crying, men pounding the wall—"

"Son—"

"*HELP ME! IF YOU LOVE ME, HELP!*" I shook him, kicked at the console. "I'm going to die!"

With a sob, Father launched himself to the lock, slapped at the hatch control. "Come here!"

Thirty seconds.

"—as the warning beacons light the front of the craft—"

Whimpering and wailing, I scuttled across the deck. Within my suit my soiled pants stuck to my rump. "Please!" I flew into his arms. "Don't let me burn!" I gasped for breath, tried not to vomit. They said if you threw up in your suit . . .

The hatch slid open.

"—callers have ceased to ring—nobody can get through and it's too late—"

Fath said, "We're moving slowly . . . I'll fling you sternward. If I push hard enough, it may overcome . . . "

"Don't let go!" Panicked, I wrapped myself around his trunk.

"PHILIP!" Desperate, he pried at my fingers. "Turn around! Aim yourself out the lock!"

I twisted round. The gaping maw of the lasers beckoned.

"I'm scared, I can't! Stop the lasers I don't want to die!"

od forgive me I'm a sinner please PLEASE . . . " I retched. I don't want to die!"

"Let GO!" He wrenched loose, slammed me against the ull, grabbed my suit.

A brilliant orange light swept across the cockpit.

"Oh, God!"

Fath braced himself against the hatch, grasped my arm and g.

My suit radio screamed. The console sparked. The radio ied. From the console, a gout of flame, instantly extin-uished. The hull around it dripped and melted.

I shrieked, a horrid endless sound that came from my lackened soul.

In slow motion, the melt moved sternward.

I broke free, leaped screaming onto Fath, clung with arms nd legs.

Father staggered, let loose the hull. Beyond frenzy, I ucked in what might have been a convulsion.

Across the cabin, a tank of oxygen exploded with a great out of silent flame.

I shrieked without end.

We toppled out the hatch. Father's desperate kick pushed s faster. We floated toward the stern of the dissolving launch.

It glided past, ever so slowly, into the cruel orange light.

I screamed my throat raw.

"Don't son. I'm with you. Hold tight. I love you. Rest our head." Somehow, the words penetrated my dread.

"Are we—is it—moving toward—"

"Yes. A few more seconds. Don't look."

I raised my head. We were less than seventy feet from the naw of a laser. Like a row of soldiers, the massive cannon ned at silent, deadly attention. "Hunngh!"

"Look away, son."

Closer we drifted. I craned my neck. Of the launch, only cattered debris remained. Pieces of the craft sailed into the ght of the second laser. They glowed, dissolved, were gone.

"I love you, Father."

"And I you."

"I'm sorry I . . . I'm sorry." I panted desperately for breath.

"I know." Almost, I could see past the edge of the deadly ube to the mystery within.

I whimpered, clung tight.

The warning light flickered.

We drifted into range. My leg would cross first. Desperately, I twisted aside, to no avail.

I crossed in front of the cannon's beam, my head buried in Father's chest.

Nothing.

I waited for agony.

None came.

From Father, a long shuddering sigh.

I looked up.

One by one, the warning beacons blinked out.

We were full in front of the first cannon.

And we lived.

"Thank You, Lord," Father whispered. "Thank You, thank You."

My suit stank, and I was desperately hot. Sick. Disoriented. Yellow light flashed in my eyes, and the red of blood. I panted.

"Fath, I'm . . . ill." I couldn't speak very well.

He looked into my face. "What's the—oh, *damn* it!"

The world spun. "Take me home." My voice was small.

"Let go. Now. This instant!"

Wearily, I unclasped my legs.

His breath rasping, Fath turned me around, fiddled with my suit. "Careless. Stupid." For a moment I thought he'd push me away, but he scissored me between his legs, held tight. "Inexcusable!"

Panting, I clawed at my helmet. Outside was fresh air. Cool, inviting. If I could only get at the clamps . . .

"Stop that!"

"It's hot . . . " But my hands fell away.

Fath grunted, twisted sharply. "There it is."

"What, Fath?"

Again he fiddled with my suit.

I floated inert, almost beyond caring.

An oxygen tank drifted past. How had it survived the hellish fire?

I panted. The stink of my waste was unendurable.

Cool air. I sucked greedily.

Fath's legs eased their grip. After a moment he came up behind me, wrapped his arms around me in a protective hug.

My head began to clear. The lights receded.

"Oh, thank you." I gasped, took in endless breaths.

We drifted past the Station. I wondered if they'd come for us.

Behind me, his head close to mine, Father began to pant.

Again, time was a blur. I recalled stabbing the unfamiliar controls of my suit caller. "I'm Philip Seafort and my father's with me, come get us he has no air for God's sake hurry we need air!"

I babbled my pleas incessantly, not knowing on what comm channel they'd be heard.

Fath's tone was reproachful. "It's one thing to . . . "

"Help us someone, bring oxygen for Captain Seafort for God's sake hurry!"

" . . . sacrifice . . . life," he panted. "But, son . . . never . . . waste it . . . "

We drifted.

It seemed eons before there came the blinking light of a thrustersuit.

We sailed to the Station, two techs guiding Father's inert form, a third hauling me along by the wrist. Fath's suit had a fresh tank, but his radio was silent, unresponsive to my pleas.

Medtechs met us at the airlock with a crashcart. They pulled his helmet the moment the lock pressurized. I leaned unnoticed against the bulkhead, weeping, until at long last Fath stirred, muttered a curse, and pawed at his oxygen mask.

It was only then that I stripped off my suit and the unspeakable clothing beneath.

Someone found a blanket, and escorted me to a washroom. I cried all the while I cleaned myself.

When I'd come out, sniffling, wrapped in my cover, someone led me by the hand to the Admiralty suite. I'd found Fath sitting with Mr. Thorne in the anteroom of the Admiral's former office.

"Not a close call, a miracle," said Thorne. "You don't know the trouble Kahn had getting through. Thanks to you, callers are out through most of Europe."

Father closed his eyes, as if exhausted.

Thorne added, "I only caught the end of his address. Until Ed rang, I . . . wasn't interested."

"Quite an about-face."

"Me? Oh, you mean Kahn." Thorne's face brightened. "He bought your whole program. U.N.A.F. pullout, pardons for all, water deliveries start Monday. Under police guard, of course. He claims the military overreaction was ordered by Leeson's crew while he was out of touch."

"Someone will have to help Chang deal with the transpops. His temper is a bit frayed."

"Yes."

"So, then." Father glanced to the closed office hatch. "Who handles my arrest? Ed Wilkes?"

"What are you talking about?"

"Don't toy with me. What will the charge be? Mutiny?"

"Well, there's the matter of the pardon. Captain Wilkes!" The office hatch slid open. "Yes, sir?"

"What was Kahn's phrasing about the pardon?"

"Let me get the printout." In a moment Wilkes was back. "' . . . grant a full and complete pardon to all persons, civil and military, for any and all acts in relation to disturbances in the City of New York and environs—' "

Fath frowned. "But I said—"

"Let me finish. 'Protests thereat, military countermeasures taken, destruction of property, death of persons, et cetera, et cetera.'"

"Excluding me! I made that clear."

"Yes. I recorded and logged our entire conversation; it's available in case anyone asks. Unfortunately, in the confusion, I failed to pass on that detail."

"You what?" Father got to his feet. "Damn it, Jeff—"

"It was an error," said Thorne testily. "Under pressure, a man can do only so much."

"An error." Father grimaced in disgust.

Thorne's eyes brimmed. He crossed the room, enfolded Fath in an embrace. "Go with God's Grace, Mr. SecGen."

"And you, Jeff."

"We'll be landing soon. How do you feel?"

"All right," I started to say, but the steward wasn't talking to me.

Fath rubbed his eyes. "I have a splitting headache."

"That's to be expected."

"Or worse. Think I still have all my brain cells?"

The steward's smile was awkward. "I'm sure you're quite well," he murmured, and moved on.

I let go of Father's hand long enough to finger my stiff new blouse. Blue wasn't my favorite color, but I was grateful not to have to travel nude.

I told Fath, "I was utterly hysterical." It was as if I spoke of someone else.

"Death is hard. It's all right."

"You weren't afraid."

"Oh, nonsense." He leaned back. "I just wasn't as . . . loud." Despite myself, I grinned.

As the shuttle's buffeting began, I said, "Why are we flying to New York instead of home?"

"I have . . . unfinished business."

"Do you think . . . " I gave Fath's hand a squeeze. "You'll be as glad to get back to the compound as I will? To the privacy of our walls?"

"Privacy. I'd like that." Father's tone was bleak. "More than anything in the world."

The heli set down on the Franjee Tower rooftop in the glare of a hundred holocamera lights. In the corner, near the elevators, Mom waited, her hand on old Mr. Chang's arm. He looked frail. She looked haggard and grim. I swallowed, fearful of the reckoning ahead.

The blades slowed. General Ruben said something behind his hand to Senator Boland, and beckoned a soldier to bring forward a stair.

As they opened the door Father took a firm grip on my arm.

"Sir, you don't have to hold me. I won't run away."

"You're sure of it?"

"I swear by Lord God, sir." I held his gaze. At length, satisfied, he let go my arm and stepped into the evening haze.

The mob of mediamen and officials surged forward. They strained to touch him, to thrust cameras and mikes in his face.

I expected him to bat them aside in fury, but he smiled and stood ramrod straight. The flash of lights redoubled.

When there was a momentary lull Senator Boland stepped forward, his son Rob watching. "Welcome back, Captain Seafort. You held the world in thrall."

Fath nodded, but moved past him. He didn't stop until he reached the outer rail. One hand on the steel, he turned to face the throng of mediamen.

"How did it feel to—"

"Did you know SecGen Kahn would back down?"

"Were you—"

"Will you—"

I fought my way through the jostling mass, to the rooftop's far corner.

Mr. Chang regarded me. "Chaco," he said.

"Naw. Peetee."

A hint of a smile. "Musta got ya confuse."

I turned to Mom. Her face was stony.

I leaned my head against her breast. My arms drew around her, locked themselves behind her back.

A full minute passed. Slowly, her hand came up to stroke my neck.

After a time, I wriggled loose. "I need to listen," I said, "I'll be right back."

I squeezed through the crowd.

"No, I wasn't sure," Fath was saying. "How could I be?" He held up a hand for silence. Drifting closer, I found myself behind Robbie Boland and his Dad.

Fath held up a hand. "No more questions. An announcement." Joeys poked and shushed each other, until there was quiet.

Father surveyed the crowd, his hair glistening in the haze of the night.

Richard Boland said softly, "Look. They hang on his every word."

"You're no slouch on a podium, Dad."

"But I'm not the . . . " He spoke the word as if strange to him. " . . . Fisherman."

"What's he up to?"

Senator Boland didn't answer.

Fath said, "I accept Mr. Kahn's assertion that he acted in

good faith throughout, and was unaware of the degree to which power was abused in his name. He's accepted the resignations of Marion Leeson and Will Banks, Secretary of Defense, and that is good."

Fath paused. "But it is the responsibility of the SecGen to supervise his aides, even if he finds himself incapable of actual leadership. In this regard I fault Mr. Kahn. Thanks to his isolation and inattention, we've suffered over fifty thousand dead, many of them in the relentless final hours of brutal laser attacks on this city."

The air was electric with tension.

"His administration is without moral authority. It is now clear his Administration has forfeited public support as well." Fath's eyes met Senator Boland's.

"Dad, he's endorsing you!" Rob Boland.

"Wait."

Fath said, "There is no candidate from either party whose prime concern is the reconciliation of our people. Therefore, I declare my candidacy for the Secretary-Generalship of the United Nations. I pledge that my Administration, when elected, will act promptly to end our cities' suffering, to integrate into our culture the hordes of urban dwellers who . . . "

The rest was lost in a roar of acclaim. The surge of the crowd nearly knocked Father from the rail, but he quickly recovered, waved to the greedy cameras.

Watching the tumult, Robert Boland stood as if crushed. After a time he said wistfully to his father, "This should have been your moment."

"Well." Somberly, Richard threw his arm around his son. "Perhaps . . . another time."

I ducked under raised holocameras, struggled until I was within a few feet of Fath. Was it a trick of the lights, or the angle from which I peered? Was I the only one who could see the tear that crept down his cheek?

Epilogue

DATESTAMP March 1, 2230
Riverview Tower School Vidclass
Greater New York, U.S.A.

Hey Mista Chang. Eng teacha say Pook s'pose ta write real letta ta someone he like, but I got two prollems. Okay, I learn ta spell my name; zarky frazzin' deal. But writin' what I think? Naw, I nevah be able ta do dat. And who I s'pose ta like? Midboss Karlo? Fah.

So I tol' teacha noway, an' she say okay ta talk a letta on vid and send it ya. I think 'bout write ta Jared Uppie, but can't fo' now. So, since Allie gone and Raulie busy wid clearin' sub, you only one I know 'sides Peetee.

Ya gotta be glitch, sendin' me Uppie school. Dunno why I 'gree in firs' place. An' why I gotta live in towah 'til vacaysh? Sub be only few block away. And if can't live dere, ya shop still stand, don' it?

Dis mornin' some snot Uppie joey make fun a me. Riddy cool me, teacha call it. Betcha he won' do it 'gain. I kicked shit outa him, threw 'im downa stair. Why teacha ack like it enda worl'? How else joeykit gonna learn? Leas' I didn' have shiv, like on streets. Gotta go ta principal office when I done here, and alla otha kits laughin', sayin' wow when he get holt a you.

Dunno, Mista Chang. Nigh'time be hardest. I lie in sof' bed lissenin' ta joeykit Winston snorin', and think a Sub, an Jared, and how Halber go out defy. Sometime make me wanna cry.

See, I can' figga what ya 'xpect a me here. Think I turn inta Uppie, all neat threads an polish? Ain' gonna happen, Mista Chang. I be Pook, of Pook lair.

Okay, I hear what ya tol' me befo'. Gotta learn how dey live, Pook, learn ta walk 'mong 'em widout be 'fraid. 'Cause trannietown changin' and we gonna need trannies can live both worl'.

Hones', I tryin'. Readin' be unzark, but I learn lettas an' soun' out stupe words. Only few joeys laugh anymore, 'cause I fix 'em when no one look. But rest a learn stuff be grody.

Who care where Belfast usetabe, or why dey drop nuke? What I wanna know, where be Washhite, and why Huds an' Rocks always so pissoff?

Peetee come ta see me once, month or so back. His motha brought him, same Uppie bitchbroad what made us take her ta sub. She sure look diff dressed like Uppie. We talk some, Peetee and I, 'bout day I firs' saw him wid Jag an' Swee.

Long time ago, he say, and guess I gotta 'gree.

Dey keepin' ya busy, Mista Chang? Maybe need help? I do watcha say, Mista Chang, hones'. Jus' gemme outa here.

Pook.

Philip Seafort
United Nations Complex
Secretary-General's Residence
Greater New York
March 18, 2230

Arlan Skeer, Dr. of Psych
Washington, D.C. USA
Dear Mr. Skeer:

Four months was a long time to be grounded, but Fath was firm and Mom backed him up. Not that I really expected otherwise, even if they're not living together. Still, it's a great relief now that I'm less of a prisoner.

I'm lonely without Mr. Tenere and Jared. Mr. Thorne is nice, but it isn't the same. He claims he's not sure how Fath persuaded him to become his Chief of Staff, though Mr. Thorne had, as he put it, nowhere else to go.

Rob Boland's adoption papers became final last week. He threw a small celebration, and Mom and I went. Jared is almost through his hormone rebalancing, but he still gets weepy and dependent from the drugs. I was surprised, given Jar's earlier claims of adulthood, to see how he let Mr. Boland comfort him. It's odd to see Robert Boland embrace parenthood. I'd thought he never cared much for Jar.

I guess Mr. Boland will have time to learn. One night after dinner, lying in Fath's study doing homework, I asked why Rob resigned as Assemblyman, especially as his Dad is now our Colonial Secretary. Fath just smiled and said I shouldn't assume Robbie is done with politics. Mr. Boland's mother is zarky. We had her to tea the other day.

When Mom came to New York we went to see Mr. Chang in the hospital. The old man fussed and growled, but I think he was pleased to see us. He seems more frail than ever, but Mom says he's still resisting a transplant. He's only allowing preop lab tests because Fath insisted he deal with the trannies until tribe councils are organized. Fath wants to make him Commissioner of Urban Affairs, even though Mr. Chang says he's too weak for it.

After, Mom took me to see the new Rodin exhibit at

ranjee Towers. When she dropped me off at home I got sort
f morose and teary. I sat outside Fath's door until he finished
vith the Admiral, and let him give me a hug. He said that
otwithstanding appearances, he wouldn't be surprised if
Mom came home to stay. Late that night I tiptoed downstairs,
nd heard him talking to her on the caller. I couldn't hear all
he words, and when he looked into the hall, I pretended to be
sleep, like I'd do in the old days.

But I'm less of a child. I'll be fourteen in a few months.
'm getting hair, and I've been rereading my downloads on
uberty. Overall, Fath has become more strict, and I don't
hink it's just the strain of politics. A few days ago I lost my
emper, and he bent me over his desk and whacked me with a
elt. Before last year he wouldn't have done that. After, when
ve made up, he said he was determined to stay in control, and
ot to let me slip into adolescent sullenness. He gave me three
hapters of astronavigation to take my mind off myself.

Now that the markets are settling down, I dabble in stocks
gain through my nets. Mom knows about it, and promises
ot to tell Fath.

It's funny how things work out. Objectively speaking—
ath says I overuse that phrase, and I ought to think of anoth-
r—I'm still rather upset. You helped a lot, even though I see
ou less often. Thanks for your home number; it gives me a
ice feeling of security.

It's kind of fun being just a joeykid again. But at night, in
ed, I think about how our lives were wrenched apart. That's
vhen I try hard not to rev. Was the rebellion my fault? Was I
esponsible for Jared, and the terrible work of the lasers? You
nd Fath say absolutely not, I'm just a child and mustn't blame
nyself.

I think they're wrong, but we'll see. Maybe I can escape
ne blame I feel. I'm not sure yet.

Filmatleven.

Philip Tyre Seafort

Coming Fall 1997
The Still
by David Feintuch

In Caledon, where the very walls strain to
hear one's whispered thoughts, only one may
wield the mighty Power of the Land. And an
uncrowned prince must tread warily in the
Halls of Kings.

Can Young Rodrigo restrain the cruelty and
temptation that beset him, to wield his Power
and seize his throne?

Don't miss David Feintuch's epic new fantasy,
The Still, coming from Warner Aspect in
Fall 1997.